OFF WITH H

SINGING IN TH

FALSE SCENT

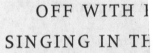

Dame Ngaio Marsh was born in New Zealand in 1895 and died in February 1982. She wrote over 30 detective novels and many of her stories have theatrical settings, for Ngaio Marsh's real passion was the theatre. Both actress and producer, she almost single-handedly revived the New Zealand public's interest in the theatre. It was for this work that the received what she called her 'damery' in 1966.

'The finest writer in the English language of the pure, classical puzzle whodunit. Among the crime queens, Ngaio Marsh stands out as an Empress.'   *The Sun*

'Ngaio Marsh transforms the detective story from a mere puzzle into a novel.'   *Daily Express*

'Her work is as nearly flawless as makes no odds. Character, plot, wit, good writing, and sound technique.'   *Sunday Times*

'She writes better than Christie!'   *New York Times*

'Brilliantly readable . . . first class detection.'   *Observer*

'Still, quite simply, the greatest exponent of the classical English detective story.'   *Daily Telegraph*

'Read just one of Ngaio Marsh's novels and you've got to read them al . . .'   *Daily Mail*

NGAIO MARSH

Off With His Head

Singing in the Shrouds

False Scent

AND

My Poor Boy

HARPER

HARPER
an imprint of HarperCollins*Publishers*
1 London Bridge Street,
London SE1 9GF
www.harpercollins.co.uk

HarperCollins*Publishers*
Macken House, 39/40 Mayor Street Upper,
Dublin 1, D01 C9W8, Ireland

This omnibus edition 2009

Off With His Head first published in Great Britain by Collins 1957
Singing in the Shrouds first published in Great Britain by Collins 1958
False Scent first published in Great Britain by Collins 1960
My Poor Boy first published in Great Britain in
Death on the Air and Other Stories by HarperCollins*Publishers* 1995

Ngaio Marsh asserts the moral right to
be identified as the author of these works

Copyright © Ngaio Marsh Ltd 1956, 1958, 1960
My Poor Boy copyright © Ngaio Marsh (Jersey) Ltd 1989

ISBN 978 0 00 732875 8

Printed and bound in the UK using 100%
Renewable Electricity at CPI Group (UK) Ltd

This book is produced from independently certified FSC™
paper to ensure responsible forest management.
For more information visit: www.harpercollins.co.uk/green

CONTENTS

Off With His Head

Contents

Cast of Characters

Mrs Bünz	
Dame Alice Mardian	*Of Mardian Castle*
The Rev. Samuel Stayne	*Rector of East Mardian,*
	her great-nephew by marriage
Ralph Stayne	*Her great-great-nephew and son*
	to the Rector
Dulcie Mardian	*Her great-niece*
William Andersen	*Of Copse Forge, blacksmith*
Daniel Andersen	
Andrew Andersen	
Nathaniel Andersen	*His sons*
Christopher Andersen	
Ernest Andersen	
Camilla Campion	*His granddaughter*
Bill Andersen	*His grandson*
Tom Plowman	*Landlord of the Green Man*
Trixie Plowman	*His daughter*
Dr Otterly	*Of Yowford, General Practitioner*
Simon Begg	*Of Simmy-Dick's Petrol Station*
Superintendent Carey	*Of the Yowford Constabulary*
Police Sergeant Obby	*Of the Yowford Constabulary*
Superintendent Roderick Alleyn	
Detective-Inspector Fox	*Of the CID*
Detective-Sergeant Bailey	*New Scotland Yard*
Detective-Sergeant Thompson	

Author's Note

To anybody with the smallest knowledge of folklore it will be obvious that the Dance of the Five Sons is a purely imaginary synthesis combining in most unlikely profusion the elements of several dances and mumming plays. For information on these elements I am indebted, among many other sources, to *England's Dances* by Douglas Kennedy and *Introduction to English Folklore* by Violet Alford.

N.M.

CHAPTER 1

Winter Solstice

Over that part of England the Winter Solstice came down with a bitter antiphony of snow and frost. Trees, minutely articulate, shuddered in the north wind. By four o'clock in the afternoon the people of South Mardian were all indoors.

It was at four o'clock that a small dogged-looking car appeared on a rise above the village and began to sidle and curvet down the frozen lane. Its driver, her vision distracted by wisps of grey hair escaping from a headscarf, peered through the fan-shaped clearing on her windscreen. Her woolly paws clutched rather than commanded the wheel. She wore, in addition to several scarves of immense length, a handspun cloak. Her booted feet tramped about over brake and clutch-pedal, her lips moved soundlessly and from time to time twitched into conciliatory smiles. Thus she arrived in South Mardian and bumped to a standstill before a pair of gigantic gates.

They were of wrought-iron and beautiful but they were tied together with a confusion of shopkeeper's twine. Through them, less than a quarter of a mile away, she saw on a white hillside, the shell of a Norman castle, theatrically erected against a leaden sky. Partly encircled by this ruin was a hideous Victorian mansion.

The traveller consulted her map. There could be no doubt about it. This was Mardian Castle. It took some time in that deadly cold to untangle the string. Snow had mounted up the far side and she had to shove hard before she could open the gates wide enough to admit her car. Having succeeded and driven through, she climbed out again to shut them.

'"St Agnes Eve, ach bitter chill it was!"' she quoted in a faintly Teutonic accent. Occasionally, when fatigued or agitated, she turned her short o's into long ones and transposed her v's and w's.

'But I see no sign,' she added to herself, 'of hare nor owl, nor of any living creature, godamercy.' She was pleased with this improvisation. Her intimate circle had lately adopted 'godamercy' as an amusing expletive.

There arose from behind some nearby bushes a shrill cachinnation and out waddled a gaggle of purposeful geese. They advanced upon her, screaming angrily. She bundled herself into the car, slammed the door almost on their beaks, engaged her bottom gear and ploughed on, watched from the hillside by a pair of bulls. Her face was pale and calm and she hummed the air (from her Playford album) of 'Sellinger's Round.'

As the traveller drew near the Victorian house she saw that it was built of the same stone as the ruin that partly encircled it. 'That is something, at least,' she thought. She crammed her car up the final icy slope, through the remains of a Norman archway and into a courtyard. There she drew in her breath in a series of gratified little gasps.

The courtyard was a semi-circle bounded by the curve of old battlemented walls and cut off by the new house. It was littered with heaps of rubble and overgrown with weeds. In the centre, puddled in snow, was a rectangular slab supported by two pillars of stone. 'Eureka!' cried the traveller.

For luck she groped under her scarves and fingered her special necklace of red silk. Thus fortified, she climbed a flight of steps that led to the front door.

It was immense and had been transferred, she decided with satisfaction, from the ruin. There was no push-button, but a vast bell, demonstrably phoney and set about with cast-iron pixies, was bolted to the wall. She tugged at its chain and it let loose a terrifying rumpus. The geese, which had reappeared at close quarters, threw back their heads, screamed derisively and made for her at a rapid waddle.

With her back to the door she faced them. One or two made unsuccessful attempts to mount and she tried to quell them, collectively, with an imperious glare. Such was the din they raised that she did not hear the door open.

'You are in trouble!' said a voice behind her. 'Nip in, won't you, while I shut the door. Be off, birds.'

The visitor was grasped, turned about and smartly pulled across the threshold. The door slammed behind her and she found herself face to face with a thin, ginger-haired lady who stared at her in watery surprise.

'Yes?' said the lady. 'Yes, well, I don't think – and in any case, what weather!'

'Dame Alice Mardian?'

'My great-aunt. She's ninety-four and I don't think – '

With an important gesture the visitor threw back her cloak, explored an inner pocket and produced a card.

'This is, of course, a surprise,' she said. 'Perhaps I should have written first but I must tell you – frankly, frankly – that I was so transported with curiosity – no, not that, not curiosity – rather with the zest of the hunter, that I could not contain myself. Not for another day, another hour even!' She checked. Her chin trembled. 'If you will glance at the card,' she said. Dimly, the other did so.

'Mrs Anna Bünz,' she read.

FRIENDS OF BRITISH FOLKLORE
GUILD OF ANCIENT CUSTOMS
THE HOBBY HORSES

Morisco Croft,
Bapple-under-Baccomb,
Warwickshire

'Oh dear!' said the ginger-haired lady, and added: 'But in any case, come in, of course.' She led the way from a hall that was scarcely less cold than the landscape outside into a drawing-room that was, if anything, more so. It was jammed up with objects. Mediocre portraits reached from the ceiling to the floor, tables were smothered in photographs and ornaments, statuettes peered over each other's shoulders. On a vast hearth dwindled a shamefaced little fire.

'Do sit down,' said the ginger-haired lady doubtfully, 'Mrs – ah – Buns.'

'Thank you, but excuse me – Bünz. Eü, eü,' said Mrs Bünz, thrusting out her lips with tutorial emphasis, 'or if eü is too difficult,

Bins or *Burns* will suffice. But nothing *edible!*' She greeted her own joke with the cordial chuckle of an old acquaintance. 'It's a German name, of course. My dear late husband and I came over before the war. Now I am saturated, I hope I may say, in the very sap of old England. But,' Mrs Bünz added, suddenly vibrating the tip of her tongue as if she anticipated some delicious titbit, 'to our muttons. To our muttons, Miss – ah – '

'Mardian,' said Miss Mardian, turning a brickish pink.

'Ach, that name!'

'If you wouldn't mind – '

'But of course. I come immediately to the point. It is this, Miss Mardian, I have driven three hundred miles to see your great-aunt.'

'Oh dear! She's resting, I'm afraid – '

'You are, of course, familiar with the name of Rekkage.'

'Well, there was old Lord Rekkage who went off his head.'

'It cannot be the same.'

'He's dead now. Warwickshire family, near Bapple.'

'It is the same. As to his sanity I feel you must be misinformed. A great benefactor. He founded the Guild of Ancient Customs.'

'That's right. And left all his money to some too-extraordinary society.'

'The Hobby Horses. I see, my dear Miss Mardian, that we have dissimilar interests. Yet,' said Mrs Bünz, lifting her voluminous chins, 'I shall plod on. So much at stake. So much.'

'I'm afraid,' said Miss Mardian vaguely, 'that I can't offer you tea. The boiler's burst.'

'I don't take it. Pray, Miss Mardian, what are Dame Alice's interests? Of course, at her wonderfully great age – '

'Aunt Akky? Well, she likes going to sales. She picked up nearly all the furniture in this room at auctions. Lots of family things were lost when Mardian Place was burnt down. So she built this house out of bits of the old castle and furnished it from sales. She likes doing that, awfully.'

'Then there *is* an antiquarian instinct. Ach!' Mrs Bünz exclaimed excitedly, clapping her hands and losing control of her accent. 'Ach, sank Gott!'

'Oh crumbs!' Miss Mardian cried, raising an admonitory finger. 'Here *is* Aunt Akky.'

She got up self-consciously. Mrs Bünz gave a little gasp of anticipation and, settling her cloak portentously, also rose.

The drawing-room door opened to admit Dame Alice Mardian.

Perhaps the shortest way to describe Dame Alice is to say that she
resembled Mrs Noah. She had a shapeless, wooden appearance and
her face, if it was expressive of anything in particular, looked dimly
jolly.

'What's all the row?' she asked, advancing with the inelastic toddle of old age. 'Hallo! Didn't know you had friends, Dulcie.'

'I haven't,' said Miss Mardian. She waved her hands. 'This is Mrs
– Mrs – '

'Bünz,' said that lady. 'Mrs Anna Bünz. Dame Alice, I am so inex-
pressibly overjoyed – '

'What about? How de do, I'm sure,' said Dame Alice. She had
loose-fitting false teeth which of their own accord chopped off the
ends of her words and thickened her sibilants. 'Don't see strangers,'
she added. 'Too old for it. Dulcie ought to've told yer.'

'It seems to be about old Lord Rekkage, Aunt Akky.'

'Lor'! Loony Rekkage. Hunted with the Quorn till he fell on his
head. Like you, Dulcie. Went as straight as the best, but mad. Don't
you 'gree?' she asked Mrs Bünz, looking at her for the first time.

Mrs Bünz began to speak with desperate rapidity. 'When he died,'
she gabbled, shutting her eyes, 'Lord Rekkage assigned to me, as
vice-president of the Friends of British Folklore, the task of examining certain papers.'

'Have you telephoned about the boilers, Dulcie?'

'Aunt Akky, the lines are down.'

'Well, order a hack and ride.'

'Aunt Akky, we haven't any horses now.'

'I keep forgettin'.'

'But allow me,' cried Mrs Bünz, 'allow me to take a message on
my return. I shall be so delighted.'

'Are you ridin'?'

'I have a little car.'

'Motorin'? Very civil of you, I must say. Just tell William
Andersen at the Copse that our boiler's burst, if you will. Much
obliged. Me niece'll see you out. Ask you to 'scuse me.'

She held out her short arm and Miss Mardian began to haul at it.

'No, no! Ach, *please*. I implore you!' shouted Mrs Bünz, wringing her hands. 'Dame Alice! Before you go! I have driven for two days. If you will listen for one minute. On my knees – '

'If you're beggin',' said Dame Alice, 'it's no good. Nothin' to give away these days. Dulcie.'

'But, no, no, no! I am not begging. Or only,' urged Mrs Bünz, 'for a moment's attention. Only for von liddle vord.'

'Dulcie, I'm goin'.'

'Yes, Aunt Akky.'

'Guided as I have been – '

'I don't like fancy religions,' said Dame Alice, who with the help of her niece had arrived at the door and opened it.

'Does the Winter Solstice mean nothing to you? Does the Mardian Mawris Dance of the Five Sons mean nothing? Does – ' Something in the two faces that confronted her caused Mrs Bünz to come to a stop. Dame Alice's upper denture noisily capsized on its opposite number. In the silence that followed this mishap there was an outbreak from the geese. A man's voice shouted and a door slammed.

'I don't know,' said Dame Alice with difficulty and passion, 'I don't know who yar or what chupter. But you'll oblige me by takin' yerself off.' She turned on her great-niece. 'You,' she said, 'are a blitherin' idiot. I'm angry. I'm goin'.'

She turned and toddled rapidly into the hall.

'Good evening, Aunt Akky. Good evening, Dulcie,' said a man's voice in the hall. 'I wondered if I – '

'I'm angry with you, too. I'm goin' upshtairs. I don't want to shee anyone. Bad for me to get fusshed. Get rid of that woman.'

'Yes, Aunt Akky.'

'And you behave yershelf, Ralph.'

'Yes, Aunt Akky.'

'Bring me a whishky and shoda to my room, girl.'

'Yes, Aunt Akky.'

'Damn theshe teeth.'

Mrs Bünz listened distractedly to the sound of two pairs of retreating feet. All by herself in that monstrous room she made a wide gesture of frustration and despair. A large young man came in.

'Oh, sorry,' he said. 'Good evening. I'm afraid something's happened. I'm afraid Aunt Akky's in a rage.'

'Alas! Alas!'

'My name's Ralph Stayne. I'm her nephew. She's a bit tricky, is Aunt Akky. I suppose being ninety-four, she's got a sort of right to it.'

'Alas! Alas!'

'I'm most frightfully sorry. If there's anything one could do?' offered the young man. 'Only I might as well tell you I'm pretty heavily in the red myself.'

'You are her nephew?'

'Her great-great-nephew actually. I'm the local parson's son. Dulcie's my aunt.'

'My poor young man,' said Mrs Bünz, but she said it absent-mindedly: there was speculation in her eye. 'You could indeed help me,' she said. 'Indeed, indeed, you could. Listen. I will be brief. I have driven here from Bapple-under-Baccomb in Warwickshire. Owing partly to the weather, I must admit, it has taken me two days. I don't grudge them, no, no, no. But I digress. Mr Stayne, I am a student of the folk dance, both central European and – particularly – English. My little monographs on the Abram Circle Bush and the symbolic tea-pawt have been praised. I am a student, I say, and a performer. I can still cut a pretty caper, Mr Stayne. Ach yes, godamercy.'

'I beg your pardon?'

'Godamercy. It is one of your vivid sixteenth century English ejaculations. My little circle has revived it. For fun,' Mrs Bünz explained.

'I'm afraid I – '

'This is merely to satisfy you that I may in all humility claim to be something of an expert. My status, Mr Stayne, was indeed of such a degree as to encourage the late Lord Rekkage – '

'Do you mean Loony Rekkage?'

' – to entrust no less than three Saratoga trunkfuls of precious *precious* family documents to my care. It was one of these documents, examined by myself for the first time the day before yesterday, that has led me to Mardian Castle. I have it with me. You shall see it.'

Ralph Stayne had begun to look extremely uncomfortable.

'Yes, well now, look here, Mrs – '

'Bünz.'

'Mrs Burns, I'm most awfully sorry but if you're heading the way I think you are then I'm terribly afraid it's no go.'

Mrs Bünz suddenly made a magnificent gesture towards the windows.

'Tell me this,' she said. 'Tell me. Out there in the courtyard, mantled in snow and surrounded at the moment by poultry, I can perceive, and with emotion I perceive it, a slighly inclined and rectangular shape. Mr Stayne, is that object the Mardian Stone? The dolmen of the Mardians?'

'Yes,' said Ralph. 'That's right. It is.'

'The document to which I have referred concerns itself with the Mardian Stone. And with the Dance of the Five Sons.'

'Does it, indeed?'

'It suggests, Mr Stayne, that unknown to research, to experts, to folk dancers and to the societies, the so-called Mardian Mawris (the richest immeasurably of all English ritual dance-plays) was being performed annually at the Mardian Stone during the Winter Solstice up to as recently as fifteen years ago.'

'Oh,' said Ralph.

'And not only that,' Mrs Bünz whispered excitedly, advancing her face to within twelve inches of his, 'there seems to be no reason why it should not have survived to this very year, *this* Winter Solstice, Mr Stayne – *this very week*. Now, do you answer me? Do you tell me if this is so?'

Ralph said: 'I honestly think it would be better if you forgot all about it. Honestly.'

'But you don't deny?'

He hesitated, began to speak and checked himself.

'All right,' he said. 'I certainly don't deny that a very short, very simple and not, I'm sure, at all important sort of dance-play is kept up once a year in Mardian. It is. We just happen to have gone on doing it.'

'Ach, blessed Saint Use and Wont.'

'Er – yes. But we have been rather careful not to sort of let it be known because everyone agrees it'd be too ghastly if the artsy-craftsy boys – I'm sure,' Ralph said, turning scarlet, 'I don't mean to be offensive but you know what can happen. Ye olde goings-on all over the village. Charabancs even. My family have all felt awfully strongly about it and so does the Old Guiser.'

Mrs Bünz pressed her gloved hands to her lips. 'Did you, *did* you say "Old Guiser"?'

'Sorry. It's a sort of nickname. He's William Andersen, really. The local smith. A perfectly marvellous old boy,' Ralph said and inexplicably again turned scarlet. 'They've been at the Copse Smithy for centuries, the Andersens,' he added. 'As long as we've been at Mardian if it comes to that. He feels jolly strongly about it.'

'The Old Man? The Guiser?' Mrs Bünz murmured. 'And he's a smith? And his forefathers perhaps made the hobby horse?'

Ralph was uncomfortable.

'Well – ' he said and stopped.

'Ach! Then there is a hobby!'

'Look, Mrs Burns, I – I do ask you as a great favour not to talk about this to anyone, or – or write about it. And for the love of Mike not to bring people here. I don't mind telling you I'm in pretty bad odour with my aunt *and* old William and, really, if they thought – look, I think I can hear Dulcie coming. Look, may I really *beg* you – '

'Do not trouble yourself. I am very discreet,' said Mrs Bünz with a reassuring leer. 'Tell me, there is a pub in the district, of course? You see I use the word pub. Not inn or tavern. I am not,' said Mrs Bünz, drawing her hand-woven cloak about her, 'what you describe as artsy-crafty.'

'There's a pub about a mile away. Up the lane to Yowford. The Green Man.'

'The Green Man. A-a-ach! Excellent.'

'You're *not* going to stay there!' Ralph ejaculated involuntarily.

'You will agree that I cannot immediately drive to Bapple-under-Baccomb. It is 300 miles away: I shall not even start. I shall put up at the pub.'

Ralph, stammering a good deal, said: 'It sounds the most awful cheek, I know, but I suppose you wouldn't be terribly kind and – if you *are* going there – take a note from me to someone who's staying there. I – I – my car's broken down and I'm on foot.'

'Give it to me.'

'It's most frightfully sweet of you.'

'Or I can drive you.'

'Thank you most terribly but if you'd just take the note. I've got it on me. I was going to post it.' Still blushing he took an envelope from his breast-pocket and gave it to her. She stowed it away in a business-like manner.

'And in return,' she said, 'you shall tell me one more thing. What do you do in the Dance of the Five Sons? For you are a performer. I feel it.'

'I'm the Betty,' he muttered.

'A-a-a-ch! The fertility symbol, or in modern parlance – ' She tapped the pocket where she had stowed the letter. 'The love interest. Isn't it?'

Ralph continued to look exquisitely uncomfortable. 'Here comes Dulcie,' he said. 'If you don't mind I really think it would be better – '

'If I made away with myself. I agree. I thank you, Mr Stayne. Good evening.'

Ralph saw her to the door, drove off the geese, advised her to pay no attention to the bulls as only one of them ever cut up rough, and watched her churn away through the snow. When he turned back to the house Miss Mardian was waiting for him.

'You're to go up,' she said. 'What have you been doing? She's furious.'

II

Mrs Bünz negotiated the gateway without further molestation from livestock and drove through what was left of the village. In all, it consisted only of a double row of nondescript cottages, a tiny shop, a church of little architectural distinction and a Victorian parsonage: Ralph Stayne's home, no doubt. Even in its fancy dress of snow it was not a picturesque village. It would, Mrs Bünz reflected, need a lot of pepping-up before it attracted the kind of people Ralph Stayne had talked about. She was glad of this because in her own way, she too was a purist.

At the far end of the village itself and a little removed from it she came upon a signpost for East Mardian and Yowford and a lane leading off in that direction.

But where, she asked herself distractedly, was the smithy? She was seething with the zeal of the explorer and with an itching curiosity that Ralph's unwilling information had exacerbated rather than assuaged. She pulled up and looked about her. No sign of a smithy. She was certain she had not passed one on her way in. Though her interest was academic rather than romantic, she fastened on smithies with the fervour of a runaway bride. But no. All was twilight and desolation. A mixed group of evergreen and deciduous trees, the signpost, the hills and a great blankness of snow. Well, she would inquire at the pub. She was about to move on when she saw simultaneously a column of smoke rise above the trees and a short man, followed by a dismal dog, come round the lane from behind them.

She leaned out and in a cloud of her own breath shouted: 'Good evening. Can you be so good as to direct me to the Corpse?'

The man stared at her. After a long pause he said: 'Ar?' The dog sat down and whimpered.

Mrs Bünz suddenly realized she was dead-tired. She thought: 'This frustrating day! So! I must now embroil myself with the village natural.' She repeated her question. 'Vere,' she said, speaking very slowly and distinctly, 'is der corpse?'

'Oo's corpse?'

'Mr William Andersen's?'

'Ee's not a corpse. Not likely. Ee's my dad.' Weary though she was she noted the rich local dialect. Aloud, she said: 'You misunderstand me. I asked you where is the smithy. His smithy. My pronunciation was at fault.'

'Copse Smithy be my dad's smithy.'

'Precisely. Where is it?'

'My dad don't rightly fancy wummen.'

'Is that where the smoke is coming from?'

'Ar.'

'Thank you.'

As she drove away she thought she heard him loudly repeat that his dad didn't fancy women.

'He's going to fancy *me* if I die for it,' thought Mrs Bünz.

The lane wound round the copse and there, on the far side, she found that classic, that almost archaic picture – a country blacksmith's shop in the evening.

The bellows were in use. A red glow from the forge pulsed on the walls. A horse waited, half in shadow. Gusts of hot iron and seared horn and the sweetish reek of horse-sweat drifted out to mingle with the tang of frost. Somewhere in a dark corner beyond the forge a man with a lantern seemed to be bent over some task. Mrs Bünz's interest in folklore, for all its odd manifestations, was perceptive and lively. Though now she was punctually visited by the, as it were, off-stage strains of the Harmonious Blacksmith, she also experienced a most welcome quietude of spirit. It was as if all her enthusiasms had become articulate. This was the thing itself, alive and luminous.

The smith and his mate moved into view. The horseshoe, lunar symbol, floated incandescent in the glowing jaws of the pincers. It was lowered and held on the anvil. Then the hammer swung, the sparks showered, and the harsh bell rang. Three most potent of all charms were at work – fire, iron and the horseshoe.

Mrs Bünz saw that while his assistant was a sort of vivid enlargement of the man she had met in the lane and so like him that they must be brothers, the smith himself was a surprisingly small man: small and old. This discovery heartened her. With renewed spirit she got out of her car and went to the door of the smithy. The third man, in the background, opened his lantern and blew out the flame. Then, with a quick movement he picked up some piece of old sacking and threw it over his work.

The smith's mate glanced up but said nothing. The smith, apparently, did not see her. His branch-like arms, ugly and graphic, continued their thrifty gestures. He glittered with sweat and his hair stuck to his forehead in a white fringe. After perhaps half a dozen blows the young man held up his hand and the other stopped, his chest heaving. They exchanged rôles. The young giant struck easily and with a noble movement that enraptured Mrs Bünz.

She waited. The shoe was laid to the hoof and the smith in his classic pose crouched over the final task. The man in the background was motionless.

'Dad, you're wanted,' the smith's mate said. The smith glanced at her and made a movement of his head. 'Yes, ma'am?' asked the son.

'I come with a message,' Mrs Bünz began gaily. 'From Dame Alice Mardian. The boiler at the castle has burst.'

They were silent. 'Thank you, then, ma'am,' the son said at last. He had come towards her but she felt that the movement was designed to keep her out of the smithy. It was as if he used his great torso as a screen for something behind it.

She beamed into his face. 'May I come in?' she asked. 'What a wonderful smithy.'

'Nobbut old scarecrow of a place. Nothing to see.'

'Ach!' she cried jocularly, 'but that's just what I like. Old things are by way of being my business, you see. You'd be' – she made a gesture that included the old smith and the motionless figure in the background – 'you'd *all* be surprised to hear how much I know about blackschmidts.'

'Ar, yes, ma'am?'

'For example,' Mrs Bünz continued, growing quite desperately arch, 'I know *all* about those spiral irons on your lovely old walls there. They're fire charms, are they not? And, of course, there's a horseshoe above your door. And I see by your beautifully printed little notice that you are Ander*sen*, not Ander*son*, and that tells me so exactly just what I want to know. Everywhere, there are evidences for me to read. Inside, I dare say – ' She stood on tiptoe and coyly dodged her large head from side to side, peeping round him and making a mocking face as she did so. 'I dare say there are all sorts of things – '

'*No, there bean't then.*'

The old smith had spoken. Out of his little body had issued a great roaring voice. His son half turned and Mrs Bünz, with a merry laugh, nipped past him into the shop.

'It's Mr Andersen, senior,' she cried, 'is it not? It is – dare I? – the Old Guiser himself? Now I *know* you don't mean what you've just said. You are much too modest about your beautiful schmiddy. And so handsome a horse! Is he a hunter?'

'Keep off. 'Er be a mortal savage kicker. See that naow,' he shouted as the mare made a plunging movement with the near hind leg which he held cradled in his lap. 'She's fair moidered already. Keep off of it. Keep aout. There's nobbut men's business yur.'

'And I had heard so much,' Mrs Bünz said gently, 'of the spirit of hospitality in this part of England. Zo! I was misinformed, it seems. I have driven over two hundred – '

'Blow up, there, you, Chris. Blow up! Whole passel's gone cold while she've been nattering. Blow up, boy.'

The man in the background applied himself to the bellows. A vivid glow pulsed up from the furnace and illuminated the forge. Farm implements, bits of harness, awards won at fairs flashed up. The man stepped a little aside and in doing so, he dislodged the piece of sacking he had thrown over his work. Mrs Bünz cried out in

German. The smith swore vividly in English. Grinning out of the shadows was an iron face, half-bird, half-monster, brilliantly painted, sardonic, disturbing and, in that light, strangely alive.

Mrs Bünz gave a scream of ecstasy.

'The Horse!' she cried, clapping her hands like a mad woman. 'The Old Hoss. The Hooden Horse. I have found it. *Gott sie danke,* what joy is mine!'

The third man had covered it again. She looked at their unsmiling faces.

'Well, that *was* a treat,' said Mrs Bünz in a deflated voice. She laughed uncertainly and returned quickly to her car.

CHAPTER 2

Camilla

Up in her room at the Green Man, Camilla Campion arranged herself in the correct relaxed position for voice exercise. Her diaphragm was gently retracted and the backs of her fingers lightly touched her ribs. She took a long, careful deep breath and as she expelled it, said in an impressive voice:

'Nine Men's Morris is filled up with mud.' This she did several times, muttering to herself, in imitation of her speechcraft instructor whom she greatly admired, 'On the breath dear child: *on* the breath.'

She glanced at herself in the looking-glass on the nice old dressing-table and burst out laughing. She laughed partly because her reflection looked so solemn and was also slightly distorted and partly because she suddenly felt madly happy and in love with almost everyone in the world. It was glorious to be eighteen, a student at the West London School of Drama and possibly in love, not only with the whole world, but with one young man as well. It was heaven to have come alone to Mardian and put up at the Green Man like a seasoned traveller. 'I'm as free as a lark,' thought Camilla Campion. She tried saying the line about Nine Men's Morris with varying inflexions. It was *filled up* with mud. Then it was filled up with *mud,* which sounded surprised and primly shocked and made her laugh again. She decided to give up her practice for the moment, and feeling rather magnificent helped herself to a cigarette. In doing so she unearthed a crumpled letter from her bag. Not for the first time she re-read it.

21

Dear Niece,

Dad asked me to say he got your letter and far as he's concerned you'll be welcome up to Mardian. There's accommodation at the Green Man. No use bringing up the past I reckon
and us all will be glad to see you. He's still terrible bitter against
your mother's marriage on account of it was to a R.C. So kindly
do not refer to same although rightly speaking her dying ought
to make all things equal in the sight of her Maker and us creatures here below.

Your affec. uncle
Daniel Andersen

Camilla sighed, tucked away the letter and looked along the lane
towards Copse Forge.

'I've got to be glad I came,' she said.

For all the cold she had opened her window. Down below a man
with a lanthorn was crossing the lane to the pub. He was followed by
a dog. He heard her and looked up. The light from the bar windows
caught his face.

'Hallo, Uncle Ernest,' called Camilla. 'You *are* Ernest, aren't you?
Do you know who I am? Did they tell you I was coming?'

'Ar?'

'I'm Camilla. I've come to stay for a week.'

'Our Bessie's Camilla?'

'That's me. Now, do you remember?'

He peered up at her with the slow recognition of the mentally
retarded. 'I did yur tell you was coming. Does Guiser know?'

'Yes. I only got here an hour ago. I'll come and see him tomorrow.'

'He doan't rightly fancy wummen.'

'He will me,' she said gaily. 'After all he's my grandfather! He
asked me to come.'

'Noa!'

'Yes, he did. Well – almost. I'm going down to the parlour. See
you later.'

It had begun to snow again. As she shut her window she saw the
headlights of a dogged little car turn into the yard.

A roundabout lady got out. Her head was encased in a scarf, her body
in a mauve handicraft cape and her hands in flowery woollen gloves.

'Darling, what a make-up!' Camilla apostrophized under her breath. She ran downstairs.

The bar-parlour at the Green Man was in the oldest part of the pub. It lay at right angles to the Public which was partly visible and could be reached from it by means of a flap in the bar counter. It was a singularly unpretentious affair, lacking any display of horse-brasses, warming-pans or sporting prints. Indeed the only item of anything but utilitarian interest was a picture in a dark corner behind the door; a faded and discoloured photograph of a group of solemn-faced men with walrus moustaches. They had blackened faces and hands and were holding up, as if to display it, a kind of openwork frame built up from short swords. Through this frame a man in clownish dress stuck his head. In the background were three figures that might have been respectively a hobby-horse, a man in a voluminous petticoat and somebody with a fiddle.

Serving in the private bar was the publican's daughter, Trixie Plowman, a fine ruddy young woman with a magnificent figure and bearing. When Camilla arrived there was nobody else in the Private, but in the Public beyond she again saw her uncle, Ernest Andersen. He grinned and shuffled his feet.

Camilla leant over the bar and looked into the Public. 'Why don't you come over here, Uncle Ernie?' she called.

He muttered something about the Public being good enough for him. His dog, invisible to Camilla, whined.

'Well, fancy!' Trixie exclaimed. 'When it's your own niece after so long and speaking so nice.'

'Never mind,' Camilla said cheerfully. 'I expect he's forgotten he ever had a niece.'

Ernie could be heard to say that no doubt she was too upperty for the likes of them-all, anyhow.

'No I'm not,' Camilla ejaculated indignantly. 'That's just what I'm *not*. Oh dear!'

'Never mind,' Trixie said, and made the kind of face that alluded to weakness of intellect. Ernie smiled and mysteriously raised his eyebrows.

'Though of course,' Trixie conceded, 'I must say it *is* a long time since we seen you,' and she added with a countrywoman's directness: 'Not since your poor mum was brought back and laid to rest.'

'Five years,' said Camilla nodding.

'That's right.'

'Ar,' Ernie interjected loudly, 'and no call for that if she'd bided homealong and wed one of her own. Too mighty our Bessie was, and brought so low's dust as a consequence.'

'That may be one way of looking at it,' Trixie said loftily. 'I must say it's not mine. That dog of yours stinks,' she added.

'Same again,' Ernie countered morosely.

'She wasn't brought as low as dust,' Camilla objected indignantly. 'She was happily married to my father who loved her like anything. He's never really got over her death.'

Camilla, as brilliantly sad as she had been happy, looked at Trixie and said: 'They were in love. They married for love.'

'So they did, then, and a wonderful thing it was for her,' Trixie said comfortably. She drew a half-pint and pointedly left Ernie alone with it.

'Killed 'er, didn't it?' Ernie demanded of his boots. 'For all 'is great 'ordes of pelf and unearthly pride, 'e showed 'er the path to the grave.'

'No. Oh, *don't!* How can you!'

'Never you heed,' Trixie said and beckoned Camilla with a jerk of her head to the far end of the Private bar. 'He's queer,' she said. 'Not soft, mind, but queer. Don't let it upset you.'

'I had a message from Grandfather saying I could come. I thought they wanted to be friendly.'

'And maybe they do. Ernie's different. What'll you take, maid?'

'Cider, please. Have one yourself, Trixie.'

There was a slight floundering noise on the stairs outside; followed by the entrance of Mrs Bünz. She had removed her cloak and all but one of her scarves and was cosy in Cotswold wool and wooden beads.

'Good evening,' she said pleasantly. 'And *what* an evening! Snowing again!'

'Good evening, ma'am,' Trixie said, and Camilla, brightening up because she thought Mrs Bünz such a wonderful 'character make-up', said:

'I *know.* Isn't it *too* frightful!'

Mrs Bünz had arrived at the bar and Trixie said: 'Will you take anything just now?'

'Thank you,' said Mrs Bünz. 'A noggin *will* buck me up. Am I right in thinking that I am in the Mead Country?'

Trixie caught Camilla's eye and then, showing all her white teeth in the friendliest of grins, said: 'Us don't serve mead over the bar, ma'am, though it's made hereabouts by them that fancies it.'

Mrs Bünz leant her elbow in an easy manner on the counter. 'By the Old Guiser,' she suggested, 'for example?'

She was accustomed to the singular little pauses that followed her remarks. As she looked from one to the other of her hearers she blinked and smiled at them and her rosy cheeks bunched themselves up into shiny knobs. She was like an illustration to a tale by the brothers Grimm.

'Would that be Mr William Andersen you mean, then?' Trixie asked.

Mrs Bünz nodded waggishly.

Camilla started to say something and changed her mind. In the Public, Ernie cleared his throat.

'I can't serve you with anything then, ma'am?' asked Trixie.

'Indeed you can. I will take zider,' decided Mrs Bünz, carefully regional. Camilla made an involuntary snuffling noise and, to cover it up, said: 'William Andersen's my grandfather. Do you know him?'

This was not comfortable for Mrs Bünz, but she smiled and smiled and nodded and, as she did so, she told herself that she would never never master the extraordinary vagaries of class in Great Britain.

'I have had the pleasure to meet him,' she said. 'This evening. On my way. A beautiful old gentleman,' she added firmly.

Camilla looked at her with astonishment.

'Beautiful?'

'Ach, yes. The spirit,' Mrs Bünz explained, waving her paws, 'the raciness, the élan!'

'Oh,' said Camilla dubiously. 'I see.' Mrs Bünz sipped her cider and presently took a letter from her bag and laid it on the bar. 'I was asked to deliver this,' she said, 'to someone staying here. Perhaps you can help me?'

Trixie glanced at it. 'It's for you, dear,' she said to Camilla. Camilla took it. Her cheeks flamed like poppies and she looked with wonder at Mrs Bünz.

'Thank you,' she said, 'but I don't quite – I mean – are you – ?'

'A chance encounter,' Mrs Bünz said airily. 'I was delighted to help.'

Camilla murmured a little politeness, excused herself and sat down in the inglenook to read her letter.

Dear Enchanting Camilla (she read),

Don't be angry with me for coming home this week. I know you said I mustn't follow you, but truly I had to because of the Mardian Morris and Christmas. I shan't come near you at the pub and I won't ring you up. But please be in church on Sunday. When you sing I shall see your breath going up in little clouds and I shall puff away too like a train so that at least we shall be doing *something* together. From this you will perceive that I love you.

Ralph

Camilla read this letter about six times in rapid succession and then put it in the pocket of her trousers. She would have liked to slip it under her thick sweater but was afraid it might fall out at the other end.

Her eyes were like stars. She told herself she ought to be miserable because after all she had decided it was no go about Ralph Stayne. But somehow the letter was an antidote to misery, and there went her heart singing like a lunatic.

Mrs Bünz had retired with her cider to the far side of the inglenook where she sat gazing – rather wistfully, Camilla thought – into the fire. The door of the Public opened. There was an abrupt onset of male voices; blurred and leisurely; unformed country voices. Trixie moved round to serve them, and her father, Ron Plowman, the landlord, came in to help. There was a general bumble of conversation. 'I had forgotten,' Camilla thought, 'what they sound like. I've never found out about them. Where do I belong?'

She heard Trixie say: 'So she is, then, and setting in yonder.'

A silence and a clearing of throats. Camilla saw that Mrs Bünz was looking at her. She got up and went to the bar. Through in the Public on the far side of Trixie's plump shoulder she could see her five uncles: Dan, Andy, Nat, Chris and Ernie, and her grandfather, old William. There was something odd about seeing them like that, as if they were images in a glass and not real persons at all. She found this impression disagreeable and to dispel it called out loudly:

'Hallo, there! Hallo, Grandfather!'

Camilla's mother, whose face was no longer perfectly remembered, advanced out of the past with the smile Dan offered his niece. She was there when Andy and Nat, the twins, sniffed at their knuckles as if they liked the smell of them. She was there in Chris's auburn fringe of hair. Even Ernie, strangely at odds with reality, had his dead sister's trick of looking up from under his brows.

The link of resemblance must have come from the grandmother whom Camilla had never seen. Old William himself had none of these signs about him. Dwarfed by his sons he was less comely and looked much more aggressive. His face had settled into a fixed churlishness.

He pushed his way through the group of his five sons and looked at his granddaughter through the frame made by shelves of bottles.

'You've come, then,' he said, glaring at her.

'Of course. May I go through, Trixie?'

Trixie lifted the counter flap and Camilla went into the Public. Her uncles stood back a little. She held out her hand to her grandfather.

'Thank you for the message,' she said. 'I've often wanted to come but I didn't know whether you'd like to see me.'

'Us reckoned you'd be too mighty for your mother's folk.'

Camilla told herself that she would speak very quietly because she didn't want the invisible Mrs Bünz to hear. Even so, her little speech sounded like a bit of diction exercise. But she couldn't help that.

'I'm an Andersen as much as I'm a Campion, Grandfather. Any "mightiness" has been on your side, not my father's or mine. We've always wanted to be friends.'

'Plain to see you're as deadly self-willed and upperty as your mother before you,' he said, blinking at her. 'I'll say that for you.'

'I am *very* like her, aren't I? Growing more so, Daddy says.' She turned to her uncles and went on, a little desperately, with her prepared speech. It sounded, she thought, quite awful. 'We've only met once before, haven't we? At my mother's funeral. I'm not sure if I know which is which, even.' Here, poor Camilla stopped, hoping that they might perhaps tell her. But they only shuffled their feet and made noises in their throats. She took a deep breath and went on. ('Voice pitched too high,' she thought.) 'May I try and guess? You're the eldest, You're my Uncle Dan, aren't you, and you're a widower with a son. And there are Andy and Nat, the twins. You're both married but I don't know what families you've got. And then came Mummy. And then you, Uncle Chris, the one she liked so much, and I don't know if you're married.'

Chris, the ruddy one, looked quickly at Trixie, turned the colour of his own hair and shook his head.

'And I've already met Uncle Ernie,' Camilla ended, and heard her voice fade uneasily.

There seemed little more to say. It had been a struggle to say as much as that. There they were with their countrymen's clothes and boots, their labourers' bodies and their apparent unreadiness to ease a situation that they themselves, or the old man, at least, had brought about.

'Us didn't reckon you'd carry our names so ready,' Dan said and smiled at her again.

'Oh,' Camilla cried, seizing at this, 'that was easy. Mummy used to tell me I could always remember your names in order because they spelt DANCE: Dan, Andy, Nat, Chris, Ernie. She said she thought Grandfather might have named you that way because of Sword Wednesday and the Dance of the Five Sons. Did you, Grandfather?'

In the inglenook of the Private, Mrs Bünz, her cider half-way to her lips, was held in ecstatic suspension.

A slightly less truculent look appeared in old William's face.

'That's not a maid's business,' he said. 'It's man's gear, that is.'

'I know. She told me. But we can look on, can't we? Will the swords be out on the Wednesday after the 21st, Grandfather?'

'Certain sure they'll be out.'

'I be Whiffler,' Ernie said very loudly. 'Bean't I, chaps?'

'Hold your noise then. Us all knows you be Whiffler,' said his father irritably, 'and going in mortal dread of our lives on account of it.'

'And the Wing-Commander's "Crack",' Ernie said monotonously pursuing his theme. 'Wing-Commander Begg, that is. Old 'Oss, that is. 'E commanded my crowd 'e did: I was 'is servant, I was. Wing-Commander Simon Begg, only we called 'im Simmy-Dick, we did. 'E'll be Old 'Oss, 'e will.'

'Ya-a-as, ya-a-as,' said his four brothers soothingly in unison. Ernie's dog came out from behind the door and gloomily contemplated its master.

'We can't have that poor stinking beast in here,' Trixie remarked.

'Not healthy,' Tom Plowman said. 'Sorry, Ern, but there you are. Not healthy.'

'No more 'tis,' Andy agreed. 'Send it back home, Ern.'

His father loudly ordered the dog to be removed, going so far as to say that it ought to be put out of its misery, in which opinion his sons heartily concurred. The effect of this pronouncement upon Ernie was disturbing. He turned sheet-white, snatched up the dog and, looking from one to the other of his relations, backed towards the door.

'I'll be the cold death of any one of you that tries,' he said violently.

A stillness fell upon the company. Ernie blundered out into the dark, carrying his dog.

His brothers scraped their boots on the floor and cleared their throats. His father said: 'Damned young fool, when all's said.' Trixie explained that she was as fond of animals as anybody but you had to draw the line.

Presently Ernie returned, alone, and after eyeing his father for some moments, began to complain like a child.

'A chap bean't let 'ave nothin' he sets his fancy to,' Ernie whined. 'Nor let do nothin' he's a notion to do. Take my case. Can't 'ave me dog. Can't do Fool's act in the Five Sons. I'm the best lepper and caperer of the lot of you. I'd be a proper good Fool, I would.' He pointed to his father. 'You're altogether beyond it, as the doctor in 'is wisdom 'as laid down. Why can't you heed 'im and let me take over?'

His father rejoined with some heat: 'You're lucky to whiffle. Hold your tongue and don't meddle in what you don't understand. Which reminds me,' he added, advancing upon Trixie. 'There was a foreign wumman up along to Copse Forge. Proper old nosey besom. If so be – Ar?'

Camilla had tugged at his coat and was gesturing in the direction of the hidden Mrs Bünz. Trixie mouthed distractedly. The four senior brothers made unhappy noises in their throats.

'In parlour, is she?' William bawled. 'Is she biding?'

'A few days,' Trixie murmured. Her father said firmly: 'Don't talk so loud, Guiser.'

'I'll talk as loud as I'm minded. Us doan't want no furreignesses hereabouts – '

'Doan't, then Dad,' his sons urged him.

But greatly inflamed, the Guiser roared on. Camilla looked through into the Private and saw Mrs Bünz wearing an expression of artificial abstraction. She tiptoed past the gap and disappeared.

'Grandfather!' Camilla cried out indignantly, 'she heard you! How could you! You've hurt her feelings dreadfully and she's not even English – '

'Hold your tongue, then.'

'I don't see why I should.'

Ernie astonished them all by bursting into shouts of laughter.

'Like mother, like maid,' he said, jerking his thumb at Camilla. 'Hark to our Bessie's girl.'

Old William glowered at his granddaughter. 'Bad blood,' he said darkly.

'Nonsense! You're behaving,' Camilla recklessly continued, 'exactly like an over-played "heavy". Absolute ham, if you don't mind my saying so, Grandather!'

'What kind of loose talk's that?'

'Theatre slang, actually.'

'Theatre!' he roared. 'Doan't tell me you're shaming your sex by taking up with that trash. That's the devil's counting-house, that is.'

'With respect, Grandfather, it's nothing of the sort.'

'My granddaughter!' William said, himself with considerable histrionic effort, 'a play-actress! Ar, well! Us might have expected it, seeing she was nossled at the breast of the Scarlet Woman.'

Nat and Andy with the occasional unanimity of twins groaned: 'Ar, dear!'

The landlord said: 'Steady, souls.'

'I really don't know what you mean by that,' Camilla said hotly. 'If you're talking about Daddy's Church you must know jolly well that it isn't mine. He and Mummy laid that on before I was born. I *wasn't* to be a Roman and if my brother had lived he *would* have been one. I'm C. of E.'

'That's next door as bad,' William shouted. 'Turning your back on Chapel and canoodling with Popery.'

He had come quite close to her. His face was scored with exasperation. He pouted, too, pushing out his lips at her and making a piping sound behind them.

To her own astonishment Camilla said: 'No, honestly! You're nothing but an old baby after all,' and suddenly kissed him.

'There now!' Trixie ejaculated, clapping her hands.

Tom Plowman said: 'Reckon that calls for one all round on the house.'

The outside door was pushed open and a tall man in a duffle coat came in.

'Good evening, Mr Begg,' said Trixie.

'How's Trix?' asked Wing-Commander Simon Begg.

II

Later on, when she had seen more of him, Camilla was to think of the first remark she heard Simon Begg make as completely typical of him. He was the sort of man who has a talent for discovering the Christian names of waiters and waitresses and uses them continually. He was powerfully built and not ill-looking, with large blue eyes, longish hair and a blond moustache. He wore an RAF tie, and a vast woollen scarf in the same colours. He had achieved distinction (she was to discover) as a bomber pilot during the war.

The elder Andersens, slow to recover from Camilla's kiss, greeted Begg confusedly, but Ernie laughed with pleasure and threw him a crashing salute. Begg clapped him on the shoulder. 'How's the corporal?' he said. 'Sharpening up the old whiffler, what?'

'Crikey!' Camilla thought, 'he isn't half a cup of tea, is the Wing-Commander.' He gave her a glance for which the word 'practised' seemed to be appropriate and ordered his drink.

'Quite a party tonight,' he said.

'Celebration, too,' Trixie rejoined. 'Here's the Guiser's grand-daughter come to see us after five years.'

'No!' he exclaimed. 'Guiser! Introduce me, please.'

After a fashion old William did so. It was clear that for all his affectation of astonishment, Begg had heard about Camilla. He began to ask her questions that contrived to suggest that they belonged to the same world. Did she by any chance know a little spot called 'Phipps' near Shepherd's Market – quite a bright little spot, really. Camilla, to whom he seemed almost elderly, thought that somehow he was also pathetic. She felt she was a failure with him and decided that she ought to slip away from the Public where she now seemed out of place. Before she could do so, however, there was a further arrival: a pleasant-looking elderly man in an old-fashioned covert-coat with a professional air about him.

There was a chorus of 'Evenin', Doctor.' The newcomer at once advanced upon Camilla and said: 'Why, bless my soul, there's no need to tell me who this is: I'm Henry Otterly, child. I ushered your mama into the world. Last time I spoke to her she was about your age and as like as could be. How very nice to see you.'

They shook hands warmly. Camilla remembered that five years ago when a famous specialist had taken his tactful leave of her mother, she had whispered: 'All the same, you couldn't beat Dr Otterly up to Mardian.' When she had died, they carried her back to Mardian and Dr Otterly had spoken gently to Camilla and her father.

She smiled gratefully at him now and his hand tightened for a moment round hers.

'What a lucky chap you are, Guiser,' said Dr Otterley: 'with a granddaughter to put a bit of warmth into your Decembers. Wish I could say as much for myself. Are you staying for Christmas, Miss Camilla?'

'For the Winter Solstice anyway,' she said. 'I want to see the swords come out.'

'Aha! So you know all about that.'

'Mummy told me.'

'I'll be bound she did. I didn't imagine you people nowadays had much time for ritual dancing. Too "folksy" – is that the word? – or "artsy-craftsy" or "chi-chi". No?'

'Ah no! Not the genuine article like this one,' Camilla protested. 'And I'm sort of specially interested because I'm working at a drama school.'

'Are you now?'

Dr Otterly glanced at the Andersens but they were involved in a close discussion with Simon Begg. 'And what does the Guiser say to *that*?' he asked and winked at Camilla.

'He's livid.'

'Ha! And what do you propose to do about it? Defy him?'

Camilla said: 'Do you know, I honestly didn't think anybody was left who thought like he does about the theatre. He quite pitched into me. Rather frightening when you come to think of it.'

'Frightening? Ah!' Dr Otterly said quickly. 'You don't really mean that. That's contemporary slang, I dare say. What did you say to the Guiser?'

'Well, I didn't *quite* like,' Camilla confided, 'to point out that after all *he* plays the lead in a pagan ritual that is probably chock full of improprieties if he only knew it.'

'No,' agreed Dr Otterly drily, 'I shouldn't tell him that if I were you. As a matter of fact, he's a silly old fellow to do it at all at his time of life. Working himself into a fizz and taxing his ticker up to the danger-mark. I've told him so but I might as well speak to the cat. Now, what do *you* hope to do, child? What rôles do you dream of playing? Um?'

'Oh, Shakespeare if I could. If *only* I could.'

'I wonder. In ten years' time? Not the giantesses, I fancy. Not the Lady M. nor yet The Serpent of Old Nile. But a Viola, now, or – what do you say to a Cordelia?'

'Cordelia?' Camilla echoed doubtfully. She didn't think all that much of Cordelia.

Dr Otterly contemplated her with evident amusement and adopted an air of cosy conspiracy.

'Shall I tell you something? Something that to *me* at least is *immensely* exciting? I believe I have made a really significant discovery: *really* significant about – you'd never guess – about *Lear*. There now!' cried Dr Otterly with the infatuated glee of a White Knight. 'What do you say to that?'

'A discovery?'

'About *King Lear*. And I have been led to it, I may tell you, through playing the fiddle once a year for thirty years at the Winter Solstice on Sword Wednesday for our Dance of the Five Sons.'

'Honestly?'

'As honest as the day. And do you want to know what my discovery is?'

'Indeed I do.'

'In a nutshell, this; here, my girl, in our Five Sons is nothing more nor less than a variant of the Basic Theme: Frazer's theme: The King of the Wood, The Green Man, The Fool, The Old Man Persecuted by his Young: the theme, by gum, that reached its full stupendous blossoming in Lear. Do you *know* the play?' Dr Otterly demanded.

'Pretty well, I think.'

'Good. Turn it over in your mind when you've seen the Five Sons, and if I'm right you'd better treat that old grandpapa of yours with respect, because on Sword Wednesday, child, he'll be playing what I take to be the original version of King Lear. There now!'

Dr Otterly smiled, gave Camilla a little pat and made a general announcement.

'If you fellows want to practise,' he shouted, 'you'll have to do it now. I can't give you more than half an hour. Mary Yeoville's in labour.'

'Where's Mr Ralph?' Dan asked.

'He rang up to say he might be late. Doesn't matter, really. The Betty's a freelance after all. Everyone else is here. My fiddle's in the car.'

'Come on, then, chaps,' said old William. 'Into the barn.' He had turned away and taken up a sacking bundle when he evidently remembered his granddaughter.

'If you bean't too proud,' he said, glowering at her, 'you can come and have a tell up to Copse Forge tomorrow.'

'I'd love to. Thank you, Grandfather. Good luck to the rehearsal.'

'What sort of outlandish word's that? We're going to practise.'

'Same thing. May I watch?'

'You can *not*. 'Tis men's work, and no female shall have part nor passel in it.'

'Just too bad,' said Begg, 'isn't it, Miss Campion? I think we ought to jolly well make an exception in this case.'

'No. No!' Camilla cried, 'I was only being facetious. It's all right, Grandfather. Sorry. I wouldn't dream of butting in.'

'Doan't go nourishing and 'citing thik old besom, neither.'

'No, no, I promise. Goodnight, everybody.'

'Goodnight, Cordelia,' said Dr Otterly.

The door swung to behind the men. Camilla said goodnight to the Plowmans and climbed up to her room. Tom Plowman went out to the kitchen.

Trixie, left alone, moved round into the bar-parlour to tidy it up. She saw the envelope that Camilla in the excitement of opening her letter had let fall.

Trixie picked it up and, in doing so, caught sight of the super-scription. For a moment she stood very still, looking at it. The tip of her tongue appearing between her teeth as if she thought to herself: 'This is tricky.' Then she gave a rich chuckle, crumpled the envelope and pitched it into the fire. She heard the door of the Public Bar open and returned there to find Ralph Stayne staring unhappily at her.

'Trixie – '

'I reckin,' Trixie said, 'you'm thinking you've got yourself into a terrible old pickle.'

'Look – Trixie – '

'Be off,' she said.

'All right. I'm sorry.'

He turned away and was arrested by her voice, mocking him.

'I will say, however, that if she takes you, she'll get a proper man.'

III

In the disused barn behind the pub, Dr Otterly's fiddle gave out a tune as old as the English calendar. Deceptively simple, it bounced and twiddled, insistent in its reiterated demand that whoever heard it should feel in some measure the impulse to jump.

Here, five men jumped: cleverly, with concentration and variety. For one dance they had bells clamped to their thick legs and, as they capered and tramped, the bells jerked positively with an overtone of irrelevant tinkling. For another, they were linked, as befitted the sons of a blacksmith, by steel: by a ring made of five swords. They pranced and leapt over their swords. They wove and unwove a con-centric pattern. Their boots banged down to the fiddle's rhythm and with each down-thump a cloud of dust was bumped up from the floor. The men's faces were blank with concentration: Dan's, Andy's, Nat's, Chris's and Ernie's. On the perimeter of the figure and moving round it danced the Old Guiser, William Andersen. On his head was a rabbit-skin cap. He carried the classic stick-and-bladder. He didn't dance with the vigour of his sons but with dedication. He made curious, untheatrical gestures that seemed to have some kind of significance. He also chided his sons and sometimes called them to a halt in order to do so.

Independent of the Guiser but also moving as an eccentric satellite to the dance was 'Crack', the Hobby Horse, with Wing-Commander Begg inside him. 'Crack' had been hammered out at Copse Forge, how many centuries ago none of the dancers could tell. His iron head, more bird-like than equine, was daubed with paint after the fashion of a witch-doctor's mask. It appeared through a great, flat, drumlike body: a circular frame that was covered to the ground with canvas and had a tiny horsehair tail stuck through it. 'Crack' snapped his iron jaws and executed a solo dance of some intricacy.

Presently Ralph Stayne came in, shaking the snow off his hat and coat. He stood watching for a minute or two and then went to a corner of the barn where he found, and put on, a battered crinoline-like skirt. It was enormously wide and reached to the floor.

Now, in the character of the man-woman, and wearing a face of thunder, Ralph, too, began to skip and march about the Dance of the Five Sons. They had formed the Knot or Glass – an emblem made by the interlacing of their swords. Dan and Andy displayed it, the Guiser approached, seemed to look in it at his reflection and then dashed it to the ground. The dance was repeated and the knot reformed. The Guiser mimed, with clumsy and rudimentary gestures, an appeal to the clemency of the Sons. He appeared to write and show his will, promising this to one and that to another. They seemed to be mollified. A third time they danced and formed their knot. Now, mimed old William, there is no escape. He put his head in the knot. The swords were disengaged with a clash. He dropped his rabbit cap and fell to the ground.

Dr Otterly lowered his fiddle.

'Sorry,' he said. 'I must be off. Quite enough anyway for you, Guiser. If I knew my duty I wouldn't let you do it at all. Look at you,

you old fool, puffing like your own bellows. There's no need, what's more, for you to extend yourself like that. Yours is not strictly a dancing role. Now, don't go on after I've left. Sit down and play for the others if you like. Here's the fiddle. But no more dancing, understand? 'Night, boys.'

He shrugged himself into his coat and went out. They heard him drive away.

Ernie practised 'whiffling'. He executed great leaps, slashing with his sword at imaginary enemies and making a little boy's spaceman noise between his teeth. The Hobby Horse performed an extraordinary and rather alarming antic which turned out merely to be the preparatory manœuvre of Simon Begg divesting himself of his trappings.

'Damned if I put this bloody harness on again tonight,' he said. 'It cuts my shoulders and it stinks.'

'So does the Betty,' said Ralph. 'They must have been great sweaters, our predecessors. However: *toujours l'art,* I suppose.'

'Anything against having them washed, Guiser?' asked Begg.

'You can't wash Old 'Oss,' the Guiser pointed out. 'Polish iron and leather and hot up your pail of pitch. Dip Crack's skirt into it last thing as is what is proper and right. Nothin' like hot pitch to smell.'

'True,' Ralph said: 'you have the advantage of me, Begg. I can't turn the Betty into a tar-baby, worse luck.'

Begg said: 'I'd almost forgotten the hot pitch. Queer sort of caper when you come to think of it. Chasing the lovely ladies and dabbing hot tar on 'em. Funny thing is, they don't run away as fast as all that, either.'

'Padstow 'Oss,' observed Chris, 'or so I've 'eard tell, catches 'em up and overlays 'em like a candle-snuff.'

''Eathen licentiousness,' rejoined his father, 'and no gear for us chaps, so doan't you think of trying it on, Simmy-Dick.'

'Guiser,' Ralph said, 'you're superb. Isn't the whole thing heathen?'

'No, it bean't then. It's right and proper when it's done proper and proper done by us it's going to be.'

'All the same,' Simon Begg said, 'I wouldn't mind twenty seconds under the old tar barrel with that very snappy little job you introduced to us tonight, Guiser.'

Ernie guffawed and was instantly slapped down by his father. 'You hold your noise. No way to conduct yourself when the maid's your niece. You should be all fiery hot in 'er defence.'

'Yes, indeed,' Ralph said quietly.

Begg looked curiously at him. 'Sorry, old man,' he said. 'No offence. Only a passing thought and all that. Let's change the subject: when are you going to let us have that smithy, Guiser?'

'Never. And you might as well make up your mind to it. Never.'

'Obstinate old dog, isn't he?' Begg said at large.

Dan, Chris and the twins glanced uncomfortably at their father.

Dan said: 'Us chaps are favourably disposed as we've mentioned, Simmy-Dick, but, the Dad won't listen to us, no more than to you.'

'Look, Dad,' Chris said earnestly, 'it'd be in the family still. We know there's a main road going through in the near future. We know a service station'd be a little gold mine yur on the cross-roads. We know the company'd be behind us. I've seen the letters that's been wrote. We can still *have* the smithy. Simmy-Dick can run the servicing side on his own to begin with. Ernie can help. Look, it's cast-iron – certain sure.' He turned to Ralph. '*Isn't* it? *Isn't it?*'

Before Ralph could answer Ernie paused in his whiffling and suddenly roared out, 'I'd let you 'ave it, Wing-Commander, sir. So I would too.'

The Guiser opened his mouth in anger but, before he could speak, Dan said: 'We here to practise or not? Come on, chaps. One more dash at the last figure. Strike up for us, Dad.'

The five brothers moved out into the middle of the floor. The Guiser, muttering to himself, laid the fiddle across his knees and scraped a preliminary call-in.

In a moment they were at it again. Down thumped their boots striking at the floor and up bounced the clouds of dust.

And outside in the snow, tied up with scarves, her hand-woven cloak enveloping her, head and all, Mrs Bünz peered through a little cobwebby window, ecstatically noting the steps and taking down the tunes.

CHAPTER 3

Preparation

All through the following week snow and frost kept up their antiphonal ceremony. The two Mardians were mentioned in the press and on the air as being the coldest spots in England.

Up at the castle, Dame Alice gave some hot-tempered orders to what remained nowadays of her staff: a cook, a house-parlourmaid, a cleaning woman, a truculent gardener and his boy. All of them except the boy were extremely old. Preparations were to be put in hand for the first Wednesday evening following the 21st December. A sort of hot cider punch must be brewed in the boiler-house. Cakes of a traditional kind must be baked. The snow must be cleared away in the courtyard and stakes planted to which torches would subsequently be tied. A bonfire must be built. Her servants made a show of listening to Dame Alice and then set about these preparations in their own fashion. Miss Mardian sighed and may have thought all the disturbance a bit of a bore but took it, as did everybody else in the village, as a complete matter of course. 'Sword Wednesday,' as the date of the Five Sons was sometimes called, made very little more stir than Harvest Festival in the two Mardians.

Mrs Bünz and Camilla Campion stayed on at the Green Man. Camilla was seen to speak in a friendly fashion to Mrs Bünz, towards whom Trixie also maintained an agreeable manner. The landlord, an easy man, was understood to be glad enough of her custom, and to be charging her a pretty tidy sum for it. It was learned that her car had broken down and the roads were too bad for it to be towed to Simon Begg's garage, an establishment that advertised itself as

'Simmy-Dick's Service Station.' It was situated at Yowford, a mile beyond East Mardian, and was believed to be doing not too well. It was common knowledge that Simon Begg wanted to convert Copse Forge into a garage and that the Guiser wouldn't hear of it.

Evening practices continued in the barn. In the bedrooms of the pub the thumping boots, jingling bells and tripping insistences of the fiddle could be clearly heard. Mrs Bünz had developed a strong vein of cunning. She would linger in the bar-parlour, sip her cider and write her voluminous diary. The thumps and the scraps of fiddling would tantalize her almost beyond endurance. She would wait for at least ten minutes and then stifle a yawn, excuse herself and ostensibly go upstairs to bed. She had, however, discovered a back stairs by which, a few minutes later, she would secretly descend, a perfect mountain of handweaving, and let herself out by a side door into a yard. From here a terribly slippery brick path led directly to the near end of the barn which the landlord used as a store-room.

Mrs Bünz's spying window was partly sheltered by overhanging thatch. She had managed to clean it a little. Here, shuddering with cold and excitement, she stood, night after night, making voluminous notes with frozen fingers.

From this exercise she derived only modified rapture. Peering through the glass which was continually misted over by her breath, she looked through the store-room and its inner doorway into the barn proper. Her view of the dancing was thus maddeningly limited. The Andersen brothers would appear in flashes. Now they would be out of her range, now momentarily within it. Sometimes the Guiser, or Dr Otterly or the Hobby Horse would stand in the doorway and obstruct her view. It was extremely frustrating.

She gradually discovered that there was more than one dance. There was a Morris, for which the men wore bells that jangled most provocatively, and there was also sword-dancing, which was part of a mime or play. And there was one passage of this dance-play which was always to be seen. This was when the Guiser in his rôle of Fool or Old Man, put his head in the knot of swords. The Five Sons were grouped about him, the Betty and the Hobby Horse were close behind. At this juncture, it was clear that the Old Man spoke. There was some fragment of dialogue, miraculously presenved, perhaps, from heaven knew what ancient source. Mrs Bünz saw his lips move, always at the same point and always, she was certain, to the same effect. Really, she would have given anything in her power to hear what he said.

She learnt quite a lot about the dance-play. She found that, after the Guiser had acted out his mock-decapitation, the Sons danced again and the Betty and Hobby Horse improvised. Sometimes the Hobby Horse would come prancing and shuffling into the store-room quite close to her. It was strange to see the iron beak-like mouth snap and bite the air on the other side of the window. Sometimes the Betty would come in, and the great barrel-like dress would brush up clouds of dust from the store-room floor. But always the Sons danced again and, at a fixed point, the Guiser rose up as if resurrected. It was on this 'Act', evidently, that the whole thing ended.

After the practice they would all return to the pub. Once, Mrs Bünz denied herself the pleasures of her peepshow in order to linger as unobtrusively as possible in the bar-parlour. She hoped that, pleasantly flushed with exercise, the dancers would talk of their craft. But this ruse was a dead failure. The men at first did indeed talk, loudly and freely at the far end of the Public, but they all spoke together and Mrs Bünz found the Andersens' dialect exceedingly difficult. She thought that Trixie must have indicated her presence because they were all suddenly quiet. Then Trixie, always pleasant, came through and asked her if she wanted anything further that evening in such a definite sort of way that somehow even Mrs Bünz felt impelled to get up and go.

Then Mrs Bünz had what she hoped at the time might be a stroke of luck.

One evening at half past five she came into the bar parlour in order to complete a little piece she was writing for an American publication on 'The Hermaphrodite in European Folklore.' She found Simon Begg already there, lost in gloomy contemplation of a small notebook and the racing page of an evening paper.

She had entered into negotiations with Begg about repairing her car. She had also, of course, had her secret glimpses of him in the character of 'Crack'. She greeted him with her particularly Teutonic air of camaraderie. 'So!' she said, 'you are early this evening, Wing Commander.'

He made a sort of token movement, shifting a little in his chair and
eyeing Trixie. Mrs Bünz ordered cider. 'The snow,' she said cosily,
'continues, does it not?'

'That's right,' he said, and then seemed to pull himself together.
'Too bad we still can't get round to fixing that little bus of yours,
Mrs – er – er – Bünz, but there you are! Unless we get a tow – '

'There is no hurry. I shall not attempt the return journey before
the weather improves. My baby does not enjoy the snow.'

'You'd be better off, if you don't mind my saying so, with something that packs a bit more punch.'

'I beg your pardon?'

He repeated his remark in less idiomatic English. The merits of a
more powerful car were discussed: it seemed that Begg had a car of
the very sort he had indicated which he was to sell for an old lady
who had scarcely used it. Mrs Bünz was by no means poor. Perhaps
she weighed up the cost of changing cars with the potential result in
terms of inside information on ritual dancing. In any case, she
encouraged Begg, who became nimble in sales talk.

'It is true,' Mrs Bünz meditated presently, 'that if I had a more
robust motor car I could travel with greater security. Perhaps, for
example, I should be able to ascend in frost with ease to Mardian
Castle – '

'Piece of cake,' Simon Begg interjected.

'I beg your pardon?'

'This job I was telling you about laughs at a stretch like that.
Laughs at it.'

' – I was going to say, to Mardian Castle on Wednesday evening.
That is, if onlookers are permitted.'

'It's open to the whole village,' Begg said uncomfortably. 'Open
house.'

'Unhappily – most unhappily – I have antagonized your Guiser.
Also, alas, Dame Alice.'

'Not to worry,' he muttered and added hurriedly, 'it's only a bit of
fun, anyway.'

'Fun? Yes. It is also,' Mrs Bünz added, 'an antiquarian jewel, a
precious survival. For example, five swords instead of six, have I
never before seen. Unique! I am persuaded of this.'

'Really?' he said politely. 'Now, Mrs Bünz, about this car – '

Each of them hoped to placate the other. Mrs Bünz did not, therefore, correct his pronunciation.

'I am interested,' she said genially, 'in your description of this auto.'

'I'll run it up here tomorrow and you can look it over.'

They eyed each other speculatively.

'Tell me,' Mrs Bünz pursued, 'in this dance you are, I believe, the Hobby Horse?'

'That's right. It's a wizard little number, you know, this job – '

'You are a scholar of folklore, perhaps?'

'*Me?* Not likely.'

'But you perform?' she wailed.

'Just one of those things. The Guiser's as keen as mustard and so's Dame Alice. Pity, in a way, I suppose, to let it fold up.'

'*Indeed, indeed.* It would be a tragedy. Ach! A sin! I am, I must tell you, Mr Begg, an expert. I wish so much to ask you – ' Here, in spite of an obvious effort at self-control, Mrs Bünz became slightly tremulous. She leant forward, her rather prominent blue eyes misted with anxiety, her voice unconvincingly casual. 'Tell me,' she quavered, 'at the moment of sacrifice, the moment when the Fool beseeches the Sons to spare him: something is spoken, is it not?'

'I say!' he ejaculated, staring at her, 'you *do* know a lot about it, don't you?'

She began in a terrific hurry to explain that all European mumming had a common origin: that it was only reasonable to expect a little dialogue.

'We're not meant to talk out of school,' Simon muttered. 'I think it's all pretty corny, mind. Well, childish, really. After all, what the heck's it matter?'

'I *assure* you, I *beg* you to rest assured of my discretion. There is dialogue, no?'

'The Guiser sort of natters at the others.'

Mrs Bünz, clutching frantically at straws of intelligence on a high wind of slang, flung out her fat little hands at him.

'Ach, my good, kind young motor salesman,' she pleaded, reminding him of her potential as a customer, 'of your great generosity, *tell* me what are the words he natters to the ozzers?'

'Honest, Mrs Bünz,' he said with evident regret, 'I don't know. Honest! It's what he's always said. Seems all round the bend to me. I doubt if the boys themselves know. P'raps it's foreign or something.'

Mrs Bünz looked like a cover-picture for a magazine called 'Frustration'. 'If it is foreign I would understand. I speak six European languages. *Gott im Himmel*, Mr Begg – *what is it*?'

His attention had wandered to the racing edition on the table before him. His face lit up and he jabbed at the paper with his finger.

'Look at this!' he said. 'Here's a turn-up! Could you beat it?'

'I have not on my glasses.'

'Running next Thursday,' he read aloud, 'in the three-fifteen. "Teutonic Dancer by Subsidize out of Substiteuton!" Laugh that off.'

'I do not understand you.'

'It's a horse,' he explained. 'A race-horse. Talk about coincidence! Talk about omens!'

'An omen?' she asked, catching at a familiar word.

'Good enough for me, anyway. You're Teutonic, aren't you, Mrs Bünz?'

'Yes,' she said patiently. 'I am Teuton, yes.'

'And we've been talking about *Dancers*, haven't we? And I've suggested you *Substitute* another car for the one you've got? And if you have the little job I've been telling you about, well, I'll be sort of *Subsidized*, won't I? Look, it's uncanny.'

Mrs Bünz rummaged in her pockets and produced her spectacles. 'Ach, I understand. You will bet upon this horse?'

'You can say that again.'

' "Teutonic Dancer by Subsidize out of Sustiteuton!" ' she read slowly, and an odd look came over her face. 'You are right, Mr Begg, it *is strange*. It may, as you say, be an omen.'

II

On the Sunday before Sword Wednesday, Camilla went after church to call upon her grandfather at Copse Forge. As she trudged through the snow she sang until the cold in her throat made her cough and then whistled until the frost on her lips made them too stiff. All through the week she had worked steadily at a part she was to play in next term's showing and had done all her exercises every day. She had seen Ralph in church. They had smiled at each other, after which the organist, who was also the village postman, might have been the progeny of Orpheus and Saint Cecilia, so heavenly sweet did his piping sound to Camilla. Ralph had kept his promise not to come near her but she hurried away from church because she had the feeling that he might wait for her if he left before she did. And until she got her emotions properly sorted out, thought Camilla, that would never do.

The sun came out. She met a robin redbreast, two sparrows and a magpie. From somewhere beyond the woods came the distant unalarming plop of a shot-gun. As she plodded down the lane she saw the spiral of smoke that even on Sundays wavered up over the copse from the hidden forge.

Her grandfather and his two unmarried sons would be home from chapel-going in the nearby village of Yowford.

There was a footpath through the copse making a short cut from the road to the smithy. Camilla decided to take it, and had gone only a little way into the trees when she heard a sound that is always most deeply disturbing. Somewhere, hidden in the wood, a grown man was crying.

He cried boisterously without making any attempt to restrain his distress and Camilla guessed at once who he must be. She hesitated for a moment and then went forward. The path turned a corner by a thicket of evergreens and on the other side Camilla found her uncle, Ernie Andersen, lamenting over the body of his mongrel dog.

The dog was covered with sacking but its tail, horridly dead, stuck out at one end. Ernie crouched beside it, squatting on his heels with his great hands dangling, splay-fingered, between his knees. His face was beslobbered and blotched with tears. When he saw Camilla he cried, like a small boy, all the louder.

'Why, Ernie!' Camilla said, 'you poor old thing.'

He broke into an angry torrent of speech, but so confusedly and in such a thickened dialect that she had much ado to understand him. He was raging against his father. His father, it seemed, had been saying all the week that the dog was unhealthy and ought to be put down. Ernie had savagely defied him and had kept clear of the forge, taking the dog with him up and down the frozen lanes. This morning, however, the dog had slipped away and gone back to the forge. The Guiser, finding it lying behind the smithy, had shot it there and then. Ernie had heard the shot. Camilla pictured him, blundering through the trees, whimpering with anxiety. His father met him with his gun in his hand and told him to take the carcass away and bury it. At this point, Ernie's narrative became unintelligible. Camilla could only guess at the scene that followed. Evidently, Chris had supported his father, pointing out that the dog was indeed in a wretched condition and that it had been from motives of kindness that the Guiser had put it out of its misery. She supposed that Ernie, beside himself with rage and grief, had thereupon carried the body to the wood.

'It's God's truth,' Ernie was saying, as he rubbed his eyes with the heels of his hands and became more coherent. 'I tell 'ee, it's God's truth I'll be quits with 'im for this job. Bad 'e is: rotten bad and so grasping and cruel's a blasted li'l old snake. Done me down at every turn: a murdering thief if ever I see one. Cut down in all the deathly pride of his sins, 'e'll be, if doctor knows what he'm talking about.'

'What on earth do you mean?' cried Camilla.

'I be a better guiser nor him. I do it betterer nor him: neat as pin on my feet and every step a masterpiece. Doctor reckons he'll kill hisself. By God, I hope 'e does.'

'Ernie! Be quiet. You don't know what you're saying. Why do you want to do the Fool's act? It's an Old Man's act. You're a Son.'

Ernie reached out his hand. With a finicky gesture of his flat red thumb and forefinger, he lifted the tip of his dead dog's tail. 'I got the fancy,' he said, looking at Camilla out of the corners of his eyes, 'to die and be rose up agin. That's why.'

Camilla thought: 'No, honestly, this is *too* mummerset.' She said: 'But that's just an act. It's just an old dance-play. It's like having mistletoe and plum pudding. Nothing else happens, Ernie. Nobody dies.'

Ernie twitched the sacking off the body of his dog. Camilla gave a protesting cry and shrank away.

'What's thik, then?' Ernie demanded. 'Be thik a real dead corpse or bean't it?'

'Bury it!' Camilla cried out. 'Cover it up, Ernie, and forget it. It's horrible.'

She felt she could stand no more of Ernie and his dog. She said: 'I'm sorry. I can't help you,' and walked on past him and along the path to the smithy. With great difficulty she restrained herself from breaking into a run. She felt sick.

The path came out at a clearing near the lane and a little above the smithy.

A man was waiting there. She saw him at first through the trees and then, as she drew nearer, more clearly.

He came to meet her. His face was white and he looked, she couldn't help feeling, wonderfully determined and romantic.

'Ralph!' she said, 'you mustn't! You promised. Go away, quickly.'

'I won't. I can't, Camilla. I saw you go into the copse, so I hurried up and came round the other way to meet you. I'm sorry, Camilla. I just couldn't help myself, and, anyway, I've decided it's too damn silly not to. What's more, there's something I've got to say.'

His expression changed. 'Hi!' he said, 'Darling, what's up? I haven't frightened you, have I? You look frightened.'

Camilla said with a little wavering laugh: 'I know it sounds the purest corn but I've just seen something beastly in the copse and it's made me feel sick.'

He took her hands in his. She would have dearly liked to put her head on his chest. 'What did you see, my poorest?' asked Ralph.

'Ernie,' she said, 'with a dead dog and talking about death.'

She looked up at him and helplessly began to cry. He gave an inarticulate cry and gathered her into his arms.

A figure clad in decent blacks came out of the smithy and stood transfixed with astonishment and rage. It was the Guiser.

III

On the day before Sword Wednesday, Dame Alice ordered her septuagenarian gardener to take his slasher and cut down a forest of dead thistles and briar that poked up through the snow where the Dance of the Five Sons was to be performed. The gardener, a fearless Scot with a will of iron and a sour disposition, at once informed her that the slasher had been ruined by unorthodox usage.

'Dame,' he said, for this was the way he chose to address his mistress, 'It canna be. I'll no' soil ma hands nor scald ma temper nor lay waste ma bodily health wi' any such matter.'

'You can sharpen your slasher, man.'

'It should fetch the blush of shame to your countenance to ask it.'

'Send it down to William Andersen.'

'And get insultit for ma pains? Yon godless old devil's altogether sunkit in heathen clamjamphries.'

'If you're talkin' about Sword Wednesday, McGlashan, you're talkin' bosh. Send down your slasher to the forge. If William's too busy one of the sons will do it.'

'I'll hae nane but the smith lay hands on ma slasher. They'd ruin it. Moreover, they are as deep sunk in depravity as their auld mon.'

'Don't you have sword dances in North Britain?'

'I didna come oot here in the cauld at the risk o' ma ain demise to be insultit.'

'Send the slasher to the forge and get the courtyard cleared. That will do, McGlashan.'

In the end, the slasher was taken down by Dulcie Mardian, who came back with the news that the Guiser was away for the day. She had given the slasher to Ernie with strict instructions that his father, and nobody else, was to sharpen it.

'Fancy, Aunt Akky, it's the first time for twenty years that William has been to Biddlefast. He got Dan Andersen to drive him to the bus. Everyone in the village is talking about it and wondering if he's gone to see Stayne and Stayne about his will. I suppose Ralph would know.'

'He's lucky to have somethin' to leave. I haven't and you might as well know it, Dulcie.'

'Of course, Aunt Akky. But everybody says old William is really as rich as possible. He hides it away, they say, like a miser. Fancy!'

'I call it shockin' low form, Dulcie, listenin' to village gossip.'

'And, Aunt Akky, that German woman *is* still at the Green Man. She tries to pump everybody about the Five Sons.'

'She'll be nosin' up here to see it. Next thing she'll be startin' some beastly guild. She's one of those stoopid women who turn odd and all that in their fifties. She'll make a noosance of herself.'

'That's what the Old Guiser says, according to Chris.'

'He's perfectly right. William Andersen is a sensible fellow.'

'Could you turn her away, Aunt Akky, if she comes?'

Dame Alice merely gave an angry snap of her false teeth.

'Is that young woman still at the Green Man?' she demanded.

'Do you mean William Andersen's granddaughter?'

'Who the deuce else should I mean?'

'Yes she is. Everyone says she's awfully nice and – well – you know – '

'If you mean she's a ladylike kind of creeter, why not say so?'

'One doesn't say that somehow, nowadays, Aunt Akky.'

'More fool you.'

'One says she's a "lidy".'

'Nimby-pimby shilly-shallyin' and beastly vulgar into the bargain. Is the gel more of a Campion than an Andersen?'

'She's got quite a look of her mother, but of course, Ned Campion brought her up as a Campion. Good schools and all that. She went to that awfully smart finishing school in Paris.'

'And learnt a lot more than they bargained for, I dare say. Is she keepin' up with the smithy?'

'She's quite cultivating them, it seems, and everybody says old William, although he pretends to disapprove, has really taken a great fancy to her. They say that she seems to like being with them. I suppose it's the common side coming out.'

'Lor', what a howlin' snob you are, Dulcie. All the more credit to the gel. But I won't have Ralph gettin' entangled.'

'What makes you think – ?'

Dame Alice looked at her niece with contempt. 'His father told me. Sam.'

'The rector?' Dulcie said automatically.

'Yes, he's the rector, Dulcie. He's also your brother-in-law. Are you goin' potty? It seems Ralph was noticed with the gel at Sandown and all that. He's been payin' her great 'tention. I won't have it.'

'Have you spoken to Ralph, Aunt Akky?'

''Course I have. 'Bout that and 'bout somethin' else,' said Dame Alice with satisfaction, 'that he didn't know I'd heard about. He's a Mardian, is Master Ralph, if his mother *did* marry a parson. Young rake.'

Dulcie looked at her aunt with a kind of dim, watery relish. 'Goodness!' she said. 'Is Ralph a rake, Aunt Akky?'

'Oh, go and do yer tattin',' said Dame Alice contemptuously, 'you old maiden.'

But Dulcie paid little attention to this insult. Her gaze had wandered to one of the many clocks in her aunt's drawing-room.

'Sword Wednesday tomorrow,' she said romantically, 'and in twenty-four hours they'll be doing the Dance of the Five Sons. Fancy!'

IV

Their final practice over, the eight dancers contemplated each other with the steady complacency of men who have worked together in a strenuous job. Dr Otterly sat on an upturned box, laid his fiddle down and began to fill his pipe.

'Fair enough,' said Old William. 'Might be better, mind.' He turned on his youngest son. 'You, Ernie,' he said, 'you'm Whiffler as us all knows to our cost. But that don't say you'm toppermost item. Altogether too much biostrosity in your whiffling. No need to lay about like a madman. Show me your sword.'

'No, I won't, then,' Ernie said. 'Thik's mine.'

'Have you been sharpening up again? Come on. Have you?'

'Thik's a sword, bean't 'er?'

Ernie's four brothers began to expostulate with him. They pointed out, angrily, that the function of the Whiffler was merely to go through a pantomime of making a clear space for the dance that was to follow. His activities were purest make-believe. Ralph and Dr Otterly joined in to point out that in other counties the whiffling was often done with a broom, and that Ernie, laying excitedly about him with a sword which, however innocuous at its point, had been made razor-sharp farther down, was a menace at once to his fellow-mummers and to his audience. All of them began shouting. Mrs Bünz at her lonely vigil outside the window, hugged herself in ecstasy. It was the ritual of purification that they shouted about. Immensely and thrillingly, their conversation was partly audible and entirely up her street. She died to proclaim her presence, to walk in, to join, blissfully, in the argument.

Ernie made no answer to any of them. He stared loweringly at his father and devotedly at Simon Begg, who merely looked bored and slightly worried. At last, Ernie, under pressure, submitted his sword for examination and there were further ejaculations. Mrs Bünz could see it, a steel blade, pierced at the tip. A scarlet ribbon was knotted through the hole.

'If one of us 'uns misses the strings and catches hold be the blade,' old Andersen shouted, 'as a chap well might in the heat of his exertions, he'd be cut to the bloody bone. Wouldn't he, Doctor?'

'And I'm the chap to do it,' Chris roared out. 'I come next, Ern. I might get me fingers sliced off.'

'Not to mention my yed,' his father added.

'Here,' Dr Otterly said quietly, 'let's have a squint at it.'

He examined the sword and looked thoughtfully at its owner. 'Why,' he asked, 'did you make it so sharp, boy?'

Ernie wouldn't answer. He held out his hand for the sword. Dr Otterly hesitated and then gave it to him. Ernie folded his arms over it and backed away cuddling it. He glowered at his father and muttered and snuffled.

'You damned dunderhead,' old William burst out, 'hand over thik rapper. Come on. Us'll take the edge off of it afore you gets loose on it again. Hand it over.'

'I won't, then.'

'You will!'

'Keep off of me.'

Simon Begg said: 'Steady, Ern. Easy does it.'

'Tell him not to touch me, then.'

'Naow, naow, naow!' chanted his brothers.

'I think I'd leave it for the moment, Guiser,' Dr Otterly said.

'Leave it! Who's boss hereabouts! I'll not leave it, neither.'

He advanced upon his son. Mrs Bünz, peering and wiping away her breath, wondered momentarily if what followed could be yet another piece of histrionic folklore. The Guiser and his son were in the middle of her peepshow, the other Andersens out of sight. In the background only partly visible, their faces alternately hidden and revealed by the leading players, were Dr Otterly, Ralph and Simon Begg. She heard Simon shout: 'Don't be a fool!' and saw rather than heard Ralph admonishing the Guiser. Then, with a kind of darting movement, the old man launched himself at his son. The picture was masked out for some seconds by the great bulk of Dan Andersen. Then arms and hand appeared, inexplicably busy. For a moment or two, all was confusion. She heard a voice and recognized it, high-pitched though it was, for Ernie Andersen's.

'Never blame me if you're bloody-handed. Bloody-handed by nature you are: what shows, same as what's hid. Bloody murderer, both ways, heart and hand.'

Then Mrs Bünz's peepshow re-opened to reveal the Guiser, alone.

His head was sunk between his shoulders, his chest heaved as if it had a tormented life of its own. His right arm was extended in exposition. Across the upturned palm there was a dark gash. Blood slid round the edge of the hand and, as she stared at it, began to drip.

Mrs Bünz left her peepshow and returned faster than usual to her back stairs in the pub.

V

That night, Camilla slept uneasily. Her shallow dreams were beset with dead dogs that stood watchfully between herself and Ralph or horridly danced with bells strapped to their rigid legs. The Five Sons of the photograph behind the bar parlour door also appeared to her with Mrs Bünz mysteriously nodding and the hermaphrodite who slyly offered to pop his great skirt over Camilla and carry her off. Then 'Crack', the Hobby Horse, came hugely to the fore. His bird-like head enlarged itself and snapped at Camilla. He charged out of her dream, straight at her. She woke with a thumping heart.

The Mardian church clock was striking twelve. A blob of light danced on the window curtain. Down in the yard somebody must be walking about with a lanthorn. She heard the squeak of trampled snow accompanied by a drag and a shuffle. Camilla, now wide awake, listened uneasily. They kept early hours at the Green Man. Squeak, squelch, drag, shuffle and still the light dodged on the curtain. Cold as it was, she sat up in the bed, pulled aside the curtain and looked down.

The sound she made resembled the parched and noiseless scream of a sleeper. As well it might: for there below by the light of a hurricane lanthorn her dream repeated itself. 'Crack', the Hobby Horse, was abroad in the night.

CHAPTER 4

The Swords Are Out

On Sword Wednesday, early in the morning, there was another heavy fall of snow. But it stopped before noon and the sun appeared, thickly observable, like a live coal in the western sky.

There had been a row about the slasher. Nobody seemed to know quite what had happened. The gardener, McGlashan, had sent his boy down to the forge to demand it. The boy had returned with a message from Ernie Andersen to say the Guiser wasn't working but the slasher would be ready in time and that, in any case, he and his brothers would come up and clear a place in the courtyard. The gardener, although he had objected bitterly and loudly to doing the job himself, instantly took offence at this announcement and retired to his noisomely stuffy cottage down in the village, where he began a long fetid sulk.

In the morning Nat and Chris arrived at Mardian Castle to clear the snow. McGlashan had locked his tool-shed, but, encouraged by Dame Alice, who had come down heavily on their side, they very quickly picked the lock and helped themselves to whatever they needed. Simon Begg arrived in his breakdown van with the other three Andersen brothers and a load of brushwood, which they built up into a bonfire outside the old battlemented wall. Here it would be partially seen through a broken-down archway and would provide an extra attraction for the village when the Dance of the Sons was over.

Torches, made at the forge from some ancient recipe involving pitch, resin and tow, were set up round the actual dancing area.

Later in the morning the Andersens and Simon Begg were entertained in the servants' hall with a generous foretaste of the celebrated Sword Wednesday Punch, served out by Dame Alice herself, assisted by Dulcie and the elderly maids.

In that company there was nobody of pronounced sensibility. Such an observer might have found something distressing in Simon Begg's attempts to detach himself from his companions, to show an ease of manner that would compel an answering signal from their hostesses. It was such a hopeless business. To Dame Alice (who if she could be assigned to any genre derived from that of Surtees) class was unremarkable and existed in the way that continents and races exist. Its distinctions were not a matter of preference but of fact. To play at being of one class when you were actually of another was as pointless as it would be for a Chinese to try and pass himself off as a Zulu. Dame Alice possessed a certain animal shrewdness but she was fantastically insensitive and not given to thinking of abstract matters. She was ninety-four and thought as little as possible. She remembered that Simon Begg's grandfather and father had supplied her with groceries for some fifty years and that he therefore was a local boy who went away to serve in the war and had, presumably, returned to do so in his father's shop. So she said something vaguely seigniorial and unconsciously cruel to him and paid no attention to his answer except to notice that he called her Dame Alice instead of Madam.

To Dulcie, who was aware that he kept a garage and had held a commission in the Air Force, he spoke a language that was incomprehensible. She supposed vaguely that he preferred petrol to dry goods and knew she ought to feel grateful to him because of the Battle of Britain. She tried to think of remarks to make to him but was embarrassed by Ernie, who stood at his elbow and laughed very loudly at everything he said.

Simon gave Dulcie a meaning smile and patted Ernie's arm. 'We're a bit above ourselves, Miss Mardian,' he said. 'We take ourselves very seriously over this little show tonight.'

Ernie laughed and Dulcie said: 'Do you?' not understanding Simon's playful use of the first person plural. He lowered his voice and said: 'Poor old Ernie! Ernie was my batman in the old days, Miss Mardian. Weren't you, Corp? How about seeing if you can help these girls, Ernie.'

Ernie, proud of being the subject of his hero's attention, threw one of his crashing salutes and backed away. 'It's pathetic really,' Simon said. 'He follows me round like a dog. God knows why. I do what I can for him.'

Dulcie repeated, 'Do you?' even more vaguely and drifted away. Dan called his brothers together, thanked Dame Alice and began to shepherd them out.

'Here!' Dame Alice shouted. 'Wait a bit. I thought you were goin' to clear away those brambles out there.'

'So we are, ma'am,' Dan said. 'Ernie do be comin' up along after dinner with your slasher.'

'Mind he does. How's your father?'

'Not feeling too clever today, ma'am, but he reckons he'll be right again for tonight.'

'What'll you do if he can't dance?'

Ernie said instantly, 'I can do Fool. I can do Fool's act better nor him. If he'm not able, I am. Able and willing.'

His brothers broke into their habitual conciliatory chorus. They eased Ernie out of the room and into the courtyard. Simon made rather a thing of his goodbye to Dame Alice and thanked her elaborately. She distressed him by replying: 'Not't all, Begg. Shop doin' well, I hope? Compliments to your father.'

He recovered sufficiently to look with tact at Dulcie, who said: 'Old Mr Begg's dead, Aunt Akky. Somebody else has got the shop.'

Dame Alice said: 'Ah? I'd forgotten,' nodded to Simon and toddled rapidly away.

She and Dulcie went to their luncheon. They saw Simon's van surrounded by infuriated geese go past the window with all the Andersens on board.

The courtyard was now laid bare of snow. At its centre the Mardian Dolmen awaited the coming of the Five Sons. Many brambles and thistles were still uncut. By three o'clock Ernie had not returned with the slasher and the afternoon had begun to darken. It was half past four that Dulcie, fatigued by preparation and staring out of the drawing-room window, suddenly ejaculated: 'Aunt Akky! Aunt Akky, they've left something on the stone.'

But Dame Alice had fallen into a doze and only muttered indistinguishably.

Dulcie peered and speculated and at last went into the hall and flung an old coat over her shoulders. She let herself out and ran across the courtyard to the stone. On its slightly tilted surface which, in the times before recorded history, may have been used for sacrifice, there was a dead goose, decapitated.

II

By eight o'clock almost all the village was assembled in the court-yard. On Sword Wednesday, Dame Alice always invited some of her neighbours in the county to Mardian, but this year, with the lanes deep in snow, they had all preferred to stay at home. They were unable to ring her up and apologize as there had been a major break-down in the telephone lines. They told each other, rather nervously, that Dame Alice would 'understand'. She not only understood but rejoiced.

So it was entirely a village affair attended by not more than fifty onlookers. Following an established custom, Dr Otterly had dined at the castle and so had Ralph and his father. The Honourable and Reverend Samuel Stayne was Dame Alice's great-nephew-in-law. Twenty-eight years ago he had had the temerity to fall in love with Dulcie Mardian's elder sister, then staying at the castle, and, subsequently, to marry her. He was a gentle, unworldy man who attempted to follow the teaching of the gospels literally and was des-pised by Dame Alice not because he couldn't afford, but because he didn't care, to ride to hounds.

After dinner, which was remarkable for its lamentable food and excellent wine, Ralph excused himself. He had to get ready for the Dance. The others sipped coffee essence and superb brandy in the drawing-room. The old parlourmaid came in at a quarter to nine to say that the dancers were almost ready.

'I really think you'd better watch from the windows, you know,' Dr Otterly said to his hostess. 'It's a devil of a cold night. Look, you'll see to perfection. May I?'

He pulled back the curtains.

It was as if they were those of a theatre and had opened on the first act of some flamboyant play. Eight standing torches in the courtyard and the bonfire beyond the battlements, flared into the night. Flames danced on the snow and sparks exploded in the frosty air. The onlookers stood left and right of the cleared area and their shadows leapt and pranced confusedly up the walls beyond them. In the middle of this picture stood the Mardian dolmen, unencumbered now, glinting with frost as if, incongruously, it had been tinselled for the occasion.

'That youth,' said Dame Alice, 'has *not* cleared away the thistles.'

'And I fancy,' Dr Otterly said, 'that I know why. Now, how about it? You get a wonderful view from here. Why *not* stay indoors?'

'No, thankee. Prefer out.'

'It's not wise, you know.'

'Fiddle.'

'All right! That's the worst of you young things: you're so damned headstrong.'

She chuckled. Dulcie had begun to carry in a quantity of coats and shawls.

'Old William,' Dr Otterly went on, 'is just as bad. He oughtn't to be out tonight with his heart what it is and he certainly oughtn't to be playing the Fool – by the way, Rector, has it ever occurred to you that the phrase probably derives from one of these mumming plays? But, there you are: I ought to refuse to fiddle for the old goat. I would if I thought it'd stop him, but he'd fiddle and fool too, no doubt. If you'll excuse me I must join my party. Here are your programmes, by the way. That's *not* for me, I *trust.'*

The parlour-maid had come in with a piece of paper on her tray. 'For Dr Otterly, madam,' she said.

'*Now,* who the hell can be ill?' Dr Otterly groaned and unfolded the paper.

It was one of the old-fashioned printed bills that the Guiser sent out to his customers. Across it was written in shaky pencil characters: 'Cant mannage it young Ern will have to. W. A.'

'There now!' Dr Otterly exclaimed. 'He *has* conked out.'

'The Guiser!' cried the Rector.

'The Guiser. I must see what's to be done. Sorry, Dame Alice. We'll manage, though. Don't worry. Marvellous dinner. 'Bye.'

'Dear me!' the Rector said, 'what *will* they do?'

'Andy Andersen's boy will come in as a Son,' Dulcie said. 'I know that's what they planned if it happened.'

'And I s'pose,' Dame Alice added, 'that idiot Ernie will dance the Fool. What a bore.'

'Poor Ernie, yes. A catastrophe for them,' the Rector murmured.

'Did I tell you, Sam, he killed one of my geese?'

'We don't know it was Ernie, Aunt Akky.'

'Nobody else dotty enough. I'll tackle 'em later. Come on,' Dame Alice said. 'Get me bundled. We'd better go out.'

Dulcie put her into coat after coat and shawl after shawl. Her feet were thrust into fur-lined boots, her hands into mitts and her head into an ancient woollen cap with a pom-pom on the top. Dulcie and the Rector hastily provided for themselves and finally the three of them went out through the front door to the steps.

Here chairs had been placed with a brazier glowing in front of each. They sat down and were covered with rugs by the parlour-maid, who then retired to an upstairs room from which she could view the proceedings cosily.

Their breath rose up in three columns. The onlookers below them were wreathed in mist. From the bonfire on the other side of the battlements, smoke was blown into the courtyard and its lovely smell was mixed with the pungent odour of tar.

The Mardian Dolmen stood darkly against the snow. Flanking it the torches flared boldly upon a scene which – almost of itself, one might have thought – had now acquired an air of disturbing authenticity.

Dame Alice, with a wooden gesture of her muffled arm shouted: 'Evenin', everybody.' From round the sides of the courtyard they all answered raggedly: 'Evening. Evening, ma'am,' dragging out the soft vowels.

Behind the Mardian Stone was the archway in the battlements through which the performers would appear. Figures could be seen moving in the shadows beyond.

The party of three consulted their programmes, which had been neatly typed.

'WINTER SOLSTICE'

The Mardian Morris of the Five Sons

The Morris Side: *Fool,* William Andersen
  Betty, Ralph Stayne
  Crack, Simon Begg
  Sons, Daniel, Andrew, Nathaniel, Christopher
    and Ernest (Whiffler) Andersen

The Mardian Morris, or perhaps more strictly, Morris Sword Dance and Play, is performed annually on the first Wednesday after the Winter Solstice. It is probably the survival of an ancient fertility rite and combines, in one ceremony, the features of a number of other seasonal dances and mumming plays.

ORDER OF EVENTS

1 General Entry The Five Sons
2 The Mardian Morris
3 Entry of The Betty and Crack
4 Improvisation Crack
5 Entry of the Fool
6 First Sword Dance (a) The Glass is Broken
  (b) The Will is Read
  (c) The Death
7 Improvisation The Betty
8 Solo D. Andersen
9 Second Sword Dance
10 The Resurrection of the Fool.

Dulcie put down her programme and looked round. '*Everybody* must be here, I should think,' she said. 'Look, Aunt Akky, there's Trixie from the Green Man and her father and that's old William's granddaughter with them.'

'Camilla?' the Rector said. 'A splendid girl. We're all delighted with her.'

'Trousers,' said Dame Alice.

'Ski-ing trousers, I *think*, Aunt Akky. Quite suitable really.'

'Is that woman here? The German woman?'

'Mrs Bünz?' the Rector said gently. 'I don't *see* her, Aunt Akky, but it's rather difficult – She's a terrific enthusiast and I'm sure – '

'If I could have stopped her comin', Sam, I would. She's a pest.'

'Oh, surely – '

'Who's this, I wonder?' Dulcie intervened.

A car was labouring up the hill in bottom gear under a hard drive and hooting vigorously. They heard it pull up outside the gateway into the courtyard.

'Funny!' Dulcie said after a pause. 'Nobody's come in. Fancy!'

She was prevented from any further speculation by a general stir in the little crowd. Through the rear entrance came Dr Otterly with his fiddle. There was a round of applause. The hand-clapping sounded desultory and was lost in the night air.

Beyond the wall, men's voices were raised suddenly and apparently in excitement. Dr Otterly stopped short, looked back, and returned through the archway.

'Doctor's too eager,' said a voice in the crowd. There was a ripple of laughter, through which a single voice beyond the wall could be heard shouting something indistinguishable. A clock above the old stables very sweetly tolled nine. Then Dr Otterly returned and this time, after a few preliminary scrapes, struck up on his fiddle.

The air for the Five Sons had never been lost. It had jigged down through time from one Mardian fiddler to another, acquiring an ornament here, an improvisation there, but remaining essentially itself. Nobody had rediscovered it, nobody had put it in a collection. Like the dance itself, it had been protected by the commonplace character of the village and the determined reticence of generation after generation of performers. It was a good tune and well suited to its purpose. After a preliminary phrase or two it ushered in the Whiffler.

Through the archway came a blackamoor with a sword. He had bells on his legs and wore white trousers with a kind of kilt over them. His face was perfect black and a dark cap was on his head. He leapt and pranced and jingled, making complete turns as he did so and 'whiffling' his sword so that it sang in the cold air. He slashed at the thistles and brambles and they fell before him. Round and round the Mardian Stone he pranced and jingled while his blade whistled and glinted. He was the purifier, the acolyte, the precursor.

'That's why Ernie wouldn't clear the thistles,' Dame Alice muttered.

'Oh, *dear*!' Dulcie said, 'aren't they *queer*? Why not *say* so? I *ask* you.' She stared dimly at the jigging blackamoor. 'All the same,' she said, 'this can't be Ernie. He's the Fool, now. Who is it, Sam? The boy?'

'Impossible to tell in that rig,' said the Rector. 'I would have thought from his exuberance that it *was* Ernie.'

'Here come the rest of the Sons.'

There were four of them dressed exactly like the Whiffler. They ran out into the torchlight and joined him. They left their swords by Dr Otterly and with the Whiffler performed the Mardian Morris. Thump and jingle: down came their boots with a strike at the frozen earth. They danced without flourish but with the sort of concentration that amounts to style. When they finished there was a round of applause, sounding desultory in the open courtyard. They took off their pads of bells. The Whiffler threaded a scarlet cord through the tip of his sword. His brothers, whose swords were already adorned with these cords, took them up in their black hands. They waited in a strange rococo group against the snow. The fiddler's tune changed. Now came 'Crack', the Hobby Horse and the Betty. Side by side they pranced. The Betty was a man-woman, black-faced, masculine to the waist and below the waist fantastically feminine. Its great hooped skirt hung from the armpits and spread like a bell-tent to the ground. On the head was a hat, half topper, half floral toque. There was a man's glove on the right hand and a woman's on the left, a boot on the left foot, a slipper on the right.

'Really,' the Rector said, 'how Ralph can contrive to make such an appalling-looking object of himself, I do not know.'

'Here comes "Crack".'

'You don't need to tell us who's comin', Dulcie,' Dame Alice said irritably. 'We can see,'

'I always like "Crack",' Dulcie said serenely.

The iron head, so much more resembling that of a fantastic bird than a horse, snapped its jaws. Beneath it the great canvas drum dipped and swayed. Its skirts left a trail of hot tar on the ground. The rat-like tail stuck up through the top of the drum and twitched busily.

'Crack' darted at the onlookers. The girls screamed unconvincingly and clutched each other. They ran into the arms of their boyfriends and out again. Some of the boys held their girls firm and let the swinging canvas daub them with tar. Some of the girls, affecting not to notice how close 'Crack' had come, allowed themselves to be tarred. They then put up a great show of indignation and astonishment. It was the age-old pantomime of courtship.

'Oh, *do* look, Aunt Akky! He's chasing the Campion girl and she's really *running,*' cried Dulcie.

Camilla was indeed running with a will. She saw the great barbaric head snap its iron beak at her and she smelt hot tar. Both the dream and the reality of the previous night were repeated. The crowd round her seemed to have drawn itself back into a barrier. The cylindrical body of the horse swung up. She saw trousered legs and a pair of black hands. It was unpleasant and, moreover, she had no mind to be daubed with tar. So she ran and 'Crack' ran after her. There was a roar of voices.

Camilla looked for some way of escape. Torchlight played over a solid wall of faces that were split with laughter.

'No!' shouted Camilla. 'No!'

The thing came thundering after her. She ran blindly and as fast as she could across the courtyard and straight into the arms of Ralph Stayne in his preposterous disguise.

'It's all right, my darling,' Ralph said. 'Here I am.'

Camilla clung to him, panting and half-crying.

'Oh, I *see*,' said Dulcie Mardian, watching.

'You don't see anythin' of the sort,' snapped her great-aunt. 'Does she, Sam?'

'I hope not,' said the Rector worriedly.

'Here's the Fool,' said Dulcie, entirely unperturbed.

III

The Fool came out of the shadows at a slow jog-trot. On his appearance 'Crack' stopped his horseplay and moved up to the near exit. The Betty released a flustered Camilla.

'Aunt Akky, do look! The German woman – '

'Shut up, Dulcie. I'm watchin' the Fool.'

The Fool, who is also the Father, jogged quietly round the court-yard. He wore wide pantaloons, tied in at the ankle, and a loose tunic. He wore also his cap fashioned from a flayed rabbit with the head above his own and the ears flopping. He carried a bladder on a stick. His mask was an old one, very roughly made from a painted bag that covered his head and was gathered and tied under his chin. It had holes cut for eyes and was painted with a great dolorous grin.

Dr Otterly had stopped fiddling. The Fool made his round in silence. He trotted in contracting circles, a course that brought him finally to the dolmen. This he struck three times with the bladder. All movements were quite undramatic and without any sense, as Camilla noted, of style. But they were not ineffectual. When he had completed his course, the Five Sons ran into the centre of the court-yard. 'Crack' reappeared through the back exit. The Fool waited beside the dolmen.

Then Dr Otterly, after a warning scrape, broke with a flourish into the second dance, the Sword Dance of the Five Sons.

Against the snow and flames and sparks they made a fine picture, all black-faced and black-handed, down-beating with their feet as if the ground was a drum for their dancing. They made their ring of steel, each holding another's sword by its red ribbon and they wove their knot and held it up before the Fool who peered at it as if it were a looking-glass. 'Crack' edged closer. Then the Fool made his undra-matic gesture and broke the knot.

'Ernie's doing quite well,' said the Rector.

The dance and its sequel were twice repeated. On the first repeti-tion, the Fool made as if he wrote something and then offered what he had written to his Sons. On the second repetition, 'Crack' and the Betty came forward. They stood to the left and right of the Fool, who, this time, was behind the Mardian Dolmen. The Sons, in front of it, again held up their knot of locked swords. The Fool leant across the stone and put his head within the knot. The Hobby Horse moved in behind him and stood motionless, looking in that flickering light, like some monstrous idol. The fiddling stopped dead. The onlookers were very still. Beyond the wall the bonfire crackled.

Then the Sons drew their swords suddenly with a great crash. Horridly the rabbit's head dripped on the stone. A girl in the crowd screamed. The Fool slithered down behind the stone and was hidden.

'Really,' Dulcie said, 'it makes one feel quite odd, don't you think, Aunt Akky?'

A kind of interlude followed. The Betty went round with an object like a ladle into which everybody dropped a coin.

'Where's it goin'?' Dame Alice asked.

'The belfry roof, this year,' the Rector replied, and such is the comfortable attitude of the Church towards the remnants of fertility ritual-dancing in England that neither he nor anybody else thought this at all remarkable.

Ralph, uplifted perhaps by his encounter with Camilla, completed his collection and began a spirited impromptu. He flirted his vast crinoline and made up to several yokels in his audience. He chucked one under the chin, tried to get another to dance with him and threw his crinoline over a third. He was a natural comedian and his antics raised a great roar of laughter. With an elaborate pantomime, laying his finger on his lips, he tiptoed up behind the Whiffler, who stood swinging his sword by its red ribbon. Suddenly Ralph snatched it away. The Hobby Horse, who was behind the dolmen, gave a shrill squeak and went off. The Betty ran and the Whiffler gave chase. These two grotesques darted here and there, disappeared behind piles of stones and flickered uncertainly through the torchlight. Ralph gave a series of falsetto screams, dodged and feinted, and finally hid behind a broken-down buttress near the rear entrance. The Whiffler plunged past him and out into the dark. One of the remaining Sons now came forward and danced a short formal solo with great exactness and spirit. 'That'll be Dan,' said Dulcie Mardian.

'He cuts a very pretty caper,' said the Rector.

From behind the battlemented wail at the back a great flare suddenly burst upwards with a roar and a crackle.

'They're throwin' turpentine on the fire,' Dame Alice said. 'Or somethin'.'

'Very naughty,' said the Rector.

Ralph, who had slipped out by the back entrance, now returned through an archway near the house, having evidently run round behind the battlements. Presently, the Whiffler, again carrying his sword, reappeared through the back entrance and joined his brothers.

The solo completed, the Five Sons then performed their final dance. 'Crack' and the Betty circled in the background, now approaching and now retreating from the Mardian Dolmen.

'This,' said Dulcie, 'is where the Old Man rises from the dead. Isn't it, Sam?'

'Ah – yes. Yes. Very strange,' said the Rector, broadmindedly.

'Exciting.'

'Well – ' he said uneasily.

The Five Sons ended their dance with a decisive stamp. They stood with their backs to their audience pointing their swords at the Mardian Dolmen. The audience clapped vociferously.

'He rises up from behind the stone, doesn't he, Aunt Akky?'

But nobody rose up from behind the Mardian Dolmen. Instead, there was an interminable pause. The swords wavered, the dancers shuffled awkwardly and at last lowered their weapons. The jigging tune had petered out.

'Look, Aunt Akky. Something's gone wrong.'

'Dulcie, for God's sake hold your tongue.'

'My dear Aunt Akky.'

'Be quiet, Sam.'

One of the Sons, the soloist, moved away from his fellows. He walked alone to the Mardian Dolmen and round it. He stood quite still and looked down. Then he jerked his head. The brothers moved in, They formed a semi-circle and they, too, looked down: five glistening and contemplative blackamoors. At last their faces lifted and turned, their eyeballs showed white and they stared at Dr Otterly.

His footfall was loud and solitary in the quietude that had come upon the courtyard.

The Sons made way for him. He stooped, knelt, and in so doing disappeared behind the stone. Thus, when he spoke, his voice seemed disembodied like that of an echo.

'Get back! All of you. Stand away!'

The five Sons shuffled back. The Hobby Horse and the Betty, a monstrous couple, were motionless.

Dr Otterly rose from behind the stone and walked forward. He looked at Dame Alice where she sat enthroned. He was like an actor coming out to bow to the Royal Box, but he trembled and his face was livid. When he had advanced almost to the steps he said loudly:

'Everyone must go. At once. There has been an accident.' The crowd behind him stirred and murmured.

'What's up?' Dame Alice demanded. 'What accident? Where's the Guiser?'

'Miss Mardian, will you take your aunt indoors? I'll follow as soon as I can.'

'I will if she'll come,' said Dulcie, practically.

'Please, Dame Alice.'

'I want to know what's up.'

'And so you shall.'

'Who is it?'

'The Guiser. William Andersen.'

'But he wasn't dancing,' Dulcie said foolishly. 'He's ill.'

'Is he dead?'

'Yes.'

'Wait a bit.'

Dame Alice extended her arm and was at once hauled up by Dulcie. She addressed herself to her guests.

'Sorry,' she said. 'Must 'pologize for askin' you to leave, but as you've heard there's bin trouble. Glad if you'll just go. Now. Quietly. Thankee. Sam, I don't want you.'

She turned away and without another word went indoors, followed by Dulcie.

The Rector murmured, 'But what a shocking thing to happen! And so dreadful for his sons. I'll just go to them, shall I? I suppose it was his heart, poor old boy.'

'Do you?' Dr Otterly asked.

The Rector stared at him. 'You look dreadfully ill,' he said, and then: 'What's happened?'

Dr Otterly opened his mouth but seemed to have some difficulty in speaking.

He and the Rector stared at each other. Villagers still moved across the courtyard and the dancers were still suspended in immobility. It was as if something they all anticipated had not quite happened.

Then it happened.

The Whiffler was on the Mardian Dolmen. He had jumped on the stone and stood there, fantastic against the snow. He paddled his feet in ecstasy. His mouth was redly open and he yelled at the top of his voice.

'What price blood for the stone! What price the Old Man's 'ead? Swords be out, chaps, and 'eads be off. What price blood for the stone?'

His sword was in his hand. He whiffled it savagely and then pointed it at someone in the crowd.

'Ax 'er,' he shouted. 'She knows. She'm the one what done it. Ax 'er.'

The stragglers in the crowd parted and fell back from a solitary figure thickly encased in a multiplicity of hand-woven garments.

It was Mrs Bünz.

CHAPTER 5

Aftermath

'Has it ever occurred to you,' Alleyn said, 'that the progress of a case is rather like a sort of thaw? Look at that landscape.'

He wiped the mist from their carriage window. Sergeants Bailey and Thompson, who had been taking gear from the rack, put on their hats, sat down again and stared out with the air of men to whom all landscapes are alike. Mr Fox, with slightly raised brows, also contemplated the weakly illuminated and dripping prospect.

'Like icing,' he said, 'running off a wedding cake. Not that I suppose it ever does.'

'Such are the pitfalls of analogy. All the same, there is an analogy. When you go out on our sort of job everything's covered with a layer of cagey blamelessness. No sharp outlines anywhere. The job itself sticks up like that phony ruin on the skyline over there but even the job tends to look different under snow. Blurred.'

Mr Fox effaced a yawn. 'So we wait for the thaw!'

'With luck, Brer Fox, we produce it. This is our station.'

They alighted on a platform bordered with swept-up heaps of grey slush. The train which had made an unorthodox halt for them, pulled out at once. They were left with a stillness broken by the drip of melting snow. The outlines of eaves, gutters, rails, leaves, twigs, slid copiously into water.

A man in a belted mackintosh, felt hat and gumboots came forward.

'That'll be the Super,' said Fox.

'Good morning, gentlemen,' said the man.

He was a big chap with a serio-comic face that, when it tried to look grave, only succeeded in achieving an expression of mock-solemnity. His name was Yeo Carey and he had a roaring voice.

The ceremonial handshaking completed, Superintendent Carey led the way out of the little station. A car waited, its wheels fitted with a suit of chains.

'Still need them, up to Mardians,' Carey said when they were all on board. 'They're not thawed out proper thereabouts, though if she keeps mild this way they'll ease off considerably come nightfall.'

'You must have had a nice turn-up with this lot,' Fox said, indicating the job in hand.

'Terrible. Terrible! I was the first to say it was a matter for you gentlemen. We're not equipped for it and no use pretending we are. First capital crime hereabouts I do believe since they burned Betsey Andersen for a witch.'

'What!' Alleyn ejaculated.

'That's a matter of three hundred years as near as wouldn't matter and no doubt the woman never deserved it.'

'Did you say "Andersen"?'

'Yes, sir, I did. There've been Andersens at Copse Forge for quite a spell in South Mardian.'

'I understand,' Fox said sedately, 'the old man who was decapitated was called Andersen.'

'So he was then. He was one of them, was William.'

'I think,' Alleyn said, 'we'll get one of you to tell us the whole story, Carey. Where are we going?'

'Up to East Mardian, sir. The Chief Constable thought you'd like to be as near as possible to the scene of the crime. They've got rooms for you at the Green Man. It's a case of two rooms for four men seeing there's a couple of lodgers there already. But as they might be witnesses, we didn't reckon to turn them out.'

'Fair enough. Where's your station, then?'

'Up to Yowford. Matter of two mile. The Chief Constable's sent you this car with his compliments. I've only got a motor-bike at the station. He axed me to say he'd have come hisself but is bedbound with influenza. We're anxious to help, of course. Every way we can.'

'Everthing seems to be laid on like central heating,' Alleyn was careful to observe. He pointed to the building on the skyline that they had seen from the train. 'What's that, up there?'

'Mardian Castle, Mr Alleyn. Scene of crime.'

'It looks like a ruin.'

'So 'tis in parts. Present residence is on t'other side of those walls. Now, sir, shall I begin, to the best of my ability, to make my report or shall we wait till we're stationary in the pub? A matter of a few minutes only and I can then give my full attention to my duty and refer in order to my notes.'

Alleyn agreed that this would be much the best course, particularly as the chains were making a great noise and the driver's task was evidently an exacting one. They churned along a deep lane, turned a corner and looked down on South Mardian: squat, unpicturesque, unremarkable and as small as a village could be. As they approached, Alleyn saw that, apart from its church and parsonage, it contained only one building that was not a cottage. This was a minute shop. 'Beggs for Everything,' was painted vaingloriously in faded blue letters across the front. They drove past the gateway to Mardian Castle. A police constable with his motor-bicycle nearby stood in front of it.

'Guarding,' explained Carey, 'against sightseers,' and he waved his arms at the barren landscape.

As they approached the group of trees at the far end of the village, Carey pointed it out. 'The Copse,' he said, 'and a parcel farther on behind it, Copse Forge, where the deceased is assembled, Mr Alleyn, in a lean-to shed, it being his own property.'

'I see.'

'We turn right, however, which I will now do, to the hamlet of East Mardian. There, sir, is your pub, ahead and on the right.'

As they drove up, Alleyn glanced at the sign, a pleasant affair painted with a foliated green face.

'That's an old one, isn't it?' he said. 'Although it looks as if it's been rather cleverly touched up.'

'So it has, then. By a lady at present resident in the pub by the name of Bünz.'

'Mrs Buns, the baker's wife,' Alleyn murmured involuntarily.

'No, sir. Foreign. And requiring, by all 'counts, to be looked into.'

'Dear me!' said Alleyn mildly.

They went into the pub, leaving Bailey and Thompson to deal with their luggage. Superintendent Carey had arranged for a small room behind the private bar to be put at their disposal. 'Used to be the Missus's parlour,' he explained, 'but she's no further use for it.'

'Are you sure?'

'Dead these five years.'

'Fair enough,' said Alleyn.

Trixie was there. She had lit a roaring fire and now put a dish of bacon and eggs, a plate of bread-and-cheese and a bottle of pickled onions on the table.

'Hour and a half till dinner,' she said, 'and you'm no doubt starved for a bite after travelling all night. Will you take something?'

They took three pints, which were increased to five on the arrival of Bailey and Thompson. They helped themselves to the hunks of food and settled down, finally, to Superintendent Carey's report.

It was admirably succinct.

Carey, it appeared, had been present at the Dance of the Five Sons. He had walked over from Yowford, more out of habit than enthusiasm and not uninfluenced, Alleyn gathered, by the promise of Dame Alice's Sword Wednesday punch.

Like everybody else, he had heard rumours of the Guiser's indisposition and he had supposed that the Fool was played by Ernie. When he heard Dr Otterly's announcement, he concluded that the Guiser had, after all, performed his part and that on his mock decapitation, which Mr Carey described vividly, he had died of a heart attack.

When, however, the Whiffler (now clearly recognizable as Ernie) had made his appalling announcement from the Mardian Dolmen, Carey had gone forward and spoken to Dr Otterly and the Rector. At the same time, Ernie's brothers had hauled him off the stone. He then, without warning, collapsed into a fit from which he was recovered by Dr Otterly and, from then onwards, refused to speak to anybody.

After a word with the doctor, Carey had ordered the stragglers off the place and had then, and not till then, walked round the dolmen and seen what lay on the ground beyond it.

At this point Carey, quite obviously, had to take a grip of himself. He finished his pint and squared his shoulders.

'I've seen things, mind,' he said. 'I had five years of it on active service and I didn't reckon to be flustered. But this flustered me, proper. Partly, no doubt, it was the way he was got up. Like a clown with the tunic thing pulled up. It'd have been over his head if – well, never mind. He didn't paint his face but he had one of these masks. It ties on like a bag and it hadn't fallen off. So he looked, if you can follow me, gentlemen, like a kind of doll that the head had come off of. There was the body, sort of doubled up, and there was the head two feet away, grinning, which was right nasty, until Rector took the bag off, which he did, saying it wasn't decent. And there was old Guiser's face. And Rector put, as you may say, the pieces together, and said a prayer over them. I beg your pardon, Mr Alleyn?'

'Nothing. Go on.'

'Now, Ernie Andersen had made this statement, which I have repeated to the best of my memory, about the German lady having "done it". I came out from behind where the remains was and there, to my surprise, the German lady stood. Kind of bewildered, if you can understand, she seemed to be, and axing *me* what had happened. "What is it? What has happened? Is he ill?" she said.

'Now, Mr Alleyn, this chap, Ernie Andersen, is not what you'd call right smart. He's a bit touched. Not simple exactly but not right. Takes funny turns. He was in a terrible state, kind of half frightened and half pleased with himself. *Why* he said what he did about Mrs Bünz, I can't make out, but *how* a lady of, say, fifty-seven or so, could step out of the crowd and cut the head off a chap at one blow in full view of everybody and step back again without being noticed takes a bit of explaining. Still, there it was. I took a statement from her. She was very much put about.'

'Well she might be.'

'Just so. Denied knowing anything about it, of course. It seems she was latish getting to the castle. She's bought a new car from Simmy-Dick Begg up to Yowford and couldn't start it at first. Over-choked would be my bet. Everybody in the pub had gone early, Trixie, the barmaid, and the pot-boy having to help the Dame's maids. Well, Mrs Bünz started her car at last and, when she gets to the corner, who should she see but the old Guiser himself.'

'Old Guiser?'

'That's what we called William Andersen hereabouts. There he was, seemingly, standing in the middle of the lane shaking his fist and swearing something ghastly. Mrs Bünz stops and offers a lift. He accepts, but with a bad grace, because, as everybody knows, he's taken a great unliking for Mrs Bünz.'

'Why?'

'On account of her axing questions about Sword Wednesday. The man was in mortal dread of it getting made kind of public and fretted accordingly.'

'A purist, was he?'

'That may be the word for it. He doan't pass a remark of any kind going up to the castle and, when she gets there, he bolts out of the car and goes round behind the ruins to where the others was getting ready to begin. She says she just walked in and stood in the crowd which, to my mind, is no doubt what the woman did. I noticed her there myself, I remember, during the performance!'

'Did you ask her if she knew why Ernie Andersen said she'd done it?'

'I did, then. She says she reckons he's turned crazy-headed with shock, which is what seems to be the general view.'

'Why was the Guiser so late starting?'

'Ah! Now! He'd been sick, had the Guiser. He had a bad heart and during the day he hadn't felt too clever. Seems Dr Otterly, who played the fiddle for them, was against the old chap doing it at all. The boys (I call them boys but Daniel's sixty if he's a day) say their father went and lay down during the day and left word not to be disturbed. They'd fixed it up that Ernie would come back and drive his dad up in an old station-wagon they've got there, leaving it till the last so's not to get him too tired.'

'Ernie again,' Alleyn muttered.

'Well, axacly so, Mr Alleyn, and when Ernie returns it's with a note from his dad which he found pinned to his door, that being the old Guiser's habit, to say he can't do it and Ernie had better. So they send the note in to Dr Otterly, who is having dinner with the Dame.'

'What?' Alleyn said, momentarily startled by this apparent touch of transatlantic realism. 'Oh, I see, yes. Dame Alice Mardian?'

'Yes, sir.'

'Have you got the note?'

'The doctor put it in his pocket, luckily, and I have.'

'Good.'

Carey produced the old-fashioned billhead with its pencilled message: 'Cant mannage it young Ern will have to. W. A.'

'It's his writing all right,' he said. 'No doubt of it.'

'And are we to suppose he felt better, and decided to play his part after all and hitch-hiked with the lady?'

'That's what his sons reckon. It's what they say he told them when he turned up.'

'Do they, now!'

'Pointing out that there wasn't much time to say *anything*. Ernie was dressed up for his dad's part . . . It's what they call the Fool. So he had to get out of his clothes quick and dress up for his own part and Daniel's boy, who was going to do Ernie's part, was left looking silly. So he went round and joined the onlookers. And he confirms the story. He says that's right, that's what happened when the old chap turned up.'

'And it's certain that the old man did dance throughout the show?'

'Must be, Mr Alleyn, mustn't it? Certain sure. There they were, five Sons, a Fiddler, a Betty, a Horse and a Fool. The Sons were the real sons all right. They wiped the muck off their faces while I was taking over. The Betty was the Dame's great-nephew, young Mr Stayne. He's a lawyer from Biddlefast and staying with the parson, who's his father. The Hoss, they call it "Crack", was Simmy-Dick Begg, who has the garage up to Yowford. They all took off their silly truck there and then in my presence as soon's they had the wit to do so. So the Fool must have been the Guiser all the time, Mr Alleyn. There's nobody left but him to be it. We've eight chaps ready to swear he dressed himself up for it and went out with the rest.'

'And stayed there in full view until – '

Mr Carey took a long pull at his tankard, set it down, wiped his mouth and clapped his palm on the table.

'There you are!' he declaimed. 'Until they made out in their dance or play or whatever you like to call it, that they were cutting his head off. Cripes!' Mr Carey added in a changed voice, 'I can see him as if it was now. Silly clown's mask sticking through the knot of swords and then – k-r-r-ring – they've drawn their swords. Down drops the rabbit's head and down goes Guiser, out of sight behind the stone. You wouldn't credit it, would you? In full view of up to sixty persons.'

'Are you suggesting – ? No,' Alleyn said, 'you can't be.'

'I was going to ask you, Super,' Fox said. 'You don't mean to say you think they may actually have beheaded the old chap then and there!'

'How could they!' Carey demanded angrily, as if Fox and Alleyn themselves advanced this theory. 'Ask yourself, Mr Fox. The idea's comical, of course they didn't. The thing is: when did they? If they did.'

'They?' Alleyn asked.

'Well now, no. No. It was done, so the doctor says, and so a chap can see for himself if he's got the stomach to look, by one weapon with one stroke by one man.'

'What about their swords? I'll see them, of course, but what are they like?'

'Straight. About two foot long. Wooden handle one end and a hole t'other through which they stick a silly-looking bit of red cord.'

'Sharp?'

'Blunt as a backside, all but one.'

'Which one?' asked Fox.

'Ernie's,' Alleyn said. 'I'll bet.'

'And you're dead right, sir. Ernie's it is and so sharp's a razor still, never mind how he whiffled down the thistles.'

'So are we forced to ask ourselves if Ernie could have whiffled his old man's head off?'

'*And* we answer ourselves, no, he danged well couldn't of. For why? For because, after his old man dropped behind the stone, there was Ernie doing a comic act with the Betty: that is, Mr Ralph Stayne, as I was telling you. Mr Ralph having taken up a collection, snatched Ernie's sword and they had a sort of chase round the courtyard and in and out through the gaps in the back of the wall. Ernie didn't get his sword back till Mr Ralph give it him. After that, Dan Andersen did a turn on his own. He always does. You could tell it was Dan anyway on account of him being bow-legged. Then the five Sons did another dance and that was when the Old Man should have risen up and didn't and there we are.'

'What was the Hobby Horse doing all this time?'

'Cavorting round chasing the maids. Off and on.'

'And this affair,' Fox said, 'this man-woman-what-have-you-Betty, who was the clergyman's son: he'd collared the sharp sword, had he?'

'Yes, Mr Fox, he had. And was swiping it round and playing the goat with it.'

'Did he go near the stone?' Alleyn asked.

'Well – yes, I reckon he did. When Ernie was chasing him. No doubt of it. But further than that – well, it's just not believable,' said Carey and added: 'He must have given the sword back to Ernie because, later on, Ernie had got it again. There's nothing at all on the sword but smears of sap from the plants Ernie swiped off. Which seems to show it hadn't been wiped on anything.'

'Certainly,' said Alleyn. 'Jolly well observed.'

Mr Carey gave a faint simper.

'Did any of them look behind the stone after the old man had fallen down?' Alleyn asked.

'Mr Ralph – that's the Betty – was standing close up when he fell behind it and reckons he just slid down and lay. There's a kind of hollow there as you'll see and it was no doubt in shadow. Two of them came prancing back to the stone during the last dance; first Simmy-Dick and then Mr Ralph, and they both think he was laying there then. Simmy-Dick couldn't see very clear because his face is in the neck of the horse and the body of the thing hides any object that's nearby on the ground. But he saw the whiteness of the Fool's clothing in the hollow, he says. Mr Ralph says he did, too, without sort of paying much attention.'

'The head – '

'They never noticed. They never noticed another thing till he was meant to resurrect and didn't. Then Dan went to see what was wrong and called up his brothers. He says – it's a funny sort of thing *to* say – but he says he thought, at first, it was some kind of joke and someone had put a dummy there and the head had come off. But, of course,' Carey said, opening his extremely blue eyes very wide, 'it was no such matter.'

There was a long silence. The fire crackled; in a distant part of the pub somebody turned up the volume of a wireless set and turned it down again.

'Well,' Alleyn said, 'there's the story, and very neatly reported if I may say so, Carey. Let's have a look at the place.'

II

The courtyard at Mardian Castle looked dismal in the thaw. The swept-up snow, running away into dirty water, was much trampled, the courtyard itself was greasy and the Mardian Dolmen a lump of wet rock standing on two other lumps. Stone and mud glistened alike in sunlight that merely lent a kind of pallor to the day and an additional emphasis to the north wind. The latter whistled through the slits in the old walls with all the venom of the arrows they had originally been designed to accommodate. Eight burnt-out torches on stakes stood in a semi-circle roughly following that of the wall but set some twelve feet inside it. In the middle of this scene stood a police sergeant with his mackintosh collar turned up and his shoulders hunched. He was presented by Carey – 'Sergeant Obby.'

Taking in the scene, Alleyn turned from the semi-circle of old wall to the hideous façade of the Victorian house. He found himself being stared at by a squarish, wooden old lady behind a ground-floor window. A second lady, sandy and middle-aged, stood behind her.

'Who's that?' he asked.

'The Dame,' said Carey. 'And Miss Mardian.'

'I suppose I ought to make a polite noise.'

'She's not,' Carey muttered, 'in a wonderful good mood today.'

'Never mind.'

'And Miss Mardian's – well – er – well, she's not right smart, Mr Alleyn.'

'Like Ernie?'

'No, sir. Not exactly. It may be,' Carey ventured, 'on account of in-breeding which is what's been going on hot and strong in the Mardian family for a great time. Not that there's anything like that about the Dame, mind. She's ninety-four and a proper masterpiece.'

'I'd better try my luck. Here goes.'

He walked past the window, separated from the basilisk glare by two feet of air and a panel of glass. As he mounted the steps between dead braziers half full of wet ash, the door was opened by Dulcie.

Alleyn said: 'Miss Mardian? I wonder if I may have two words with Dame Alice Mardian?'

'Oh, dear!' Dulcie said. 'I don't honestly know if you can. I expect I ought to remember who you are, oughtn't I, but with so many new people in the county these days it's a bit muddly. Ordinarily I'm sure Aunt Akky would love to see you. She adores visitors. But this morning she's awfully upset and says she won't talk to anybody but policemen.'

'I am a policeman.'

'Really? How very peculiar. You are sure,' Dulcie added, 'that you are not just pretending to be one in order to find out about the Mardian Morris and all that?'

'Quite sure. Here's my card.'

'Goodness! Well, I'll ask Aunt Akky.'

As she forgot to shut the door Alleyn heard the conversation. 'It's a man who says he's a policeman, Aunt Akky, and here's his card. He's a gent.'

'I won't stomach these filthy 'breviations.'

'Sorry, Aunt Akky.'

''Any case you're talkin' rot. Show him in.'

So Alleyn was admitted and found her staring at his card.

'Morning to yer,' said Dame Alice. 'Sit down.'

He did so.

'This is a pretty kettle-of-fish,' she said. 'Ain't it?'

'Awful.'

'What are you, may I ask? 'Tective?'

It wouldn't have surprised him much if she'd asked if he were a Bow Street Runner.

'Yes,' he said. 'A plain-clothes detective from Scotland Yard.'

'Superintendent?' she read, squinting at the card.

'That's it.'

'Ha! Are you goin' to be quick about this? Catch the feller?'

'I expect we shall.'

'What'd yer want to see me for?'

'To apologize for making a nuisance of myself, to say I hope you'll put up with us and to ask you, at the most, six questions.'

She looked at him steadily over the top of her glasses.

'Blaze away,' she said at last.

'You sat on the steps there, last night, during the performance?'

'Certainly.'

'What step exactly?'

'Top. Why?'

'The top. So you had a pretty good view. Dame Alice, could William Andersen, after the mock-killing, have left the courtyard without being seen?'

'No.'

'Not under cover of the last dance of the Five Sons?'

'No.'

'Not if he crawled out?'

'No.'

'As he lay there could he have been struck without your noticing?'

'No.'

'No?'

'No.'

'Could his body have been brought in and put behind the stone without the manœuvre attracting your attention?'

'No.'

'You're sure?'

'Yes.'

He looked at Dulcie, who hovered uncertainly near the door. 'You were with Dame Alice, Miss Mardian. Do you agree with what she says?'

'Oh yes,' Dulcie said a little vaguely, and added – 'rather!' with a misplaced show of enthusiasm.

'Was anyone else with you?'

'Sam,' Dulcie said in a hurry.

'Fat lot of good that is, Dulcie. She means the Rector, Sam Stayne, who's my great-nephew-in-law. Bit of a milksop.'

'Right. Thank you so much. We'll bother you as little as possible. It was kind of you to see me.'

Alleyn got up and made her a little bow. She held out her hand. 'Hope you find,' she said as he took it.

Dulcie, astonished, showed him out.

There were three chairs in the hall that looked as if they didn't belong there. They had rugs safety-pinned over them. Alleyn asked Dulcie if these were the chairs they had sat on and, learning that they were, got her startled permission to take one of them out again.

He put it on the top step, sat in it and surveyed the courtyard. He was conscious that Dame Alice, at the drawing-room window, surveyed him.

From here, he could see over the top of the dolmen to within about two feet of its base and between its standing legs. An upturned box stood on the horizontal stone and three others, which he could just see, on the ground beyond and behind it. The distance from the dolmen to the rear archway in the old semi-circular wall – the archway that had served as an entrance and exit for the performers – was perhaps twenty-five feet. The other openings into the courtyard were provided at the extremities of the old wall by two further archways that joined it to the house. Each of these was about twenty feet distant from the dolmen.

There was, on the air, a tang of dead fire and through the central archway at the back Alleyn could see a patch of seared earth, damp now, but bearing the scar of heat.

Fox, who with Carey, Thompson, Bailey and the policeman, was looking at the dolmen, glanced up at his chief.

'You have to come early,' he remarked, 'to get the good seats.'

Alleyn grinned, replaced his chair in the hall and picked up a crumpled piece of damp paper. It was one of last night's programmes. He read it through with interest, put it in his pocket and went down into the courtyard.

'It rained in the night, didn't it, Carey?'

'Mortal hard. Started soon after the fatality. I covered up the stone and place where he lay, but that was the best we could do.'

'And with a team of Morris men, if that's what you call them, galumphing like baby elephants over the terrain there wouldn't be much hope anyway. Let's have a look, shall we, Obby?'

The sergeant removed the inverted box from the top of the dolmen. Alleyn examined the surface of the stone.

'Visible prints where Ernie stood on it,' he said. 'Rubber soles. It had a thin coat of rime, I should think, at the time. Hallo! What's this, Carey?'

He pointed a long finger at a small darkness in the grain of the stone. 'Notice it? What is it?'

Before Carey could answer there was a vigorous tapping on the drawing-room window. Alleyn turned in time to see it being opened by Dulcie evidently under orders from her great-aunt, who, from within, leant forward in her chair, shouted: 'If you want to know what that is, it's blood,' and leant back again.

'How do you know?' Alleyn shouted in return. He had decided that his only hope with Dame Alice was to meet her on her own ground. 'What blood?'

'Goose's. One of mine. Head cut off yesterday afternoon and left on the stone.'

'Good lord!'

'You may well say so. Guess who did it.'

'Ernie?' Alleyn asked involuntarily.

'How d'yer know?'

'I guessed. Dame Alice, where's the body?'

'In the pot.'

'Damn!'

'Why?'

'It doesn't matter.'

'Shut the window, Dulcie.'

Before Dulcie had succeeded in doing so, they heard Dame Alice say: 'Ask that man to dinner. He's got brains.'

'You've made a hit, Mr Alleyn,' said Fox.

Carey said: 'My oath!'

'Did you know about this decapitated bird?'

'First I heard of it. It'll be one of that gang up on the hill there.'

'Near the bulls?' Fox asked sombrely.

'That's right. You want to watch them geese, Mr Fox,' the sergeant said, 'they so savage as lions and tricksy as snakes. I've been minded myself, off and on this morning, to slaughter one and all.'

'I wonder,' Alleyn said, 'if it *was* Ernie. Get a shot of the whole dolmen, will you, Thompson, and some details of the top surface.'

Sergeant Thompson moved in with his camera and Alleyn walked round to the far side of the dolmen.

'What,' he asked, 'are these black stains all over the place? Tar?'

'That's right, sir,' Obby said, 'off of old "Crack's" skirts.'

Carey explained. 'Good lord!' Alleyn said mildly and turned to the area behind the dolmen.

The upturned boxes that they had used to cover the ground here were bigger. Alleyn and Fox lifted them carefully and stood away from the exposed area. It was a shallow depression into which had collected a certain amount of the fine gravel that had originally been spread over the courtyard. The depression lay at right angles to the dolmen. It was six feet long and shelved up to the level of the surrounding area. At the farthest end of the dolmen there was a dark viscous patch, about four inches in diameter, overlying a little drift of gravel. A further patch, larger, lay about a foot from it, nearer the dolmen and still in the hollow.

'You know, Carey,' Alleyn said under his breath and out of the sergeant's hearing, 'he should never have been moved: never.'

Carey, scarlet-faced, said loudly: 'I know's well as the next man, sir, the remains didn't ought to have been shifted. But shifted they were before us chaps could raise a finger to stop it. Parson comes in and says, "it's not decent as it is," and, with 'is own hands, Mr Ralph assisting, takes off mask and lays out the pieces tidy-like while Obby, here, and I were still ordering back the crowd.'

'You were here too, Sergeant?'

'Oh, ya-as, Mr Alleyn. All through.'

'And seeing, in a manner of speaking, the damage was done and rain setting in, we put the remains into his own car, which is an old station wagon. Simmy-Dick and Mr Stayne gave us a hand. We took them back to the forge. They're in his lean-to coach-house, Mr Alleyn, locked up proper with a police seal on the door and the only other constable in five mile on duty beside it.'

'Yes, yes,' Alleyn said. 'All right. Now, tell me, Carey, you did actually see how it was before the parson tidied things up, didn't you?'

'I did, then, and not likely to forget it.'

'Good. How was it?'

Carey drew the back of his hand across his mouth and looked hard at the shallow depression. 'I reckon,' he said, 'those two patches show pretty clear. One's blood from head and t'other's blood from trunk.'

Fox was squatting above them with a rule in his hands. 'Twenty-three inches apart,' he said.

'How was the body lying?' Alleyn asked. 'Exactly.'

'Kind of cramped up and on its left side, sir. Huddled. Knees to chin.'

'And the head?'

'That was what was so ghasshley,' Carey burst out. 'T'other way round.'

'Do you mean the crown of the head and not the neck was towards the trunk?'

'Just so, Mr Alleyn. Still tied up in that there bag thing with the face on it.'

'I reckoned,' Sergeant Obby ventured, 'that it must of been kind of disarranged in the course of the proceedings.'

'By the dancers?'

'I reckoned so, sir. Must have been.'

'In the final dance, after the mock beheading, did the Five Sons go behind the stone?'

There was silence. The superintendent and the sergeant eyed each other.

'I don't believe they did, you know, Sarge,' Carey said.

'Put it that way, no more don't I, then.'

'But the other two. The man-woman and the Hobby Horse?'

'They were every which-way,' Carey said.

Alleyn muttered: 'If they'd come round here they could hardly fail to see what was lying there. What colour were his clothes?'

'Whitish, mostly. And they reckon they *did* see them.'

'There you are,' Fox said.

'Well, Thompson, get on with it. Cover the area again. When he's finished we'll take specimens of the stains, Fox. In the meantime, what's outside the wall there?'

Carey took him through the rear archway. 'They waited out here before the performance started,' he said.

It was a bleak enough spot, now: an open field that ran up to a ragged spinney and the crest of the hill. On the higher slopes the snow still lay pretty thick but down near the wall it had melted and, to one side of the archway, there was the great scar left by the bonfire. It ran out from the circular trace of the fire itself in a blackened streak about fourteen feet long.

'And here?' Alleyn said, pointing his stick at a partially burnt out drum, lying on its side in the fire-scar. 'We have the tar barrel?'

'That's so, Mr Aleyn. For "Crack".'

'Looks as if it caught fire.'

'Reckon it might have got overturned when all the skylarking was going on between Mr Ralph and Ernie. They ran through here. There was a mighty great blaze sprung up about them. The fire might have spread to it.'

'Wouldn't the idea be to keep the fire as an extra attraction, though?'

'Maybe they lit it early for warmth? One of them may have got excited-like and poured tar on it.'

'Ernie, for instance,' Alleyn said patiently, and Carey replied that it was very likely.

'And this?' Alleyn went on. 'Look at this, Carey.'

Round the burnt-out scar left by the bonfire lay a fringe of green brushwood that had escaped complete destruction. A little inside it, discoloured and deadened by the heat, its wooden handle a mere blackened stump, was a steel blade about eighteen inches long.

'That's a slasher,' Alleyn said.

III

'That's Copse Forge,' Carey said. 'Stood there a matter of four hundred year and the smith's been an Andersen for as long as can be reckoned.'

'Not so profitable,' Fox suggested, 'nowadays, would it be?'

'Nothing like. Although he gets all the shoeing for the Mardian and adjacent hunts and any other smith's job for miles around. Chris has got a mechanic's ticket and does a bit with cars. A big oil company's offered to back them if they convert to a service station. I believe Simmy-Dick Begg's very anxious to run it. The boys like the idea but the Guiser wouldn't have it at any price. There's a main road to be put through too.'

'Do they all work here?' Alleyn asked. 'Surely not?'

'No, no. Dan, the eldest, and the twins, Andy and Nat, are on their own. Farming. Chris and Ernie work at the forge. Hallo, that's Dr Otterly's car. I axed him to be here and the five boys beside. Mr Ralph and Simmy-Dick Begg are coming up to the pub at two. If that suits, of course.'

Alleyn said it did. As they drew up, Dr Otterly got out of his car and waited for them. His tweed hat was pulled down over his nose and his hands were thrust deep in the pockets of his covert-coat.

He didn't wait to be introduced but came up and looked in at the window of their car.

'Morning,' he said. 'Glad you've managed to get here. Morning, Carey. Expect you are, too.'

'We're damn' pleased to see *you*,' Alleyn rejoined. 'It's not every day you get police officers and a medical man to give what almost amounts to eye-witness's evidence of a capital crime.'

'There's great virtue in that "almost", however,' Dr Otterly said, and added: 'I suppose you want to have a look at him.'

'Please.'

'Want me to come?'

'I think so. Don't you, Carey?'

They went through the smithy. There was no fire that morning and no heat in the place. It smelt of cold iron and stale horse-sweat. Carey led the way out by a back door into a yard. Here stood a small ramshackle cottage, and, alongside it, the lean-to coach-house.

'He lived in the cottage, did he?' Alleyn asked.

'Chris and Ern keep there. The old chap slept in a little room off the smithy. They all ate in the cottage, however.'

'They're in there now,' Dr Otterly said, 'waiting.'

'Good,' Alleyn said. 'They won't have to wait much longer. Will you open up, Carey?'

With some evidence of gratification, Carey broke the seal he had put on the double-doors of the coach-house and opened them wide enough to make an entry.

It was a dark place filled with every imaginable kind of junk but a space had been cleared in the middle and an improvised bier made up from boxes and an old door covered by a horsecloth.

A clean sheet had been laid over the Guiser. When Dr Otterly turned this down it was a shock, after the conventional decency of the arrangements to see an old dead man in the dirty dress of a clown. For collar there was a ragged blood-stained and slashed frill, and this had been pulled up to hide the neck. The face was smudged with black on the nose, forehead, cheek-bones and chin.

'That's burnt cork,' Dr Otterly said. 'From inside his mask, you know. Ernie had put it on over his black makeup when he thought he was going to dance the Fool.'

The Guiser's face under these disfigurements was void of expression. The eyes had been closed, but the mouth gaped. The old hands, chopped and furrowed, were crossed heavily over the breastbone. The tunic was patched with bloodstains. And above the Guiser, slung on wooden pins, were the shells of his fellow mummers: 'Crack', the Hobby Horse, was there. Its hinged jaw had dropped as if in burlesque of the head below it. The harness dangled over its flat drum-shaped carcass, which was propped against the wall. Nearby, hung the enormous crinoline of the Betty, and, above it, as if they belonged to each other, the Guiser's bag-like and dolorous mask, hanging upside down by its strings. It was stained darkly round the strings and also at the other end, at the apex of the scalp. This interested Alleyn immensely. Lower down, caught up on a nail, was the rabbit-cap. Farther away hung the clothes and sets of bells belonging to the Five Sons.

From the doorway, where he had elected to remain, Carey said: 'We thought best to lock all their gear in here, Mr Alleyn. The swords are in that sacking there, on the bench.'

'Good,' Alleyn said.

He glanced up at Fox. 'All right,' he said, and Fox, using his great hands very delicately, turned down the rag of the frilling from the severed neck.

'One swipe,' Dr Otterly's voice said.

'From slightly to the right of front centre to slightly left of back centre, would you say?' Alleyn asked.

'I would.' Dr Otterly sounded surprised. 'I suppose you chaps get to know about things.'

'I'm glad to say that this sort of thing doesn't come even our way very often. The blow must have fallen above the frill on his tunic and below the strings that tied the bag-mask. Would you say he'd been upright or prone when it happened?'

'Your Home Office man will know better than I about that. If it was done standing I'd say it was by somebody who was just slightly taller than the poor old Guiser.'

'Yes. Was there anybody like that in the team?'

'No. They're all much taller.'

'And there you are. Let's have a look at that whiffler, Fox.'

Fox came back with Ernie's sword, holding it by the red cord that was threaded through the tip. 'You can see the stains left by all that green stuff,' he said. 'And sharp! You'd be astounded.'

'We'd better put Bailey on it for dabs though I don't fancy there's much future there. What do you think, Dr Otterly? Could this be the weapon?'

'Without closer examination of the wound, I wouldn't like to say. It would depend – but no,' Dr Otterly said, 'I can't give an opinion.'

Alleyn had turned away and was looking at the garments hanging on the wall. 'Tar over everything. On the Betty's skirt, the Sons' trousers and I suppose on a good many village maidens' stockings and shoes to say nothing of their coats.'

'It's a cult,' Dr Otterly said.

'Fertility rite?'

'Of course.'

'See old Uncle T. Frazer and all,' Alleyn muttered. He turned to the rabbit. 'Recently killed and gutted with head left on. Strings on it. What for?'

'He wore it on his head.'

'How very undelicious. Why?'

'Helped the decapitation effect. He put his head through the lock of swords, untied the strings and, as the Sons drew the swords, he let the rabbit's head drop. They do it in the Grenoside sword dance too, I believe. It's quite startling – the effect.'

'I dare say. In this case, rather overshadowed by the subsequent event,' Alleyn said drily.

'All right!' Dr Otterly ejaculated with some violence. 'I know it's beastly. All right.'

Alleyn glanced at him and then turned to look at 'Crack's' harness. 'This must weigh a tidy lump. How does he wear it?'

'The head is on a sort of rod. His own head is inside the canvas neck. It was made in the smithy.'

'The century before last?'

'Or before that. The body too. It hangs from the yoke. His head goes through a hole into the canvas tube, which has got a sort of window in it. "Crack's" head is on top again and joined to the yoke by the flexible rod inside the neck. By torchlight it looks quite a thing.'

'I believe you,' Alleyn said absently. He examined the harness and then turned to the Betty's crinoline. 'How does this go on? It's a mountain of a garment.'

'It hangs from a kind of yoke, too. But in this case, the arms are free. The frame, as you see, is made of withies like basket-work. In the old days there used to be quite a lot of fairly robust fun with the Betty. The chap who was acting her would chase some smaller fellow round the ring and pop the crinoline thing right over him and go prancing off with the little chap hidden under his petticoats as it were. You can imagine the sort of barracking that went on.'

'Heaps of broad bucolic fun,' Alleyn said, 'was doubtless had by all. It's got a touch of the tarbrush, too, but not much.'

'I expect Ralph kept clear of "Crack" as well as he could.'

'And the Guiser?' Alleyn returned to the bier and removed the sheet completely.

'A little tar on the front of the tunic and – ' He stooped. 'Quite a lot on the hands,' he said. 'Did he handle the tar barrel, do you know?'

'Earlier in the day perhaps. But no. He was out of action, earlier. Does it matter?'

'It might,' Alleyn said, it might matter very much indeed. Then again not. Have you noticed this fairly recent gash across the palm of his right hand?'

'I saw it done.' Dr Otterly's gaze travelled to the whiffler which Fox still held by the ribbons. He looked away quickly.

'With that thing,' Alleyn asked, 'by any chance?'

'Actually, yes.'

'How did it happen?'

'It was nothing, really. A bit of a dust-up about it being too sharp. He – ah – he tried to grab it away from – well from – '

'Don't tell me,' Alleyn said. 'Ernie.'

IV

The shutters were down over the Private Bar and the room was deserted. Camilla went in and sat by the fire. Since last night she had felt the cold. It was as if some of her own natural warmth had deserted her. When the landlord had driven her and Trixie back to the pub from Mardian Castle, Camilla shivered so violently that they gave her a scalding toddy and two aspirins and Trixie put three stone hot-jugs in her bed. Eventually, she had dropped into a doze and was running away again from 'Crack'. He was the big drum in a band. Somebody beat him with two swords making a sound like a fiddle. His jaws snapped, dreadfully close. She experienced the dream of frustrated escape. His breath was hot on her neck and her feet were leaden. Then there was Ralph with his arms strapped close about her, saying: 'It's all right. I'll take care of you.' That was heaven at first, but even that wasn't quite satisfactory because Ralph was trying to stop her looking at something. In the over-distinct voice of nightmare, he said: 'You don't want to watch Ernie because it's not most awfully nice.' But Ernie jumped up on the dolmen and shouted at the top of his voice: 'What price blood for the stone?' Then all the Morris bells began to jingle like an alarm clock and she woke.

Awake, she remembered how Ralph had, in fact, run to where she and Trixie stood and had told them to go to the car at once. That was after Ernie had fainted and Dame Alice had made her announcement. The landlord, Tom Plowman, had gone up to the stone and had been ordered away by Dr Otterly and Superintendent Carey. He drove the girls back to the pub and, on the way, told them in great detail what he had seen. He was very excited and pleased with himself for having looked behind the stone. In one of her dreams during the night, Camilla thought he made her look too.

Now she sat by the fire and tried to get a little order into her thoughts. It was her grandfather who had been murdered, dreadfully and mysteriously, and it was her uncle who had exulted and collapsed. She herself, therefore, must be said to be involved. She felt as if she was marooned and deserted. For the first time since the event she was inclined to cry.

The door opened and she turned, her hand over her mouth. 'Ralph!' she said.

He came to her quickly and dragged up a chair so that he could sit and hold both her hands.

'You want me now, Camilla,' he said. 'Don't you?'

CHAPTER 6

Copse Forge

Ralph had big hands. When they closed like twin shells over Camilla's, her own felt imprisoned and fluttery like birds.

She looked at his eyes and hair, which were black, at his face, which was lean and at his ears, which were protuberant and, at that moment, scarlet. 'I am in love with Ralph,' thought Camilla.

She said: 'Hallo, you. I thought we'd agreed not to meet again. After last Sunday.'

'Thing of the past,' Ralph said grandly.

'You promised your father.'

'I've told him I consider myself free. Under the circs.'

'Ralph,' Camilla said, 'you mustn't cash in on murder.'

'Is that a very kind thing to say?'

'Perhaps it's not. I don't mean I'm not glad to see you – but – well, you know.'

'Look,' he said, 'there are one or two things I've got to know. Important things. I've *got* to know them, Camilla. The first is: are you *terribly* upset about last night? Well, of course you are, but so much upset, I mean, that one just mustn't bother you about anything. Or are you – oh, God, Camilla, I've never so much as kissed you and I do love you so much.'

'Do you? No, never mind. About your first question: I just don't know *how* I feel about Grandfather and that's a fact. As far as it's a personal thing – well, I scarcely even knew him ten days ago. But, since I got here, we've seen quite a lot of each other and – this is what you may find hard to believe – we kind of clicked, Grandfather and I.'

Ralph said on an odd inflexion: 'You certainly did that,' and then looked as if he wished he hadn't.

Camilla, frowning with concentration, unconsciously laced her fingers through his.

'You, of course,' she said, 'just think of him as a bucolic character. The Old Guiser. Wonderful old boy in his way. Not many left. Didn't have much truck with soap and water. Half *me* felt like that about him: the Campion half. Smelly old cup of tea, it thought. But then I'd see my mother look out of his eyes.'

'Of course,' he said. 'I know.'

'Do you? You can't quite know, dear Ralph. You're all of a piece: half Mardian, half Stayne. I'm an alloy.'

'You're a terrible old inverted snob,' he said fondly, but she paid no attention to this.

'But as for sorrow – personal grief,' she was saying, 'no. No. *Not* exactly that. It doesn't arise. It's the awful *grotesquerie* that's so night-marish. It's like something out of Webster or Marlowe: horror-plus. It gives one the horrors to think of it.'

'So you know what happened. Exactly, I mean?'

She made a movement of her head indicating the landlord. 'He saw. He told us: Trixie and me.'

She felt a stillness in his hands: almost as if he would draw them away, but he didn't do that. 'The whole thing!' she exclaimed. 'It's so outlandish and sickening and ghastly. The way he was dressed and everything. And then one feels such pity.'

'He couldn't have known anything about it.'

'Are you sure? How can you tell?'

'Dr Otterly says so.'

'And then – worst of all, unthinkably worst – the – what it was – the crime. You see, I can't use the word.'

'Yes,' Ralph said. 'There's that.'

Camilla looked at him with panic in her eyes. 'The boys!' she said. 'They couldn't. Any of them. Could they?' He didn't answer, and she cried out: 'I know what you're thinking. You're thinking about Ernie and – what he's like. You're remembering what I told you about the dog. And what you said happened with his sword? Aren't you?'

'All right,' Ralph said. 'I am. No, darling. Wait a bit. Suppose, just suppose it *is* that. It would be quite dreadful and Ernie would have to go through a very bad time and probably spend several years in a criminal lunatic asylum. But there'd be no question of anything worse than that happening to him. It's perfectly obvious, if you'll excuse me, darling, that old Ernie's only about fifteen and fourpence in the pound.'

'Well, I dare say it is,' Camilla said, looking very white. 'But to do that!'

'Look,' he said, 'I'm going on to my next question. Please, answer it.'

'I can guess – '

'All right. Wait a bit. I've told you I love you. You said you were not sure how you felt and wanted to get away and think about it. Fair enough. I respected that and I'd have held off and not waited for you on Sunday if it hadn't been for seeing you in church and – well, you know.'

'Yes, well, we disposed of that, didn't we?'

'You were marvellously understanding. I thought everything was going my way. But then you started up *this* business. Antediluvian hooey! Because you're what you choose to call an "alloy" you say it wouldn't do for us to marry. Did you, by any chance, come down here to see your mother's people with the idea of facing up to that side of it?'

'Yes,' Camilla said, 'I did.'

'You wanted to glower out of the smithy at the county riding by.'

'In effect. Though it's not the most attractive way of putting it.'

'Do you love me, blast you?'

'Yes,' Camilla said wildly. 'I do. So shut up.'

'Not bloody likely! Camilla, how marvellous! How frightfully, *frightfully* nice of you to love me. I can't get over it,' said Ralph who, from emotion and rapture, had also turned white.

'But I stick to my point,' she said. 'What's your great-aunt going to say? What's your father going to think? Ralph, can you look me in the eye and tell me they wouldn't mind?'

'If I look you in the eye I shall kiss you.'

'Ah! You see? You can't. And now – now when this has happened! There'll be the most ghastly publicity, won't there? What about that? What sort of fiancée am I going to be to a rising young county solicitor? Can you see the headlines? "History Repeats Itself!"

"Mother ran away from Smithy to marry Baronet!" "Granddaughter of murdered Blacksmith weds Peer's Grandson!" "Fertility Rite Leads to Engagement" Perhaps – perhaps – "Niece of – " What are you doing?'

Ralph had got up and, with an air of determination, was buttoning his mackintosh. 'I'm going,' he said, 'to send a telegraph to Auntie Times. Engagement announced between –'

'You're going to do nothing of the sort.' They glared at each other. 'Oh!' Camilla exclaimed, flapping her hands at him, 'what *am* I going to do with you? And how *can* I feel so happy?'

She made an exasperated noise and bolted into his arms.

Alleyn walked in upon this scene and with an apologetic ejaculation hurriedly walked out again.

Neither Ralph nor Camilla was aware either of his entry or of his withdrawal.

II

When they had left Bailey and Thompson to deal with certain aspects of technical routine in the old coach-house, Alleyn and Fox, taking Carey and Dr Otterly with them, had interviewed the Guiser's five sons.

They had found them crammed together in a tiny kitchen-living-room in the cottage next door to the coach-house. It was a dark room, its two predominant features being an immense iron range and a table covered with a plush cloth. Seated round this table in attitudes that were somehow on too large a scale for their environment, were the five Andersen sons: Daniel, Andrew, Nathaniel, Christopher and Ernest.

Dr Otterly had knocked and gone in, and the others had followed him. Dan had risen, the others merely scraped their chair legs and settled back again. Carey introduced them.

Alleyn was greatly struck by the close family resemblance among the Andersens. Even the twins were scarcely more like to each other than to the other three brothers. They were all big, sandy, blue-eyed men with fresh colour in their cheeks: heavy and powerful men whose muscles bulged hard under their countrymen's clothing. Dan's eyes were red and his hands not perfectly steady. Andy sat with raised brows as if in a state of guarded astonishment. Nat looked bashful and Chris angry. Ernie kept a little apart from his brothers. A faint, foolish smile was on his mouth and he grimaced; not broadly, but with a portentous air as if he was possessed of some hidden advantage.

Alleyn and Fox were given a chair at the table. Carey and Dr Otterly sat on a horsehair sofa against the wall and were thus a little removed from the central party.

Alleyn said: 'I'm sorry to have to worry you when you've already had to take so much, but I'm sure that you'll all want the circumstances of your father's death to be cleared up as quickly as possible.'

They made cautious sounds with their throats. He waited, and presently Dan said: 'Goes without saying, sir. We want to get to the bottom of this. We'm kind of addleheaded and over-set, one way and t'other, and can't seem to take to *any* notion.'

'Look at it how you like,' Andy said, 'it's fair fantastical.'

There was a strong smell of stale tobacco smoke in the room. Alleyn threw his pouch and a packet of cigarettes on the table. 'Let's take our pipes to it,' he said. 'Help yourselves.'

After a proper show of deprecation they did so: Ernie alone preferred a cigarette and rolled his own. He grimaced over the job, working his mouth and eyebrows. While they were still busy with their pipes and tobacco, Alleyn began to talk to them.

'Before we can even begin to help,' he said, 'we'll have to get as clear an account of yesterday's happenings as all of you can give us. Now, Superintendent Carey has already talked to you and he's given me a damn' good report on what was said. I just want to take up one or two of his points and see if we can carry them a bit further. Let's go back, shall we, to yesterday evening. About half an hour before the Dance of the Five Sons was due to start. All right?'

They were lighting their pipes now. They looked up at him guardedly and waited.

'I understand,' Alleyn went on, 'that would be about half past eight. The performers were already at Mardian Castle with the exception of Mr William Andersen himself and his youngest son, Mr Ernest Andersen. That right?'

Silence. Then Dan, who looked like becoming the spokesman, said: 'Right enough.'

'Mr William Andersen – may I for distinction use the name by which I'm told he was universally known – the Guiser? That means "The Mummer", doesn't it?'

'Literally,' Dr Otterly said from the sofa, 'it means "The Disguised One".'

'Lord, yes! Of course. Well, the Guiser, at half past eight, was still down here at the forge. And Mr Ernest Andersen was either here, too, or shortly to return here, because he was to drive his father up to the castle. Stop me if I go wrong.'

Silence.

'Good. The Guiser was resting in a room that opens off the smithy itself. When did he go there, if you please?'

'I can answer that one,' Dr Otterly said. 'I looked in at midday to see how he was and he wasn't feeling too good. I told him that, if he wanted to appear at all, he'd have to take the day off – I said I'd come back later on and have another look at him. Unfortunately, I got called out on an urgent case and found myself running late. I dined at the castle and it doesn't do to be late there. I'd had a word with the boys about the Guiser and arranged to have a look at him when he arrived and – '

'Yes,' Alleyn said. 'Thank you so much. Can we just take it from there. So he rested all day in his room. Any of you go and see how he was getting on?'

'Not us!' Chris said. 'He wouldn't have nobody anigh him when he was laying-by. Told us all to keep off.'

'So you went up to the castle without seeing him?'

Dan said: 'I knocked on the door and says "We're off then," and "hoping to see you later," and Dad sings out "Send Ern back at half-past. I'll be there." So we all went up along and Ern drove back at half past like he'd said.'

'Right.' Alleyn turned to Ernie and found him leaning back in his chair with his cigarette in his mouth and his hands clasped behind his neck. There was something so strained in this attitude that it suggested a kind of clumsy affectation. 'Now, will you tell us just what happened when you came back for your father?'

'A-a-a-aw!' Ernie drawled, without looking at him. 'I dunno. Nuthin.'

'Naow, naow, naow!' counselled his brothers anxiously.

'Was he still in his room?'

'Reckon so. Must of been,' Ernie said and laughed.

'Did you speak to him?'

'Not me.'

'What did you do?'

Nat said: 'Ernie seen the message – '

'Wait a bit,' Alleyn said. 'I think we'll have it from him, if we may. What did you do, Ernie? What happened? You went into the forge, did you – and what?'

'He'd no call,' Ernie shouted astonishingly without changing his posture or shifting his gaze, 'he'd no call to treat me like 'e done. Old sod.'

'Answer what you're axed, you damned young fool,' Chris burst out, 'and don't talk silly.' The brothers all began to tell Alleyn that Ernie didn't mean what he said.

Alleyn held up his hand and they stopped. 'Tell me what happened,' he said to Ernie. 'You went into the forge and what did you see?'

'Ar?' He turned his head and looked briefly at Alleyn. 'Like Nat says. I seen the message pinned to his door.'

Alleyn drew from his coat pocket the copper-plate billhead with its pencilled message. It had been mounted between two sheets of glass by Bailey. He said: 'Look at this, will you? Is this the message?'

Ernie took it in his hand and gave a great laugh. Fox took it away from him.

'What did you do then?' Alleyn asked.

'Me? Like what it says. "Young Ern," that's me, "will have to." There was his things hanging up ready: mask, clothes and old rabbity cap. So I puts 'em on; quick.'

'Were you already dressed as the whiffling son?'

'Didn't matter. I put 'em on over. Quiet like. 'Case he heard and changed his mind. Out and away, quick. Into old bus and up the road. *Whee-ee-ee!*' Ernie gave a small boy's illustration of excessive speed. 'I bet I looked right clever. I was the Fool I was. Driving fast to the dance. Whee-ee-ee!'

Dan suddenly buried his face in his hands. ''Tain't decent,' he said.

Alleyn took them through the scene after Ernie's arrival. They said they had passed round the note and then sent it in to Dr Otterly by Dan's young son, Bill, who was then dressed and black-faced in his role as understudy. Dr Otterly came out. The brothers added some last-minute instructions to the boy. When the clock struck nine, Dr Otterly went into the courtyard with his fiddle. It was at that moment they all heard Mrs Bünz's car hooting and labouring up the drive. As they waited for their entrance music, the car appeared round the outer curve of the old wall with the Guiser rampant in the passenger's seat. Dr Otterly heard the subsequent rumpus and went back to see what had happened.

It appeared that, during the late afternoon, the Guiser had fallen deeply asleep and had woken refreshed and fighting fit, only to hear his son driving away without him. Speechless with rage, he had been obliged to accept a hitch-hike from his enemy, Mrs Bünz.

'He was jibbering when he got to us,' Otterly said, 'and pretty well incoherent. He grabbed Ernie and began hauling his Fool's clothes off him.'

'And how,' Alleyn said to Ernie, 'did you enjoy that?'

Ernie, to the evident perturbation of his brothers, flew into a retrospective rage. As far as Alleyn could make out, he had attempted to defy his father but had been hurriedly quelled by his brothers.

'Ern didn't want to whiffle,' Dan said and they all confirmed this eagerly. Ernie had refused to dance if he couldn't dance the Fool. Simon Begg had finally prevailed on him.

'I done it for the Wing-Commander and not for another soul. He axed me and I done it. I went out and whiffled.'

From here, what they had to tell followed without addition the account Alleyn had already heard from Carey. None of the five sons had, at any stage of their performance, gone behind the dolmen to the spot where their father lay hidden. They were all positive the Guiser could neither have left the courtyard nor returned to it, alive or dead. They were equally and mulishly positive that no act of violence could have been done upon him during the period begun by his mock fall and terminated by the discovery of his decapitated body. They stuck to this, loudly repeating their argument and banging down their great palms on the table. It was impossible.

'I take it,' said Mr Fox during a pause, 'that we don't believe in fairies.' He looked mildly round the table.

'Not at the bottom of this garden, anyway,' Alleyn muttered.

'My Dad did, then,' Ernie shouted.

'Did what?' Alleyn asked patiently.

'Believe in fairies.'

Fox sighed heavily and made a note.

'Did he,' Alleyn continued, 'believe in sacrifices too?'

The Guiser's five sons fidgeted and said nothing.

'The old idea,' Alleyn said. 'I may have got it wrong but in the earliest times, didn't they sacrifice something – a bird, wasn't it – on some of these old stones? At certain times of the year?'

After a further and protracted silence, Dr Otterly said: 'No doubt they did.'

'I take it that this Morris dance – cum-sword-dance-cum-mumming play – forgive me if I've got the terms muddled – is a survival of some such practice?'

'Yes, yes, of course,' Dr Otterly said impatiently, and yet with the air of a man whose hobby horse is at the mounting-block. 'Immeasurably the richest survival we have.'

'Really? The ritual death of the Fool is the old mystery of sacrifice, isn't it, with the promise of renewal behind it?'

'Exactly.'

'And, at one time, there would have been actual bloodshed? Or well might have been?'

To this there was no answer.

'Who,' Alleyn asked, 'killed Dame Alice's goose yesterday afternoon and put it on the dolmen?'

Through the pipe-smoke that now hung thick over the table he looked round the circle of reddened faces. 'Ernie,' he said. 'Was it you?'

A slow grin stretched Ernie's mouth until he looked remarkably like a bucolic Fool himself.

'I whiffled 'un,' he said.

III

As Ernie was not concerned to extend this statement and returned very foolish answers to any further questions, Alleyn was obliged to listen to his brothers who were eager in explanation.

Throughout yesterday morning, they said, while they erected the torches and prepared the bonfire, they had suffered a number of painful and determined assaults from Dame Alice's geese. One male, in particular, repeatedly placing himself in the van, had come hissing down upon them. Damaging stabs and sidelong slashes had been administered, particularly upon Ernie, who had greatly resented them. He had been sent up again in the afternoon with the gardener's slasher which he had himself sharpened, and had been told to cut down the brambles on the dancing area. In the dusk, the gander had made a final assault and an extremely painful one. Irked beyond endurance, Ernie had swiped at him with the slasher. When they arrived in the evening the brothers were confronted with the corpse and taken to task by Miss Mardian. Subsequently, they had got the whole story out of Ernie. He now listened to their recital with a maddening air of complacency.

'Do you agree that is what happened?' Alleyn asked him and he clasped his hands behind his head, rocked to and fro and chuckled. 'That's right,' he said. 'I whiffled 'im proper.'

'Why did you leave the bird on the dolmen?'

Ernie said conceitedly: 'You foreign chaps wouldn't rightly catch on. I know what for I done it.'

'Was it blood for the stone?'

He ducked his head low between his shoulders and looked sideways at Alleyn. 'Happen it was, then. And happen 'twasn't enough, however.'

'Wanted more?' Alleyn asked and mentally crossed his thumbs.

'Wanted and got it, then.'

('Naow, naow, naow!')

Ernie unclasped his hands and brought them down on the table. He gripped the edge so hard that the table quivered. 'His own fault,' he gabbled, 'and not a soul else's. Blood axes for blood and always will. I told him. Look what he done on me, Sunday. Murdered my dog, he did, murdered my dog on me when my back was turned. What he done Sunday come home on him Wednesday, and not a soul to answer for it but himself. Bloody murderer, he was, and paid in his own coin.'

Chris Anderson reached out and gripped his brother's arm. 'Shut your mouth,' he said.

Dan said: 'You won't stop him that fashion. Take thought for yourself, Ernie. You're not right smart in the head, boy. Your silly ways is well known: no blame to you if you're not so clear-minded as the rest of us. Keep quiet then or, in your foolishness, you'll bring shame on the family.' His brothers broke into a confused chorus of approval.

Alleyn listened, hoping to glean something from the general rumpus, but the brothers merely reiterated their views with increased volume, no variation, and little sense.

Ernie suddenly jabbed his forefinger at Chris. 'You can't talk, Chrissie,' he roared. 'What about what happened yesterday? What about what you said you'd give 'im if he crossed you over you know – what – '

There was an immediate uproar. Chris and his three elder brothers shouted in unison and banged their fists down on the table.

Alleyn stood up. This unexpected movement brought about an instant quiet.

'I'm sorry, men,' he said, 'but from the way things are shaping there can be no point in my keeping you round this table. You will stay either here or hereabouts, if you please, and we shall in due course see each of you alone. Your father's body will be taken to the nearest mortuary for an examination which will be made by the Home Office pathologist. As soon as we can allow the funeral to take place you will be told all about it. There will, of course, be an inquest which you'll be asked to attend. If you think it wise to do so, you may be legally represented, individually or as a family.' He stopped, looked at each of them in turn and then said: 'I'm going to do something that is unorthodox. Before I do so, however, I warn you that to conspire – that is, to act together and in collaboration for the purpose of withholding vital evidence in a case of murder – can be an extremely serious offence. I may be wrong, but I believe there is some such intention in your minds. You will do well to give it up. Now. Before more harm can come of it.'

He waited but they said nothing.

'All right,' said Alleyn, 'we'll get on with it.' He turned to Ernie. 'Last night, after your father's body had been found, I'm told you leapt on the stone where earlier in the day you had put the dead gander. I'm told you pointed your sword at the German lady who was standing not very far away and you said, "Ask her. She's the one that did it." Did you do this?'

A half smile touched Ernie's mouth, but he said nothing. 'Did you?' Alleyn insisted.

'Ernie took a queer turn,' Andy said. 'He can't rightly remember after his turns.'

'Let him answer for himself. Did you do this, Ernie?'

'I might and I might not. If they say so, I might of.'

'Do you think the German lady killed your father?'

'*Course* she didn't,' Chris said angrily. 'She couldn't.'

'I asked Ernie if he thought she did.'

'*I* dunno,' Ernie muttered and laughed.

'Very well then,' Alleyn said and decided suddenly to treat them to a rich helping of ham. 'Here, in the presence of you all – you five sons of a murdered father – I ask you, Ernest Andersen, if you cut off that father's head.'

Ernie looked at Alleyn, blinked and opened his mouth: but whether to speak or horridly to laugh again would never be known. A shadow had fallen across the little room. A voice from the doorway said:

'I'd keep my mouth shut on that one if I were you, Corp.'

It was Simon Begg.

IV

He came forward easily. His eyes were bright as if he enjoyed the effect he had made. His manner was very quietly tough.

'Sorry if I intrude,' Simon said, 'I'm on my way to the pub to be grilled by the cops and thought I'd look in. But perhaps you *are* the cops. Are you?'

'I'm afraid so,' Alleyn said. 'And you, I think, must be Mr Simon Begg.'

'He's my Wing-Commander, he is,' Ernie cut in. 'We was in the same crowd, him and me.'

'OK, boy, OK,' Simon said and, passing round the table, put his hand on Ernie's shoulder. 'You talk such a lot,' he said good-naturedly. 'Keep your great trap shut, Corp, and you'll come to no harm.' He cuffed

Ernie lightly over the head and looked brightly at Alleyn. 'The Corp,' he said, 'is just a great big baby: not quite with us, shall we say. Maybe you like them that way. Anything I can do for you?'

Alleyn said: 'If you'll go ahead we'll be glad to see you at the Green Man. Or – can we give you a lift?'

'Thanks, I've got my heap out there.'

'We'll be hard on your heels, then.'

Begg went through the motion of whistling.

'Don't wait for me,' he said, 'I'll follow you.'

'No,' Alleyn said very coolly, 'you won't. You'll go straight on, if you please.'

'Is that an order or a threat, Mr – I'm afraid I don't know your rank.'

'We're not allowed to threaten. My rank couldn't matter less. Off you go.'

Simon looked at him, raised his eyebrows, said, with a light laugh, 'Well, *really*!' and walked out. They heard him start up his engine. Alleyn briefly surveyed the brothers Andersen.

'You chaps,' he said, 'had better reconsider your position a bit. Obviously you've talked things over. Now, you'd do well to think them over and jolly carefully at that. In the meantime, if any of you feel like making a sensible statement about this business, I'll be glad to hear what it is.' He moved to the door, where he was joined by Fox and Carey.

'By the way,' he said, 'we shall have to find out the terms of your father's will, if he made one.'

Dan, a picture of misery and indecision, scratched his head and gazed at Alleyn.

Andy burst out: 'We was right fond of the old man. Stood together, us did, father and sons, so firm as a rock.'

'A united family?'

'So we was, then,' Nat protested. Chris added: 'And so we are.'

'I believe you,' Alleyn said.

'As for his will,' Dan went on with great simplicity, 'we can't tell you, sir, what we don't know our own selves. Maybe he made one and maybe not.'

Carey said: 'You haven't taken a look round the place at all, then?'

Andy turned on him. 'It's our father what's been done to death, Mr Carey. It's his body laying out there, not as an old man's did ought – peaceful and proper – but ghassly as a sacrifice and crying aloud for – for – ' He looked round wildly, saw his youngest brothers, hesitated and then broke down completely.

' – for justice?' Alleyn said. 'Were you going to say?'

'He's beyond earthly justice,' Nat put in. 'Face to face with his Maker and no doubt proud to be there.'

Superintendent Carey said: 'I did hear tell he was up to Biddlefast on Tuesday to see lawyer Stayne.'

'So he was, then, but none of us knows why,' Chris rejoined.

'Well,' Alleyn said, 'we'll be off. I'm very sorry but I'm afraid we'll have to leave somebody here. Whoever it is will, I'm sure, be as considerate as possible. You see, we may have to poke back into the past. I can fully understand,' he went on, talking directly to Andy, 'how you feel about your father's death. It's been – of course it has – an appalling shock. But you will, no doubt, have a hunt round for any papers or instructions he may have left. I can get an expert search made or, if you'd rather, just leave an officer here to look on. In case something turns up that may be of use to us. We really do want to make it as easy for you as we can.'

They took this without much show of interest. 'There'll be cash, no doubt,' Dan said. 'He was a great old one for putting away bits of cash. Proper old jackdaw, us used to call him.' He caught back his breath harshly.

Alleyn said: 'I'm sorry it has to be like this.' Dan was the one nearest to him. 'He's an elderly chap himself,' Alleyn thought, and touched him lightly on the shoulder. 'Sorry,' he repeated and looked at Fox and Carey. 'Shall we move on?'

'Do you want me again?' Dr Otterly asked.

'If I can just have a word with you.'

They all went out through the forge. Alleyn paused and looked round.

'What a place for a search. The collection of generations. There's the door, Fox, where Ernie says the note was pinned. And his room's beyond that.'

He went down a narrow pathway between two heaped-up benches of litter and opened the door in the end wall. Beyond it was a tiny room with a bed that had been pulled together rather than made and gave clear evidence of use. The room was heaped up with boxes, piles of old newspapers and all kinds of junk. A small table had evidently served as a desk and bore a number of account books, files and the Guiser's old-fashioned copper-plate bills. 'In Dr to W. Andersen, Blacksmith, Copse Forge, South Mardian.' A pencil lay across a folded pile of blotting paper.

'Hard lead,' Alleyn said to Fox, who stood in the doorway. 'The message was written with a hard point. Wonder if the paper lay here. Let's have a look.'

He held the blotting paper to the light and then took out his pocket lens. 'Yes,' he grunted, 'it's there all right. A faint trace but it could be brought out. It's the trace of the note we've already got, my hearties. We'll put Bailey and Thompson on to this lot. Hallo!'

He had picked up a sheet of paper. Across it, in blue indelible pencil, was written 'Wednesday, W. Andersen. Kindly sharpen my slasher at once if not all ready done do it yourself mind and return by bearer to avoid further trouble as urgently require and oblige JNO McGlashan. PS – I will have none but yourself on this job.'

'Carey!' Alleyn called out, and the superintendent looked up behind Fox. 'Who's J. N. O. McGlashan? Here, take a look at this. Will this be the slasher in question?'

'That'll be the one surely,' Carey agreed. 'McGlashan's the gardener up along.'

'It was written yesterday. Who would the bearer be?'

'His boy, no doubt.'

'Didn't they tell us Ernie sharpened the slasher? And took it up late yesterday afternoon? And whiffled the goose's head off with it?'

'That's right, sir. That's what they said.'

'So the boy, if the boy was the bearer, was sent empty away.'

'Must of been.'

'And the slasher comes to a sticky end in the bonfire. Now, all of this,' Alleyn said, rubbing his nose, 'is hellish intriguing.'

'Is it?' Fox asked stolidly.

'My dear old chap, of course it is. Nip back to the coach-house and tell Bailey and Thompson to move in here as soon as they're ready and do their stuff.' Fox went sedately off and Alleyn shut the door of the bedroom behind him. 'We'll have this room sealed,

Carey. And will you check up on the slasher story? Find out who spoke to the boy. And, Carey, I'll leave you in charge down here for the time being. Do you mind?'

Superintendent Carey, slightly bewildered by this mode of approach, said that he didn't.

'Right. Come on.'

He led the way outside where Dr Otterly waited in his car.

Carey, hanging off and on, said: 'Will I seal the room now, sir? Or what?'

'Let the flash and dabs chaps in first. Fox is fixing them. Listen as inconspicuously as you can to the elder Andersen boy's general conversation. How old is Dan, by the way? Sixty, do you say?'

'Turned sixty, I reckon.'

'And Ernie?'

'He came far in the rear which may account for him being not right smart.'

'He's smart enough,' Alleyn muttered, 'in a way. Believe me, he's only dumb nor'-nor' west, and yesterday, I fancy, the wind was in the south.'

'It shifted in the night,' Carey said and stared at him. 'Look, Mr Alleyn,' he burst out, 'I can't help but ask. Do you reckon Ernie Andersen's our chap?'

'My dear man, I don't know. I think his brothers are determined to stop him talking. So's this man Begg, by the way. I would cheerfully have knocked Begg's grinning head off his shoulders. Sorry! Unfortunate phrase. But I believe Ernie was going to give me a straight answer, one way or the other.'

'Suppose,' Carey said, 'Ernie lost his temper with the old chap, and gave a kind of swipe, or suppose he was just fooling with that murderous sharp whiffler of his and – and – well, without us noticing while the Guiser was laying doggo behind the stone – Ar, hell!'

'Yes,' Alleyn said grimly, 'and it'll turn out that the only time Ernie might have waltzed behind the stone was the time when young Stayne pinched his sword. And what about the state of the sword, Carey? Nobody had time to clean it and restain it with green sap, had they? And, my dear man, what about blood? Blood, Carey, which reminds me we are keeping the doctor waiting. Leave Bailey and Thompson here while you arrange with Obby or that PC by the castle gates to take your place when you want to get off. I'll bring extra men in if we need them. I'll leave you the car and ask Dr Otterly to take us up to the pub. OK?'

'OK, Mr Alleyn. I'll be up along later then?'

'Right. Here's Fox. Come on Foxkin. Otterly, will you give us a lift?'

Carey turned back into the forge and Alleyn and Fox got into Dr Otterly's car.

Dr Otterly said: 'Look here, Alleyn, before we go on I want to ask you something.'

'I bet I know what it is. Do we or do we not include you on our list of suspects?'

'Exactly so,' Otterly said rather stiffly. 'After all, one would prefer to know. Um?'

'Of course. Well, at the moment, unless you can explain how you fiddled unceasingly in full view of a Superintendent of Police, a P.C, a Dame of the British Empire, a parson and about fifty other witnesses during the whole of the period when this job must have been done and, at the same time, *did* it, you don't look to be a likely starter.'

'Thank you,' said Dr Otterly.

'On the other hand, you look to be a damn' good witness. Did you watch the dancers throughout?'

'Never took my eyes off 'em. A conscientious fiddler doesn't.'

'Wonderful. Don't let's drive up for a moment, shall we? Tell me this. Would you swear that it was in fact the Guiser who danced the rôle of Fool?'

Dr Otterly stared at him. 'Good lord, of course it was! I thought you understood. I'd gone out to start proceedings, I heard the rumpus, I went back and found him lugging his clothes off Ernie. I had a look at him, not a proper medical look, because he wouldn't let me, and I told him if he worked himself up any more he'd probably crock up anyway. So he calmed down, put on the Fool's clothes and the bag-mask, and, when he was ready, I went out. Ernie followed and did his whiffling. I could see the others waiting to come on. The old man appeared last, certainly, but I could see him just beyond the gate, watching the others. He'd taken his mask off and only put it on at the last moment.'

'Nobody, at any stage, could have taken his place?'

'Utterly impossible,' Otterly said impatiently.

'At no time could he have gone off-stage and swapped with somebody?'

'Lord, lord, lord, how many more times! *No!*'

'All right. So he danced and lay down behind the stone. You fiddled and watched and fiddled and watched. Stayne and Ernie fooled and Stayne collared Ernie's sword. Begg, as the Hobby Horse, retired. These three throughout the show were all over the place and dodged in and out of the rear archway. Do you know exactly when and for how long any of them was out of sight?'

'I do not. I doubt if they do. Begg dodged out after his first appearance when he chivvied the girls, you know. It's damn' heavy, that gear he wears, and he took the chance, during the first sword dance, to get the weight off his shoulders. He came back before they made the lock. He had another let-up after the "death". Ralph Stayne was all over the shop. In and out. So was Ernie during their interlude.'

'Right. And at some stage Stayne returned the sword to Ernie. Dan did a solo. The Sons danced and then came the dénouement. Right?'

'It hasn't altered,' Dr Otterly said drily, 'since the last time you asked.'

'It's got to alter some time, somehow,' Fox observed unexpectedly.

'Would you also swear,' Alleyn said, 'that at no time did either Ernie or Ralph Stayne prance round behind the stone and make one great swipe with the sword that might have done the job?'

'I know damn' well neither of them did.'

'Yes? Why?'

'Because, my dear man, as I've told you, I never took my eyes off them. I knew the old chap was lying there. I'd have thought it a bloody dangerous thing to do.'

'Is there still another reason why it didn't happen that way?'

'Isn't it obvious that there is?'

'Yes,' Alleyn said, 'I'd have thought it was. If anybody had killed him in that way he'd have been smothered in blood?'

'Exactly.'

'But, all the same, Otterly, there could be one explanation that would cover that difficulty.'

Dr Otterly slewed round in his seat and stared at Alleyn. 'Yes,' he said. 'Yes, you're right. I'd thought of it, of course. But I'd still swear that neither of them did.'

'All the same it is, essentially, I'm sure, the explanation nearest to the truth.'

'And, in the meantime,' Mr Fox observed, 'we still go on believing in fairies.'

CHAPTER 7

The Green Man

Before they set off for the Green Man, Alleyn asked Dr Otterly if he could arrange for the Guiser's accommodation in a suitable mortuary.

'Curtis, the Home Office man, will do the PM,' Alleyn said, 'but he's two hundred odd miles away across country and, the last time I heard of him, he was held up on a tricky case. I don't know how or when he'll contrive to get here.'

'Biddlefast would offer the best facilities. It's twenty miles away. We've a cottage hospital at Yowford where we could fix him up straight away – after a fashion.'

'Do, will you? Things are very unsatisfactory as they are. Can we get a mortuary van or an ambulance?'

'The latter. I'll fix it up.'

'Look,' Alleyn said, 'I want you to do something else, if you will. I'm going, now, to talk to Simon Begg, young Stayne, the German lady and the Guiser's granddaughter who, I hear, is staying at the pub. Will you sit in on the interviews? Will you tell me if you think anything they may say is contrary to the facts as you observed them? Will you do that, Otterly?'

Dr Otterly stared at the dripping landscape and whistled softly through his teeth. 'I don't know,' he said at last.

'Don't you? Tell me, if this is deliberate homicide, do you want the man run in?'

'I suppose so.' He pulled out his pipe and opened the door to knock it out on the running-board. When he reappeared he was very red in the face. 'I may as well tell you,' he said, 'that I disapprove strongly and vehemently of the McNaughton Rules and would never voluntarily bring anybody who was a border-line case under their control.'

'And you look upon Ernie Andersen as such a case.'

'I do. He's an epileptic. *Petit mal.* Very rare attacks but he had one, last night, after he saw what had happened to his father. I won't fence with you but I tell you that, if I thought Ernie Andersen stood any chance of being hanged for the murder of his father, I wouldn't utter a syllable that might lead to his arrest.'

'What would you do?'

'Bully a couple of brother-medicos into certifying him and have him put away.'

Alleyn said: 'Why don't you chaps get together and make a solid medical front against the McNaughton Rules? But, never mind that now. Perhaps if I tell you exactly what I'm looking for in this case, you'll feel more inclined to sit in. Mind you, I may be looking for something that doesn't exist. The theory, if it can be graced with the title, is based on such slender evidence that it comes jolly close to being guesswork and, when you find a cop guessing you kick him in the pants. Still, here, for what it's worth, is the line of country.'

Dr Otterly stuffed his pipe, lit it, threw his head back and listened. When Alleyn had finished, he said: 'By God, I wonder!' and then: 'All right. I'll sit in.'

'Good. Shall we set about it?'

It was half past twelve when they reached the pub. Simon and Ralph were eating a snack at the bar. Mrs Bünz and Camilla sat at a table before the parlour fire, faced with a meal that Camilla, for her part, had been quite unable to contemplate with equanimity. Alleyn and Fox went to their private room where they found that cold meat and hot vegetables awaited them. Dr Otterly returned from the telephone to say he had arranged for the ambulance to go to Copse Forge and for his partner to take surgery alone during the early part of the afternoon.

While they ate their meal, Alleyn asked Dr Otterly to tell him something of the history of the Dance of the Five Sons.

'Like most people who aren't actively interested in folklore, I'm afraid I'm inclined to associate it with flushed ladies imperfectly braced for violent exercise and bearded gentlemen dressed like the glorious Fourth of June gone elfin. A philistine's conception, I'm sure.'

'Yes,' Dr Otterly said, 'it is. You're confusing the "sports" with the true generic strain. If you're really interested, ask the German lady. Even if you don't ask, she'll probably tell you.'

'Couldn't you give me a succinct résumé? Just about this particular dance?'

'Of course I could. I don't want any encouragement, I assure you, to mount on my hobby horse. And there, by the way, you are! Have you thought how many everyday phrases derive from the folk drama? Mounting one's hobby-horse! Horseplay! Playing the fool! Cutting capers! Midsummer madness! Very possibly "horn mad", though I recognize the more generally known application. This pub, the Green Man, gets its name from a variant of the Fool, the Robin Hood, the Jack-in-the-Green.'

'What does the whole concept of the ritual dance go back to? Frazer's King of the Sacred Grove?'

'Certainly. And the Dionysian play about the Titans who killed their old man.'

'Fertility rite-cum-sacrifice-death-and-resurrection?'

'That's it. It's the oldest manifestation of the urge to survive and the belief in redemption through sacrifice and resurrection. It's as full of disjointed symbolism as a surrealist's dream.'

'Maypoles, corn-babies, ladles – all that?'

'Exactly. And, being a folk manifestation, the whole thing changes all the time. It's full of cross-references. The images overlap and the characters swap roles. In the few places in England where it survives in its traditional form, you get, as it were, different bits of the kaleidoscopic pattern. The lock of the swords here, the rabbitcap there, the blackened faces somewhere else. Horns at Abbots Bromley, Old Hoss in Kent and Old Tup in Yorkshire. But always, however much debased and fragmentary, the central idea of the death and resurrection of the Fool who is also the Father, Initiate, Medicine Man, Scapegoat and King. At its lowest, a few scraps of half-remembered jargon. At its highest – '

'Not – by any chance – Lear?'

'My dear fellow,' Dr Otterly cried, and actually seized Alleyn by the hand, 'you don't mean to say you've spotted that! My dear fellow, I really am *delighted* with you. You must let me bore you again and at greater length. I realize now is *not* the time for it. No. No, we must confine ourselves for the moment to the Five Sons.'

'You're far from boring me but I'm afraid we must. Surely,' Alleyn said, 'this particular dance-drama is unusually rich? Doesn't it present a remarkable number of elements?'

'I should damn' well say it does. Much the richest example we have left in England and, luckily for us, right off the beaten track. Generally speaking, traditional dancing and mumming (such of it as survives) follows the line of the original Danish occupation but here we're miles off it.'

'The spelling of the Andersen name, though?'

'Ah! There you are! In my opinion, they're a Danish family who, for some reason, drifted across to this part of the world and brought their Winter Solstice ritual with them. Of course, the trade of smith has always been particularly closely associated with folklore.'

'And, originally, there was an actual sacrifice?'

'Of some sort, I have no doubt.'

'Human?'

Dr Otterly said: 'Possibly.'

'This lock, or knot, of swords, now. Five swords, you'd expect it to be six.'

'So it is everywhere else that I know of. Another element that makes the Five Sons unique.'

'How do they form it?'

'While they dance. They've got two methods. The combination of a cross interwoven with an A or a sort of monogram of an X and an H. Both of them take quite a bit of doing.'

'And Ernie's was as sharp as hell.'

'Absolutely illicit, but it was.'

'I wonder,' Alleyn said, 'if Ernie expected this particular Old Man to resurrect.'

Dr Otterly laid down his knife and fork. '*After* what happened?' He gave a half laugh. 'I wouldn't be surprised.'

'What's their attitude to the dance? All of them? Why do they go on with it, year after year?'

Dr Otterly hesitated. 'Come to that, Doctor,' Fox said, 'why do you?'

'Me? I suppose I'm a bit of a crank about it. I've got theories. Anyway, I enjoy fiddling. My father, and his before him and his before that have been doctors at Yowford and the two Mardians and we've all fiddled. Before that, we were yeomen and before that tenant farmers. One in the family has always been a fiddler. I try not to be cranky. The Guiser was a bigger crank in his way than I. I can't tell you *why* he was so keen. He just inherited the Five Sons habit. It runs in his blood like poaching does in Old Moley Moon's up to Yowford Bridge or hunting in Dame Alice Mardian's, or doctoring, if you like, in mine.'

'Do you think any of the Andersens pay much attention to the ritualistic side of the thing? Do you think they believe, for instance, that anything tangible comes of the performance?'

'Ah, now! You're asking me just how superstitious they are, you know.' Dr Otterly placed the heels of his well-kept hands against the edge of his plate and delicately pushed it away. 'Hasn't every one of us,' he asked, 'a little familiar shame-faced superstition?'

'I dare say,' Alleyn agreed. 'Cosseted but reluctantly acknowledged. Like the bastard sons of Shakespearian papas.'

'Exactly. I know, *I've* got a little Edmund. As a man of science, I scorn it, as a countryman I give it a kind of heart service. It's a particularly ridiculous notion for a medical man to harbour.'

'Are we to hear what it is?'

'If you like. I always feel it's unlucky to see blood. Not, may I hasten to say, to see it in the course of my professional work, but fortuitously. Someone scratches a finger in my presence, say, or my own nose bleeds. Before I can stop myself I think: "Hallo. Trouble coming." No doubt it throws back to some childish experience. I don't let it affect me in the slightest. I don't believe it. I merely get an emotional reflex. It's – ' He stopped short. 'How very odd,' he said.

'Are you reminded that the Guiser cut his hand on Ernie's sword during your final practice?'

'I was, yes.'

'Your hunch wasn't so far wrong that time,' Alleyn observed. 'But what are the Andersens' superstitious reflexes? Concerning the Five Sons?'

'I should say pretty well undefined. A feeling that it would be unlucky not to do the dance. A feeling, strong perhaps in the Guiser, that, in doing it, something is placated, some rhythm kept ticking over.'

'And in Ernie?'

Dr Otterly looked vexed. 'Any number of crackpot notions, no doubt,' he said shortly.

'Like the headless goose on the dolmen?'

'I am persuaded,' Dr Otterly said, 'that he killed the goose accidentally and in a temper and put in on the dolmen as an afterthought.'

'Blood, as he so tediously insists, for the stone?'

'If you like. Dame Alice was furious. She's always been very kind to Ernie, but this time – '

'He's killed the goose,' Fox suggested blandly, 'that lays the golden eggs?'

'You're in a bloody whimsical mood, aren't you?' Alleyn inquired idly, and then, after a long silence: 'What a very disagreeable case this is, to be sure. We'd better get on with it, I suppose.'

'Do you mind,' Dr Otterly ventured, 'my asking if you two are typical CID officers?'

'I am,' Alleyn said. 'Fox is a sport.'

Fox collected their plates, stacked all the crockery neatly on a tray and carried it out into the passage where he was heard to say: 'A very pleasant meal, thank you, Miss. We've done nicely.'

'Tell me,' Alleyn asked. 'Is the Guiser's granddaughter about eighteen with dark reddish hair cut short and very long fingers? Dressed in black ski-ing trousers and a red sweater?'

'I really can't tell you about the fingers, but the other part's right. Charming child. Going to be an actress.'

'And is young Stayne about six feet? Dark. Long back. Donegal tweed jacket with a red fleck and brown corduroy bags?'

'That's right, I think. He's got a scar on his cheekbone.'

'I couldn't see his face,' Alleyn said. 'Or hers.'

'Oh?' Dr Otterly murmured. 'Really?'

'What's her name?'

'Camilla Campion.'

'Pretty,' Alleyn said absently. 'Nice name.'

"Isn't it?'

'Her mum was the Guiser's daughter, was she?'

'That's right.'

'There's a chap,' Alleyn ruminated, 'called Camillo Campion, who's an authority on Italian primitives. Baronet. Sir Camillo.'

'Her father. Twenty years ago, his car broke an axle coming too fast down Dame Alice's drive. He stopped at Copse Forge, saw Bess Andersen, who was a lovely creature, fell like a plummet and married her.'

'Lor'!' said Fox mildly, returning from the passage. 'Sudden!'

'She had to run away. The Guiser wouldn't hear of it. He was an inverted snob and a bigoted Nonconformist, and, worst of all, Campion's a Roman Catholic. '

'I thought I remembered some story of that kind,' Alleyn said. 'Had he been staying at Mardian Castle?'

'Yes. Dame Alice was livid because she'd made up her mind he was to marry Dulcie. Indeed, I rather fancy there was an unofficial engagement. She never forgave him and the Guiser never forgave Bess. She died five years ago. Campion and Camilla brought her back here to be buried. The Guiser didn't say a word to them. The boys, I imagine, didn't dare. Camilla was thirteen and like enough to her mama at that age to give the old man a pretty sharp jolt.'

'So he ignored her?'

'That's right. We didn't see her again for five years, and then the other day she turned up, determined to make friends with her mother's people. She managed to get round him. She's a dear child, in my opinion.'

'Let's have her in,' said Alleyn.

II

When they had finished their lunch, of which Camilla ate next to nothing and Mrs Bünz, who normally had an enormous appetite, not much more, they sat *vis-à-vis* by the parlour fire and found very little to say to each other. Camilla was acutely conscious of Simon Begg and, in particular, of Ralph Stayne, consuming their counter lunches in the Public Bar. Camilla had dismissed Ralph with difficulty when Mrs Bünz came in. Now she was in a rose-coloured flutter only slightly modified by the recurrent horror of her grandfather's death. From time to time, gentle Camilla reproached herself with

heartlessness and as often as she attempted this pious exercise the
memory of Ralph's kisses made nonsense of her scruples.

In the midst of her preoccupations she noticed that Mrs Bünz was
much quieter than usual and seemed, in some indefinable way, to have
diminished in size. She noticed, too, that Mrs Bünz had a monstrous
cold, characterized by heavy catarrhal noises of a most irritating nature.
In addition to making these noises, Mrs Bünz sighed very often and
kept moving her shoulders uneasily as if her clothes prickled them.

Trixie came round occasionally from the Public Bar into the
Private. It was Trixie who had been entrusted by Alleyn with the
message that the police would be obliged if Mrs Bünz and Miss
Campion would keep the early afternoon free.

'Which was exactly the words he used,' Trixie said. 'A proper
gentleman if a policeman, and a fine deep voice, moreover, with a
powerful kind of smack in it.'

This was not altogether reassuring.

Mrs Bünz said unexpectedly: 'It is not pleasant to be told to await
the police. I do not care for policemen. My dear husband and I were
anti-Nazi. It is better to avoid such encounters.'

Camilla, seeing a look of profound anxiety in Mrs Bünz's eyes,
said: 'It's all right, Mrs Bünz. They're here to take care of us. That's
what we keep them for. Don't worry.'

'Ach!' Mrs Bünz said, 'you are a child. The police do not look after
anybody. They make investigations and arrests. They are not sympathetic. Dar,' she added, making one of her catarrhal noises.

It was upon this sombre note that Inspector Fox came in to say
that if Miss Campion had finished her luncheon Mr Alleyn would be
very pleased to have a word with her.

Camilla told herself it was ridiculous to feel nervous but she
continued to do so. She followed the enormous bulk of Mr Fox
down the narrow passage. Her throat became dry and her heart
thumped. 'Why?' she thought. 'What have I got to get flustered
about? This is ridiculous.'

Fox opened the door into the little sitting-room and said: 'Miss
Campion, Mr Alleyn.' He beamed at Camilla and stepped aside for
her. She walked in and was immeasurably relieved to find her friend
Dr Otterly. Beyond him, at the far side of a table, was a tall dark man
who stood up politely as she came in.

'Ah!' Dr Otterly said, 'here's Camilla.'

Alleyn came round the table and Camilla found herself offering him her hand as if they had been introduced at a party.

'I hope,' he said, 'you don't mind giving us a few minutes.'

'Yes,' murmured Camilla, 'I mean, no.'

Alleyn pushed forward a chair.

'Don't worry,' he said, 'it won't be as bad as all that, and Dr Otterly's here to see fair play. The watchword is "routine".'

Camilla sat down. Like a good drama student, she did it beautifully without looking at the chair. 'If I could pretend this was a mood-and-movement exercise,' she thought, 'I'd go into it with a good deal more poise.'

Alleyn said: 'We're checking the order of events before and during the Dance of the Five Sons. You were there, weren't you, for the whole time? Would you be very patient and give us an account of it? From your point of view.'

'Yes, of course. As well as I can. I don't expect I'll be terribly good.'

'Let's see, anyway,' he suggested comfortably. 'Now, here goes.'

Her account tallied in every respect with what he had already been told. Camilla found it easier than she would have expected and hadn't gone very far before she had decided with correct professional detachment that Alleyn had 'star quality'.

When she arrived at the point where Simon Begg as 'Crack', the hobby horse, did his improvisation, Camilla hesitated for the first time and turned rather pink.

'Ah, yes,' Alleyn said. 'That was the tar-baby thing after the first general entrance, wasn't it? What exactly *is* "Crack's" act with the tar?'

'It's all rather ham, I'm afraid,' Camilla said grandly. 'Folksey-hokum.' She turned a little pinker still and then said honestly: 'I expect it isn't really. I expect it's quite interesting but I didn't much relish it because he came thundering after me and, for some ridiculous reason, I got flustered.'

'I've seen the head. Enough to fluster anybody in that light, I should imagine.'

'It did me, anyway. And I wasn't all that anxious to have my best ski-ing trousers ruined. So I ran. It came roaring after me. I couldn't get away because of all the people. I felt kind of cornered and faced it. Its body swung up – it hangs from a frame, you know. I could see his legs: he was wearing lightish coloured trousers.'

'Was he?' Alleyn said with interest.

'Yes. Washed-out cords. Almost white. He always wears them. It *was* silly,' Camilla said, 'to be rattled. Do you know I actually yelled. Wasn't it shaming? In front of all those village oafs.' She checked herself. 'I don't mean that. I'm half village myself and I dare say that's why I yelled. Anyway I did.'

'And then?'

'Well,' Camilla said, half laughing, 'well then I kind of made a bee-line for the Betty and that was all right because it was Ralph Stayne, who's not at all frightening.'

'Good,' Alleyn said, smiling at her. 'And he coped with the situation, did he?'

'He was just the job. Masterful type: or he would have been if he hadn't looked so low comedy. Anyway, I took refuge in his bombasine bosom and "Crack" sort of sloped off.'

'Where to?'

'He went sort of cavorting and frisking out at the back and everybody laughed. Actually, Begg does get pretty well into the skin of that character,' Camilla said with owlish professionalism.

Alleyn led her through the rest of the evening and was told nothing that he hadn't already heard from Dr Otterly. It was oddly touching to see how Camilla's natural sprightliness faltered as she approached the moment of violence in her narrative. It seemed to Alleyn she was still so young that her spirit danced away from any but the most immediate and direct shock. 'She's vulnerable only to greenstick fracture of the emotion,' he thought. But, as they reached the point when her grandfather failed to reappear and terror came upon the five sons, Camilla turned pale and pressed her hands together between her knees.

'I didn't know in the slightest what had happened, of course. It was queer. One sort of felt there was something very much amiss and yet one didn't exactly know, one felt it. Even when Dan called them and they all went and looked – I – it was so silly, but I think I sort of wondered if he'd just gone away.'

'Ah!' Alleyn said quickly. 'So he could have gone away during the dance and you mightn't have noticed?'

Dr Otterly sighed ostentatiously.

'Well – no,' Camilla said. 'No, I'm sure he couldn't. It would have been quite impossible. I was standing right over on the far side and rather towards the back of the stage. About OP second entrance, if you know where that is.'

Alleyn said he did. 'So you actually could see behind the stone?'

'Sort of,' Camilla agreed and added in a worried voice:

'I must stop saying "sort of". Ralph says I do it all the time. Yes, I could see behind the stone.'

'You could see him lying there?'

She hesitated, frowning. 'I saw him crouch down after the end of the dance. He sat there for a moment, and then lay down. When he lay down, he – I mean I really couldn't see him. I expect that was the idea. He meant to hide. I think he must have been in a bit of a hollow. So I'd have noticed like anything if he'd got up.'

'Or, for the sake of argument, if anybody had offered him any kind of violence?'

'Good heavens, yes!' she said, as if he'd suggested the ridiculous. 'Of *course.*'

'What happened immediately after he sank out of sight? At the end of the dance?'

'They made a stage picture. The Sons had drawn their swords out of the lock. "Crack" stood behind the stone looking like a sort of idol. Ralph stood on the prompt side and the Sons separated. Two of them stood on one side, near me, and two on the other, and the fifth, the Whiffler – I knew afterwards it was Ernie – wandered away by himself. Ralph went round with the collecting thing and then Ralph snatched Ernie's sword away and they had a chase. Ralph's got rather a nice sense of comedy, actually. He quite stole the show. I remember "Crack" was behind the dolmen about then so he ought to be able to tell you if there was anything – anything – wrong – '

'Yes. What did he do while he was there?'

'Nothing. He just stood. Anyway,' Camilla said rapidly, 'he couldn't do anything much, could he, in that harness? Nothing – nothing that would – '

'No,' Alleyn said, 'he couldn't. What *did* he do, in fact?'

'Well, he sort of played up to Ralph and Ernie. He gave a kind of falsetto neigh, and he went off at the back.'

'Yes? And then?'

'Then Ralph pretended to hide. He crouched down behind a heap of rubble and he'd still got Ernie's sword. And Ernie went off-stage looking for him.'

'You're sure all this is in the right order?'

'I think so. One looked at it in terms of theatre,' said Camilla. 'So, of course, one wouldn't forget.'

'No,' Alleyn agreed with careful gravity, 'one wouldn't, would one. And then?'

'Then Uncle Dan did his solo and I rather think that was when the bonfire flared up.' She looked at Dr Otterly. 'Do you?'

'It was then. I was playing "Lord Mardian's Fancy," which is Dan's tune.'

'Yes. And Ralph came out of his hiding-place and went off at the back. He must have returned his sword to Ernie and walked round behind the wall because he came on at the O.P. entrance. I *call* it "O.P."'

'Precisely.'

'And I think, at about the same time, Ernie and "Crack" must have come back together through the centre entrance at the back.'

'And Ernie had got his sword?'

'Yes, he had. I remember thinking: "So Ralph's given him back his sword," and anyway, I'd noticed that Ralph hadn't got it any longer.'

Camilla had a very direct way of looking at people. She looked now straight at Alleyn and frowned a little. Then, a curious thing happened to her face. It turned ashen white without changing its expression. 'About the sword,' she said. 'About the sword – ?'

'Yes?'

'It wasn't – it couldn't have been – could it?'

'There's no saying,' Alleyn said gently, 'what the weapon was. We're just clearing the ground, you know.'

'But it couldn't. No. Nobody went near with the sword. I swear nobody went near. I swear.'

'Do you? Well, that's a very helpful thing for us to know.'

Dr Otterly said: 'I do, too, you know, Alleyn.'

Camilla threw a look of agonized gratitude at him and Alleyn thought: 'Has she already learnt at her drama school to express the maximum of any given emotion at any given time? Perhaps, but she hasn't learned to turn colour in six easy lessons. She was frightened, poor child, and now she's relieved and it's pretty clear to me she's fathoms deep in love with Master Stayne.'

He offered Camilla a cigarette and moved round behind her as he struck a match for it.

'Dr Otterly,' he said, 'I wonder if you'd be terribly kind and ring up Yowford about the arrangements there? I've only just thought of it, fool that I am. Fox will give you the details. Sorry to be such a bore.'

He winked atrociously at Dr Otterly, who opened his mouth and shut it again.

'There, now!' said Mr Fox, 'and I'd meant to remind you. 'T, 't, 't! Shall we fix it up, now, Doctor? No time like the present.'

'Come back,' Alleyn said, 'when it's all settled, won't you?'

Dr Otterly looked fixedly at him, smiled with constraint upon Camilla and suffered Mr Fox to shepherd him out of the room.

Alleyn sat down opposite Camilla and helped himself to a cigarette.

'All wrong on duty,' he said, 'but there aren't any witnesses. *You* won't write a complaint to the Yard, will you?'

'No,' Camilla said and added: 'Did you send them away on purpose?'

'How did you guess?' Alleyn asked admiringly.

'It had all the appearance of a piece of full-sized hokum.'

'Hell, how shaming! Never mind, I'll press on. I sent them away because I wanted to ask you a personal question and, having no witnesses makes it unofficial. I wanted to ask you if you were about to become engaged to be married.'

Camilla choked on her cigarette.

'Come on,' Alleyn said. 'Do tell me, like a nice comfortable child.'

'I don't know. Honestly, I don't.'

'Can't you make up your mind?'

'There's no reason that *I* can see,' Camilla said, with a belated show of spirit, 'why I should tell you anything at all about it.'

'Nor there is, if you'd rather not.'

'Why do you want to know?'

'It makes it easier to talk to people,' Alleyn said, 'if you know about their preoccupations. A threatened engagement is a major preoccupation, as you will allow and must admit.'

'All right,' Camilla said. 'I'll tell you. I'm not engaged but Ralph wants us to be.'

'And you? Come,' Alleyn said, answering the brilliant look she suddenly gave him. 'You're in love with him, aren't you?'

'It's not as easy as all that.'

'Isn't it?'

'You see, my mother was Bess Andersen. She was the feminine counterpart of Dan and Andy and Chris and Nat, and talked and thought like them. She was their sister. I loved my mother,' Camilla said fiercely, 'with all my heart. And my father, too. We should have been a happy family, and, in a way, we were, in our attachment for each other. But my mother wasn't really happy. All her life she was homesick for South Mardian and she never learned to fit in with my father's setting. People tell you differences of that sort don't matter any more. Not true. They matter like hell.'

'And that's the trouble?'

'That's it.'

'Anything more specific?'

'Look,' Camilla said, 'forgive my asking, but did you get on in the Force by sheer cheek or sheer charm or what?'

'Tell me your trouble,' Alleyn said, 'and I'll tell you my success story. Of course, there's your pride, isn't there?'

'All right. Yes. And there's also the certainty of the past being rehashed by the more loathsome daily newspapers in the light of this ghastly crime. I don't know,' Camilla burst out, 'how I can *think* of Ralph and I *am* thinking all the time of him, after what has happened.'

'But why shouldn't you think of him?'

'I've told you. Ralph's a South Mardian man. His mother was a Mardian. His aunt was jilted by my papa when he ran away with my mum. My Mardian relations are the Andersen boys. If Ralph married me, there'd be hell to pay. Every way there'd be hell. He's Dame Alice's heir, after his aunt, and, although I agree that doesn't matter so much – he's a solicitor and able to make his own way – she'd undoubtedly cut him off.'

'I wonder. Talking of wills, by the way, do you know if your grandfather made one?'

Camilla caught back her breath. 'Oh, God!' she whispered. 'I hope not. Oh, I *hope* not.'

Alleyn waited.

'He talked about it,' Camilla said, 'last time I saw him. Four days ago. We had a row about it.'

'If you'd rather not tell me, you needn't.'

'I said I wouldn't touch a penny of his money, ever, and that, if he left me any, I'd give it to the Actors' Benevolent Fund. That rocked him.'

'He'd spoken of leaving you something?'

'Yes. Sort of back-handedly. I didn't understand, at first. It was ghastly. As if I'd come here to – ugh! – to sort of worm my way into his good books. Too frightful it was.'

'The day before yesterday,' Alleyn said, watching her, 'he visited his solicitors in Biddlefast.'

'He *did?* Oh, my goodness me, how awful. Still, perhaps it was about something else.'

'The solicitors are Messrs Stayne and Stayne.'

'That's Ralph's office,' Camilla said instantly. 'How funny. Ralph didn't say anything about it.'

'Perhaps,' Alleyn suggested lightly, 'it was a secret.'

'What do you mean?' she said quickly.

'A professional secret.'

'I see.'

'Is Mr Ralph Stayne your own solicitor, Miss Campion?'

'Lord, no,' Camilla said. 'I haven't got one.'

The door opened and a dark young man, wearing a face of thunder, strode into the room.

He said in a magnificent voice: 'I consider it proper and appropriate for me to be present at any interviews Miss Campion may have with the police.'

'Do you?' Alleyn said mildly. 'In what capacity?'

'As her solicitor.'

'My poorest heavenly old booby!' Camilla ejaculated, and burst into peals of helpless laughter.

'Mr Ralph Stayne,' Alleyn said, 'I presume.'

III

The five Andersens, bunched together in their cold smithy, contemplated Sergeant Obby. Chris, the belligerent brother, slightly hitched his trousers and placed himself before the sergeant. They were big men and of equal height.

'Look yur,' Chris said, 'Bob Obby. Us chaps want to have a tell. Private.'

Without shifting his gaze, which was directed at some distant object above Chris's head, Obby very slightly shook his own. Chris reddened angrily and Dan intervened:

'No harm in that now, Bob: natural as the day, seeing what's happened.'

'You know us,' the gentle Andy urged. 'Soft as doves so long's we're easy-handled. Harmless.'

'But mortal set,' Nat added, 'on our own ways. That's us. Come on, now, Bob.'

Sergeant Obby pursed his lips and again shook his head.

Chris burst out: 'If you're afraid we'll break one of your paltry by-laws you can watch us through the bloody winder.'

'But out of earshot, in simple decency,' Nat pursued, 'for ten minutes you're axed to shift. Now!'

After a longish pause and from behind an expressionless face, Obby said: 'Can't be done, souls.'

Ernie broke into aimless laughter.

'Why, you damned fool,' Chris shouted at Obby, 'what's gone with you? D'you reckon one of us done it!'

'Not for me to say,' Obby primly rejoined, 'and I'm sure I hope you're all as innocent as new-born babes. But I got my duty which is to keep observation on the whole boiling of you guilty or not, as the case may be.'

'We got to talk PRIVATE!' Chris shouted. 'We got to.' Sergeant Obby produced his notebook.

'No got about it,' he said. 'Not in the view of the law.'

'To oblige, then?' Andy urged.

'The suggestion,' Obby said, 'is unworthy of you, Andrew.'

He opened his book and licked his pencil.

'What's that for?' Chris demanded.

Obby looked steadily at him and made a note.

'Get out!' Chris roared.

'That's a type of remark that does an innocent party no good,' Obby told him. 'Let alone a guilty.'

'What the hell d'you mean be that?'

'Ax yourself.'

'Are you trying to let on you reckon one of us is a guilty party? Come on. Are you?'

'Any such caper on my part would be dead against the regulations,' Obby said stuffily.

'Then why do you pick on me to take down in writing? What 'ave I done?'

'Only yourself and your Maker,' Obby remarked, 'knows the answer to that one.'

'And me,' Ernie announced unexpectedly. 'I know.'

Sergeant Obby became quite unnaturally still. The Andersens, too, seemed to be suspended in a sudden, fierce attentiveness. After a considerable pause, Obby said: 'What might you know, then, Ernest?'

'Ar-ar-ar! That'd be telling!'

'So it would,' Chris said shortly. 'So shut your big silly mouth and forget it.'

'No, you don't, Christopher,' Obby rejoined. 'If Ern's minded to pass a remark, he's at liberty to do so. Speak up, Ernest. What was you going to say? You don't,' Obby added hastily, 'have to talk, if you don't want to. I'm here to see fair play. What's on your mind, Ernest?'

Ernie dodged his head and looked slyly at his brothers. He began to laugh with the *grotesquerie* of his kind. He half shut his eyes and choked over his words. 'What price Sunday, then? What price Chrissie and the Guiser? What price you know who?'

He doubled himself up in an ecstasy of bucolic enjoyment. 'How's Trix?' he squeaked and gave a shrill cat-call. 'Poor old Chrissie.' He exulted.

Chris said savagely: 'Do you want the hide taken off you?'

'When's the wedding, then?' Ernie asked, dodging behind Andy. 'Nothing to hold you now, is there?'

'By God – !' Chris shouted and lunged forward. Andy laid his hands on Chris's chest.

'Steady, naow, Chris, boy, steady,' Andy begged him.

'And you, Ernie,' Dan added, 'you do like what Chris says and shut your mouth.' He turned to Obby. 'You know damn well what he's like. Silly as a sheep. You didn't ought to encourage him. 'Tain't neighbourly.'

Obby completed his notes and put up his book. He looked steadily from one of the Andersens to another. Finally, he addressed himself to them collectively.

'Neighbourliness,' he said, 'doesn't feature in this job. I don't say I like it that way, but that's the way it is. I don't say if I could get a transfer at this moment I wouldn't take it and pleased to do so. But I can't, and that being so, souls, here I stick according to orders.' He paused and buttoned his pocket over his notebook. 'Your dad,' he said, 'was a masterpiece. Put me up for the Lodge did your dad. Worth any two of you, if you'll overlook the bluntness. And, unpleasant though it may be to contemplate, whoever done him in, ghastly and brutal, deserves what he'll get. I said "whoever",' Sergeant Obby repeated with sledgehammer emphasis and let his gaze dwell in a leisurely manner, first on Ernest Andersen and then on Chris.

'All right. *All* right,' Dan said disgustedly. 'Us all knows you're a monument.'

Nat burst out: 'What d'you think *we* are, then? Don't you reckon we're all burning fiery hot to lay our hands on the bastard that done it? Doan't you!'

'Since you ax me,' Sergeant Obby said thoughtfully, 'no. Not all of you. No, I don't.'

IV

'I am not in the least embarrassed,' Ralph said angrily. 'You may need a solicitor, Camilla, and, if you do, you will undoubtedly consult me. My firm has acted for your family – ah – for many years.'

'There you are!' Alleyn said cheerfully. 'The point is, did your firm act for Miss Campion's family in the person of her grandfather, the day before yesterday?'

'That,' Ralph said grandly, 'is neither here nor there.'

'Look,' Camilla said, 'darling. I've told Mr Alleyn that grandfather intimated to me that he was thinking of leaving me some of his cash and that I said I wouldn't have it at any price.'

Ralph glared doubtfully at her. It seemed to Alleyn that Ralph was in that degree of love which demands of its victim some kind of emphatic action. 'He's suffering,' Alleyn thought, 'from ingrowing knight-errantry. And I fancy he's also very much worried about something.' He told Ralph that he wouldn't at this stage press for information about the Guiser's visit but that, if the investigation seemed to call for it, he could insist.

Ralph said that, apart from professional discretion and propriety, there was no reason at all why the object of the Guiser's visit should not be revealed and he proceeded to reveal it. The Guiser had called on Ralph, personally, and told him he wished to make a will. He had been rather strange in his manner, Ralph thought, and beat about the bush for some time.

'I gathered,' Ralph said to Camilla, 'that he felt he wanted to atone – although he certainly didn't put it like that – for his harshness to your mama. It was clear enough you had completely won his heart and I must say,' Ralph went on in a rapid burst of devotion, 'I wasn't surprised at that.'

'Thank you, Ralph,' said Camilla.

'He also told me,' Ralph continued, addressing himself with obvious difficulty to Alleyn, 'that he believed Miss Campion might refuse a bequest and it turned out that he wanted to know if there was some legal method of tying her up so that she would be obliged to accept it. Of course I told him there wasn't.' Here Ralph looked at Camilla and instantly abandoned Alleyn. 'I said – I knew, dar – I knew you would want me to – that it might be better for him to think it over and that, in any case, his sons had a greater claim, surely, and that you would never want to cut them out.'

'Darling, I'm terribly glad you said that.'

'Are you? I'm so glad.'

They gazed at each other with half smiles. Alleyn said: 'To interrupt for a moment your mutual rejoicing – ' and they both jumped slightly.

'Yes,' Ralph said rapidly. 'So then he told me to draft a will on those lines, all the same, and he'd have a look at it and then make up his mind. He also wanted some stipulation made about keeping Copse Forge on as a smithy and not converting it into a garage which the boys, egged on by Simon Begg, rather fancy. He asked me if I'd frame a letter that he could sign, putting it to Miss Campion – '

'Darling, I have *told* Mr Alleyn we're in love, only not engaged on account I've got scruples.'

'Camilla, darling! Putting it to her that she ought to accept for his ease of spirit, as it were, and for the sake of the late Mrs Elizabeth Campion's memory.'

'My mum,' Camilla said in explanation.

'And then he went. He proposed, by the way, to leave Copse Forge to his sons and everything else to Camilla.'

'Would there be much else?' Alleyn asked, remembering what Dan Andersen had told him. Camilla answered him almost in her uncle's words. 'All the Andersens are great ones for putting away. They used to call Grandfather an old jackdaw.'

'Did you, in fact, frame a draft on those lines?' Alleyn asked Ralph.

'No. It was only two days ago. I was a bit worried about the whole thing.'

'Sweetest Ralph, why didn't you ask *me?*'

'Darling *(a)* because you'd refused to see me at all and *(b)* because it would have been grossly unprofessional.'

'Fair enough,' said Camilla.

'But you already knew, of course,' Alleyn pointed out, 'that your grandfather was considering this step?'

'I told you. We had a row about it.'

'And you didn't know he'd gone to Biddlefast on Tuesday?'

'No,' she said, 'I didn't go down to the forge on Tuesday. I didn't know.'

'All right,' Alleyn said and got up. 'Now I want to have a word or two with your young man, if I'm allowed to call him that. There's no real reason why you should leave us, except that I seem to get rather less than two-fifths of his attention while you are anywhere within hail.' He walked to the door and opened it. 'If you see Inspector Fox and Dr Otterly,' he said, 'would you be very kind and ask them to come back?'

Camilla rose and walked beautifully to the door.

'Don't you want to discover Ralph's major preoccupation?' she asked and fluttered her eyelashes.

'It declares itself abundantly. Run along and render love's awakening. Or don't you have that one at your drama school?'

'How did you know I went to drama school?'

'I can't imagine. Star quality, or something.'

'What a heavenly remark!' she said.

He looked at Camilla. There she was; loving, beloved, full of the positivism of youth, immensely vulnerable, immensely resilient. 'Get along with you,' he said. No more than a passing awareness of something beyond her field of observation seemed to visit Camilla. For a moment she looked puzzled. 'Stick to your own preoccupation,' Alleyn advised her, and gently propelled her out of the room.

Fox and Dr Otterly appeared at the far end of the passage. They stood aside for Camilla who, with great charm, said: 'Please, I was to say you're wanted.'

She passed them. Dr Otterly gave her an amiable buffet. 'All right, Cordelia?' he asked. She smiled brilliantly at him. 'As well as can be expected, thank you,' said Camilla.

When they had rejoined Alleyn, Dr Otterly said: 'An infallible sign of old age is a growing inability to understand the toughness of the young. I mean toughness in the nicest sense,' he added, catching sight of Ralph.

'Camilla,' Ralph said, 'is quite fantastically sensitive.'

'My dear chap, no doubt. She is a perfectly enchanting girl in every possible respect. What I'm talking about is a purely physiological matter. Her perfectly enchanting little inside mechanisms react youthfully to shock. My old machine is in a different case. That's all, I assure you.'

Ralph thought to himself how unamusing old people were when they generalized about youth. 'Do you still want me, sir?' he asked Alleyn.

'Please. I want your second-to-second account of the Dance of the Five Sons. Fox will take notes and Dr Otterly will tell us afterwards whether your account tallies with his own impressions.'

'I see,' Ralph said, and looked sharply at Dr Otterly.

Alleyn led him along the now familiar train of events and at no point did his account differ from the others. He was able to elaborate a little. When the Guiser ducked down after the mock beheading, Ralph was quite close to him. He saw the old man stoop, squat and then ease himself cautiously down into the depression. 'There was nothing wrong with him,' Ralph said. 'He saw me and made a signal with his hand and I made an answering one, and then went off to take up the collection. He'd planned to lie in the hollow because he thought he would be out of sight there.'

'Was anybody else as close to him as you were?'

'Yes, "Crack" – Begg, you know. He was my opposite number just before the breaking of the knot. And after that he stood behind the dolmen for a bit and – ' Ralph stopped.

'Yes?'

'It's just that – no, really, it's nothing.'

'May I butt in?' Dr Otterly said quickly from the fireside. 'I think perhaps I know what Ralph is thinking. When we rehearsed, "Crack" and the Betty – Ralph – stood one on each side of the dolmen and then while Ralph took up the collection, "Crack" was meant to cavort round the edge of the crowd, repeating his girl-scaring act. He didn't do that last night. Did he, Ralph?'

'I don't think so,' Ralph said, and looked very disturbed. 'I don't, of course, know which way your mind's working, but the best thing we can do is to say that, wearing the harness he does, it'd be quite impossible for Begg to do – well, to do what must have been done. Wouldn't it, Dr Otterly?'

'Impossible. He can't so much as see his own hands. They're under the canvas body of the horse. Moreover, I was watching him and he stood quite still.'

'When did he move?'

'When Ralph stole Ernie Andersen's sword. Begg squeaked like a neighing filly and jogged out by the rear exit.'

'Was it in order for him to go off then?'

'Could be,' Ralph said. 'The whole of that part of the show's an improvisation. Begg probably thought Ernie's and my bit of fooling would do well enough for him to take time off. That harness is damned uncomfortable. Mine's bad enough.'

'You, yourself, went out through the back exit a little later, didn't you?'

'That's right,' Ralph agreed very readily. 'Ernie chased me, you know, and I hid. In full view of the audience. He went charging off by the back exit, hunting me. I thought to myself, Ernie *being* Ernie, that the joke had probably gone far enough, so I went out, too, to find him.'

'What *did* you find, out there? Behind the wall?'

'What you'd expect. "Crack" squatting there like a great clucky hen. Ernie looking absolutely furious. I gave him back his sword and he said – ' Ralph scratched his head.

'What did he say?'

'I think he said something about it being too late to be any use. He was pretty bloody-minded. I suppose it *was* rather a mistake to bait him but it went down well with the audience.'

'Did Begg say anything?'

'Yes. From inside "Crack". He said Ernie was a bit rattled and it'd be a good idea if I left him alone. I could see that for myself, so I went off round the outside wall and came through the archway by the house. Dan finished his solo. The Sons began their last dance. Ernie came back with his sword and "Crack" followed him.'

'Where to?'

'Just up at the back somewhere, I fancy. Behind the dancers.'

'And you, yourself? Did you go anywhere near the dolmen on your return?'

Ralph looked again at Dr Otterly and seemed to be undecided. 'I'm not sure,' he said. 'I don't really remember.'

'Do you remember, Dr Otterly?'

'I think,' Otterly said quietly, 'that Ralph did make a round trip during the dance. I suppose that would bring him fairly close to the stone.'

'Behind it?'

'Yes, behind it.'

Ralph said: 'I remember now. Damn' silly of me. Yes, I did a trip round.'

'Did you notice the Guiser lying in the hollow?'

Ralph lit himself a cigarette and looked at the tip. He said: 'I don't remember.'

'That's a pity.'

'Actually, at the time, I was thinking of something quite different.'

'Yes?'

'Yes. I'd caught sight of Camilla,' said Ralph simply.

'Where was she?'

'At the side and towards the back. The left side, as you faced the dancing arena. OP, she calls it.'

'By herself?'

'Yes, then.'

'But not earlier? Before she ran away from "Crack"?'

'No.' Ralph's face slowly flooded to a deep crimson. 'At least, I don't think so.'

'Of course she wasn't,' Dr Otterly said in some surprise. 'She came up with the party from this pub. I remember thinking what a picture the two girls made, standing there together in the torchlight.'

'The *two* girls?'

'Camilla was there with Trixie and her father.'

'Was she?' Alleyn asked Ralph.

'I – ah – I – yes, I believe she was.'

'Mr Stayne,' Alleyn said, 'you will think my next question impertinent and you may refuse to answer it. Miss Campion has been very frank about your friendship. She has told me that you are fond of each other but that, because of her mother's marriage and her own background, in its relation to yours, she feels an engagement would be a mistake.'

'Which is most utter and besotted bilge,' Ralph said hotly. 'Good God, what age does she think she's living in! Who the hell cares if her mum was a blacksmith's daughter?'

'Perhaps she does.'

'I never heard such a farrago of unbridled snobbism.'

'All right. I dare say not. You said, just now, I think, that Miss Campion had refused to see you. Does that mean you haven't spoken to each other since you've been in South Mardian?'

'I really fail to understand – '

'I'm sure you don't. See here, now. Here's an old man with his head off, lying on the ground behind a sacrificial stone. Go back a bit in time. Here are eight men, including the old man, who performed a sort of playdance as old as sin. Eight men,' Alleyn repeated and vexedly rubbed his nose. 'Why do I keep wanting to say "nine". Never mind. On the face of it, the old man never leaves the arena or dance floor or stage or whatever the hell you like to call it. On the face of it, nobody offered him any violence. He dances in full view. He has his head cut off in pantomime and in what for want of a better word, we must call fun. But it isn't really cut off. You exchanged signals with him after the fun so we know it isn't. He hides in a low depression. Eight minutes later, when he's meant to resurrect and doesn't, he is found to be genuinely decapitated. That's the story everybody gives us. Now, as a reasonably intelligent chap and a solicitor into the bargain, don't you think that we want to know every damn' thing we can find out about these eight men and anybody connected with them?'

'You mean – just empirically. Hoping something will emerge?'

'Exactly. You know very well that where nothing apropos does emerge, nothing will be made public.'

'Oh, no, no, no,' Ralph ejaculated irritably. 'I suppose I'm being tiresome. What was this blasted question? Have I spoken to Camilla since we both came to South Mardian? All right, I have. After church on Sunday. She'd asked me not to, but I did because the sight of her in church was too much for me.'

'That was your only reason?'

'She was upset. She'd come across Ernie howling over a dead dog in the copse.'

'Bless my soul!' Alleyn ejaculated. 'What next in South Mardian? Was the dog called Keeper?'

Ralph grinned. 'I suppose it is all a bit Brontë. The Guiser had shot it because he said it wasn't healthy, which was no more than God's truth. But Ernie cut up uncommonly rough and it upset Camilla.'

'Where did you meet her?'

'Near the forge. Coming out of the copse.'

'Did you see the Guiser on this occasion?'

After a very long pause, Ralph said: 'Yes. He came up.'

'Did he realize that you wanted to marry his granddaughter?'

'Yes.'

'And what was his reaction?'

Ralph said: 'Unfavourable.'

'Did he hold the same views that she does?'

'More or less.'

'You discussed it there and then?'

'He sent Camilla away first.'

'Will you tell me exactly all that was said?'

'No. It was nothing to do with his death. Our conversation was entirely private.'

Fox contemplated the point of his pencil and Dr Otterly cleared his throat.

'Tell me,' Alleyn said abruptly, 'this thing you wear as the Betty – it's a kind of stone age crinoline to look at, isn't it?'

Ralph said nothing.

'Am I dreaming it, or did someone tell me that it's sometimes used as a sort of extinguisher? Popped over a girl so that she can be carried off unseen? Origin,' he suggested facetiously, 'of the phrase "undercover girl"? Or "undercover man", of course.'

Ralph said quickly and easily: 'They used to get up to some such capers, I believe, but I can't see how they managed to carry anybody away. My arms are *outside* the skirt thing, you know.'

'I thought I noticed openings at the sides.'

'Well – yes. But with the struggle that would go on – '

'Perhaps,' Alleyn said, 'the victim didn't struggle.'

The door opened and Trixie staggered in with two great buckets of coal.

'Axcuse me, sir,' she said. 'You-all must be starved with cold. Boy's never handy when wanted.'

Ralph had made a movement towards her as if to take her load, but had checked awkwardly.

Alleyn said: 'That's much too heavy for you. Give them to me.'

'Let be, sir,' she said, 'no need.'

She was too quick for him. She set one bucket on the hearth and, with a sturdy economy of movement, shot half the contents of the other on the fire. The knot of reddish hair shone on the nape of her neck. Alleyn was reminded of a Brueghel peasant. She straightened herself easily and turned. Her face, blunt and acquiescent, held, he thought, its own secrets and, in its mode, was attractive.

She glanced at Ralph and her mouth widened.

'You don't look too clever yourself, then, Mr Ralph,' she said. 'Last night's ghastly business has overset us all, I reckon.'

'I'm all right,' Ralph muttered.

'Will there be anything, sir?' Trixie asked Alleyn pleasantly.

'Nothing at the moment, thank you. Later on in the day some time, when you're not too busy, I might ask for two words with you.'

'Just ax,' she said. 'I'm willing if wanted.'

She smiled quite broadly at Ralph Stayne. 'Bean't I, Mr Ralph?' she asked placidly and went away, swinging her empty bucket.

'Oh, *God*!' Ralph burst out, and, before any of them could speak, he was gone, slamming the door behind him.

'Shall I?' Fox said and got to his feet.

'Let him be.'

They heard an outer door slam.

'*Well*!' Dr Otterly exclaimed with mild concern, 'I must say I'd never thought of *that*!'

'And nor, you may depend upon it,' Alleyn said, 'has Camilla.'

CHAPTER 8

Question of Fact

When afternoon closing-time came, Trixie pulled down the bar shutters and locked them. Simon Begg went into the Private. There was a telephone in the passage outside the Private and he had put a call through to his bookmaker. He wanted, if he could, to get the results of the 1.30 at Sandown. Teutonic Dancer was a rank outsider. He'd backed it both ways for a great deal more than he could afford to lose and had already begun to feel that if he did lose, it would be in some vague way Mrs Bünz's fault. This was both ungracious and illogical.

For many reasons, Mrs Bünz was the last person he wanted to see and for an equal number of contradictory ones she was the first. And there she was, the picture of uncertainty and alarm, huddled, snuffling, over the parlour fire with her dreadful cold and her eternal notebooks.

She had bought a car from Simon, she might be his inspiration in a smashing win. One way and another, they had done business together. He produced a wan echo of his usual manner.

'Hallo–'llo! And how's Mrs B today?' asked Simon.

'Unwell. I have caught a severe cold in the head. Also, I have received a great shawk. Last night in the pawk was a terrible, terrible shawk.'

'You can say that again,' he agreed glumly, and applied himself to the *Sporting News*.

Suddenly they both said together: 'As a matter of fact – ' and stopped, astonished and disconcerted.

'Ladies first,' said Simon.

136

'Thank you. I was about to say that, as a matter of fact, I would suggest that our little transaction – ach! How shall I say it? Should remain, perhaps – '

'Confidential?' he ventured eagerly.

'That is the word for which I sought. Confidential.'

'I'm all for it, Mrs B. I was going to make the same suggestion myself. Suits me.'

'I am immensely relieved. Immensely. I thank you, Wing-Commander. I trust, at the same time – you do not think – it would be so shawkink – if – '

'Eh?' He looked up from his paper to stare at her. 'What's that? No, no, no, Mrs B. Not to worry. Not a chance. The idea's laughable.'

'To me it is not amusink but I am glad you find it so,' Mrs Bünz said stuffily. 'You read something of interest, perhaps, in your newspaper?'

'I'm waiting. Teutonic Dancer. Get me? The 1.30?'

Mrs Bünz shuddered.

'Oh, well!' he said. 'There you are. I follow the form as a general thing. Don't go much for gimmicks. Still! Talk about a coincidence! You couldn't go past it really, could you?' He raised an admonitory finger. The telephone had begun to ring in the passage. 'My call,' he said. 'This is it. Keep your fingers crossed, Mrs B.'

He darted out of the room.

Mrs Bünz, left alone, breathed uncomfortably through her mouth, blew her nose and clocked her tongue against her palate. 'Dar,' she breathed.

Fox came down the passage past Simon, who was saying: 'Hold the line, please, miss, for Pete's sake. Hold the line,' and entered the parlour.

'Mrs Burns?' he asked.

Mrs Bünz, though she eyed him with evident misgivings, rallied sufficiently to correct him: '*E*ü, *e*ü, *e*ü,' she demonstrated windingly through her cold. 'Bünz.'

'Now, that's *very* interesting,' Fox said, beaming at her. 'That's a noise, if you will excuse me referring to it as such, that we don't make use of in English, do we? Would it be the same, now, as the sound in the French "eu"?' He arranged his sedate mouth in an agonized pout. '*Deux diseuses*,' said Mr Fox by way of illustration. 'Not that I got beyond a very rough approximation, I'm afraid.'

'It is not the same at all. "Bünz."'

'Bünz,' mouthed Mr Fox.

'Your accent is not perfect.'

'I know that,' he agreed heavily. 'In the meantime, I'm forgetting my job. Mr Alleyn presents his compliments and wonders if you'd be kind enough to give him a few minutes.'

'Ach! I too am forgetting. You are the police.'

'You wouldn't think so, the way I'm running on, would you?'

(Alleyn had said: 'If she was an anti-Nazi refugee, she'll think we're ruthless automatons. Jolly her along a bit.')

Mrs Bünz gathered herself together and followed Fox. In the passage, Simon Begg was saying: 'Look, old boy, *all* I'm asking for is the gen on the 1.30. Look, old boy – '

Fox opened the door of the sitting-room and announced her.

'Mrs Bünz,' he said quite successfully.

As she advanced into the room Alleyn seemed to see, not so much a middle-aged German, as the generalization of a species. Mrs Bünz was the lady who sits near the front of lectures and always asks questions. She has an enthusiasm for obscure musicians, stands nearest to guides, keeps handicraft shops of the better class and reads Rabindranath Tagore. She weaves, forms circles, gives talks, hand-throws pots and designs book-plates. She is sometimes a vegetarian, though not always a crank. Occasionally she is an expert.

She walked slowly into the room and kept her gaze fixed on Alleyn. 'She is afraid of me,' he thought.

'This is Mr Alleyn, Mrs Bünz,' Dr Otterly said.

Alleyn shook hands with her. Her own short stubby hand was tremulous and the palm was damp. At his invitation, she perched warily on a chair. Fox sat down behind her and palmed his notebook out of his pocket.

'Mrs Bünz,' Alleyn said, 'in a minute or two I'm going to throw myself on your mercy.'

She blinked at him.

'Zo?' said Mrs Bünz.

'I understand you're an expert on folklore and, if ever anybody needed an expert, we do.'

'I have gone a certain way.'

'Dr Otterly tells me,' Alleyn said, to that gentleman's astonishment, 'that you have probably gone as far as anyone in England.'

'Zo,' she said, with a magnificent inclination towards Otterly.

'But, before we talk about that, I suppose I'd better ask you the usual routine questions. Let's get them over as soon as possible. I'm told that you gave Mr William Andersen a lift – '

They were off again on the old trail, Alleyn thought dejectedly, and not getting much farther along it. Mrs Bünz's account of the Guiser's hitch-hike corresponded with what he had already been told.

'I was so delighted to drive him,' she began nervously. 'It was a great pleasure to me. Once or twice I attempted, tactfully, to a little draw him out but he was, I found, angry, and not inclined for cawn-versation.'

'Did he say anything at all, do you remember?'

'To my recollection he spoke only twice. To begin with, he invited me by gesture to stop and, when I did so, he asked me in his splendid, *splendid* rich dialect, "Be you goink up-alongk?" *On* the drive, he remarked that, when he found Mr Ernie Andersen he would have the skin off of his body. Those, however, were his only remarks.'

'And when you arrived?'

'He descended and hurried away.'

'And what,' Alleyn asked, 'did you do?'

The effect of the question, casually put, upon Mrs Bünz was extraordinary. She seemed to flinch back into her clothes as a tortoise into its shell.

'When you got there, you know,' Alleyn gently prompted her, 'what did you do?'

Mrs Bünz said in a cold-thickened voice: 'I became a spectator. Of course.'

'Where did you stand?'

Her head sank a little further into her shoulders.

'Inside the archway.'

'The archway by the house as you come in?'

'Yes.'

'And from there you watched the dance?'

Mrs Bünz wetted her lips and nodded.

'That must have been an absorbing experience. Had you any idea of what was in store for you?'

'Ach! No! No, I swear it! No!' She almost shouted.

'I meant,' Alleyn said, 'in respect of the dance itself.'

'The dance,' Mrs Bünz said in a strangulated croak, 'is unique.'

'Was it all that you expected?'

'But of course!' She gave a little gasp and appeared to be horror stricken. 'Really,' Alleyn thought, 'I seem to be having almost too much success with Mrs Bünz. Every shy a coconut.'

She had embarked on an elaborate explanation. All folk dance and drama had a common origin. One expected certain elements. The amazing thing about the Five Sons was that it combined so rich an assortment of these elements as well as some remarkable features of its own. 'It has everythink. But everythink,' she said and was plagued by a gargantuan sneeze.

'And did they do it well?'

Mrs Bünz said they did it wonderfully well. The best performance for sheer execution in England. She rallied from whatever shock she had suffered and began to talk incomprehensibly of galleys, split-jumps and double capers. Not only did she remember every move of the Five Sons and the Fool in their twice-repeated dance, but she had noted the positions of the Betty and Hobby. She remembered how these two pranced round the perimeter and how, later on, the Betty chased the young men and flung his skirts over their heads and the Hobby stood as an image behind the dolmen. She remembered everything.

'This is astonishing,' he said, 'for you to retain the whole thing, I mean, after seeing it only once. Extraordinary. How do you do it?'

'I – I – have a very good memory,' said Mrs Bünz, and gave an agonized little laugh. 'In such matters my memory is phenomenal.' Her voice died away. She looked remarkably uncomfortable. He asked her if she took notes and she said at once she didn't, and then seemed in two minds whether to contradict herself.

Her description of the dance tallied in every respect with the accounts he had already been given, with one exception. She seemed to have only the vaguest recollection of the Guiser's first entrance when, as Alleyn had already been told, he had jogged round the arena and struck the Mardian Dolmen with his clown's bladder. But, from then onwards, Mrs Bünz knew everything right up to the moment when Ralph stole Ernie's sword. After that, for a short period, her memory seemed again to be at fault. She remembered that, somewhere about this time, the Hobby Horse went off, but had apparently forgotten that Ernie gave chase after Ralph and only had the vaguest recollection, if any, of Ralph's improvised fooling with Ernie's sword. Moreover, her own uncertainty at this point seemed to embarrass her very much. She blundered about from one fumbled generalization to another.

'The solo was interesting – '

'Wait a bit,' Alleyn said. She gulped and blinked at him. 'Now look here, Mrs Bünz. I'm going to put it to you that from the time the first dance ended with the mock death of the Fool until the solo began, you didn't watch the proceedings at all. Now is that right?'

'I was not interested – '

'How could you know you wouldn't be interested if you didn't even look? *Did* you look, Mrs Bünz?'

She gaped at him with an expression of fear. She was elderly and frightened and he supposed that, in her mind, she associated him with monstrous figures of her past. He was filled with compunction.

Dr Otterly appeared to share Alleyn's feeling. He walked over to her and said: 'Don't worry, Mrs Bünz. Really, there's nothing to be frightened about, you know. They only want to get at the facts. Cheer up.'

His large doctor's hand fell gently on her shoulder.

She gave a falsetto scream and shrank away from him.

'Hallo!' he said good-humouredly, 'what's all this? Nerves? Fibrositis?'

'I – yes – yes. The cold weather.'

'In your shoulders?'

'Ja. Both.'

'Mrs Bünz,' Alleyn said, 'will you believe me when I remind you of something I think you must already know? In England the Police Code has been most carefully framed to protect the public from any kind of bullying or overbearing behaviour on the part of investigating officers. Innocent persons have nothing to fear from us. Nothing. Do you believe that?'

It was difficult to hear what she said. She had lowered her head and spoke under her breath.

'. . . because I am German. It does not matter to you that I was anti-Nazi; that I am naturalized. Because I am German, you will think I am capable. It is different for Germans in England.'

The three men raised a little chorus of protest. She listened without showing any sign of being at all impressed.

'They think I am capable,' she said, 'of anything.'

'You say that, don't you, because of what Ernie Andersen shouted out when he stood last night on the dolmen?'

Mrs Bünz covered her face with her knotty little hands.

'You remember what that was, don't you?' Alleyn asked.

Dr Otterly looked as if he would like to protest but caught Alleyn's eye and said nothing.

Alleyn went on: 'He pointed his sword at you, didn't he, and said, "Ask her. She knows. She's the one that did it." Something like that, wasn't it?' He waited for a moment but she only rocked herself a little with her hands still over her face.

'Why do you think he said that, Mrs Bünz?' Alleyn asked.

In a voice so muffled that they had to strain their ears to hear her, she said something quite unexpected.

'It is because I am a woman,' said Mrs Bünz.

II

Try as he might, Alleyn could get no satisfactory explanation from Mrs Bünz as to what she implied by this statement or why she had made it. He asked her if she was thinking of the exclusion of women from ritual dances and she denied this with such vehemence that it was clear the question had caught her on the raw. She began to talk rapidly, excitedly and, to Mr Fox at least, embarrassingly, about the sex element in ritual dancing.

'The man-woman!' Mrs Bünz shouted. 'An age-old symbol of fertility. And the Hobby, also, without a doubt. There must be the Betty to lover him and the Hobby to – '

She seemed to realize that this was not an acceptable elucidation of her earlier statement and came to a halt. Dr Otterly, who had heard all about her arrival at Copse Forge, reminded her that she had angered the Guiser in the first instance by effecting an entrance into the smithy. He asked her if she thought Ernie had some confused idea that, in doing this, she had brought ill-luck to the performance.

Mrs Bünz seized on this suggestion with feverish intensity. 'Yes, yes,' she cried. That no doubt was what Ernie had meant. Alleyn was unable to share her enthusiasm and felt quite certain it was assumed. She eyed him furtively. He realized, with immense distaste, that any forbearance or consideration that he might show her would probably be taken by Mrs Bünz for weakness. She had her own ideas about investigating officers.

Furtively, she shifted her shoulders under their layers of woollen clothes. She made a queer little arrested gesture as if she was about to touch them and thought better of it.

Alleyn said: 'Your shoulders *are* painful, aren't they? Why not let Dr Otterly have a look at them? I'm sure he would.'

Dr Otterly made guarded professional noises, and Mrs Bünz behaved as if Alleyn's suggestion was tantamount to the Usual Warning. She shook her head violently, became grey-faced and speechless and seemed to contemplate a sudden break-away.

'I won't keep you much longer,' Alleyn said. 'There are only one or two more questions. This is the first. At any stage of the proceedings last night did the Hobby Horse come near you?'

At this she did get up, but slowly and with the uncoordinated movements of a much older woman. Fox looked over the top of his spectacles at the door. Alleyn and Dr Otterly rose and on a common impulse moved a little nearer to her. It occurred to Alleyn that it would really be rather a pleasant change to ask Mrs Bünz a question that did *not* throw her into a fever.

'*Did* you make any contact at all with the Hobby?' he insisted.

'I think. Once. At the beginning, during his chasinks.' Her eyes were streaming, but whether with cold or distress, it was impossible to say. 'In his flirtinks he touched me,' she said. 'I think.'

'So you have no doubt got tar on your clothes?'

'A little on my coat. I think.'

'Do the Hobby and Betty rehearse, I wonder.'

Dr Otterly opened his mouth and shut it again.

'I know nothing of that,' Mrs Bünz said.

'Do you know where they rehearsed?'

'Nothink. I know nothink.'

Fox, who had his eye on Dr Otterly, gave a stentorian cough, and Alleyn hurried on.

'One more question, Mrs Bünz, and I do ask you very seriously to give me a frank answer to it. I beg you to believe that, if you are innocent of this crime, you can do yourself nothing but good by speaking openly and without fear. Please believe it.'

'I am completely, *completely* innocent.'

'Good. Then here is the question. Did you after the end of the first Morris leave the courtyard for some reason and not return to it until the beginning of the solo dance? *Did* you, Mrs Bünz?'

'No,' said Mrs Bünz very loudly.

'Really?'

'No.'

Alleyn said after a pause: 'All right. That's all. You may be asked later on to sign a statement. I'm afraid I must also ask you to stay in East Mardian until after the inquest.' He went to the door and opened it. 'Thank you,' he said.

When she reached the door, she stood and looked at him. She seemed to collect herself and, when she spoke, it was with more composure than she had hitherto shown.

'It is the foolish son who has done it,' she said. 'He is epileptic. Ritual dancing has a profound effect upon such beings. They are carried back to their distant origins. They become excited. Had not this son already cut his father's hand and shed his blood with his sword? It is the son.'

'How do you know he had already cut his father's hand?' Alleyn asked.

'I have been told,' Mrs Bünz said, looking as if she would faint.

Without another word and without looking at him again, she went out and down the passage.

Alleyn said to Fox: 'Don't let her talk to Begg. Nip out, Fox, and tell him that, as we'll be a little time yet, he can go up to his garage and we'll look in there later. Probably suits him better, anyway.'

Fox went out and Alleyn grinned at Dr Otterly.

'You can go ahead, now,' he said, 'if you want to spontaneously combust.'

'I must say I feel damn' like it. What's she up to, lying right and left? Good God, I never heard anything like it! Not know when we rehearsed. Good God! They could hear us all over the pub.'

'Where did you rehearse?'

'In the old barn at the back, here.'

'Very rum. But I fancy,' Alleyn muttered, 'we know why she went away during the show.'

'Are you sure she did?'

'My dear chap, yes. She's a fanatic. She's a folk-lore hound with her nose to the ground. She remembered the first and last parts of your programme with fantastic accuracy. *Of course*, if she'd been there she'd have watched the earthy antics of the comics. If they are comics. Of course. She'd have been on the look-out for all the fertility fun that you hand out. If she'd been there she'd have looked and she'd have remembered in precise detail. She doesn't remember because she didn't look and she didn't look because she wasn't there. I'd bet my boots on it and I bet I know why.'

Fox returned, polishing his spectacles, and said: 'Do you know what I reckon, Mr Alleyn? I reckon Mrs B. leaves the arena, just after the first dance, is away from it all through the collection and the funny business between young Mr Stayne and daft Ernie and gets back before Dan Andersen does a turn on his own. Is that your idea?'

'Not altogether, Brer Fox. If my tottering little freak of an idea is any good, she leaves her observation post *before* the first dance.'

'Hey?' Fox ejaculated. 'But it's the first dance that she remembers so well.'

'I must say – ' Dr Otterly agreed and flapped his hands.

'Exactly,' Alleyn said. 'I know. Now. Let me explain.' He did so at some length and they listened to him with the raised eyebrows of assailable incredulity.

'Well,' they said, 'I suppose it's possible.' And: 'It might be, but how'll you prove it?' And: 'Even so, it doesn't get us all that much further, does it?' And: 'How are you to find out?'

'It gets us a hell of a lot further,' Alleyn said hotly, 'as you'd find out pretty quickly if you could take a peep at Mrs Bünz in the rude nude. However, since that little treat is denied us, let's visit Mr Simon Begg and see what he can provide. What was he up to, Fox?'

'He was talking on the telephone about horse-racing,' Fox said. 'Something called Teutonic Dancer in the 1.30 at Sandown. That's funny,' Mr Fox added, 'I never thought of it at the time. Funny!'

'Screamingly. You might see if Bailey and Thompson are back, Fox, and if there's anything. They'll need a meal, poor devils. Trixie'll fix that, I dare say. Then we'll take a drive up the road to Begg's garage.'

While Fox was away Alleyn asked Dr Otterly if he could give him a line on Simon Begg.

'He's a local,' Dr Otterly said. 'Son of the ex-village shopkeeper. Name's still up over the shop. He did jolly well in the war with the RAF. Bomber pilot. He was brought down over Germany, tackled a bunch of Huns single-handed and got himself and two of his crew back through Spain. They gave him the DFC for it. He'd been a bit of a problem as a lad but he took to active service like a bird.'

'And since the war?'

'Well – in a way, a bit of a problem again. I feel damn' sorry for him. As long as he was in uniform with his ribbons up he was quite a person. That's how it was with those boys; wasn't it? They lived high, wide and dangerous and they were everybody's heroes. Then he was demobilized and came back here. You know what county people are like: it takes a flying bomb to put a dent in their class-consciousness, and then it's only temporary. They began to say how ghastly the RAF slang was and to ask each other if it didn't rock you a bit when you saw them out of uniform. It's quite true that Simon bounded sky high and used an incomprehensible and irritating jargon and that some of his waistcoats were positively terrifying. All the same.'

'I know,' Alleyn said.

'I felt rather sorry for him. Neither fish, nor flesh, nor stock-broker's tudor. That was why I asked him to come into the Sword Wednesday show. Our old Hobby was killed in the raids. He was old Begg from Yowford, a relation of Simon's. There've been Beggs for Hobbies for a very long time.'

'*So* this Begg has done it – how many times?'

'About nine. Ever since the war.'

'What's he been up to all that time?'

'He's led rather a raffish kind of life for the last nine years. Constantly changing his job. Gambling pretty high, I fancy. Hanging round the pubs. Then, about three years ago his father died and he bought a garage up at Yowford. It's not doing too well, I fancy. He's said to be very much in the red. The boys would have got good backing from one of the big companies if they could have persuaded the Guiser to let them turn Copse Forge into a filling-station. It's at a cross-roads and they're putting a main road through before long, more's the pity. They were very keen on the idea and wanted Simon to go in with them. But the Guiser wouldn't hear of it.'

'They may get it – now,' Alleyn said without emphasis. 'And Simon may climb out of the red.'

'He's scarcely going to murder William Andersen,' Dr Otterly pointed out acidly, 'on the off-chance of the five sons putting up five petrol pumps. Apart from the undoubted fact that, wherever Begg himself may have got to last night, the Guiser certainly didn't leave the stage after he walked on to it and I defy you to perform a decapitation when you're trussed up in "Crack's" harness. Besides, I *like* Begg, ghastly as he is, I like him.'

'All right. I know. I didn't say a thing.'

'You are not, I hope,' Dr Otterly angrily continued, 'putting on that damned superior-sleuth act: "You have the facts, my dear whatever-the-stooge's-name-is."'

'Not I.'

'Well, you've got some damned theory up your sleeve, haven't you?'

'I'm ashamed of it.'

'*Ashamed?*'

'Utterly, Otterly.'

'Ah, hell!' Dr Otterly said in disgust.

'Come with us to Begg's garage. Keep on listening. If anything doesn't tally with what you remember, don't say a word unless I tip you the wink. All right? Here we go.'

III

In spite of the thaw, the afternoon had grown deadly cold. Yowford lane dripped greyly between its hedgerows and was choked with mud and slush. About a mile along it they came upon Simmy-Dick's Service

Station in a disheartened-looking shack with Begg's car standing outside it. Alleyn pulled up at the first pump and sounded his horn.

Simon came out, buttoning up a suit of white overalls with a large monogram on the pocket: sad witness, Alleyn suspected, to a grandiloquent beginning. When he saw Alleyn he grinned sourly and raised his eyebrows.

'Hallo,' Alleyn said. 'Four, please.'

'Four what? Coals of fire?' Simon said, and moved round to the petrol tank.

It was an unexpected opening and made things a good deal easier for Alleyn. He got out of the car and joined Simon.

'Why coals of fire?' he asked.

'After me being a rude boy this morning.'

'That's all right.'

'It's just that I know what a clot Ernie can make of himself,' Simon said, and thrust the nose of the hosepipe into the tank. 'Four, you said?'

'Four. And this *is* a professional call, by the way.'

'I'm not all that dumb,' Simon grunted.

Alleyn waited until the petrol had gone in and then paid for it. Simon tossed the change up and caught it neatly before handing it over. 'Why not come inside?' he suggested. 'It's bloody cold out here, isn't it?'

He led the way into a choked-up cubby-hole that served as his office. Fox and Dr Otterly followed Alleyn and edged in sideways.

'How's the Doc!' Simon said. 'Doing a Watson?'

'I'm beginning to think so,' said Dr Otterly. Simon laughed shortly.

'Well,' Alleyn began cheerfully, 'how's the racing news?'

'Box of birds,' Simon said.

'Teutonic Dancer do any good for herself?'

Simon looked sharply at Fox. 'Who's the genned-up type?' he said. 'You?'

"That's right, Mr Begg. I heard you on the telephone.'

'I see.' He took out his cigarettes, frowned over lighting one and then looked up with a grin. 'I can't keep it to myself,' he said. 'It's the craziest thing. Came in at 27 to 1. Everything else must have fallen down.'

'I hope you had something on.'

'A wee flutter,' Simon said and again the corners of his mouth twitched. 'It was a dicey do but was it worth it! How's the Doc?' he repeated, again aware of Dr Otterly.

'Quite well, thank you. How's the garage proprietor?' Dr Otterly countered chillily.

'Box of birds.'

As this didn't seem to be getting them anywhere, Alleyn invited Simon to give them his account of the Five Sons.

He started off in a very business-like way, much, Alleyn thought as he must have given his reports in his bomber pilot days. The delayed entrance, the arrival of the Guiser, 'steamed-up' and roaring at them all. The rapid change of clothes and the entrance. He described how he began the show with his pursuit of the girls.

'Funny! Some of them just about give you the go-ahead signal. I could see them through the hole in the neck. All giggles and girlishness. Half windy, too. They reckon it's lucky or something.'

'Did Miss Campion react like that?'

'The fair Camilla? I wouldn't have minded if she *had*. I made a very determined attempt, but not a chance. She crash-landed in the arms of another bod. Ralphy Stayne. Lucky type!'

He grinned cheerfully round. '*But*, still!' he said. It was a sort of summing up. One could imagine him saying it under almost any circumstances.

Alleyn asked him what he did after he'd finished his act and before the first Morris began. He said he went up to the back archway and had a bit of a breather.

'And during the Morris?'

'I just sort of bummed around on my own.'

'With the Betty?'

'I think so. I don't remember exactly. I'm not sort of officially "on" in that scene.'

'But you didn't go right off?'

'No, I'm meant to hang around. I'm the animal-man. God knows what it's all in aid of but I just sort of trot around on the outskirts.'

'And you did that last night?'

'That's the story.'

'You didn't go near the dancers?'

'I don't think so.'

'Nor the dolmen?'

'No,' he said sharply.

'You couldn't tell me, for instance, exactly what the Guiser did when he slipped down to hide?'

'Disappeared as usual behind the stone, I suppose, and lay doggo.'

'Where were you at that precise moment?'

'I don't remember exactly.'

'Nowhere near the dolmen?'

'Absolutely. Nowhere near.'

'I see,' Alleyn said, and was careful not to look at Dr Otterly. 'And then? After that? What did you do?'

'I just hung around for a bit and then wandered up to the back.'

'What was happening in the arena?'

'The Betty did an act and after that Dan did his solo.'

'What was the Betty's act?'

'Kind of ad lib. In the old days, they tell me, "she" used to hunt down some bod in the crowd and tuck them under her petticoats. Or she'd come on screeching and, presently, there'd be a great commotion under the crinoline and out would pop some poor type. You can imagine. A high old time was had by all.'

'Mr Stayne didn't go in for that particular kind of clowning?'

'Who – Ralph? Only very mildly. He's much too much the gentleman, if you know what I mean.'

'What *did* he do?' Alleyn persisted.

'Honest, I've forgotten. I didn't really watch. Matter of fact, I oozed off to the back and had a smoke.'

'When did you begin to watch again?'

'After Dan's solo. When the last dance began. I came back for that.'

'And then?'

After that, Simon's account followed the rest. Alleyn let him finish without interruption and was then silent for so long that the others began to fidget and Simon Begg stood up.

'Well,' he said, 'if that's all – '

'I'm afraid it's nothing like all.'

'Hell!'

'Let us consider,' Alleyn said, 'your story of your own movements during and immediately after the first dance – this dance that was twice repeated and ended with the mock decapitation. Why do you suppose that your account of it differs radically from all the other accounts we have had?'

Simon glanced at Dr Otterly and assumed a tough and mulish expression.

'Your guess,' he said, 'is as good as mine.'

'We don't want to guess. We like to know. We'd like to know, for instance, why you say you trotted round on the outskirts of the dance and that you didn't go near the dancers or the dolmen. Dr Otterly here, and all the other observers we have consulted, say that, as a matter of fact, you went up to the dolmen at the moment of climax and stood motionless behind it.'

'Do they?' he said. 'I don't remember everything I did. Perhaps they don't either. P'r'aps you've been handed a lot of duff gen.'

'If that means,' Dr Otterly said, 'that I may have laid false information, I won't let you get away with it. I am absolutely certain that you stood close behind the dolmen and therefore so close to where the Guiser lay that you couldn't fail to notice him. Sorry, Alleyn. I've butted in.'

'That's all right. You see, Begg, that's what they all say. Their accounts agree.'

'Too bad,' Simon said.

'If, in fact, you did stand behind the dolmen when he hid behind it you must have seen exactly what the Guiser did.'

'I didn't see what the Guiser did. I don't remember being behind the stone. I don't think I was near enough to see.'

'Would you make a statement, on oath, to that effect?'

'Why not?'

'And that you don't remember exactly what the clowning act was between the Betty and Ernest Andersen?'

'Didn't he and Ralphy have a row about his whiffler? Come to think of it, I believe I oozed off before they got going.'

'No, you didn't. Sorry, Alleyn,' said Dr Otterly.

'We are told that "Crack", who was watching them, gave a sort of neighing sound before he went off by the rear archway. Did you do that?'

'I might have. Dare say. Why the heck should I remember?'

'Because, up to the point when you finished tarring the village maidens and the dance proper began, you remember everything

very clearly. Then we get this period when you're overtaken by a
sort of mental miasma, a period that covers the ritual of the Father
and the Five Sons culminating in the mock death. Everybody else
agrees about where you were at the moment of the climax: behind
the dolmen, they tell us, standing stock still. You insist that you don't
remember going near the dolmen.'

'That's right,' Simon said very coolly and puckered his lips in a
soundless whistle. 'To the best of my remembrance, you know.'

'I think I'd better tell you that, in my opinion, this period, from
the end of your improvisation until your return (and incidentally,
the return of your memory), covers the murder of William
Andersen.'

'I didn't hand him the big chop,' Simon said. 'Poor old bastard.'

'Have you any notion who did?'

'No.'

'I do *wish*,' Alleyn said vexedly, 'you wouldn't be such an ass – if
you are being an ass, of course.'

'Will that be all, teacher?'

'No. How well do you know Mrs Bünz?'

'I never met her till she came down here.'

'You've sold her a car, haven't you?'

'That's right.'

'Any other transactions?'

'What the hell do you mean?' Simon asked very quietly.

'Did you come to any understanding about Teutonic Dancer?'

Simon shifted his shoulders with a movement that reminded
Alleyn of Mrs Bünz herself. 'Oh,' he said. 'That.' He seemed to
expand and the look of irrepressible satisfaction appeared again.
'You might say the old dear brought me that bit of luck. I mean to
say: could you beat it? Teutonic Dancer by Subsidize out of
Substituteon? Piece of cake!'

'Subsidize?'

'Yes. Great old sire, of course, but the dam isn't so hot.'

'Did they give you any other ideas?'

'Who?'

'Subsidize and Substituteon?'

'I don't,' Simon said coolly, 'know what you mean.'

'Let it go then. What clothes did you wear last night?'

'Clothes? Oldest I've got. By the time the party was over, I looked pretty much like the original tar-baby myself.'

'What were they?'

'A heavy RAF sweater and a pair of old cream slacks.'

'Good,' Alleyn said. 'May we borrow them?'

'Look here, I don't much like this. Why?'

'Why do you think? To see if there's any blood on them.'

'Thanks,' said Simon, turning pale, 'very much!'

'We'll be asking for everybody's.'

'Safety in numbers?' He hesitated and then looked again at Dr Otterly. 'Not my job,' he muttered, 'to try and teach the experts. I know that. All the same – '

'Come on,' Alleyn said. 'All the same, what?'

'I just happen to know. Anybody buys his bundle that way, there isn't just a *little* blood.'

'I see. How do you happen to know?'

'Show I was in. Over Germany.'

'Can you elaborate a bit?'

'It's not all that interesting. We got clobbered and I hit the silk the same time as she exploded.'

'His bomber blew up and they parachuted down,' Dr Otterly translated drily.

'That's the story,' Simon agreed.

'Touch and go?' Alleyn hazarded.

'You can say that again.' Simon drew his brows together. His voice was unemphatic and without dramatic values, yet had the authentic colour of vivid recollection.

'I could see the Jerries before I hit the deck. Soon as I did they bounced me. Three of them. Two went the hard way. But the third, a little old tough-looking type, he was, with a hedge-cutter, came up behind while I was still busy with his cobs. I turned and saw him. Too late to cope. I'd have bought it if one of my own crew hadn't come up and got operational. He used his knife.' Simon made an all too graphic gesture. 'That's how I know,' he said. 'OK, isn't it, Doc? Buckets of blood?'

'Yes,' Dr Otterly agreed. 'There would be.'

'Yes. Which ought to make it a simple story,' Simon said and turned to Alleyn. 'Oughtn't it?'

'The story,' Alleyn said, 'would be a good deal simpler if everyone didn't try to elaborate it. Now, keep still. I haven't finished with you yet. Tell me this. As far as I can piece it out, you were either up at the back exit or just outside it when Ernie Andersen came back-stage.'

'Just outside it's right.'

'What happened?'

'I told you. After the Morris, I left Ralphy to it. I could hear him squeaking away and the mob laughing. I had a drag at a gasper and took the weight off my boots. Then the old Corp – that's Ernie, he was my batman in the war – came charging out in one of his tantrums. I couldn't make out what was biting him. After a bit, Ralphy turned up and gave Ernie his whiffler. Ralphy started to say "I'm sorry," or something like that, but I told him to beat it. So he did.'

'And then?'

'Well, then it was just about time for me to go back. So I did. Ernie went back, too.'

'Who threw tar on the bonfire?'

'Nobody. I knocked the drum over with the edge of "Crack's" body. It's a dirty big clumsy thing. Swings round. I jolly nearly went on fire myself,' Simon reflected with feeling. 'By God, I did.'

'So you went back to the arena? You and Ernie?'

'That's the story.'

'Where exactly did you go?'

'I don't know where Ernie got to. Far as I remember, I went straight in.' He half shut his eyes and peered back through the intervening hours. 'The boys had started their last dance. I think I went fairly close to the dolmen that time because I seem to remember it between them and me. Then I sheered off to the right and took up my position there.'

'Did you notice the Guiser lying behind the dolmen?'

'Sort of. Poor visibility through the hole in that canvas neck. And the body sticks out like a great shelf just under your chin. It hides the ground for about three feet all round you.'

'Yes, I see. Do you think you could have kicked anything without realizing you'd done it?'

Simon stared, blinked and looked sick. 'Nice idea I *must* say,' he said with some violence.

'Do you remember doing so?'

He stared at his hands for a moment, frowning.

'God, I don't know. I don't know. I *hadn't* remembered.'

'Why did you stop Ernie Andersen answering me when I asked if he'd done this job?'

'Because,' Simon said at once, 'I know what Ernie's like. He's not more than nine and fivepence in the pound. He's queer. I sort of kept an eye on him in the old days. He takes fits. I knew. I fiddled him in as a batman.' Simon began to mumble. 'You know, same as the way he felt about his ghastly dog, I felt about him, poor old bastard. I know him. What happened last night got him all worked up. He took a fit after it happened, didn't he, Doc? He'd be just as liable to say he'd done it as not. He's queer about blood and he's got some weird ideas about this dance and the stone and what-have-you. He's the type that rushes in and confesses to a murder he hasn't done just for the hell of it.'

'Do you think he did it?' Alleyn said.

'I do not. How could he? Only time he might have had a go, Ralphy had pinched his whiffler. I certainly do not.'

'All right. Go away and think over what you've said. We'll be asking you for a statement and you'll be subpoenaed for the inquest. If you'd like, on consideration, to amend what you've told us, we'll be glad to listen.'

'I don't *want* to amend anything.'

'Well, if your memory improves.'

'Ah, hell!' Simon said disgustedly and dropped into his chair.

'You never do any good,' Alleyn remarked, 'by fiddling with the facts.'

'Don't you just,' Simon rejoined with heartfelt emphasis, and added: 'You lay off old Ern. He hasn't got it in him: he's the mild one in that family.'

'Is he? Who's the savage one?'

'They're all mild,' Simon said, grinning. 'As mild as milk.'

And on that note they left him.

When they were in the car, Dr Otterly boiled up again.

'What the devil does that young bounder think he's up to! I never heard such a damned farrago of lies. By God, Alleyn, I don't like it. I don't like it at all.'

'Don't you?' Alleyn said absently.

'Well, damn it, do you?'

'Oh,' Alleyn grunted. 'It sticks out a mile what Master Simon's up to. Doesn't it, Fox?'

'I'd say so, Mr Alleyn,' Fox agreed cheerfully.

Dr Otterly said: 'Am I to be informed?'

'Yes, yes, of course. Hallo, who's this?'

In the hollow of the lane, pressed into the bank to make way for the oncoming car, were a man and a woman. She wore a shawl pulled over her head and he a woollen cap and there was a kind of intensity in their stillness. As the car passed the woman looked up. It was Trixie Plowman.

'Chris hasn't lost much time,' Dr Otterly muttered.

'Are they engaged?'

'They were courting,' Dr Otterly said shortly. 'I understood it was all off.'

'Because of the Guiser?'

'I didn't say so.'

'You said Chris hadn't lost much time, though. Did the Guiser disapprove?'

'Something of the sort. Village gossip.'

'I'll swap Simon's goings-on for your bit of gossip.'

Dr Otterly shifted in his seat. 'I don't know so much about that,' he said uneasily. 'I'll think it over.'

They returned to the fug and shadows of their room in the pub. Alleyn was silent for some minutes and Fox busied himself with his notes. Dr Otterly eyed them both and seemed to be in two minds whether or not to speak. Presently, Alleyn walked over to the window. 'The weather's hardening. I think it may freeze tonight,' he said.

Fox looked over the top of his spectacles at Dr Otterly, completed his notes and joined Alleyn at the window.

'Woman,' he observed. 'In the lane. Looks familiar. Dogs.'

'It's Miss Dulcie Mardian.'

'Funny how they will do it.'

'What?'

'Go for walks with dogs.'

'She's coming into the pub.'

'All that fatuous tarradiddle,' Dr Otterly suddenly fulminated, 'about where he was during the triple sword dance! Saying he didn't go behind the dolmen. Sink me, he *stood* there and squealed like a colt when he saw Ralph grab the sword. I don't understand it and I don't like it. Lies.'

Alleyn said: 'I don't think Simon lied.'

'What!'

'He says that during the first dance, the triple sword dance, he was nowhere near the dolmen. I believe that to be perfectly true.'

'But rot my soul, Alleyn – I swear – '

'Equally, I believe that he didn't see Ralph Stayne grab Ernest Andersen's sword.'

'Now, look here – '

Alleyn turned to Dr Otterly. 'Of *course*, he didn't. He was well away from the scene of action. He'd gone off-stage to keep a date with a lady friend.'

'A *date?* What lady friend for pity's sake?'

Trixie came in.

'Miss Dulcie Mardian,' she said, 'to see Mr Alleyn, if you please.'

CHAPTER 9

Question of Fancy

Alleyn found it a little hard to decide quite how addle-pated Dulcie Mardian was. She had a strange vague smile and a terribly inconsequent manner. Obviously, she was one of those people who listen to less than half of what is said to them. Yet, could the strangeness of some of her replies be attributed only to this?

She waited for him in the tiny entrance hall of the Green Man. She wore a hat that had been mercilessly sat upon, an old hacking waterproof and a pair of down-at-heel Newmarket boots. She carried a stick. Her dogs, a bull-terrier and a spaniel, were on leashes and had wound them round her to such an extent that she was tied up like a parcel.

'How do you do,' she said, 'I won't come in. Aunt Akky asked me to say she'd be delighted if you'd dine tonight. Quarter past eight for half past and don't dress if it's a bother. Oh, yes, I nearly forgot. She's sorry it's such short notice. I hope you'll come because she gets awfully cross if people don't, when they're asked. Goodbye.'

She plunged a little but was held firmly pinioned by her dogs and Alleyn was able to say: 'Thank you very much,' collect his thoughts and accept.

'And I'm afraid I can't change,' he added.

'I'll tell her. *Don't*, dogs.'

'May I – ?'

'It's all right, thank you. I'll kick them a little.'

She kicked the bull-terrier, who rather half-heartedly snapped back at her.

'I suppose,' Dulcie said, 'you ran away to be a policeman when you were a boy.'

'Not exactly.'

'Isn't it awful about old William? Aunt Akky's furious. She was in a bad mood anyway because of Ralph, and this has put her out more than ever.'

Trixie came through the passage and went into the Public Bar.

'Which reminds me,' Dulcie said, but didn't elucidate what reminded her of what. It was much too public a place for Alleyn to pursue the conversation to any professional advantage, if there was any to be had. He asked her if she'd come into their improvised office for a few minutes, and she treated the suggestion as if it was an improper advance.

'No, thank you,' she said, attempting to draw herself up but greatly hampered by her dogs. 'Quite impossible, I'm afraid.'

Alleyn said: 'There are one or two points about this case that we'd like to discuss with you. Perhaps, if I came a little early tonight? Or if Dame Alice goes to bed early, I might – '

'I go up at the same time as my aunt. We shall be an early party, I'm afraid,' Dulcie said stiffly. 'Aunt Akky is sure you'll understand.'

'Of course, yes. But if I might have a word or two with you in private – '

He stopped, noticing her agitation.

Perhaps her involuntary bondage to the bull-terrier and the spaniel had put into Dulcie's head some strange fantasy of jeopardized maidenhood. A look of terrified bravado appeared on her face. There was even a trace of gratification.

'You don't,' Dulcie astoundingly informed him, 'follow with the South Mardian and Adjacent Hunts without learning how to look after yourself. No, by Jove!'

The bull-terrier and the spaniel had begun to fight each other. Dulcie beat them impartially and was forced to accept Alleyn's help in extricating herself from a now quite untenable position.

'Hands off,' she ordered him brusquely as soon as it was remotely possible for him to leave her to her own devices. 'Behave yourself,' she advised him, and was suddenly jerked from his presence by the dogs.

Alleyn was left rubbing his nose.

When he rejoined the others, he asked Dr Otterly how irresponsible he considered Miss Mardian to be.

'Dulcie?' Dr Otterly said. 'Well – '

'In confidence.'

'Not certifiable. No. Eccentric, yes. Lots of in-breeding there. She
took a bad toss in the hunting-field about twenty years ago. Kicked
on the head. Never ridden since. She's odd, certainly.'

'She talked as if she rode to hounds every day of the week.'

'Did she? Odd, yes. Did she behave as if you were going to make
improper proposals?'

'Yes.'

'She does that occasionally. Typical spinster's hallucination. Dame
Alice thinks she waxes and wanes emotionally with the moon. I'd
give it a more clinical classification but you can take your choice.
And now, if you don't mind, Alleyn, I really am running terribly
late.'

'Yes, of course.'

'I won't ask you for an explanation of your extraordinary pronouncement just now. Um?'

'Won't you? That's jolly big of you.'

'You go to hell,' Dr Otterly said without much rancour and took
himself off.

Fox said: 'Bailey and Thompson have rigged up a workroom
somewhere in the barn and got cracking on dabs. Carey saw the gardener's boy from the castle. He went down yesterday with the note
from the gardener himself about the slasher. He didn't see the
Guiser. Ernie took the note in to him and came back and said the
Guiser would do the job if he could.'

'I thought as much.'

'Carey's talked to the lad who was to stand in for Ernie: Dan's boy,
he is. He says his granddad arrived on the scene at the last moment.
Ernie was dressed up in the Guiser's clothes and this boy was wearing Ernie's. The Guiser didn't say much. He grabbed Ernie and tried
to drag the clothes off him. Nobody explained anything. They just
changed over and did the show.'

'Yes, I see. Let's take another gollop of fresh air, Fox, and then I
think I'll have a word with the child of nature.'

'Who? Trixie?'

'That, as Mr Begg would say, is the little number. A fine cheerful job straight out of the romps of Milk Wood. Where's the side door?'

They found it and walked out into the backyard.

'And there,' Alleyn said, 'is the barn. They rehearsed in here. Let's have a look, shall we?'

They walked down the brick path and found themselves by a little window in the rear of the barn. A raincoat had been hung over it on the inside. 'Bailey's,' Alleyn said. 'They'll be hard at it.'

He stood there, filling his pipe and looking absently at the small window. 'Somebody's cleaned a peep-hole on the outside,' he said. 'Or it looks like a peep-hole.'

He stooped down while Fox watched him indulgently. Between the brick path and the wall of the barn there was a strip of unmelted snow.

'Look,' Alleyn said and pointed.

Mrs Bünz had worn rubber overboots with heels. Night after night she had stood there and, on the last night, the impressions she made had frozen into the fresh fall of snow. It was a bitterly cold, sheltered spot and the thaw had not yet reached it. There they were, pointing to the wall, under the window: two neat footprints over the ghosts of many others.

'Size six. Not Camilla Campion and Trixie's got smallish feet, too. I bet it was the Teutonic folklorist having a sly peep at rehearsals. Look here, now. Here's a nice little morsel of textbook stuff for you.'

A naked and ragged thorn bush grew by the window. Caught up in one of its twigs was a tuft of grey-blue woollen material.

'Handspun,' Alleyn said, 'I bet you.'

'Keen!' Fox said, turning his back to a razor-like draught.

'If you mean the lady,' Alleyn rejoined, 'you couldn't be more right, Brer Fox. As keen as a knife. A fanatic, in fact. Come on.'

They moved round to the front of the barn and went in. The deserted interior was both cold and stuffy. There was a smell of sacking, cobwebs and perhaps the stale sweat of the dancers. Cigarettes had been trodden out along the sides. The dust raised by the great down-striking capers had settled again over everything. At the far end, double doors led into an inner room and had evidently been dragged together by Bailey and Thompson, whose voices could be heard on the other side.

'We won't disturb them,' Alleyn said, 'but, if those doors were open as I should say they normally are, there'd be a view into this part of the barn from the little window.'

'It'd be a restricted view, wouldn't it?'

'It'd be continually interrupted by figures coming between the observer and the performers and limited by the size of the opening. I tell you what, Foxkin,' Alleyn said, 'unless we can "find" as the Mardian ladies would say, pretty damn' quickly, we'll have a hell of a lot of deadwood to clear away in this case.'

'Such as?'

'Such as the Andersen boys' business instincts, for one thing. And tracking down Master Ralph's peccadillos for another. And the Bünz for a third. And just what Ernie got up to before the show. And Chris's love pangs. All that and more and quite likely none of it of any account in the long run.'

'None?'

'Well – there's one item that I think may ring the bell.'

Bailey, hearing their voices, wrenched open one of the double doors and stuck his head out.

'No dabs anywhere that you wouldn't expect, Mr Alleyn,' he reported. 'A few stains that look like blood on the Andersens' dancing pants and sleeves. Nothing on their swords. They handled the body, of course. The slasher's too much burnt for anything to show, and the harness on the horse affair's all mucked up with tar.'

Bailey was a man of rather morose habit, but when he had this sort of report to make he usually grinned. He did so now. 'Will I get Mr Begg's clothes off him?' he asked.

'Yes. I've told him we want them. You may have the car for the next hour.'

Bailey said: 'The local sergeant looked in. Obby. Pretty well asleep in his boots. He says when you left this morning the Andersens had a bit of a set-to. Seems Ernie reckons there was something about Chris Andersen. He kept saying "What about Chris and the Guiser and you-know-who?" Obby wrote it all down and left his notes. It doesn't sound anything much.'

'I'll look at it,' Alleyn said, and, when Bailey produced the note-book, read it carefully.

'All right,' he said. 'Carry on finding out nothing you wouldn't expect. Glad you're enjoying yourself.'

Bailey looked doubtful and withdrew his head.

'I'm going to see Trixie.' Alleyn announced.

'If you get frightened,' Mr Fox said, 'scream.'

'I'll do that, Fox. Thank you.'

II

Trixie was behind the shutter tidying the Public Bar. Tucked away behind the shelves of bottles, she had a snuggery with a couple of chairs and an electric fire. Into this retreat she invited Alleyn, performed the classic geture of dusting a chair and herself sat down almost knee to knee with him, calmly attentive to whatever he might choose to say.

'Trixie,' Alleyn began, 'I'm going to ask you one or two very personal questions and you're going to think I've got a hell of a cheek. If your answers are no help to us then I shall forget all about them. If they are of help, we shall have to make use of them; but, as far as possible, we will treat them as confidential. All right?'

'I reckon so,' Trixie said readily.

'Good. Before we tackle the personalities, I want you to tell me what you saw last night, up at the castle.'

Her description of the dance tallied with Dr Otterly's except at moments when her attention had obviously strayed. Such a moment had occurred soon after the entry of the Guiser. She had watched 'Crack's' antics and had herself been tarred by him. 'It's lucky to get touched,' Trixie said with her usual broad smile. She had wonderfully strong white teeth and her fair skin had a kind of bloom over it. She remembered in detail how 'Crack' had chased Camilla and how Camilla had run into the Betty's arms. But, at the moment when the Guiser came in, it seemed, Trixie's attention had been diverted. She had happened to catch sight of Mrs Bünz.

'Were you standing anywhere near her?' Alleyn asked.

'So I was, then, but she was powerful eager to see and get tar-touched and crept in close.'

'Yes?'

'But after Guiser come in I see her move back in the crowd and, when I looked again, she wasn't there.'

'Not anywhere in the crowd?'

'Seemingly.'

Knowing how madly keen Mrs Bünz was to see the dance, Trixie was good-naturedly concerned and looked round for her quite persistently. But there was no sign of her. Then Trixie herself became interested in the performance and forgot all about Mrs Bünz. Later on, when Dan was already embarked on his solo, Trixie looked round again and, lo and behold, there was Mrs Bünz after all, standing inside the archway and looking, Trixie said, terribly put-about. After that, the account followed Dr Otterly's in every respect.

Alleyn said: 'This has been a help. Thank you, Trixie. And now, I'm afraid, for the personalities. This afternoon when you came into our room and Mr Ralph Stayne was there, I thought from your manner and from his that there has been something – some understanding between you. Is that right?'

Trixie's smile widened into quite a broad grin. A dimple appeared in her cheek and her eyes brightened.

'He's a proper lad,' she said, 'is Mr Ralph.'

'Does he spend much time at home, here?'

'During the week he's up to Biddlefast lawyering, but most weekends he's to home.' She chuckled. 'It's kind of slow most times hereabouts,' said Trixie. 'Up to rectory it's so quiet's a grave. No place for a high-mettled chap.'

'Does he get on well with his father?'

'Well enough. I reckon passon's no notion what fancies lay hold on a young fellow or how powerful strong and masterful they be.'

'Very likely not.'

Trixie smoothed her apron and, catching sight of her reflection in a wall-glass, tidied her hair. She did this without coquetry and yet, Alleyn thought, with a perfect awareness of her own devastating femininity.

'And so – ?' he said.

'It was a bit of fun. No harm come of it. Or didn't ought to of. He's a proper good chap.'

'Did something come of it?'

She giggled. 'Sure enough. Ernie seen us. Last spring, 'twas one evening up to Copse Forge.'

She looked again at the wall-glass but abstractedly as if she saw in it not herself as she was now but as she had been on the evening she evoked. ''Twasn't nothing for him to fret hisself over, but he's a bit daft-like, is Ern.'

'What did he do about it?'

Nothing, it seemed, for a long time. He had gaped at them and then turned away. They had heard him stumble down the path through the copse. It was Trixie's particular talent not so much to leave the precise character of the interrupted idyll undefined as to suggest by this omission that it was of no particular importance. Ernie had gone, Ralph Stayne had become uneasy and embarrassed. He and Trixie parted company and that was the last time they had met, Alleyn gathered, for dalliance. Ralph had not returned to South Mardian for several weekends. When summer came, she believed him to have gone abroad during the long vacation. She answered all Alleyn's questions very readily and apparently with precision.

'In the end,' Alleyn suggested, 'did Ernie make mischief, or what?'

'So he did, then. After Camilla came back, 'twas.'

'Why then, particularly?'

'Reckon he knew what was in the wind. He's not so silly but what he doesn't notice. Easy for all to see Mr Ralph's struck down powerful strong by her.'

'But were they ever seen together?'

'No, not they.'

'Well, then – '

'He'd been courting her in London. Maids up to castle heard his great-auntie giving him a terrible rough-tonguing and him saying if Camilla would have him he'd marry her come fine or foul.'

'But where,' Alleyn asked patiently, 'does Ernie come in?'

Ernie, it appeared, was linked up with the maids at the castle. He was in the habit of drifting up there on Sunday afternoon when, on their good-natured sufferance, he would stand inside the door of the servants' hall, listening to their talk and, occasionally, contributing an item himself. Thus he had heard all about Dame Alice's strictures upon her great-nephew's attachment to Camilla. Ernie had been able, as it were, to pay his way by describing his own encounter with Ralph and Trixie in the copse. The elderly parlourmaid, a gossip of Trixie's, lost no time in acquainting her of the whole conversation. Thus the age-old mechanics of village inter-communication were neatly demonstrated to Alleyn.

'Did you mind,' he asked, 'about this tittle-tattle?'

'Lor', no,' she said. 'All they get out of life, I reckon, them old maidens.'

'Did anyone else hear of these matters?'

She looked at him with astonishment.

'Certain sure. Why wouldn't they?'

'Did the Guiser know, do you think?'

'He did, then. And so full of silly notions as a baby; him being chapel and terrible narrow in his views.'

'Who told him?'

'Why,' she said, 'Ernie, for sure. He told, and his Dad went raging and preachifying to Dame Alice and to Mr Ralph, saying he'd tell passon. Mr Ralph come and had a tell with me, axing what he did ought to do. And I told him pay no 'tention; hard words break no bones and no business of Guiser's when all's said. 'Course,' Trixie added, 'Mr Ralph was upset for fear his young lady might get to hear of it.'

'Did she?'

'I don't reckon she did. Though, if she had, it mightn't have made all that differ between them. She'm a sensible maid for all her grand bringing up: a lovely nature, true's steel and a lady. But proper proud of her mother's folk, mind. She's talked to me since she come back: nobody else to listen, I dessay, and when a maid's dizzy with love like Camilla she's a mighty need to be talking.'

'And you don't think she knew about you and Mr Ralph?'

'Not by my reckoning, though Mr Ralph got round to thinking maybe he should tell her. Should he make a clean breast of it to Camilla and I dunno what else beside. I told him it were best left unsaid. Anyway, Camilla had laid it down firm they was not to come anigh each other. But, last Sunday, he seen her in church and his natural burning desire for the maid took a-hold of him and he followed her up to Copse Forge and kissed her, and the Guiser come out of the smithy and seen them. Camilla says he ordered her off and

Mr Ralph told her it would be best if she went. So she did and left them together. I reckon Guiser gave Mr Ralph a terrible tonguing, but Camilla doesn't know what 'twas passed between them.'

'I see. Do you think the Guiser may have threatened to tell Camilla about you?'

Trixie thought this extremely likely. It appeared that, on the Monday, the Guiser had actually gone down to the Green Man and tackled Trixie herself, declaiming that Ralph ought to make an honest woman of her. For this extreme measure, Trixie said, perhaps a thought ambiguously, there was no need whatever. The Guiser had burst into a tirade saying that he wouldn't hear of his grand-daughter marrying so far 'above her station', and repeating the improper pattern of her mother's behaviour. It could lead, he said, to nothing but disaster. He added, with superb inconsistency, that, anyway, Ralph was morally bound to marry Trixie.

'What did you say to all that?' Alleyn asked her.

'I said I'd other notions.'

He asked her what had been the outcome of her interview with the Guiser and gathered that a sort of understanding had been arrived at between them. An armed neutrality was to be observed until after Sword Wednesday. Nobody could do the Betty's act as well as Ralph, and for the Guiser this was a powerful argument. Towards the end of their talk, the old man had become a good deal calmer. Trixie could see that a pleasing thought had struck him.

'Did you discover what this was?'

'So I did, then. He was that tickled with his own cunning, I reckon he had to tell me.'

'Yes?'

'He said he'd make his will and leave his money to Camilla. He said he'd make Mr Ralph do it for him and that'd stop his nonsense.'

'But why?'

'Because he'd make him lay it down that she'd only get the money if she didn't marry him,' said Trixie.

There was a long silence.

'Trixie,' Alleyn said at last, 'do you mind telling me if you were ever in love with Ralph Stayne?'

She stared at him and then threw back her head. The muscles in her neck swelled sumptuously and she laughed outright.

'Me! He's a nice enough young fellow and no harm in him but he's not my style and I'm not his. It were a bit of fun, like I said, and natural as birds in May: no offence taken either side.'

Thinking, evidently, that the interview was over, she stood up and, setting her hands at her waist, pulled down her dress to tidy it.

'Have you got a man of your own?' Alleyn asked.

'So I have then, and a proper man, too.'

'May I know who he is?'

'I don't see why for not,' she said slowly. 'It's Chris Andersen. Reckon you saw us a while back in the lane.'

'What did the Guiser have to say about that?'

For the first time since he spoke to her, Trixie looked uneasy. An apple-blossom blush spread over her face and faded, Alleyn thought, to an unusual pallor.

'You tell me,' he said, 'that the Guiser thought Mr Stayne should marry you. Did the Guiser know about Chris?'

She hesitated and then said: 'Reckon he knew, all right.'

'And objected?'

'He wasn't all that pleased, no doubt,' she said.

'Did he have an argument about it with Chris?'

She put her hand over her mouth and would say no more.

Alleyn said: 'I see you can keep things to yourself and I hope you'll decide to do so now. There's something else I want you to do.'

Trixie listened. When he'd finished she said: 'I reckon I can but try and try I will.'

He thanked her and opened the door for her to go out.

'A remarkable young woman,' he thought.

III

Fox, who had enjoyed a substantial high tea, sat on the edge of the bed, smoked his pipe and watched his chief get ready for his dinner-party.

'The water's hot,' Alleyn said. 'I'll say that for the Green Man or Trixie or whoever stokes the boilers.'

'What happened, if it's not indiscreet, of course, with Trixie?'

Alleyn told him.

'Fancy!' Mr Fox commented placidly. 'So the old boy asks the young solicitor to make out the will that's planned to put the kybosh on the romance. What a notion!'

'I'm afraid the Guiser was not only a bloody old tyrant but a bloody old snob into the bargain.'

'And the young solicitor,' Mr Fox continued, following his own line of thought, 'although he talks to us quite freely about the proposed will, doesn't mention this bit of it. Does he?'

'He doesn't.'

'Ah!' said Fox calmly. 'I dare say. And how was Trixie, Mr Alleyn?'

'From the point of view of sex, Brer Fox, Trixie's what nice women call a-moral. That's what *she* is.'

'Fancy!'

'She's a big, capable, good-natured girl with a code of her own and I don't suppose she's ever done a mean thing in her life. Moreover, she's a generous woman.'

'So it seems.'

'In every sense of the word.'

'That's right. And this morning,' Fox continued, 'Ernie let on that there were words between Chris and the old man. On account of Trixie, would you think?'

'I wouldn't be surprised.'

'Ah! before you go up to the castle, Mr Alleyn, would there be time for a quick survey of this case?'

'It'll have to be damn' quick. To put it your way, Fox, the case is going to depend very largely on a general refusal to believe in fairies. We've got the Guiser alive up to the time he ducks down behind the dolmen and waves to Ralph Stayne (if, of course, he did wave). About eight minutes later, we've got him still behind the dolmen, dead and headless. We've got everybody swearing blue murder he didn't leave the spot and offering to take Bible oaths nobody attacked him. And, remember, the presumably disinterested onlookers, Carey and the sergeant, agree about this. We've got to find an answer that will cover their evidence. I can only think of one and it's going to be a snorter to bring home.'

'You're telling me.'

'Consider the matter of bloodstains, for instance, and I wish to hell Curtis would get here and confirm what we suppose. If the five brothers, Begg, Otterly and Stayne had blood all over their clothes it wouldn't get us much nearer because that old ass Carey let them go milling round the corpse. As it is, Bailey tells me they've been over the lot and can't find anything beyond some smears on their trousers and sleeves. Begg, going on his own cloak-and-dagger experience in Germany, points out that the assailant in such cases is well enough bloodied to satisfy the third murderer in Macbeth. And he's right of course.'

'Yes, but we think we know the answer to that one,' said Fox. 'Don't we?'

'So we do. But it doesn't get us any closer to an arrest.'

'Motive?'

'I *despise* motive. (Why, by the way, don't we employ that admirable American usage?) I *despise* it. The case is lousy with motive. Everybody's got a sort of motive. We can't ignore it, of course, but it won't bring home the bacon, Brer Fox. Opportunity's the word, my boy. Opportunity.'

He shrugged himself into his jacket and attacked his head violently with a pair of brushes.

Fox said: 'That's a nice suit, Mr Alleyn, if I may say so. Nobody'd think you'd travelled all night in it.'

'It ought to be Victorian tails and a red silk handkerchief for the Dame of Mardian Castle. What'll you do, Fox? Could you bear to go down to the forge and see if the boys have unearthed the Guiser's wealth? Who's on duty there, by the way?'

'A fresh PC Carey got up by the afternoon bus from Biddlefast. The ambulance is coming from Yowford for the remains at nine. I ought to go down and see that through.'

'Come on, then. I'll drop you there.'

They went downstairs and, as they did so, heard Trixie calling out to some invisible person that the telephone lines had broken down.

'That's damn' useful,' Alleyn grumbled.

They went out to their car, which already had a fresh ledge of snow on it.

'Listen!' Alleyn said and looked up to where a lighted and partially opened window glowed theatrically beyond a light drift of falling snow. Through the opening came a young voice. It declaimed with extraordinary detachment and great attention to consonants:

' *"Nine men's morris is filled up with mud"*.'

'Camilla,' Alleyn said.

'What's she saying?' Fox asked, startled. Alleyn raised a finger. The voice again announced:

' *"Nine men's morris is filled up with mud"*.'

'It's a quotation. "Nine men's morris." Is that why I kept thinking it ought to be nine and not eight? Or did I – ?'

The voice began again, using a new inflexion.

' *"Nine men's morris is filled up with MUD"*.'

'So was ours this morning,' Alleyn muttered.

'I thought, the first time, she said "blood",' Fox ejaculated, greatly scandalized.

'Single track minds: that's what's the matter with us.' He called out cheerfully: 'You can't say "the human mortals want their winter here",' and Camilla stuck her head out of the window.

'Where are you off to?' she said, 'or doesn't one ask?'

'One doesn't ask. Goodnight, Titania. Or should it be Juliet?'

'Dr Otterly thinks it ought to be Cordelia.'

'He's got a thing about her. Stick to your fairy tales while you can,' Alleyn said. She gave a light laugh and drew back into her room.

They drove cautiously down the lane to the crossroads. Alleyn said: 'We've got to get out of Ernie what he meant by his speech from the dolmen, you know. And his remark about Chris and the old man. If a propitious moment presents itself, have a shot.'

'Tricky, a bit, isn't it?'

'Very. Hallo! Busy night at the smithy.'

Copse Forge was alert in the snowbound landscape. The furnace glowed and lights moved about in the interior: there was a suggestion of encrusted Christmas cards that might open to disclose something more disturbing.

When Alleyn and Fox arrived, however, it was to discover Simon Begg's car outside and a scene of semi-jubilant fantasy within. The five Andersen brothers had been exceedingly busy. Lanthorns, lighted candles and electric torches were all in play. A trestle-table had been rigged up in the middle of the smithy and, on it, as if they bore

witness to some successful parish féte, were many little heaps of
money. Copper, silver, paper: all were there; and, at the very
moment of arrival, Alleyn and Fox found Dan Andersen with his
brothers clustered round him, shining their torches on a neat golden
pile at one end of the table.

'Sovereigns,' Dan was saying. 'Eleven golden sovereigns. There
they be! Can you believe your eyes, chaps?'

'Gold,' Ernie said loudly, 'ain't it? Gold.'

'It'll 've been the granddad's, surely,' Andy said solemnly. 'He
were a great saver and hoarder and the dad after him: so like's two
cherrystones. As has always been recognized.'

A little worshipful chorus mounted above the totem brightness of
the sovereigns. A large policeman moved nearer the table and out of
the shadows behind the forge came Simon Begg, wearing the broad
and awkward smile of an onlooker at other people's good fortune.

They heard Alleyn and Fox and they all looked up, preoccupied
and perhaps a little wary.

Dan said: 'Look at this, sir. This is what we've found and never
thought to see. My father's savings and his dad's before him and no
doubt his before that. There's crown pieces here with a King's head
on them and sovereigns and bank notes so old and dirty it's hard to
say what they're worth. We're flabbergasted.'

'I'm not surprised,' Alleyn said, 'it's a fabulous sight. Where did
you find it all?'

Dan made a comprehensive sweep of his arm.

'Everywhere. Iron boxes under his bed. Mouldy old tins and pots
along the top shelves. Here it's been, as you might say, laughing at
us, I dunknowmany years. We've not touched on the half of it yet,
however. No doubt there'll be lashings more to come.'

'I can't credit!' Andy said. 'It's unnatural.'

'We're made, chaps,' Nat said doubtfully. 'Bean't we?'

'Have you found a will?' Alleyn asked.

'So we have, then,' they chanted. They were so much alike in
appearance and in manner that, again, Alleyn couldn't help thinking of them as chorus to the action.

'May I see it?'

Dan produced it quite readily. It had been found in a locked iron
box under the bed and was twenty years old.

Andy, who was gradually emerging as the least rugged and most sentimental of the Andersens, embarked with some relish on a little narrative.

'April the second, 1936. That was the day our Bess ran away to marry. Powerful angered he was that night. Wouldn't go to bed. Us could hear him tramping about in yur, all hours.'

'Stoked up the fire, he did,' Dan chipped in and he also adopted the story-teller's drone, 'and burnt all her bits of finery and anything else she left behind. Ah-huh!'

Ernie laughed uproariously and hit his knees.

Chris said: 'He must of wrote it that night. Next day when two chaps come in with a welding job, he axed 'em into his room and when they come out I yurd 'em laughing and telling each other they didn't reckon what the old chap left would make a millionaire of nobody. There's their names put to it in witness.'

'More fools them as it turns out,' Dan said amiably. 'Not to say "millionaire", mind, but handsome.'

They all murmured together and the policeman from Biddlefast cleared his throat.

Simon said: 'Funny how things work out, though, isn't it.'

Alleyn was reading the will. It was a very short document: the whole of the Guiser's estate was to be divided equally among his sons; 'on condition that they do not give any to my daughter Elizabeth or to any child she may bear on account of what she done this day. Signed W. Andersen.'

'Terrible bitter,' Andy pointed out and sighed heavily.

Nat, addressing himself to Alleyn, asked anxiously: 'But how do us chaps stand, sir? Is this here document a proper testymant? Will it hold up afore a coroner? Is it *law?*'

Alleyn had much ado not to reply: '"Aye, marry is't. Crowner's quest law!"' So evocative of those other countrymen were the Andersens, peering up at him, red-faced and bright-eyed in the lamplight.

He said: 'Your solicitor will be the man to talk to about that. Unless your father made a later will, I should think this one ought to be all right.'

'And then us'll have enough to turn this old shop into a proper masterpiece of a garridge, won't us, chaps?' Ernie demanded excitedly.

Dan said seriously: 'It's not the occasion to bring that up now, Ern. It'll come due for considering at the proper time.'

Chris said: 'Why not consider it now? It's at the back of what we're thinking. And with all this great heap of cash – well!'

Andy said: 'I don't fancy talking about it, knowing how set he was agin it.' He turned to Alleyn. 'Seems to me, sir, we ought to be axing you what's the right thing to do with all this stuff.'

'You should leave everything as it is until the will is proved. But I don't really know about these things and I've got to be off. Inspector Fox will stay here until the ambulance comes. I'd suggest that when your – your astonishing search is completed, you do very carefully count and lock away all this money. Indeed, if I may say so, I think you should keep a tally as you go. Goodnight.'

They broke into a subdued chorus of acknowledgement. Alleyn glanced at Fox and turned to go out. Simon said: 'Don't do anything you wouldn't do if I was watching you, all you bods. Cheery-ho-ho,' and accompanied Alleyn to the cars. Fox walked down with them.

'Like a lot of great big kids, really, aren't they?' Simon said.

Alleyn was non-committal.

'Well, Ern is, anyway,' Simon said defensively. 'Just a great big kid.' He opened the door for Alleyn and stood with his hand still on it. He looked at his boots and kicked the snow; at the moment rather like a small boy, himself.

'You all seem to pick on the old Corp,' Simon mumbled.

'We only want the facts from him, you know. As from everybody else.'

'But he's not *like* everybody else. He'll tell you *anything*. Irresponsible.'

('He's going to say it again,' Alleyn thought.)

'Just like a great big kid,' Simon added punctually.

'Don't worry,' Alleyn said. 'We'll try not to lose our heads.'

Simon grinned and looked at him sideways.

'It's nice for them, all the same,' he said. He rubbed his fingers and thumb together.

'Oh!' Alleyn said, 'the Guiser's hoard. Yes. Grand for them, isn't it? I must get on.'

He started his engine. It was cold and sluggish and he revved it up noisily. Ernie appeared in the pool of light outside the smithy door. He came slowly towards the car and then stopped. Something in his demeanour arrested Alleyn.

'Hi-ya, Corp,' Simon called out cheerfully. It was characteristic of him to bestow perpetual greetings.

Alleyn suddenly decided to take a chance. 'See here,' he said hurriedly to Simon, 'I want to ask Ernie something. I could get him by himself but I've a better chance of a reasonable answer if you stand by. Will you?'

'Look here, though – '

'Ernie,' Alleyn called, 'just a second, will you?'

Ernie moved forward.

'If you're trying to catch him out – ' Simon began.

'Do you suggest there's anything to catch?'

'No.'

'Ernie,' Alleyn said, 'come here a moment.'

Ernie walked slowly towards them, looking at Simon.

'Tell me,' Alleyn said, 'why did you say the German lady killed your father?'

Chris Andersen had come into the smithy doorway. Ernie and Simon had their backs turned to him.

Ernie said: 'I never. What I said, she *done* it.'

'Ah, for Pete's sake!' Simon ejaculated. 'Go on! Go right ahead. I dare say he knows, and, anyway, it couldn't matter less. Go on.'

But Ernie seemed to have been struck by another thought. 'Wummen!' he observed. 'It's them that's the trouble, all through, just like what the Guiser reckoned. Look at our Chris.'

The figure standing in the over-dramatic light from the smithy turned its head, stirred a little and was still again.

'What about him?' Alleyn asked very quietly and lifted a warning finger at Simon.

Ernie assumed a lordly off-hand expression. 'You can't,' he said, 'tell me nothing I don't know about them two,' and incontinently began to giggle.

Fox suddenly said: 'Is that so? Fancy!'

Ernie glanced at him. 'Ar! That's right. Him and Trix.'

'And the Guiser?' Alleyn suggested under his breath.

Ernie gave a long affirmative whistle.

Chris moved down towards them and neither Simon nor Ernie heard him. Alleyn stamped in the snow as if to warm his feet, keeping time with Chris.

Simon appealed to Alleyn. 'Honest to God,' he said, 'I don't know what this one's about. Honest to God.'

'All right,' Alleyn rejoined. 'Ask him. Quietly.'

'What's it all about, Corp?' Simon began obediently. 'Where did the Guiser come into it? What's the gen? Come on.'

Ernie, always more reasonable with Simon than with anyone else, said at once: 'Beg pardon, sir. I was meaning about Trix and what I told the Guiser I seen. You know. Her and Mr Ralph.'

Simon said: 'Hell!' And to Alleyn: 'I can't see this is of any interest to you, you know.'

Chris was close behind his brother.

'Was there a row about it?' Alleyn asked Ernie. 'On Sunday?'

Ernie whistled again, piercingly.

Chris's hand closed on his brother's arm. He twisted Ernie round to face him.

'What did I tell you?' he said, and slapped him across the face.

Ernie made a curious sound, half whimper, half giggle. Simon, suddenly very tough indeed, shouldered between them.

'Was that necessary?' he asked Chris.

'You mind your own bloody business,' Chris rejoined. He turned on his heel and went back into the smithy. Fox, after a glance at Alleyn, followed him.

'By God!' Simon said thoughtfully. He put his arm across Ernie's shoulders.

'Forget it, Corp,' he said. 'It's like what I said: nobody argues with the dumb. You talk too much, Corp.' He looked at Alleyn. 'Give him a break, sir,' Simon said. 'Can't you?'

But Ernie burst out in loud lamentation. 'Wummen!' he declared. 'There you are! Like what the old man said. They're all the same, that lot. Look what the foreigness done on us. Look what she done.'

'All right,' Alleyn said. 'What *did* she do?'

'Easy on, easy now, Corp. What did I tell you?' Simon urged very anxiously and looked appealing at Alleyn. 'Have a heart,' he begged.

He moved towards Ernie and checked abruptly. He stared at something beyond the rear of Alleyn's car.

Out of range of the light from the smithy, but visible against the background of snow and faintly illuminated by a hurricane lanthorn that one of them carried, were three figures. They came foward slowly into the light and were revealed.

Dr Otterly, Mrs Bünz and Ralph Stayne.

IV

Mrs Bünz's voice sounded lonely and small on the night air and had no more endurance than the jets of frozen breath that accompanied it. It was like the voice of an invalid.

'What is he saying about me? He is speaking lies. You must not believe what he tells you. It is because I was a German. They are in league against me. They think of me as an enemy, still.'

'Go on, Ernie,' Alleyn said.

'No!' Ralph Stayne shouted, and then, with an air that seemed to be strangely compounded of sheepishness and defiance, added:

'She's right. It's not fair.'

Dr Otterly said: 'I really do think, Alleyn – '

Mrs Bünz gabbled: 'I thank you. I thank you, gentlemen.' She moved forward.

'You keep out of yur,' Ernie said and backed away from her. 'Don't you go and overlook us 'ns.'

He actually threw up his forearm as if to protect himself, turned aside and spat noisily.

'There you are!' Simon said angrily to Alleyn. 'That's what *that* all adds up to.'

'All right, all right,' Alleyn said.

He looked past Simon at the smithy. Fox had come out and was massively at hand. Behind him stood the rest of the Andersen brothers, fitfully illuminated. Fox and one of the other men had torches and, whether by accident or design, their shafts of light reached out like fingers to Mrs Bünz's face.

It was worth looking at. As the image from a lantern slide that is being withdrawn may be momentarily overlaid by its successor, so alarm modulated into fanaticism in Mrs Bünz's face. Her lips moved. Out came another little jet of breath. She whispered: 'Wunderbar!' She advanced a pace towards Ernie, who at once retired upon his brothers. She clasped her hands and became lyrical.

'It is incredible,' Mrs Bünz whispered, 'and it is very, *very* interesting and important. He believes me to have the Evil Eye. It is remarkable.'

Without a word, the five brothers turned away and went back into the smithy.

'You are determined, all of you,' Alleyn said with unusual vehemence, 'to muck up the course of justice, aren't you? What are you three doing here?'

They had walked down from the pub, it appeared. Mrs Bünz wished to send a telegram and to buy some eucalyptus from the village shop, which she had been told would be open. Ralph was on his way home. Dr Otterly had punctured a tyre and was looking for an Andersen to change the wheel for him.

'I'm meant to be dining with you at the castle,' he said. 'Two nights running, I may tell you, which is an acid test, metaphorically and clinically, for any elderly stomach. I'll be damn' late if I don't get moving.'

'I'll drive you up.'

'Like me to change your wheel, Doc?' Simon offered.

'I didn't expect you'd be here. Yes, will you, Begg? And do the repair? I'll pick the car up on my way back and collect the wheel from your garage tomorrow.'

'Okey-doke, sir,' Simon said. 'I'll get cracking, then.' He tramped off, whistling self-consciously.

'Well,' Ralph Stayne said from out of the shadows behind Alleyn's car. 'I'll be off too, I think. Goodnight.'

They heard the snow squeak under his boots as he walked away.

'I also,' said Mrs Bünz.

'Mrs Bünz,' Alleyn said. 'Do you really believe it was only the look in your eye that made Ernie say what he did about you?'

'But yes. It is one of the oldest European superstitions. It is fascinating to find it. The expression "overlooking" proves it. I am immensely interested,' Mrs Bünz said rather breathlessly.

'Go and send your telegram,' Alleyn rejoined crossly. 'You are behaving foolishly, Mrs Bünz. Nobody, least of all the police, wants to bully you or dragoon you or brainwash you, or whatever you're frightened of. Go and get your eucalyptus and snuff it up and let us hope it clears your head for you. *Guten abend*, Mrs Bünz.'

He walked quickly up the path to Fox.

'I'll hand you all that on a plate, Fox,' he said. 'Keep the tabs on Ernie. If necessary, we'll have to lock him up. What a party! All right?'

'All right, Mr Alleyn.'

'Hell, we must go! Where's Otterly? Oh, there you are. Come on.'

He ran down the path and slipped into the car. Dr Otterly followed slowly.

Fox watched them churn off in the direction of Mardian Castle.

CHAPTER 10

Dialogue for a Dancer

The elderly parlourmaid put an exquisite silver dish filled with puckered old apples on the table. Dame Alice, Dulcie, Alleyn and Dr Otterly removed their mats and finger bowls from their plates. Nobody helped themselves to apples.

The combined aftermath of pallid soup, of the goose that was undoubtedly the victim of Ernie's spleen, and of queen's pudding, lingered in the cold room together with the delicate memory of a superb red wine. The parlour-maid returned, placed a decanter in front of Dame Alice, and then withdrew.

'Same as last night,' Dame Alice said. She removed the stopper and pushed the decanter towards Dr Otterly.

'I can scarcely believe my good fortune,' he replied. He helped himself and leant back in his chair. 'We're greatly honoured, believe me, Alleyn. A noble wine.'

The nobility of the port was discussed for some time. Dame Alice, who was evidently an expert, barked out information about it, no doubt in much the same manner as that of her male forebears. Alleyn changed down (or up according to the point of view) into the appropriate gear and all the talk was of vintage, body and aroma. Under the beneficent influence of the port even the dreadful memory of wet Brussels sprouts was gradually effaced.

Dulcie, who was dressed in brown velveteen with a lace collar, had recovered her usual air of vague acquiescence, though she occasionally threw Alleyn a glance that seemed to suggest that she knew a trick worth two of his and could look after herself if the need arose.

In the drawing-room, Alleyn had seen an old copy of one of those publications that are dedicated to the profitable enshrinement of family relationships. Evidently, Dame Alice and Dulcie had consulted this work with reference to himself. They now settled down to a gruelling examination of the kind that leaves not a second-cousin unturned nor a collateral unexplored. It was a pastime that he did not particularly care for and it gave him no opportunity to lead the conversation in the direction he had hoped it would take.

Presently, however, when the port had gone round a second time, some execrable coffee had been offered and a maternal great-aunt of Alleyn's had been tabulated and dismissed, the parlourmaid went out and Dame Alice suddenly shouted:

'Got yer man?'

'Not yet,' Alleyn confessed.

'Know who did it?'

'We have our ideas.'

'Who?'

'It's a secret.'

'Why?'

'We might be wrong and then what fools we'd look.'

'I'll tell yer who I'd back for it.'

'Who?' asked Alleyn in his turn.

'Ernest Andersen. He took the head off that goose you've just eaten and you may depend upon it he did as much for his father. Over-excited. Gets above himself on Sword Wednesday, always. Was it a full moon last night, Otters?'

'I – yes, I rather think – yes. Though, of course, one couldn't see it.'

'There yar! All the more reason. They always get worse when the moon's full. Dulcie does, don't you, Dulcie?' asked her terrible aunt.

'I'm sorry, Aunt Akky. I wasn't listening.'

'There yar! I said you always get excited when the moon's full.'

'Well, I think it's awfully *pretty,*' Dulcie said, putting her head on one side.

'How,' Alleyn intervened rather hurriedly, 'do you think Ernie managed it, Dame Alice?'

'That's for you to find out.'

'True.'

'Pass the port. Help yourself.'

Alleyn did so.

'Have you heard about the great hoard of money that's turned up at Copse Forge?' he asked.

They were much interested in this news. Dame Alice said the Andersens had hoarded money for as long as they'd been at the forge, a matter of four centuries and more, and that Dan would do just the same now that his turn had come.

'I don't know so much about that, you know,' Dr Otterly said, squinting at his port. 'The boys and Simon Begg have been talking for a long time about converting the Forge into a garage and petrol station. Looking forward to when the new road goes through.'

This, as might have been expected, aroused a fury in Dame Alice. Alleyn listened to a long diatribe, during which her teeth began to play up, against new roads, petrol pumps and the decline of proper feeling in the artisan classes.

'William,' she said (she pronounced it Will'm), 'would never've had it. Never! He told me what his fools of sons were plottin'. Who's the feller that's put 'em up to it?'

'Young Begg, Aunt Akky.'

'Begg? Begg? What's he got to do with it? He's a grocer.'

'No, Aunt Akky, he left the shop during the war and went into the Air Force and now he's got a garage. He was here yesterday.'

'You don't have to tell me that, Dulcie. Of course I know young Begg was here. I'd have given him a piece of my mind if you'd told me what he was upter.'

'When did you see William Andersen, Dame Alice?'

'What? When? Last week. I sent for 'im. Sensible old feller, Will'm Andersen.'

'Are we allowed to ask why you sent for him?'

'Can if yer like. I told 'im to stop his granddaughter makin' sheep's eyes at my nephew.'

'Goodness!' Dulcie said, 'was she? Did Ralph like it? Is that what you meant, Aunt Akky, when you said Ralph was a rake?'

'No.'

'If you don't mind my cutting in,' Dr Otterly ventured, 'I don't believe little Miss Camilla made sheep's eyes at Ralph. She's a charming child with very nice manners.'

'Will'm 'greed with me. Look what happened when his girl 'loped with young Campion. That sort of mix-up never answers and he knew it.'

'One can't be too careful, can one, Aunt Akky,' Dulcie said, 'with men?'

'Lor', Dulcie, what a stoopid gel you are. When,' Dame Alice asked brutally, 'have you had to look after yerself, I'd like to know?'

'Ah-ha, Aunt Akky!'

'Fiddlesticks!'

The parlourmaid reappeared with cigarettes and, surprisingly, a great box of cigars.

'I picked 'em up,' Dame Alice said, 'at old Tim Combardale's sale. We'll give you ten minutes. You can bring 'em to the drawin'-room. Come on, Dulcie.'

She held out her arm. Dulcie began to collect herself.

'Let me haul,' Alleyn said, 'may I?'

'Thanks. Bit groggy in the fetlocks, these days. Go with the best, once I'm up.'

He opened the door. She toddled rapidly towards it and looked up at him.

'Funny world,' she said. 'Ain't it?'

'Damned odd.'

'Don't be too long over your wine. I've got a book to show you and I go up in half an hour. Don't keep 'im now, Otters.'

'Wouldn't dream of it,' Dr Otterly said. When the door had shut he placed his hand on his diaphragm and muttered: 'By heaven, that was an athletic old gander. But what a cellar, isn't it?'

'Wonderful,' Alleyn said abstractedly.

He listened to Dr Otterly discoursing on the Mardian family and its vanished heyday. 'Constitutions of oxes and heads of cast-iron, the lot of them,' Dr Otterly declared. 'And arrogant!' He wagged a finger. ''Nuff said.' It occurred to Alleyn that Dr Otterly's head was not perhaps of the same impregnability as the Mardians'.

'Join the ladies?' Dr Otterly suggested, and they did so.

Dame Alice was established in a bucket-shaped armchair that cut her off in some measure from anybody that wasn't placed directly in front of her. Under her intructions, Alleyn drew up a hideous Edwardian stool to a strategic position. Dulcie placed a newspaper

parcel on her grandmother's knee. Alleyn saw with some excitement
a copy of *The Times* for 1871.

'Time someone got some new wrappin' for this,' Dame Alice said
and untied the tape with a jerk.

'By heaven,' Dr Otterly said, waving his cigar, 'you're highly
favoured, Alleyn. By heaven, you are!'

'There yar,' said Dame Alice. 'Take it. Give him a table, Dulcie, it's
fallin' to bits.'

Dr Otterly brought up a table and Alleyn laid down the book she
had pushed into his hands. It was one of the kind that used to
be called 'commonplace' and evidently of a considerable age. The
leather binding had split down the back. He opened it and found that
it was the diary of one 'Ambrose Hilary Mardian of Mardian Place,
nr. Yowford, written in the year 1798.'

'My great-grandfather,' said Dame Alice. 'I was born Mardian and
married a Mardian. No young. Skip to the Wednesday before Christmas.'

Alleyn turned over the pages. 'Here we are,' he said.

The entry, like all the others, was written in an elaborate copper-
plate. The ink had faded to a pale brown.

'Sword Wednesday,' he read. '1798. A note on the Mardian
Morris of 5 Sons.' Alleyn looked up for a second at Dame Alice and
then began to read.

'This evening being the occasion of the Mardian Mumming
or Sword Dance (which is perhaps the more proper way of
describing it than as a Morisco or Morris) I have thought to set
down the ceremony as it was performed in my childhood for I
have perceived since the death of old Yeo Andersen at Copse
Forge there has been an abridgement of the doggerel which I
fear either through indifference, forgetfulness or sheepishness
on the part of the morris side – if morris or morisco it can be
named – may become altogether neglected and lost. This were
a pity as the ceremony is curious and I believe in some aspects
unique. For in itself it embraces divers others, as the mummers' play in which the father avoids death from his sons by
breaking the glass or knot and then by showing his Will and
the third time is in mockery beheaded. Also from this source is
derived the Sword Dance itself in three parts and from yet

another the quaint device of the rabbit cap. Now, to leave all
this, my purpose here is to set down what was always said by
Yeo Andersen the smith and his forebears who had enacted the
part of the Fool. Doubtless the words have been changed as
time goes by but here they are, as given to me by Yeo. These
words are not spoken out boldly but rather are they mumbled
under the breath. Sorry enough stuff it is, no doubt, but perhaps of interest to those who care for these old simple pastimes
of our country people.

'At the end of the first part of the Sword Dance as he breaks
the glass, the Fool says:

> *Once for a looker and all must agree*
> *If I bashes the looking-glass so I'll go free.*"

'At the end of the second part he shows them his Will and
says:

> *Twice for a Testament. Read it and see*
> *If you look at the leavings then so I'll go free.*"

'At the end of the third part, he puts his head in the Lock
and says:

> *Here comes the rappers to send me to bed*
> *They'll rapper my head off and then I'll be dead.*"

'And after that he says:

> *Betty to lover me*
> *Hobby to cover me*
> *If you cut off my head*
> *I'll rise from the dead.*"

'NB I believe the word "rapper" to be a corruption of
"rapier", though in other parts it is used of wooden swords.
Some think it refers to a practice of rapping or hitting with
them after the manner of Harlequin in his dancing. Yet in the
Mardian dance the swords are of steel pierced for cords at the
point.'

There the entry for Sword Wednesday ended.

'Extraordinarily interesting,' Alleyn said. 'Thank you.' He shut the book and turned to Dr Otterly. 'Did the Guiser speak any of this verse?'

'I believe he did, but he was very cagey about it. He certainly used to mutter something at those points in the dance but he wouldn't tell anybody what it was. The boys were near enough to hear but they don't like talking about it, either. Damn' ridiculous when you come to think of it,' Dr Otterly said, slightly running his words together. 'But interesting all the same.'

'Did he ever see this diary, Dame Alice?'

'I showed it to him. One of the times when he'd come to mend the boiler. He put on a cunnin' look and said he knew all about it.'

'Would you think these lines, particularly the last four, are used in other places where folk dancing thrives?'

'Definitely not,' Dr Otterly said, perhaps rather more loudly than he had intended. 'They're not in the Revesby text nor anywhere else in British ritual mumming. Purely local. Take the word "lover" used as a verb. You still heard it hereabouts when I was a boy, but I doubt if it's ever been found elsewhere in England. Certainly not in that context.'

Alleyn put his hand on the book and turned to his hostess. 'Clever of you,' he said 'to think of showing me this. I congratulate you.' He got up and stood looking at her. She turned her Mrs Noah's face up to him and blinked like a lizard.

'Not goin', are yer?'

'Isn't it your bedtime?'

'Most certainly it is,' said Dr Otterly, waving his cigar.

'Aunt Akky, it's after ten.'

'Fiddlededee. Let's have some brandy. Where's the grog-tray? Ring the bell, Otters.'

The elderly parlourmaid answered the bell at once, like a servant in a fairy tale, ready-armed with a tray, brandy-glasses, and a bottle of fabulous cognac.

'I 'fer it at this stage,' Dame Alice said, 'to havin' it with the coffee. Papa used to say: "When dinner's dead in yer and bed is still remote, ring for the brandy." Sound advice in my 'pinion.'

It was eleven o'clock when they left Mardian Castle.

Fox, running through his notes with a pint of beer before the fire, looked up over his spectacles when his chief came in. There was an unusual light in Alleyn's eyes.

'You're later than I expected, sir,' said Fox. 'Shall I order you a pint?'

'Not unless you feel like carrying me up to bed after it. I've been carousing with the Dame of Mardian Castle. She may be ninety-four, Fox, but she carries her wine like a two-year-old, does that one.'

'God bless my soul! Sit down, Mr Alleyn.'

'I'm all right. I must say I wonder how old Otterly's managing under his own steam. He was singing the "Jewel Song" from Faust in a rousing falsetto when we parted.'

'What did you have for dinner? To eat, I mean.'

'Ernie's victim and sodden Brussels sprouts. The wine, however, was something out of this world. Laid down by one of the gods in the shape of Dame Alice's papa. But the *pièce de résistance*, Brer Fox, the wonder of the evening, handed to me, as it were, on a plate by Dame Alice herself, was – what do you suppose?'

'I *don't* suppose, sir,' Fox said, smiling sedately.

'The little odd golden morsel of information that clicks down into the pattern and pulls it together. The key to the whole damn' set-up, my boy. Don't look scandalized, Brer Fox, I'm not so tight that I don't know a crucial bit of evidence when it's shoved under my nose. Have you heard the weather report?'

Mr Fox began to look really disturbed. He cleared his throat and said warmer and finer weather had been predicted.

'Good,' Alleyn cried and clapped him on the back. 'Excellent. You're in for a treat.'

'What sort of treat,' Mr Fox said, 'for heaven's sake?'

'A touch of the sword and fiddle, Brer Fox. A bit of hey-nonny-no. A glimpse of Merrie England with bells on. Nine men's morris, mud and all. Repeat *nine*.'

'Eh?'

'We're in for a reconstruction, my boy, and I'll tell you why. Now, listen.'

II

The mid-winter sun smiled faint as an invalid over South and East Mardian on the Friday after Sword Wednesday. It glinted on the breakfast tables of the Reverend Mr Samuel Stayne and his aunt,

Dame Alice Mardian. It touched up the cruet-stand and the Britannia metal in the little dining-room at the Green Man and an emaciated ray even found its way to the rows of bottles in the bar and to the anvil at Copse Forge. A feeble radiance it was but there was something heartening about it nevertheless. Up at Yowford, Dr Otterly surveyed the scene with an uplifting of his spirit that he would have found hard to explain. Also at Yowford, Simon Begg, trundling out Dr Otterly's wheel with its mended puncture, remembered his winning bet, assured himself that he stood a fair chance now of mending his fortune with an interest in a glittering petrol station at Copse Forge, reminded himself it wouldn't, under the circumstances, look nice to be too obviously pleased about this, and broke out, nevertheless, into a sweet and irresponsibly exultant whistling.

Trixie sang and the potboy whistled louder but less sweetly than Simon. Camilla brushed her short hair before her open window and repeated a voice-control exercise. 'Bibby bobby bounced a ball against the wall.' She thought how deeply she was in love, and, like Simon, told herself it wasn't appropriate to be so obviously uplifted. Then the memory of her grandfather's death suddenly flooded her thoughts and her heart was filled with a vast pity and love, not only for him but for all the world. Camilla was eighteen and a darling.

Dame Alice woke from a light doze and felt for a moment quite desperately old. She saw a robin on her window-sill. Sharp as a thorn were its bright eyes and quick as thought the turn of its sun-polished head. Down below, the geese were in full scream. Dulcie would be pottering about in the dining-room. The wave of depression receded. Dame Alice was aware of her release but not, for a moment, of its cause. Then she remembered her dinner-party. Her visitor had enjoyed himself. It was, she thought, thirty years – more – since she had been listened to like that. He was a pretty fellow, too. By 'pretty' Dame Alice meant 'dashing'. And what was it he'd said when he left? That with her permission they would revive the Mardian Morris that afternoon. Dame Alice was not moved by the sort of emotions that the death of the Guiser had aroused in younger members of Wednesday's audience. The knowledge that his decapitated body had been found in

her courtyard did not fill her with horror. She was no longer sus-
ceptible to horror. She merely recognized in herelf an unusual
feeling of anticipation and connected it with her visitor of last
night. She hadn't felt so lively for ages.

'Breakfast,' she thought, and jerked at the tapestry bell-pull by
her bed.

Dulcie in the dining-room heard the bell jangling away in the servants' hall. She roused herself, took the appropriate dishes off the
hot plate and put them on the great silver tray. Porridge. Kedgeree.
Toast. Marmalade. Coffee. The elderly parlourmaid came in and took
the tray up to Dame Alice.

Dulcie was left to push crumbs about the tablecloth and hope that
the police wouldn't find the murderer too soon. Because if they did,
Mr Alleyn, to whom she had shown herself as a woman of the
world, would go somewhere else.

III

Ralph Stayne looked down the table at his father, who had, he
noticed, eaten no breakfast.

'You're looking a bit poorly, Pop,' he said. 'Anything wrong?'

His father stared at him in pale bewilderment.

'My dear chap,' he said, 'no. Not with me. But the – the events of
the night before last – '

'Oh!' Ralph said, 'that! Yes, of course. As long as it's only that – I
mean,' he went on hurriedly, answering the look in his father's eye,
'as long as it's not anything actually *wrong* with you. Yes, I *know* it
was ghastly about the poor old Guiser. It was. Quite frightful.'

'I can't get it out of my head. Forgive me, old boy, but I really
don't know how you contrive to be so – so resilient.'

'I? I expect this sounds revoltingly tough to you – but, you see,
Pop, if one's seen rather a lot of that particular kind of horror – well,
it's a hell of a sight different. I have. On the deck of a battleship
among other places. I'm damn' – blast, I keep swearing! – I couldn't
be sorrier about the Guiser but the actual look of the thing wasn't all
that much of a horror to me.'

'I suppose not. I suppose not.'

'One'd go mad,' Ralph said, 'if one didn't get tough. When there's a war on. Simmy-Dick Begg would agree. So would Ernie and Chris. Although it *was* their father. Any returned chap would agree.'

'I suppose so.'

Ralph got up. He squared his shoulders, looked steadily at his father and said: 'Camilla's the one who really did get an appalling shock.'

'I know. Poor child. I wondered if I should go and see her, Ralph.'

'Yes,' Ralph said. 'I wish you would. I'm going, now, and I'll tell her. She'll be awfully pleased.'

His father, looking extremely disturbed, said: 'My dear old man, you're not – ?'

'Yes, Pop,' Ralph said, 'I'm afraid I am. I've asked Camilla to marry me.'

His father got up and walked to the windows. He looked out on the dissolving whiteness of his garden.

'I wish this hadn't happened,' he said. 'Something was suggested last night by Dulcie that seemed to hint at it. I – as a churchman, I hope I'm not influenced by – by – well, my dear boy, by any kind of snob's argument. I'm sure I'm not. Camilla is a dear child and, other things being equal, I should be really delighted.' He rubbed up his thin hair and said ruefully: 'It'll worry Aunt Akky most awfully.'

'Aunt Akky'll have to lump it, I'm afraid,' Ralph said, and his voice hardened. 'She evidently heard that I've been seeing a good deal of Camilla in London. She's already tried to bulldoze me about it. But honestly, Pop, what, after all, has it got to do with Aunt Akky? I know Aunt Akky's marvellous. I adore her. But I refuse to accept her as a sort of animated tribal totem though I admit she looks very much like one.'

'It's not only that,' his father said miserably. 'There's – forgive me, Ralph, I really detest having to ask you this, but isn't there – some-one – '

Mr Stayne stopped and looked helplessly at his son. 'You see,' he said, 'I've listened to gossip. I tried not to, but I listened.'

Ralph said: 'You're talking about Trixie Plowman, aren't you?'

'Yes.'

'Who gossiped? Please tell me.'

'It was old William Andersen.'

Ralph drew in his breath. 'I was afraid of that,' he said.

'He was genuinely worried. He thought it his duty to talk to me. You know how adamant his views were. Apparently Ernie had seen you and Trixie Plowman together. Old William was the more troubled because, on last Sunday morning – '

'It appears to be my fate,' Ralph said furiously, 'to be what the Restoration dramatists call "discovered" by the Andersens. It's no good trying to explain, Pop. It'd only hurt you. I know you would look on this Trixie thing as – well – '

'As a sin? I do, indeed.'

'But – it was so brief and so much outside the general stream of my life. And hers – Trixie's. It was just a sort of natural thing; a little kindness of hers.'

'You can't expect me to take that view of it.'

'No,' Ralph said. 'I'll only sound shallow or something.'

'It's not a question of how you sound. It's a question of wrong-doing, Ralph. There's the girl – Trixie herself.'

'She's all right. Honestly. She's going to be tokened to Chris Andersen.'

The Rector momentarily shut his eyes. 'Oh, Ralph!' he said and then: 'William Andersen forbade it. He spoke to Chris on Sunday.'

'Well, anyway, *now* they can,' Ralph said, and then looked rather ashamed of himself. 'I'm sorry, Pop. I shouldn't have put it like that, I suppose. Look: it's all *over*, that thing. It was before I knew Camilla. I did regret it very much, after I loved Camilla. Does that help?'

The Rector made a most unhappy gesture. 'I am talking to a stranger,' he said. 'I have failed you, dreadfully, Ralph. It's quite dreadful.'

A bell rang distantly.

'They've fixed the telephone up,' the Rector said miserably.

'I'll go.'

Ralph went out and returned looking bewildered.

'It was Alleyn,' he said. 'The man from the Yard. They want us to go up to the castle this afternoon.'

'To the *castle?*'

'To do the Five Sons again. They want you, too, Pop.'

'Me. But why?'

'You were an observer.'

'Oh *dear!*'

'Apparently they're calling everybody up: Mrs Bünz included.'

Ralph joined his father in a kind of half companionable dissonance and looked across the rectory tree-tops towards East Mardian,
where a column of smoke rose gracefully from the pub.

Trixie had done her early chores and seen that the fires were
burning brightly.

She had also taken Mrs Bünz's breakfast up to her.

At this moment, Trixie was behaving oddly. She stood with a can
of hot water outside Mrs Bünz's bedroom door, intently listening.
The expression of her face was not at all sly, rather it was grave and
attentive. On the other side of the door, Mrs Bünz clicked her knife
against her plate and her cup on its saucer. Presently there was a
more complicated clatter as she put her tray down on the floor
beside her bed. This was followed by the creak of a wire mattress, a
heavy thud and the pad of bare feet. Trixie held her breath, listened
feverishly and, then, without knocking, quickly pushed open the
door and walked in.

'I'm sure I do ax your pardon, ma'am,' Trixie said. 'Axcuse me,
please.' She crossed the room to the wash-stand, set down her can
of water, returned past Mrs Bünz and went out again. She shut the
door gently behind her and descended to the back parlour, where
Alleyn, Fox, Thompson and Bailey had finished their breakfasts and
were setting their course for the day.

'Axcuse me, sir,' Trixie said composedly.

'All right, Trixie. Any news for us?'

'So there is, then.' She crossed her plump arms and laid three
fingers of each hand on the opposite shoulder. 'So broad's that,' she
said, 'and proper masterpieces for colour: blue and red and yaller
and all puffed up angrily-like, either side.'

'You're a clever girl. Thank you very much.'

'Have you in the force yet, Miss Plowman,' Fox said, beaming at
her.

Trixie gave them a tidy smile, cleared the breakfast things away,
asked if that would be all and left the room.

'Pity,' Thompson said to Bailey. 'There isn't the time.'

Bailey, who was a married man, grinned sourly.

'Have we got through to everybody, Fox?' Alleyn asked.

'Yes, Mr Alleyn. All set for four o'clock at the castle. The weather report's still favourable, the telephone's working again, and Dr Curtis has rung up to say he hopes to get to us by this evening.'

'Good. Before we go any further, I think we'd better have a look at the general set-up. It'll take a bit of time but I'll be glad of a chance to try and get some sort of shape out of it.'

'It'd be a nice change to come up against something unexpected, Mr Alleyn,' Thompson grumbled. 'We haven't struck a thing so far.'

'We'll see if we can surprise you. Come on.'

Alleyn put his file on the table, walked over to the fireplace and began to fill his pipe. Fox polished his spectacles. Bailey and Thompson drew chairs up and produced their notebooks. They had the air of men who had worked together for a long time and who understood each other's ways.

'You know,' Alleyn said, 'if this case had turned up three hundred years ago, nobody would have had any difficulty in solving it. It'd have been regarded by the villagers, at any rate, as an open-and-shut affair.'

'Would it, now?' Fox said placidly. 'How?'

'Magic.'

'Hell!' Bailey said, and looked faintly disgusted.

'Ask yourselves. Look how the general case echoes the pattern of the performance. Old Man. Five Sons. Money. A will. Decapitation. The only thing that doesn't tally is the poor old boy's failure to come to life again.'

'You reckon, do you, sir,' Thompson asked, 'that, in the olden days, they'd have taken a superstitious view of the death?'

'I do. The initiates would have thought that the god was dissatisfied or that the gimmick had misfired, or that Ernie's offering of the goose had roused the bloodlust of the stone or that the rites had been profaned and the Guiser punished for sacrilege. Which again tallies, by the way.'

'Does it?' Bailey asked, and added: 'Oh, yes. What you said, Mr Alleyn. That's right.'

'The authorities, on the other hand,' Alleyn went on, 'would have plumped at once for witchcraft and the whole infamous machinery of seventeenth century investigation would have begun to tick over.'

'Do you reckon,' Thompson said, 'that any of these chaps take the superstitious view? Seems hardly credible but – well?'

'Ernie?' Fox suggested rather wearily.

'He's dopey enough, isn't he, Mr Fox?'

'He's not so dopey,' Alleyn said strongly, 'that he can't plan an extremely cunning leg-pull on his old man, his four brothers, Simon Begg, Dr Otterly and Ralph Stayne. And jolly nearly bring it off, what's more.'

'Hal-*lo*,' Bailey said under his breath to Thompson. 'Here comes the "R. A." touch.'

Fox, who overheard him, bestowed a pontifical but not altogether disapproving glance upon him. Bailey, aware of it, said: 'Is this going to be one of your little surprises, Mr Alleyn?'

Alleyn said: 'Damn' civil of you to play up. Yes, it is, for what it's worth. Bring out that chit the Guiser's supposed to have left on his door, saying he wouldn't be able to perform.'

Bailey produced it, secured between two sheets of glass and clearly showing a mass of finger-prints where he had brought them up.

'The old chap's prints,' he said, 'and Ernie's. I got their dabs after you left yesterday afternoon. Nobody objected, although I don't think Chris Andersen liked it much. He's tougher than his brothers. There's a left and right thumb of Ernie's on each side of the tack hole. And all the rest of the gang, which is what you'd expect, isn't it, if they handed it round?'

'Yes,' Alleyn said. 'And do you remember where Ernie said he found it?'

'Tacked to the door. There's the tack-hole.'

'And where are the Guiser's characteristic prints? Suppose he pushed the paper over the head of the existing tack which the nature of the hole seems to suggest? You'd get a right and left thumb print on each side of the hole, wouldn't you? And what *do* you get? A right and left thumb print, sure enough. But whose?'

Bailey said: 'Ah *hell*! Ernie's.'

'Yes, Ernie's. So Ernie shoved it over the tack. But Ernie says he found it there when he came down to get the Guiser. So what's Ernie up to?'

'Rigging the old man's indisposition?' Fox said.

'I think so.'

Fox raised his eyebrows and read the Guiser's message aloud.

'"Can't mannage it young Ern will have to. W. A."'

'It's the old man's writing, isn't it, Mr Alleyn?' Thompson said. 'Wasn't that checked?'

'It's his writing all right, but, in my opinion, it wasn't intended for his fellow-mummers, it wasn't originally tacked to the door, it doesn't refer to the Guiser's inability to perform and it doesn't mean young Ern will have to go on in his place.'

There was a short silence.

'Speaking for self,' Fox said, 'I am willing to buy it, Mr Alleyn.' He raised his hand. 'Wait a bit, though,' he said. 'Wait a bit! I've started.'

'Away you go.'

'The gardener's boy went down on Tuesday afternoon with a note for the Guiser telling him he'd got to sharpen that slasher himself and return it by bearer. The Guiser was in Biddlefast. Ernie took the note. Next morning, wasn't it? – the boy comes for the slasher. It isn't ready and he's told by Ernie that it'll be brought up later. Any good?'

'You're away to a pretty start.'

'All right, all right. So Ernie does sharpen the slasher and, on the Wednesday, he does take it up to the castle. Now Ernie didn't give the boy a note from the Guiser, but that doesn't mean the Guiser didn't write one. How's that?'

'You're thundering up the straight.'

'It means Ernie kept it and pushed it over that tack and pulled it off again and, when he was sent down to fetch his dad, he didn't go near him. He dressed himself up in the Guiser's rig while the old boy was snoozing on his bed and he lit off for the castle and showed the other chaps this ruddy note. Now then!'

'You've breasted the tape, Brer Fox, and the trophy is yours.'

IV

'Not,' Alleyn said dubiously, observing his colleagues, 'that it gets us all that much farther on. It gets us a length or two nearer but that's all.'

'What *does* it do for us?' Fox ruminated.

'It throws a light on Ernie's frame of mind before the show. He's told us himself he went hurtling up the hill in their station wagon dressed in the Guiser's mummery and feeling wonderful. His dearest ambition was about to be raised: he was to act the leading rôle: literally to "Play the Fool", in the Dance of the Sons. He was exalted. Ernie's not the village idiot: he's an epileptic with all the characteristics involved.'

'Exaggerated moods, sort of?'

'That's it. He gets up there and hands over the note to his brothers. The understudy's bundled into Ernie's clothes, the note is sent in to Otterly. It's all going Ernie's way like a charm. The zeal of the folk dance sizzles in his nervous ganglions or wherever fanaticism does sizzle. I wouldn't mind betting he remembered his sacrifice of our last night's dinner upon the Mardian Stone and decided it had brought him luck. Or something.'

Alleyn stopped short and then said in a changed voice: ' "It will have blood, they say. Blood will have blood." I bet Ernie subscribes to that unattractive theory.'

'Bringing him in pretty close to the mark, aren't you, Mr Alleyn?'

'Well, of course, he's close to the mark, Brer Fox. He's as hot as hell, is Ernie. Take a look at him. All dressed up and somewhere to go with his audience waiting for him. Dr Otterly, tuning his fiddle. Torches blazing. It doesn't matter whether it's Stratford-upon-Avon with all the great ones in waiting behind the curtain or the Little Puddleton Mummers quaking in their borrowed buskins; no, by heaven, nor the Andersen brothers listening for the squeal of a fiddle in the snow: there's the same kind of nervous excitement let loose. And, when you get a chap like Ernie – well, look at him. At the zero hour, when expectation is ready to topple over into performance, who turns up?'

The Guiser.'

'The Guiser. Like a revengeful god. Driven up the hill by Mrs Bünz. The Old Man himself, in what the Boys would call a proper masterpiece of a rage. Out he gets, without a word to his driver, and wades in. He didn't say much. If there was any mention of the hanky-panky with the written message, it didn't lead to any explanation. He seems merely to have launched himself at Ernie, practically lugged the

clothes off him, forced him to change back to his own gear and herded them on for the performance. All right. And how did Ernie feel?
Ernie, whose pet dog the old man had put down, Ernie who'd
manoeuvred himself into the major role in this bit of prehistoric pantomime, Ernie who was on top of the world? How did he feel?'

'Murderous?' Thompson offered.

'I think so. Murderous.'

'Yes,' said Fox and Bailey and Thompson. 'Yes. Well. What?'

'He goes on for their show, doesn't he, with the ritual sword
that he's sharpened until half-way down it's like a razor: the
sword that cut the Guiser's hand in a row they had at their last
practice, which was first blood to Ernie, by the way. On he goes
and takes it out on the thistles. He slashes their heads off with
great sweeps of his sword: Ernie is a thistle whiffler and he whif-
fles thistles with a thistle whiffler. Diction exercise for Camilla
Campion. He prances about and plays the savage. After that he
gets warmed up still more effectively by dancing and going
through the pantomime of cutting the Fool's head off. And
remember he's in a white hot rage with the Fool. What happens
next to Ernie? Nothing that's calculated to soothe his nerves or
sweeten his mood. When the fun is at its height and he's looking
on with his sword dangling by its red cord from his hand, young
Stayne comes creeping up behind and collars it. Ernie loses his
temper and gives chase. Stayne hides in view of the audience and
Ernie plunges out at the back. He's dithering with rage. Simon
Begg says he was incoherent. Stayne, having done the damage,
comes out and gives him back the whiffler. Stayne re-enters by
another archway. Ernie comes back complete with sword and
takes part in the final dance. If you consider Ernie like that, in
continuity, divorced for the moment from the trimmings, you get
a picture of mounting fury, don't you? The dog, the Guiser's cut
hand, the decapitated goose, the failure of the great plan, the
Guiser's rage, the stolen sword. A sort of crescendo.'

'Ending,' Fox mused, 'in what?'

'Ending, in my opinion, with his performing in deadly reality, the
climax of their play.'

'*Hey?*' Bailey ejaculated.

'Ending in him taking his Old Man's head off.'

'Ernie?'

'Ernie.'

'Then – well, cripes,' Thompson said, 'so Ernie's our chap, after all?'

'No.'

'Look – Mr Alleyn – '

'He's not our chap, because when he took his Old Man's head off, his Old Man was already dead.'

V

Mr Fox, as was his custom, glanced complacently at his subordinates. He had the air of drawing their attention to their chief's virtuosity.

'Not enough blood,' he explained. 'On anybody.'

'Yes, but if it was done from the rear,' Bailey objected.

'Which it wasn't.'

'The character of the wound gives us that,' Alleyn said.

'Otterly agrees and I'm sure Curtis will. It was done from the front. You'll see when you look. Of course, the PM will tell us definitely. If decapitation was the cause of death, I imagine there would be a considerable amount of internal bleaching. I feel certain, though, that Curtis will find there is none.'

'Any other reasons, Mr Alleyn? Apart from nobody being bloody enough?' Thompson asked.

'If it had happened where he was lying and he'd been alive, there'd have been much more blood on the ground.'

Bailey suddenly said: 'Hey!'

Mr Fox frowned at him.

'What's wrong, Bailey?' Alleyn asked.

'Look, sir, are you telling us it's not homicide at all? That the old chap died of heart failure or something and Ernie had the fancy to do what he did? After? Or what?'

'I think that may be the defence that will be raised. I don't think it's the truth.'

'You think he was murdered?'

'Yes.'

'Pardon me,' Thompson said politely, 'but any idea *how?*'

'An idea, but it's only a guess. The post-mortem will settle it.'

'Laid out cold somehow and then beheaded,' Bailey said, and added most uncharacteristically, 'Fancy.'

'It couldn't have been the Whiffler,' Thompson sighed. 'Not that it seems to matter.'

'It wasn't the Whiffler,' Alleyn said, 'It was the slasher.'

'Oh! But he was dead?'

'Dead.'

'Oh.'

CHAPTER 11

Question of Temperament

Camilla sat behind her window. When Ralph Stayne came into the inn-yard, he stood there with his hands in his pockets and looked up at her. The sky had cleared and the sun shone quite brightly, making a dazzle on the window-pane. She seemed to be reading.

He scooped up a handful of fast-melting snow and threw it at the glass. It splayed out in a wet star. Camilla peered down through it and then pushed open the window.

'Romeo, Romeo,' she said, 'wherefore art thou Romeo?'

'I can't remember any of it to quote,' Ralph rejoined. 'Come for a walk, Camilla. I want to talk to you.'

'OK. Wait a bit.'

He waited. Bailey and Thompson came out of the side door of the pub, gave him good morning and walked down the brick path in the direction of the barn. Trixie appeared and shook a duster. When she saw Ralph she smiled and dimpled at him. He pulled self-consciously at the peak of his cap. She jerked her head at him. 'Come on over, Mr Ralph,' she said.

He walked across the yard to her, not very readily.

'Cheer up, then,' Trixie said. 'Doan't look at me as if I was going to bite you. There's no bones broke, Mr Ralph. I'll never say a word to her, you may depend, if you ax me not. My advice, though, is to tell the maid yourself and then there's nothing hid betwixt you.'

'She's only eighteen,' Ralph muttered.

'That don't mean she's silly, however. Thanks to Ernie and his dad, everybody hereabouts knows us had our bit of fun. The detective gentleman axed me about it and I told him yes.'

'Good God, Trixie!'

'Better the truth from me than a great blowed-up fairy tale from elsewhere and likewise better for Camilla if she gets the truth from you. Here she comes.'

Trixie gave a definite flap with her duster and returned indoors. Ralph heard her greet Camilla, who now appeared with the freshness of the morning in her cheeks and eyes and a scarlet cap on her head.

Alleyn, coming out to fetch the car, saw them walk off down the lane together.

'And I fancy,' he muttered, 'he's made up his mind to tell her about his one wild oat.'

'Camilla,' Ralph said, 'I've got something to tell you. I've been going to tell you before and then – well, I suppose I've funked it. I don't know what you feel about this sort of thing and – I – well – I – '

'You're not going to say you've suddenly found it's all been a mistake and you're not in love with me after all?'

'Of course I'm not, Camilla. What a preposterous notion to get into your head. I love you more every minute of the day: I adore you, Camilla.'

'I'm *delighted* to hear it, darling. Go ahead with your story.'

'It may rock you a bit.'

'Nothing can rock me really badly unless – you're *not* secretly married, I *hope!*' Camilla suddenly ejaculated.

'Indeed I'm not. The things you think of!'

'And of course (forgive me for mentioning it) you didn't murder my grandfather, did you?'

'Camilla!'

'Well, I know you didn't.'

'If you'd just let me – '

'Darling Ralph, you can see by this time that I've given in about not meeting you. You can see I've come over to your opinion: my objections were immoderate.'

'Thank God, darling. But – '

'All the same, darling, *darling* Ralph, you must understand that although I go to sleep thinking of you, and wake in a kind of pink paradise because of you, I am still determined to keep my head. People may say,' Camilla went on, waving a knitted paw, 'that class is *vieux jeu* but they're only people who haven't visited South Mardian. So what I propose – '

'Sweetheart, it is I who propose. I do so now, Camilla. Will you marry me?'

'Yes, thank you, I will indeed. Subject to the unequivocal consent of your papa and your great-aunt and, of course, my papa who I would expect would prefer an R.C., although I'm not one. Otherwise, I can guarantee he would be delighted. He fears I might contract an alliance with a drama student,' Camilla explained and turned upon Ralph a face eloquent with delight at her own absurdities. She was in that particular state of intoxication that attends the young woman who knows she is beloved and is therefore moved to show off for the unstinted applause of an audience of one.

'I adore you,' Ralph repeated unsteadily and punctually. 'But, sweetest, darling Camilla, I've got, I repeat, something that I ought to tell you about.'

'Yes, of course you have. You began by saying so. Is it,' Camilla hazarded suddenly, 'that you've had an affair?'

'As a matter of fact, in a sort of way, it is but – '

Camilla began to look owlish. 'I'm not much surprised by that,' she said. 'After all you are thirty and I'm eighteen. Even people of my vintage have affairs, you know, although, personally, I don't care for the idea at all. But I've been given to understand it's different for the gentlemen.'

'Camilla, stop doing an act and listen to me.'

Camilla looked at him and the impulse to show off for him suddenly left her. 'I'm sorry,' she said. 'Well, go on.'

He went on. They walked up the road to Yowford, and for Camilla, as she listened, some of the brightness of the morning fell from the sky and was gone. When he had finished she could find nothing to say to him.

'Well,' Ralph said presently, 'I see it has made a difference.'

'No, not at all,' Camilla rejoined politely. 'I mean not really. It couldn't, could it? It's just that somehow it's strange because – well, I suppose because it's here and someone I know.'

'I'm sorry,' Ralph said.

'I've been sort of buddies with Trixie. It seems impossible. Does she mind? Poor Trixie.'

'No, she doesn't. Really, she doesn't. I'm not trying to explain anything away or to excuse myself, but they've got quite a different point of view in the villages. They think on entirely different lines about that sort of thing.'

' "They?" Different from whom?'

'Well – from us,' Ralph said and saw his mistake. 'It's hard to understand,' he mumbled unhappily.

'I ought to understand, oughtn't I? Seeing I'm half "them".'

'Camilla, *darling* – '

'You seem to have a sort of predilection for "them", don't you? Trixie. Then me.'

'That *did* hurt,' Ralph said after a pause.

'I don't want to be beastly about it.'

'There was no question of anything serious – it was just – it just happened. Trixie was – kind. It didn't mean a thing to either of us.'

They walked on and stared blankly at dripping trees and dappled hillsides.

'Isn't it funny,' Camilla said, 'how this seems to have sort of thrown me over on "their" side. On Trixie's side.'

'Are you banging away about class again?'

'But *you* see it in terms of class yourself. "They" are different about that sort of thing, you say.'

He made a helpless gesture.

'Do other people know?' Camilla asked.

'I'm afraid so. There's been gossip. You know what – ' He pulled himself up.

'What *they* are?'

Ralph swore violently.

Camilla burst into tears.

'I'm so sorry,' Ralph kept repeating, 'I'm so terribly sorry you mind.'

'Well,' Camilla sobbed, 'it's not much good going on like this and I dare say I'm being very silly.'

'Do you think you'll get over it?' he asked anxiously.

'One can but try.'

'Please try very hard,' Ralph said.

'I expect it all comes of being an only child. My papa is extremely old-fashioned.'

'Is he a roaring inverted snob like you?'

'Certainly not.'

'Here comes the egregious Simmy-Dick. You'd better not be crying, darling, if you can manage not to.'

'I'll pretend it's the cold air,' Camilla said, taking the handkerchief he offered her.

Simon Begg came down the lane in a raffish red sports car. When he saw them he skidded to a standstill.

'Hallo-allo!' he shouted. 'Fancy meeting you two. And how are we!'

He looked at them both with such a knowing air, compounded half of surprise and half of a rather debased sort of comradeship, that Camilla found herself blushing.

'I didn't realize you two knew each other,' Simon went on. 'No good offering you a lift, I suppose. I can just do three if we're cosy.'

'This is meant to be a hearty walk,' Ralph explained.

'Quite, quite,' Simon said, beaming. 'Hey, what's the gen on this show this afternoon? Do you get it?'

'I imagine it's a reconstruction, isn't it?'

'We're all meant to do what we all did on Wednesday?'

'I should think so, wouldn't you?'

'Are the onlookers invited?'

'I believe so. Some of them.'

'The whole works?' Simon looked at Camilla, raised his eyebrows and grinned, 'Including the ad libs?'

Camilla pretended not to understand him.

'Better put my running shoes on this time,' he said.

'It's not going to be such a very amusing party after all,' Ralph pointed out stiffly, and Simon agreed, very cheerfully, that it was not. 'I'm damn' sorry about the poor old Guiser,' he declared. 'And I can't exactly see what they hope to get out of it. Can you?'

Ralph said coldly that he supposed they hoped to get the truth out of it. Simon was eyeing Camilla with unbridled enthusiasm. 'In a moment,' she thought, 'he will twiddle those awful moustaches.'

'I reckon it's a lot of bull,' Simon confided. 'Suppose somebody did do something – well, is he going to turn it all on again like a good boy for the police? Like hell, he is!'

'We ought to move on, Camilla, if we're to get back for lunch.'

'Yes,' Camilla said. 'Let's.'

Simon said earnestly: 'Look, I'm sorry. I keep forgetting the relationship. It's – well, it's not all that easy to remember, is it? Look, Cam. Hell, I *am* sorry.'

Camilla, who had never before been called Cam, stared at him in bewilderment. His cheeks were rosy, his eyes were impertinent and blue and his moustache rampant. A half-smile hovered on his lips. 'I *am* a goon,' said Simon, ruefully. *'But*, still – '

Camilla, to her surprise, found she was not angry with him. 'Never mind,' she said. 'No bones broken.'

'Honest? You *are* a pal. Well, be good, children,' said Simon and started up his engine. It responded with deafening alacrity. He waved his hand and shot off down the lane.

'He is,' Ralph said, looking after him, 'the definite and absolute rock bottom.'

'Yes. But I find him rather touching,' said Camilla.

II

The five Andersen boys were in the smithy. The four younger brothers sat on upturned boxes and stools. A large tin trunk stood on a cleared bench at the far end of the smithy. Dan turned the key in the padlock that secured it. Sergeant Obby, who was on duty, had slipped into a light doze in a dark corner. He was keen on his job but unused to late hours.

'Wonderful queer to think of, hearts,' Dan said. 'The Guiser's savings. All these years.' He looked at Chris. 'And you'd no notion of it?'

'I wouldn't say that,' Chris said. 'I knew he put it by, like. Same as granddad and his'n, before him.'

'I knew,' Ernie volunteered. 'He was a proper old miser, he was. Never let me have anything, not for a wireless nor a telly nor nothing, he wouldn't. I knew where he put it by, I did, but he kept watch over it like a bloody mastiff, so's I dussn't let on. Old tyrant, he was. Cruel hard and cranktankerous.'

Andy passed his great hand across his mouth and sighed. 'Doan't talk that way,' he said, lowering his voice and glancing towards Sergeant Obby. 'What did we tell you?'

Dan agreed strongly. 'Doan't talk that way, you, Ern. You was a burden to him with your foolishness.'

'And a burden to us,' Nat added, 'as it turns out. Heavy and anxious.'

'Get it into your thick head,' Chris advised Ernie, 'that you're born foolish and not up to our level when it comes to great affairs. Leave everything to us chaps. Doan't say nothing and doan't do nothing but what you was meant to do in the beginning.'

'Huh!' Ernie shouted. 'I'll larn 'em! Whang!' He made a wild swiping gesture.

'What'll we do?' Andy asked, appealing to the others. 'Listen to him!'

Ernie surveyed his horrified brothers with the greatest complacency. 'You doan'i need to fret yourselves, chaps,' he said. 'I'm not so silly as what you all think I am. I can keep my tongue behind my teeth, fair enough. I be one too many for they coppers. Got 'em proper baffled, I 'ave.'

'Shut up,' Chris whispered savagely.

'No, I won't then.'

'You will, if I have to lay you out first,' Chris muttered. He rose and walked across to his youngest brother. Chris was the biggest of the Andersens, a broad, powerful man. He held his clenched fist in front of Ernie's face as if it was an object of virtue. 'You know me, Ern,' he said softly. 'I've give you a hiding before this and never promised you one but what I've kept my word and laid it on solid. You got a taste last night. If you talk about you know what, or open your silly damn' mouth on any matter at all when we're up-along, I'll give you a masterpiece. Won't I? *Won't I?*'

Ernie wiped his still-smiling mouth and nodded.

'You'll whiffle and you'll dance and you'll go where you went and you'll hold your tongue and you'll do no more nor that. Right?'

Ernie nodded and backed away.

'It's for the best, Ernie-boy,' the gentle Andy said. 'Us knows what's for the best.'

Ernie pointed at Chris and continued to back away from him.

'You tell him to lay off of me,' he said. 'I know *him*. Keep him off of me.'

Chris made a disgusted gesture. He turned away and began to examine the tools near the anvil.

'You keep your hands off of me,' Ernie shouted after him. Sergeant Obby woke with a little snort.

'Don't talk daft. There you go, see!' Nat ejaculated. 'Talking proper daft.'

Dan said: 'Now, listen, Ern. Us chaps doan't want to know nothing but what was according to plan. What you done, Wednesday, was what you was meant to do: whiffle, dance, bit of larking with Mr Ralph, wait your turn and dance again. Which you done. And that's *all* you done. Nothing else. Doan't act as if there was anything else. There *wasn't*.'

'That's right,' his brothers counselled, 'that's how 'tis.'

They were so much alike, they might indeed have been a sort of rural chorus. Anxiety looked in the same way out of all their faces: they had similar mannerisms, their shared emotion ran a simple course through Dan's elderly persistence, Andy's softness, Nat's despair and Chris's anger. Even Ernie himself, half-defiant, half-scared, reflected something of his brothers' emotion.

And when Dan spoke again, it was as if he gave expression to this general resemblance.

'Us Andersens,' he said, 'stick close. Always have and always will, I reckon. So long as we stay that fashion, all together, we're right souls. The day any of us cuts loose and sets out to act on his own, agin the better judgement of the others, will be the day of disaster. Mind that.'

Andy and Nat made sounds of profound agreement.

'All right!' Ernie said, 'all right. I never said nothing.'

'Keep that way,' Dan said, 'and you'll do no harm. Mind that. And stick together, souls.'

There was a sudden metallic clang. Sergeant Obby leapt to his feet. Chris, moved by some impulse of violence, had swung his great hammer and struck the cold anvil.

It was as if the smithy had spoken with its own voice in support of Dan Andersen.

III

Mrs Bünz made a long entry in her journal. For this purpose she employed her native language and it calmed her a little to form the words and see them, old familiars, stand in their orderly ranks across her pages. Mrs Bünz had an instinctive respect for regimentation – a respect and a fear. She laid down her pen, locked away her journal and began to think about policemen: not about any specific officer but about the *genus policeman* as she saw it and believed it to be. She remembered all the things that had happened to her husband and herself in Germany before the war and the formalities that had attended their arrival in England. She remembered the anxieties and discomforts of the first months of the war when they had continually to satisfy the police of their innocuous attitude, and she remembered their temporary incarceration while this was going on.

Mrs Bünz did not put her trust in policemen.

She thought of Trixie's inexplicable entrance into her room that morning at a moment when Mrs Bünz had every reason not to desire a visit. Was Trixie, perhaps, a police agent? A most disturbing thought.

She went downstairs and ate what was, for her, a poor breakfast. She tried to read but was unable to concentrate. Presently, she went out to the shed where she kept the car she had bought from Simon Begg and, after a bit of a struggle, started up the engine. If she had intended to use the car she now changed her mind and, instead, took a short walk to Copse Forge. But the Andersen brothers were gathered in the doorway and responded very churlishly to the forced *bonhomie* of her greeting. She went to the village shop, purchased two faded postcards and was looked at sideways by the shopkeeper.

Next, Mrs Bünz visited the church but, being a rationalist, received and indeed sought no spiritual solace there. It was old but, from her point of view, not at all interesting. A bas-relief of a four-teenth-century Mardian merely reminded her unpleasingly of Dame Alice.

As she was leaving, she met Sam Stayne coming up the path in his cassock. He greeted her very kindly. Encouraged by this manifestation, Mrs Bünz pulled herself together and began to question him about the antiquities of South Mardian. She adopted a somewhat patronizing tone that seemed to suggest a kind of intellectual unbending on her part. Her cold was still very heavy and lent to her manner a fortuitous air of complacency. 'I have been looking at your little church,' she said.

'I'm glad you came in.'

'Of course, for me it is not, you will excuse me, as interestink as, for instance, the Corpse Forge.'

'Isn't it? It's nothing of an archaeological "find", of course.'

'Perhaps you do not interest yourself in ritual dancing?' Mrs Bünz suggested with apparent irrelevance but following up her own line of thought.

'Indeed I do,' Sam Stayne said warmly. 'It's of great interest to a priest, as are all such instinctive gestures.'

'But it is pagan.'

'Of course it is,' he said, and began to look distressed. 'As I see it,' he went on, choosing his words very carefully, 'the Dance of the Sons is a kind of child's view of a great truth. The church, more or less, took the ceremony under her wing, you know, many years ago.'

'How! Ach! Because, no doubt there had been a liddle licence? A liddle too much freedom?'

'Well,' he said, 'I dare say. Goings-on, of sorts. Anyway, somewhere back in the nineties, a predecessor of mine took possession of "Crack's" trappings and the Guiser's and the Betty's dresses and "props", as I think they call them in the theatre. He locked them up in the vestry. Ever since then the parson has handed them out a week or so before the winter solstice to be looked over and repaired and used for the final practices and performance.'

Mrs Bünz stared at him and sneezed violently. She said in her cold-stricken voice: 'Id is *bost* peculiar. I believe you because I have evidence of other cases. But for these joyous, pagan, and indeed albost purely phallig objects to be lodged in an Aglicud church is, to say the least of it, adobalous.' She blew her nose with Teutonic thoroughness. 'Rebarkable!' said Mrs Bünz.

'Well, there it is,' he said, 'and now if you'll excuse me, I must go about my job.'

'You are about to hold a service?'

'No,' he said, 'I've come to say my prayers.'

She blinked at him. 'Ach, so! Tell me, Mr Stayne. In your church you do not, I believe, pray for the dead? That is dot your customb?'

'*I* do,' Sam said. 'That's what I'm here for now: to say a prayer or two for old William's soul.' He looked mildly at her. Something prompted him to add: 'And for another and unhappier soul.'

Mrs Bünz blew her nose again and eyed him over the top of her handkerchief. 'Beaningk?' she asked.

'Meaning his murderer, you know,' the rector said.

Mrs Bünz seemed to be so much struck by this remark that she forgot to lower her handkerchief. She nodded her head two or three times, however, and said something that sounded like: 'No doubt.' She wished the rector good morning and returned to the Green Man.

There she ran into Simon Begg. Alleyn and Fox witnessed their encounter from behind the window curtain. Simon contemplated Mrs Bünz with, apparently, some misgiving. His very blue eyes stared out of his pink face and he climbed hurriedly from his car. Mrs Bünz hastened towards him. He stood with his hands in his pockets and looked down at her. Alleyn saw her speak evidently with some urgency. Simon pulled at his flamboyant moustaches and listened with his head on one side. Mrs Bünz glanced hastily at the pub as if she would have preferred not to be seen. She turned her back towards it and her head moved emphatically. Simon answered her with equal emphasis and presently with a reassuring gesture clapped his great hand down on her shoulder. Even through the window, which was shut, they heard her yelp of pain. It was clearly to be seen that Simon was making awkward apologies. Presently he took Mrs Bünz by the elbow – he was the sort of man who habitually takes women by the elbow – and piloted her away towards the car she had bought from him. He lifted the bonnet and soon they had their heads together talking eagerly over the engine.

Fox said dubiously to Alleyn: 'Is *that* what it was all about?'

'Don't you believe it, Brer Fox. Those two are cooking up a little plot, the burden of which may well be: "For O, for O, the Hobby Horse is forgot."'

'Shakespeare,' Fox said, 'I suppose.'

'And why not? This case smacks of the Elizabethan. And I don't altogether mean Hamlet or Lear. Or Nine Men's Morris, though there's a flavour of all of them to be sure. But those earlier plays of violence when people kill each other in a sort of quintessence of spleen and other people cheer each other up by saying things like: "And now, my lord, to leave these doleful dumps." Shall you be glad to leave these doleful dumps, Fox?'

'So-so,' Fox said. 'It's always nice to get a case cleared up. There's not all that much variety in murder.'

'You've become an epicure of violence which is as much as to say a "bloody snob".'

Fox chuckled obligingly.

Mrs Bünz had drawn away from the car. She now approached the pub. They stood back in the room and they watched her. So did Simon Begg. Simon looked extremely worried and more than a little dubious. He scowled after Mrs Bünz and scratched his head. Then, with the sort of shrug that suggests the relinquishment of an insoluble problem, he slammed down the bonnet of her car. Alleyn grinned. He could imagine Simon saying out loud: '*But* still,' and giving it up.

Mrs Bünz approached the pub and as if she felt that she was observed, glanced up at the windows. Her weathered face was patchy and her lips were set in a determined line.

'It's a very odd temperament,' Alleyn muttered. 'Her particular kind of Teutonic female temperament, I mean. At her sort of age and with her sort of background. Conditioned, if that's the beastly word, by violence and fear and full of curiosity. And persistence.'

'Persistence?' Fox repeated, savouring the idea.

'Yes. She's a very thorough sort of woman, is Mrs Bünz. Look what she did on Wednesday night.'

'That's right.'

'Yes,' Alleyn repeated, more to himself than to Fox, 'she's a thorough sort of woman, is Mrs Bünz.'

IV

The sun continued to shine upon South Mardian and upon the surrounding countryside. The temperature rose unseasonably. Bigger and bigger patches emerged, dark and glistening, from the dismantled landscape. Dr Curtis, driving himself across-country, slithered and skidded but made better time. At noon, he rang through to say he expected to be with them before three. Alleyn directed him to Yowford, where the Guiser waited for him in the cottage hospital mortuary.

At half past one a police car arrived with five reinforcements.

Alleyn held a sort of meeting in the back parlour and briefed his men for the afternoon performance. Carey, who had been down at Copse Forge, came in and was consulted with fitting regard for his rank and local importance.

'We haven't the faintest notion if we'll make an arrest,' Alleyn said. 'With luck we might. I'd feel much happier about it if the results of the PM were laid on, but I've decided not to wait for them. The chances of success in a show of this sort rest on the accuracy of the observers' memories. With every hour they grow less dependable. We're taking pretty considerable risks and may look damn' silly for damn all at the end of it. However, I think it's worth trying and Mr Fox agrees with me. Now this is what happens.'

He laid out his plan of action, illustrating what he said with a rough sketch of the courtyard at Mardian Castle.

Dame Alice, Dulcie Mardian and the rector would again sit on the steps. The rest of the audience would consist of Trixie, her father, Camilla, Carey, Sergeant Obby and Mrs Bünz. The events of Wednesday night would be re-enacted in their order. At this point it became clear that Superintendent Carey was troubled in his mind. Seeing this, Alleyn asked him if he had any suggestions to make.

'Well! Naow!' Carey said. 'I was just asking myself, Mr Alleyn. If everybody, in a manner of speaking, is going to act their own parts over again, who would – er – who would – ?'

'Act the principal part?'

'That's right. The original,' Mr Carey said reasonably, 'not being available.'

'I wanted to consult you about that. What sort of age is the boy – Andy's son, isn't it? – who was the understudy?'

'Young Bill? Thirteen – fourteen or thereabouts. He's Andrew's youngest.'

'Bright boy?'

'Smart enough little lad, far's I know.'

'About the same height as his grandfather?'

'Just, I reckon.'

'Could we get hold of him?'

'Reckon so. Andrew Andersen's farm's up to Yowford. Matter of a mile.'

'Is Andy himself still down at the Forge?'

'Went home for his dinner, no doubt, at noon. There's been a great family conference all morning at the smithy,' Carey said. 'My sergeant was on duty there. Obby. I don't say he was as alert as we might prefer: not used to late hours and a bit short of sleep. As a matter of fact, the silly danged fool dozed off and had to admit it.'

The Yard men were at pains not to catch each other's eyes.

'He came forward, however, with the information that a great quantity of money was found and locked away, and that all the boys seem very worried about what Ern may say or do. Specially Chris. He's a hot-tempered chap is Chris Andersen, and not above using his hands, which he knows how to, having been a commando in the war.'

'Hardly suitable as a mild corrective technique,' Alleyn said dryly.

'Well, no. Will I see if I can lay hold of young Bill, Mr Alleyn? Now?'

'Would you, Carey? Thank you so much. Without anything being noticed. You'll handle it better than we will, knowing them.'

Carey, gratified, set about this business.

They heard him start up his motor-bicycle and churn off along Yowford Lane.

'He's all right,' Alleyn said to the Yard men. 'Sound man, but he's feeling shy about his sergeant going to sleep on duty.'

'So he should,' Fox said, greatly scandalized. 'I never heard such a thing. Very bad. Carey ought to have stayed there himself if he can't trust his chaps.'

'I don't think it's likely to have made all that difference, Brer Fox.'

'It's the principle.'

'Of course it is. Now, about this show – here's where I want everyone to stand. Mr Fox up at the back by the archway through which
they made their exits and entrances. Bailey and Thompson are coming off their specialists' perches and keeping observation again.
There' – he pointed on his sketch – 'by the entrance to the castle,
that is to say the first archway that links the semi-circular ruined
wall to the new building and here, by its opposite number at the
other end of the wall. That's the way Ralph Stayne came back to the
arena. The bonfire was outside the wall and to the right of the central archway. I want three men there. The remaining two will stand
among the onlookers, bearing in mind what I've said we expect to
find. We may be involved with more than one customer if the pot
comes to the boil. Carey will be there with his sergeant and his PC
of course, and if the sergeant dozes off at *this* show it'll be because
he's got sleeping sickness.'

Fox said: 'May we inquire where you'll be yourself, Mr Alleyn?'

'Oh,' Alleyn said, 'here and there, Brer Fox. Roaring up and down
as a raging lion seeking whom I may devour. To begin with, in the
Royal Box with the nobs, I dare say.'

'On the steps with Dame Alice Mardian?'

'That's it. Now, one word more.' Alleyn looked from Fox, Bailey
and Thompson to the five newcomers. 'I suggest that each of us
marks one particular man and marks him well. Suppose you, Fox,
take Ernie Andersen. Bailey takes Simon Begg as "Crack", the
Hobby. Thompson takes Ralph Stayne as the Betty, and the rest of
you parcel out between you the boy in his grandfather's rôle as the
Fool and the other four sons as the four remaining dancers. That'll
be one each for us, won't it? A neat fit.'

One of the newcomers, a Sergeant Yardley, said: 'Er – beg pardon.'

'Yes, Yardley?'

'I must have lost count, sir. There's nine of us, counting yourself,
and I understood there's only eight characters in this play affair, or
dance or whatever it is.'

'Eight characters,' Alleyn said, 'is right. Our contention will be
that there were nine performers, however.'

'Sorry, sir. Of course.'

'I,' Alleyn said blandly, 'hope to keep my eye on the ninth.'

V

Young Bill Andersen might have sat to the late George Clauson for one of his bucolic portraits. He had a shock of tow-coloured hair, cheeks like apples and eyes as blue as periwinkles. His mouth stretched itelf into the broadest grin imaginable and his teeth were big, white and far apart.

Carey brought him back on the pillion of his motorbicycle and produced him to Alleyn as if he was one of the natural curiosities of the region.

'Young Bill,' Carey said, exhibiting him. 'I've told him what he's wanted for and how he'll need to hold his tongue and be right smart for the job, and he says he's able and willing. Come on,' he added, giving the boy a business-like shove. 'That's right, isn't it? Speak up for yourself.'

'Ar,' said young Bill. He looked at Alleyn through his thick white lashes and grinned. 'I'd like it,' he said.

'Good. Now, look here, Bill. What we want you to do is quite a tricky bit of work. It's got to be cleverly done. It's important. One of us would do it, actually, but we're all too tall for the job as you can see for yourself. You're the right size. The thing is: do you know your stuff!'

'I know the Five Sons, sir, like the back of meyand.'

'You do? You know the Fool's act, do you? Your grandfather's act.'

'Certain sure.'

'You watched it on Wednesday night, didn't you?'

'So I did, then.'

'And you remember exactly what he did?'

'Ya-as.'

'How can you be so sure?'

Bill scratched his head. 'Reckon I watched him, seeing what a terrible rage he was in. After what happened, like. And what was said.'

'What did happen?'

Bill very readily gave an account of the Guiser's arrival and the furious change-over: 'I 'ad to strip off Uncle Ern's clothes and he 'ad to strip off Granfer's. Terrible quick.'

'And what *was* said?'

'Uncle Ern reckoned it'd be the death of Granfer, dancing. So did Uncle Chris. He'll kill himself, Uncle Chris says, if he goes capering in the great heat of his rages. The silly old b–'ll fall down dead, he says. So I was watching Granfer to see.'

Bill passed the tip of his tongue round his lips. 'Terrible queer,' he muttered, 'as it turned out because so 'e did, like. Terrible queer.'

Alleyn said: 'Sure you don't mind doing this for us, Bill?'

The boy looked at him. 'I don't mind,' he declared and sounded rather surprised. 'Suits me, all right.'

'And you keep it as a dead secret between us? Not a word to anybody: top security.'

'Ya-as,' Bill said. 'Surely.' A thought seemed to strike him.

'Yes?' Alleyn said. 'What's up?'

'Do I have to dress up in bloody clothes of his'n?'

'No,' Alleyn said after a pause.

'Nor wear his ma-ask?'

'No.'

'I wouldn't fancy thik.'

'There's no need. Weil fix you up with something light-coloured to wear and something over your face to look like the mask.'

He nodded, perfectly satisfied. The strange and innocent cruelty of his age and sex was upon him.

'Reckon I can fix that,' he said. 'I'll get me a set of pyjammers and I got a ma-ask of me own. Proper clown's ma-ask.'

And then with an uncanny echo of his Uncle Ernie, he said: 'Reckon I can make a proper old Fool of myself.'

'Good. And now, young Bill, you lay your ears back and listen to me. There's something else we'll ask you to do. It's something pretty tricky, it may be rather frightening and the case for the police may hang on it. How do you feel about that?'

'Bettn't I know what 'tis first?'

'Fair enough,' Alleyn said and looked pleased. 'Hold tight, then, and I'll tell you.'

He told young Bill what he wanted.

The blue eyes opened wider and wider. Alleyn waited for an expostulation but none came. Young Bill was thirteen. He kept his family feeling, his compassion and his enthusiasms in separate compartments. An immense grin converted his face into the likeness of a bucolic Puck. He began to rub the palms of his hands together.

Evidently he was, as Superintendent Carey had indicated, a smart enough lad for the purpose.

CHAPTER 12

The Swords Again

The afternoon had begun to darken when the persons concerned in the Sword Wednesday Morris of the Five Sons returned to Mardian Castle.

Dr Otterly came early and went indoors to present his compliments to Dame Alice and find out how she felt after last night's carousal. He found the Rector and Alleyn were there already, while Fox and his assistants were to be seen in and about the courtyard.

At four o'clock the Andersens, with Sergeant Obby in attendance, drove up the hill in their station wagon from which they unloaded torches and a fresh drum of tar.

Superintendent Carey arrived on his motor-bike.

Simon appeared in his breakdown van with a new load of brushwood for the bonfire.

Ralph Stayne and his father walked up the hill and were harried by the geese, who had become hysterical.

Trixie and her father drove up with Camilla, looking rather white and strained, as their passenger.

Mrs Bünz, alone this time, got her new car halfway up the drive and was stopped by one of Alleyn's men, who asked her to leave the car where it was until further orders and come the rest of the way on foot. This she did quite amenably.

From the drawing-room window Alleyn saw her trudge into the courtyard. Behind him Dame Alice sat in her bucket chair. Dulcie and the Rector stood further back in the room. All of them watched the courtyard.

The preparations were almost complete. Under the bland scrutiny of Mr Fox and his subordinates, the Andersens had re-erected the eight torches: four on each side of the dolmen.

'It looks *just* like it did on Sword Wednesday,' Dulcie pointed out, 'doesn't it, Aunty Akky? Fancy!'

Dame Alice made a slight contemptuous noise.

'Only, of course,' Dulcie added, 'nobody's beheaded a goose this time. There is that, isn't there, Aunt Akky?'

'Unfortunately,' her great-aunt agreed savagely. She stared pointedly at Dulcie, who giggled vaguely.

'What's that ass Ernie Andersen up to?' Dame Alice demanded.

'Dear me, yes,' the Rector said. 'Look at him.'

Ernie, who had been standing apart from his brothers, apparently in a sulk, now advanced upon them. He gesticulated and turned from one to the other. Fox moved a little closer. Ernie pointed at his brothers and addressed himself to Fox.

'I understand,' Alleyn said, 'that he's been cutting up rough all the afternoon. He wants to play the Father's part.'

'Mad!' Dame Alice said. 'What did I tell you? He'll get himself into trouble before it's all over, you may depend 'pon it.'

It was clear that Ernie's brothers had reacted in their usual way to his tantrums and were attempting to silence him. Simon came through the archway from the back, carrying 'Crack's' head, and walked over to the group. Ernie listened. Simon clapped him good-naturedly on the shoulder and in a moment Ernie had thrown his customary crashing salute.

'That's done the trick,' Alleyn said.

Evidently Ernie was told to light the torches. Clearly mollified, he set about this task and presently bright fans of crimson and yellow consumed the cold air. Their light quivered over the dolmen and dramatized the attentive faces of the onlookers.

'It's a strange effect,' the Rector said uneasily. 'Like the setting for a barbaric play – *King Lear*, perhaps.'

'Otterly will agree with your choice,' Alleyn said, and Dr Otterly came out of the shadow at the back of the room. The Rector turned to him but Dr Otterly didn't show his usual enthusiasm for his pet theory.

'I suppose I'd better go out,' he said. 'Hadn't I, Alleyn?'

'I think so. I'm going back now.' Alleyn turned to Dulcie, who at once put on her expression of terrified jocosity.

'I wonder,' Alleyn said, 'if I could have some clean rag? Enough to make a couple of thick pads about the size of my hand? And some first-aid bandages, if you have them?'

'Rag!' Dulcie said. 'Fancy! Pads! Bandages!' She eyed him face-tiously. 'Now, I *wonder*.'

"Course he can have it,' Dame Alice said. 'Don't be an ass, Dulcie. Get it.'

'Very well, Aunt Akky,' Dulcie said in a hurry. She plunged out of the room and in a surprisingly short space of time returned with a handful of old linen and two bandages. Alleyn thanked her and stuffed them into his overcoat pocket.

'I don't think we shall be long now,' he said. 'And when you're ready, Dame Alice – '

'*I'm* ready. Haul me up, will yer? Dulcie! Bandle!'

As this ceremony would evidently take some considerable time, Alleyn excused himself. He and Dr Otterly went out to the court-yard.

Dr Otterly joined his colleagues and they all took up their posi-tions off-stage behind the old wall. Alleyn paused on the house steps and surveyed the scene.

The sky was clear now and had not yet completely darkened: to the west it was still faintly green. Stars exploded into a wintry glit-ter. There was frost in the air.

The little party of onlookers stood in their appointed places at the side of the courtyard and would have almost melted into darkness if it had not been for the torchlight. The Andersens had evidently strapped their pads of bells on their thick legs. Peremptory jangles could be heard off-stage.

Alleyn's men were at their stations and Fox now came forward to meet him.

'We're all ready, Mr Alleyn, when you are.'

'All right. What was biting Ernie?'

'Same old trouble. Wanting to play the Fool.'

'Thought as much.'

Carey moved out from behind the dolmen,

'I suppose it's all right,' he murmured uneasily. 'You know. Safe.'

'Safe?' Fox repeated, and put his head on one side as if Carey had advanced a quaintly original theory.

'Well, *I* dunno, Mr Fox,' Carey muttered. 'It seems a bit uncanny-like and with young Ern such a queer, excitable chap – he's been saying he wants to sharpen up that damned old sword affair of his. 'Course we won't let him *have* it, but how's he going to act when we don't! Take one of his fits like as not.'

'We'll have to keep a nice sharp observation over him, Mr Carey,' Fox said.

'Over all of them,' Alleyn amended.

'Well,' Carey conceded, 'I dare say I'm fussy.'

'Not a bit,' Alleyn said. 'You're perfectly right to look upon this show as a chancy business. But they've sent us five very good men who all know what to look for. And with you,' Alleyn pointed out wickedly, 'in a key position I don't personally think we're taking too big a risk.'

'Ar, no-no-no,' Carey said quickly and airily. 'No, I wasn't suggesting we were, you know. I wasn't suggesting *that.*'

'We'll just have a final look round, shall we?' Alleyn proposed.

He walked over to the dolmen, glanced behind it and then moved on through the central arch at the back.

Gathered together in a close-knit group, rather like a bunch of carol singers, with lanthorns in their hands, were the five Andersens. As they changed their positions in order to eye the new arrivals, their bells clinked. Alleyn was reminded unexpectedly of horses that stamped and shifted in their harness. Behind them, near the unlit bonfire, stood Dr Otterly and Ralph, who was again dressed in his great hooped skirt. Simon stood by the cylindrical cheese-shaped body of the Hobby Horse. 'Crack's' head grinned under his arm. Beyond these again were three of the extra police officers. The hedge-slasher with its half-burnt handle and heat-distempered blade leant against the wall with the drum of tar nearby. There was a strong tang of bitumen on the frosty air.

'We'll light the bonfire,' Alleyn said, 'and then I'll ask you all to come into the courtyard while I explain what we're up to.'

One of the Yard men put a match to the paper. It flared up. There was a crackle of brushwood and a pungent smell rose sweetly with smoke from the bonfire.

They followed Alleyn back, through the archway, past the dolmen and the flaring torches and across the arena.

Dame Alice was enthroned at the top of the steps, flanked, as before, by Dulcie and the Rector. Rugged and shawled into a quadrel with a knob on top, she resembled some primitive totem and appeared to be perfectly immovable.

Alleyn stood on a step below and a little to one side of this group. His considerable height was exaggerated by the shadow that leapt up behind him. The torchlight lent emphasis to the sharply defined planes on his face and fantasticated it. Below him stood the Five Sons with Simon, Ralph and Dr Otterly. Alleyn looked across to the little group on his right.

'Will you come nearer?' he said. 'What I have to say concerns all of you.'

They moved out of the shadows, keeping apart, as if each was anxious to establish a kind of disassociation from the others: Trixie, the landlord, Camilla, and, lagging behind, Mrs Bünz. Ralph crossed over to Camilla and stood beside her. His conical skirt looked like a giant extinguisher, and Camilla, in her flame-coloured coat, like a small candle flame beside him.

Fox, Carey and their subordinates waited attentively in the rear.

'I expect,' Alleyn said, 'that most of you wonder just why the police have decided upon this performance. I don't suppose any of you enjoy the prospect and I'm sorry if it causes you anxiety or distress.'

He waited for a moment. The faces upturned to his were misted by their own breath. Nobody spoke or moved.

'The fact is,' he went on, 'that we're taking an unusual line with a very unusual set of circumstances. The deceased man was in full sight of you all for as long as he took an active part in this dance-play of yours and he was still within sight of some of you after he lay down behind that stone. Now, Mr Carey has questioned every man, woman and child who was in the audience on Wednesday night. They are agreed that the Guiser did not leave the arena or move from his hiding-place and that nobody offered him any violence as he lay behind the stone. Yet, a few minutes *after* he lay down there came the appalling discovery of his decapitated body.'

'We've made exhaustive inquiries but each of them has led us slap up against this apparent contradiction. We want, therefore, to see for ourselves exactly what did happen.'

Dr Otterly looked up at Alleyn as if he was about to interrupt but seemed to change his mind and said nothing.

'For one reason or another,' Alleyn went on, 'some of you may feel disinclined to repeat some incident or occurrence. I can't urge you too strongly to leave nothing out and to stick absolutely to fact. "Nothing extenuate,"' he found himself saying, '"nor set down ought in malice." That's as sound a bit of advice on evidence as one can find anywhere and what we're asking you to do is, in effect, to provide visual evidence. To *show* us the truth. And by sticking to the whole truth and nothing but the truth, each one of you will establish the innocent. You will show us who *couldn't* have done it. But don't fiddle with the facts. Please don't do that. Don't leave out anything because you're afraid we may think it looks a bit fishy. We won't think so if it's not. And what's more,' he added, and raised an eyebrow, 'I must remind you that any rearrangement would probably be spotted by your fellow-performers or your audience.'

He paused. Ernie broke into aimless laughter and his brothers shifted uneasily and jangled their bells.

'Which brings me,' Alleyn went on, 'to my second point. If at any stage of this performance any one of you notices anything at all, however slight, that is different from what you remember, you will please say so. There and then. There'll be a certain amount of noise, I suppose, so you'll have to give a clear signal. Hold up your hand. If you're a fiddler,' Alleyn said and nodded at Dr Otterly, 'stop fiddling and hold up your bow. If you're the Hobby Horse,' he glanced at Simon, 'you can't hold up your hand but you can let out a yell, can't you?'

'Fair enough,' Simon said. 'Yip-ee!'

The Andersens and the audience looked scandalized.

'And similarly,' Alleyn said, 'I want any member of this very small audience who notices any discrepancy to make it clear, at once, that he does so. Sing out or hold up your hand. Do it there and then.'

'Dulcie.'

'Yes, Aunt Akky?'

'Get the gong.'

'The gong, Aunt Akky?'

'The one I bought at that jumble sale. And the hunting-horn from the gun-room.'

'Very well, Aunt Akky.'

Dulcie got up and went indoors.

'You,' Dame Alice told Alleyn, 'can bang if you want them to stop. I'll have the horn.'

Alleyn said apologetically: 'Thank you very much, but as it happens I've got a whistle.'

'Sam can bang, then, if he notices anything.'

The Rector cleared his throat and said he didn't think he'd want to.

Alleyn, fighting hard against this rising element of semi-comic activity, addressed himself again to the performers.

'If you hear my whistle,' he said, 'you will at once stop whatever you may be doing. Now, is all this perfectly clear? Are there any questions?'

Chris Andersen said loudly: 'What say us chaps won't?'

'You mean, won't perform at all?'

'Right. What say we won't?'

'That'll be that,' Alleyn said coolly.

'Here!' Dame Alice shouted, peering into the little group of men. 'Who was that? Who's talkin' about will and won't?'

They shuffled and jangled.

'Come on,' she commanded. 'Daniel! Who was it?'

Dan looked extremely uncomfortable. Ernie laughed again and jerked his thumb at Chris. 'Good old Chrissy,' he guffawed.

Big Chris came tinkling forward. He stood at the foot of the steps and looked full at Dame Alice.

'It was me, then,' he said. 'Axcuse me, ma'am, it's our business whether this affair goes on or don't. Seeing who it was that was murdered. We're his sons.'

'Pity you haven't got his brains!' she rejoined. 'You're a hot-headed, blunderin' sort of donkey, Chris Andersen, and always have been. Be a sensible feller, now, and don't go puttin' yourself in the wrong.'

'What's the sense of it?' Chris demanded. 'How can we do what was done before when there's no Fool? What's the good of it?'

'Anyone'd think you wanted your father's murderer to go scot free.'

Chris sank his head a little between his shoulders and demanded of Alleyn: 'Will it be brought up again' us if we won't do it?'

Alleyn said, 'Your refusal will be noted. We can't use threats.'

'Mamby-pamby nonsense,' Dame Alice announced.

Chris stood with his head bent. Andy and Nat looked out of the corners of their eyes at Dan. Ernie did a slight kicking step and roused his bells.

Dan said: 'As I look at it, there's no choice, souls. We'll dance.'

'Good,' Alleyn said. 'Very sensible. We begin at the point where the Guiser arrived in Mrs Bünz's car. I will ask Mrs Bünz to go down to the car, drive it up, park it where she parked it before and do exactly what she did the first time. You will find a police constable outside, Mrs Bünz, and he will accompany you. The performers will wait off-stage by the bonfire. Dr Otterly will come on-stage and begin to play. Right, Mrs Bünz?'

Mrs Bünz was blowing her nose. She nodded and turned away. She tramped out through the side archway and disappeared.

Dan made a sign to his brothers. They faced about and went tinkling across the courtyard and through the centre archway. Ralph Stayne and Simon followed. The watchers took up their appointed places and Dr Otterly stepped out into the courtyard and tucked his fiddle under his chin.

The front door burst open and Dulcie staggered out bearing a hunting-horn and a hideous gong slung between two tusks. She stumbled and, in recovering, struck the gong smartly with the horn. It gave out a single and extremely strident note that echoed forbiddingly round the courtyard.

As if this was an approved signal, Mrs Bünz, half-way down the drive, started up the engine of her car and Dr Otterly gave a scrape on his fiddle.

'Well,' Alleyn thought, 'it's a rum go and no mistake, but we're off.'

II

Mrs Bünz's car, with repeated blasts on the horn, churned in low gear up the drive and turned to the right behind the curved wall. It stopped. There was a final and prolonged hoot. Dr Otterly lowered his bow.

'This was when I went off to see what was up,' he said.

'Right. Do so, please.'

He did so, a rather lonely figure in the empty courtyard.

Mrs Bünz, followed by a constable, returned and stood just within the side entrance. She was as white as a sheet and trembling.

'We could hear the Guiser,' Dame Alice informed them, 'yellin'.'

Nobody was yelling this time. On the far side of the semi-circular wall out of sight of their audience and lit by the bonfire, the performers stood and stared at each other. Dr Otterly faced them. The police hovered anonymously. Mr Fox, placidly bespectacled, contemplated them all in turn. His notebook lay open on his massive palm.

'This,' he said, 'is where the old gentleman arrived and found *you*' – he jabbed a forefinger at Ernie – 'dressed up for his part and young Bill, dressed up for yours. He grabbed *his* clothes off *you*' – another jab at Ernie – 'and got into them himself. And you changed with young Bill. Take all that as read. What was said?'

Simon, Dr Otterly and Ralph Stayne all spoke together. Mr Fox pointed his pencil at Dr Otterly. 'Yes, thank you, Doctor?' he prompted.

'When I came out,' Dr Otterly said, 'he was roaring like a bull but you couldn't make head or tail of it. He got hold of Ernie and practically lugged the clothes off him.'

Ernie swore comprehensively. 'Done it to spite me,' he said. 'Old bastard!'

'Was any explanation given?' Fox pursued, 'about the note that had been handed round saying Ernie could do it?'

There was no answer. 'Nobody,' Fox continued, 'spotted that it hadn't been written about the dance but about that slasher there?'

Ernie, meeting the flabbergasted gaze of his brothers, slapped his knees and roared out: 'I foxed the lot of you proper, I did. Not so silly as what I let on to be, me!'

Nat said profoundly: 'You *bloody* great fool.'

Ernie burst into his high rocketing laugh.

Fox held up his hand. 'Shut up,' he said and nodded to one of his men who came forward with the swords in a sacking bundle and gave them out to the dancers.

Ernie began to swing and slash with his sword.

'Where's mine?' he demanded. 'This 'un's not mine. Mine's sharp.'

'That'll do you,' Fox said. 'You're not having a sharp one this time. Places, everyone. In the same order as before *if* you please.'

Dr Otterly nodded and went out through the archway into the arena.

'Now,' Dulcie said, 'they *really* begin, don't they, Aunt Akky?'

A preliminary scrape or two and then the jiggling reiterant tune. Out through the archway came Ernie, white-faced this time instead of black, but wearing his black cap and gloves. His movements at first were less flamboyant than they had been on Wednesday, but perhaps he gathered inspiration from the fiddle for they soon became more lively. He pranced and curveted and began to slash out with his sword.

'This, I take it, is whiffling,' Alleyn said. 'A kind of purification, isn't it, Rector?'

'I believe so. Yes.'

Ernie completed his round and stood to one side. His brothers came out at a run, their bells jerking. Ernie joined them and they performed the Mardian Morris together, wearing their bells and leaving their swords in a heap near Dr Otterly. This done, they removed their bells and took up their swords. Ernie threaded his red ribbon. They stared at each other and, furtively, at Alleyn.

Now followed the entry of the hermaphrodite and the Hobby Horse. Ralph Stayne's extinguisher of a skirt suspended from his armpits, swung and bounced. His man's jacket spread over it. His hat, half-topper, half floral toque, was jammed down over his forehead. The face beneath was incongruously grave.

'Crack's' iron head poked and gangled monstrously on the top of its long canvas neck. The cheese-shaped body swung rhythmically and its skirt trailed on the ground. 'Crack's' jaws snapped and its ridiculous rudiment of a tail twitched busily. Together these two came prancing in.

Dulcie again said, 'Here comes "Crack",' and her aunt looked irritably at her as if she, too, was bent on a complete pastiche.

'Crack' finished his entry dead centre, facing the steps. A voice that seemed to have no point of origin, but to be merely *there*, asked anxiously:

'I say, sorry, but do you want *all* the fun and games?'

'Crack's' neck opened a little, rather horridly, and Simon's face could be seen behind the orifice.

'Everything,' Alleyn said.

'Oh righty-ho. Look out, ladies, here I come,' the voice said. The neck closed. 'Crack' swung from side to side as if the monster ogled its audience and made up its mind where to hunt. Camilla moved closer to Trixie and looked apprehensively from Alleyn to Ralph Stayne. Ralph signalled to her, putting his thumb up as if to reassure her of his presence.

'Crack's' jaws snapped. It began to make pretended forays upon an imaginary audience. Dr Otterly, still fiddling, moved nearer to Camilla and nodded to her encouragingly. 'Crack' darted suddenly at Camilla. She ran like a hare before it, across the courtyard and into Ralph's arms. 'Crack' went off at the rear archway.

'Just what they did before,' Dulcie ejaculated. 'Isn't it, Aunt Akky? Isn't it, Sam?'

The Rector murmured unhappily and Dame Alice said: 'I do wish to goodness you'd shut up, Dulcie.'

'Well, I'm sorry, Aunt Akky, but – *ow!*' Dulcie ejaculated.

Alleyn had blown his whistle.

Dr Otterly stopped playing. The Andersen brothers turned their faces towards Alleyn.

'One moment,' Alleyn said.

He moved to the bottom step and turned a little to take in both the party of three above him and the scattered groups in the courtyard.

'I want a general check, here,' he said. 'Mrs Bünz, are you satisfied that so far this was exactly what happened?'

Bailey had turned his torchlight on Mrs Bünz. Her mouth was open. Her lips began to move.

'I'm afraid I can't hear you,' Alleyn said. 'Will you come a little nearer?'

She came very slowly towards him.

'Now,' he said.

'*Ja.* It is what was done.'

'And what happened next?'

She moistened her lips. 'There was the entry of the Fool,' she said.

'What did he do, exactly?'

She made an odd and very ineloquent gesture.

'He goes round,' she said. 'Round and round.'

'And what else does he do?'

'Aunt Akky – '

'No,' Alleyn said so strongly that Dulcie gave another little yelp. 'I want Mrs Bünz to show us what he did.'

Mrs Bünz was, as usual, much enveloped. As she moved forward, most reluctantly, a stiffish breeze sprang up. She was involved in a little storm of billowing handicraft.

In an uncomfortable silence she jogged miserably round the outside of the courtyard, gave two or three dejected skips and came to a halt in front of the steps. Dame Alice stared at her implacably and Dulcie gaped. The Rector looked at his boots.

'That is all,' said Mrs Bünz.

'You have left something out,' said Alleyn.

'I do not remember everything,' Mrs Bünz said in a strangulated voice.

'And I'll tell you why,' Alleyn rejoined. 'It is because you have never seen what he did. Not even when you looked through the window of the barn.'

She put her woolly hand to her mouth and stepped backwards.

'I'll be bloody well danged!' Tom Plowman loudly ejaculated, and was silenced by Trixie.

Mrs Bünz said something that sounded like ' . . . interests of scientific research –'

'Nor, I suggest, will you have seen what the Guiser did on his first entrance on Wednesday night. Because on Wednesday night you left the arena at the point we have now reached. Didn't you, Mrs Bünz?'

She only moved her head from side to side as if to assure herself that it was on properly.

'Do you say that's wrong?'

She flapped her woollen paws and nodded.

'Yes, but you know, Aunt Akky, she *did.*'

'Hold your tongue, Dulcie, do,' begged her great-aunt.

'No,' Alleyn said. 'Not at all. I want to hear from Miss Mardian.'

'Have it your own way. It's odds on she don't know what she's talkin' about.'

'Oh,' Dulcie cried, 'but I *do*. I *said* so to *you*. Aunt Akky. I said: "Aunt Akky, do look at the German woman going away." I said so to Sam. Didn't I, Sam?'

The Rector, looking startled and rather guilty, said to Alleyn, 'I believe she did.'

'And what *was* Mrs Bünz doing, Rector?'

'She – actually – I really had quite forgotten – she *was* going out.'

'Well, Mrs Bünz?'

Mrs Bünz now spoke with the air of a woman who has had time to make up her mind.

'I had unexpected occasion,' she said, choosing *her* words, 'to absent myself. Delicacy,' she added, 'excuses me from further cobbent.'

'Rot,' said Dame Alice.

Alleyn said: 'And when did you come back?'

She answered quickly: 'During the first part of the sword dance.'

'Why didn't you tell me all this yesterday when we had such difficulty over the point?'

To that she had nothing to say.

Alleyn made a signal with his hand and Fox, who stood in the rear archway, turned to 'Crack' and said something inaudible. They came forward together.

'Mr Begg,' Alleyn called out, 'will you take your harness off if you please?'

'What say? Oh, righty-ho,' said Simon's voice. There was a strange and uncanny upheaval. 'Crack's' neck collapsed and the iron head retreated after it into the cylindrical body. The whole frame tilted on its rim and presently Simon appeared.

'Good. Now. I suggest that on Wednesday evening while you waited behind the wall at the back, you took off your harness as you have just done here.'

Simon began to look resigned. 'And I suggest,' Alleyn went on, 'that when you, Mrs Bünz, left the arena by the side arch, you went round behind the walls and met Mr Begg at the back.'

Mrs Bünz flung up her thick arms in a gesture of defeat.

Simon said clumsily: 'Not to worry, Mrs B,' and dropped his hands on her shoulders.

She screamed out: 'Don't touch me!'

Alleyn said: 'Your shoulders *are* sore, aren't they? But then "Crack's" harness is very heavy, of course.'

After that, Mrs Bünz had nothing to say.

III

A babble of astonishment had broken out on the steps and a kind of suppressed hullabaloo among the Andersens.

Ernie shouted: 'What did I tell you, then, chaps? I said it was a wumman what done it, didn't I? No good comes of it when a wumman mixes 'erself up in this gear. Not it. Same as curing hams,' he astonishingly added. 'Keep 'em out when it's men's gear same as the old baarstard said.'

'Ah, shut up, Corp. Shut your trap, will you?' Simon said wearily.

'Very good, sir,' Ernie shouted and flung himself into a salute.

Alleyn said: 'Steady now, and attend to me. I imagine that you, Begg, accepted a sum of money from Mrs Bünz in consideration of her being allowed to stand-in as "Crack" during the triple sword dance. You came off after your tarring act and she met you behind the wall near the bonfire and you put your harness on her and away she went. I think that, struck by the happy coincidence of names, you probably plonked whatever money she gave you, and I dare say a whole lot more, on Teutonic Dancer by Subsidize out of Substiteuton. The gods of chance are notoriously unscrupulous and, without deserving in the least to do so, you won a packet.'

Simon grinned and then looked as if he wished he hadn't. He said: 'How can you be so sure you haven't been handed a plateful of duff gen?'

'I can be perfectly sure. Do you know what the Guiser's bits of dialogue were in the performance?'

'No,' Simon said. 'I don't. He always mumbled whatever it was. Mrs B asked me, as a matter of fact, and I told her I didn't know.'

Alleyn turned to the company at large.

'Did any of you ever tell Mrs Bünz anything about what was said?'

Chris said angrily: 'Not bloody likely.'

'Very well. Mrs Bünz repeated a phrase of the dialogue in conversation with me. A phrase that I'm sure she heard with immense satisfaction for the first time on Wednesday night. That's why you bribed Mr Begg to let you take his part, wasn't it, Mrs Bünz? You were on the track of a particularly sumptuous fragment of folklore. You didn't dance as you were meant to do round the edge of the arena. Disguised as "Crack" you got as close as you could to the Guiser and you listened-in.'

Alleyn hesitated for a moment and then quoted: '"Betty to lover me." Do you remember how it goes on?'

'I answer nothing.'

'Then I'm afraid I must ask you to act.' He fished in his pockets and pulled out the bandages and two handfuls of linen. 'These will do to pad your shoulders. We'll get Dr Otterly to fix them.'

'What will you make me do?'

'Only what you did on Wednesday.'

Chris shouted violently: 'Doan't let 'er. Keep the woman out of it. Doan't let 'er.'

Dan said: 'And so I say. If that's what happened 'twasn't right and never will be. Once was too many: let alone her doing it again deliberate.'

'Hold hard, chaps,' Andy said, with much less than his usual modesty. 'This makes a bit of differ, all the same. None of us knew about this, did we?' He jerked his head at Ernie. 'Only young Ern seemingly. He knew the woman done this on us? Didn't you, Ern?'

'Keep your trap shut, Corp,' Simon advised him.

'Very good. Sir.'

Chris suddenly roared at Simon: 'You leave Ern alone, you Simmy-Dick. You lay off of him, will you? Reckon you're no better nor a damned traitor, letting a woman in on the Five Sons.'

'So he is, then,' Nat said. 'A bloody traitor, don't you heed him, Ern.'

'Ah, put a sock in it, you silly clots,' Simon said disgustedly. 'Leave the poor sod alone. You don't know what you're talking about. Silly bastards!'

Dan, using a prim voice, said: 'Naow! Naow! Language!'

They all glanced self-consciously at Dame Alice.

It had been obvious to Alleyn that behind him Dame Alice was getting up steam. She now let it off by means literally of an attenuated hiss. The Andersens stared at her apprehensively.

She went for them with a mixture of arrogance and essential understanding that must derive, Alleyn thought, from a line of coarse, aristocratic, overbearing landlords. She was The Old Englishwoman not only of Surtees but of Fielding and Wycherley and Jonson: a bully, and a harridan, but one who spoke with authority. The Andersens listened to her, without any show of servility but rather with the air of men who recognize a familiar voice among foreigners. She had only one thing to say to them and it was to the effect that if they didn't perform she, the police, and everyone else would naturally conclude that they had united to make away with their father. She ended abruptly with an order to get on with it before she lost patience. Chris still refused to go on but his brothers, after a brief consultation, overruled him.

Fox, who had been writing busily, exchanged satisfied glances with his chief.

Alleyn said: 'Now, Mrs Bünz. Are you ready?'

Dr Otterly had been busy with the bandages and the pads of linen which now rested on Mrs Bünz's shoulders like a pair of unwieldly epaulets.

'You're prepared, I see,' Alleyn said, 'to help us.'

'I have not said.'

Ernie suddenly bawled out: 'Don't bloody well let 'er. There'll be trouble.'

'That'll do,' Alleyn said, and Ernie was silent. 'Well, Mrs Bünz?'

She turned to Simon. Her face was the colour of lard and she smiled horridly. 'Wing-Commander Begg, you as much as I, are implicated in this idle prank. Should I repeat?'

Simon took her gently round the waist. 'I don't see why not, Mrs B.,' he said. 'You be a good girl and play ball with the cops. Run along now.'

He gave her a facetious pat. 'Very well,' she said, and produced a sort of laugh. 'After all, why dot?'

So she went out by the side archway and Simon by the centre one. Dr Otterly struck up his fiddle again.

It was the tune that had ushered in the Fool. Dr Otterly played the introduction and, involuntarily, performers and audience alike looked at the rear archway where on Sword Wednesday the lonely figure in its dolorous mask had appeared. The archway gaped enigmatically upon the night. Smoke from the bonfire drifted across the background and occasional sparks crossed it like fireflies. It had an air of expectancy.

'But this time there won't be a Fool,' Dulcie pointed out. 'Will there, Aunt Akky?'

Dame Alice had opened her mouth to speak. It remained open but no voice came out. The Rector ejaculated sharply and rose from his chair. A thin, shocking sound, half laughter and half scream, wavered across the courtyard. It had been made by Ernie and was echoed by Trixie.

Through the smoke, as if it had been evolved from the same element, came the white figure: jog, jog, getting clearer every second. Through the archway and into the arena: a grinning mask, limp arms, a bauble on a stick, and bent legs.

Dr Otterly, after an astonished discord, went into the refrain of Lord Mardian's Fancy. Young Bill, in the character of the Fool, began to jog round the courtyard. It was as if a clockwork toy had been rewound.

Alleyn joined Fox by the rear archway. From here he could still see the Andersens. The four elder brothers were reassuring each other. Chris looked angry, and the others mulish and affronted. But Ernie's mouth gaped and his hands twitched and he watched the Fool like a fury. Offstage, through the archway, Alleyn was able to see Mrs Bünz's encounter with Simon. She came round the outside curve of the wall and he met her at the bonfire. He began to explain sheepishly to Alleyn.

'We'd fixed it up like this,' Simon said. 'I met her here. We'd plenty of time.'

'Why on earth didn't you tell us the whole of this ridiculous story at once?' Alleyn asked.

Simon mumbled. 'i don't expect you to credit it but I was cobs with the boys. They're a good shower of bods. I knew how they'd feel if it ever got out. And anyway it doesn't look so hot, does it? For all I knew, you might get thinking things.'

'What sort of things?'

'Well, *you* know. With murder about.'

'You *have* been an ass,' Alleyn said.

'I wouldn't have done it only I wanted the scratch like hell.' He added impertinently: 'Come to that, why didn't you tell us you were going to rig up an understudy? Nasty jolt he gave us, didn't he, Mrs B? Come on, there's a big girl. Gently does it.'

Mrs Bünz, who seemed to be shattered into acquiescence, sat on the ground. He tipped up the great cylinder of 'Crack's' body, exposing the heavy shoulder straps under the canvas top and the buckled harness. He lowered it gently over Mrs Bünz. 'Arms through the leathers,' he said.

The ringed canvas neck which lay concertina-ed on the top of the cylinder now swelled at the base. Simon leant over and adjusted it, and Mrs Bünz's pixie cap appeared through the top. He lifted the head on its flexible rod and then introduced the rod into the neck. 'Here it comes,' he said. Mrs Bünz's hands could be seen grasping the end of the rod.

'It fits into a socket in the harness,' Simon explained. The head now stood like some monstrous blossom on a thin stalk above the body. Simon drew up the canvas neck. The pixie cap disappeared. The top of the neck was made fast to the head and Mrs Bünz contemplated the world through a sort of window in the canvas.

'The hands are free underneath,' Simon said, 'to work the tail string.' He grinned. 'And to have a bit of the old woo if you catch your girlie. I didn't, worse luck. There you are. The Doc's just coming up with the tune for the first sword dance. On you go, Mrs B. Not to worry. We don't believe in spooks, do we?'

And Mrs Bünz, subdued to the semblance of a prehistoric bad dream, went through the archway to take part in the Mardian Sword Dance.

Simon squatted down by the bonfire and reached for a burning twig to light his cigarette.

'Poor old B.,' he said, looking after Mrs Bünz. *'But* still.'

IV

Camilla had once again run away from the Hobby into Ralph Stayne's arms and once again he stayed beside her.

She had scarcely recovered from the shock of the Fool's entrance and kept looking into Ralph's face to reassure herself. She found his great extinguisher of a skirt and his queer bi-sexual hat rather off-putting. She kept remembering stories Trixie had told her of how in earlier times the Betties had used the skirt. They had popped it over village girls, Trixie said, and had grabbed hold of them through the slits in the sides and carried them away. Camilla would have jeered at herself heartily if she had realized that even though Ralph had only indulged in a modified form of this piece of horseplay, she intensely disliked the anecdote. Perhaps it was because Trixie had related it.

She looked at Ralph now and, after the habit of lovers, made much of the qualities she thought she saw in him. His mouth was set and his eyebrows were drawn together in a scowl. 'He's terribly sensitive, really,' Camilla told herself. 'He's hating this business as much in his way as I am in mine. And,' she thought, 'I dare say he's even angrier because Simon Begg chased me again.' This thought cheered her immensely.

They watched young Bill doing his version of his grandfather's first entry and the ceremonial trot round the courtyard. He repeated everything quite correctly and didn't forget to slap the dolmen with his clown's bauble.

'And *that's* what Mrs Bünz didn't know about,' Ralph muttered.

'Who is it?' Camilla wondered. 'He knows it all, doesn't he? It's horrible.'

'It's that damned young Bill,' Ralph muttered. 'There's nobody else who does know. By heaven, when I get hold of him – '

Camilla said: 'Darling, you don't think – ?'

He turned his head and looked steadily at Camilla for a moment before answering her.

'I don't know what to think,' he said at last. 'But I know damn' well that if the Guiser had spotted Mrs Bünz dressed up as "Crack" he'd have gone for her like a fury.'

'But nothing *happened*,' Camilla said. 'I stood here and I looked and nothing *happened*.'

'I know,' he said.

'Well then – how? Was he carried off? Or something?' Ralph shook his head.

Dr Otterly had struck up a bouncing introduction. The Five Sons, who had removed their bells, took up their swords and came forward into position. And through the central archway jogged the Hobby Horse, moving slowly.

'Here she comes,' Camilla said. 'You'd never guess, would you?'

Alleyn and Fox reappeared and stood inside the archway. Beyond them lit by the bonfire was Simon.

The Sons began the first part of the Triple Sword Dance.

They had approached their task with a lowering and reluctant air. Alleyn wondered if there was going to be a joint protest about the re-enactment of the Fool. Ernie hadn't removed his gaze from the dolorous mask. His eyes were unpleasantly brilliant and his face glistened with sweat. He came forward with his brothers and had an air of scarcely knowing what he was about. But there was some compulsion in the music. They had been so drilled by their father and so used to executing their steps with a leap and a flourish that they were unable to dance with less than the traditional panache. They were soon hard at it, neat and vigorous, rising lightly and coming down hard. The ring of steel was made. Each man grasped his successor's sword by its red ribbon. The lock or knot was formed. Dan raised it aloft to exhibit it and it glittered in the torchlight. Young Bill approached and looked at the knot as if at his reflection in a glass.

A metallic rumpus broke out on the steps. It was Dame Alice indulging in a wild cachinnation on her hunting-horn.

Dr Otterly lowered his bow. The dancers, the Betty and the Hobby Horse were motionless.

'Yes, Dame Alice?' Alleyn asked.

'The Hobby ain't close enough,' she said. 'Nothin' like. It kept sidlin' up to Will'm. D'you 'gree?' she barked at the Rector.

'I rather think it did.'

'What does everybody else say to this?' Alleyn asked.

Dr Otterly said he remembered noting that 'Crack' kept much closer than usual to the Fool.

'So do I,' Ralph said. 'Undoubtedly it did. Isn't that right?' he added, turning to the Andersens.

'So 'tis, then, Mr Ralph,' Dan said. 'I kind of seed it was there when we was hard at it dancing. And afterwards in all the muck up, I reckon I forgot. Right?' He appealed to his brothers.

'Reckon so,' they said, glowering at the Hobby, and Chris added angrily: 'Prying and sneaking and none of us with the sense to know. What she done it for?'

'In order to hear what the Fool said when he looked in the "glass"?' Alleyn suggested. '*Was* it, Mrs Bünz?' he shouted, standing over the Hobby Horse and peering at its neck. 'Did you go close because you wanted to hear?'

A muffled sound came through the neck. The great head swayed in a grotesque nod.

> '*Once for a looker,*' Alleyn quoted, '*and all must agree,*
> *If I bashes the looking-glass so I'll go free.*'

'Was that what he said?'

The head nodded again.

'Stand closer then, Mrs Bünz. Stand as you did on Wednesday.'

The Hobby Horse stood closer.

'Go on,' Alleyn said. 'Go on, Fool.'

Young Bill, using both hands, took the knot of swords by the hilts and dashed it to the ground. Dr Otterly struck up again, the Sons retrieved their swords and began the second part of the dance which was an exact repetition of the first. They now had the air of being fiercely dedicated. Even Ernie danced with concentration though he continually threw glances of positive hatred at the Fool.

And the Hobby Horse stood close.

It swayed and fidgeted as if the being at its centre was uneasy. Once, as the head moved, Alleyn caught a glimpse of eyes behind the window in its neck.

The second sword-knot was made and exhibited by Dan. Then young Bill leant his mask to one side and mimed the writing of the will and the offer of the will to the Sons.

Alleyn quoted again:

> '*Twice for a Testament. Read it and see*
> *If you look at the leavings then so I'll go free:*'

The Betty drew nearer. The Hobby and the Betty now stood right and left of the dolmen.

The Sons broke the knot and began the third part of the dance.

To the party of three on the steps, to the watching audience and the policemen and to Camilla who looked on with a rising sensation of nausea, it seemed as if the Five Sons now danced on a crescendo that thudded like a quickening pulse towards its climax.

For the last and the third time their swords were interlaced and Dan held them aloft. The Fool was in his place behind the dolmen, the hermaphrodite and the horse stood like crazy acolytes to left and right of the stone. Dan lowered the knot of swords to the level of the Fool's head. Each of the Sons laid hold of his own sword-hilt. The fiddling stopped.

'I can't look,' Camilla thought, and then: 'But that's not how it was. They've gone wrong again.'

At the same time the gong, the hunting-horn and Alleyn's whistle sounded. Ralph Stayne, Tom Plowman and Trixie all held up their hands and Dr Otterly raised his bow.

It was the Hobby Horse again. It should, they said, have been close behind the Fool, who was now leaning across the dolmen towards the sword-lock.

Very slowly the Hobby moved behind the Fool.

'And then,' Alleyn said, 'came the last verse:

> *'Here comes the rappers to send me to bed*
> *They'll rapper my head off and then I'll be dead.'*

'Now.'

Young Bill leant over the dolmen and thrust his head with its rabbit cap and mask into the lock of swords. There he was, grinning through a steel halter.

> *'Betty to lover me*
> *Hobby to cover me*
> *If you cut off my head*
> *I'll rise from the dead.'*

The swords flashed and sang. The rabbit head dropped on the dolmen. The Fool slid down behind the stone out of sight.

'Go on,' Alleyn said. He stood beside the Hobby Horse. The Fool lay at their feet. Alleyn pointed at Ralph Stayne. 'It's your turn,' he said. 'Go on.'

Ralph said apologetically: 'I can't very well without any audience.'

'Why not?'

'It was an ad lib. It depended on the audience.'

'Never mind. You've got Mr Plowman and Trixie and a perambu-
lation of police. Imagine the rest.'

'It's so damn' silly,' Ralph muttered.

'Oh, get *on*,' Dame Alice ordered. 'What's the matter with the
boy!'

From the folds of his crate-like skirt Ralph drew out a sort of ladle
that hung on a string from his waist. Rather half-heartedly he made
a circuit of the courtyard and mimed the taking up of a collection.

'That's all,' he said and came to a halt.

Dame Alice tooted. 'No, it bean't all, neither.'

'I mean it's all of that bit,' Ralph said to Alleyn.

'What comes next? Keep going.'

With rather a bad grace he embarked on his fooling. He flirted his
crinoline and ran at two or three of the stolidly observant policemen.

His great-aunt shouted, 'Use yer skirt, boy!'

Ralph made a sortie upon a large officer and attempted without
success to throw the crinoline over his head.

"*Yah!*' jeered his great-aunt. 'Go for a little 'un. Go for the gel.'

This was Trixie.

She smiled broadly at Ralph: 'Come on, then, Mr Ralph. I doan't
mind,' said Trixie.

Camilla turned away quickly. The Andersens stared, bright-eyed,
at Ralph.

Alleyn said: 'Obviously the skirt business only works if the
victim's very short and slight. Suppose we resurrect the Fool for the
moment.'

Young Bill got up from behind the dolmen. Ralph ran at him and
popped the crinoline over his head. The crinoline heaved and
bulged. It was not difficult, Alleyn thought, to imagine the hammer
blows of bucolic wit that this performance must have inspired in the
less inhibited days of Merrie England.

'Will *that* do?' Ralph asked ungraciously.

'Yes,' Alleyn said. 'Yes. I think it will.'

Young Bill rolled out from under the rim of the crinoline and
again lay down between dolmen and 'Crack'.

'Go on,' Alleyn said. 'Next.'

Ralph set his jaw and prepared grimly for a revival of his Ernie-baiting. Ernie immediately showed signs of resentment and of wishing to anticipate the event.

'Not this time, yer won't,' he said, showing his teeth and holding his sword behind him. 'Not me. I know a trick worth two nor that.'

This led to a general uproar.

At last, when the blandishments of his brothers, Dame Alice's fury, Alleyn's patience and the sweet reasonableness of Dr Otterly had all proved fruitless, Alleyn fetched Simon from behind the wall.

'Will you,' he said, 'get him to stand facing his brothers and holding his sword by the ribbons, which I gather is what he did originally?'

'I'll give it a whirl if you say so but don't depend on it. He's blowing up for trouble, is the Corp.'

'Try.'

'Roger. But he may do *anything*. Hey! Corp!'

He took Ernie by the arm and murmured wooingly in his ear. Ernie listened but when it came to the point, remained truculent. 'No bloody fear,' he said. He pulled away from Simon and turned on Ralph. 'You keep off.'

'Sorry,' Simon muttered. 'N.b.g.'

'Oh well,' Alleyn said. 'You go back, will you.'

Simon went back.

Alleyn had a word with Ralph, who listened without any great show of enthusiasm but nodded agreement. Alleyn went up to Ernie.

He said: 'Is that the sword you were making such a song about? The one you had on Wednesday?'

'Not it,' Ernie said angrily. 'This un's a proper old blunt 'un. Mine's a whiffler, mine is. So sharp's a knife.'

'You must have looked pretty foolish when the Betty took it off you.'

'No, I did not, then.'

'How did he get it? If it's so sharp why didn't he cut his hand?'

'You mind your own – business.'

'Come on, now. He ordered you to give it to him and you handed it over like a good little boy.'

Ernie's response to this was furious and unprintable.

Alleyn laughed. 'All right. Did he smack your hand or what? Come on.'

'He wouldn't of took it,' Ernie spluttered, 'if I'd seen. He come sneaking up be'ind when I wo-n't noticing, like. *Didn't* you?' he demanded of Ralph. 'If I'd held thik proper you wouldn't 'ave done it.'

'Oh,' Alleyn said offensively. 'And how *did* you hold it? Like a lady's parasol?'

Ernie glared at him. A stillness had fallen over the courtyard. The bonfire could be heard crackling cheerfully beyond the wall. Very deliberately Ernie reversed his sword and swung it by the scarlet cord that was threaded through the tip.

'Now!' Alleyn shouted and Ralph pounced.

'Crack' screamed: a shrill wavering cry. Mrs Bünz's voice could be heard within protesting, apparently, in German and the Hobby, moving eccentrically and very fast, turned and bolted through the archway at the rear. At the same time Ralph, with the sword in one hand and his crinoline gathered up in the other, fled before the enraged Ernie. Round and round the courtyard they ran. Ralph dodged and feinted, Ernie roared and doubled and stumbled after him.

But Alleyn didn't wait to see the chase.

He ran after the Hobby. Through the archway he ran, and there behind the old wall in the light of the bonfire was 'Crack' the Hobby Horse, plunging and squealing in the strangest manner. Its great cylinder of a body swung and tilted. Its skirt swept the muddy ground, its canvas top bulged, and its head gyrated wildly. Fox and three of his men stood by and watched. There was a final mammoth upheaval. The whole structure tipped and fell over. Mrs Bünz, terribly dishevelled, bolted out and was caught by Fox.

She left behind her the strangest travesty of the Fool. His clown's face was awry and his pyjama jacket in rags. His hands were scratched and he was covered in mud. He stepped out of the wreckage of 'Crack' and took off his mask.

'Nice work, young Bill,' Alleyn said. 'And that, my hearties, is how the Guiser got himself off-stage.'

V

There was no time for Mrs Bünz or Simon to remark upon this state-ment. Mrs Bünz whimpered in the protective custody of Mr Fox. Simon scratched his head and stared uncomfortably at young Bill.

And young Bill, for his part, as if to clear his head, first shook it, then lowered it and finally dived at Simon and began to pummel his chest with both fists.

Simon shouted: 'Hey! What the hell!' and grabbed the boy's wrists.

Simultaneously Ernie came plunging through the archway from the arena.

'Where is 'e?' Ernie bawled. 'Where the hell is the bastard?'

He saw Simon with the Fool's figure in his grip. A terrible stillness came upon them all.

Then Ernie opened his mouth indecently wide and yelled: 'Let 'im have it, then. I'll finish 'im.'

Simon loosed his hold as if to free himself rather than his captive.

The boy in Fool's clothing fell to the ground and lay there, mask upwards.

Ernie stumbled towards him. Alleyn and the three Yard men moved in.

'Leave 'im to me!' Ernie said.

'You clot,' Simon said. 'Shut your great trap, you *bloody* clot. Corp! *Do you hear me? Corp!*'

Ernie looked at his own hands.

'I've lost my whiffler. Where's t'other job?'

He turned to the wall and saw the charred slasher. 'Ar!' he said. 'There she is.' He grabbed it, turned and swung it up. Alleyn and one of his men held him.

'Lemme go!' he said, struggling. 'I got my orders. Lemme go.'

Mrs Bünz screamed briefly and shockingly.

'What orders?'

'My Wing-Commander's orders. Will I do it again, sir? Will I do it, like you told me? Again?'

Looking larger than human in the smoke of the bonfire, five men moved forward. They closed in about Simon.

Alleyn stood in front of him.

'Simon Richard Begg,' he said, 'I am going to ask you for a statement but before I do so I must warn you – '

Simon's hand flashed. Alleyn caught the blow on his forearm instead of on his throat. 'Not again,' he said.

It was well that there were five men to tackle Simon. He was experienced in unarmed combat and he was a natural killer.

CHAPTER 13

The Swords Go In

'He's a natural killer,' Alleyn said. 'This is the first time, as far as we know, that it's happened since he left off being a professional. If it *is* the first time it's because until last Wednesday nobody had happened to annoy him in just the way that gingers up his homicidal reflexes.'

'Yes, but *fancy*!' Dulcie said, coming in with a steaming grog tray. 'He had *such* a good war record. You know he came down in a parachute and killed *quantities* of Germans with his bare hands all at once and escaped and got decorated.'

'Yes,' Alleyn said dryly, 'he's had lots of practice. He told us about that. That was the last time.'

'D'you meantersay,' Dame Alice asked, handing Alleyn a bottle of rum and a corkscrew, 'that he killed Will'm Andersen out of temper and nothin' else?'

'Out of an accumulation of spleen and frustrated ambition and on a snap assessment of the main chance.'

'Draw that cork and begin at the beginnin'.'

'Aunt Akky, shouldn't you have a rest –'

'No.'

Alleyn drew the cork. Dame Alice poured rum and boiling water into a saucepan and began to grind up nutmeg. 'Slice the lemons,' she ordered Fox.

Dr Otterly said: 'Frustrated ambition because of Copse Forge and the filling-station?'

'That's it.'

'Otters, don't interrupt.'

'I dare say,' Alleyn said, 'he'd thought often enough that if he could hand the old type the big chop, and get by, he'd give it a go. The boys were in favour of his scheme, remember, and he wanted money very badly.'

'But he didn't plan this thing?' Dr Otterly interjected and added: 'Sorry, Dame Alice.'

'No, no. He only planned the substitution of Mrs Bünz as "Crack" and she gave him, she now tells us, thirty pounds for the job and bought a car from him into the bargain. He'd taken charge of "Crack" and left the thing in the back of her car. She actually crept out when the pub was bedded down for the night and put it on to see if she could support the weight. They planned the whole thing very carefully. What happened was this. At the end of his girl-chase he went off-stage and put Mrs Bünz into "Crack's" harness. She went on for the triple sword dance and was meant to come off in time for him to change back before the finale. La Bella Bünz, however, hell-bent on picking up a luscious morsel of folksy dialogue, edged up as close to the dolmen as she could get. She thought she was quite safe. The tar-daubed skirts of the Hobby completely hid her. Or almost completely.'

'Completely. No almost about it,' Dame Alice said. 'I couldn't see her feet.'

'No. But you would have seen them if you'd lain down in a shallow depression in the ground a few inches away from her. As the Guiser did.'

'Hold the pot over the fire for a bit, one of you. Go on.'

'The Guiser, from his worm's viewpoint, recognized her. There she was, looming over him, with "Crack's" carcass probably covering the groove where he lay and her rubber overshoes and hairy skirts showing every time she moved. He reached up and grabbed her. She screamed at the top of her voice and you all thought it was Begg trying to neigh. The Guiser was a very small man and a very strong one. He pinioned her arms to her body, kept his head down and ran her off.'

'That was when Ralph pinched Ernie's sword?' Dr Otterly ventured.

'That's it. Once off-stage, while he was still, as it were, tented up with her, the Guiser hauled her out of "Crack's" harness. He was gibbering with temper. As soon as he was free, a matter of seconds, he turned on Begg, who of course was waiting there for her. The Guiser went for Begg like a fury. It was over in a flash. Mrs Bünz saw Begg hit him across the throat. It's a well-known blow in unarmed combat, and it's deadly. She also saw Ernie come charging off-stage without his whiffler and in a roaring rage himself. Then she bolted.

'What happened after that, Ernie demonstrated for us tonight. He saw his god fell the Guiser. Ernie was in a typical epileptic's rage and, as usual, the focal point of his rage was his father. The Old Man, who had killed his dog, frustrated his god's plans and snatched the role of Fool away from Ernie himself at the last moment. He was additionally inflamed by the loss of his sword.

'But the slasher was there. He'd sharpened it and brought it up himself and he grabbed it as soon as he saw it.

'He said tonight that he was under orders and I'm sure he was. Begg saw a quick way out. He said something like this: "He tried to kill me. Get him, Corp!" And Ernie, his mind seething with a welter of emotions and superstitions, did what he'd done to the aggressive gander earlier that day.'

'Gracious! Aunt Akky, fancy! *Ernie!*'

'Very nasty,' said Mr Fox, who was holding the saucepan of punch over the drawing-room fire.

'A few moments later, Ralph Stayne came out with Ernie's whiffler. He found Ernie and he found "Crack", sitting there, he says, like a great broody hen. Begg was hiding the decapitated Guiser with the only shield available — "Crack".

'He told Stayne that Ernie was upset and he'd better leave him alone. Stayne returned the whiffler and went on round the wall to the O.P. entrance.

'Begg knew that if the body was found where it lay Stayne would remember how he saw him squatting there. He did the only thing possible. He sent Ernie back to the arena, threw the slasher on the fire and overturned the drum of tar to obliterate any traces of blood. It caught fire. Then he hitched "Crack's" harness over his own shoulders and returned to the arena. He carried the body in his arms and held the head by the strings of its bag-like mask, both ends of which became bloodstained. All this under cover of the great canvas body.

'At this time the final dance was in progress and the Five Sons were between their audience and the dolmen. "Crack" was therefore

masked by the stone and the dancers. Not that he needed any masking. He dropped the body – laid it, like an egg, in the depression
behind the dolmen. This accounts for the state it was in when the
Andersens found it. Begg leapt with suspicious alacrity at my suggestion that he might have tripped over it or knocked it with the edge
of "Crack's" harness.'

'Oh dear, Aunt Akky!'

'He was careful to help with the removal of the body in order to
account for any bloodstains on his clothes. When I told him we
would search his clothes for bloodstains, he made his only mistake.
His vanity tripped him up. He told us the story of his ferocious
exploits in Germany and how, if a man was killed as the Guiser was
supposed to have been killed his assailant would be covered in
blood. Of course we knew that, but the story told us that Begg had
once been involved in unarmed combat with an old peasant and that
he had been saved by one of his own men. A hedge-slasher had been
involved in that story, too.'

Alleyn glanced at Dame Alice and Dulcie. 'Is this altogether too
beastly for you?' he asked.

'Absolutely *ghastly*,' Dulcie said. 'Still,' she added in a hurry, 'I'd
rather *know*.'

'Don't be 'ffected, Dulcie. 'Course you would. So'd I. Go on,'
Dame Alice ordered.

'There's not much more to tell. Begg hadn't time to deliberate but
he hoped, of course, that with all those swords about it would be
concluded that the thing was done while the Guiser lay behind the
dolmen. He and Dr Otterly were the only two performers who
would be at once ruled out if this theory were accepted. He's completely callous. I don't suppose he minded much who might be
accused, though he must have known that the only two who would
really look likely would be Ernie, with the sharp sword, and Ralph
Stayne, who pinched it and made great play slashing it round.'

'But he stuck up for Ernie,' Dr Otterly said. 'All through. Didn't
he?'

Fox sighed heavily. Dame Alice pointed to a magnificent silver
punch bowl that was blackening in the smoke on the hearth. He
poured the fragrant contents of the saucepan into it and placed it
before her.

Alleyn said: 'Begg wanted above all things to prevent us finding out about Ernie and the slasher. Once we had an inkling that the Guiser was killed off-stage his improvised plan would go to pot. We would know that *he* was off-stage and must have been present. He would be able, of course, to say that Ernie killed the Guiser and that he himself, wearing "Crack's" harness, was powerless to stop him. But there was no knowing how Ernie would behave: Ernie, filled with zeal and believing he had saved his god and wiped out that father-figure who so persistently reappeared, always to Begg's and Ernie's undoing. Moreover, there was Mrs Bünz, who had seen Begg strike his blow though she didn't realize he had struck to kill. He fixed Mrs Bünz by telling her that we suspected her and that there was a lot of feeling against her as a German. Now he's been arrested, she's come across with a full statement and will give evidence.'

'What'll happen?' Dame Alice asked, beginning to ladle out her punch.

'Oh,' Alleyn said, 'we've a very groggy case, you know. We've only got the undeniable fact, based on medical evidence, that he was dead before Ernie struck. Moreover, in spite of Ernie, there may with luck be the evidence of the actual injury.'

'Larynx,' Dr Otterly said.

'Exactly.'

'What,' Dr Otterly asked, 'will he plead?'

'His counsel may plump for self-defence. The Guiser went for him and his old unarmed combat training took over. He defended himself instinctively.'

'Mightn't it be true?'

'The Guiser,' Alleyn said, 'was a very small and very old man. But as far as that goes I think Begg's training *did* reassert itself. Tickle a dog's ribs and it scratches itself. There's Begg's temperament, make-up, and experience. There are his present financial doldrums, there are his prospects if he can start his petrol station. There's the Guiser, standing in his path. The Guiser comes at him like an old fury. Up goes the arm in goes the edge of the hand. It was unpremeditated but in my opinion he hit to kill.'

'Will he get off?' Dr Otterly asked.

'How the bloody hell should I know!' Alleyn said with some violence. 'Sorry, Dame Alice.'

'Have some punch,' said Dame Alice. She looked up at him out of her watery old eyes. 'You're an odd sort of feller,' she remarked. 'Anybody'd think you were squeamish.'

II

Ralph took Camilla to call on his great-aunt.

'We'll have to face it sooner or later,' he said, 'and so will she.'

'I can't pretend I'm looking forward to it.'

'Darling, she'll adore you. In two minutes she'll adore you.'

'Come off it, my sweet.'

Ralph beamed upon his love and untied the string that secured the wrought-iron gates.

'Those geese!' Camilla said.

They were waiting in a solid phalanx.

'I'll protect you. They know me.'

'And the two bulls on the skyline. The not very distant skyline.'

'Dear old boys, I assure you. Come on.'

'Up the Campions!' Camilla said, if not the Andersens.'

'Up, emphatically, the Andersens,' Ralph said and held out his hand.

She went through the gates.

The geese did menacing things with their necks. Ralph shook his stick and they hissed back at him.

'Perhaps, darling, if you hurried and I held them at bay – '

Camilla panted up the drive. Ralph fought a rearguard action. The bulls watched with interest.

Ralph and Camilla stumbled breathless and hand-fast through the archway and across the courtyard. They mounted the steps. Ralph tugged at the phoney bell. It set up a clangour that caused the geese to scream, wheel and waddle indignantly away.

'That's done it,' Ralph said and put his arm round Camilla.

They stood with their backs to the door and looked across the courtyard. The snow had gone. Grey and wet were the walls and wet the ground. Beyond the rear archway stood a wintry hill, naked trees and a windy sky.

And in the middle of the courtyard was the dolmen; very black, one heavy stone supported by two others. It looked expectant.

'*Nine men's morris is filled up with mud,*y Camilla murmured.

'There *were* nine,' Ralph said. 'Counting Mrs Bünz.'

'Well,' she said under her breath, 'that's the last of the Mardian Morris of the Five Sons, isn't it?'

'Think so?'

'*Ralph!* No one, not the boys, or you or Dr Otterly can ever want to do it again: ever, ever, ever. Can you? *Can* you?'

Ralph was saved from answering by Dulcie, who opened the great door behind them.

'How do you do?' Dulcie said to Camilla. 'Do come in. Aunt Akky'll be delighted. She's been feeling rather flat after all the excitement.' Ralph gently propelled Camilla into the hall. Dulcie shut the door.

'Aunt Akky,' she said, 'does so like things to happen. She's been saying what a long time it seems to next Sword Wednesday.'

Singing in the Shrouds

FOR

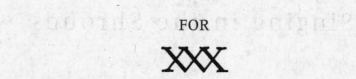

XXX

Contents

Cast of Characters

PC Moir
A Taxi-driver
A Sailor
Mrs Dillington-Blick
Her Friend
Mr Cuddy   *A draper*
Mrs Cuddy   *His wife*
Miss Katherine Abbott   *An authority on church music*
Mr Philip Merryman   *A retired schoolmaster*
Father Jourdain   *An Anglo-Catholic priest*
His Fellow-Cleric
Jemima Carmichael
Dr Timothy Makepiece   *Medical Officer,* Cape Farewell
Mr Aubyn Dale   *A celebrity of commercial television*
His dearest friend
Their dearest male friend
Their dearest female friend
Mr Donald McAngus   *A philatelist*
Dennis   *A steward*
A Wireless Officer
Captain Bannerman   *Master,* Cape Farewell
Superintendent Roderick Alleyn   *CID, New Scotland Yard*

CHAPTER 1

Prologue with Corpse

In the Pool of London and farther east all through the dockyards the fog lay heavy. Lights swam like moons in their own halos. Insignificant buildings, being simplified, became dramatic. Along the Cape Line Company's stretch of wharfage the ships at anchor loomed up portentously: *Cape St Vincent*, Glasgow. *Cape Horn*, London. *Cape Farewell*, Glasgow. The cranes that served these ships lost their heads in the fog. Their gestures as they bowed and turned became pontifical.

Beyond their illuminated places the dockyards vanished. The gang loading the *Cape Farewell* moved from light into nothingness. Noises were subdued and isolated and a man's cough close at hand was more startling than the rattle of winches.

Police Constable Moir, on duty until midnight, walked in and out of shadows. He breathed the soft cold smell of wet wood and heard the slap of the night tide against the wharves. Acres and acres of shipping and forests of cranes lay around him. Ships, he thought romantically, were, in a sort of way, like little worlds. Tied up to bollards and lying quiet enough but soon to sail over the watery globe as lonely as the planets wandering in the skies. He would have liked to travel. He solaced himself with thoughts of matrimony, promotion and, when the beat was getting him down a bit, of the Police Medal and sudden glory. At a passageway between buildings near the *Cape Farewell* he walked slower because it was livelier there. Cars drove up: in particular an impressive new sports car with a smashing redhead at the wheel and three passengers, one of whom he recognized with interest as the great TV personality, Aubyn Dale. It was evident that the others, a man and woman, also belonged to that mysterious world of glaring lights, trucking cameras and fan mails. You could tell by the way they shouted 'darling' at each other as they walked through the passageway.

PC Moir conscientiously moved himself on. Darkness engulfed him, lights revealed him. He had reached the boundary of his beat and was walking along it. A bus had drawn up at the entry to the water-front and he watched the passengers get out and plod, heads down and suitcases in hand, towards the *Cape Farewell* – two clergymen, a married couple, a lush bosomy lady and her friend, a benevolent-looking gentleman, a lovely young lady with a miserable expression and a young gentleman who lagged behind and looked as if he'd like to ask her to let him carry her luggage. They walked into the fog, became phantoms and disappeared down the passageway in the direction of the wharf.

For the next two and a half hours PC Moir patrolled the area. He kept an eye on occasional drunks, took a look at parked vehicles, observed ships and pubs and had an instinctive ear open for any untoward sounds. At half past eleven he took a turn down the waterfront and into a region of small ambiguous ships, ill-lit and silent, scarcely discernible in the fog that had stealthily accumulated about them.

'Quiet,' he thought. 'Very quiet, this stretch.'

By a strange coincidence (as he was afterwards and repeatedly to point out) he was startled at this very moment by a harsh mewing cry.

'Funny,' he thought. 'You don't often seem to hear seagulls at night. I suppose they go to sleep like Christians.'

The cry sounded again but shortly as if somebody had lifted the needle from a record. Moir couldn't really tell from what direction the sound had come but he fancied it was from somewhere along the Cape Company's wharf. He had arrived at the farthest point of his beat and he now returned. The sounds of activity about the *Cape Farewell* grew clear again. She was still loading.

When he got back to the passageway he found a stationary taxi wreathed in fog and looking desolate. It quite surprised him on drawing nearer to see the driver, motionless over the wheel. He was so still that Moir wondered if he was asleep. However he turned his head and peered out.

'Evening, mate,' Moir said. 'Nice night to get lost in.'

'And that's no error,' the driver agreed hoarsely. ' 'Ere!' he continued, leaning out and looking fixedly at the policeman. 'You seen anybody?'

'How d'you mean, seen?'

'A skirt. Wiv a boxerflahs.'

'No,' Moir said. 'Your fare, would it be?'

'Ah! My fare! 'Alf a minute at the outside she says, and nips off lively. 'Alf a minute! 'Alf a bloody ar, more likely.'

'Where'd she go? Ship?' asked Moir, jerking his head in the direction of the *Cape Farewell*.

' 'Course. Works at a flah shop. Cartin' rahnd bokays to some silly bitch wot'll frow 'em to the fishes, like as not. Look at the time: arpas eleven. Flahs!'

'P'raps she couldn't find the recipient,' PC Moir ventured, using police-court language out of habit.

'P'raps she couldn't find the flippin' ship nor yet the ruddy ocean! P'raps she's drahned,' said the taxi driver in a passion.

'Hope it's not all that serious, I'm sure.'

'Where's my fare comin' from? Twelve and a tanner gone up and when do I get it? Swelp me Bob if I don't cut me losses and sling me 'ook.'

'I wouldn't do that,' PC Moir said. 'Stick it a bit longer, I would. She'll be back. Tell you what, Aubyn Dale's on board that ship.'

'The TV bloke that does the Jolyon Swimsuits commercial and the "Pack up Your Troubles" show?'

'That's right. Dare say she's spotted him and can't tear herself away. They go nuts over Aubyn Dale.'

'Silly cows,' the taxi driver muttered. '*Telly!*'

'Why don't you stroll along to the ship and get a message up to her?'

'Why the hell should I!'

'Come on. I'll go with you. I'm heading that way.'

The driver muttered indistinguishably but he clambered out of his taxi and together they walked down the passageway. It was a longish passage and very dark, but the lighted wharf showed up mistily at the far end. When they came out they were almost alongside the ship. Her stern loomed up through the fog with her name across it.

CAPE FAREWELL
GLASGOW

Her after and amidships hatches had been shut down and, forward, her last load was being taken. Above her lighted gangway stood a sailor, leaning over the rails. PC Moir looked up at him.

'Seen anything of a young lady who brought some flowers on board, mate?' he asked.

'Would that be about two hours back?'

'More like half an hour.'

'There's been nobody like that since I first come on and that's eight bells.'

' 'Ere!' said the driver. 'There must of.'

'Well, there wasn't. I been on duty here constant. No flowers come aboard after eight bells.'

PC Moir said: 'Well, thanks, anyway. P'raps she met someone on the wharf and handed them over.'

'No flowers never came aboard with nobody. Not since when I told you. Eight bells.'

'Awright, awright, we 'eard,' said the driver ungratefully. *'Bells!'*

'Are your passengers all aboard?' Moir asked.

'Last one come aboard five minutes back. All present and correct including Mr Aubyn Dale. You'd never pick him, though, now he's slaughtered them whiskers. What a change! Oh, dear!' The sailor made a gesture that might have indicated his chin; or his neck. 'I reckon he'd do better to grow again,' he said.

'Anyone else been about? Anyone you couldn't place, at all?'

'Hallo-allo! What's wrong, anyway?'

'Nothing so far as I know. Nothing at all.'

The sailor said: 'it's been quiet. The fog makes it quiet.' He spat carefully overboard. 'I heard some poor sod singing,' he said. 'Just the voice: funny sort of voice too. Might of been a female and yet I don't reckon it was. I didn't rekkernize the chune.'

Moir waited a moment and then said: 'Well, thanks again, sailor, we'll be moving along.'

When he had withdrawn the driver to a suitable distance he said, coughing a little because a drift of fog had caught him in the throat: 'What was she like, daddy? To look at?'

The taxi driver gave him a jaundiced and confused description of his fare in which the only clear glimpse to emerge was of a flash piece with a lot of yellow hair done very fancy. Pressed further the driver remembered pin-heels. When she left the taxi the girl had caught her foot in a gap between two planks and had paused to adjust her shoe.

Moir listened attentively.

'Right you are,' he said. 'Now, I think I'll just take a wee look round, daddy. You go back to your cab and wait. *Wait*, see?'

This suggestion evoked a fresh spate of expostulation but Moir became authoritative and the driver finally returned to his cab. Moir looked after him for a moment and then walked along to the forward winch where he was received by the shore gang with a degree of guarded curiosity that in some circles is reserved for the police. He asked them if they had seen the girl and repeated the driver's description. None of them had done so.

As he was turning away one of the men said: 'What seems to be the trouble anyway, Copper?'

'Not to say trouble,' Moir called back easily. A second voice asked derisively: 'Why don't you get the Flower Killer, Superintendent?'

Moir said good-naturedly: 'We're still hoping, mate.' And walked away: a man alone on his job.

He began to look for the girl from the flower shop. There were many dark places along the wharf. He moved slowly, flashing his lamp into the areas under platforms, behind packing-cases, between buildings and dumps of cargo and along the dark surface of the water where it made unsavoury but irrelevant discoveries.

It was much quieter now aboard the *Farewell*. He heard the covers go down on the forward hatch and glancing up could just see the Blue Peter hanging limp in the fog. The gang that had been loading the ship went off through one of the sheds and their voices faded into silence.

He arrived back at the passageway. Beyond its far end the taxi still waited. On their way through here to the wharf he and the driver had walked quickly; now he went at a snail's pace, using his flashlight. He knew that surfaces which in the dark and fog looked like unbroken walls, were in fact the rear ends of sheds with a gap between them. There was an alley opening off the main passage and this was dark indeed.

It was now one minute to midnight and the *Cape Farewell*, being about to sail, gave a raucous unexpected hoot like a gargantuan belch. It jolted PC Moir in the pit of his stomach.

With a sudden scrabble a rat shot out and ran across his boots. He swore, stumbled and lurched sideways. The light from his flashlamp darted eccentrically up the side alley, momentarily exhibiting a high-heeled shoe with a foot in it. The light fluttered, steadied and returned. It crept from the foot along a leg, showing a red graze through the gap in its nylon stocking. It moved on and came to rest at last on a litter of artificial pearls and fresh flowers scattered over the breast of a dead girl.

CHAPTER 2

Embarkation

At seven o'clock on that same evening an omnibus had left Euston Station for the Royal Albert Docks.

It had carried ten passengers, seven of whom were to embark in the *Cape Farewell*, sailing at midnight for South Africa. Of the remainder, two were seeing-off friends while the last was the ship's doctor, a young man who sat alone and did not lift his gaze from the pages of a formidable book.

After the manner of travellers, the ship's passengers had taken furtive stock of each other. Those who were escorted by friends speculated in undertones about those who were not.

'My dear!' Mrs Dillington-Blick ejaculated. *'Honestly? Not one!'*

Her friend made a slight grimace in the direction of the doctor and raised her eyebrows. 'Not bad?' she mouthed. 'Noticed?'

Mrs Dillington-Blick shifted her shoulders under their mantling of silver fox and turned her head until she was able to include the doctor in an absent-minded glance.

'I *hadn't* noticed,' she confessed and added, 'Rather nice? But the others! My dear! Best forgotten! Still – '

'There *are* the officers,' the friend hinted slyly.

'My dear!'

They caught each other's eyes and laughed again, cosily. Mr and Mrs Cuddy in the seat in front of them heard their laughter. The Cuddys could smell Mrs Dillington-Blick's expensive scent. By turning their heads slightly they could see her reflection in the window-pane, like a photomontage richly floating across street lamps and the façades of darkened buildings. They could see the ghosts of her teeth, the feather in her hat, her earrings, the orchids on her great bust and her furs.

Mrs Cuddy stiffened in her navy overcoat and her husband smiled thinly. They, too, exchanged glances and thought of derisive things to say to each other when they were private in their cabin.

In front of the Cuddys sat Miss Katherine Abbott; alone, neat and composed. She was a practised traveller and knew that the first impression made by fellow-passengers is usually contradicted by experience. She rather liked the rich sound of Mrs Dillington-Blick's laughter and deplored what she had heard of the Cuddy accent. But her chief concern at the moment was for her own comfort: she disliked being ruffled and had chosen her seat in the middle of the bus because people would be unlikely to brush past her and she was out of the draught when the door opened. In her mind she checked over the contents of her two immaculately packed suitcases. She travelled extremely light because she loathed what she called the 'fussation' of heavy luggage. With a single exception she carried nothing that was not positively essential. She thought now of the exception, a photograph in a leather case. To her fury her eyes began to sting. 'I'll throw it overboard,' she thought. 'That'll larn her.'

The man in front of her turned a page of his newspaper and through her unshed tears Miss Abbott read a banner headline: 'Killer Who Says It With Flowers. Still no arrest.' She had longish sight and by casually leaning forward she was able to read the paragraph underneath.

'The identity of the sex-murderer who sings as he kills and leaves flowers by the bodies of his victims is still unknown. Investigations leading to hundreds of interviews have proved clueless. Here (left) is a new snapshot of piquant Beryl Cohen, found strangled on the 15th January, and (right) a studio portrait of Marguerite Slatters, the second victim of a killer who may well turn out to be the worst of his kind since Jack the Ripper. Superintendent Alleyn (inset) refuses to make a statement, but says the police will welcome information about Beryl's movements during her last hours (see page 6, 2nd column).'

Miss Abbott waited for the owner of the newspaper to turn to page 6 but he neglected to do so. She stared greedily at the enlarged snapshot of piquant Beryl Cohen and derisively at the inset.

Superintendent Alleyn, grossly disfigured by the exigencies of reproduction in newsprint, stared dimly back at her.

The owner of the paper began to fidget. Suddenly he turned his
head, obliging Miss Abbott to throw back her own and stare vaguely
at the luggage rack where she immediately spotted his suitcase with
a dangling label: 'P. Merryman, Passenger, S.S. *Cape Farewell.*' She
had an uncomfortable notion that Mr Merryman knew she had been
reading over his shoulder and in this she was perfectly right.

Mr Philip Merryman was fifty years old and a bachelor. He was a
man of learning and taught English in one of the less distinguished
of the smaller public schools. His general appearance, which was
highly deceptive, corresponded closely with the popular idea of a
schoolmaster, while a habit of looking over the tops of his spectacles
and ruffling his hair filled in the outlines of this over-familiar
picture. To the casual observer Mr Merryman was perfect Chips. To
his intimates he could be hell.

He was fond of reading about crime, whether fictitious or actual,
and had dwelt at some length on the *Evening Herald*'s piece about
The Flower Killer as, in its slipshod way, it called this undetected
murderer. Mr Merryman deplored journalese and had the poorest
possible opinion of the methods of the police but the story itself
quite fascinated him. He read slowly and methodically, wincing at
stylistic solecisms and bitterly resentful of Miss Abbott's trespassing
glances. 'Detested kite!' Mr Merryman silently apostrophized her.
'Blasts and fogs upon you! Why in the names of all the gods at once,
can you not buy your own disnatured newspaper!'

He turned to page six, moved the *Evening Herald* out of Miss
Abbott's line of sight, read column two as quickly as possible, folded
the newspaper, rose and offered it to her with a bow.

'Madam,' Mr Merryman said, 'allow me. No doubt you prefer, as
I confess I do, the undisputed possession of your chosen form of
literature.'

Miss Abbott's face darkened into a rich plum colour. In a startling-
ly deep voice she said: 'Thank you: I don't care for the evening
paper.'

'Perhaps you have already seen it?'

'No,' said Miss Abbott loudly. 'I haven't and what's more I don't
want to. Thank you.'

Father Charles Jourdain muttered whimsically to his brother-cleric: 'Seeds of discord! Seeds of discord!' They were in the seat opposite and could scarcely escape noticing the incident.

'I do *hope*,' the brother-cleric murmured, 'that you find someone moderately congenial.'

'In my experience there is always someone.'

'And you *are* an experienced traveller,' the other sighed, rather wistfully.

'Would you have liked the job so much, Father? I'm sorry.'

'No, no, no, please don't think it for a moment, really. I would carry no weight in Durban. Father Superior, as always, has made the wisest possible choice. And you are glad to be going – I hope?'

Father Jourdain waited for a moment and then said: 'Oh, yes. Yes. I'm glad to go.'

'It will be so interesting. The Community in Africa – '

They settled down to talk Ango-Catholic shop.

Mrs Cuddy, overhearing them, smelt Popery.

The remaining ship's passenger in the bus took no notice at all of her companions. She sat in the front seat with her hands thrust deep into the pockets of her camel-hair coat. She had a black zouave hat on the back of her head and a black scarf wound skilfully about her neck and a great studded black belt round her waist. She was so good-looking that all the tears she had shed still left her attractive. She was not crying now. She tucked her chin into her scarf and scowled at the bus driver's back. Her name was Jemima Carmichael. She was twenty-three and had been crossed in love.

The bus lurched up Ludgate Hill. Dr Timothy Makepiece put down his book and leant forward, stooping, to see the last of St Paul's. There it was, fabulous against the night sky. He experienced a sensation which he himself would have attributed, no doubt correctly, to a disturbance of the nervous ganglions but which laymen occasionally describe as a turning over of the heart. This must be, he supposed, because he was leaving London. He had come to that conclusion when he found he was no longer staring at the dome of St Paul's but into the eyes of the girl in the front seat. She had turned, evidently with the same intention as his own, to look out and upwards.

Father Jourdain was saying: 'Have you ever read that rather exciting thing of GKC's: *The Ball and the Cross?*'

Jemima carefully made her eyes blank and faced front. Dr Makepiece returned uneasily to his book. He was filled with a kind of astonishment.

II

At about the same time as the bus passed by St Paul's a very smart sports car had left a very smart mews flat in Mayfair. In it were Aubyn Dale, his dearest friend (who owned the car and sat at the wheel in a mink coat) and their two dearest friends who were entwined in the back seat. They had all enjoyed an expensive farewell dinner and were bound for the docks. 'The form,' the dearest friend said, 'is unlimited wassail, darling, in your stateroom. Drunk, I shall be less disconsolate.'

'But, *darling*!' Mr Dale rejoined tenderly, 'you shall be *plastered*! I promised! It's all laid on.'

She thanked him fondly and presently turned into the Embankment where she drove across the bows of an oncoming taxi whose driver cursed her very heartily. His fare, a Mr Donald McAngus, peered anxiously out of the window. He also was a passenger for the *Cape Farewell*.

About two and a half hours later a taxi would leave The Green Thumb flower shop in Knightsbridge for the East End. In it would be a fair-haired girl and a box of flowers which was covered with Cellophane, garnished with a huge bow of yellow ribbon and addressed to Mrs Dillington-Blick. The taxi would head eastward. It, too, was destined for the Royal Albert Docks.

III

From the moment she came aboard the *Cape Farewell*, Mrs Dillington-Blick had automatically begun to practise what her friends, among themselves, called her technique. She had turned her attention first upon the steward. The *Farewell* carried only nine passengers and one steward attended them all. He was a pale, extremely plump young man with blond hair that looked crimped, liquid eyes, a mole at the corner of his mouth and a voice that was both strongly Cockney, strangely affected and indescribably familiar. Mrs Dillington-Blick took no end of trouble with him. She asked him his name (it was Dennis) and discovered that he also served in the bar. She gave him three pounds and hinted that this was merely an initial gesture. In less than no time she had discovered that he was twenty-five, played the mouth-organ and had taken a dislike to Mr and Mrs Cuddy. He showed a tendency to linger but somehow or another, and in the pleasantest manner, she contrived to get rid of him.

'You are wonderful!' her friend exclaimed.

'My dear!' Mrs Dillington-Blick returned, 'he'll put my make-up in the fridge when we get to the tropics.'

Her cabin was full of flowers. Dennis came back with vases for them and suggested that the orchids also should be kept in the refrigerator. The ladies exchanged glances. Mrs Dillington-Blick unpinned the cards on her flowers and read out the names with soft little cries of appreciation. The cabin, with its demure appointments and sombre decor seemed to be full of her – of her scent, her furs, her flowers and herself.

'Steward!' a querulous voice, at this juncture, had called in the passage. Dennis raised his eyebrows and went out.

'He's your slave,' the friend said. *'Honestly!'*

'I like to be comfortable,' said Mrs Dillington-Blick.

It was Mr Merryman who had shouted for Dennis. When it comes to separating the easygoing from the exacting passenger, stewards are not easily deceived. But Dennis had been taken in by Mr Merryman. The spectacles, the rumpled hair and cherubic countenance had led him to diagnose absence-of-mind, benevolence and timidity. He was bitterly disappointed when Mr Merryman now gave unmistakable signs of being a Holy Terror. Nothing, it seemed, was right with the cabin. Mr Merryman had stipulated the port side and found himself on the starboard. His luggage had not been satisfactorily stowed and he wished his bed to be made up in the manner practised on land and not, he said, like an unstuck circular.

Dennis had listened to these complaints with an air of resignation; just not casting up his eyes.

'Quite a chapter of accidents,' he said when Mr Merryman paused. 'Yerse. Well, we'll see what we can do for you.' He added: 'Sir,' but not in the manner required by Mr Merryman at his minor public school.

Mr Merryman said: 'You will carry out my instructions immediately. I am going to take a short walk. When I return I shall expect to find it done.' Dennis opened his mouth. Mr Merryman said: 'That will do.' Rather pointedly he then locked a case on his dressing-table and walked out of the cabin.

'And I'll take me oaf,' Dennis muttered pettishly, 'he's TT into the bargain. What an old bee.'

Father Jourdain's brother-priest had helped him to bestow his modest possessions about his room. This done they had looked at each other with the hesitant and slightly self-conscious manner of men who are about to take leave of each other.

'Well – ' they both said together and Father Jourdain added: 'It was good of you to come all this way. I've been glad of your company.'

'Have you?' his colleague rejoined. 'And I, needless to say, of yours.' He hid his hands under his cloak and stood modestly before Father Jourdain. 'The bus leaves at eleven,' he said. 'You'd like to settle down, I expect.'

Father Jourdain asked, smiling: 'Is there something you want to say to me?'

'Nothing of the smallest consequence. It's just – well, I've suddenly realized how very much it's meant to me having the great benefit of your example.'

'My dear man!'

'No, really! You strike me, Father, as being quite tremendously sufficient (under God and our Rule, of course) to yourself. All the brothers are a little in awe of you, did you know? I think we all feel that we know much less about you than we do about each other. Father Bernard said the other day that although ours is not a Silent Order you kept your own rule of spiritual silence.'

'I don't know that I am altogether delighted by Father Bernard's aphorism.'

'Aren't you? He meant it awfully nicely. But I really do chatter much too much. I should take myself in hand and do something about it, I expect. Goodbye, Father. God bless you.'

'And you, my dear fellow. But I'll walk with you to the bus.'

'No – please – '

'I should like to. '

They had found their way down to the lower deck. Father Jourdain said a word to the sailor at the head of the gangway and both priests went ashore. The sailor watched them pace along the wharf towards the passageway at the far end of which the bus waited. In their black cloaks and hats they looked fantastic. The fog swirled about them as they walked. Half an hour had gone by before Father Jourdain returned alone. It was then a quarter past eleven.

Miss Abbott's cabin was opposite Mrs Dillington-Blick's. Dennis carried the suitcases to it. Their owner unpacked them with meticulous efficiency, laying folded garments away as if for some ceremonial robing. They were of a severe character. At the bottom of the second suitcase there was a stack of music in manuscript. In a pocket of the suitcase was the photograph. It was of a woman of about Miss Abbott's own age, moderately handsome but with a heavy dissatisfied look. Miss Abbott stared at it and, fighting back a painful sense of desolation and resentment, sat on the bed and pressed clumsy hands between large knees. Time went by. The ship moved a little at her moorings. Miss Abbott heard Mrs Dillington-Blick's rich laughter and was remotely and very slightly eased. There was the noise of fresh arrivals, of footsteps overhead and of dockside activities. From a more distant part of the passengers' quarters came sounds of revelry and of a resonant male voice that was somehow familiar. Soon Miss Abbott was to know why. The cabin door had been hooked ajar so that when Mrs Dillington-Blick's friend came into the passage she was very clearly audible. Mrs Dillington-Blick stood in her own open doorway and said through giggles: 'Go on, then, I dare you,' and the friend went creaking down the passage. She returned evidently in high excitement saying: 'My dear, it is! He's shaved it off! The steward told me. It's Aubyn Dale! My dear, how perfectly gorgeous for you.'

There was another burst of giggling through which Mrs Dillington-Blick said something about not being able to wait for the tropics to wear her Jolyon swimsuit. Their further ejaculations were cut off by the shutting of their door.

'Silly fools,' Miss Abbott thought dully, having not the smallest interest in television personalities. Presently she began to wonder if she really would throw the photograph overboard when the ship was out at sea. Suppose she were to tear it up now and drop the pieces in the waste-paper basket? Or into the harbour? How lonely she would be then! The heavily-knuckled fingers drummed on the bony knees and their owner began to think about things going overboard into the harbour. The water would be cold and dirty: polluted by the excreta of ships: revolting!

'Oh, *God!*' Miss Abbott said, 'how hellishly unhappy I am.'

Dennis knocked at her door.

'Telegram, Miss Abbott,' he fluted.

'Telegram? For me? Yes?'

He unhooked the door and came in.

Miss Abbott took the telegram and shakily opened it. It fluttered between her fingers.

'Darling Abbey so miserable do please write or if not too late telephone, F.'

Dennis had lingered. Miss Abbott said shakily: 'Can I send an answer?'

'Well – ye-ees. I mean to say – '

'Or telephone? Can I telephone?'

'There's a phone on board but I seen a queue lined up when I passed.'

'How long before we sail?'

'An hour, near enough, but the phone goes off earlier.'

Miss Abbott said distractedly: 'It's very important. Very urgent, indeed.'

' 'Tch, 'tch.'

'Wait. Didn't I see a call box on the dock? Near the place where the bus stopped?'

'That's correct,' he said appreciatively. 'Fancy you noticing!'

'I've time to go off, haven't I?'

'Plenty of *time*, Miss Abbott. Oodles.'

'I'll do that. I'll go at once.'

'There's coffee and sandwiches on in the dining-room.'

'I don't want them. I'll go now.'

'Cold outside. Proper freezer. Need a coat, Miss Abbott, won't you?'

'It doesn't matter. Oh, very well. Thank you.'

She took her coat out of the wardrobe, snatched up her handbag, and hurried out.

'Straight ahead, down the companionway and turn right,' he called after her and added: 'Don't get lost in the fog, now.'

Her manner had been so disturbed that it aroused his curiosity. He went out on the deck and was in time to see her running along the wharf into the fog. 'Runs like a man,' Dennis thought. 'Well, it takes all sorts.'

Mr and Mrs Cuddy sat on their respective beds and eyed each other with the semi-jocular family air that they reserved for intimate occasions. The blowers on the bulkhead were pouring hot air into the cabin, the porthole was sealed, the luggage was stowed and the Cuddys were cosy.

'All right so far,' Mrs Cuddy said guardedly.

'Satisfied, dear?'

'Can't complain. Seems clean.'

'Our own shower and toilet,' he pointed out, jerking his head at a narrow door.

'They've all got that,' she said. 'I wouldn't fancy sharing.'

'What did you make of the crowd, though? Funny lot, I thought.'

'RC priests.'

'Only the one. The other was seeing-off. Do you reckon, RC?'

'Looked like it, didn't it?'

Mr Cuddy smiled. He had a strange thin smile, very broad and knowing. 'They look ridiculous to me,' he said.

'We're moving in high society, it seems,' Mrs Cuddy remarked. 'Notice the furs?'

'And the *perfume!* Phew!'

'I'll have to keep my eye on you, I can see that.'

'Could you catch what was said?'

'Quite a bit,' Mrs Cuddy admitted. 'She may talk very la-de-dah but her ideas aren't so refined.'

'Reely?'

'She's a man-eater.'

Mr Cuddy's smile broadened. 'Did you get the flowers?' he asked. 'Orchids. Thirty bob each, they are.'

'Get on!'

'They are! It's a fact. Very nice, too,' Mr Cuddy said with a curious twist in his voice.

'Did you see what happened with the other lady reading over the elderly chap's shoulder? In the bus?'

'Did I what! Talk about a freezer! Phew!'

'He was reading about those murders. You know. The flower murderer. They make out he leaves flowers all scattered over the breasts of his victims. And sings.'

'Before or after?'

'After, isn't it awful?' Mrs Cuddy asked with enormous relish.

Mr Cuddy made an indefinite noise.

His wife ruminated: 'It gives me the creeps to think about. Wonder what makes him go on so crazy.'

'Women.'

'That's right. Put it all on the ladies,' she said good-naturedly. 'Just like a man.'

'Well, ask yourself. Was there much in the paper?'

'I couldn't see properly but I think so. It's on all the placards. They haven't got him, of course.'

'Wish we'd got a paper. Can't think how I forgot.'

'There might be one in the lounge.'

'What a hope!'

'The old chap left his in the bus. I noticed.'

'Did you? You know,' Mr Cuddy said, 'I've got quite a fancy for the evening paper. I might stroll back and see if it's there. The bus doesn't go till eleven. I can just do it.'

'Don't be long. You know what I'm like. If you missed the boat – '

'We don't sail till midnight, dear, and it's only ten to eleven now. I won't be more than a few minutes. Think I'd let you go out to sea with all these fascinatin' sailors?'

'Get along with you!'

'Won't be half a tick. I've got the fancy for it.'

'I know I'm silly,' Mrs Cuddy said, 'but whenever you go out – to the Lodge or anything – I always get that *nervous*.'

'Silly girl. I'd say come too, but it's not worth it. There's coffee on down below.'

'Coffee essence, more like.'

'Might as well try it when I get back. Behave yourself now.'

He pulled a steel-grey felt hat down almost to his ears, put on a belted raincoat and, looking rather like the film director's idea of a private detective, he went ashore.

Mrs Cuddy remained, anxious and upright on her bunk.

Aubyn Dale's dearest friend looking through the porthole said with difficulty: 'Darling: it's boiling up for a pea-shuper-souper. I think perhaps we ought to weep ourselves away.'

'Darling, are you going to drive?'

'Naturally.'

'You *will* be all right, *won't* you?'

'Sweetie,' she protested, 'I'm never safer than when I'm plastered. It just gives me that little something other drivers haven't got.'

'How terrifying.'

'To show you how completely in control I am, I suggest that it might be better to leave before we're utterly fogged down. Oh, dear! I fear I am going into a screaming weep. Where's my hanky?'

She opened her bag. A coiled mechanical snake leapt out at her, having been secreted there by her lover who had a taste for such drolleries.

This prank, though it was received as routine procedure, a little delayed their parting. Finally, however, it was agreed that the time had come.

' 'Specially,' said their dearest male friend, 'as we've killed the last bottle. Sorry, old boy. Bad form. Poor show.'

'Come on,' said their dearest girl friend. 'It's been smashing, actually. Darling Auby! But we ought to go.'

They began elaborate leave-takings but Aubyn Dale said he'd walk back to the car with them.

They all went ashore, talking rather loudly, in well trained voices, about the fog which had grown much heavier.

It was now five past eleven. The bus had gone, the solitary taxi waited in its place. Their car was parked farther along the wharf. They stood round it, still talking, for some minutes. His friends all told Dale many times how much good the voyage would do him, how nice he looked without his celebrated beard, how run down he was and how desperately the programme would sag without him. Finally they drove off waving and trying to make hip-hip-hooray with their horn.

Aubyn Dale waved, shoved his hands down in the pockets of his camel-hair coat and walked back towards the ship. A little damp breeze lifted his hair, eddies of fog drifted past him. He thought how very photogenic the wharves looked. The funnels on some of the ships were lit from below and the effect, blurred and nebulous though it now had become, was exciting. Lights hung like globes in the murk. There were hollow indefinable sounds and a variety of smells. He pictured himself down here doing one of his special features and began to choose atmospheric phrases. He would have looked rather good, he thought, framed in the entrance to the passageway. His hand strayed to his naked chin and he shuddered. He must pull himself together. The whole idea of the voyage was to get away from his job: not to think of it, even. Or of anything else that was at all upsetting. Such as his dearest friend, sweetie though she undoubtedly was. Immediately, he began to think about her. He ought to have given her something before she left. Flowers? No, no. Not flowers. They had an unpleasant association. He felt himself grow cold and then hot. He clenched his hands and walked into the passageway.

About two minutes later the ninth and last passenger for the *Cape Farewell* arrived by taxi at the docks. He was Mr Donald McAngus, an elderly bachelor, who was suffering from a terrible onset of ship-fever. The fog along the Embankment had grown heavier. In the City it had been atrocious. Several times his taxi had come to a stop, twice it had gone off its course and finally, when he was really feeling physically sick with anxiety the driver had announced that this was as far as he cared to go. He indicated shapes, scarcely perceptible, of roofs and walls and the faint glow beyond them. That, he said, was where Mr McAngus's ship lay. He had merely to make for the glow and he would be aboard. There ensued a terrible complication over the fare, and the tip: first Mr McAngus under-tipped and then, in a frenzy of apprehension, he over-tipped. The driver adopted a pitying attitude. He put Mr McAngus's fibre suitcases into their owner's grip and

tucked his cardboard box and his brown paper parcel under his arms.
Thus burdened Mr McAngus disappeared at a shambling trot into the
fog and the taxi returned to the West End of London.

The time was now eleven-thirty. The taxi from the flower shop was
waiting for his fare and PC Moir was about to engage him in conversation. The last hatch was covered, the *Cape Farewell* was cleared and
Captain Bannerman, Master, awaited his pilot.

At one minute to twelve the siren hooted.

PC Moir was now at the police call-box. He had been put through
to the CID.

'There's one other thing, sir,' he was saying, 'beside the flowers.
There's a bit of paper clutched in the right hand, sir. It appears to be
a fragment of an embarkation notice, like they give passengers. For
the *Cape Farewell*.'

He listened, turning his head to look across the tops of half-seen
roofs at the wraith of a scarlet funnel, with a white band. It slid away
and vanished smoothly into the fog.

'I'm afraid I can't board her, sir,' he said. 'She's sailed.'

CHAPTER 3

Departure

At regular two-minute intervals throughout the night, *Cape Farewell* sounded her siren. The passengers who slept were still, at times, conscious of this noise; as of some monster blowing monstrous raspberries through their dreams. Those who waked listened with varying degrees of nervous exasperation. Aubyn Dale, for instance, tried to count the seconds between blasts, sometimes making them come to as many as one hundred and thirty and at others, by a deliberate tardiness, getting them down to one hundred and fifteen. He then tried counting his pulse but this excited him. His heart behaved with the greatest eccentricity. He began to think of all the things it was better not to think of, including the worst one of all: the awful debacle of the Midsummer Fair at Melton Medbury. This was just the sort of thing that his psychiatrist had sent him on the voyage to forget. He had already taken one of his sleeping-pills. At two o'clock he took another and it was effective.

Mr Cuddy also was restive. He had recovered Mr Merryman's *Evening Herald* from the bus. It was in a somewhat dishevelled condition but when he got into bed he read it exhaustively, particularly the pieces about the Flower Murderer. Occasionally he read aloud for Mrs Cuddy's entertainment but presently her energetic snores informed him that this exercise was profitless. He let the newspaper fall to the deck and began to listen to the siren. He wondered if his fellow-travellers would exhibit a snobbish attitude towards Mrs Cuddy and himself. He thought of Mrs Dillington-Blick's orchids, heaving a little at their superb anchorage, and himself gradually slipped into an uneasy doze.

Mr Merryman, on the other hand, slept heavily. If he was visited by dreams of a familiar steward or an inquisitive spinster, they were of too deeply unconscious a nature to be recollected. Like many people of an irascible temperament, he seemed to find compensation for his troubles in the profundity of his slumber.

So, too, did Father Jourdain, who on finishing his prayers, getting into bed and putting himself through one or two pretty stiff devotional hoops, fell into a quiet oblivion that lasted until morning.

Mr Donald McAngus took a little time to recover from the circumstances that attended his late arrival. However he had taken coffee and sandwiches in the dining-room and had eyed his fellow-passengers with circumspection and extreme curiosity. His was the not necessarily malicious but all-absorbing inquisitiveness of the Lowland Scot. He gathered facts about other people as an indiscriminate philatelist gathers stamps: merely for the sake of adding to his collection. He had found himself at the same table as the Cuddys – the passengers had not yet been given their official places – and had already discovered that they lived in Dulwich and that Mr Cuddy was 'in business' though of what nature Mr McAngus had been unable to divine. He had told them about his trouble with the taxi. Distressed by Mrs Cuddy's unwavering stare he had tied himself up in a tangle of parentheses and retired unsatisfied to his room and his bed.

There he lay tidily all night in his gay crimson pyjamas, occupied with thoughts so unco-ordinated and feckless that they modulated imperceptibly into dreams and were not at all disturbed by the re-iterated booming of the siren.

Miss Abbott had returned from the call box on the wharf, scarcely aware of the fog and with a dull effulgence under her darkish skin. The sailor at the gangway noticed, and was afterwards to remember, her air of suppressed excitement. She went to bed and was still wide-awake when the ship sailed. She watched blurred lights slide past the porthole and felt the throb of the engines at dead slow. At about one o'clock in the morning she fell asleep.

Jemima Carmichael hadn't paid much attention to her companions: it took all her determination and fortitude to hold back her tears. She kept telling herself angrily that crying was a voluntary physical process, entirely controllable and in her case absolutely without justification. Lots of other people had their engagements broken off at the last minute and were none the worse for it: most of them without her chance of cutting her losses and bolting to South Africa.

It had been a mistake to peer up at St Paul's. That particular kind of beauty always got under her emotional guard; and there she went again with the man in the opposite seat looking into her face as if he'd like to be sorry for her. From then onwards the bus journey had seemed intolerable but the walk through the fog to the ship had been better. It was almost funny that her departure should be attended by such obvious gloom. She had noticed Mrs Dillington-Blick's high-heeled patent leather shoes tittupping ahead and had heard scraps of the Cuddys' conversation. She had also been conscious of the young man walking just behind her. When they had emerged from the passageway to the wharf he said:

'Look, do let me carry that suitcase,' and had taken it out of her hand before she could expostulate. 'My stuff's all on board,' he said. 'I feel unimportant with nothing in my hand. Don't you hate feeling unimportant?'

'Well, no,' Jemima said, surprised into an unconventional reply. 'At the moment, I'm not minding it.'

'Perhaps it's a change for you.'

'Not at all,' she said hurriedly.

'Or perhaps women are naturally shrinking creatures, after all. "Such," you may be thinking, "is the essential vanity of the human male." And you are perfectly right. Did you know that Aubyn Dale is to be a passenger?'

'Is he?' Jemima said without much interest. 'I would have thought a luxury liner and organized fun would be more his cup-of-tea.'

'I understand it's a rest cure. Far away from the madding camera and I bet you anything you like that in no time he'll be missing his spotlights. I'm the doctor, by the way, and this is my first long voyage.

My name's Timothy Makepiece. You must be either Miss Katherine
Abbott or Miss Jemima Carmichael and I can't help hoping it's the
latter.'

'You'd be in a bit of a spot if it wasn't,' Jemima said.

'I risked everything on the one throw. Rightly, I perceive. Is it
your first long voyage?'

'Yes.'

'You don't sound as excited as I would have expected. This is the
ship, looming up. It's nice to think we shall be meeting again. What
is your cabin number? I'm not being fresh: I just want to put your
bag in it.'

'It's 4. Thank you very much.'

'Not at all,' said Dr Makepiece politely. He led the way to her
cabin, put her suitcase into it, made her a rather diffident little bow
and went away.

Jemima thought without much interest: 'The funny thing is that
I don't believe that young man was putting on an act,' and at once
stopped thinking about him.

Her own predicament came swamping over her again and she
began to feel a great desolation of the spirit. She had begged her parents and her friends not to come to the ship, not to see her off at all
and already it seemed a long time ago that she had said goodbye to
them. She felt very much alone.

The cabin was without personality. Jemima heard voices and the
hollow sounds of footsteps on the deck overhead. She smelt the
inward rubbery smell of a ship. How was she to support five weeks of
the woman with the pin-heels and the couple with Clapham
Common voices and that incredibly forbidding spinster? She
unpacked the luggage which was already in her cabin. Dennis looked
in and she thought him quite frightful. Then she took herself to task
for being bloody-minded and beastly. At that moment she found in
her cabin-trunk a parcel from a wonderful shop with a very smart
dress in it and a message from her mother and at this discovery she
sat down on her bunk and cried like a small girl.

By the time she had got over that and finished her unpacking she
was suddenly quite desperately tired and went to bed.

Jemima lay in her bed and listened to the sounds of the ship and
the port. Gradually the cabin acquired an air of being her own and

somewhere at the back of all the wretchedness there stirred a very slight feeling of anticipation. She heard a pleasant voice saying again: 'You don't sound as excited as I would have expected,' and then she was so sound asleep that she didn't hear the ship sail and was only very vaguely conscious of the fog signal, booming at two-minute intervals all night.

By half past twelve all the passengers were in bed, even Mrs Dillington-Blick who had given her face a terrific workout with a new and complicated beauty treatment.

The officers of the watch went about their appointed ways and the *Cape Farewell*, sailing dead slow, moved out of the Thames estuary with a murderer on board.

II

Captain Jasper Bannerman stood on the bridge with the pilot. He would be up all night. Their job was an ancient one and though they had radar and wireless to serve them, their thoughts as they peered into the blank shiftiness of the fog were those of their remote predecessors. An emergency warning come through with its procession of immemorial names – Dogger, Dungeness, Outer Hebrides, Scapa Flow, Portland Bill and the Goodwin Sands. 'She's a corker,' said the pilot alluding to the fog. 'Proper job, she's making of it.'

The voices of invisible shipping, hollow and desolate, sounded at uneven distances. Time passed very slowly.

At two-thirty the wireless officer came to the bridge with two messages.

'I thought I'd bring these up myself, sir,' he said, referring obliquely to his cadet. 'They're in code. Urgent.'

Captain Bannerman said: 'All right. You might wait, will you,' and went into his room. He got out his code book and deciphered the messages. After a considerable interval he called out: 'Sparks.'

The wireless officer tucked his cap under his arm, entered the captain's cabin and shut the door.

'This is a damned perishing bloody turn-up,' Captain Bannerman said. The wireless officer waited, trying not to look expectant. Captain Bannerman walked over to the starboard porthole and silently re-read the decoded messages. The first was from the Managing Director of the Cape Line Company:

'Very secret. Directors compliments stop confident you will show every courtesy to Superintendent Alleyn boarding you off Portsmouth by pilot cutter stop will travel as passenger stop suggest uses pilots room stop please keep me personally advised all developments stop your company relies on your discretion and judgment stop Cameron stop message ends.'

Captain Bannerman made an indeterminate but angry noise and re-read the second message.

'Urgent immediate and confidential stop Superintendent R. Alleyn will board you off Portsmouth by pilot cutter stop he will explain nature of problem stop this department is in communication with your company stop C.A. Majoriebanks Assistant Commissioner Criminal Investigation Department Scotland Yard message ends.'

'I'll give you the replies,' Captain Bannerman said, glaring at his subordinate. 'Same for both! "Instructions received and noted Bannerman." And you'll oblige me, Sparks, by keeping the whole thing under your cap.'

'Certainly, sir.'

'Dead under.'

'Certainly, sir.'

'Very well.'

'Thank you, sir.'

When the wireless officer had gone Captain Bannerman remained in a sort of scandalized trance for half a minute and then returned to the bridge.

Throughout the rest of the night he gave the matter in hand, which was the pilotage of his ship through the worst fog for ten years, his sharpest attention. At the same time and on a different level, he speculated about his passengers. He had caught glimpses of them from the bridge. Like every man who so much as glanced at her, he had received a very positive impression of Mrs Dillington-Blick. A fine woman. He had also noticed Jemima Carmichael who came under the general heading of Sweet Young Girl and as they approached the tropics would probably cause a ferment among his officers. At another level he was aware of, and disturbed by the two radiograms. Why the suffering cats, he angrily wondered, should he have to take in at the last second, a plain-clothes detective? His mind ranged through an assortment of possible reasons. Stowaway? Escaping criminal? Wanted man in the crew? Perhaps, merely, a last-minute assignment at Las Palmas but if so, why didn't the fellow fly? It would be an infernal bore to have to put him up: in the pilot's room of all places where one would be perpetually aware of his presence. At four o'clock, the time of low vitality, Captain Bannerman was visited by a premonition that this was going to be an unlucky voyage.

III

All the next morning the fog still hung over the English Channel. As she waited off Portsmouth the *Farewell* was insulated in obscurity. Her five male passengers were on deck with their collars turned up. In the cases of Messrs Merryman, McAngus and Cuddy and Father Jourdain they wore surprised-looking caps on their heads and wandered up and down the boat-deck or sat disconsolately on benches that would probably never be used again throughout the voyage. Before long Aubyn Dale came back to his own quarters. He had, in addition to his bedroom, a little sitting-room: an arrangement known in the company's offices as The Suite. He had asked Mrs Dillington-Blick and Dr Timothy Makepiece to join him there for a drink before luncheon. Mrs Dillington-Blick had sumptuously appeared on deck at about eleven o'clock and, figuratively speaking with one hand tied behind her back, had achieved this invitation by half past. Dr Makepiece had accepted, hoping that Jemima Carmichael, too, had been invited but Jemima spent the morning walking on the boat-deck and reading in a chilly but undiscovered little shelter aft of the centrecastle.

Mr McAngus, too, remained but a short time on deck and soon retired to the passengers' drawing-room, where, after peering doubtfully at the bookcases, he sat in a corner and fell asleep. Mrs Cuddy was also there and also asleep. She had decided in the teeth of the weather forecast that it was going to be rough and had taken a pill. Miss Abbott was tramping up and down the narrow lower deck having, perhaps instinctively, hit upon that part of the ship which, after the first few hours, is deserted by almost everyone. In the plan shown to passengers it was called the promenade deck.

It was Jemima who first noticed the break in the weather. A kind of thin warmth fell across the page of her book: she looked up and saw that the curtain of fog had grown threadbare and that sunlight had weakly filtered through. At the same moment the *Farewell* gave her noonday hoot and then Jemima heard the sound of an engine. She went over to the port side and there, quite close, was the pilot cutter. She watched it come alongside the rope ladder. A tall man stood amidships, looking up at the *Farewell*. Jemima was extremely critical of men's clothes and she noticed his with absentminded approval. A sailor at the head of the ladder dropped a line to the cutter and hauled up two cases. The pilot went off and the tall man climbed the ladder very handily and was met by the cadet on duty who took him up to the bridge.

On his way he passed Mr Merryman and Mr Cuddy who looked up from their crime novels and were struck by the same vague notion, immediately dismissed, that they had seen the new arrival before. In this they were not altogether mistaken: on the previous evening they had both looked at his heavily distorted photograph in the *Evening Herald.* He was Superintendent R. Alleyn.

IV

Captain Bannerman put his hands in his jacket pockets and surveyed his latest passenger. At the outset Alleyn had irritated Captain Bannerman by not looking like his own conception of a plain-clothes detective and by speaking with what the Captain, who was an inverted snob, considered a bloody posh accent entirely unsuited to a cop. He himself had been at some pains to preserve his own Midland habit of speech.

'Well,' he said. 'Superintendent A*'leen* is it? – I take it you'll tell me what all this is in aid of and I don't mind saying I'll be glad to know.'

'I suppose, sir,' Alleyn said, 'you've been cursing ever since you got whatever signals they sent you.'

'Well – not to say cursing.'

'I know damn' well what a bore this must be. The only excuse 1 can offer is one of expedience: and I must say of extreme urgency.'

Captain Bannerman, deliberately broadening his vowels said: 'Sooch a-a-s?'

'Such as murder. Multiple murder.'

'Mooltipul murder? Here: you don't mean this chap that says it with flowers and sings.'

'I do, indeed.'

'What the hell's he got to do with my ship?'

'Tve every reason to believe,' Alleyn said, 'that he's aboard your ship.'

'Don't talk daft.'

'I dare say it does sound preposterous.'

Captain Bannerman took his hands out of his pockets, walked over to a porthole and looked out. The fog had lifted and the *Farewell* was underway. He said, with a change of voice: 'There you are! That's the sort of crew they sign on for you these days. Murderers!'

'My bosses,' Alleyn said, 'don't seem to think he's in the crew.'

'The stewards have been in this ship three voyages.'

'Nor among the stewards. Unless sailors or stewards carry embarkation notices.'

'D'you mean to stand there and tell me we've shipped a murdering passenger?'

'It looks a bit like it at the moment.'

'Here!' Captain Bannerman said with a change of voice. 'Sit down. Have a drink. I might have known it'd be a passenger.'

Alleyn sat down but declined a drink, a circumstance that produced the usual reaction from his companion. 'Ah!' Captain Bannerman said with an air of gloomy recognition. 'I suppose not. I suppose not.'

His manner was so heavy that Alleyn felt impelled to say: 'That doesn't mean, by the way, that I'm about to arrest you.'

'I doubt if you could, you know. Not while we're at sea. I very much question it.'

'Luckily, the problem doesn't at the moment arise.'

'I should have to look up the regulations,' sighed Captain Bannerman.

'Look here,' Alleyn suggested, 'may I try to give you the whole story, as far as it affects my joining your ship?'

'That's what I've been waiting for, isn't it?'

'Yes,' Alleyn agreed, 'I'm sure it is. Here goes then!'

He looked full at Captain Bannerman who seated himself, placed his hands on his knees, raised his eyebrows and waited.

'You know about these cases, of course,' Alleyn said, 'as far as they're being reported in the papers. During the last thirty days up to about eleven o'clock last night there have been two homicides which we believe to have been committed by the same person, and which may be part of a larger pattern. In each case the victim was a woman and in each case she had been strangled and flowers had been left on the body. I needn't worry you with any other details at the moment. Last night, a few minutes before this ship sailed, a third victim was found. She was in a dark side-alley off the passageway between the place where the bus and taxis put down passengers and the actual wharf where you were moored. She was a girl from a flower-shop who was bringing a box of hyacinths to one of your passengers: a Mrs Dillington-Blick. Her string of false pearls had been broken and the flowers had been scattered, in the usual way, over the victim.'

'Any singing?'

'What? Oh, that. That's an element that has been very much played up by the Press. It certainly does seem to have occurred on the first occasion. The night of the fifteenth of last month. The victim you may remember was Beryl Cohen who ran a cheapjack stall in Warwick Road and did a bit of the older trade on the side. She was found in her bed-sitting-room in a side street behind Paddington. The lodger in the room above seems to have heard the visitor leaving at about ten o'clock. The lodger says the visitor was singing.'

'What a dreadful thing,' Captain Bannerman said primly. 'What sort of song, for God's sake?'

'The Jewel Song,' Alleyn said, 'from *Faust*. In an alto voice.'

'I'm a bass-baritone, myself,' the Captain said absently. 'Oratorio,' he gloomily added.

'The second victim,' Alleyn went on, 'was a respectable spinster called Marguerite Slatters, who was found similarly strangled in a street in Fulham on the night of the 25th January. A nightwatchman on duty in a warehouse nearby says he heard someone rendering "The Honeysuckle and the Bee" in a highish voice at what may have been the appropriate time.'

Alleyn paused, but Captain Bannerman merely glowered at him.

'And it appears that the sailor on duty at the head of our gang-way last night heard singing in the fog. A funny sort of voice, he said. Might mean anything, of course, or nothing. Drunken seaman. Anything. He didn't recognize the tune.'

'Here! About last night. How d'you know the victim was – ' Captain Bannerman began and then said: 'All right. Go on.'

'In her left hand, which was clenched in cadaveric spasm, was a fragment of one of the embarkation notices your company issues to passengers. I believe the actual ticket is usually pinned to this notice and torn off by the officer whose duty it is to collect it. He hands the embarkation notice back to the passenger: it has no particular value but I dare say a great many passengers think it constitutes some kind of authority and stick to it. Unfortunately this fragment only showed part of the word *Farewell* and the date.'

'No name?'

'No name.'

'Doesn't amount to much, in that case,' said Captain Bannerman.

'It suggests that the victim struggling with her murderer grasped this paper, that it was torn across and that the rest of it may have remained in the murderer's possession or may have been blown somewhere about the wharf.'

'The whole thing might have been blowing about the wharf when the victim grabbed it.'

'That's a possibility of course.'

'Probability, more like. What about the other half then?'

'When I left for Portsmouth this morning it hadn't been found.'

'There you are!'

'But if all the others have kept their embarkation notices – '

'Why should they?'

'May we tackle that one a bit later? Now, the body was found by the PC on that beat, five minutes before you sailed. He's a good chap and kept his head admirably, it seems, but he couldn't do anything about boarding you. You'd sailed. As he talked to me on the dock telephone he saw your funnel slip past into the fog. A party of us from the Yard went down and did the usual things. We got in touch with your Company, who were hellishly anxious that your sailing shouldn't be delayed.'

'I'll be bound!' Captain Bannerman ejaculated.

' – and my bosses came to the conclusion that we hadn't got enough evidence to justify our keeping you back while we held a full-scale inquiry in the ship.'

'My Gawd!'

'So it was decided that I should sail with you and hold it, as well as I can, under the counter.'

'And what say,' Captain Bannerman asked slowly and without any particular signs of bad temper, 'what say I won't have it? There you are! How about that?'

'Well,' Alleyn said, 'I hope you don't cut up rough in that particular direction and I'm sure you won't. But suppose you did and suppose I took it quietly, which, by the way, I wouldn't: the odds are you'd have another corpse on your hands before you made your next landfall.'

Captain Bannerman leant forward, still keeping his palms on his knees, until his face was within a few inches of Alleyn's. His eyes were of that piercing, incredible blue that landsmen so correctly associate with sailors and his face was the colour of old bricks.

'Do you mean,' he asked furiously, 'to tell me you think this chap's not had enoof to satisfy him for the voyage?'

'So far,' Alleyn said, 'he's been operating at ten-day intervals. That'll carry him, won't it, to somewhere between Las Palmas and Cape Town?'

'I don't believe it. I don't believe he's aboard.'

'Don't you?'

'What sort of chap is he? Tell me that.'

Alleyn said: 'You tell me. You've got just as good a chance of being right.'

'Me!'

'You or anyone else: may I smoke?'

'Here – ' the Captain began and reached for a cigarette box.

' – a pipe, if you don't mind.' Alleyn pulled it out and as he talked, filled it.

'These cases,' he said, 'are the worst of the lot from our point of view. We can pick a card-sharp or a con-man or a sneak-thief or a gunman or a dozen other bad lots by certain mannerisms and tricks of behaviour. They develop occupational habits and they generally keep company with their own kind. But not the man who, having never before been in trouble with the police, begins, perhaps latish in life, to strangle women at ten-day intervals and leave flowers on their faces. He's a job for the psychiatrist if ever there was one and he doesn't go in for psychiatry. He's merely an example. But of what? The result of bad housing conditions, or a possessive mother or a kick on the head at football or a bullying schoolmaster or a series of regrettable grandparents? Again, your guess is as good as mine. He is. He exists. He may behave with perfect propriety in every possible aspect of his life but this one. He may be, and often is, a colourless little fellow who trots to and fro upon his lawful occasions for, say fifty years, seven months and a day. On the day after that he trots out and becomes a murderer. Probably there have been certain eccentricities of behaviour which he's been at great pains to conceal and which have suddenly become inadequate. Whatever compulsion it is that hounds him into his appointed crime, it now takes over. He lets go and becomes a monster.'

'Ah!' Captain Bannerman said, 'a monster. There's unnatural things turn up where you'd least expect to find them in most human souls. That I will agree to. But not in my ship.'

The two men looked at each other, and Alleyn's heart sank. He knew pigheadedness when he met it.

The ship's engines, now at full speed, drove her, outward bound, upon her course. There was no more fog: a sunny seascape accepted her as its accident. Her wake opened obediently behind her and the rhythm of her normal progress established itself. England was left behind and the *Farewell*, sailing on her lawful occasions, set her course for Las Palmas.

V

'What,' Captain Bannerman asked, 'do you want me to do? The thing's flat-out ridiculous but let's hear what you want. I can't say fairer than that, can I? Come on.'

'No,' Alleyn agreed, 'that's fair enough and more than I bargained for. First of all, perhaps I ought to tell you what I don't want. Particularly, I don't want to be known for what I am.'

'Is that so?'

'I gather that supercargoes are a bit out-of-date, so I'd better not be a supercargo. Could I be an employee of the company going out to their Durban office?'

Captain Bannerman stared fixedly at him and then said: 'It'd have to be something very senior.'

'Why? On account of age? – '

'It's nothing to do with age. Or looks. Or rather,' Captain Bannerman amended, 'it's the general effect.'

'I'm afraid I don't quite – '

'You don't look ill, either. Voyage before last, outward bound, we carried a second cousin of the managing director's. Getting over D.T.'s, he was, after taking one of these cures. You're not a bit like him. You're not a bit like a detective either if it comes to that,' Captain Bannerman added resentfully.

'I'm sorry.'

'Have you always been a 'tec?'

'Not absolutely.'

'I know,' Captain Bannerman said, 'leave it to me. You're a cousin of the chairman and you're going out to Canberra via Durban to one of these legations or something. There's all sorts of funny jobs going in Canberra. Anybody'll believe anything, almost.'

'Will they?'

'It's a fact.'

'Fair enough. Who *is* your chairman?'

'Sir Graeme Harmond.'

'Do you mean a little fat man with pop eyes and a stutter?'

'Well,' said Captain Bannerman, staring at Alleyn, 'if you care to put it that way.'

'I know him.'

'You don't tell me!'

'He'll do.'

'Do!'

'I'd better not use my own name. There's been something in the papers. How about C.J. Roderick?'

'Roderick?'

'It happens to be the first chunk of my own name but it's never appeared in print. When you do this sort of thing you answer more readily to a name you're used to.' He thought for a moment. 'No,' he said. 'Let's play safer and make it Broderick.'

'Wasn't your picture in last night's *Herald?*'

'*Was* it? Hell!'

'Wait a bit.'

The Captain went into his stateroom and came back with a copy of the paper that had so intrigued Mr Cuddy. He folded it back at the snapshot of piquant Beryl Cohen and Superintendent R. Alleyn (inset).

'Is that like me?' Alleyn said.

'No.'

'Good.'

'There may be a very slight resemblance. It looks as if your mouth was full.'

'It was.'

'I see,' said Captain Bannerman heavily.

'We'll have to risk it.'

'I suppose you'll want to keep very much to yourself?'

'On the contrary. I want to mix as much as possible with the passengers.'

'Why?'

Alleyn waited for a moment and then asked: 'Have you got a good memory for dates?'

'*Dates.*'

'Could you, for instance, provide yourself with a cast-iron alibi plus witnesses for the fifteenth of last month between ten and eleven p.m., the twenty-fifth between nine p.m. and midnight and for last night during the half-hour before you sailed?'

Captain Bannerman breathed stertorously and whispered to himself. At last he said: 'Not all three, I couldn't.'

'There you are, you see.'

Captain Bannerman removed his spectacles and again advanced his now empurpled face to within a short distance of Alleyn's.

'Do I look like a Sex-Monster?' he furiously demanded.

'Don't ask *me*,' Alleyn rejoined mildly. 'I don't know what they look like. That's part of the trouble. I thought I'd made it clear.'

As Captain Bannerman had nothing to say to this, Alleyn went on. 'I've got to try and check those times with all your passengers and – please don't misunderstand me, sir – I can only hope that most of them manage to turn in solider alibis than, on the face of it, yours looks to be.'

'Here! I'm clear for the 15th. We were berthed in Liverpool and I was aboard with visitors till two in the morning.'

'If that can be proved we won't pull you in for murder.'

Captain Bannerman said profoundly: 'That's a queer sort of style to use when you're talking to the Master of the ship.'

'I mean no more than I say, and that's not much. After all, you don't come aboard your own ship, clutching an embarkation notice.'

Captain Bannerman said: 'Not as a rule. No.'

Alleyn stood up. 'I know,' he said, 'what a bind this is for you and I really am sorry. I'll keep as quiet as I reasonably may.'

'I'll bet you anything you like he hasn't shipped with us. Anything you like! Now!'

'If we'd been dead certain we'd have held you up until we got him.'

'It's all some perishing mistake.'

'It may be.'

'Well,' Captain Bannerman said grudgingly as he also rose. 'I suppose we'll have to make the best of it. No doubt you'd like to see your quarters. This ship carries a pilot's cabin. On the bridge. We can give you that if it suits.'

Alleyn said it would suit admirably. 'And if I can just be treated as a passenger – '

'I'll tell the Chief Steward.' He went to his desk, sat down behind it, pulled a slip of paper towards him and wrote on it, muttering as he did so. 'Mr C. J. Broderick, relative of the chairman, going out to a Commonwealth Relations Office job in Canberra. That it?'

'That's it. I don't, of course, have to tell you anything about the need for complete secrecy.'

'You do not. I've no desire to make a fool of myself, talking daft to my ship's complement.'

A fresh breeze had sprung up and was blowing through the starboard porthole. It caught the memorandum that the Captain had just completed. The paper fluttered, turned over and was revealed as a passenger's embarkation notice for the *Cape Farewell*.

Staring fixedly at Alleyn, the Captain said: 'I used it yesterday in the offices. For a memo.' He produced a curiously uncomfortable laugh. 'It's not been torn, anyway,' he said.

'No,' Alleyn said, 'I noticed that.'

An irresponsible tinkling on a xylophonic gong announced the first luncheon on board the *Cape Farewell*, outward bound.

CHAPTER 4

Hyacinths

Having watched Alleyn mount the companionway Jemima Carmichael returned to her desolate little veranda aft of the centre-castle and to her book.

She had gone through the morning in a kind of trance, no longer inclined to cry or to think much of her broken engagement and the scenes that had attended it or even of her own unhappiness. It was as if the face of departure had removed her to a spiritual distance quite out-of-scale with the night's journey down the estuary and along the Channel. She had walked until she was tired, tasted salt on her lips, read a little, heard gulls making their BBC atmospheric noises and watched them fly mysteriously in and out of the fog. Now in the sunshine she fell into a half-doze.

When she opened her eyes it was to find that Doctor Timothy Makepiece stood not far off, leaning over the rail with his back towards her. He had, it struck her, a pleasant nape to his neck: his brown hair grew tidily into it. He was whistling softly to himself. Jemima, still in a strange state of inertia, idly watched him. Perhaps he sensed this for he turned and smiled at her.

'Are you all right?' he asked. 'Not sea-sick or anything?'

'Not at all. Only ridiculously sleepy.'

'I expect that *is* the sea. They tell me it does have that effect on some people. Did you see the pilot go off and the arrival of the dark and handsome stranger?'

'Yes, I did. Had he missed the ship last night do you suppose?'

'I've no idea. Are you going for drinks with Aubyn Dale before lunch?'

'Not I.'

'I hoped you were. Haven't you met him yet?' He didn't seem to expect an answer to this question but wandered over and looked sideways at Jemima's book.

'Elizabethan Verse?' he said. 'So you don't despise anthologies. Which is your favourite – Bard apart?'

'Well – Michael Drayton, perhaps, if he wrote "Since there's no help".'

'I'll back the Bard for that little number every time.' He picked up the book, opened it at random and began to chuckle.

' "*O yes, O yes, if any maid*
Whom leering Cupid hath betrayed," ' he read.

'Isn't *that* a thing, now? Leering Cupid! They really were wonderful. Do you – but no,' Tim Makepiece said, interrupting himself, 'I'm doing the thing I said to myself I wouldn't do.'

'What was that?' Jemima asked, not with any great show of interest.

'Why, forcing my attentions on you to be sure.'

'What an Edwardian expression.'

'None the worse for that.'

'Shouldn't you be going to your party?'

'I expect so,' he agreed moodily. 'I don't really like alcohol in the middle of the day and am far from being one of Mr Aubyn Dale's fans.'

'Oh.'

'I've yet to meet a man who is.'

'All jealous of him, I dare say,' Jemima said idly.

'You may be right. And a very sound reason for disliking him. It's the greatest mistake to think that jealousy is necessarily a fault. On the contrary, it may very well sharpen the perception.'

'It didn't sharpen Othello's.'

'But it did. It was his *interpretation* of what he saw that was at fault. He *saw*, with an immensely sharpened perception.'

'I don't agree.'

'Because you don't want to.'

'Now, look here – ' Jemima said, for the first time giving him her full attention.

'He saw Cassio, doing his sophisticated young Venetian act over Desdemona's hand. He saw him at it again after he'd blotted his copy-book. He was pathologically aware of every gallantry that Cassio showed his wife.'

'Well,' Jemima said, 'if you're pathologically aware of every attention Aubyn Dale shows his however-many-they-may-be female fans, I must say I'm sorry for you.'

'All right, Smartie,' Tim said amiably, 'you win.'

'After all, it's the interpretation that matters.'

'There's great virtue in perception alone. Pure scientific observation that is content to set down observed fact after observed fact – '

'Followed by pure scientific interpretation that adds them all up and makes a nonsense.'

'Why should you say that?' he asked gently. 'It's you that's making a nonsense.'

'Well, I must say!'

'To revert to Aubyn Dale. What about his big thing on TV? – "Pack Up Your Troubles". In other words "Come to me everybody that's got a bellyache and I'll put you before my public and pay you for it." If I were a religious man I'd call it blasphemy.'

'I don't say I *like* what he does – '

'Still, he does make an ass of himself good and proper on occasions. Witness the famous Molton Medbury Midsummer Muck-up.'

'I never heard exactly what happened.'

'He was obviously plastered. He went round televising the Molton Medbury flower show with old Lady Agatha Panthing. You could see he was plastered before he spoke and when he did speak he said the first prize in the competition went to Lady Agatha's umbilicus globular. He meant,' Timothy explained, 'Agapanthus Umbellatus globosus. I suppose it shattered him because after that a sort of rot set in and at intervals he broke into a recrudescence of Spoonerisms. It went on for weeks. Only the other day he was going all springlike over a display of hyacinths and said that in arranging them all you really needed was a "turdy stable". '

'Oh, *no*! Poor chap. How too shaming for him!'

'So he shaved off his fetching little imperial and I expect he's taking a long sea voyage to forget. He's in pretty poor shape, I fancy.'

'Do you? What sort of poor shape?'

'Oh, neurosis,' Timothy said shortly, 'of some sort, I should think.'

The xylophonic gong began its inconsequent chiming in the bridge-house.

'Good lord, that's for *eating!*' Timothy exclaimed.

'What *will* you say to your host?'

'I'll say I had an urgent case among the greasers. But I'd better just show up. Sorry to have been such a bore. Goodbye, now,' said Tim attempting a brogue.

He walked rapidly away.

To her astonishment and slightly to her resentment Jemima found that she was ravenously hungry.

II

The Cape Company is a cargo line. The fact that six of its ships afford accommodation for nine passengers each does not in any way modify the essential function of the company. It merely postulates that in the case of these six ships there shall be certain accommodation. There will also be a Chief Steward without any second string, a bar-and-passengers' steward and an anomalous offsider who may be discovered by the passengers polishing the taps in their cabins at unexpected moments. The business of housing, feeding and, within appropriate limits, entertaining the nine passengers is determined by Head Office and then becomes part of the Captain's many concerns.

On the whole, Captain Bannerman preferred to carry no passengers, and always regarded them as potential troublemakers. When, however, somebody of Mrs Dillington-Blick's calibre appeared in his ship, his reaction corresponded punctually with that of ninety per cent of all other males whom she encountered. He gave orders that she should be placed at his table (which luckily was all right anyway because she carried VIP letters) and, until Alleyn's arrival, had looked forward to the voyage with the liveliest anticipation of pleasurable interludes. He was, he considered, a young man for his age.

Aubyn Dale he also took at his table because Dale was famous and Captain Bannerman felt that in a way he would be bunching Mrs Dillington-Blick by presenting her with a No. I Personality. Now he decided, obscurely and resentfully, that Alleyn also would be an impressive addition to the table. The rest of the seating he left to his Chief Steward who gave the Cuddys and Mr Donald McAngus to the First Mate, whom he disliked; Jemima Carmichael and Dr Makepiece to the Second Mate and the Wireless Officer of whom he approved, and Miss Abbott, Father Jourdain and Mr Merryman to the Chief Engineer towards whom his attitude was neutral.

This, the first luncheon on board, was also the first occasion at which the senior ship's officers with the exception of those on duty were present. At a long table in a corner sat a number of young men presenting several aspects of adolescence and all looking a trifle sheepish. These were the electrical and engineering junior officers and the cadets.

Alleyn arrived first at the table and was carefully installed by the Captain's steward. The Cuddys, already seated hard by, settled down to a good long stare and so, more guardedly, did Mr McAngus. Mrs Cuddy's burning curiosity manifested itself in a dead-pan glare which was directed intermittently at the objects of her interest. Its mechanics might be said to resemble those of a lighthouse whose different frequencies make its signal recognizable far out at sea.

Mr Cuddy, on the contrary, kept observation under cover of an absent-minded smile while Mr McAngus quietly rolled his eyes in the direction of his objective and was careful not to turn his head.

Miss Abbott, at the Chief Engineer's table, gave Alleyn one sharp look and no more. Mr Merryman rumpled his hair, opened his eyes very wide and then fastened with the fiercest concentration upon the menu. Father Jourdain glanced in a civilized manner at Alleyn and turned with a pleasant smile to his companions.

At this juncture Mrs Dillington-Blick made her entrance rosy with achievement, buzzing with femininity, and followed by the Captain, Aubyn Dale and Timothy Makepiece.

The Captain introduced Alleyn – 'Mr Broderick, who joined us today – '

The men made appropriate wary noises at each other. Mrs Dillington-Blick, who might have been thought to be already in full flower, awarded herself a sort of bonus in effulgence. Everything about her blossomed madly. 'Fun!' she seemed to be saying. 'This is what I'm really good at. We're all going to like this.'

She bathed Alleyn in her personality. Her eyes shone, her lips were moist, her small hands fluttered at the ends of her Rubenesque arms. 'But I *watched* you!' she cried. 'I watched you with my heart in my mouth! Coming on board! Nipping up that Frightful Thing! Do tell me. Is it as Terrifying as it looks or am I being silly?'

'It's plain murder,' Alleyn said, 'and you're not being silly at all. I was all of a tremble.'

Mrs Dillington-Blick cascaded with laughter. She raised and lowered her eyebrows at Alleyn and flapped her hands at the Captain. 'There now!' she cried. 'Just what I supposed. How you dared! If it was a choice of feeding the little fishes or crawling up that ladder I swear I'd pop thankfully into the shark's maw. And don't you look so superior,' she chided Captain Bannerman.

This was exactly how he had hoped she would talk. A fine woman who enjoyed a bit of chaff. And troubled though he was, he swelled a little in his uniform.

'We'll have you shinning down it like an old hand,' he teased, 'when you go ashore at Las Palmas.' Aubyn Dale looked quizzically at Alleyn who gave him the shadow of a wink. Mrs Dillington-Blick was away to a magnificent start. Three men, one a celebrity, two good-looking and all teasing her. Las Palmas? Did they mean . . .? Would she have to . . . ? Ah *no*! She didn't believe them.

A number of rococo images chased each other improperly through Alleyn's imagination. 'Don't give it another thought,' he advised, 'you'll make the grade. I understand that if the sea's at all choppy they rig a safety net down below. Same as trapeze artistes have when they lose their nerve.'

'I won't listen.'

'It's the form, though, I promise you,' Alleyn said. 'Isn't it, sir?'

'Certainly.'

'Not true! Mr Dale, they're being *beastly* to me!'

Dale said: 'I'm on your side.' It was a phrase with which he often reassured timid subjects on television. He was already talking to Mrs Dillington-Blick as if they were lifelong friends and yet with that touch of deference that lent such distinction to his programmes and

NGAIO MARSH

filled Alleyn, together with eighty per cent of his male viewers, with a vague desire to kick him. There was a great deal of laughter at the Captain's table. Mrs Cuddy was moved to stare at it so fixedly that at one moment she completely missed her mouth.

A kind of restlessness was engendered in the passengers, a sense of being done out of something and, in two of the women, of resentment. Miss Abbott felt angry with Mrs Dillington-Blick because she was being silly over three men. Mrs Cuddy felt angry with her because three men were being silly over her and also because of a certain expression that had crept into Mr Cuddy's wide smile. Jemima Carmichael wondered how Mrs Dillington-Blick could be bothered and then took herself to task for being a humbug: the new passenger, she thought, was quite enough to make any girl do her stuff. She found that Dr Makepiece was looking at her and to her great annoyance she blushed. For the rest of luncheon she made polite conversation with the second mate who was Welsh and bashful and with the Wireless Officer who wore that wild and lonely air common to his species.

After luncheon Alleyn went to see his quarters. The pilot's cabin had a door and porthole opening on to the bridge. He could look down on the bows of the ship, thrust arrow-like into the sea and at the sickle-shaped and watery world beyond. Under other circumstances, he thought, he would have enjoyed this trip. He unpacked his suitcases, winked at a photograph of his wife, went below and carried out a brief inspection of the passengers' quarters. These were at the same level as the drawing-room and gave on to a passage that went through from port to starboard. The doors were all shut with the exception of that opening into the cabin aft of the passage on the port side. This was open and the cabin beyond resembled an overcrowded flower-shop. Here Dennis was discovered, sucking his thumb and lost in contemplation. Alleyn knew that Dennis, of whom this was his first glimpse, might very well become a person of importance. He paused by the door.

'Afternoon,' he said. 'Are you the steward for the pilot's cabin?'

Evidently Dennis had heard about Alleyn. He hurried to the door, smiled winsomely and said: 'Not generally, but I'm going to have the pleasure of looking after *you*, Mr Broderick.'

Alleyn tipped him five pounds. Dennis said: 'Oh, you shouldn't sir, really,' and pocketed the note. He indicated the flowers and said, 'I just can't make up my mind, sir: Mrs Dillington-Blick said I was to take some into the dining-room and lounge and as soon as I've finished in the bar I'm going to but I *don't* know which to choose. Such an umberance-der-riches! What would you say for the *lounge*, sir? The décor's dirty *pink*.'

Alleyn was so long answering that Dennis gave a little giggle. 'Isn't it *diffy*!' he sympathized.

Alleyn pointed a long finger. 'That,' he said, 'I should certainly make it that one,' and went on his way to the passengers' lounge.

III

It was a modest combination of bar, smoking-room and card-room and in it the passengers were assembled for coffee. Already by the curious mechanism of human attraction and repulsion they had begun to sort themselves into groups. Mr McAngus having found himself alongside the Cuddys at luncheon was reappropriated by them both and seemed to be not altogether at ease in their company, perhaps because Mrs Cuddy stared so very fixedly at his hair which, Alleyn noticed, was of an unexpected shade of nutbrown with no parting and a good deal of overhang at the back. He drew a packet of herbal cigarettes from his pocket and lit one, explaining that he suffered from asthma. They began to chat more cosily about diseases. Mr McAngus confided that he was but recently recovered from an operation and Mr Cuddy returned this lead with a lively account of a suspected duodenal ulcer.

Father Jourdain and Mr Merryman had discovered a common taste in crime fiction and smiled quite excitedly at each other over their coffee cups. Of all the men among the passengers, Alleyn thought, Father Jourdain had the most arresting appearance. He wondered what procession of events had led this man to become an Anglo-Catholic celibate priest. There was intelligence and liveliness in the face whose pallor, induced no doubt by the habit of his life, emphasized rather than concealed the opulence of the mouth and watchfulness of the dark eyes. His short white hands were muscular and his hair thick and glossy. He was infinitely more vivid than his companion, whose baby-faced petulance, Alleyn felt, was probably the outward wall of the conventional house-master. He caught himself up. 'Conventional?' Was Mr Merryman the too-familiar pedant who cultivates the eccentric to compensate himself for the deadly boredom of scholastic routine? A don *manqué*? Alleyn took himself mildly to task for indulgence in idle speculation and looked elsewhere.

Dr Timothy Makepiece stood over Jemima Carmichael with the slightly mulish air of a young Englishman in the early stages of an attraction. Alleyn noted the formidable lines of Dr Makepiece's jaw and mouth and, being at the moment interested in hands, the unusual length of the fingers.

Miss Abbott sat by herself on a settee against the wall. She was reading. The hands that held her neatly-covered book were large and muscular. Her face, he reflected, would have been not unhandsome if it had been only slightly less inflexible and if there had not been the suggestion of – what was it? – harshness? – about the jaw.

As for Aubyn Dale, there he was, with Mrs Dillington-Blick who had set herself up with him hard-by the little bar. When she saw Alleyn she beckoned gaily to him. She was busy establishing a coterie. As Alleyn joined them Aubyn Dale laid a large beautifully tended hand over hers and burst into a peal of all-too-infectious laughter. 'What a perfectly marvellous person you are!' he cried boyishly and appealed to Alleyn. 'Isn't she wonderful?'

Alleyn agreed fervently and offered them liqueurs.

'You take the words out of my mouth, dear boy,' Dale exclaimed.

'I oughtn't to!' Mrs Dillington-Blick protested. 'I'm on an *inquisitorial* diet!' She awarded her opulence a downward glance and Alleyn an upward one. She raised her eyebrows. 'My dear!' she cried. 'You can see for yourself. I oughtn't.'

'But you're going to,' he rejoined and the drinks were served by the ubiquitous Dennis who had appeared behind the bar. Mrs Dillington-Blick, with a meaning look at Dale, said that if she put on another ounce she would never get into her Jolyon swimsuit and they began to talk about his famous session on commercial television. It appeared that when he visited America and did a specially sponsored half-hour, he had been supported by a great mass of superb models all wearing Jolyon swimsuits. His hands eloquently sketched their curves. He leant towards Mrs Dillington-Blick and whispered. Alleyn noticed the slight puffiness under his eyes and the blurring weight of flesh beneath the inconsiderable jaw which formerly his beard had hidden. 'Is this the face,' Alleyn asked himself, 'that launched a thousand hips?' and wondered why.

'You haven't forgotten the flowers?' Mrs Dillington-Blick asked Dennis and he assured her that he hadn't.

'As soon as I've a spare *sec* I'll pop away and fetch them,' he promised and smiled archly at Alleyn. 'They're all chosen and ready.'

As Aubyn Dale's conversation with Mrs Dillington-Blick tended to get more and more confidential Alleyn felt himself at liberty to move away. At the far end of the lounge Mr Merryman was talking excitedly to Father Jourdain who had begun to look uncomfortable. He caught Alleyn's eye and nodded pleasantly. Alleyn dodged round the Cuddys and Mr McAngus and bypassed Miss Abbott. There was a settee near the far end but as he made for it Father Jourdain said: 'Do come and join us. These chairs are much more comfortable and we'd like to introduce ourselves.'

Alleyn said: 'I should be delighted,' and introductions were made. Mr Merryman looked sharply at him over the tops of his spectacles and said: 'How do you do, sir.' He added astonishingly: 'I perceived that you were effecting an escape from what was no doubt an excruciating situation.'

'I?' Alleyn said. 'I don't quite – '

'The sight,' Mr Merryman continued in none too quiet a voice, 'of yonder popinjay ruffling his dubious plumage at the bar is singularly distasteful to me and no doubt intolerable to you.'

'Oh, come, now!' Father Jourdain protested.

Alleyn said: 'He's not as bad as all that, is he?'

'You know who he is, of course.'

'Yes, indeed.'

'Yes, yes,' said Father Jourdain. 'We know. Ssh!'

'Have you witnessed his weekly exhibitions of indecent exposure on the television?'

'I'm not much of a viewer,' Alleyn said.

'Ah! You show your good judgment. As an underpaid pedagogue it has been my hideous lot to sit on Tuesday evenings among upper middle-class adolescents of low intelligence, "looking in" (loathsome phrase) at this man's antics. Let me tell you what he does, sir. He advertises women's bathing clothes and in another programme he incites – arrogant presumption – he incites members of the public to bring their troubles to him! And the fools do! Conceive!' Mr Merryman invited. 'Picture to yourself! A dupe is discovered. Out of focus, unrecognizable, therefore. Facing this person and us, remorselessly illuminated, and elevated in blasphemous (you will appreciate that in clerical company I use the adjective advisedly) in blasphemous supremacy is or was the countenance you see before you, but garnished with a hirsute growth which lent it a wholly spurious distinction.'

Alleyn glanced with amusement at Mr Merryman and thought what bad luck it was for him that he was unable to give visual expression to his spleen. For all the world he looked like an indignant baby.

'If you will believe me,' he continued angrily whispering, 'a frightful process known as "talking it over" now intervenes. The subject discloses to That Person and to however many thousands of listening observers there may be, some intimate predicament of her (it is, I repeat, usually a woman) private life. *He* then propounds a solution, is thanked, applauded, preens himself and is presented with a fresh sacrifice. Now! What do you think of *that*!' whispered Mr Merryman.

'I think it all sounds very embarrassing,' Alleyn said.

Father Jourdain made a comically despairing face at him. 'Let's talk about something else,' he suggested. 'You were saying, Mr Merryman, that the psychopathic murderer – '

'You heard of course,' Mr Merryman remorselessly interjected, 'what an exhibition he made of himself at a later assignment. "Lady Agatha's umbilicus globular",' he quoted, and broke into a shrill laugh.

'You know,' Father Jourdain remarked, 'I'm on holiday and honestly *don't* want to start throwing my priestly weight about.' Before Mr Merryman could reply he raised his voice a little and added: To go back, as somebody, was it Humpty Dumpty? said, to the last conversation but one: I'm immensely interested in what you were saying about criminals of the Heath type. What was the book you recommended? By an American psychiatrist, I think you said.'

Mr Merryman muttered huffily: 'I don't recollect.'

Alleyn asked: 'Not, by any chance, *The Show of Violence*, by Frederick Wertham?'

Father Jourdain turned to him with unconcealed relief. 'Ah!' he said. 'You're an addict, too, and a learned one, evidently.'

'Not I. The merest amateur. Why, by the way, is everybody so fascinated by crimes of violence?' He looked at Father Jourdain. 'What do you think, sir?'

Father Jourdain hesitated and Mr Merryman cut in.

'I am persuaded,' he said, 'that people read about murder as an alternative to committing it.'

'A safety valve?' Alleyn suggested.

'A conversion. The so-called anti-social urge is fed into a socially acceptable channel: we thus commit our crimes of violence at a safe remove. We are all,' Mr Merryman said tranquilly folding his hands over his stomach, 'savages at heart.' He seemed to have recovered his good humour.

'Do you agree?' Alleyn asked Father Jourdain.

'I fancy,' he rejoined, 'that Mr Merryman is talking about something I call original sin. If he is, I do of course agree.'

An accidental silence had fallen on the little assembly. Into this silence with raised voice, as a stone into a pool, Alleyn dropped his next remark.

'Take for instance, this strangler – the man who "says it with" – what are they? Roses? What, do you suppose, is behind all that?'

The silence continued for perhaps five seconds.

Miss Abbott said: 'Not roses. Hyacinths. Flowers of several kinds.'

She had lifted her gaze from her book and fixed it on Mrs Dillington-Blick. 'Hot-house flowers,' she said. 'It being winter. The first time it was snowdrops, I believe.'

'And the second,' Mr Merryman said, 'hyacinths.'

Aubyn Dale cleared his throat.

'Ah yes!' Alleyn said. 'I remember now. Hyacinths.'

'Isn't it awful?' Mrs Cuddy gloated.

'Shocking,' Mr Cuddy agreed. 'Hyacinths! Fancy!' Mr McAngus said gently: 'Poor things.'

Mr Merryman with the falsely innocent air of a child that knows it's being naughty asked loudly: 'Hasn't there been something on

television about these flowers? Something rather ludicrous? Of what
can I be thinking?'

Everybody avoided looking at Aubyn Dale, but not even Father
Jourdain found anything to say.

It was at this juncture that Dennis staggered into the room with a
vast basket of flowers which he set down on the central table.

'Hyacinths!' Mrs Cuddy shrilly pointed out. 'What a coincidence!'

IV

It was one of those naïve arrangements which can give nothing but
pleasure to the person who receives them unless, of course, that
person is allergic to scented flowers. The hyacinths were rooted
and blooming in a mossy bed. They trembled slightly with the
motion of the ship, shook out their incongruous fragrance and filled
the smoking-room with reminiscences of the more expensive kinds
of shops, restaurants and women.

Dennis fell back a pace to admire them.

'Thank you, Dennis,' Mrs Dillington-Blick said.

'It's a pleasure, Mrs Dillington-Blick,' he rejoined. 'Aren't they
gorgeous?'

He retired behind the bar. The passengers stared at the growing
flowers and the flowers, quivering, laid upon them a further burden
of sweetness.

Mrs Dillington-Blick explained hurriedly: 'There isn't room
for all one's flowers in one's cabin. I thought we'd enjoy them
together.'

Alleyn said: 'But what a charming gesture.' And was barely
supported by a dilatory murmur.

Jemima agreed quickly: 'Isn't it? Thank you so much, they're
quite lovely.'

Tim Makepiece murmured: 'What nice manners you've got,
Grandmama.'

'I do hope,' Mrs Dillington-Blick said, 'that nobody finds the scent
too much. Me, I simply wallow in it.' She turned to Aubyn Dale. He
rejoined: 'But of course. You're so wonderfully exotic.' Mr Merryman
snorted.

Mrs Cuddy said loudly: 'I'm afraid we're going to be spoilsports: Mr Cuddy can't stay in the same room with flowers that have a heavy perfume. He's allergic to them.'

'Oh, I *am* so sorry,' Mrs Dillington-Blick cried. 'Then, of course, they must go.' She waved her hands helplessly.

'I'm sure there's no need for that,' Mrs Cuddy announced. 'We don't want to make things uncomfortable. We were going to take a turn on deck anyway. Weren't we, dear?'

Alleyn asked: 'Do you suffer from hay fever, Mr Cuddy?'

Mrs Cuddy answered for her husband. 'Not exactly hay fever, is it, dear? He just comes over queer.'

'Extraordinary,' Alleyn murmured.

'Well, it's quite awkward sometimes.'

'At weddings and funerals for instance it must be.'

'Well on our *silver* wedding some of the gentlemen from Mr Cuddy's Lodge brought us a gorgeous mixed booky of hothouse flowers and he had to say how much he appreciated it and all the time he was feeling peculiar and when they'd gone he said: "I'm sorry, Mum, but it's me or the booky" and we live opposite a hospital so he took them across and had to go for a long walk afterwards to get over it, didn't you, dear?'

'*Your* silver wedding,' Alleyn said, and smiled at Mrs Cuddy. 'You're not going to tell us you've been married twenty-five years!'

'Twenty-five years and eleven days to be exact. Haven't we, dear?'

'That's correct, dear.'

'He's turning colour,' Mrs Cuddy said, exhibiting her husband with an air of triumph. 'Come on, love. Walky-walky.'

Mr Cuddy seemed unable to look away from Mrs Dillington-Blick. He said: 'I don't notice the perfume too heavy. It isn't affecting me.'

'That's what *you* say,' his wife replied, ominously bluff. 'You come into the fresh air, my man.' She took his arm and turned him towards the glass doors that gave on to the deck. She opened them. Cold, salt air poured into the heated room and the sound of the sea and of the ship's engines. The Cuddys went out. Mr Cuddy shut the doors and could be seen looking back into the room. His wife removed him and they walked away, their grey hair lifting in the wind.

'They'll die of cold!' Jemima exclaimed. 'No coats or hats.'

'Oh, dear!' Mrs Dillington-Blick lamented and appealed in turn to the men. 'And I expect it's all my fault.' They murmured severally.

Mr McAngus, who had peeped into the passage, confided: 'It's all right. They've come in by the side door and I *think* they've gone to their cabin.' He sniffed timidly at the flowers, gave a small apologetic laugh and made a little bobbing movement to and from Mrs Dillington-Blick. '*I* think we're all most awfully lucky,' he ventured. He then went out into the passage, putting on his hat as he did so.

'That poor creature dyes its hair,' Mr Merryman observed calmly.

'Oh come!' Father Jourdain protested and gave Alleyn a helpless look. 'I seem,' he said under his breath, 'to be saying nothing but "Oh, come." A maddening observation.'

Mrs Dillington-Blick blossomed at Mr Merryman: 'Aren't you *naughty*!' She laughed and appealed to Aubyn Dale: '*Not* true. *Is* it?'

'I honestly can't see, you know, that if he does dye his hair, it's anybody's business but his,' Dale said, and gave Mr Merryman his celebrated smile. 'Can you?' he said.

'I entirely agree with you,' Mr Merryman rejoined, grinning like a monkey. 'I must apologize. In point of fact I abominate the public elucidation of private foibles.'

Dale turned pale and said nothing.

'Let us talk about flowers instead,' Mr Merryman suggested and beamed through his spectacles upon the company.

Mrs Dillington-Blick at once began to do so. She was supported, unexpectedly, by Miss Abbott. Evidently they were both experienced gardeners. Dale listened with a stationary smile. Alleyn saw him order himself a second double brandy.

'I suppose,' Alleyn remarked generally, 'everybody has a favourite flower.'

Mrs Dillington-Blick moved into a position from which she could see him. 'Hallo, you!' she exclaimed jollily. 'But of course they have. Mine's magnolias.'

'What are yours?' Tim Makepiece asked Jemima.

'Distressingly obvious – roses.'

'Lilies,' Father Jourdain smiled, 'which may also be obvious.'

'Easter?' Miss Abbott barked.

'Exactly.'

'What about you?' Alleyn asked Tim.

'The hop,' he said cheerfully.

Alleyn grinned. 'There you are. It's all a matter of association. Mine's lilac and throws back to a pleasant childhood memory. But if beer happened to make you sick or my nanny, whom I detested, had worn lilac in her nankeen bosom or Father Jourdain associated lilies with death, we'd have all hated the sight and smell of these respective flowers.'

Mr Merryman looked with pity at him. 'Not,' he said, 'a remarkably felicitous exposition of a somewhat elementary proposition, but, as far as it goes, unexceptionable.'

Alleyn bowed. 'Have you, sir,' he asked, 'a preference?'

'None, none. The topic, I confess, does not excite me.'

'I think it's a *heavenly* topic,' Mrs Dillington-Blick cried. 'But then I adore finding out about people and their preferences.' She turned to Dale and at once his smile reprinted itself. 'Tell me your taste in flowers,' she said, 'and I'll tell you your type in ladies. Come clean, now. Your favourite flower? Or shall I guess?'

'Agapanthas?' Mr Merryman loudly suggested. Dale clapped his glass down on the bar and walked out of the room.

'Now *look* here, Mr Merryman!' Father Jourdain said and rose to his feet.

Mr Merryman opened his eyes very wide and pursed his lips: 'What's up?' he asked.

'You know perfectly well what's up. You're an extremely naughty little man and although it's none of my business I think fit to tell you so.'

Far from disconcerting Mr Merryman this more or less public rebuke appeared to afford him enjoyment. He clapped his hands lightly, slapped them on his knees and broke into elfish laughter.

'If you'll take my advice,' Father Jourdain continued, 'you will apologize to Mr Dale.'

Mr Merryman rose, bowed and observed in an extremely high-falutin' manner: '*Consilia formiora sunt de divinis locis.*'

The priest turned red.

Alleyn, who didn't see why Mr Merryman should be allowed to make a corner in pedantry, racked his own brains for a suitable tag. ' "*Consilium inveniunt multi se docti explicant*", however,' he said.

'Dear me!' Mr Merryman observed. 'How often one has cause to remark that a platitude sounds none the better for being uttered in an antique tongue. I shall now address myself to my post-prandial nap.'

He trotted towards the door, paused for a moment to stare at Mrs Dillington-Blick's pearls and then went out.

'For pity's sake!' she ejaculated. 'What is all this! What's happening? What's the matter with Aubyn Dale? Why agapanthas?'

'Can it be possible,' Tim Makepiece said, 'that you don't know about Lady Agatha's umbilicus globula and the hyacinths on the turdy stable?' and he retold the story of Aubyn Dale's misfortunes.

'How *frightful*!' Mrs Dillington-Blick exclaimed, laughing until she cried. 'How too tragically frightful! And how *naughty* of Mr Merryman.'

Tim Makepiece said: 'We don't 'alf look like being a happy family. What will Mr Chips's form be, one asks oneself, when he enters the Torrid Zone?'

'He may look like Mr Chips,' Alleyn remarked. 'He behaves like Thersites.'

Jemima said: 'I call it the rock-bottom of him. You could see Aubyn Dale minded most dreadfully. He went as white as his teeth. What could have possessed Mr Chips?'

'Schoolmaster,' Miss Abbott said, scarcely glancing up from her book. 'They often turn sour at his age. It's the life.'

She had been quiet for so long they had forgotten her. 'That's right,' she continued, 'isn't it, Father?'

'It may possibly, I suppose, be a reason. It's certainly not an excuse.'

'I think,' Mrs Dillington-Blick lamented, 'I'd better throw my lovely hyacinths overboard, don't you?' She appealed to Father Jourdain. 'Wouldn't it be best? It's not only poor Mr Dale.'

'No,' Jemima agreed. 'Mr Cuddy, we must remember, comes over queer at the sight of them.'

'Mr Cuddy,' Miss Abbott observed, 'came over queer but not, in my opinion, at the sight of the hyacinths.' She lowered her book and looked steadily at Mrs Dillington-Blick.

'My dear!' Mrs Dillington-Blick rejoined and began to laugh again.

'Well!' Father Jourdain said with the air of a man who refuses to recognize his nose before his face. 'I think I shall see what it's like on deck.'

Mrs Dillington-Blick stood between him and the double doors and he was quite close to her. She beamed up at him. His back was turned to Alleyn. He was still for a moment and then she moved aside and he went out. There was a brief silence.

Mrs Dillington-Blick turned to Jemima.

'My dear!' she confided. 'I've *got* that man. He's a reformed rake.'

Mr McAngus re-entered from the passage still wearing his hat. He smiled diffidently at his five fellow passengers.

'All settling down?' he ventured, evidently under a nervous compulsion to make some general remark.

'Like birds in their little nest,' Alleyn agreed cheerfully.

'Isn't it delicious,' Mr McAngus said, heartened by this response, 'to think that from now on it's going to get warmer and warmer and warmer?'

'Absolutely enchanting.'

Mr McAngus made the little *chassé* with which they were all to become familiar, before the basket of hyacinths.

'Quite intoxicating,' he said. 'They are my favourite flowers.'

'Are they!' cried Mrs Dillington-Blick. 'Then do please, *please* have them. Please do. Dennis will take them to your room. Mr McAngus, I should adore you to have them.'

He gazed at her in what seemed to be a flutter of bewildered astonishment. 'I?' Mr McAngus said. 'But why? I beg your pardon, but it's so very kind, and positively I can't believe you mean it.'

'But I do, indeed. Please have them.'

Mr McAngus hesitated and stammered. 'I'm quite overcome. Of course I should be delighted.' He gave a little giggle and tilted his head over to one side. 'Do you know,' he said, 'this is the first occasion, the *very* first, on which a lady has ever, of her own free will, offered me her flowers? And my favourites, too. Thank you. Thank you very much indeed.'

Alleyn saw that Mrs Dillington-Blick was touched by this speech. She smiled kindly and unprovocatively at him and Jemima laughed gently.

'I'll carry them myself,' Mr McAngus said. 'Of course I will. I shall put them on my little table and they'll be reflected in my looking-glass.'

'Lucky man!' Alleyn said lightly.

'Indeed, yes. May I, really?' he asked. Mrs Dillington-Blick nodded gaily and he advanced to the table and grasped the enormous basket with his reddish bony hands. He was an extremely thin man and, Alleyn thought, very much older than his strange nutbrown hair would suggest.

'Let me help you,' Alleyn offered.

'No, no! I'm really very strong, you know. Wiry.'

He lifted the basket and staggered on bent legs with it to the door. Here he turned, a strange figure, his felt hat tilted over his nose, blinking above a welter of quivering hyacinths.

'*I* shall think of something to give *you*,' he promised Mrs Dillington-Blick, 'after Las Palmas. There must be a reciprocal gesture.'

He went groggily away.

'He may dye his hair a screaming magenta if he chooses,' Mrs Dillington-Blick said. 'He's a sweetie-pie.'

From behind her covered book Miss Abbott remarked in that not very musical voice: 'Meanwhile we await his reciprocal gesture. After Las Palmas.'

CHAPTER 5

Before Las Palmas

Alleyn sat in the pilot's cabin looking at his file of the case in question. Captain Bannerman was on the bridge outside. At regular intervals he marched past Alleyn's porthole. The weather, as Mr McAngus had predicted, was getting warmer and in two days *Cape Farewell* would sight Las Palmas. She steamed now through a heavy swell. A tendency to yawn, doze and swap panaceas against seasickness had broken out among the passengers.

'January 15th. 13 Hop Lane. Paddington,' Alleyn read. 'Beryl Cohen. Jewess. Cheapjack. Part-time prostitute. Showy. Handsome. About 26. 5 feet 6 inches. Full figure. Red (dyed) hair. Black skirt. Red jersey. Artificial necklace (green glass). Found January 16th: 10.5 a.m. by fellow lodger. Estimated time of death: between 10 and 11 p.m. previous night. On floor, face upward. Broken necklace. Flowers (snowdrops) on face and breast. Cause: manual strangulation but necklace probably first. Lodger states she heard visitor leave about 10.45. Singing. Jewel Song, *Faust*. High-pitched male voice.'

A detailed description of the room followed. He skipped it and read on.

'January 25th. Alleyway off Ladysmith Crescent, Fulham. Marguerite Slatters, of 36A Stackhouse Street, Fulham, London. Floral worker. Respectable. Quiet. 37. 5 feet 8 inches. Slight. Homely. Dark brown hair. Sallow complexion. Brown dress. Artificial pearls and teeth. Brown beret, gloves and shoes. Returning home from St Barnabas' Parish Church. Found 11.55 by Stanley Walker, chauffeur. Estimated time of death between 9 and 12 p.m. By doorstep of empty

garage. Face upward. Broken necklace. Torn dress. Manual strangulation. Flowers (hyacinths) on face and breast. Had no flowers when
last seen alive. Alfred Bates, nightwatchman in warehouse next door,
says he heard a light voice singing "Honeysuckle and the Bee."
Thinks the time was about 10.45.'

Alleyn sighed and looked up. Captain Bannerman bobbed past
the porthole. The ship was heaved upward and forward, the horizon
tilted, rose and sank.

'February 1st. Passageway between sheds, Cape Company's No. 2
wharf Royal Albert Dock. Coralie Kraus of 16 Steep Lane, Hampstead.
Assistant at Green Thumb, Knightsbridge. 18. Naturalized Austrian.
Lively. Well-conducted, 5 feet $4^3/4$ inches. Fair hair. Pale complexion.
Black dress, gloves and shoes. No hat. Pink artificial jewellery.
(Earrings, bracelet, necklace, clips.) Taking box of hyacinths to Mrs
Dillington-Blick, passenger, *Cape Farewell*. Found 11.48 p.m. by PC
Martin Moir. Body warm. Death estimated between 11.15 and 11.48
p.m. Face upwards. Stocking torn. Jewellery broken. Ears torn.
Manual strangulation. Fragment of embarkation notice for S.S. *Cape
Farewell* in right hand. Flowers (hyacinths) on face and breast. Seaman
(on duty. *Cape Farewell* gangway) mentioned hearing high male voice
singing. Very foggy conditions. All passengers went ashore (ref. above
seaman) except Mr Donald McAngus who arrived last.'

Alleyn shook his head, pulled towards him a half-finished letter
to his wife and after a moment, continued it.

'– so instead of drearily milling over these grisly, meagre and
infuriating bits of information-received I offer them, my darling, to
you: together with any developments that may, as Fox says in his
more esoteric flights of fancy, accrue. There they are, then, and for
the first time you will have the fun, God help you, of following a
case as it develops from the casebook. The form, I suppose, is to ask
oneself what these three wretched young women had in common
and the answer is: very nearly damn' all unless you feel inclined to
pay any attention to the fact that in common with ninety per cent
of their fellow females, they all wore false jewellery. Otherwise
they couldn't physically, racially or morally be less like each other.
On the other hand they all met their death in exactly the same
fashion and each was left with her broken necklace and ghastly little floral tribute. By the way, I imagine I've spotted one point of

resemblance which didn't at first jump to the eye. Wonder if you have?

'As for the fragment of embarkation notice in Miss Kraus's right hand, that's all I've got to justify my taking this pleasure cruise and if it was blowing about the wharf and she merely happened to clutch it in her death throes, it'll be another case of public money wasted. The Captain, egged on by me, got the steward (a queer little job called Dennis) to collect the embarkation notices as if it was the usual procedure. With this result:

Mrs Dillington-Blick. Has lost it.

Mr and Mrs Cuddy. Joint one. Names written in. Just possible he could have fiddled in 'Mr and' when he found he'd lost his own. Room for fiddle. Can check office procedure.

Mr Merryman. Had it in waistcoat pocket and now accuses steward of pinching it (!).

Father Jourdain. Chucked it overboard.

Mr McAngus. Can't find it but says he's sure he kept it. Frantic search – fruitless.

Dr Makepiece. Wasn't given one.

Aubyn Dale. Thinks his sweetie took it. Doesn't know why.

Miss Abbott. Put it in wastepaper basket. (Gone.)

Miss Carmichael. Has got.

So that's not much cop. No torn embarkation notice.

'I've told you about getting the D-B's hyacinths planted in the lounge. Dazzling reactions from Dale and Cuddy. Pity it was both. Explanation for Dale's megrim (spoonerism on TV) very persuasive. Note Cuddy's wedding anniversary date. Am I or am I not playing fair? Darling Troy, how very much, by the way, I love you.

'On a sea voyage, you may remember, human relationships undergo a speeding-up process. People get to know each other after a fashion very quickly, and often develop a kind of intimacy. They lose their normal sense of responsibility and become suspended, like the ship, between two worlds. They succumb to infatuations. Mr Cuddy is succumbing to an infatuation for Mrs D-B and so, in a vague rarified way, is Mr McAngus. The Captain belongs to the well-known nautical group "middle-aged sea-dog". High blood-pressure.

Probably soaks in the tropics. Amorous. (Do you remember your theory about men of a certain age?) Has also set his course for Mrs D-B. Makepiece has got his eye on Jemima Carmichael and so have all the junior officers. She's a nice child with some sort of chip on her shoulder. The D-B is a tidy armful and knows it. Mrs Cuddy is a network of subfusc complications and Miss Abbott is unlikely on the face of it, to release the safety catch in even the most determined sex-monster. But I suppose I shouldn't generalize. She shaves.

'As for the men: I've told you enough about our *Mr Merryman* to indicate what a cup-of-tea *he* is. It may help to fill in the picture if I add that he is the product of St Chads, Cantor, and Caius, looks a bit like Mr Pickwick and much more like Mr Chips and resembles neither in character. He's retired from teaching but displays every possible pedagogic eccentricity from keeping refuse in his waistcoat pocket to laying down the law in and out of season. He despises policemen, seems to have made a sort of corner in acerbity and will, I bet you, cause a real row before the journey's over.

'*Aubyn Dale:* Education, undivulged. ? Non-U. So like himself on TV that one catches oneself supposing him to be two-dimensional. His line is being a thoroughly nice chap and he drinks about three times as much as is good for him. For all I know, he may be a thoroughly nice chap. He has a distressing predilection for practical jokes and has made a lifelong enemy of Merryman by causing the steward to serve him with a plastic fried egg at breakfast.

'*Jourdain:* Lancing and BNC. On a normal voyage would be a pleasant companion. To me, the most interesting of the men but then I always want to find out at what point in an intelligent priest's progress PC Faith begins to direct the traffic. I'll swear in this one there's still a smack of the jay-walker.

'*Cuddy:* Methodist School. Draper. Not very delicious. Inquisitive. Conceited. A bit mean. Might be a case for a psychiatrist.

'*Makepiece:* Felsted, New College and St Thomas's. *Is* a psychiatrist. The Orthodox BMA class. Also MD. Wants to specialize in criminal psychiatry. Gives the impression of being a sound chap.

'*McAngus:* Scottish High School. Philatelist. Amiable eunuch: but I don't mean literally; a much-too-facile label. May, for all one knows, be a seething mass of "thing". Also very inquisitive. Gets in a tizzy over details. Dyes, as you will have gathered, his hair.

'Well, my dear love, there you are. The night before Las Palmas, with the connivance of Captain Bannerman, who is only joining in because he hopes I'll look silly, I am giving a little party. You have just read the list of guests. It's by way of being an experiment and may well turn out to be an unproductive bore. But what the hell, after all, am I to do? My instructions are not to dive in, boots and all, declare myself and hold a routine investigation, but to poke and peer and peep about and try to find out if any of these men has *not* got an alibi for one of the three vital occasions. My instructions are also to prevent any further activities, and not antagonize the Master who already turns purple with incredulity and rage at the mere suggestion of our man being aboard his ship. On the face of it the D-B and Miss C. look the likeliest candidates for strangulation, but you never know. Mrs Cuddy may have a *je ne sais quoi* which has escaped me but I fancy that as a potential victim Miss Abbott is definitely out. However that may be, you can picture me, as we approach the tropics, muscling in on any cosy little party à *deux* that breaks out in the more secluded corners of the boat deck and thus becoming in my own right a likely candidate for throttling. (Not really, so don't agitate yourself.) Because the ladies must be protected. At Las Palmas there should be further reports from headquarters, following Fox's investigations at the Home end. One can only hope they'll cast a little beam. At the moment there's not a twinkle but – '

There was a tap at the door and, on Alleyn's call, the wireless cadet, a wan youth, came in with a radiogram.

'In code, Mr Broderick,' he said.

When he had gone Alleyn decoded the message and after an interval continued his letter.

'Pause indicating suspense. Signal from Fox. It appears that a young lady from the hardware department in Woolworth's called Bijou Browne, after thirty days' disastrous hesitation, has coyly informed the Yard that she was half-strangled near Strand-on-the-Green on January 5th. The assailant offered her a bunch of hellebore (Christmas roses to you) and told her there was a spider on her neck. He started in on her rope of beads which, being poppets, broke; was interrupted by the approach of a wayfarer and bolted. It was a dark night and all she can tell Fox about her assailant is that he too was dark, spoke very nice, and wore gloves and ever such a full dark beard.'

II

Alleyn's suggestion that he should give a dinner party was made, in the first instance, to Captain Bannerman.

'It may be unorthodox,' Alleyn said, 'but there's just a chance that it may give us a lead about these people.'

'I can't say I see how you work that out.'

'I hope you will, though, in a minute. And, by the by, I'll want your collaboration, sir, if you'll agree to give it.'

'Me! Now then, now then, what is all this?'

'Let me explain.'

Captain Bannerman listened with an air of moody detachment. When Alleyn had finished the Captain slapped his palms on his knees and said: 'It's a damn' crazy notion but if it proves once and for all that you're on a wild goose chase it'll be worth the trouble. I won't say no. Now!'

Fortified by this authority Alleyn interviewed the Chief Steward, who expressed astonishment. Any parties that were given aboard this ship, the Chief Steward explained, were traditionally cocktail parties for which Dennis, always helpful, made very dainty little savouries and records were played over the loudspeaker.

However, before Alleyn's vast prestige as a supposed VIP and relation of the Managing Director, objections dissolved. Dennis became flushed with excitement, the stewards were gracious and the chef, a Portuguese whose almost moribund interest in his art revived under a whacking great tip, enthusiastic. Tables were run together and decorated, wine was chosen and at the appointed hour the eight passengers, the mate, the chief engineer, Alleyn and Tim Makepiece, having first met for drinks in the lounge, were assembled in the dining-room at a much later hour than was usually observed for dinner at sea.

Alleyn sat at one end of the table with Mrs Cuddy on his right and Miss Abbott on his left. The Captain sat at the other between Mrs Dillington-Blick and Jemima: an arrangement that broke down his last resistance to so marked a departure from routine and fortified him against the part he had undertaken to play.

Alleyn was a good host; his professional knack of getting other people to talk, coupled with the charm to which his wife never alluded without using the adjective indecent, generated an atmos-phere of festivity. He was enormously helped by Mrs Dillington-Blick whose genuine enthusiasm and plunging neckline were, in their separate modes, provocative of jollity. She looked so dazzling that she sounded brilliant. Father Jourdain, who sat next to her, was admirable. Aubyn Dale, resplendent in a velvet dinner-jacket, corus-cated with bonhomie and regaled his immediate neighbours with stories of practical jokes that he had successfully inflicted upon his chums, as he called them, in the world of admass. These anecdotes met with a gay response in Mrs Dillington-Blick.

Mr McAngus wore a hyacinth in his buttonhole. Tim Makepiece was obviously enjoying himself and Jemima had an air of being astonished at her own gaiety. Mr Merryman positively blossomed or, at any rate, sprouted a little, under the influence of impeccably chosen wines and surprisingly good food while Miss Abbott relaxed and barked quite jovially across the table at Mr Cuddy. The two officers rapidly eased off their guarded good manners.

The Cuddys were the tricky ones. Mrs Cuddy looked as if she wasn't going to give herself away if she knew it and Mr Cuddy's smile suggested that he enjoyed secret information about something slightly discreditable to everyone else. They exchanged looks occasionally.

However as the Montrachet was followed by Pierrier Jouet in a lordly magnum, even the Cuddys shed some of their caginess. Mrs Cuddy, having assured Alleyn that they never touched anything but a drop of port wine on anniversaries, was persuaded to modify her austerity and did so with abandon. Mr Cuddy cautiously sipped and asked sharp questions about the wine, pointing out with tedious iteration that it was all above his head, he being a very simple-living person and not used to posh meals. Alleyn was unable to like Mr Cuddy very much.

Nevertheless it was he who provided a means of introducing the topic that Alleyn had planned to exploit. There were no flowers on the table. They had been replaced by large bowls of fruit and shaded lamps, in deference, Alleyn pointed out, to Mr Cuddy's idiosyncrasy. It was an easy step from here to the flower murderer. 'Flowers,' Alleyn suggested, 'must have exactly the opposite effect on him to the one they have on you, Mr Cuddy. A morbid attraction. Wouldn't you say so, Makepiece?'

'It might be so,' Tim agreed cheerfully. 'From the standpoint of clinical psychiatry there is probably an unconscious association – '

He was young enough and had drunk enough good wine to enjoy airing his shop and, it seemed, essentially modest enough to pull himself up after a sentence or two. 'But really very little is known about these cases,' said he apologetically. 'I'm probably talking through my hat.'

But he had served Alleyn's purpose, and the talk was now concentrated on the flower murderer. Theories were advanced. Famous cases were quoted. Arguments abounded. Everybody seemed to light up pleasurably on the subject of the death by strangulation of Beryl Cohen and Marguerite Slatters. Even Mr Merryman became animated and launched a full-scale attack on the methods of the police who, he said, had obviously made a complete hash of their investigation. He was about to embroider his theme when the Captain withdrew his right hand from under the tablecloth without looking at Mrs Dillington-Blick, raised his glass of champagne and proposed Alleyn's health. Mrs Cuddy shrilly and unexpectedly ejaculated, 'Speech, speech!' and was supported by the Captain, Aubyn Dale, the officers and her husband. Father Jourdain murmured: 'By all means, speech.' Mr Merryman looked sardonic and the others, politely apprehensive, tapped the table.

Alleyn stood up. His great height and the circumstances of his face being lit from below like an actor's in the days of footlights, may have given point to the silence that fell upon the room. The stewards had retired into the shadows, there was a distant rattle of crockery. The anonymous throb of the ship's progress re-established itself.

'It's very nice of you,' Alleyn said, 'but I'm no hand at all at speeches and would make a perfect ass of myself if I tried, particularly in this distinguished company: – The Church! Television! Learning! No, no. I shall just thank you all for making this, I hope I may say, such a good party and sit down.' He made as if to do so when to everybody's amazement, and judging by his extraordinary expression, his own as well, Mr Cuddy suddenly roared out in the voice of a tone-deaf bull: 'For – or – '

The sound he made was so destitute of anything remotely resembling any air that for a moment everybody was at a loss to know what ailed him. Indeed it was not until he had got as far as 'Jolly

Good Fellow', that his intention became clear and an attempt was made by Mrs Cuddy, the Captain and the officers to support him. Father Jourdain then good-humouredly struck in but even his pleasant tenor could make little headway against the deafening atonalities of Mr Cuddy's ground-swell. The tribute ended in confusion and a deadly little silence. '

Alleyn hastened to fill it. He said, 'Thank you very much,' and caught Mr Merryman's eye.

'You were saying,' he prompted, 'that the police have made a hash of their investigations: in what respect, exactly?'

'In every possible respect, my dear sir. What have they done? No doubt they have followed the procedure they bring to bear upon other cases which they imagine are in the same category. This procedure having failed they are at a loss. I have long suspected that our wonderful police methods, so monotonously extolled by a too-complacent public, are in reality cumbersome, inflexible and utterly without imaginative direction. The murderer has not obliged them by distributing pawn tickets, driving licences or visiting cards about the scenes of his activities and they are left therefore gaping.'

'Personally,' Alleyn said, 'I can't imagine how they even begin to tackle their job. I mean what *do* they do?'

'You may well ask!' cried Mr Merryman now pleasurably uplifted. 'No doubt they search the ground for something they call, I understand, occupational dust, in the besotted hope that their man is a bricklayer, knifegrinder or flour-miller. Finding none, they accost numbers of blameless individuals who have been seen in the vicinity and, weeks after the event, ask them to produce alibis. Alibis!' Mr Merryman ejaculated and threw up his hands.

Mrs Dillington-Blick, opening her eyes very wide, said: 'What would *you* do, Mr Merryman, if *you* were the police?'

There was a fractional pause after which Mr Merryman said with hauteur that as he was not in fact a detective the question was without interest.

The Captain said: 'What's wrong with alibis? If a chap's got an alibi he's out of it, isn't he? So far so good.'

'Alibis,' Mr Merryman said grandly, 'are in the same category as statistics: in the last analysis they prove nothing.'

'Oh, come now!' Father Jourdain protested. 'If I'm saying compline in Kensington with the rest of my community at the time a crime is committed in Bermondsey, I'm surely incapable of having committed it.'

Mr Merryman had begun to look very put out and Alleyn came to his rescue.

'Surely,' he said, 'a great many people don't even remember exactly what they were doing on a specific evening at a specific time. I'm jolly certain I don't.'

'Suppose, for instance, now – just for the sake of argument,' Captain Bannerman said, and was perhaps a trifle too careful not to look at Alleyn, 'that all of us had to produce an alibi for one of these crimes. By gum, I wonder if we could do it. I wonder.'

Father Jourdain, who had been looking very steadily at Alleyn, said: 'One might try.'

'One might,' Alleyn rejoined. 'One might even have a bet on it. What do you say, Mr Merryman?'

'Normally,' Mr Merryman declared, 'I am not a betting man. However: *dissipet Euhius curos edaces:* I would be prepared to wager some trifling sum upon the issue.'

'Would you?' Alleyn asked. 'Really? All right, then. Propose your bet, sir.'

Mr Merryman thought for a moment. 'Coom on, now,' urged the Captain.

'Very well. Five shillings that the majority, here, will be unable to produce, on the spot, an acceptable alibi for any given date.'

'I'll take you!' Aubyn Dale shouted. 'It's a bet!'

Alleyn, Captain Bannerman and Tim Makepiece also said they would take Mr Merryman's bet.

'And if there's any argument about the acceptability of the alibi,' the Captain announced, 'the non-betters can vote on it. How's that?'

Mr Merryman inclined his head.

Alleyn asked what was to be the given date and the Captain held up his hand. 'Let's make it,' he suggested, 'the first of the Flower Murders?'

There was a general outbreak of conversation through which Mr Cuddy could be heard smugly asserting that he couldn't understand anybody finding the slightest difficulty over so simple a matter. An argument developed between him and Mr Merryman and was hotly continued over coffee and liqueurs in the lounge. Gently fanned by Alleyn it spread through the whole party. He felt that the situation had ripened and should be harvested before anybody, particularly the Captain and Aubyn Dale, had anything more to drink.

'What about this bet?' he asked in a temporary lull. 'Dale has taken Mr Merryman. We've all got to find alibis for the first Flower Murder. I don't even remember when it was. Does anybody remember? Mr McAngus?'

Mr McAngus at once launched himself upon the uncertain bosom of associated recollections. He was certain, he declared, that he read about it on the morning when his appendix, later to perforate, subjected him to a preliminary twinge. This, he was persuaded, had been on Friday the sixteenth of January. And yet – was it? His voice sank to a whisper. He began counting on his fingers and wandered disconsolate amidst a litter of parentheses.

Father Jourdain said, 'I believe, you know, that it *was* the night of the fifteenth.'

' – and only five days afterwards,' Mr McAngus could be heard, droning pleasurably, 'I was whisked into Saint Bartholomew's Hospital where I hung between life and death – '

'Cohen!' Aubyn Dale shouted. 'Her name was Beryl Cohen. Of course!'

'Hop Lane, Paddington,' Tim Makepiece added with a grin. 'Between ten and eleven.'

The Captain threw an altogether much too conspiratorial glance at Alleyn. 'Coom on!' he said. 'There you are! We're off! Ladies first.'

Mrs Dillington-Blick and Jemima at once protested that they hadn't a hope of remembering what they did on any night-in-question. Mrs Cuddy said darkly and confusedly that she preferred to support her husband and refused to try.

'You see!' Mr Merryman gleefully ejaculated. 'Three failures at once.' He turned to Father Jourdain. 'And what can the Church produce?'

Father Jourdain said quietly that he was actually in the neighbourhood of the crime on that night. He had been giving a talk at a boys' club in Paddington. 'One of the men there drove me back to the Community. I remember thinking afterwards that we must have been within a stone's throw of Hop Lane.'

'Fancy!' Mrs Cuddy ejaculated with ridiculous emphasis. 'Fred! Fancy!'

'Which would, I suppose,' Father Jourdain continued, 'constitute my alibi, wouldn't it?' He turned to Alleyn.

'I must say I'd have thought so.'

Mr Merryman, whose view of alibis seemed to be grounded in cantankerousness rather than logic, pointed out that it would all have to be proved and that in any case the result would be inconclusive.

'Oh,' Father Jourdain said tranquilly. 'I could *prove* my alibi quite comfortably. And conclusively,' he added.

'More than I could,' Alleyn rejoined. 'I fancy I was at home that night but I'm blowed if I could prove it.'

Captain Bannerman loudly announced that he had been in Liverpool with his ship and could prove it up to the hilt. 'Now then!' he exhorted, absent-mindedly seizing Mrs Dillington-Blick by the elbow, 'what's everybody else got to say for themselves? Any murderers present?' He laughed immoderately at this pleasantry and stared at Alleyn who became a prey to further grave misgivings. 'What about you, Mr Cuddy? You, no doubt, *can* account for yourself?'

The passengers' interest had been satisfactorily aroused. If only, Alleyn thought, Captain Bannerman would pipe down, the conversation might go according to plan. Fortunately, at this juncture, Mrs Dillington-Blick murmured something that caught the Captain's ear. He became absorbed and everybody else turned their attention upon Mr Cuddy.

Mr Cuddy adopted an attitude that seemed to be coloured by gratification at finding himself the centre of interest and a suspicion that in some fashion he was being got at by his fellow passengers. He was maddening but in a backhanded sort of way rewarding. The fifteenth of January, he said, consulting a pocketbook and grinning meaninglessly from ear to ear, was a Tuesday and Tuesday was his Lodge night. He gave the address of his Lodge (Tooting) and on being asked by Mr Merryman if he had, in fact, attended that night, appeared to take umbrage and was silent.

'Mr Cuddy,' his wife said, 'hasn't missed for twenty years. They made him an Elder Bison for it and gave him ever such a nice testimonial.'

Jemima and Tim Makepiece caught each other's eyes and hurriedly turned aside.

Mr Merryman who had listened to Mr Cuddy with every mark of the liveliest impatience began to question him about the time he left his Lodge but Mr Cuddy grew lofty and said he wasn't feeling quite the thing, which judging by his ghastly colour was true enough. He retired, accompanied by Mrs Cuddy, to the far end of the lounge. Evidently Mr Merryman looked upon this withdrawal as a personal triumph for himself. He straightened his shoulders and seemed to inflate.

'The discussion,' he said, looking about him, 'is not without interest. So far we have been presented with two allegedly provable alibis,' he made a facetious bob at the Captain and Father Jourdain: 'and otherwise, if the ladies are to be counted, with failures.'

'Yes, but look here,' Tim said, 'a little further examination – '

Mr Merryman blandly and deliberately misunderstood him. 'By all means!' he ejaculated. 'Precisely. Let us continue. Miss Abbott – '

'What about yourself?' Mr Cuddy suddenly bawled from the far end of the room.

'Ah!' Mrs Cuddy rejoined and produced a Rabelaisian laugh: 'Ho, ho, ho,' she said, without moving a muscle of her face. 'What about yourself, Mr Merryband?'

'Steady, Ethel,' Mr Cuddy muttered.

'Good God!' Tim muttered to Jemima. 'She's tiddly!'

'She was tossing down bumpers at dinner – probably for the first time in her life.'

'That's it. Tiddly. How wonderful.'

'Ho, ho, ho!' Mrs Cuddy repeated, 'And where was Merryband when the lights went out?'

'Eth!'

'Fair enough,' Aubyn Dale exclaimed. 'Come along, Mr Merryman. Alibi, please.'

'With all the pleasure in life,' Mr Merryman said, 'I have none. I join the majority. On the evening in question,' he continued didactically, as if he expected them all to start taking dictation, 'I attended

a suburban cinema. The Kosy, spelt (abominable vulgarism) with a K.
In Bounty Street, Chelsea. By a diverting coincidence the film was
The Lodger. I am totally unable to prove it,' he ended triumphantly.

'Very fishy!' Tim said, shaking his head owlishly. 'Oh, very fishy
indeed, I fear, sir!'

Mr Merryman gave a little crowing laugh.

'I know!' Mr McAngus abruptly shouted. 'I have it! Tuesday!
Television!' And at once added, 'No, no, wait a moment. *What* did
you say the date was?'

Alleyn told him and he became silent and depressed.

'What about Miss Abbott, now,' Captain Bannerman asked. 'Can
Miss Abbott find an alibi? Come along, Miss Abbott. January 15th.'

She didn't answer at once but sat, unsmiling and staring straight
before her. A silence fell upon the little company.

'I was in my flat,' she said at last and gave the address. There
was something uncomfortable in her manner. Alleyn thought,
'Damn! The unexpected. In a moment somebody will change the
conversation.'

Aubyn Dale was saying waggishly: 'Not good enough! Proof, Miss
Abbott, proof.'

'Did anybody ring up or come in?' Jemima prompted with a
friendly smile for Miss Abbott.

'My friend – the person I share my flat with – came in at ten
thirty-five.'

'How clever to remember!' Mrs Dillington-Blick murmured and
managed to suggest that she herself was enchantingly feckless.

'And before that?' Mr Merryman demanded.

A faint dull red settled above Miss Abbott's cheekbones. 'I
watched television,' she said.

'Voluntarily?' Mr Merryman asked in astonishment.

To everybody's surprise Miss Abbott shuddered. She wetted her
lips: 'It passed – it – sometimes helped to pass the time – '

Tim Makepiece, Father Jourdain and Jemima, sensing her discomfiture, tried to divert Mr Merryman's attention but he was evidently one
of those people who are unable to abandon a conversation before they
have triumphed. ' "Pass the time," ' he ejaculated, casting up his eyes.
' Was ever there a more damning condemnation of this bastard, this
emasculate, this enervating peepshow. What was the programme?'

Miss Abbott glanced at Aubyn Dale who was looking furiously at Mr Merryman. 'In point of fact – ' she began.

Dale waved his hands. 'Ah – ah! I knew it. Alas, I knew it! Nine to nine-thirty. Every Tuesday night, God help me. I knew.' He leant forward and addressed himself to Mr Merryman. 'My session you know. The one you dislike so much. "Pack Up Your Troubles" which, oddly enough, appears to create a slightly different reaction in its all-time high viewing audience. Very reprehensible, no doubt, but there it is. They seem quite to like it.'

'Hear, hear!' Mrs Cuddy shouted vaguely from the far end of the lounge and stamped approval.

' "Pack Up Your Troubles," ' Mrs Dillington-Blick ejaculated. 'Of *course*!'

'Madam,' Mr Merryman continued looking severely at Miss Abbott. 'Will you be good enough to describe the precise nature of the predicaments that were aired by the – really, I am at a loss for the correct term to describe these people – the protagonist will no doubt enlighten me – '

'The subjects?' Father Jourdain suggested.

'The victims?' Tim amended.

'Or the guests? I like to think of them as my guests,' said Aubyn Dale.

Mrs Cuddy said rather wildly: 'That's a lovely *lovely* way of putting it!'

('Steady, Eth!')

Miss Abbott, who had been twisting her large hands together said: 'I remember nothing about the programme. Nothing.'

She half rose from her seat and then seemed to change her mind and sank back. 'Mr Merryman, you're not to badger Miss Abbott,' Jemima said quickly and turned to Aubyn Dale. 'You, at any rate, have got your alibi, it seems.'

'Oh, yes!' he rejoined. He finished his double brandy and, in his turn, slipped his hand under Mrs Dillington-Blick's forearm. 'God, yes! I've got the entire Commercial TV admass between me and Beryl Cohen. Twenty million viewers can't be wrong! In spite of Mr Merryman.'

Alleyn said lightly: 'But isn't the programme over by nine-thirty? What about the next half-hour?'

'Taking off the war-paint, dear boy, and meeting the chums in the jolly old local.'

It had been generally agreed that Aubyn Dale's alibi was established when Mr McAngus said diffidently: 'Do you know – I may be quite wrong – but I had a silly notion someone said that particular session was done at another time – I mean – if of course it *was* that programme.'

'Ah?' Mr Merryman ejaculated pointing at him as if he'd held his hand up. 'Explain yourself. Filmed? Recorded?'

'Yes. But, of course I may be – '

But Mr Merryman pounced gleefully on Aubyn Dale. 'What do you say, sir? Was the session recorded?'

Dale collected everybody else's attention as if he invited them to enjoy Mr Merryman with him. He opened his arms and enlarged his smile and he patted Mr McAngus on the head.

'Clever boy,' he said. 'And I thought I'd got away with it. I couldn't resist pulling your leg, Mr Merryman: you will forgive me won't you?'

Mr Merryman did not reply. He merely stared very fixedly at Aubyn Dale and, as Jemima muttered to Tim, may have been restraining himself from saying he would see him in his study after prep.

Dale added to this impression by saying with uneasy boyishness, 'I swear, by the way, I was just about to come clean. Naturally.'

'Then,' Alleyn said, 'it was not a live transmission?'

'Not that one. Usually is but I was meant to be on my way to the States so we filmed it.'

'Indeed?' Mr Merryman said. 'And *were* you on your way to the United States, sir?'

'Actually, no. One of those things. There was a nonsense made over dates. I flew three days later. Damn' nuisance. It meant I didn't get back till the day before we sailed.'

'And your alibi?' Mr Merryman continued ominously.

'Well – ah – well – don't look at me, padre. I spent the evening with my popsey. Don't ask me to elaborate, will you? No names, no pack-drill.'

'And no alibi,' said Mr Merryman neatly.

There was a moment's uneasy suspense during which nobody looked at anybody else and then Mr McAngus unexpectedly surfaced.

'I remember it all quite perfectly,' he announced. 'It *was* the evening before my first hint of trouble and I *did* watch television!'

'Programme?' Mr Merryman snapped. Mr McAngus smiled timidly at Aubyn Dale. 'Oh,' he tittered, 'I'm no end of a fan, you know.'

It turned out that he had, in fact, watched 'Pack Up Your Troubles'. When asked if he could remember it, he said at once: 'Very clearly.' Alleyn saw Miss Abbott close her eyes momentarily as if she felt giddy. 'There was a lady,' Mr McAngus continued, 'asking, I recollect, whether she ought to get married.'

'There almost always is,' Dale groaned and made a face of comic despair.

'But this was very complicated because, poor thing, she felt she would be deserting her great friend and her great friend didn't know about it and would be dreadfully upset. There!' Mr McAngus cried. 'I've remembered! If only one could be sure which evening. The twenty-fifth, I ask myself? I mean the fifteenth, of course.'

Dale said: 'I couldn't tell you which programme but, ah, poor darling: I remember her. I think I helped her. I hope I did!'

'Perhaps,' Captain Bannerman suggested, 'Miss Abbott remembers now you've mentioned it. That'd fix your alibi for you.'

'*Do* you, Miss Abbott?' Mr McAngus asked anxiously.

Everybody looked at Miss Abbott and it was at once apparent to everybody but Mr McAngus that she was greatly upset. Her lips trembled. She covered them with her hand in a rather dreadful parody of cogitation. She shook her head and her eyes overflowed.

'No?' Mr McAngus said wistfully oblivious and shortsightedly, blinking, 'Do try, Miss Abbott. She was a dark, rather *heavy* lady. I mean, of course, that was the impression one had. Because one doesn't see the face and the back of the head is rather out of focus, isn't it, Mr Dale? But she kept saying (and I think they must distort the voice a little, too) that she knew her friend would be dreadfully hurt because apart from herself, she had so few to care for her.' He made a little bob at Aubyn Dale. 'You were wonderful,' he said, 'so tactful. About loneliness. I'm sure, if you saw it, Miss Abbott, you must remember. Mr Dale made such practical and helpful suggestions. I don't remember exactly what they were but – '

Miss Abbott rounded on him and cried out with shocking violence, 'For God's sake stop talking. "Helpful suggestions"! What "suggestions" can help in that kind of hell!' She looked round at them all with an expression of evident despair. 'For some of us,' she said, 'there's no escape. We are our own slaves. No escape or release.'

'Nonsense!' Mr Merryman said sharply. 'There is always an escape and a release. It is a matter of courage and resolution.'

Miss Abbott gave a harsh sob. 'I'm sorry,' she muttered. 'I'm not myself. I shouldn't have had so much champagne.' She turned away.

Father Jourdain said quickly: 'You know, Mr McAngus, I'm afraid you haven't quite convinced us.'

'And that's the last alibi gone overboard,' said the Captain. 'Mr Merryman wins.'

He made a great business of handing over his five shillings. Alleyn, Tim Makepiece and Aubyn Dale followed suit.

They all began to talk at once and with the exception of the Cuddys avoided looking at Miss Abbott. Jemima moved in front of her and screened her from the others. It was tactfully done and Alleyn was confirmed in his view that Jemima was a nice child. Mrs Dillington-Blick joined her and automatically a group assembled round Mrs Dillington-Blick. So between Miss Abbott and the rest of the world there was a barrier behind which she trumpeted privately into her handkerchief.

Presently she got up, now mistress of herself, thanked Alleyn for his party and left it.

The Cuddys came forward, clearly agog, eager, by allusion and then by direct reference, to speculate upon Miss Abbott's distress. Nobody supported them. Mr McAngus merely looked bewildered. Tim talked to Jemima and Captain Bannerman and Aubyn Dale talked to Mrs Dillington-Blick. Mr Merryman looked once at the Cuddys over his spectacles, rumpled his hair and said something about *'Hoc morbido cupiditatis'* in a loud voice to Alleyn and Father Jourdain. Alleyn was suddenly visited by an emotion that is unorthodox in an investigating officer: he felt a liking and warmth for these people. He respected them because they refused to gossip with the Cuddys about Miss Abbott's unhappiness and because they had behaved with decency and compassion when she broke down.

He saw Jemima and Mrs Dillington-Blick speak together and then slip out of the room and he knew they had gone to see if they could help Miss Abbott. He was very much troubled.

Father Jourdain came up to him and said: 'Shall we move over here?' He led Alleyn to the far end of the room.

'That was unfortunate,' he said.

'I'm sorry about it.'

'You couldn't possibly know it would happen. She is a very unhappy woman. She exhales unhappiness.'

'It was the reference to that damn' spiritual striptease session of Dale's,' Alleyn said. 'I suppose something in the programme had upset her.'

'Undoubtedly,' Father Jourdain smiled. 'That's a good description of it: a spiritual striptease. I suppose you'll think I'm lugging in my cloth but you know I really do think it's better to leave confession to the professional.'

'Dale would call himself a professional.'

'What he does,' Father Jourdain said, with warmth, 'is vulgar, dangerous and altogether odious. But he's not a bad chap, of course. At least I don't think so. Not a bad sort of chap, at all.'

Alleyn said: 'There's something else you want to say to me, isn't there?'

'There is, but I hesitate to say it. I am not sure of myself. Will you laugh at me if I tell you that, by virtue of my training perhaps, and perhaps because of some instinct, I am peculiarly sensitive to – to spiritual atmospheres?'

'I don't know that I – '

Father Jourdain interrupted him.

'I mean that when I feel there is something really out-of-joint, spiritually – I use this word because I'm a priest, you know – with a group of people, I'm usually right.'

'And do you feel it now?'

'Very strongly. I suspect it's a sense of unexpressed misery,' said Father Jourdain. 'But I can't hunt it home.'

'Miss Abbott?'

'I don't know. I don't know.'

'Even that,' Alleyn said, 'is not what you want to say.'

'You're very perceptive yourself,' Father Jourdain looked steadily at him. 'When the party breaks up, will you stay behind for a moment?'

'Certainly.'

Father Jourdain said so softly that Alleyn could barely hear him, 'You *are* Roderick Alleyn, aren't you?'

III

The deserted lounge smelt of dead cigarettes and forgotten drinks. Alleyn opened the doors to the deck outside, the stars were careering in the sky: the ship's mast swung against them and the night sea swept thudding and hissing past her flanks.

'I'm sorry to have kept you waiting,' said Father Jourdain behind him.

Alleyn shut the doors again and they sat down.

'Let me assure you at once,' Father Jourdain said, 'that I shall respect your – I suppose anonymity is not the right word. Your incognito, shall we say?'

'I'm not particularly bothered about the choice of words,' Alleyn said drily.

'Nor need you be bothered about my recognizing you. It's by the oddest of coincidences. Your wife may be said to have effected the introduction.'

'Really?'

'I have never met her but I admire her painting. Some time ago I went to a one-man show of hers and was very much impressed by a small portrait. It too was anonymous, but a brother-priest, Father Copeland of Winton St Giles who knows you both, told me it was a portrait of her husband who was the celebrated Inspector Alleyn. I have a very long memory for faces and the likeness was striking. I felt sure I was not mistaken.'

'Troy,' Alleyn said, 'will be enormously gratified.'

'And then: that bet of Mr Merryman's was organized, wasn't it?'.

'Lord, Lord! I do seem to have made an ass of myself.'

'No, no. Not you. You were entirely convincing. It was the Captain.'

'His air of spontaneity *was* rather massive, perhaps.'

'Exactly.' Father Jourdain leant forward and said: 'Alleyn: why was that conversation about the Flower Murderer introduced?'

Alleyn said: 'For fun. Why else?'

'So you are not going to tell me.'

'At least,' Alleyn said lightly, 'I've got your alibi for January the fifteenth.'

'You don't trust me, of course.'

'It doesn't arise. As you have discovered, I am a policeman.'

'I beg you to trust me. You won't regret it. You can check my alibi, can't you? And the other time: the other poor child who was going to church – when was that? The twenty-fifth. Why, on the twenty-fifth I was at a conference in Paris. You can prove it at once. No doubt you're in touch with your colleagues. Of course you can.'

'I expect it can be done.'

'Then do it. I urge you to do it. If you are here for the fantastic reason I half-suspect, you will need someone you can trust.'

'It never comes amiss.'

'These women must not be left alone.' Father Jourdain had arisen and was staring through the glass doors. 'Look,' he said.

Mrs Dillington-Blick was taking a walk on deck. As she passed the lighted windows above the engine-rooms she paused. Her earrings and necklace twinkled, the crimson scarf she had wrapped about her head fluttered in the night breeze. A man emerged from the shadow of the centrecastle and walked towards her. He took her arm. They turned away and were lost to view. He was Aubyn Dale. 'You see,' Father Jourdain said. 'If I'm right, that's the sort of thing we mustn't allow.'

Alleyn said: 'Today is the seventh of February. These crimes have occurred at ten-day intervals.'

'But there have only been two.'

'There was an attempt on January fifth. It was not publicized.'

'Indeed! The fifth, the fifteenth and the twenty-fifth. Why then, ten days have already passed since the last crime. If you are right (and the interval after all may be a coincidence) the danger is acute.'

'On the contrary, if there's anything in the ten-day theory, Mrs Dillington-Blick at the moment is in no danger.'

'But – ' Father Jourdain stared at him. 'Do you mean there's been another of these crimes? Since we sailed? Why then – ?'

'About half an hour before you sailed and about two hundred yards away from the ship. On the night of the fourth. He was punctual almost to the minute.'

'Dear God!' said Father Jourdain.

'At the moment, of course, none of the passengers except the classic *one*, knows about this and unless anybody takes the trouble to cable the news to Las Palmas they won't hear about it there.'

'The fourteenth,' Father Jourdain muttered. 'You think we may be safe until the fourteenth.'

'One simply hopes so. All the same: shall we take the air before we turn in? I think we might.' Alleyn opened the doors. Father Jourdain moved towards them.

'It occurs to me,' he said, 'that you may think me a busybody. It's not that. It is, quite simply, that I have a nose for evil and a duty to prevent, if I can, the commission of sin. I am a spiritual policeman, in fact. You may feel that I'm talking professional nonsense.'

'I respect the point of view,' Alleyn said. For a moment they looked at each other. 'And, sir, I am disposed to trust you.'

'That, at least, is a step forward,' said Father Jourdain. 'Shall we leave it like that until you have checked my alibis?'

'If you're content to do so.'

'I haven't much choice,' Father Jourdain observed. He added, after a moment, 'and at any rate it *does* appear that we have an interval. Until February the fourteenth?'

'Only if the time theory is correct. It may not be correct.'

'I suppose – a psychiatrist – ?'

'Dr Makepiece, for instance. He's one. I'm thinking of consulting him.'

'But – '

'Yes?'

'He had no alibi. He said so.'

'They tell us,' Alleyn said, 'that the guilty man in a case of this sort never says he has no alibi. They say he always produces an alibi. Of some sort. Shall we go out?'

They went out on deck. A light breeze still held but it was no longer cold. The ship, ploughing through the dark, throbbed with her own life and with small orderly noises and yet was compact of a larger quietude. As they moved along the starboard side of the welldeck a bell sounded in four groups of two.

'Midnight,' Alleyn said. Sailors passed them, quiet-footed. Mrs Dillington-Blick and Aubyn Dale appeared on the far side of the hatch, making for the passengers' quarters. They called out good-night and disappeared.

Father Jourdain peered at his watch. 'And this afternoon we arrive at Las Palmas,' he said.

CHAPTER 6

Broken Doll

Las Palmas is known to tourists for its walkie-talkie dolls. They stare out of almost every shop-window, and sit in rows in the street bazaars near the wharves. They vary in size, cost and condition. Some have their garments cynically nailed to their bodies and others wear hand-sewn dresses of elaborate design. Some are bald under their bonnets, others have high Spanish wigs of real hair crowned with real lace mantillas. The most expensive of all are adorned with necklaces, bracelets and even rings and have masses of wonderful petticoats under their flowered and braided skirts. They can be as tall as a child or as short as a woman's hand.

Two things the dolls have in common. If you hold any one of them by the arm it may be induced to jerk its legs to and fro in a parody of walking and as it walks it also jerks its head from side to side and from within its body it ejaculates: 'Ma-ma.' They all squeak in the same way with voices that are shockingly like those of infants. Nearly everybody who goes to Las Palmas remembers either some little girl who would like a walkie-talkie doll or, however misguidedly, some grown woman who might possibly be amused by one.

The Company placed an open car at the disposal of Captain Bannerman and in it he put Mrs Dillington-Blick, looking like a piece of Turkish Delight. They drove about Las Palmas stopping at shops where the driver had a profitable understanding with the proprietor. Mrs Dillington-Blick bought herself a black lace near-mantilla with a good deal of metal in it, a comb to support it, some Portuguese jewellery and a fan. Captain Bannerman bought her a lot of artificial magnolias because they didn't see any real ones. He felt proud because all the Las Palmanians obviously admired her very much indeed. They came to a shop where a wonderful dress was displayed, a full Spanish dress made of black lace and caught up to display a foam of petticoats, scarlet, underneath. The driver kissed his fingers over and over again and intimated that if Mrs Dillington-Blick were to put it on she would look like the Queen of Heaven. Mrs Dillington-Blick examined it with her head on one side.

'Do you know,' she said, 'allowing for a little Latin exaggeration, I'm inclined to agree with him.'

Tim Makepiece and Jemima came along the street and joined them. Jemima said: '*Do* try it on. You'd look absolutely marvellous. Do. For fun.'

'Shall I? Come in with me, then. Make me keep my head.'

The Captain said he would go to his agents' offices where he had business to do and return in twenty minutes. Tim, who very much wanted to buy some roses for Jemima, also said he'd come back. Greatly excited, the two ladies entered the shop.

The stifling afternoon wore into evening. Dusk was rapidly succeeded by night, palm trees rattled in an enervated breeze and at nine o'clock, by arrangement, Captain Bannerman and Mrs Dillington-Blick were to meet Aubyn Dale at the grandest hotel in Las Palmas for dinner.

Mrs Dillington-Blick had been driven back to the ship where she changed into the wonderful Spanish dress which of course she had bought. She was excitedly assisted by Jemima: 'What did I tell you?' Jemima shouted triumphantly. 'You ought to be sitting in a box looking at a play by Lope de Vega with smashing caballeros all round you. It's a riot.' Mrs Dillington-Blick, who had never heard of Lope de Vega, half-smiled, opened her eyes very wide, turned and turned again to watch the effect in her looking-glass and said: 'Not bad. Really, it's not bad,' and pinned one of the Captain's artificial magnolias in her decolletage. She gave Jemima the brilliant look of a woman who knows she is successful.

'All the same,' she murmured, 'I can't help *rather* wishing it was the GB who was taking me out.'

'The GB?'

'My dear, the Gorgeous Brute. Glamorous Broderick, if you like. I dropped hints like thunder-bolts but no luck, alas.'

'Never mind,' Jemima said, 'you'll have a terrific success, anyway. I promise you.'

She ran off to effect her own change. It was when she fastened one of Tim Makepiece's red roses in her dress that it suddenly occurred to Jemima she hadn't thought of her troubles for at least six hours. After all, it *was* rather fun to be dining out in a foreign city on a strange island with a pleasant young man.

It all turned out superbly: an enchanted evening suspended like a dream, between the strange intervals of a sea voyage. The streets they drove through and the food they ate; the music they danced to, the flowers, the extremely romantic lighting and the exotic people were all, Jemima told Tim, 'out of this world'. They sat at their table on the edge of the dance floor, talked very fast about the things that interested them and were delighted to find how much they liked each other.

At half past nine Mrs Dillington-Blick arrived with the Captain and Aubyn Dale. She really was, as Jemima pointed out to Tim, sensational. Everybody looked at her. A kind of religious gravity impregnated the deportment of the head waiter. Opulence and observance enveloped her like an expensive scent. She *was* terrific.

'I admire her,' Jemima said, 'enormously. Don't you?'

Jemima's chin rested in the palm of her hand. Her forearm, much less opulent than Mrs Dillington-Blick's, shone in the candlelight and her eyes were bright.

Tim said: 'She's the most suffocatingly feminine job I've ever seen, I think. An all-time-high in what it takes. If, of course, that happens to be your line of country. It's not mine.'

Jemima found this answer satisfactory. 'I like her,' she said. 'She's warm and uncomplicated.'

'She's all that. Hallo! Look who's here!'

Alleyn came in with Father Jourdain. They were shown to a table at some distance from Tim's and Jemima's.

' "Distinguished visitors"!' Jemima said, gaily waving to them.

They are rather grand-looking, aren't they? I must say I like Broderick. Nice chap, don't you think?'

'Yes, I do,' Jemima said emphatically. 'What about Father Jourdain?'

'I wouldn't know. Interesting face: not typically clerical.'

'*Is* there a typically clerical face or are you thinking of comic curates at the Players Theatre Club?'

'No,' said Tim slowly. 'I'm not. But look at the mouth and the eyes. He's a celibate, isn't he? I bet it's been a bit of a hurdle.'

'Suppose,' Jemima said, 'you wanted advice very badly and had to go to one of those two. Which would it be?'

'Oh, Broderick. Every time. *Do* you by any chance want advice?'

'No.'

'If you did, I'd take it very kindly if you came to me.'

'Thank you,' said Jemima. 'I'll bear it in mind.'

'Good. Let's trip a measure.'

'Nice young couple,' said Father Jourdain as they danced past him and he added: 'I do hope you're right in what you say.'

'About – '

'About alibis.'

The band crashed and was silent. The floor cleared and two spotlights introduced a pair of tango dancers, very fierce, like game birds. They strutted and stalked, clattered their castanets, and frowned ineffably at each other. 'What an angry woo,' Tim said.

When they had finished they moved among the tables followed by their spotlight.

'Oh, *no*!' Father Jourdain exclaimed. 'Not *another* doll!'

It was an enormous and extraordinarily realistic one, carried by the woman dancer. Evidently it was for sale. She flashed brilliant smiles and proudly showed it off, while her escort stood moodily by. '*Senors e Senoras,*' announced a voice over the loudspeaker and added, they thought, something about have the honour to present '*La Esmeralda*' which was evidently the name of the doll.

'Curious!' Alleyn remarked.

'What!'

'It's dressed exactly like Mrs D-B.'

And so it was – in a flounced black lace dress and a mantilla. It even had a green necklace and earrings and lace gloves and its fingers were clamped round the handle of an open fan. It was a woman-doll with a bold, handsome face and a flashing smile like the dancer's. It looked terrifyingly expensive. Alleyn watched with some amusement as it approached the table where Mrs Dillington-Blick sat with the Captain and Aubyn Dale.

The dancers had of course noticed the resemblance and so had the head waiter. They all smiled and ejaculated and admired as the doll waddled beguilingly towards Mrs Dillington-Blick.

'Poor old Bannerman,' Alleyn said, 'he's sunk, I fear. Unless Dale – '

But Aubyn Dale extended his hands in his well-known gesture and with a smile of rueful frankness was obviously saying it was no good them looking at him, while the Captain, ruby-faced, stared in front of him with an expression of acute unconcern. Mrs Dillington-Blick shook her head and beamed and shook it again. The dancers bowed, smiled and moved on, approaching the next table. The woman stooped and with a kind of savage gaiety, induced the doll to walk. 'Ma-ma!' squeaked the doll. 'Ma-ma!'

'Ladies and Gentlemen,' the loudspeaker repeated and continued, this time in English, 'we have the honour to present Mees Esmeralda, Queen of Las Palmas.'

From somewhere in the shadows at the back of the room a napkin fluttered. The woman snatched up the doll and swept between the tables, followed by her escort. The spotlight settled on them. Heads were turned. One or two people stood up. It was impossible to see the person at the distant table. After a short delay the dancer returned, holding the doll aloft.

'She *hasn't* sold it,' Father Jourdain remarked.

'On the contrary,' Alleyn rejoined, 'I think she has. Look.'

The doll was borne in triumph to the Captain's table and with a magnificent curtsy, presented to Mrs Dillington-Blick.

At the other side of the room Tim said: 'Look at that, now!'

'What a triumph!' Jemima exclaimed delightedly.

'Who's the poor fish, do you suppose?'

'I can't see. It'll be some superb grandee with flashing eyes and a crimson cummerbund. What *fun* for Mrs Dillington-Blick.'

The dancers were making gestures in the direction of their customer. Mrs Dillington-Blick, laughing and triumphant holding the doll, strained round to see. The spotlight probed into the distant corner. Somebody stood up.

'Oh, *look!*' cried Jemima.

'Well, blow me down flat!' said Tim.

'How very surprising,' observed Father Jourdain, 'it's Mr McAngus!'

'He has made his reciprocal gesture,' said Alleyn.

II

The *Cape Farewell* sailed at two in the morning and the passengers were all to be aboard by half past one. Alleyn and Father Jourdain had returned at midnight and Alleyn had gone to his cabin to have another look at his mail. It included a detailed report from the Yard of the attack that had been made upon Miss Bijou Browne on January fifth and a letter from his senior saying nothing had developed that suggested alteration in Alleyn's plan of action. Alleyn had telephoned the Yard from Police Headquarters in Las Palmas and had spoken to Inspector Fox. Following Alleyn's radiogram of the previous night, the Yard had at once tackled the passengers' alibis. Father Jourdain was, Fox said, as good as gold. Mr Merryman's cinema had in fact shown *The Lodger* on the night in question as the first half of a double bill. The name of Aubyn Dale's sweetie so far eluded the Yard but Fox hoped to get it before long and would, he said, dream up some cock-and-bull story that might give him an excuse to question her about the night of the fifteenth. The rest of Dale's statement had been proved. Fox had got in touch with Mr Cuddy's Lodge and had told them the Police were making inquiries about a valuable watch. From information received they believed it had been stolen from Mr Cuddy near the Lodge premises on the night of the fifteenth. A record of attendances showed that Mr Cuddy had signed in but the secretary remembered that he left very early, feeling unwell. Apart from Mr McAngus having perforated his appendix four days after the date in question, Fox drily continued, it would be impossible to check his litter of disjointed reminiscence. They would, however, poke about and see if anything cropped up. An inquiry at Dr Makepiece's hospital gave conclusive evidence that he had been on duty there until midnight.

Captain Bannerman, it appeared, had certainly been in Liverpool on the night of the fifteenth and a routine check completely cleared the other officers. In any case it was presumed that the ship's complement didn't go aboard clutching passengers' embarkation notices.

The missing portion of the embarkation notice had not been found.

A number of psychiatric authorities had been consulted and all agreed that the ten-day interval would probably be maintained and that the fourteenth February, therefore, might be anticipated as a deadline. One of them added, however, that the subject's homicidal urge might be exacerbated by an untoward event. Which meant, Inspector Fox supposed drily, that he might cut up for trouble before the fourteenth: if a bit of what he fancied turned up in the meantime and did the trick.

Fox concluded the conversation by inquiring about the weather and on being told it was semi-tropical remarked that some people had all the luck. Alleyn had rejoined that if Fox considered a long voyage with a homicidal maniac (identity unknown and boiling up for trouble) and at least two eminently suitable victims, was a bit of luck, he'd be glad to swap jobs with him. On this note they rang off.

Alleyn had also received a cable from his wife which said: 'Lodging petition for desertion do you want anything sent anywhere love darling Troy.'

He put his papers away and went down to the well-deck. It was now twenty minutes past midnight but none of the passengers had gone to bed. The Cuddys were in the lounge telling Dennis, with whom they were on informal terms, about their adventures ashore. Mr Merryman reclined in a deck-chair with his arms folded and his hat over his nose. Mr McAngus and Father Jourdain leant on the taffrail and stared down at the wharf below. The after-hatch was open and the winch that served it still in operation. The night was oppressively warm.

Alleyn strolled along the deck and looked down into the after-hatch, yawning black, and at the dramatically lit figures that worked it. The rattle of the winch, the occasional voices and the pulse of the engines made a not unattractive accompaniment to the gigantic fishing operation. He had watched and listened for some minutes before he became aware of another and most unexpected sound. Quite close at hand was someone singing in Latin: an austere, strangely measured and sexless chant.

> *Procul recedant somnia*
> *Et noctium phantasmata*
> *Hostemque nostrum comprime*
> *Ne polluantur corpora.*

Alleyn moved across the after end of the deck. In the little veran-dah, just visible in reflected light, sat Miss Abbott, singing. She stopped at once when she saw him. She had under her hands what appeared to be many sheets of paper; perhaps an immensely long letter.

'That was lovely,' Alleyn said, 'I wish you hadn't stopped. It was extraordinarily – what? – tranquil?'

She said, more it seemed to herself than to him: 'Yes. Tranquil and devout. It's music designed against devils.'

'What *were* you singing?'

She roused herself suddenly and became defensive. It seemed incredible that her speaking voice could be so harsh.

'A Vatican plainsong,' she said.

'What a fool I was to blunder in and stop you. Would it be – seventh century?'

'Six-fifty-five. Printed from manuscript in the *Liber Gradualis*, 1883,' she barked and got up.

Alleyn said: 'Don't move. I'll take myself off.'

'I'm going anyway.' She walked straight past him. Her eyes were dark with excitement. She strode along the deck to the lighted area where the others were congregated, sat in a deck-chair a little apart from them and began to read her letter.

After a minute or two Alleyn also returned and joined Mr McAngus. 'That was a charming gesture of yours this evening,' he said.

Mr McAngus made a little tittering sound. 'I was so lucky!' he said. 'Such a happy coincidence, wasn't it? And the resemblance, you know, is complete. I *promised* I'd find something and *there* it was. So very appropriate, I felt.' He hesitated for a moment and added rather wistfully, 'I was invited to join their party but of course, I thought, better to decline. She seemed quite delighted. At the doll, I mean. The doll delighted her.'

'I'm sure it did.'

'Yes,' Mr McAngus said. 'Yes.' His voice had trailed away into a murmur. He was no longer aware of Alleyn but looked past him and down towards the wharf.

It was now twenty past one. A taxi had come along the wharf. Out of it got Jemima Carmichael and Tim Makepiece, talking busily and obviously on the best possible terms with each other and the world at large. They came up the gangway smiling all over their faces. 'Oh!' Jemima exclaimed to Alleyn. 'Isn't Las Palmas Heaven? We *have* had such fun.'

But it was not at Jemima that Mr McAngus stared so fixedly. An open car had followed the taxi and in it were Mrs Dillington-Blick, the Captain and Aubyn Dale. They too were gay but with a more ponderous gaiety than Tim's and Jemima's. The men's faces were darkish and their voices heavy. Mrs Dillington-Blick still looked marvellous. Her smile, if not exactly irrepressible, was full of meaning and if her eyes no longer actually sparkled they were still extremely expressive and the tiny pockets underneath them, scarcely noticeable. The men helped her up the gangway. The Captain went first. He carried the doll and held Mrs Dillington-Blick's elbow while Aubyn Dale put his hands on her waist and made a great business of assisting her from the rear. There were jokes and a lot of suppressed laughter.

When they arrived on deck the Captain went up to the bridge and Mrs Dillington-Blick held court. Mr McAngus was made much of, Father Jourdain appealed to and Alleyn given a great many side-long glances. The doll was exhibited and the Cuddys came out to see it. Mrs Cuddy said she supposed the dolls were produced with sweated labour but Mr Cuddy stared at Mrs Dillington-Blick and said, with an odd inflection, that there were some things that couldn't be copied. Alleyn was made to walk with the doll and Mrs Dillington-Blick went behind, imitating its action, jerking her head and squeaking: 'Ma-ma!'

Miss Abbott put down her letter and stared at Mrs Dillington-Blick with a kind of hungry amazement.

'Mr Merryman!' cried Mrs Dillington-Blick. 'Wake up! Let me introduce my twin sister Donna Esmeralda.'

Mr Merryman removed his hat, gazed at the doll with distaste and then at its owner.

'The resemblance,' he said, 'is too striking to arouse any emotion but one of profound misgiving.'

'Ma-ma!' squeaked Mrs Dillington-Blick.

Dennis trotted out on deck, plumply smiling, and approached her. 'A night-lettergram for *you*, Mrs Dillington-Blick. It came after you'd gone *ashore*. I've been looking out for you. Oh, mercy!' he added, eyeing the doll, 'isn't she *twee*!'

Mr Merryman contemplated Dennis with something like horror and replaced his hat over his nose.

Mrs Dillington-Blick gave a sharp ejaculation and fluttered her open night-lettergram.

'My dears!' she shouted. 'You'll never credit this! How too frightful and murky! My dears!'

'Darling!' Aubyn Dale exclaimed. 'What?'

'It's from a man, a friend of mine. You'll *never* believe it. Listen! "Sent masses of hyacinths to ship but shop informs me young female taking them latest victim flower murderer stop card returned by police stop what a thing stop have lovely trip Tony"!'

III

Her fellow-passengers were so excited by Mrs Dillington-Blick's news that they scarcely noticed their ship's sailing. *Cape Farewell* separated herself from Las Palmas with an almost imperceptible gesture and moved away into the dark, taking up the rhythm of her voyage, while Mrs Dillington-Blick held the stage.

They all gathered round her and Mr Cuddy managed to get close enough to look sideways at the night-lettergram. Mr Merryman, with an affectation of stretching his legs, strolled nearer, his head thrown back at an angle that enabled him to stare superciliously from under his hat brim at Mrs Dillington-Blick. Even Miss Abbott leant forward in her chair, grasping her crumpled letter, her large hands dangling between her knees. Captain Bannerman, who had come down from the bridge, looked much too knowing for Alleyn's peace of mind, and repeatedly attempted to catch his eye. Alleyn avoided him, plunged into the mêlée and was himself loud in ejaculation and comment. There was much speculation as to where and when the girl who brought the flowers could have been murdered. Out of the general conversation Mrs Cuddy's voice rose shrilly: 'And it was hyacinths again, too. Fancy! What a coincidence.'

'My dear madam,' Dr Makepiece testily pointed out, 'the flowers are in season. No doubt the shops are full of them. There is no esoteric significance in the circumstance.'

'Mr Cuddy never fancied them,' said Mrs Cuddy. 'Did you dear?'

Mr Merryman raised his hands in a gesture of despair, turned his back on her and ran slap into Mr McAngus. There was a clash of spectacles and a loud oath from Mr Merryman. The two gentlemen began to behave like simultaneous comedians. They stooped, crashed heads, cried out in anguish and rose clutching each other's spectacles, hat and hyacinth.

'I am so very sorry,' said Mr McAngus, holding his head. 'I hope you're not hurt.'

'I am hurt. That is my hat, sir, and those are my glasses. Broken.'

'I do trust you have a second pair.'

'The existence of a second pair does not reduce the value of the first which is, I see at a glance, irrevocably shattered,' said Mr Merryman. He flung down Mr McAngus's hyacinth and returned to his chair.

The others still crowded about Mrs Dillington-Blick. As they all stood there, so close together that the smell of wine on their breath mingled with Mrs Dillington-Blick's heavy scent, there was, Alleyn thought, a classic touch, a kind of ghastly neatness in the situation if indeed one of them was the murderer they all so eagerly discussed.

Presently Jemima and Tim moved away and then Father Jourdain walked aft and leant on the rails. Mrs Cuddy announced that she was going to bed and took Mr Cuddy's arm. The whole thing, she said, had given her quite a turn. Her husband seemed reluctant to follow her but on Mrs Dillington-Blick and Aubyn Dale going indoors the whole party broke up and disappeared severally through doors or into shadows.

Captain Bannerman came up to Alleyn. 'How about that one?' he said. 'Upsets your little game a bit, doesn't it?' and loudly belched. 'Pardon me,' he added. 'It's the fancy muck we had for dinner.'

'Eight of them don't know where it happened and they don't know exactly when,' Alleyn pointed out. 'The ninth knows everything anyway. It doesn't matter all that much.'

'It matters damn' all seeing the whole idea's an error.' The Captain made a wide gesture. 'Well – look at them. I ask you. Look at the way they behave and everything.'

'How do you expect him to behave? Go about in a black sombrero making loud animal noises? Heath had very nice manners. Still, you may be right. By the way, Father Jourdain and Makepiece seem to be in the clear. And you, sir. I thought you'd like to know. The Yard's been checking alibis.'

'Ta,' said the Captain gloomily and began to count on his fingers. 'That leaves Cuddy, Merryman, Dale and that funny old bastard what's-'is-name.'

'McAngus.'

'That's right. Well, I ask you! I'm turning in,' added the Captain. 'I'm a wee bit plastered. She's a wonderful woman though. Goodni'.'

'Goodnight, sir.'

The Captain moved away, paused and came back.

'I had a signal from the Company,' he said. 'They don't want any kind of publicity and in my opinion they're right. They reckon it's all my eye. They don't want the passengers upset for nothing and n'more do I. You might 'member that.'

'I'll do my best.'

'At sea – Master's orders.'

'Sir.'

'Ver' well.' The Captain made a vague gesture and climbed carefully up the companionway to the bridge.

Alleyn walked aft to where Father Jourdain, still leaning on the taffrail, his hands loosely folded, stared out into the night.

'I've been wondering,' Alleyn said, 'if you played Horatio's part just now.'

'I? Horatio?'

'Observing with the very comment of your soul.'

'Oh, that! If that's to be my role! I did, certainly, watch the men.'

'So did I. How about it?'

'Nothing. Nothing at all. Unless you count Mr Merryman keeping his hat over his face or his flying into a temper.'

'Or Mr Cuddy's overt excitement.'

'Or Mr McAngus's queer little trick of dancing backwards and forwards. No!' Father Jourdain exclaimed strongly. 'No! I can't believe it of any of them. And yet – '

'Do you still smell evil?'

'I begin to ask myself if I merely imagine it.'

'As well you may,' Alleyn agreed. 'I ask myself continually if we're building a complete fantasy round the fragment of paper clutched in that wretched girl's hand. But then – You see, you all had your embarkation notices when you came aboard. Or so it seems. Could one of the lost ones – yours, for instance, have blown through the porthole to the dock and into her hand? No. The portholes were all shut as they always are when the ship's tied up. Let's take a turn, shall we?'

They walked together down the well-deck on the port side. When they reached the little verandah aft of the engine house they stopped while Alleyn lit his pipe. The night was still very warm but they had run into a stiff breeze and the ship was alive with it. There was a high thrumming sound in the shrouds.

'Someone singing,' Alleyn said.

'Isn't it the wind in those ropes? Shrouds, don't they call them? I wonder why.'

'No. Listen. It's clearer now.'

'So it is. Someone singing.'

It was a high rather sweet voice and seemed to come from the direction of the passengers' quarters.

' "The Broken Doll," ' Alleyn said.

'A strangely old-fashioned choice.'

> ' "You'll be sorry some day
> You left behind a Broken Doll." '

The thin commonplace tune evaporated.

'It's stopped, now,' said Alleyn.

'Yes. Should these women be warned, then?' Father Jourdain asked as they continued their walk. 'Before the deadline approaches?'

'The Shipping Company is all against it and so's the Captain. My bosses tell me, as far as possible to respect their wishes. They think the women should be protected without knowing it, which is all bloody fine for them. Makepiece, by the way, seems OK. We'll tell him, I think. He'll be delighted to protect Miss Carmichael.'

Like the Captain, Father Jourdain said: 'That leaves Dale, Merryman, Cuddy and McAngus.' But unlike the Captain he added: 'I suppose it's possible. I suppose so.' He put his hand on Alleyn's arm. 'You'll think I'm ridiculously inconsistent: it's only that I've remembered – ' He stopped for a moment, and his fingers closed over Alleyn's coatsleeve.

'Yes?' Alleyn said.

'You see, I'm a priest: an Anglo-Catholic priest. I hear confessions. It's a humbling and an astonishing duty. One never stops being dumbfounded at the unexpectedness of sin.'

Alleyn said: 'I suppose in a way the same observation might apply to my job.'

They walked on in silence, rounded the end of the hatch and returned to the port side. The lights in the lounge were out and great pools of shadow lay about the deck.

'It's an awful thing to say,' Father Jourdain observed abruptly, 'but do you know, for a moment I almost found myself wishing that rather than go in such frightful uncertainty, we knew, positively, that this murderer was on board.' He turned aside to sit on the hatch. The hatch-coaming cast a very deep shadow along the deck. He seemed to wade into it as if it were a ditch.

'Ma-ma!'

The voice squeaked horridly from under his feet. He gave a stifled ejaculation and lurched against the hatch.

'Good Heavens, what have I done!' cried Father Jourdain.

'By the sound of it,' Alleyn said, 'I should say you've trodden on Esmeralda.'

He stooped. His hands encountered lace, a hard dead surface and something else. 'Don't move,' he said. 'Just a moment.'

He carried a pencil-thin flashlamp in his pocket. The beam darted out like a replica in miniature of PC Moir's torch.

'Have I broken it?' asked Father Jourdain, anxiously.

'It was already broken. Look.'

It was indeed broken. The head had been twisted so far and with such violence that Esmeralda now grinned over her left shoulder at a quite impossible angle. The black lace mantilla was wound tightly round the neck and lying on the rigid bosom was a litter of emerald beads and a single crushed hyacinth.

'You've got your wish,' Alleyn said. 'He's on board, all right.'

IV

Captain Bannerman pushed his fingers through his sandy hair and rose from his sitting-room table.

'It's half past two,' he said, 'and for any good the stuff I drank last night does me, I might as well have not taken it. I need a dram and I advise you gentlemen to join me.'

He dumped a bottle of whisky and four glasses on the table and was careful not to touch a large object that lay there, covered with a newspaper. 'Neat?' he asked. 'Water? Or soda?'

Alleyn and Father Jourdain had soda and Tim Makepiece water. The Captain took his neat.

'You know,' Tim said. 'I can't get myself geared to this situation. Really, it's jolly nearly impossible to believe it.'

'I don't,' said the Captain. 'The doll was a joke. A damn' nasty, spiteful kind of joke, mind. But a joke. I'll be sugared if I think I've shipped a Jack the Ripper. Now!'

'No, no,' Father Jourdain murmured. 'I'm afraid I can't agree. Alleyn?'

Alleyn said: 'I suppose the joke idea's just possible. Given the kind of person and all the talk about these cases and the parallel circumstances.'

'There you are!' Captain Bannerman said triumphantly. 'And if you ask me, we haven't got far to look for the kind of chap. Dale's a great card for practical jokes. Always at it on his own confession. Bet you what you like – '

'No, no!' Father Jourdain protested, 'I can't agree. He'd never perpetrate such an unlovely trick. No.'

Alleyn said: 'I can't agree either. In my opinion: literally it's no joke.'

Tim said slowly: 'I suppose you all noticed that – well that Mr McAngus was wearing a hyacinth in his coat.'

Father Jourdain and the Captain exclaimed but Alleyn said: 'And that he dropped it when he clashed heads with Mr Merryman. And that Mr Merryman picked it up and threw it down on the deck.'

'Ah!' said the Captain triumphantly. 'There you are! What's the good of that!'

'Where,' Tim asked, 'did she leave the doll?'

'On the hatch. She put it there when she got her cable and evidently forgot to take it indoors. It was just above the spot where we found it which was about three feet away from the place where Merryman threw down the hyacinth: everything was nice and handy.' He turned to Tim. 'You and Miss Carmichael were the first to leave the general group. I think you walked over to the starboard side, didn't you?'

Tim, pink in the face, nodded.

'Er – yes.'

'Do you mind telling me *exactly* where?'

'Er – no. No. Naturally not. It was – where was it? Well, it was sort of a bit farther along than the doorway into the passengers' quarters. There's a seat.'

'And you were there, would you say – for how long?'

'Well – er – '

'Until after the group of passengers on deck had dispersed?'

'O, lord, yes! Yes.'

'Did you notice whether any of them went in or, more importantly, came out again, by that doorway?'

'Er – no. No.'

'Gentlemen of your vintage,' Alleyn said mildly, 'from the point of view of evidence are no damn' good until you fall in love and then you're no damn' good.'

'Well, I must say!'

'Never mind. I think I know how they dispersed. Mr Merryman, whose cabin is the first on the left of the passage on the starboard side and has windows looking aft and to that side went in at the passengers' doorway near you. He was followed by Mr McAngus who has the cabin opposite his across the passage. The others all moved away in the opposite direction and presumably went in by the equivalent passengers' entrance on the port side, with the exception

of Mrs Dillington-Blick and Aubyn Dale who used the glass doors
into the lounge. Captain Bannerman and I had a short conversation
and he returned to the bridge. Father Jourdain and I then walked to
the after end or back or rear or whatever you call it of the deck
where there's a verandah and where we could see nothing. It must
have been at that moment somebody returned and garrotted
Esmeralda.'

'How d'you remember all that?' Captain Bannerman demanded.

'God bless my soul, I'm on duty.' Alieyn turned to Father
Jourdain. 'The job must have been finished before we walked back
along the starboard side.'

'Must it?'

'Don't you remember? We heard someone singing: "A Broken
Doll." '

Father Jourdain passed his hand across his eyes. 'This is, it really
is, quite beastly.'

'It appears that he always sings when he's finished.'

Tim said suddenly: 'We heard it. Jemima and I. It wasn't far off.
On the other side. We thought it was a sailor but actually it sounded
rather like a choirboy.'

'Oh, please!' Father Jourdain ejaculated and at once added,
'Sorry. Silly remark.'

'Here!' the Captain interposed, jabbing a square finger at the
newspaper-covered form on the table. 'Can't you do any of this
funny business with fingerprints? What about them?'

Alieyn said he'd try, of course, but he didn't expect there'd be any
that mattered as their man was believed to wear gloves. He very gingerly removed the newspaper and there, shockingly large, smirking,
with her detached head looking over her shoulder, was Esmeralda. In
any case, Alleyn pointed out, the mantilla had been wound so tightly
round the neck that any fingerprints would be obliterated.

'It's a right-handed job, I think,' he said. 'But as we've no
left-handed passengers that doesn't cast a blinding light on anything.' He eased away the black lace, exposing part of the pink
plastic neck. 'He tried the necklace first but he never has any luck
with beads. They break. You can see the dents in the paint.'

He dropped the newspaper over the doll and looked at Tim
Makepiece.

'This sort of thing's up your street, isn't it?'

Tim said: 'If it wasn't for the immediacy of the problem it'd be damned interesting. It still is. It looks like a classic. The repetition, the time factor – by the way the doll's out of step in that respect, isn't it?'

'Yes,' Alleyn said. 'Dead out. It's six days too soon. Would you say that made the time theory look pretty sick?'

'On the face of it – no, I don't think I would; although one shouldn't make those sorts of pronouncements. But I'd think the doll being inanimate might be – well, a kind of extra.'

'A *jeu d'esprit*?'

'Yes. Like a Donald Campbell amusing himself with a toy speed-boat. It wouldn't interfere with the normal programme. That'd be my guess. But if one could only get him to talk.'

'You can try and get all of 'em to talk,' said Captain Bannerman sardonically. 'No harm in trying.'

'It's a question, isn't it,' Alleyn said, 'of what we are going to do about it. It seems to me there are three courses open to us. A: We can make the whole situation known to everybody in the ship and hold a routine inquiry, but I'm afraid that won't get us much further. I could ask if there were alibis for the other occasions, of course, but our man would certainly produce one and there would be no imme-diate means of checking it. We know, by the way, that Cuddy hasn't got one for the other occasion.'

'Do we?' said the Captain woodenly.

'Yes. He went for a walk after leaving his silver-wedding bouquet at a hospital.'

'My God!' Tim said softly.

'On the other hand an inquiry would mean that my man is fully warned and at the cost of whatever anguish to himself goes to earth until the end of the voyage. So I don't make an arrest and at the other side of the world more girls are killed by strangulation. B: We can warn the women privately and I give you two guesses as to what sort of privacy we might hope to preserve after warning Mrs Cuddy. C: We can take such of your senior officers as you think fit, into our confidence, form ourselves into a sort of vigilance committee and try by observation and undercover inquiry to get more information before taking action.'

'Which is the only course *I'm* prepared to sanction,' said Captain Bannerman. 'And that's flat.'

Alleyn looked thoughtfully at him. 'Then it's just as well,' he said, 'that at the moment it appears to be the only one that's at all practicable.'

'That makes four suspects to watch,' Tim said after a pause.

'Four?' Alleyn said. 'Everybody says four. You may all be right, of course. I'm almost inclined to reduce the field, tentatively, you know, very tentatively. It seems to me that at least one of your four is in the clear.'

They stared at him. 'Are we to know which?' Father Jourdain asked.

Alleyn told him.

'Dear me!' he said. 'How excessively stupid of me. But of course.'

'And then, for two of the others,' Alleyn said apologetically, 'there are certain indications: nothing like certainties, you might object, and yet I'm inclined to accept them as working hypotheses.'

'But look here!' Tim said, 'that would mean – '

He was interrupted by Captain Bannerman. 'Do you mean to sit there,' he roared out, 'and tell us you think you know who done – damnation! – who did it?'

'I'm not sure. Not nearly enough, but I fancy so.'

After a long pause Father Jourdain said: 'Well – again, are we to know which? And why?'

Alleyn waited for a moment. He glanced at the Captain's face, scarlet with incredulity, and then at the other two: dubious, perhaps a little resentful.

'I think perhaps better not,' he said.

V

When at last he went to bed, Alleyn was unable to sleep. He listened to the comfortable pulse of the ship's progress and seemed to hear beyond it a thin whistle of a voice lamenting a broken doll. If he closed his eyes it was to find Captain Bannerman's face, blown with obstinacy, stupid and intractable, and Esmeralda, smirking over her shoulder. And even as he told himself that this must be the beginning of a dream, he was awake again. He searched for some exercise to discipline his thoughts and remembered Miss Abbott's plainsong chant. Suppose Mr Merryman had ordered him to do it into English verse?

> *Dismiss the dreams that sore affright*
> *Phantasmagoria of the night.*
> *Confound our carnal enemy*
> *Let not our flesh corrupted be.*

'No! *No!* NO!' Mr Merryman shouted, coming very close and handing him an embarkation notice. 'You have completely misinterpreted the poem. My compliments to the Captain and request him to lay on six of the best.'

Mr Merryman then opened his mouth very wide, turned to Mr Cuddy and jumped overboard. Alleyn began to climb a rope ladder with Mrs Dillington-Blick on his back and, thus burdened, at last fell heavily to sleep.

CHAPTER 7

After Las Palmas

The passengers always met for coffee in the lounge at eleven o'clock. On the morning after Las Palmas this ceremony marked the first appearance of Mrs Dillington-Blick and Aubyn Dale, neither of whom had come down for breakfast. It was a day with an enervating faint wind and the coffee was iced.

Alleyn had chosen this moment to present Mrs Dillington-Blick with the *disjecta membra* of Esmeralda. She had already sent Dennis to find the doll and was as fretful as a good-natured woman can be when he came back empty-handed. Alleyn told her that at a late hour he and Father Jourdain had discovered Esmeralda lying on the deck. He then indicated the newspaper parcel that he had laid out on the end of the table.

He did this at the moment when the men of the party and Miss Abbott were gathered round the coffee. Mrs Cuddy, Mrs Dillington-Blick and Jemima always allowed themselves the little ceremony of being waited upon by the gentlemen. Miss Abbott consistently lined herself up in the queue and none of the men had the temerity to question this procedure.

With the connivance of Father Jourdain and Tim Makepiece, Alleyn unveiled Esmeralda at the moment when Aubyn Dale, Mr Merryman, Mr Cuddy and Mr McAngus were hard by the table.

'Here she is,' he said, 'and I'm afraid she presents rather a sorry sight.'

He flicked the newspaper away in one jerk. Mrs Dillington-Blick cried out sharply.

Esmeralda lying on her back with her head twisted over her shoulder and the beads and dead hyacinth in position.

After its owner's one ejaculation the doll's exposure was followed by a dead silence and then by a violent oath from Mr Merryman.

Almost simultaneously Miss Abbott ejaculated: 'Don't!'

Her cup of iced coffee had tilted and the contents had fallen over Mr Merryman's hands.

Miss Abbott moistened her lips and said: 'You must have jolted my arm, Mr Merryman.'

'My dear Madam, I did nothing of the sort!' he contradicted and angrily flipped his hands. Particles of iced coffee flew in all directions. One alighted on Mr Cuddy's nose. He seemed to be quite unaware of it. Half smiling, he stared at Esmeralda and with lightly clasped fingers revolved his thumbs slowly round each other.

Aubyn Dale said loudly: 'Why have you done this! It looks disgusting.' He reached out and with a quick movement brushed the dead hyacinth off the doll. The beads fell away with a clatter and rolled about the table. Dale straightened the flashily smiling head.

Mr McAngus murmured gently: 'She looks quite herself again, doesn't she? Perhaps she can be mended.'

'I don't understand all this,' Dale said angrily to Alleyn. 'Why did you do it?'

'Do what, exactly?'

'Lay it out like that. Like – like – '

Mrs Cuddy said with relish: 'Like one of those poor girls. Flowers and beads and everything: giving us all such a turn.'

'The doll,' Alleyn said, 'is exactly as Father Jourdain and I found it: hyacinth and all. I'm sorry if it's upset anyone.'

Mrs Dillington-Blick had come to the table. It was the first time, Alleyn thought, that he had seen her without so much as a flicker of a smile on her face. 'Was it like that?' she asked. 'Why? What happened?'

Dale said: 'Don't worry, darling Ruby. Somebody must have trodden on it and broken the beads and – and the neck.'

'I trod on it,' Father Jourdain said. 'I'm most awfully sorry, Mrs Dillington-Blick, but it was lying on the deck in pitch-dark shadow.'

There you are!' Dale exclaimed. He caught Alleyn's eye and recovered something of his professional bonhomie. 'Sorry, old boy.

I didn't mean to throw a temperament. You gathered the doll up just as it was. No offence, I hope?'

'None in the wide world,' Alleyn rejoined politely.

Mrs Cuddy said: 'Yes: but all the same it's funny about the flowers, isn't it, dear?'

'That's right, dear. Funny.'

'Being a hyacinth and all. Such a coincidence.'

'That's right,' smiled Mr Cuddy. 'Funny.'

Mr Merryman, who was still fretfully drying his hands on his handkerchief, suddenly cried out in anguish.

'I was mad enough to suppose,' Mr Merryman lamented, 'that in undertaking this voyage I would escape, however briefly, from the egregious, the remorseless ambiguities of the lower school urchin. "Funny! Funny!" Will you be so kind, my good Cuddy, as to enlighten us? In what respect do you consider droll, entertaining or amusing the discovery of a wilted hyacinth upon the bosom of this disarticulated puppet? For my part,' Mr Merryman added with some violence, 'I find the obvious correlation altogether beastly. And the inescapable conclusion that I myself was, hypothetically at least, responsible for its presence, adds to my distaste. "Funny!" ' Mr Merryman concluded in a fury and flung up his hands.

The Cuddys eyed him with dawning resentment. Mr McAngus said brightly: 'But of course. I'd *quite* forgotten. It was *my* hyacinth. You took it, do you recollect? When we had our little collision? And threw it down.'

'I did *not* "take" it.'

'Accidentally, of course. I meant, accidentally.' Mr McAngus bent over the doll. His reddish knotted fingers manipulated the neck. 'I'm *sure* she can be mended,' he said.

Mrs Dillington-Blick said in a constrained voice: 'Do you know – I *hope* you'll forgive me, Mr McAngus, and I expect I'm being dreadfully silly – but do you know I don't somehow think I feel quite the same about Esmeralda. I don't believe I want her mended, or at any rate not for me. Perhaps we could think of some little girl – you may have a niece.' Her voice faded into an apologetic murmur.

With a kind of social readiness that consorted very ill with the look in his eyes, Mr McAngus said: 'But of course. I quite understand.' His hands were still closed round the neck of the doll. He looked at them, seemed to recollect himself, and turned aside. 'I quite understand,' he repeated, and helped himself to a herbal cigarette.

Mrs Cuddy, relentless as a Greek chorus, said: 'All the same it *does* seem funny.' Mr Merryman gave a strangulated cry but she went on greedily, 'The way we were all talking about those murders. You know. And then the way Mrs Blick got that cable from her gentleman-friend about the girl being murdered who brought the flowers. And the way hyacinths keep turning up. You'd almost think it was intentional, really you would.' She stared in her unwinking fashion at Mrs Dillington-Blick. 'I don't wonder you feel funny about it with the doll being dressed like you. You know. It might almost *be* you, lying there, mightn't it, Mrs Blick?'

Miss Abbott struck her big hands together. 'For God's sake!' she ejaculated, 'do we have to listen to all this. Can't someone take that thing away!'

'Of course,' Alleyn said and dropped the newspaper over the doll. 'I can.'

He gathered up the unwieldy parcel and took it to his cabin.

II

'As usual,' he wrote to his wife, 'I miss you very much. I miss – ' He paused and looked, without seeing them, at the objects in his cabin. He reflected on the odd circumstance that although his memory had been trained for a long time to retain with scrupulous accuracy the various items of human faces, it always let him down when he wanted it to show Troy to him. Her photograph was not much good, after all. It merely reminded him of features he knew but couldn't visualize: it was only a map of her face. He put something of this down in his letter, word after careful word, and then began to write about the case in hand, setting out in detail everything that had happened since his last letter had been posted in Las Palmas.

' – so you see,' he wrote, 'the nature of the predicament. I'm miles away from the point where one can even begin to think of making an arrest. All I've been able to do is whittle down the field of possibles. Do you agree? Have you arrived at the predominantly possible one? I'm sure you have. I'm making a mystery about nothing which must be the last infirmity of the police mind.

'Meanwhile we have laid a plan of action that is purely negative. The First and Second Mates and the Chief Engineer have been put wise by the Captain. They all think with him that the whole idea is completely up the pole and that our man's not on board. But they'll fall in with the general scheme and at this moment are delightedly and vigilantly keeping an eye on the ladies who, by the way, have been told that there have been thefts on board and that they'll be well advised to lock their doors, day and night. It's been made very clear that Dennis, the queer fat steward, you know, is not suspected.

'From almost every point of view,' Alleyn went on after a pause, 'these cases are the worst of the lot. One is always hag-ridden by one's personal conviction that the law is desperately inadequate in its dealings with them. One wonders what sort of frightfulness is at work behind the unremarkable face, the more-or-less unexceptionable behaviour. What *is* the reality? With a psychiatrist, a priest and a policeman all present we've got the ingredients for a Pirandello play, haven't we? Jourdain and Makepiece are due here now and no doubt I shall get two completely opposed professional opinions from them. In fact – '

There was a tap on the door. Alleyn hurriedly wrote: ' – here they are. *Au revoir*, darling,' and called out: 'Come in.'

Father Jourdain now wore a thin light-coloured suit, a white shirt and a black tie. The change in his appearance was quite startling: it was as if a stranger had walked in.

'I really *don't* feel,' he said, 'that the mortification of a dog collar in the tropics is required of me. I shall put it on for dinner and, on Sunday, I shall sweat in my decent cassock. The sight of you two in your gents' tropical suitings was too much for me. I bought this in Las Palmas and in happier circumstances would get a great deal of pleasure out of wearing it.'

They sat down and looked at Alleyn with an air of expectancy. It occurred to him that however sincerely they might deplore the presence of a homicidal monster as their fellow-traveller they were nevertheless stimulated in a way that was not entirely unpleasurable. They were both, he thought, energetic inquisitive men and each in his own mode had a professional interest in the matter in hand.

'Well,' he said, when they were settled, 'how do you feel about Operation Esmeralda?'

They agreed, it appeared, that nothing had happened to contradict Alleyn's theory. The reaction to the doll had been pretty well what he had predicted.

'Though the trouble is,' Father Jourdain added, 'that when one is looking for peculiar behaviour one seems to see it all over the place. I must confess that I found Dale's outburst, the Cuddys' really almost gloating relish, Merryman's intolerable pedantry and McAngus's manipulations equally disturbing. Of course it doesn't arise,' he added after a pause, 'but even poor Miss Abbott behaved, or so it seemed to me, with a kind of extravagance. I suppose I lost my eye.'

'Why,' Alleyn asked, 'do you call her *"poor* Miss Abbott"?'

'Oh, my dear Alleyn! I think you know very well. The problem of the unhappy spinster crops up all along the line in my job.'

Tim gave an inarticulate grunt.

'Yes,' Alleyn said, 'she *is* obviously unhappy.' He looked at Tim. 'What did that knowledgeable noise mean?'

Tim said impatiently: 'We're not concerned with Miss Abbott, I imagine, but it meant that I too recognize the type though perhaps my diagnosis would not appeal to Father Jourdain.'

'Would it not?' Father Jourdain said. 'I should like to hear it all the same.'

Tim said rapidly: 'No, really. I mustn't bore you and at any rate one has no business to go by superficial impressions. It's just that on the face of it she's a textbook example of the woman without sexual attraction who hasn't succeeded in finding a satisfactory adjustment.'

Alleyn looked up from his clasped hands. 'From your point of view isn't that also true of the sort of homicide we're concerned with?'

'Invariably, I should say. These cases almost always point back to some childish tragedy in which the old gang – fear, frustration and jealousy, have been predominant. This is true of most psychological abnormalities. For instance: as a psychotherapist I would, if I got the chance, try to discover why hyacinths make Mr Cuddy feel ill and I'd expect to find the answer in some incident that may have been thrust completely into his subconscious and that superficially may seem to have no direct reference to hyacinths. And with Aubyn Dale, I'd be interested to hunt down the basic reason for his love of practical jokes. While if Mr Merryman were my patient I'd try and find a reason for his chronic irritability.'

'Dyspepsia no good?' Alleyn asked. 'He's for ever taking sodamints.'

'All dyspeptics are not irritable woman-haters. I'd expect to find that his indigestion is associated with some very long-standing psychic disturbance.'

'Such as his nurse having snatched away his favourite rattle and given it to his papa?'

'You might not be as far out as you may think you are, at that.'

'What about Dale and McAngus?'

'Oh,' Tim said, 'I wouldn't be surprised if Dale hadn't achieved on the whole, a fairly successful sublimation with his ghastly telly-therapy. He's an exhibitionist who thinks he's made good. That's why his two public blunders upset his applecart and gave him his "nervous breakdown".'

'I didn't know he'd had one,' said Father Jourdain.

'He says he has. It's a term psychotherapists don't accept. As for McAngus, he really *is* interesting: all that timidity and absent-mindedness and losing his way in his own stories: very characteristic.'

'Of what?' Alleyn asked.

'Of an all-too-familiar type. Completely inhibited. Riddled with anxieties and frustrations. And of course he's quite unconscious of their origins. His giving Mrs D-B that damn' doll was very suggestive. He's a bachelor.'

'Oh dear!' Father Jourdain murmured and at once added: 'Pay no attention to me. Do go on.'

'Then,' Alleyn said, 'the psychiatrist's position in respect of these crimes is that they have all developed out of some profound emo-tional disturbance that the criminal is quite unaware of and is unable to control?'

'That's it.'

'And does it follow that he may, at the conscious level, loathe what he does, try desperately hard to fight down the compulsion and be filled with horror each time he fails?'

'Very likely.'

'Indeed, yes,' Father Jourdain said with great emphasis. 'Indeed, indeed!'

Alleyn turned to him. 'Then you agree with Makepiece?'

Father Jourdain passed a white hand over his dark luxuriant hair. 'I'm sure,' he said, 'that Makepiece has described the secondary cause and its subsequent results very learnedly and accurately.'

'The *secondary* cause!' Tim ejaculated.

'Yes. The repressed fear, or frustration or whatever it was – I'm afraid,' said Father Jourdain with a faint smile, 'I haven't mastered the terminology. But I'm sure you're right about all that: indeed you *know* it all as a man of science. But you see I would look upon that early tragedy and its subsequent manifestations as the – well, as the *modus operandi* of an infinitely more terrible agent.'

'I don't follow,' Tim said. 'A more terrible agent?'

'Yes. The devil.'

'I beg your pardon?'

'I believe that this poor soul is possessed of a devil.'

Tim, to Alleyn's amusement, actually blushed scarlet as if Father Jourdain had committed some frightful social solecism.

'I see,' Father Jourdain observed, 'that I have embarrassed you.'

Tim mumbled something about everybody being entitled to his opinion.

Alleyn said: 'I'm afraid I'm rather stuck for a remark, too. Forgive me, but you do mean, quite literally, exactly what you've just said? Yes, I see you do.'

'Quite literally. It is a case of possession. I've seen too many to be mistaken.'

There was a long pause during which Alleyn reminded himself that there were a great number of not unintelligent people in the world who managed, with some satisfaction to themselves, to believe in devils. At last he said:

'I must say, in that case, I very much wish you could exorcise it.'

With perfect seriousness Father Jourdain replied that there were certain difficulties. 'I shall, of course, continue to pray for him,' he said.

Tim shuffled his feet, lit a cigarette and with an air of striking out rather wildly for some kind of raft, asked Alleyn for the police view of these kinds of murderers. 'After all,' he said, 'you must be said to be experts.'

'Not at all,' Alleyn rejoined. 'Very far from it. Our job, God save the mark, is first to protect society and then as a corollary, to catch the criminal. These sorts of criminals are often our worst headache. They have no occupational habits. They resemble each other only in their desire to kill for gratification. In everyday life they may be anything: there are no outward signs. We generally get them but by no means always. The thing one looks for, of course, is a departure from routine. If there's no known routine, if your man is a solitary creature as Jack the Ripper was, your chances lessen considerably.' Alleyn paused and then added in a changed voice: 'But as to why, fundamentally, he is what he is – we are dumb. Perhaps if we knew we'd find our job intolerable.'

Father Jourdain said: 'You are, after all, a compassionate man, I see.'

Alleyn found this remark embarrassing and inappropriate. He said quickly: 'It doesn't arise. An investigating officer examining the bodies of strangled girls who have died on a crescendo of terror and physical agony is not predisposed to feel compassion for the strangler. It's not easy to remember that he may have suffered a complementary agony of the mind. In many cases he hasn't done anything of the sort. He's too far gone.'

'Isn't it a question,' Tim asked, 'of whether something might have been done about him before his obsession reached its climax?'

'Of course it is,' Alleyn agreed, very readily, 'that's where you chaps come in.'

Tim stood up. 'It's three o'clock. I'm due for a game of deck golf,' he said. 'What's the form? Watchful diligence?'

'That's it.'

Father Jourdain also rose. 'I'm going to do a crossword with Miss Abbott. She's got the new Penguin. Mr Merryman is Ximenes standard.'

'I'm a *Times* man myself,' Alleyn said.

'There's one thing about the afternoons,' Father Jourdain sighed, 'the ladies do tend to retire to their cabins.'

'For the sake of argument only,' Tim asked gloomily, 'suppose Cuddy was your man. Do you think he'd be at all liable to strangle Mrs Cuddy?'

'By thunder,' Alleyn said, 'if I were in his boots, *I* would. Come on.'

In the afternoons there were not very many shady places on deck and a good deal of quiet manoeuvring went on among the passengers to secure them. Claims were staked. Mr Merryman left his air cushion and his Panama on the nicest of the deck-chairs. The Cuddys did a certain amount of edging in and shoving aside when nobody else was about. Mr McAngus laid his plaid along one of the wooden seats, but as nobody else cared for the seats this procedure aroused no enmity. Aubyn Dale and Mrs Dillington-Blick used their own luxurious chaise-longues with rubber-foam appointments and had set them up in the little verandah which they pretty well filled. Although they were never occupied till after tea nobody liked to use them in the meantime.

So while Tim, Jemima and two of the junior officers played deck golf, Miss Abbott and five men were grouped in a shady area cast by the centrecastle between the doors into the lounge and the amidships hatch. Mr Cuddy slept noisily with a *Reader's Digest* over his face. Mr McAngus dozed, Mr Merryman and Alleyn read, Father Jourdain and Miss Abbott laboured at their crossword. It was a tranquil-looking scene. Desultory sentences and little spurts of observation drifted about with the inconsequence of a conversational poem by Verlaine.

Above their heads Captain Bannerman took his afternoon walk on the bridge, solacing the monotony with pleasurable glances at Jemima, who looked enchanting in jeans and a scarlet shirt. As he had predicted, she was evidently a howling success with his junior officers. And with his medical officer, too, reflected the Captain. Sensible perhaps of his regard, Jemima looked up and gaily waved to him. In addition to being attractive she was also what he called a thoroughly nice, unspoiled little lady; just a sweet young girl, he thought. Dimly conscious, perhaps, of some not altogether appropriate train of thought aroused by this reflection, the Captain decided to think instead of Mrs Dillington-Blick; a mental exercise that came very easy to him.

Jemima took a long swipe at her opponent's disc, scuppered her own, shouted 'Damn!' and burst out laughing. The junior officers who had tried very hard to let her win now polished off the game in an expert manner and regretfully returned to duty.

Jemima said: 'Oh, Tim, I *am* sorry! You must get another partner.'

'Are you sick of me?' Tim rejoined. 'What shall we do now? Would you like to have a singles?'

'Not very much, thank you. I need the support of a kind and forbearing person like yourself. Perhaps some of the others would play. Mr McAngus for instance. His game is about on a par with mine.'

'Mr McAngus is mercifully dozing and you know jolly well you're talking nonsense.'

'Well, who?' Jemima nervously pushed her hair back and said: 'Perhaps it's too hot after all. Don't let's play.' She looked at the little group in the shade of the centrecastle. Mr Merryman had come out of his book and was talking to Alleyn in an admonitory fashion, shaking his finger and evidently speaking with some heat.

'Mr Chips is at it again,' Tim said. 'Poor Alleyn!'

He experienced the sensation of his blood running down into his boots. He thought complicatedly of a number of things at once. Perhaps his predominant emotion was one of incredulity: surely he, Tim Makepiece, a responsible man, a man of science, a psychiatrist, could not have slipped into so feeble, so imbecile an error. Would he have to confess to Alleyn? How could he recover himself with Jemima? Her voice recalled him.

'What did you say?' she asked.

' "Poor Broderick." '

'Is he called Allan? You've got down to Christian names pretty smartly. Very chummy of you.'

Tim said after a pause: 'I don't to his face. I like him.'

'So do I. Awfully. We agreed about it before.' Jemima shook her head impatiently. 'At any rate,' she said, 'he's not the guilty one. I'm sure of that.'

Tim stood very still and after a moment wetted his lips.

'What do you mean?' he said. 'The guilty one?'

'Are you all right, Tim?'

'Perfectly.'

'You look peculiar.'

'It's the heat. Come back here, do.'

He took her arm and led her to the little verandah, pushed her down on the sumptuous footrest belonging to Mrs Dillington-Blick's chaise-longue and himself sat at the end of Aubyn Dale's. 'What guilty one?' he repeated.

Jemima stared at him. 'There's no need, really, to take it so massively,' she said. 'You may not feel like I do about it.'

'About *what?*'

'The business with the D-B's doll. It seems to me such a beastly thing to have done and I don't care what anyone says, it was done on purpose. Just treading on it wouldn't have produced that result. And then, putting the flower on its chest: a scurvy trick, I call it.'

Tim stooped down and made a lengthy business of tying his shoelace. When he straightened up Jemima said: 'You *are* all right, aren't you? You keep changing colour like a chameleon.'

'Which am I now?'

'Fiery red.'

'I've been stooping over. I agree with you about the doll. It was a silly unbecoming sort of thing to do. Perhaps it was a drunken sailor.'

'There weren't any drunken sailors about. Do you know who I think it was?'

'Who?'

'Mr Cuddy.'

'Do you, Jem?' Tim said. 'Why?'

'He kept smiling and smiling all the time that Mr Broderick was showing the doll.'

'He's got a chronic grin. It never leaves his face.'

'All the same – ' Jemima looked quickly at Tim and away again. 'In my opinion,' she muttered, 'he's a DOM.'

'A what?'

'A dirty old man. I don't mind telling you, I'd simply hate to find myself alone on the boatdeck with him after dark.'

Tim hastily said that she'd better make sure she never did. 'Take me with you for safety's sake,' he said. 'I'm eminently trustworthy.'

Jemima grinned at him absent-mindedly. She seemed to be in two minds about what she should say next.

'What is it?' he asked.

'Nothing. Nothing, really. It's just – I don't know – it's ever since Dennis brought Mrs D-B's hyacinths into the lounge on the second day out. We don't seem to be able to get rid of those awful murders. Everybody talking about them. That alibi discussion the night before Las Palmas and Miss Abbott breaking down. Not that *her* trouble had anything to do with it, poor thing. And then the awful business of the girl that brought Mrs D-B's flowers being a victim and now the doll being left like that. You'll think I'm completely dotty,' Jemima said, 'but it's sort of got me down a bit. Do you know, just now I caught myself thinking: "Wouldn't it be awful if the flower murderer was on board." '

Tim had put out a warning hand but a man's shadow had already fallen across the deck and across Jemima.

'Dear child!' said Aubyn Dale, 'what a *pathologically* morbid little notion!'

III

Tim and Jemima got up. Tim said automatically: 'I'm afraid we've been trespassing on your footrests,' and hoped this would account for any embarrassment they might have displayed.

'My dear old boy!' Dale cried, '*do* use the whole tatty works! Whenever you like, as far as I'm concerned. And I'm sure Madame would be enchanted.'

He had an armful of cushions and rugs which he began to arrange on the chaise-longues. 'Madame tends to emerge for a nice cuppa,' he explained. He punched a cushion with all the aplomb of the manservant in *Charley's Aunt* and flung it into position. 'There now!' he said. He straightened up, pulled a pipe out of his pocket, gripped it mannishly between his teeth, contrived to tower over Jemima and became avuncular.

'As for you, young woman,' he said, cocking his head quizzically at her, 'you've been letting a particularly lively imagination run away with you. What?'

This was said with such an exact reproduction of his television manner that Tim, in spite of his own agitation, felt momentarily impelled to whistle 'Pack Up Your Troubles'. However he said quickly: 'It wasn't as morbid as it sounded. Jemima and I have been having an argument about the "Alibi" bet and that led to inevitable conjectures about the flower expert.'

'M-m-m,' Dale rumbled understandingly, still looking at Jemima. '*I* see.' He screwed his face into a whimsical grimace. 'You know, Jemima, I've got an idea we've just about had that old topic. After all, it's not the prettiest one in the world, is it? What do you think? Um?'

Pink with embarrassment, Jemima said coldly: 'I feel sure you're right.'

'Good girl,' Aubyn Dale said and patted her shoulder.

Tim muttered that it was tea-time and withdrew Jemima firmly to the starboard side. It was a relief to him to be angry.

'My God, what a frightful fellow,' he fulminated. 'That egregious nice-chappery! That ineffable decency! That indescribably phoney goodwill!'

'Never mind,' Jemima said. 'I dare say he has to keep in practice. And, after all, little as I relish admitting it, he was in fact right. I suppose I have been letting my imagination run away with me.'

Tim stood over her, put his head on one side and achieved a quite creditable imitation of Aubyn Dale. 'Good girl,' he said unctuously and patted her shoulder.

Jemima made a satisfactory response to this sally and seemed to be a good deal cheered. 'Of course,' she said, 'I didn't *really* think we'd shipped a murderer: it was just one of those things.' She looked up into Tim's face.

'Jemima!' he said, and took her hands in his.

'No, don't,' she said quickly. 'Don't.'

'I'm sorry.'

'There's nothing to be sorry about. Pay no attention. Let's go and talk to Mr Chips.'

They found Mr Merryman in full cry. He had discovered Jemima's book, *The Elizabethans*, which she had left on her deck-chair, and seemed to be giving a lecture on it. It was by an author-itative writer but one, evidently, with whom Mr Merryman found himself in passionate disagreement. It appeared that Alleyn, Father Jourdain and Miss Abbott had all been drawn into the discussion while Mr McAngus and Mr Cuddy looked on, the former with admiration and the latter with his characteristic air of uninformed disparagement.

Jemima and Tim sat on the deck and were accepted by Mr Merryman as if they had come late for class but with valid excuses. Alleyn glanced at them and found time to hope that theirs, by some happy accident, was not merely a shipboard attraction. After all, he thought, he himself had fallen irrevocably in love during a voyage from the Antipodes. He turned his attention back to the matter in hand.

'I honestly *don't* understand,' Father Jourdain was saying, 'how you can put *The Duchess of Malfi* before *Hamlet* or *Macbeth*.'

'Or why,' Miss Abbott barked, 'you should think *Othello* so much better than any of them.'

Mr Merryman groped in his waistcoat pocket for a sodamint and remarked insufferably that really it was impossible to discuss criteria of taste where the rudiments of taste were demonstrably absent. He treated his restive audience to a comprehensive de-gumming of *Hamlet* and *Macbeth*. Hamlet, he said, was an inconsistent, deficient and redundant *rechauffé* of some absurd German melodrama: it was not surprising, Mr Merryman said, that Hamlet was unable to make up his mind since his creator had himself been the victim of a still greater blight of indecision. Macbeth was merely a muddle-headed blunderer. Strip away the language and what remained? A tediously ignorant expression of defeatism. ' "What's the good of anyfink? Wy nuffink", ' Mr Merryman quoted in pedantic cockney and tossed his sodamint into his mouth.

'I don't know anything about Shakepeare – ' Mr Cuddy began and was at once talked down.

'It is at least something,' Mr Merryman said, 'that you acknowledge your misfortune. May I advise you not to break your duck with *Macbeth*.'

'All the same,' Alleyn objected, 'there *is* the language.'

'I am not aware,' Mr Merryman countered, 'that I have suggested that the fellow had no vocabulary.' He went on to praise the classic structure of *Othello*, the inevitability of Webster's *The Duchess of Malfi*, and, astoundingly, the admirable directness of *Titus Andronicus*. As an afterthought he conceded that the final scene of *Lear* was 'respectable'.

Mr McAngus, who had several times made plaintive little noises, now struck in with unexpected emphasis.

'To me,' he said, '*Othello* is almost spoilt by that bit near the end when Desdemona revives and speaks and then, you know, after all, dies. A woman who has been properly strangled would *not* be able to do that. It is quite ridiculous.'

'What's the medical opinion?' Alleyn asked Tim.

'Pathological verisimilitude,' Mr Merryman interjected with more than a touch of Pooh-Bah, 'is irrelevant. One accepts the convention. It is artistically proper that she should be strangled and speak again. Therefore, she speaks.'

'All the same,' Alleyn said, 'let's have the expert's opinion.' He looked at Tim.

'I wouldn't say it was utterly impossible,' Tim said. 'Of course, her physical condition can't be reproduced by an actress and would be unacceptable if it could. I should think it's just possible that he might not have killed her instantly and that she might momentarily revive and attempt to speak.'

'But, Doctor,' Mr McAngus objected diffidently, 'I *did* say properly. Properly strangled, you know.'

'Doesn't the text,' Miss Abbott pointed out, 'say she was smothered?'

'The text!' Mr Merryman exclaimed and spread out his hands. 'What text, pray? Which text?' and launched himself into a general animadversion of Shakespearian editorship. This he followed up with an extremely dogmatic pronouncement upon the presentation of the plays. The only tolerable method, he said, was that followed by the Elizabethans themselves. The bare boards. The boy-players. It appeared that Mr Merryman himself produced the plays in this manner at his school. He treated them to a lecture upon speechcraft, costume and make-up. His manner was so insufferably cocksure that it robbed his discourse of any interest it might have had for his extremely mixed audience. Mr McAngus's eyes became glazed. Father Jourdain was resigned and Miss Abbott impatient. Jemima looked at the deck and Tim looked at Jemima. Alleyn, conscious of all this, still managed to preserve the semblance of respectful attention.

He was conscious also of Mr Cuddy who had the air of a man baulked of his legitimate prey. It was evident throughout the discussion that he had some observation to make. He now raised his voice unmelodiously and made it.

'Isn't it funny,' Mr Cuddy asked generally, 'how the conversation seems to get round to the subject of ladies being throttled? Mrs Cuddy was remarking on the same thing. Quite a coincidence, she was saying.'

Mr Merryman opened his mouth, shut it, and reopened it when Jemima cried out with some violence:

'I think it's perfectly beastly. I hate it!'

Tim put his hand over hers. 'Well, I'm sorry,' Jemima said, 'but it *is* beastly. It doesn't matter *how* Desdemona died. Othello isn't a clinical example. Shakespeare wasn't some scruffy existentialist: it's a tragedy of simplicity and – and greatness of heart being destroyed by a common smarty-smarty little placefinder. Well anyway,' Jemima mumbled, turning very pink, 'that's what I think and I suppose one can try and say what one thinks, can't one?'

'I should damn' well suppose one can,' Alleyn said warmly, 'and how right you are, what's more.'

Jemima threw him a grateful look.

Mr Cuddy smiled and smiled. 'I'm sure,' he said, 'I didn't mean to upset anyone.'

'Well, you have,' Miss Abbott snapped, 'and now you know it, don't you?'

'Thank you very much,' said Mr Cuddy.

Father Jourdain stood up. 'It's tea-time,' he said. 'Shall we go in? And shall we decide,' he smiled at Jemima, 'to take the advice of the youngest and wisest among us and keep off this not very delectable subject? I propose that we do.'

Everybody except Mr Cuddy made affirmative noises and they went in to tea.

'But the curious thing is,' Alleyn wrote to his wife that evening, 'that however much they may or may not try to avoid the subject of murder, it still crops up. I don't want to go previous about it, but really one might suppose that the presence of this expert on board generates a sort of effluvia. They are unaware of it and yet it infects them. Tonight, for instance, after the women had gone to bed, which to my great relief was early, the men got cracking again. Cuddy, Jourdain and Merryman are all avid readers of crime fiction and of the sort of book that calls itself "Classic Cases of Detection". As it happens there are two or three of that kind in the ship's little library: among them *The Wainwrights* in the admirable Notable Trials series, a very fanciful number on the Yard and an affair called: *The Thing He Loves*. The latter title derives from *The Ballad of Reading Gaol*, of course, and I give you one guess as to the subject matter.

'Well, tonight, Merryman being present, there was automatically a row. Without exception he's the most pugnacious, quarrelsome, arrogant chap I've ever met. It seemed that Cuddy had got *The Thing He Loves,* and was snuffling away at it in the corner of the lounge. Merryman spotted the book and at once said that he himself was already reading it. Cuddy said he'd taken the book from the shelves and that they were free for all. Neither would give in. Finally McAngus announced that he had a copy of *The Trial of Neil Cream* and actually succeeded in placating Merryman with an offer to lend it to him. It appears that Merryman is one of the fanatics who believes the story of Cream's unfinished confession. So peace was in a sense restored though once again we were treated to an interminable discussion on what Cuddy *will* call sex-monstrosity. Dale was full of all kinds of secondhand theories. McAngus joined in with a sort of terrified relish. Makepiece talked from the psychiatric angle and Jourdain from the religious one. Merryman contradicted everybody. Of course, I'm all for these discussions. They give one an unexampled chance to listen to the man one may be going to arrest, propounding the sort of crime with which he will ultimately be charged.

'The reactions go like this:

'McAngus does a great deal of tut-tutting, protests that the subject is too horrid to dwell upon, is nevertheless quite unable to go away while it's under discussion. He gets all the facts wrong, confuses names and dates so persistently that you'd think it was deliberate and is slapped back perpetually by Merryman.

'Cuddy is utterly absorbed. He goes over the details and incessantly harks back to Jack the Ripper, describing all the ritualistic horrors and speculating about their possible significance.

'Merryman, of course, is overbearing, didactic and argumentative. He's got a much better brain than any of the others, is conversant with the cases, never muddles the known facts and never loses a chance of blackguarding the police. In his opinion they won't catch their man and he obviously glories in the notion (Hah-hah, did he but know, sneered Hawkshaw, the Detective).

'Dale, like McAngus, puts up a great show of abhorrence but professes an interest in what he calls the "psychology of sadistic homicide". He talks like a signed article in one of the less responsible of our dailies and also, of course, like a thoroughly nice chap on television. Poor wretch! is his cry: poor, poor girls, poor everybody. Sad! Sad!

'Meanwhile, being in merry pin, he has had enough misguided energy to sew up Mr Merryman's pyjamas and put a dummy woman made from one of the D-B's tremendous nightgowns in Mr McAngus's bed and has thus by virtue of these hilarious pranks graduated as a potential victim himself. Merryman's reaction was to go straight to the Captain and McAngus's to behave as if he was a typical example from Freud's casebook.

'Well, there they are, these four precious favourites in the homicide handicap. I've told you that I fancy one in particular and, in the classic tradition, my dearest, having laid bare the facts I leave you to your deduction; always bearing in mind that the Captain and his mates may be right and there ain't no flaming murderer on board.

'Goodnight, darling. Don't miss our next instalment of this absorbing serial.'

Alleyn put his letter away, doodled absently on his blotting paper for a few minutes and then thought he'd stretch his legs before turning in.

He went down to the deck below and found it deserted. Having walked six times round it and had a word with the wireless officer who sat lonely as a cloud in his cubby hole on the starboard side, Alleyn thought he would call it a day. He passed Father Jourdain's cabin door on his way through the passengers' quarters and as he did so the handle turned and the door was opened a crack. He heard Father Jourdain's voice.

'But, of course. You must come to me whenever you want to. It's what I'm for, you know.'

A woman's voice answered harshly and undistinguishably.

'I think,' said Father Jourdain, 'you should dismiss all that from your mind and stick to your duties. Perform your penance, come to mass tomorrow, make the special intention I have suggested. Go along, now, and say your prayers. Bless you, my child. Goodnight.'

Alleyn moved quickly down the passage and had reached the stairs before Miss Abbott had time to see him.

CHAPTER 8

Sunday the Tenth

The next day, being Sunday, Father Jourdain with the Captain's permission celebrated Holy Communion in the lounge at seven o'clock. The service was attended among the passengers by Miss Abbott, Jemima, Mr McAngus and, rather surprisingly, Mr Merryman. The Third Officer, the Wireless Officer, two of the cadets and Dennis represented the ship's complement. Alleyn, at the back of the room, listened, watched and, not for the first time, felt his own lack of acceptance to be tinged with a faint regret.

When the service was over the little group of passengers went out on deck and presently were joined by Father Jourdain, wearing, as he had promised, his 'decent black cassock'. He looked remarkably handsome in it with the light breeze lifting his glossy hair. Miss Abbott, standing, characteristically, a little apart from the others, watched him, Alleyn noticed, with a look of stubborn deference. There was a Sunday morning air about the scene. Even Mr Merryman was quiet and thoughtful while Mr McAngus who, with Miss Abbott, had carried out the details of Anglo-Catholic observance like an old hand, was quite giddy and uplifted. He congratulated Jemima on her looks and did his little chassé before her with his head on one side. Mr McAngus's russet-brown hair had grown, of course, even longer at the back and something unfortunate seemed to have happened round the brow and temples. But as he always wore his felt hat out-of-doors and quite often in the lounge, this was not particularly noticeable.

Jemima responded gaily to his blameless compliments and turned to Alleyn.

'I didn't expect to see *you* about so early,' she said.

'And why not?'

'You were up late! Pacing round the deck. Wrapped in thought!' teased Jemima.

'That's all very fine,' Alleyn rejoined. 'But what I might ask were you up to yourself? From what angle of vantage did you keep all this observation?'

Jemima blushed. 'Oh,' she said with a great air of casualness, 'I was sitting in the verandah along there. We didn't like to call out as you passed, you looked so solemn and absorbed.' She turned an even brighter pink, glanced at the others who were gathered round Father Jourdain and added quickly: 'Tim Makepiece and I were talking about Elizabethan literature.'

'You were not talking very loudly about it,' Alleyn observed mildly.

'Well – ' Jemima looked into his face. 'I'm not having a shipboard flirtation with Tim. At least – at least, I don't think I am.'

'Not a flirtation?' Alleyn repeated and smiled at her.

'And not anything else. Oh, golly!' Jemima said impulsively. 'I'm in such a muddle.'

'Do you want to talk about your muddle?'

Jemima put her arm through his. 'I've arrived at the age,' Alleyn reflected, 'when charming young ladies take my arm.' They walked down the deck together.

'How long,' Jemima asked, 'have we been at sea? And, crikey!' she added, *'what* an appropriate phrase that is!'

'Six days.'

'There you are! Six days! The whole thing's ridiculous. How can anybody possibly know how they feel in six days? It's out of this world.'

Alleyn remarked that he had known how he felt in one. 'Shorter even than that,' he added. 'At once.'

'Really? And stuck to it?'

'Like a limpet. She took much longer, though.'

'But – ? Did you?'

'We are *very* happily married, thank you.'

'How lovely,' Jemima sighed.

'However,' he added hurriedly, 'don't let me raise a finger to urge you into an ill-considered undertaking.'

'You don't have to tell me anything about that,' she rejoined with feeling. 'I've made that sort of ass of myself in quite a big way, once already.'

'Really?'

'Yes, indeed. The night we sailed should have been my wedding night only he chucked me three days before. I've done a bolt from all the *brouhaha*, leaving my wretched parents to cope. Very poor show as you don't need to tell me,' said Jemima in a high uneven voice.

'I expect your parents were delighted to get rid of you. Much easier for them, I dare say, if you weren't about: throwing vapours.'

They had reached the end of the well-deck and stood, looking aft, near the little verandah. Jemima remarked indistinctly that going to church always made her feel rather light-headed and talkative and she expected that was why she was being so communicative.

'Perhaps the warm weather has something to do with it, as well,' Alleyn suggested.

'I dare say. One always hears that people get very unguarded in the tropics. But actually you're to blame. I was saying to Tim the other night that if I was ever in a real jam I'd feel inclined to go bawling to you about it. He quite agreed. And here, fantastically, I am. Bawling away.'

'I'm enormously flattered. Are you in a jam?'

'I suppose not, really. I just need to keep my eye. And see that he keeps his. Because whatever you say, I don't see how he can possibly know in six days.'

Alleyn said that people saw more of each other in six days at sea then they did in as many weeks ashore but, he was careful to add, in rather less realistic circumstances. Jemima agreed. There was no doubt, she announced owlishly, that strange things happened to one at sea. Look at her, for instance, she said with enchanting egoism. She was getting all sorts of the rummiest notions into her head. After a little hesitation and then, very much with the air of a child that screws itself up to confiding a groundless fear, Jemima said rapidly: 'I even started thinking the flower murderer was on board. Imagine!'

Among the various items of Alleyn's training as an investigating officer, the trick of wearing an impassive face in the teeth of unexpected information was not the least useful. It stood him in good stead now.

'I wonder,' he said, 'what in the world could have put that idea in your head.'

Jemima repeated the explanation she had already given Tim yesterday afternoon. 'Of course,' she said, 'he thought it as dotty as you do and so did the FNC.'

'Who,' Alleyn asked, 'is the FNC?'

'It's our name for Dale. It stands for Frightfully Nice Chap only we don't mean it frightfully nicely, I'm afraid.'

'Nevertheless you confided your fantasy to him, did you?'

'He overheard me. We were "squatting" on his and the D-B's lush chairs and he came round the corner with cushions and went all avuncular.'

'And now you've brought this bugaboo out into the light of day it's evaporated?'

Jemima swung her foot and kicked an infinitesimal object into the scuppers: 'Not altogether,' she muttered.

'No?'

'Well, it has, really. Only last night, after I'd gone to bed, something happened. I don't suppose it was anything much but it got me a bit steamed up again. My cabin's on the left hand side of the block. The porthole faces my bed. Well, you know that blissful moment when you're not sure whether you're awake or asleep but kind of floating? I'd got to that stage. My eyes were shut and I was all airborne and drifting. Then with a jerk I was wide awake and staring at that porthole.' Jemima swallowed hard. 'It was moonlight outside. Before 'I'd shut my eyes I'd seen the moon; looking in and then swinging out of sight and leaving a procession of stars and then swinging back. Lovely! Well, when I opened my eyes and looked at the porthole – somebody outside was looking in at me.'

Alleyn waited for a moment and then said: 'You're quite sure, I suppose?'

'Oh, yes. There he was, blotting out the stars and the moon and filling up my porthole with his head.'

'Do you know who it was?'

'I haven't a notion. Somebody in a hat but I could only see the outline. And it was only for a second. I called out – it was not a startling original remark – "Hallo! Who's there?" and at once it – went down. I mean it sank in a flash. He must have ducked and then bolted. The moon came whooping back and there was I, all-of-a-dither and thinking: "Suppose the flower murderer is on board and suppose after everyone else has gone to bed, he prowls and prowls around like the hosts of Midian or is it Gideon, in that blissful hymn?" So you see, I haven't quite got over my nonsense, have I?'

'Have you told Makepiece about this?'

'I haven't seen him. He doesn't go to church.'

'No, of course you haven't. Perhaps,' Alleyn said, 'it was Aubyn Dale being Puckish.'

'I must say I never thought of that. Could he hit quite such an all-time-low for unfunniness, do you suppose?'

'I would have expected him to follow it up with a dummy spider on your pillow. You do lock your door at night, don't you? And in the daytime?'

'Yes. There was that warning about things having been pinched. Oh, lord!' Jemima ejaculated, 'do you suppose that's who it was? The petty larcener? Why on earth didn't I remember before! Hoping he could fish something out through the porthole, would you think?'

'It wouldn't be the first time,' Alleyn said.

The warning gong for breakfast began to tinkle. Jemima remarked cheerfully: 'Well, that's *that*, anyway.'

Alleyn waited for a moment and then said: 'Look. In view of what you've just told me, I'd keep your curtains over your port at night. And as there evidently is a not-too-desirable character in the ship's complement, I don't think, if I were you, I'd go out walking after dark by yourself. He might come along and make a bit of a nuisance of himself.'

Jemima said: 'OK, but what a *bore*. And, by the way, you'd better hand on that piece of advice to Mrs D-B. She's the one to go out walking – or dancing, rather – by the light of the moon.' Jemima smiled reminiscently. 'I do think she's marvellous,' she said. 'All that *joie-de-vivre* at her age. Superb.'

Alleyn found time to wonder how much Mrs Dillington-Blick would relish this tribute and also how many surprises Jemima was liable to spring on him at one sitting.

He said: '*Does* she dance by the light of the moon? Who with?'

'By herself.'

'You don't tell me she goes all pixy-wixy on the boat deck? Carrying that weight?'

'On the other deck, the bottom one, nearer the sharp end. I've seen her. The weight doesn't seem to matter.'

'Do explain yourself.'

'Well, I'm afraid you're in for another night-piece – in point of fact the night before last. It was awfully hot: Tim and I had sat up rather late, *not*, I'd have you know again, for amorous dalliance but for a long muddly argument. And when I went to my cabin it was stuffy and I knew I wouldn't sleep for thinking about the argument. So I went along to the windows that look down on the lower deck – it's called the forrard well-deck, isn't it? – and wondered if I could be bothered climbing down and then along and up to the bows where I rather like to go. And while I was wondering and looking down into the forrard well-deck which was full of black shadows, a door opened underneath me and a square patch of light was thrown across the deck.'

Jemima's face, vivid and gay with the anticipation of her narrative, clouded a little.

'In point of fact,' she said, 'for a second or two it was a trifle grizzly. You see, a shadow appeared on the lighted square. And – well – it was exactly as if the doll, Esmeralda, had come to life. Mantilla, fan, wide lace skirt. Everything. I dare say it contributed to my "thing" about the Flower Murders. Anyway it gave me quite a jolt.'

'It would,' Alleyn agreed. 'What next?'

'Well, somebody shut the door and the light patch vanished. And I knew, of course, who it was. There she stood, all by herself. I was looking down on her head. And then it happened. The moon was up and just at that moment it got high enough to shine into the deck. All those lumps of covered machinery cast their inky-black shadows, but there were patches of moonshine and it was exciting to see. She ran out and flirted her fan and did little pirouettes and curtsies and even two or three of those sliding backsteps like they do with castanets in *The Gondoliers*. I think she was holding her mantilla across her face. It was the strangest sight.'

'Very rum, indeed. You're sure it was the D-B?'

'But, of course. Who else? And, do you know, I found it rather touching. Don't you agree? She only stayed for a few moments and then ran back. The door opened and her shadow flashed across the patch of light. I heard men's voices, laughing, and then it was all blanked out. But wasn't it gay and surprising of Mrs Dillington-Blick? Aren't you astonished?' asked Jemima.

'Flabbergasted. Although, one does hear, of course, of elephant dances in the seclusion of the jungle.'

Jemima said indignantly: 'She's as light as a feather on her pins. Fat people are, you know. They dance like fairies. Still, perhaps you'd better warn her not to on account of the petty larcener. Only please don't say I told you about her moonlight party. In a funny sort of way I felt like an interloper.'

'I won't,' he promised. 'And in the meantime don't take any solitary walks yourself. Tell Makepiece about it, and see if he doesn't agree with me.'

'Oh,' Jemima assured him, 'he'll agree all right.' And a dimple appeared near the corner of her mouth.

The group round Father Jourdain had moved nearer. Mr McAngus called out: 'Breakfast!' and Jemima said 'Coming!' She joined them, turned, crinkled her eyes at Alleyn and called out: 'You *have* been nice. Thank you – Allan.'

Before he could reply she had made off with the others in search of breakfast.

II

During breakfast Tim kept trying to catch Alleyn's eye and got but little response for his pains. He was waiting in the passage when Alleyn came out and said with artificial heartiness: 'I've found those books I was telling you about: would you like to come along to my room, or shall I bring them up to yours?'

'Bring them,' Alleyn said, 'to mine.'

He went straight upstairs. In five minutes there was a knock on his door and Tim came in, burdened with unwanted text-books. 'I've got something I think I ought to tell you,' he said.

'Jemima Carmichael wonders if the flower-murderer is on board and Aubyn Dale knows she does.'

'How the hell did you find out!' Tim ejaculated.

'She told me.'

'Oh.'

'And I'm rather wondering why you didn't.'

'I didn't get a chance before dinner. I was going to after dinner but you were boxed up with the D-B and Dale in the lounge and later on – well – '

'You were discussing Elizabethan literature on the verandah?'

'Exactly.'

'Very well. At what stage did you inform Miss Carmichael of my name?'

'Damn it, it's not as bad as you think. Look – did she tell you that too?'

'She merely called it out before the whole lot of them as we came down to breakfast.'

'She thinks it's your Christian name – Allan.'

'Why?'

Tim told him. 'I really am ashamed of myself,' he said. 'It just slipped out. I wouldn't have believed I could be such a *bloody* fool.'

'Nor would I. I suppose it comes of all this poodle-faking non-sense. Calling oneself by a false name! Next door to wearing false whiskers, I've always thought, but sometimes it can't be avoided.'

'She's not a notion who you are, of course.'

'That, at least, is something. And, by the way, she'll be telling you about an incident that occurred last night. I think you'll agree that it's serious. I've suggested the mythical sneak-thief as the culprit. You'd better take the same line.'

'But what's happened?'

'A Peeping Tom's happened. She'll tell you. She may also tell you how Mrs Dillington-Blick goes fey among the derricks by moonlight.'

'*What!*'

'I'm going to see the Captain. Father Jourdain's joining me there: you'd better come too, I think. You might as well know about it.'

'Of course. If I'm not confined to outer darkness.'

'Oh,' Alleyn said, 'we'll give you another chance.'

Tim said: 'I'm sorry about my gaffe, Alleyn.'

'The name is Broderick.'

'I'm sorry.'

'She's a nice child. None of my business but I hope you're not making a nonsense. She's had one bad knock and she'd better not be dealt another.'

'She seems,' Tim observed, 'to confide in you a damn' sight more freely than in me.'

'Advanced years carry their own compensation.'

'For me, this is *it*.'

'Certain?'

'Absolutely. I wish I was as certain about her.'

'Well – look after her.'

'I've every intention of doing so,' Tim said, and on that note they found Father Jourdain and went to visit Captain Bannerman.

It was not an easy interview.

Alleyn would have recognized Captain Bannerman for an obstinate man even if he had not been told as much by members of the Cape Line Company before he left. 'He's a pig-headed old b.,' one of these officials had remarked. 'And if you get up against him he'll make things very uncomfortable for you. He drinks pretty hard and is reported to be bloody-minded in his cups. Keep on the right side of him and he'll be OK.'

So far, Alleyn thought, he had managed to follow this suggestion, but when he described the episode of the moonlit figure seen by Jemima on Friday night, he knew he was in for trouble. He gave his own interpretation of this story and he suggested that steps should be taken to ensure that there was no repetition. He met with a flat refusal. He then went on to tell them of the man outside Jemima's porthole. The Captain said at once that he would detail the officer of the watch who would take appropriate steps to ensure that this episode was not repeated. He added that it was of no particular significance and that very often people behaved oddly in the tropics: an observation that Alleyn was getting a little tired of hearing. He attempted to suggest a more serious interpretation and met with blank incredulity.

As for the Dillington-Blick episode, the Captain said he would take no action either to investigate it or prevent a repetition. He treated them to a lecture on the diminishing powers of a ship's master at sea and grew quite hot on the subject. There were limitations. There were unions. Even passengers nowadays had their rights, he added regretfully. What had occurred was in no way an infringement of any of the regulations, he didn't propose to do anything about it and he must request Alleyn to follow suit. And that, he said finally, was flat.

He stood with his hands in his jacket pockets and glared through his porthole at the horizon. Even the back of his neck looked mulish. The other three men exchanged glances.

'The chap's not aboard my ship,' the Captain loudly announced without turning his head. 'I know that as well as I know you *are.* I've been master under the Cape Company's charter for twenty years and I know as soon as I look at him whether a chap'll blow up for trouble at sea. I had a murderer shipped fireman aboard me, once. Soon as I clapped eyes on him I knew he was no good. Never failed yet. And I've been observing this lot. Observing them closely. There's not a murdering look on one of their faces, not a sign of it.' He turned slowly and advanced upon Alleyn. His own face, lobster-red, wore an expression of childish complacency. 'You're on a wild goose chase,' he said blowing out gusts of whisky. Then with quite astonishing violence he drew his mottled hirsute fist from his pocket and crashed it down on his desk. 'That sort of thing,' said Captain Bannerman, 'doesn't happen in *my ship!*'

'May I say just this?' Alleyn ventured. 'I wouldn't come to you with the suggestion unless I thought it most urgently necessary. You may, indeed, be perfectly right. Our man may not, after all, be aboard. But suppose, sir, that in the teeth of all you feel about it, he is in this ship.' Alleyn pointed to the Captain's desk calendar. 'Sunday the tenth of February,' he said. 'If he's here we've got four days before his supposed deadline. Shouldn't we take every possible step to prevent him going into action? I know very well that what I've suggested sounds farfetched, cockeyed and altogether preposterous. It's a precautionary measure against a threat that may not exist. But isn't it better – ' He looked at that unyielding front and very nearly threw up his hands. ' – Isn't it better, in fact, to be sure than sorry?' said Alleyn in despair. Father Jourdain and Tim murmured agreement but the Captain shouted them down.

'Ah! So it is and it's a remark I often pass myself. But in this case it doesn't apply. What you've suggested is dead against my principles as Master and I won't have it. I don't believe it's necessary and I won't have it.'

Father Jourdain said: 'If I might just say one word – '

'You may spare yourself the trouble. I'm set.'

Alleyn said: 'Very good, sir, I hope you're right. Of course we'll respect your wishes.'

'I won't have that lady put-about by an interference or – or criticism.'

'I wasn't suggesting – '

'It'd look like criticism,' the Captain mumbled cryptically and added: 'A touch of high spirits never did anyone any harm.'

This comment, from Alleyn's point of view, was such a master-piece of meiosis that he could find no answer to it.

He said: 'Thank you, sir,' in what he hoped was the regulation manner and made for the door. The others followed him.

'Here!' Captain Bannerman ejaculated and they stopped. 'Have a drink,' said the Captain.

'Not for me at the moment, thank you very much,' said Alleyn.

'Why not?'

'Oh, I generally hold off till the sun's over the yard-arm if that's the right way of putting it.'

'You don't take overmuch then, I've noticed.'

'Well,' Alleyn said apologetically, 'I'm by the way of being on duty.'

'Ah! And nothing to show for it when it's all washed up. Not that I don't appreciate the general idea. You're following orders I dare say, like all the rest of us, never mind if it's a waste of time and the public's money.'

'That's the general idea.'

'Well – what about you two gentlemen?'

'No, thank you, sir,' said Tim.

'Nor I, thank you very much,' said Father Jourdain.

'No offence, is there?'

They hurriedly assured him there was none, waited for a moment and then went to the door. The last glimpse they had of the Captain was a square, slightly wooden figure making for the corner cupboard where he kept his liquor.

III

The rest of Sunday passed by quietly enough. It was the hottest day
the passengers had experienced and they were all subdued. Mrs
Dillington-Blick wore white and so did Aubyn Dale. They lay on their
chaise-longues in the verandah and smiled languidly at passers-by.
Sometimes they were observed to have their hands limply engaged,
occasionally Mrs Dillington-Blick's rich laughter would be heard.

Tim and Jemima spent most of the day in or near a canvas
bathing-pool that had been built on the after well-deck. They were
watched closely by the Cuddys who had set themselves up in a place
of vantage at the shady end of the promenade deck, just under the
verandah. Late in the afternoon Mr Cuddy himself took to the water
clad in a rather grisly little pair of puce-coloured drawers. He developed a vein of aquatic playfulness that soon drove Jemima out of the
pool and Tim into a state of extreme irritation.

Mr Merryman sat in his usual place and devoted himself to Neil
Cream and, when that category of horrors had reached its appointed
end, to the revolting fate that met an assortment of ladies who graced
the pages of *The Thing He Loves*. From time to time he commented
unfavourably on the literary style of this work and also on the police
methods it described. As Alleyn was the nearest target he found himself at the receiving end of these strictures. Inevitably, Mr Merryman
was moved to enlarge once again on the Flower Murders. Alleyn had
the fun of hearing himself described as 'some plodding Dogberry drest
in a little brief authority. One, Alleyn,' Mr Merryman snorted, 'whose
photograph was reproduced in the evening news-sheets – a countenance of abysmal foolishness, I thought.'

'Really?'

'Oh, shocking, I assure you,' said Mr Merryman with immense
relish. 'I imagine, if the unknown criminal saw it, he must have been
greatly consoled. I should have been, I promise you.'

'Do you believe, then,' Alleyn asked, 'that there is after all an art
"to find the mind's construction in the face"?'

Mr Merryman shot an almost approving glance at him: 'Source?'
he demanded sharply, 'and context?'

'Macbeth, 1, 4. Duncan on Cawdor,' Alleyn replied, himself
feeling like Alice in Wonderland.

'Very well. You know your way about that essentially second-rate melodrama, I perceive. Yes,' Mr Merryman went on with pedagogic condescension, 'unquestionably, there are certain facial evidences which serve as pointers to the informed observer. I will undertake for example to distinguish at first sight a bright boy among a multitude of dullards, and believe me,' Mr Merryman added drily, 'the opportunity does not often present itself.'

Alleyn asked him if he would extend this theory to include a general classification. Did Mr Merryman, for instance, consider that there was such a thing as a criminal type of face? 'I've read somewhere, I fancy, that the police say there isn't,' he ventured. Mr Merryman rejoined tartly that for once the police had achieved a glimpse of the obvious. 'If you ask me whether there are facial types indicative of brutality and low intelligence I must answer yes. But the sort of person we have been considering,' he held up his book, 'need not be exhibited in the countenance. The fact that he is possessed by his own particular devil is not written across his face that all who run may read.'

'That's an expression that Father Jourdain used in the same context,' Alleyn said. 'He considers this man must be possessed of a devil.'

'Indeed?' Mr Merryman remarked: 'That is of course the accepted view of the Church. Does he postulate the cloven hoof and toasting-fork?'

'I have no idea.'

A shadow fell across the deck and there was Miss Abbott.

'I believe,' she said, 'in a personal Devil. Firmly.'

She stood above them, her back to the setting sun, her face dark and miserable. Alleyn began to get up from his deck-chair but she stopped him with a brusque movement of her hand. She jerked herself up on the hatch where she sat bolt upright, her large feet in tennis shoes dangling awkwardly.

'How else,' she demanded, 'can you explain the cruelties? God permits the Devil to torment us for His own inscrutable purposes.'

'Dear me!' observed Mr Merryman, quite mildly for him. 'We find ourselves in a positive hive of orthodoxy, do we not?'

'You're a churchman,' Miss Abbott said, 'aren't you? You came to Mass. Why do you laugh at the Devil?'

Mr Merryman contemplated her over his spectacles and after a long pause said: 'My dear Miss Abbott, if you can persuade me of his existence I assure you I shall not treat the Evil One as a laughing matter. Far from it.'

'*I'm* no good,' she said impatiently. 'Talk to Father Jourdain. He's full of knowledge and wisdom and will meet you on your own ground. I suppose you think it very uncouth of me to butt in and shove my faith down your throats but when – ' she set her dark jaw and went on with a kind of obstinacy, 'when I hear people laugh at the Devil it raises him in me. I *know* him.'

The others found nothing to say to her. She passed her hand heavily across her eyes. 'I'm sorry,' she said. 'I don't usually throw my weight about like this. It must be the heat.'

Aubyn Dale came along the deck, spectacular in sharkskin shorts, crimson pullover and a pair of exotic espadrilles he had bought in Las Palmas. He wore enormous sun-glasses and his hair was handsomely ruffled.

'I'm going to have a dip,' he said. 'Just time before dinner and the water's absolutely superb. Madame won't hear of it, though. Any takers here?'

Mr Merryman merely stared at him. Alleyn said he'd think about it. Miss Abbott got down from the hatch and walked away. Dale looked after her and wagged his head. 'Poor soul!' he said. 'I couldn't be sorrier for her. Honestly, life's hell for some women, isn't it?'

He looked at the other two men. Mr Merryman ostentatiously picked up his book and Alleyn made a noncommittal noise. 'I see a lot of that sort of thing,' Dale went on, 'in my fantastic job. The Lonely Legion, I call them. Only to myself, of course.'

'Quite,' Alleyn murmured.

'Well, let's face it. What the hell is there for them to do – looking like that? Religion. Exploring Central Africa? Or – ask yourself. *I* dunno,' said Dale, whimsically philosophical. 'One of those things.'

He pulled out his pipe, shook his head over it, said 'Ah, well!' and meeting perhaps with less response than he had expected, walked off, trilling a stylish catch.

Mr Merryman said something quite unprintable into his book and Alleyn went in search of Mrs Dillington-Blick.

He found her, still reclining on the verandah and fanning herself: enormous but delectable. Alleyn caught himself wondering what Henry Moore would have made of her. She welcomed him with enthusiasm and a helpless flapping gesture to show how hot she was. But her white dress was uncreased. A lace handkerchief protruded crisply from her décolletage and her hair was perfectly in order.

'You look as cool as a cucumber,' Alleyn said and sat down on Aubyn Dale's footrest, 'What an enchanting dress.'

She made comic eyes at him. 'My dear!' she said.

'But then all your clothes are enchanting. You dress quite beautifully, don't you?'

'How sweet of you to think so,' she cried, delightedly.

'Ah!' Alleyn said, leaning towards her, 'you don't know how big a compliment you're being paid. I'm extremely critical of women's clothes.'

'*Are* you, indeed. And what do you like about mine, may I ask?'

'I like them because they are clever enough to express the charm of their wearer,' Alleyn said with a mental reservation to tell that one to Troy.

'Now, I do call that a *perfect* remark! In future I shall dress 'specially for you. There now!' promised Mrs Dillington-Blick.

'Will you? Then I must think about what I should like you to wear. Tonight, for instance. Shall I choose that wonderful Spanish dress you bought in Las Palmas? May I?'

There was quite a long pause during which she looked sideways at him. 'I think perhaps that'd be a little too much, don't you?' she said at last. 'Sunday night, remember.'

'Well then, tomorrow?'

'Do you know,' she said, 'I've gone off that dress. You'll think me a frightful silly-billy but all the rather murky business with poor *sweet* Mr McAngus's doll has sort of set me against it. Isn't it queer?'

'*Oh*!' Alleyn ejaculated with a great show of disappointment. '*What* a pity! And what a waste!'

'I know. All the same, that's how it is. I just *see* Esmeralda looking so like those murdered girls and all I want to do with my lovely, lovely dress is drop it overboard.'

'You haven't done that!'

Mrs Dillington-Blick gave a little giggle. 'No,' she said. 'I haven't done that.'

'Or given it away?'

'Jemima would swim in it and I can't quite see Miss Abbott or Mrs Cuddy going all flamenco, can you?'

Dale came by on his way to the bathing-pool now wearing Palm Beach trunks and looking like a piece of superb publicity for a luxury liner. *'You're* a couple of slackers,' he said heartily and shinned nimbly down to the lower deck.

'I shall go and change,' sighed Mrs Dillington-Blick.

'But not into the Spanish dress?'

'I'm afraid not. Sorry to disappoint you.' She held out her luxurious little hands and Alleyn dutifully hauled her up. 'It's too sad,' he said, 'to think we are never to see it.'

'Oh, I shouldn't be absolutely sure of that,' she said and giggled again. 'I may change my mind and get inspired all over again.'

'To dance by the light of the moon?'

She stood quite still for a few seconds and then gave him her most ravishing smile. 'You never know, do you?' said Mrs Dillington-Blick.

Alleyn watched her stroll along the deck and go through the doors into the lounge.

' – and I expect you will agree,' he wrote to his wife that evening, 'that in a subsidiary sort of way, this was a thoroughly disquieting bit of information.'

IV

Steaming down the west coast of Africa, *Cape Farewell* ran into the sort of weather that is apt to sap the resources of people who are not accustomed to it. The air through which she moved was of the land: enervated and loaded with vague impurities. A thin greyness that resembled dust rather than cloud obscured the sun but scarcely modified its potency. Mr Merryman got a 'touch' of it and looked as if he was running a temperature but refused to do anything about it. Dysentery broke out among the crew and also afflicted Mr Cuddy who endlessly consulted Tim and, with unattractive candour, anybody else who would listen to him.

Aubyn Dale drank a little more and began to look like it and so, to Alleyn's concern, did Captain Bannerman. The Captain was a heavy, steady drinker, who grew less and less tractable as his potations increased. He now resented any attempt Alleyn might make to discuss the case in hand and angrily reiterated his statement that there were no homicidal lunatics on board his ship. He became morose, unapproachable and entirely pig-headed.

Mr McAngus on the other hand grew increasingly loquacious and continually lost himself in a maze of non sequiturs. 'He suffers,' Tim said, 'from verbal dysentery.'

'With Mr McAngus,' Alleyn remarked, 'the condition appears to be endemic. We mustn't blame the tropics.'

"They seem to have exacerbated it, however,' observed Father Jourdain wearily. 'Did you know that he had a row with Merryman last night?'

'What about?' Alleyn asked.

"Those filthy medicated cigarettes he smokes. Merryman says the smell makes him feel sick.'

'He's got something there,' Tim said. 'God knows what muck they're made of.'

'They stink like a wet haystack.'

'Ah, well,' Alleyn said, 'to our tasks, gentlemen. To our unwelcome tasks.'

Since their failure with the Captain they had agreed among themselves upon a plan of campaign. As soon as night fell each of them was to 'mark' one of the women passengers. Tim said flatly that he would take Jemima and that arrangement was generally allowed to be only fair. Father Jourdain said he thought perhaps Alleyn had better have Mrs Dillington-Blick. 'She alarms me,' he remarked. 'I have a feeling that she thinks I'm a wolf in priest's clothing. If I began following her about after dark she will be sure of it.'

Tim grinned at Alleyn: 'She's got her eye on you. It'd be quite a thing if you cut the Telly King out.'

'Don't confuse me,' Alleyn said dryly, and turned to Father Jourdain. 'You can handle the double, then,' he said. 'Mrs Cuddy never leaves Cuddy for a second and – ' He paused.

'And poor Katherine Abbott is not, you feel, in any great danger.'

'What do you suppose is the matter with her?' Alleyn asked and remembered what he had heard her saying as she left Father Jourdain on Saturday night. The priest's eyes were expressionless. 'We are not really concerned,' he said, 'with Miss Abbott's unhappiness, I think.'

'Oh,' Alleyn said, 'it's a sort of reflex action for me to wonder why people behave as they do. When we had the discussion about alibis, her distress over the Aubyn Dale programme of the night of January the fifteenth was illuminating, I thought.'

'I thought it damn' puzzling,' said Tim. 'D'you know, I actually found myself wondering, I can't think why, if she was the victim and not the viewer that night.'

'I think she was the viewer.'

Father Jourdain looked sharply at Alleyn and then walked over to the porthole and stared out.

'As for the victim – ' Alleyn went on, 'the woman, do you remember, who told Dale she didn't like to announce her engagement because it would upset her great friend? – ' He broke off and Tim said: 'You're not going to suggest that Miss Abbott was the great friend?'

'At least it would explain her reactions to the programme.'

After a short silence Tim said idly: 'What does she do? Has she a job, do you know?'

Without turning his head Father Jourdain said: 'She works for a firm of music publishers. She is quite an authority on early church music, particularly the Gregorian chants.'

Tim said involuntarily: 'I imagine, with that voice, she doesn't sing them herself.'

'On the contrary,' Alleyn rejoined, 'she does. Very pleasantly. I heard her on the night we sailed from Las Palmas.'

'She has a most unusual voice,' Father Jourdain said. 'If she were a man it would be a counter tenor. She represented her firm at a conference on Church music three weeks ago in Paris. I went over for it and saw her there. She was evidently a person of importance.'

'Was she indeed?' Alleyn murmured and then, briskly: 'Well, as you say, we are not immediately concerned with Miss Abbott. The sun's going down. It's time we went on duty.'

On the evenings of the eleventh and twelfth, according to plan, Alleyn devoted himself exclusively to Mrs Dillington-Blick. This manoeuvre brought about the evident chagrin of Aubyn Dale, the amusement of Tim, the surprise of Jemima and the greedy observance of Mrs Cuddy. Mrs Dillington-Blick was herself delighted. 'My dear!' she wrote to her friend, 'I've nobbled the Gorgeous Brute! My dear, too gratifying! Nothing, to coin a phrase, *tangible*. As yet! But *marked* attention! And with the tropical moon being what it is I feel something *rather* nice may eventuate? In the meantime I promise you, I've only to wander off after dinner to my so suitable little verandah and he's after me in a flash. A.D., my dear, rapidly becoming peagreen, which is always so gratifying. Aren't I hopeless but what fun! ! !'

On the night of the thirteenth, when they were all having coffee, Aubyn Dale suddenly decided to give a supper-party in his private sitting-room. It was equipped with a radiogram on which he proposed to play some of his own records.

'Everybody invited,' he said largely, waving his brandy glass. 'I won't take no for an answer,' and indeed it would have been difficult under the circumstances for anybody to attempt to refuse, though Mr Merryman and Tim looked as if they would have liked to do so.

The 'suite' turned out to be quite a grand affair. There were a great many signed photographs of Aubyn Dale's poppet and of several celebrities and one of Aubyn Dale himself, bowing before the grandest celebrity of all. There was a pigskin writing-case and a pigskin record-carrier. There were actually some monogrammed Turkish cigarettes, a present, Dale explained with boyish ruefulness, from a potentate who was one of his most ardent fans. And almost at once there was a great deal to drink. Mr McAngus was given a trick glass that poured his drink over his chin and was not quite as amused as the Captain, the Cuddys and Mrs Dillington-Blick though he took it quite quietly. Aubyn Dale apologized with the air of a chidden child and did several very accurate imitations of his fellow celebrities in television. Then they listened to four records including one of Dale himself doing an Empire Day talk on how to be Broadminded though British in which he laid a good deal of stress on the National Trait of being able to laugh at ourselves.

'*How* proud we are of it, too,' Tim muttered crossly to Jemima.

After the fourth record most of the guests began to be overtaken by the drowsiness of the tropics. Miss Abbott was the first to excuse herself and everybody else except Mrs Dillington-Blick and the

Captain followed her lead. Jemima had developed a headache in the overcrowded room and was glad to get out into the fresh air. She and Tim sat on the starboard side under Mr McAngus's porthole. There was a small ship's lamp in the deckhead above them.

'Only five minutes,' Jemima said. 'I'm for bed after that. My head's behaving like a piano accordion.'

'Have you got any aspirins?'

'I can't be bothered hunting them out.'

'I'll get you something. Don't move, will you?' Tim said, noting that the light from Mr McAngus's porthole and from the ship's lamp fell across her chair. He could hear Mr McAngus humming to himself in a reedy falsetto as he prepared for bed. 'You will stay put,' Tim said, 'won't you?'

'Why shouldn't I? I don't feel at all like shinning up the rigging or going for a strapping walk. Couldn't we have that overhead light off? Not,' Jemima said hurriedly, 'in order to create a romantic gloom, I assure you, Tim. It shines in one's eyes, rather; that's all.'

'The switch is down at the other end. I'll turn it off when I come back,' he said. 'I shan't be half a tick, Jem.'

When he had gone, Jemima lay back and shut her eyes. She listened to the ship's engines and to the sound of the sea and to Mr McAngus's droning. This stopped after a moment and through her closed lids she was aware of a lessening of light. 'He's turned his lamp off,' she thought gratefully, 'and has tucked his poor dithering old self up in his virtuous couch.' She opened her eyes and saw the dim light in the deckhead above her.

The next moment it, too, went out.

'That's Tim coming back,' she thought. 'He *has* been quick.'

She was now in almost complete darkness. A faint breeze lifted her hair. She heard no footfall but she was conscious that someone had approached from behind her.

'Tim?' she said.

Hands came down on her shoulders. She gave a little cry. 'Oh, *don't*! You made me jump.'

The hands shifted towards her neck and she felt her chain of pearls move and twist and break. She snatched at the hands and they were not Tim's.

'*No!*' she cried out, '*No! Tim!*'

There was a rapid thud of retreating feet. Jemima struggled out of her chair and ran down the dark tunnel of the covered deck into someone's arms.

'It's all right,' Alleyn said. 'You're all right. It's me.'

V

A few seconds later, Tim Makepiece came back.

Alleyn still held Jemima in his arms. She quivered and stammered and clutched at him like a frightened child.

'What the hell – ' Tim began but Alleyn stopped him.

'Did you turn out the deckhead lights?'

'No. Jem, darling – '

'Did you meet anyone?'

'No. Jem – !'

'All right. Take over, will you? She'll tell you when she's got her second wind.'

He disengaged her arms. 'You're in clover,' he said. 'Here's your medical adviser.'

She bolted into Tim's arms and Alleyn ran down the deck.

He switched on the overhead lights and followed round the centre-castle. He looked up and down companionways, along hatch coamings, behind piles of folded chairs and into recesses. He knew, as he hunted, he was too late. He found nothing but the odd blankness of a ship's decks at night. On the excuse that he had lost his pocket-book with his passport and letters of credit, he knocked up all the men, including Mr Cuddy. Dale was still dressed and in his sitting-room. The others were in pyjamas and varying degrees of ill-temper. He told Father Jourdain, briefly, what had happened and arranged that they would go, with Tim, to the Captain.

Then he returned to Jemima's chair. Her pearls were scattered on the deck and in the loose seat. He collected them and thought at first that otherwise, he had drawn a blank. But at the last, clinging to the back of the chair, discoloured and crushed, he found a scrap of something which, when he took it to the light, declared itself plainly enough. It was a tiny fragment of a flower petal.

It still retained, very faintly, the scent of hyacinth.

CHAPTER 9

Thursday the Fourteenth

'Now,' Alleyn demanded, standing over Captain Bannerman. '*Now*, do you believe this murderer's on board? Do you?'

But as he said it he knew he was up against the unassailable opponent: the elderly man who has made up his mind and is temperamentally incapable of admitting he has made it up the wrong way.

'I'll be damned if I do,' said Captain Bannerman.

'I am appalled to hear you say so.'

The Captain swallowed the end of his drink and clapped the glass down on the table. He looked from Alleyn to Father Jourdain, wiped his mouth with the back of his hand and said: 'You've got this blasted notion into your heads and every footling little thing that takes place, you make out is something to do with it. *What* takes place? Little Miss Jemima is sitting all alone in her deck-chair. Some chap comes up and puts his hands on her shoulders. Playful, like. And what's unnatural in that? By gum, I wouldn't blame – ' He pulled himself up, turned a darker shade of brick red and continued: 'On your own statement, she's got ideas into her head about these murders. Natural enough, I dare say, seeing how the lot of you can't let the matter alone but never stop talking about it. She's startled-like, and jumps up and runs away. Again – natural enough. But you come blustering up here and try to tell me she was nigh-on murdered. You won't get anywhere with me, that road. Someone's got to hang on to his common sense in this ship and, by gum, that's going to be the Master.'

Father Jourdain said: 'But it's not the one incident, it's the whole sequence, as Alleyn has shown us only too clearly. An embarkation paper in the hand of the girl on the wharf. The incident of the doll. The fact that singing was heard. The peeping Tom at Miss Carmichael's porthole. Now this. What man among us, knowing these crimes are in all our minds, would play such a trick on her?'

'And what man among you would murder her – tell me that!'

Tim had been sitting with his head between his hands. He now looked up and said: 'Sir, even if you do think there's nothing in it, surely there can be no harm in taking every possible precaution – ?'

'What the hell have you all been doing if you haven't been taking precautions? Haven't I said just that, all along? Didn't I – ' he pointed his stubby finger at Alleyn, – 'get them all jabbering about alibis because you asked me to? Haven't I found out for you that the whole boiling went ashore the night we sailed, never mind if my own deckhand thought I was barmy? Haven't I given out there's an undesirable character in my ship's company, which there isn't, and ordered the ladies to lock their doors? What the suffering cats more could I have done? Tell me that!'

Alleyn said instantly: 'You could, you know, do something to ensure that there's no more wandering about deserted decks at night in Spanish dresses.'

'I've told you. I won't have any interference with the rights of the individual in my ship.'

'Will you let me say something unofficially about it?'

'No.'

'Will you consider a complete showdown? Will you tell the passengers who I am and why I'm here? It'll mean no arrest, of course,' Alleyn said, 'but with the kind of threat that I believe hangs over this ship I'm prepared to admit defeat. Will you do this?'

'No.'

'You realize that tomorrow is the night, when, according to the considered opinion of experts, this man may be expected to go into action again?'

'He's not aboard my ship.'

' – and that Miss Carmichael,' Father Jourdain intervened, 'naturally will speak of her fears to the other ladies.'

Tim said: 'No.'

'No?'

'No,' Alleyn said. 'She's not going to talk about it. She agrees that it might lead to a panic. She's a courageous child.'

'She's been given a shock,' Tim said angrily to the Captain, 'that may very easily have extremely serious results. I can't allow – '

'Doctor Makepiece, you'll be good enough to recollect you have signed on as a member of my ship's company.'

'Certainly, sir.'

The Captain stared resentfully about him, made a petulant ejaculation and roared out: 'Damn it, you can tell her to stay in bed all day tomorrow and the next day too, can't you? Suffering from shock? All right. That gets *her* out of the way, doesn't it? Where is she now?'

'I've given her a Nembutal. She's asleep in bed. The door's locked and I've got the key.'

'Well, keep it and let her stay there. The steward can take her meals. Unless you think *he's* the sex monster,' said the Captain with an angry laugh.

'Not in the sense you mean,' Alleyn said.

'That's enough of that!' the Captain shouted.

'Where,' Father Jourdain asked wearily, 'is Mrs Dillington-Blick?'

'In bed,' the Captain said at once, and added in a hurry: 'She left Dale's suite when I did. I saw her to her cabin.'

'They do lock their doors, don't they?'

'She did,' said the Captain morosely.

Father Jourdain got up. 'If I may be excused,' he said. 'It's very late. Past midnight.'

'Yes,' Alleyn said and he also rose. 'It's February the fourteenth. Goodnight, Captain Bannerman.'

He had a brief session with Father Jourdain and Tim. The latter was in a rage. 'That *bloody* Old Man,' he kept saying. 'Did you ever know such a *bloody* Old Man!'

'All right, all right,' Alleyn said. 'We'll just have to go on under our own steam. The suggestion, by the way, to keep Miss Carmichael in bed for twenty-four hours has its points.'

Tim said grandly that he'd consider it. Father Jourdain asked if they were to do anything about the other women. Could they not emphasize that as Jemima had had an unpleasant experience it might be as well if the ladies were particularly careful not to wander about the deck at night without an escort.

Alleyn said: 'We've done that already. But think a minute. Suppose one of them chose the wrong escort.'

'You know, it's an extraordinary thing,' Father Jourdain said after a moment, 'but I keep forgetting it's one of us. I almost believe in the legend of the unsavoury deck-hand.'

'I think it might be a good idea if you suggest a four of bridge or canasta. Mrs Dillington-Blick plays both, doesn't she? Get Mrs Cuddy and Miss Abbott to come in. Or if Dale and the other men all play you might get two fours going. Makepiece will look after Miss Carmichael.'

'What'll you do?' Tim asked.

'I?' Alleyn asked. 'Look on. Look round. Just look. Of course they may refuse to play. In which case we'll have to use our wits, Heaven help us, and improvise. In the meantime, you probably both want to go to bed.'

'And you, no doubt,' said Father Jourdain.

'Oh,' Alleyn said, 'I'm an owl by habit. See you in the morning. Goodnight.'

He was indeed trained to put up with long stretches of sleeplessness and faced the rest of the short night with equanimity. He changed into slacks, a dark shirt and rope-soled shoes and then began a systematic beat. Into the deserted lounge. Out on to the well-deck, past the little verandah where the two chaise-longues stood deserted. Round the hatch, and then to the cabin quarters and their two covered decks.

The portholes were all open. He listened outside each of them. The first, facing aft and to the starboard side, was Mr Merryman's. It appeared to be in darkness but after a moment he saw that a blue point glowed somewhere inside. It was the little nightlight above the bed. Alleyn stood near the porthole and was just able to make out Mr Merryman's tousled head on the pillow. Next came the doorway into the passage bisecting the cabin-quarters and then further along on the starboard side was Mr McAngus who could be heard whistling in his sleep. The Cuddys, in the adjoining, the last on the starboard side, snored antiphonally. He turned left and moved along the forward face of the block, past Miss Abbott's dark and silent

cabin and then on to Father Jourdain's. His light still shone and as
the porthole was uncovered Alleyn thought he would have a word
with him.

He looked in. Father Jourdain was on his knees before a crucifix,
his joined hands pressed edgeways to his lips. Alleyn turned away
and walked on to the 'suite'. Dale's light was still in his sitting-room.
Alleyn stood a little to one side of the forward porthole. The curtain
across it fluttered and blew out. He caught a brief glimpse of Dale in
brilliant pyjamas with a glass in his hand. He turned left past
Jemima's porthole with its carefully-drawn curtain and then moved
aft to Mrs Dillington-Blick's cabin. Her light too was still on. He
paused with his back to the bulkhead and close to her porthole and
became aware of a rhythmic slapping noise and a faint whiff of some
aromatic scent. 'She's coping with her neckline,' he thought.

He moved on past the darkened lounge. He had completed his
round and was back at Mr Merryman's cabin.

He approached the iron ladder leading to the forward well-deck
and climbed down it. When he had reached the bottom he waited
for a moment in the shadow of the centrecastle. On his left was the
door through which the figure in the Spanish dress had come on
Friday night. It led into a narrow passage by the chief steward's quar
ters. Above him towered the centrecastle. He knew if he walked out
into the moonlight, the second officer, keeping his watch far above
on the bridge, would see him. He did walk out. His shadow, black as
ink, splayed across the deck and up the hatch coaming.

On the fo'c'sle two bells sounded. Alleyn watched the seaman
who had rung them come down and cross the deck towards him.

'Goodnight,' he said.

'Goodnight, sir,' the man replied and sounded surprised.

Alleyn said: 'I thought I'd go up into the bows and see if I could
find a cap-full of cool air.'

'That's right, sir. A bit fresher up there.'

The man passed him and disappeared into shadow. Alleyn
climbed up to the fo'c'sle and stood in the bows. For a moment or
two he faced the emptiness of the night. Beneath him, in a pother of
phosphorescence, the waters were divided. 'There is nothing more
lonely in the world,' he thought, 'than a ship at sea.'

He turned and looked at the ship, purposeful and throbbing with her own life. Up on the bridge he could see the second officer. He waved with a broad gesture of his arm and after a moment the second officer replied slightly, perhaps ironically.

Alleyn returned to the lower deck. As he climbed down the ladder, a door beneath him, leading into the seamen's quarters in the fo'c'sle, opened and somebody came out. Alleyn looked down over his shoulder. The newcomer, barefooted and clad only in pyjama trousers, moved out, seemed to sense that he was observed and stopped short.

It was Dennis. When he saw Alleyn he made as if to return.

Alleyn said: 'You keep late hours, steward.'

'Oh, it's *you*, Mr Broderick. You quite startled me. Yes, *don't* I? I've been playing poker with the boys,' Dennis explained. 'Fancy you being up there, sir, at this time of night.'

Alleyn completed his descent. 'I couldn't sleep,' he said. 'It's the heat, I suppose.'

Dennis giggled. 'I *know*. Isn't it terrific!'

He edged away slightly.

'What's it like in your part of the world?' Alleyn asked. 'Where are your quarters?'

'I'm in the glory-hole, sir. Down below. It's *frightful*.'

'All the same, I fancy it's healthier indoors.'

Dennis said nothing.

'You want to be careful what you wear in the tropics. Particularly at night.'

Dennis looked at his plump torso and smirked.

Alleyn waited for a moment and then said: 'Well, I shall take my own advice and go back to bed. Goodnight to you.'

'Good *morning*, sir,' said Dennis pertly.

Alleyn climbed up to the bridge deck. When he got there he looked back. Dennis still stood where he had left him but after a moment turned away and went back into the fo'c'sle.

At intervals, through the rest of the night, Alleyn walked round his beat but he met nobody. When the dawn came up he went to bed and slept until Dennis, pallid, glistening and silent, brought in his morning tea.

II

That day was the hottest the passengers had experienced. For Alleyn it began with a radioed report in code from Inspector Fox who was still sweating away with his checks on alibis. Apart from routine confirmations of Mr McAngus's appendicular adventure and Aubyn Dale's departure for America, nothing new had come to hand. The Yard, Fox intimated, would await instructions which meant, Alleyn sourly and unfairly reflected, that if he made an arrest before Cape Town, somebody would be flown over with a spare pair of handcuffs or something. He made his way, disgruntled, to continue observation on the passengers.

They were all on the lower deck. Jemima, who was still rather white, had flatly refused to stay in bed and spent most of the day in or near the bathing-pool where an awning had been erected and deck-chairs set out. Here she was joined by Tim and at intervals by one or two of the others. Only Miss Abbott, Mr McAngus and Mrs Cuddy refrained from bathing, but they too sat under the awning and looked on.

At noon Mrs Dillington-Blick took to the water and the appearance was in the nature of a star turn. She wore a sort of bathing-negligee which Aubyn Dale, who escorted her, called a 'bewilderment of nonsense'. It was all compact of crisp cotton frills and black ribbons and under it Mrs Dillington-Blick was encased in her Jolyon Swimsuit which belonged to a group advertised as being 'for the Queenly Woman'. She had high-heeled thonged sandals on her feet and had to be supported down the companion-ladder by Aubyn Dale who carried her towel and sunshade. At this juncture only Jemima, Tim, Alleyn and Mr Cuddy were bathing. The others were assembled under the awning and provided an audience for Mrs Dillington-Blick. She laughed a great deal and made deprecatory *moues*. 'My dears!' she said. '*Look* at me!'

'You know,' Jemima said to Tim, 'I really *do* admire her. She actually cashes in on her size. I call that brilliant.'

'It's fascinating,' Tim agreed. 'Do look! She's standing there like a piece of baroque, waiting to be unveiled.'

Dale performed this ceremony. Alleyn, who was perched on the edge of the pool near the steps that led down into it, watched the reaction. It would have been untrue to say that anybody gasped when Mrs Dillington-Blick relinquished her bathing-robe. Rather, a kind of trance overtook her fellow-passengers. Mr Cuddy, who had been frisking in the waters, grasped the rim of the pool and grinned horridly through his wet fringe. Mr Merryman, who wore an old-fashioned gown and an equally old-fashioned bathing-dress and whose hair had gone into a damp fuzz like a baby's, stared over his spectacles, as startled as Mr Pickwick in the Maiden Lady's four-poster. Mr McAngus, who had been dozing, opened his eyes and his mouth at the same time and turned dark red in the face. On the bridge, Captain Bannerman was transfixed. Two deckhands stood idle for several seconds round a can of red lead and then self-consciously fell to work with their heads together.

Mrs Cuddy tried to catch somebody's eye but, failing to do so, stared in amazement at her infatuated husband.

Miss Abbott looked up from the letter she was writing, blinked twice and looked down again.

Father Jourdain, who had been reading, made a slight move-ment with his right hand. Alleyn told himself it was absurd to suppose that Father Jourdain had been visited by an impulse to cross himself.

Jemima broke the silence. She called out: 'Jolly good! Come in: it's Heaven.'

Mrs Dillington-Blick put on a bathing cap, removed her sandals, precariously climbed the ladder up to the rim of the pool, avoided looking at Mr Cuddy and held out her hands to Alleyn.

'Launch me,' she invited winningly and at the same moment lost her balance and fell like an avalanche into the brimming pool. The water she displaced surged over the edges. Alleyn, Mr Cuddy, Jemima and Tim bobbed about like flotsam and jetsam. Aubyn Dale was drenched. Mrs Dillington-Blick surfaced, gasping and astound-ed, and struck out for the nearest handhold.

'Ruby!' Aubyn Dale cried anxiously, as he dashed the sea-water from his face, 'what have you done?'

For the first time in the voyage Mr Merryman burst into peals of ungovernable laughter.

This incident had a serio-comic sequel. While Mrs Dillington-Blick floated in a corner of the pool, clinging to the edges, Mr Cuddy swam slyly alongside and with a quick grab pulled her under. There was a struggle from which she emerged furious and half-suffocated. Her face was streaked with mascara, her nose was running and her bathing cap was askew. She was a terrible sight. Alleyn helped her up the submerged steps. Dale received her on the far side and got her down to deck level.

'That horrible man!' she choked out. 'That horrible man!'

Mr McAngus also hurried to her side while Mr Cuddy leered over the rim of the pool.

A ridiculous and rather alarming scene ensued. Mr McAngus, in an unrecognizably shrill voice, apostrophized Mr Cuddy: 'You're an unmitigated bounder, sir,' he screamed and actually shook his fist in Mr Cuddy's wet face.

'I must say, Cuddy!' Dale said, all restraint and seemly indignation, 'you've got an extraordinary idea of humour.'

Mr Cuddy still leered and blinked. Mrs Cuddy from her deck-chair, cried anxiously: 'Dear! You're forgetting yourself.'

'You're an ape, sir!' Mr McAngus added and he and Dale simultaneously placed an arm round Mrs Dillington-Blick.

'I'll look after her,' said Dale coldly.

'Let me help you,' said Mr McAngus. 'Come and sit down.'

'Leave her alone. Ruby, darling – '

'Oh, shut up, both of you!' said Mrs Dillington-Blick. She snatched up her robe and made off: a mountain of defaced femininity.

Mr Merryman continued to laugh, the other gentlemen separated and Mr Cuddy swam quietly about the pool by himself.

It was the only incident of note in an otherwise torpid day. After luncheon all the passengers went to their respective cabins and Alleyn allowed himself a couple of hours' sleep. He woke, as he had arranged with himself to wake, at four o'clock and went down to tea. Everybody was limp and disinclined to talk. Dale, Mr McAngus and Mr Cuddy had evidently decided to calm down. Mr Merryman's venture into the pool had brought on his 'touch of the sun' again. He looked feverish and anxious and actually didn't seem to have the energy to argue with anyone. Jemima came over to him. She very prettily knelt by his chair, and begged him to let her find Tim and ask him to prescribe. 'Or at least take some aspirin,' she said. 'I'll get some for you. Will you?' She put her hand on his but he drew it away quickly.

'I think I may have a slight infection,' he said in explanation and positively added: 'But thank you, my dear.'

'You're terribly hot.' She went away and returned with the aspirin and water. He consented to take three tablets and said he would lie down for a little while. When he went out they all noticed that he was quite shaky.

'Well,' Mr Cuddy said, 'I'm sure I hope it's nothing catching.'

'It's not very considerate,' Mrs Cuddy said, 'to sit round with everybody if it is. How are you feeling, dear?'

'Good, thanks, dear. My little trouble,' Mr Cuddy said to everybody, 'has cleared up nicely. I'm a box of birds. I really quite enjoy the heat: something a bit intoxicating about the tropics, to my way of thinking.'

He himself was not urgently intoxicating. His shirt had unlovely dark areas about it, the insides of his knees were raddled with prickly heat and his enormous hands left wet patches on everything they touched. 'I'm a very free perspirer,' he said proudly, 'and that's a healthy sign, I'm told.'

This observation met with a kind of awed silence broken by Mr McAngus.

'Has everybody seen?' he asked, turning his back on Mr Cuddy. 'There's going to be a film tonight. They've just put up a notice. On the boat deck, it's going to be.'

There was a stir of languid interest. Father Jourdain muttered to Alleyn: 'That disposes of our canasta party.'

'How lovely!' Mrs Dillington-Blick said. 'Where do we sit?'

'I *think*,' Mr McAngus fluted, at once tripping up to her, 'that we all sit on deck-chairs on the top of the hatch. Such a good idea! You must lie on your chaise-longue, you know. You'll look quite wonderful,' he added with his timid little laugh. 'Like Cleopatra in her barge with all her slaves round her. Pagan, almost.'

'My dear!'

'What's the film?' Dale asked.

'*Othello*. With that large American actor.'

'Oh, God!'

'Mr Merryman *will* be pleased,' said Jemima. 'It's his favourite. If he improves, of course.'

'Well, *I* don't think he ought to come,' Mrs Cuddy at once objected. 'He should consider other people.'

'It'll be in the open air,' Miss Abbott countered, 'and there's no need, I imagine, for you to sit next to Mr Merryman.'

Mrs Cuddy smiled meaningly at her husband.

Jemima said: 'But how exciting! Orson Welles and everything! I couldn't be better pleased.'

'We'd rather have a nice musical,' said Mrs Cuddy. 'But then we're not arty, are we, dear?'

Mr Cuddy said nothing. He was looking at Mrs Dillington-Blick.

III

The film version of *Othello* began to wind up its remarkable course. Mr Merryman could be heard softly invoking the retribution of the gods upon the head of Mr Orson Welles.

In the front row Captain Bannerman sighed windily, Mrs Dillington-Blick's jaw quivered and Dale periodically muttered: 'Oh, *no!*' Alleyn, who was flabbergasted by the film, was able to give it only a fraction of his attention.

Behind the Captain's party sat the rest of the passengers, while a number of ship's officers were grouped together at one side. Dennis and his fellow-stewards watched from the back.

The sea was perfectly calm, stars glittered with explosive brilliance. The cinema screen, an incongruous accident with a sterile life of its own, glowed and gestured in the surrounding darkness.

> Put out the light, and then put out the light.
> If I quench thee, thou flaming minister,
> I can again thy former light restore,
> Should I repent me –

Jemima caught her breath and Tim reached for her hand. They were moved by a single impulse and by one thought: that it was superbly right for them to listen together to this music.

– I know not where is that Promethean heat
That can thy light relume.

'*Promethean heat,*' Father Jourdain murmured appreciatively.

The final movement emerged not entirely obscured by the treatment that had been accorded it. A huge face loomed out of the screen.

Kill me tomorrow; let me live tonight –
– But half an hour!
Being done, there is no pause.
But while I say one prayer!
It is too late.

A white cloth closed like a shroud about Desdemona's face and tightened horridly.

The screen was no longer there. At their moment of climax Othello and Desdemona were gone and their audience was in darkness. The pulse of the ship's engines emerged and the chief engineer's voice saying that a fuse had blown somewhere. Matches were struck. There was a group of men round the projector. Alleyn produced his torch, slipped out of his seat which was at the end of the row, and walked slowly along the hatch. None of the passengers had stirred but there was a certain amount of movement among the stewards, some of whom, including Dennis, had already left.

'The circuit's gone,' a voice near the projector said and another added: 'That's the story. Hold everything.' One of the figures disentangled itself and hurried away.

' "Put out the light",' a junior officer quoted derisively, ' "and then put out the light".' There was a little gust of laughter. Mrs Cuddy in the middle of the third row, tittered: 'He stifles her, doesn't he, dear? Same thing again! We don't seem to be able to get away from it, do we?'

Miss Abbott said furiously: 'Oh, for pity's *sake!*'

Alleyn had reached the edge of the hatch. He stood there, watching the backs of the passengers' chairs, now clearly discernible. Immediately in front of him were Tim and Jemima, their hands enlaced, leaning a little towards each other. Jemima was saying: 'I don't want to pull it to pieces yet. After all there *are* the words.'

A figure rose up from the chair in the middle of the row. It was Mr Merryman.

'I'm off,' he announced.

'Are you all right, Mr Merryman?' Jemima asked.

'I am nauseated,' Mr Merryman rejoined, 'but not for the reason you suppose. I can stomach no more of this. Pray excuse me.'

He edged past them and past Father Jourdain, moved round the end of the row and thus approached Alleyn.

'Had enough?' Alleyn asked.

'A bellyful, thank you.'

He sat on the edge of the hatch, his back ostentatiously presented to the invisible screen. He was breathing hard. His hand which had brushed against Alleyn's was hot and dry.

'I'm afraid you've still got a touch of your bug, whatever it is,' Alleyn said. 'Why don't you turn in?'

But Mr Merryman was implacable. 'I do not believe,' he said, 'in subjecting myself to the tyranny of indisposition. I do not, like our Scottish acquaintance, surrender to hypochondriacal speculations. On the contrary, I fight back. Besides,' he added, 'in this Stygian gloom, where is the escape? There is none. *J'y suis, et j'y reste.*'

And so in fact he remained. The fuse was repaired, the film drew to its close. An anonymous choir roared its anguish and, without benefit of authorship, ended the play. The lights went up and the passengers moved to the lounge for supper. Mr Merryman alone remained outside, seated in a deck-chair by the open doors and refusing sustenance.

Alleyn, and indeed all of them, were to remember that little gathering very vividly: Mrs Dillington-Blick had recovered her usual form and was brilliant. Dressed in black lace, though not that of her Spanish dress, and wreathed in the effulgence of an expensive scent that had by now acquired the authority of a signature tune, she held her customary court. She discussed the film: it had, she said, *really* upset her. 'My dear! That ominous man! Terrifying! But all the same — there's *something*. One could quite see why she married him.'

'I thought it disgusting,' Mrs Cuddy said. 'A black man. She deserved all she got.'

Mrs Dillington-Blick laughed. She and Aubyn Dale, Alleyn noticed, kept catching each other's eye and quickly looking away again. Neither Mr Cuddy nor Mr McAngus could remove their gaze from her. The Captain hung over her: even Miss Abbott watched her with a kind of brooding appreciation while Mrs Cuddy resentfully stared and stared. Only Jemima and Tim, bent on their common voyage of discovery, were unmindful of Mrs Dillington-Blick.

Presently she yawned, and she even managed to yawn quite fetchingly.

'I'm for my little bed,' she announced.

'Not even a stroll around the deck?' asked the Captain.

'I *don't* think so, really.'

'Or a cigarette on the verandah?' Dale suggested loudly.

'I might.'

She laughed and walked over to the open doors. Mr Merryman struggled up from his deck-chair. She wished him goodnight, looked back into the lounge and smiled intimately and brilliantly at Mr McAngus. 'Goodnight,' she repeated softly and went out on the deserted deck.

Father Jourdain caught his breath. 'All right,' Alleyn muttered. 'You carry on, here.'

Tim glanced at Alleyn and nodded. The Captain had been buttonholed by Mr McAngus and looked restive. Jemima was talking to Mr Merryman who half-rose, bestowed on her an old-fashioned bow and sank groggily back into his chair. Aubyn Dale was drinking and Mr Cuddy was in the grasp of his wife who now removed him.

Alleyn said: 'Goodnight, everybody.' He followed the Cuddys into the passageway, turned left and went to the deck by the port-side door. He was just in time to see Mrs Dillington-Blick disappear round the verandah corner of the engine house. Before he could reach it she returned, paused for a second when she saw him, and then swam gaily towards him.

'Just one gulp of fresh air,' she said rather breathlessly. She slipped her arm through his and quite deliberately leant against him.

'Help me negotiate that frightful ladder, will you? I want to go down to the lower deck.'

He glanced back at the lounge. There they all were, lit up like a distant peep show.

'Why the lower deck?'

'I don't know. A whim.' She giggled. 'Nobody will find me for one thing.'

The companion ladder was close to where they stood. She led him towards it, turned and gave him her hands.

'I'll go backwards. You follow.'

He was obliged to do so. When they reached the promenade deck she took his arm again.

'Let's see if there are ghost fires tonight.'

She looked over the side still holding him.

Alleyn said: 'You're much too dangerous a person for me, you know.'

'Do you really think so?'

'I do indeed. Right out of my class. I'm a dull dog.'

'I don't find you so.'

'How enchanting of you,' Alleyn said. 'I must tell my wife. That'll larn her.'

'Is she very attractive?'

Suddenly, in place of the plushy, the abundant, the superbly tended charms now set before him, Alleyn saw his wife's head with its clearly defined planes, its delicate bone and short not very tidy hair.

He said: 'I must leave you, I'm afraid. I've got work to do.'

'Work? What sort of work, for heaven's sake?'

'Business letters. Reports.'

'I don't believe you. In mid-ocean!'

'It's true.'

'Look! There *are* ghost fires.'

'And I don't think you'd better stay down here by yourself. Come along. I'll see you to your cabin.'

He put his hand over hers. 'Come along,' he repeated. She stared at him, her lips parted.

'All right!' she agreed suddenly. 'Let's.'

They returned by the inside stairway and he took her to her door.

'You're *rather* nice,' she whispered.

'Lock your door, won't you?'

'Oh, good *heavens!*' said Mrs Dillington-Blick and bounced into her cabin. He heard her shoot her bolt and he returned quickly to the lounge.

Only Father Jourdain, Tim and Captain Bannerman were there. Miss Abbott came in by the double doors as Alleyn arrived. Tim furtively signalled 'thumbs up', and Father Jourdain said: 'Everybody seems to be going to bed early tonight.'

'It's not all that early,' Captain Bannerman rejoined, staring resentfully at Miss Abbott.

She stopped dead in the middle of the room and with her eyes downcast seemed to take in the measure of her own unwantedness.

'Goodnight,' she said grudgingly and went out.

Father Jourdain followed her to the landing. 'By the way,' Alleyn heard him say, 'I got that word in the Ximenes. It's "holocaust".'

'How brilliant!' she said. 'That should be a great help.'

'I think so. Goodnight.'

'Goodnight.'

Father Jourdain came back: ' "Safely stowed",' he quoted and smiled at Alleyn.

Alleyn asked sharply, 'Where's everybody else?'

'It's OK,' Tim rejoined. 'The women are all in their cabins: at least I suppose you've accounted for the D-B, haven't you?'

'And the men?'

'Does it matter? Cuddy went off with his wife and McAngus, very properly, by himself. Merryman toddled off some time after that.'

'And Dale?'

'He left after the Cuddys,' Tim said.

'I think,' Father Jourdain observed, 'that someone must have gone out on deck?'

'Why?'

'Only because I thought I heard someone singing.' His voice faded and his face blanched. 'But there's nothing in that!' Father Jourdain ejaculated. 'We can't panic every time somebody sings.'

'I can!' Alleyn said grimly.

'With the women all in their cabins? Why?'

Captain Bannerman interjected, loudly scoffing: 'You may well ask why! Because Mr Ah-leen's got a bee in his bonnet. That's why!'

'What had McAngus got to say to you?' Alleyn asked him.

The Captain glowered at him. 'He reckons someone's been interfering with his hyacinths.'

'Interfering?'

'Pinching them.'

'Damnation!' Alleyn said and turned to go out.

Before he could do so, however, he was arrested by the sound of thudding feet.

It came from the deck outside and was accompanied by tortuous breathing. For a moment the brilliant square cast by the light in the lounge was empty. Then into it ran an outlandish figure, half-naked, wet, ugly, gasping.

It was Cuddy. When he saw Alleyn he fetched up short, grinning abominably. Water ran from his hair into his open mouth.

'Well?' Alleyn demanded. 'What is it?'

Cuddy gestured meaninglessly. His arm quivered like a branch.

'What is it? Speak up! Quickly.'

Cuddy lunged forward. His wet hands closed like clamps on Alleyn's arms.

'Mrs Dillington-Blick,' he stuttered and the syllables dribbled out with the water from his mouth. He nodded two or three times, came close to Alleyn and then threw back his head and broke into sobbing laughter.

'The verandah?'

'What the bloody hell are you talking about?' the Captain shouted.

Cuddy nodded and nodded.

Alleyn said: 'Captain Bannerman, will you come with me, if you please? And Dr Makepiece.' He struck up Cuddy's wet arms and thrust him aside. He started off down the deck with them both at his heels.

They had gone only a few paces when a fresh rumpus broke out behind them. Cuddy's hysterical laughter had mounted to a scream.

Father Jourdain shouted: 'Doctor Makepiece! Come back!'

There was a soft thud and silence.

Captain Bannerman said: 'Wait a bit. He's fainted.'

'Let him faint.'

'But – '

'All right. *All right.*'

He strode on down the deck. There was a light in the deckhead over the verandah. Alleyn switched it on.

The Spanish dress was spread out wide, falling in black cascades on both sides of the chaise-longue. Its wearer lay back, luxuriously, each gloved hand trailing on the deck. The head was impossibly twisted over the left shoulder. The face was covered down to the tip of the nose by part of the mantilla which had been dragged down like a blind. The exposed area was livid and patched almost to the colour of the mole at the corner of the mouth. The tongue protruded, the plump throat already was discoloured. Artificial pearls from a broken necklace lay scattered across the décolletage into which had been thrust a white hyacinth.

'All right,' Alleyn said without turning. 'It's too late, of course, but you'd better see if there's anything you can do.'

Tim had come up with Captain Bannerman behind him. Alleyn stood aside. 'Only Dr Makepiece please,' he said. 'I want as little traffic as possible.'

Tim stooped over the body.

In a moment he had straightened up.

'But, look here!' he said. 'It's not – it's – it's – '

'Exactly. But our immediate concern is with the chances of recovery. Are there any?'

'None.'

'Sure?'

'None.'

'Very well. Now, this is what we do – '

IV

Captain Bannerman and Tim Makepiece stood side-by-side exactly where Alleyn had placed them. The light in the deckhead shone down on the area round the chaise-longue. It was dappled with irregular wet patches most of which had been made by large naked feet. Alleyn found that they were overlaid by his own prints and Tim's and by others which he examined closely.

'Espadrilles,' he said, 'size nine.'

The wearer had approached the chaise-longue, stood beside it, turned and made off round the starboard side.

'Running,' Alleyn said, following the damp prints. 'Running along the deck, then stopping as he got into the light, then turning and stopping by the hatch and then carrying on round the centre-castle to the port side. Not much doubt about that one.'

He turned back towards the verandah, pausing by a tall locker near its starboard corner. He shone his torch behind this. 'Cigarette ash and a butt.'

He collected the butt and found it was monogrammed and Turkish.

'How corny can you get?' he muttered, showing it to Tim, and returned to the verandah from where he pursued the trace of the wet naked feet. Their owner had come to the port side companion-ladder from the lower deck and the swimming-pool. On the fifth step from the top there was a large wet patch.

He returned to Captain Bannerman.

'In this atmosphere,' he said, 'I can't afford to wait. I'm going to take photographs. After that we'll have to seal off the verandah. I suggest, sir, that you give orders to that effect.'

Captain Bannerman stood louring at him. 'This sort of thing,' he said at last, 'couldn't have been anticipated. It's against common sense.'

'On the contrary,' Alleyn rejoined, 'it's precisely what was to be expected.'

CHAPTER 10

Aftermath

The passengers sat at one end of the lounge behind shut doors and drawn blinds. Out of force of habit each had gone to his or her accustomed place and the scene thus was giving a distorted semblance of normality. Only Mr Merryman was absent. And, of course, Mrs Dillington-Blick.

Alleyn himself had visited the unattached men in their cabins. Mr Merryman had been peacefully and very soundly asleep, his face blank and rosy, his lips parted and his hair ruffled in a cockscomb. Alleyn decided for the moment to leave him undisturbed. Shutting the door quietly, he crossed the passage. Mr McAngus in vivid pyjamas had been doing something with a small brush to his hair which was parted in the middle and hung in dark elf locks over his ears. He had hastily slammed down the lid of an open box on his dressing-table and turned his back on it. Aubyn Dale, fully dressed, was in his sitting-room. He had a drink in his hand and apparently he had been standing close to his door which was not quite shut. His manner was extraordinary: at once defiant, terrified and expectant. It was obvious also that he was extremely drunk. Alleyn looked at him for a moment and then said:

'What have you been up to?'

'I? Have a drink, dear boy? No? What d'you mean, up to?' He swallowed the remains of his drink and poured out another.

'Where have you been since you left the lounge?'

'What the devil's that got to do with you?' He lurched towards Alleyn and peered into his face. 'Who the bloody hell,' he asked indistinctly, 'do you think you are?'

Alleyn took him in the regulation grip: 'Come along,' he said, 'and find out.'

He marched Dale into the lounge and deposited him in the nearest chair.

Tim Makepiece had fetched Jemima and Mrs Cuddy. Mr Cuddy, recovered from his faint, had been allowed to change into pyjamas and dressing-gown and looked ghastly.

Captain Bannerman, louring and on the defensive, stood beside Alleyn.

He said: 'Something's happened tonight that I never thought to see in my ship and a course of action has to be set to deal with it.'

He jerked his head at Alleyn. 'This gentleman will give the details. He's a Scotland Yard man and his name's A'leen not Broderick and he's got my authority to proceed.'

Nobody questioned or exclaimed at this announcement. It was merely accorded a general look of worried bewilderment. The Captain nodded morosely at Alleyn and then sat down and folded his arms.

Alleyn said: 'Thank you, sir.' He was filled with anger against Captain Bannerman: an anger not unmixed with compassion and no more tolerable for that. At least half the passengers were scarcely less irritating. They were irresponsible, they were helpless, two of them were profoundly silly and one of them was a murderer. He took himself sharply to task and began to talk to them.

He said: 'I shan't at the moment elaborate or explain the statement you've just heard. You will, if you please, accept it. I'm a police officer. A murder has been committed and one of the passengers in this ship, almost certainly, is responsible.'

Mr Cuddy's smile, an incredible phenomenon, was stamped across his face like a postmark. His lips moved. He said with a kind of terrified and incredulous jocosity: 'Oh, go on!' His fellow passengers looked appalled but Mrs Cuddy dreadfully and incredibly tossed her head and said: 'Mrs Blick, isn't it? I suppose it's a remark I shouldn't pass but I must say with that type of behaviour – '

'No!' Father Jourdain interposed very strongly. 'You must stop. Be quiet, Mrs Cuddy!'

'Well, I must say!' she gasped and turned to her husband. 'It *is* Mrs Blick, Fred, isn't it?'

'Yes, dear.'

Alleyn said: 'It will become quite apparent before we've gone very much further who it is. The victim was found a few minutes ago by Mr Cuddy. I am going to take statements from most of you. I'm sorry I can't confine the whole business to the men only and I hope to do so before long. Possibly it's less distressing for the ladies, who are obviously not under suspicion, to hear the preliminary examination than it would be for them to be kept completely in the dark.'

He glanced at Jemima, white and quiet, sitting by Tim and looking very young in a cotton dressing-gown and with her hair tied back. Tim had fetched her from her cabin. He had said: 'Jem: Something rather bad has happened to somebody in the ship. It's going to shock you, my dear.'

She had answered: 'You're using the doctor's voice that means somebody has died.' And after looking into his face for a moment, 'Tim – ? *Tim*, can it be the thing I've been afraid of? Is it that?'

He told her that it was and that he was not able just then to say anything more. 'I've promised not,' he had said. 'But don't be frightened. It's not as bad as you'll think at first. You'll know all about it in a few minutes and – I'm here, Jem.'

So he had taken her to join the others and she sat beside him, watching and listening to Alleyn.

He turned to her now. 'Perhaps,' he said, 'Miss Carmichael will tell me at once when she went to her cabin.'

'Yes, of course,' she said. 'It was just after you left. I went straight to bed.'

'I saw her to her door,' Tim said, 'and heard her lock it. It was still locked when I returned just now.'

'Did you hear or see anything that seemed out of the way?' Alleyn asked her.

'I heard – I heard voices in here and – somebody laughed and then screamed, and there were other voices shouting. Nothing else.'

'Would you like to go back to your cabin now? You may if you'd rather.'

She looked at Tim. 'I think I'd rather be here.'

'Then stay. Miss Abbott, I remember that you came in here from outside, on your way to your cabin. Where had you been?'

'I walked once round the deck,' she said, 'and then I leant over the rails on the, I think, starboard side. Then I came in for a few minutes.'

'Did you meet or see or hear anyone?'

'Nobody.'

'Was there anything at all, however slight, that you noticed?'

'I think not. Except – '

'Yes.'

'When I'd passed the verandah and turned, I thought I smelt cigarette smoke. Turkish. But there was nobody about.'

'Thank you. When you left here I think Father Jourdain walked to your door with you?'

'Yes. He saw me go in, I suppose. Didn't you, Father?'

'I did,' said Father Jourdain. 'And I heard you lock it. It's the same story, I imagine.'

'Yes, and I'd rather stay here, too,' said Miss Abbott.

'Are you sure?' Father Jourdain asked. 'It's not going to be very pleasant, you know. I can't help feeling, Alleyn, that the ladies – '

'It would be much less pleasant for the ladies,' Miss Abbott said grimly, 'to swelter in their cabins in a state of terrified ignorance.' Alleyn gave her an appreciative look.

'Very well,' he said. 'Now, Mrs Cuddy, if you please. Your cabin faces forward and to the starboard side and is next to Mr McAngus's. You and your husband went to it together. Is that right?' Mrs Cuddy who, unlike her husband, never smiled, turned her customary fixed stare upon Alleyn. 'I don't see that it matters,' she said, 'but I retired with Mr Cuddy, didn't I, dear?'

'That's right, dear.'

'And went to bed?'

'I did,' she said in an affronted voice.

'But your husband evidently did not go to bed?'

Mrs Cuddy said after a pause and with some constraint: 'He fancied a dip.'

'That's right. I fancied it. The prickly heat was troubling me.'

'I told you,' Mrs Cuddy said without looking at him, 'it's unwholesome in the night air and now see what's happened. Fainting. I wouldn't be surprised if you hadn't caught an internal chill and with the trouble you've been having – '

Alleyn said: 'So you changed into bathing trunks?'

'I don't usually go in fully dressed,' Mr Cuddy rejoined. His wife laughed shortly and they both looked triumphant.

'Which way did you go to the pool?'

'Downstairs, from here, and along the lower deck.'

'On the starboard side?'

'I don't know what they call it,' Mr Cuddy said contemptuously. 'Same side as our cabin.'

'Did you see anything of Miss Abbott?'

'I did not,' Mr Cuddy said and managed to suggest that there might be something fishy about it.

Miss Abbott raised her hand.

'Yes, Miss Abbott?'

'I'm sorry, but I do remember now that I noticed someone was in the pool. That was when I walked round the deck. It's a good way off and down below: I didn't see who it was. I'd forgotten.'

'Never mind. Mr Cuddy, did you go straight into the pool?'

'It's what I was there for, isn't it?'

'You must have come out almost at once.'

There was a long pause. Mr Cuddy said: 'That's right. Just a cooler and out.'

'Please tell me exactly what happened next.'

He ran the tip of his tongue round his lips. 'I want to know where I stand. I've had a shock. I don't want to go letting myself in for unpleasantness.'

'Mr Cuddy's very sensitive.'

'There's been things said here that I don't fancy. I know what the police are like. I'm not going to talk regardless. Pretending you was a cousin of the Company's!'

Alleyn said: 'Did you commit this crime?'

'There you are! Asking me a thing like that.'

Mrs Cuddy said: 'The idea!'

'Because if you didn't you'll do well to speak frankly and truthfully.'

'I've got nothing to conceal.'

'Very well, then,' Alleyn said patiently, 'don't behave as if you had. You found the body. After a fashion you reported your discovery. Now, I want the details. I suppose you've heard of the usual warning. If I was thinking of charging you I'd be obliged to give it.'

'Don't be a fool, man,' Captain Bannerman suddenly roared out. 'Behave yourself and speak up.'

'I'm ill. I've had a shock.'

'My dear Cuddy,' Father Jourdain said, 'I'm sure we all realize that you've had a shock. Why not get your story over and free yourself of responsibility?'

'That's right, dear. Tell them and get it over. It's all they deserve,' said Mrs Cuddy mysteriously.

'Come along,' Alleyn said. 'You left the pool and you started back. Presumably you didn't return by the lower deck but by one of the two companion-ladders up to this deck. Which one?'

'Left hand.'

'Port side,' the Captain muttered irritably.

'That would bring you to within a few feet of the verandah and a little to one side of it. Now, Mr Cuddy, do go on like a sensible man and tell me what followed.'

But Mr Cuddy was reluctant and evasive. He reiterated that he had had a shock, wasn't sure if he could exactly recall the sequence of events and knew better than to let himself in for a grilling. His was the sort of behaviour that is a commonplace in the experience of any investigating officer but in this instance, Alleyn was persuaded, it arose from a specific cause. He thought that Mr Cuddy hedged, not because he mistrusted the police on general grounds but because there was something he urgently wished to conceal. It became increasingly obvious that Mrs Cuddy, too, was prickly with misgivings.

'All right,' Alleyn said. 'You are on the ladder. You climb up it and your head is above the level of the upper deck. To your right, quite close and facing you, is the verandah. Can you see into the verandah?'

Mr Cuddy shook his head.

'Not at all?'

He shook his head.

'It was in darkness? Right, you stay there for some time. Long enough to leave quite a large wet patch on the steps. It was still there some minutes later when I looked at them. I think you actually may have sat down on a higher step which would bring your head below the level of the upper deck. Did you do this?'

A strange and unlovely look had crept into Mr Cuddy's face, a look at once furtive and – the word flashed up in Alleyn's thoughts – salacious.

'I do hope,' Alleyn went on, 'that you will tell me if this is in fact what happened. Surely there can be no reason why you shouldn't.'

'Go on, Fred,' Mrs Cuddy urged. 'They'll only get thinking things.'

'Exactly,' Alleyn agreed and she looked furious.

'All right, then,' Mr Cuddy said angrily. 'I did. Now!'

'Why? Was it because of something you saw? No? Or heard?'

'Heard's more like it,' he said and actually, after a fashion, began to smile again.

'Voices?'

'Sort of.'

'What the hell,' Captain Bannerman broke out, 'do you mean, sort of! You heard someone talking or you didn't.'

'Not to say talking.'

'Well, what *were* they doing. Singing?' Captain Bannerman demanded and then looked horrified.

'That,' said Mr Cuddy, 'came later.'

There was a deadly little silence.

Alleyn said: 'The first time was it one voice? Or two?'

'Sounded to me like one. Sounded to me – ' He looked sidelong at his wife, 'like hers. You know. Mrs Blick.' He squeezed his hands together and added: 'I thought at the time it was, well – just a bit of fun.'

Mrs Cuddy said: 'Disgusting. Absolutely disgusting.'

'Steady, Ethel.'

Father Jourdain made a small sound of distress. Jemima thought: 'This is the worst thing yet,' and couldn't look at the Cuddys. But Miss Abbott watched them with hatred and Mr McAngus, who had not uttered a word since he was summoned, murmured: 'Must we! Oh, must we!'

'I *so* agree,' Aubyn Dale began with an alcoholic travesty of his noblest manner. 'Indeed, *indeed* must we?'

Alleyn lifted a hand and said, 'The answer, I'm afraid, is that indeed, indeed, we must. Without interruption, if possible.' He waited for a moment and then turned again to Cuddy. 'So you sat on the steps and listened. For how long?'

'I don't know how long. Until I heard the other thing.'

'The singing?'

He nodded. 'It sort of faded out. In the distance. So I knew he'd gone.'

'Did you form any idea,' Alleyn asked him, 'who it was?'

They had all sat quietly enough until now. But at this moment, as if all their small unnoticeable movements had been disciplined under some imperative stricture, an excessive stillness fell upon them.

Mr Cuddy said loudly: 'Yes. I did.'

'Well?'

'Well, it was what he was singing. You know. The chune,' said Mr Cuddy.

'What was it?'

He turned his head and looked at Aubyn Dale. Like automata the others repeated this movement. Dale got slowly to his feet.

'You couldn't fail to pick it. It's an old favourite. "Pack Up Your Troubles". After all,' Cuddy said grinning mirthlessly at Aubyn Dale, 'it *is* your theme song, Mr Dale, isn't it?'

II

There was no outcry from any of the onlookers: not even from Aubyn Dale himself. He merely stared at Cuddy as if at some unidentifiable monster. He then turned slowly, looked at Alleyn and wetted his lips.

'You can't pay any attention to this,' he said with difficulty, running his words together. 'It's pure fantasy. I went to my cabin – didn't go out on deck.' He passed his hand across his eyes. 'I don't know that I can prove it. I – can't think of anything. But it's true, all the same. Must be some way of proving it. Because it's true.'

Alleyn said: 'Shall we tackle that one a bit later? Mr Cuddy hasn't finished his statement. I should like to know, Mr Cuddy, what you did next. At once, without evasions, if you please. What did you do?'

Cuddy gave his wife one of his sidelong glances, and then slid his gaze over to Alleyn. 'I haven't got anything to conceal,' he said. 'I went up and I thought – I mean it seemed kind of quiet. I mean – you don't want to get fanciful, Eth – I got the idea I'd see if she was OK. So I – so I went into that place and she didn't move. So I put out my hand in the dark. And she didn't move and I touched *her* hand. She had gloves on. When I touched it, it sort of slid sideways like it wasn't anything belonging to anybody and I heard it thump on the deck. And I thought she's fainted. So, in the dark, I felt around and I touched her face and – and – then I knew and – Gawd, Eth, it was ghastly!'

'Never mind, Fred.'

'I don't know what I did. I got out of it. I suppose I ran round the side. I wasn't myself. Next thing I knew I was in the doorway there and – well, I come over faint and I passed out. That's all. I never did anything else, I swear I didn't. Gawd's my judge, I didn't.'

Alleyn looked thoughtfully at him for a moment and said: 'That, then, is an account of the discovery by the man who made it. So far, of course, there's no way of checking, but in the meantime we shall use it as a working hypothesis. Now. Mr McAngus.'

Mr McAngus sat in a corner. The skirts of his dressing-gown, an unsuitably heavy one, were pulled tight over his legs and clenched between his knees. His arms were crossed over his chest and his hands buried in his armpits. He seemed to be trying to protect himself from anything anybody might feel inclined to say to him. He gazed dolorously at Alleyn as the likeliest source of assault.

'Mr McAngus,' Alleyn began, 'when did you leave this room?'

'I don't remember.'

'You were still here when I left. That was after Mrs Dillington-Blick had gone. Did you leave before or after Mr and Mrs Cuddy?' He added: 'I would rather Mr McAngus was not prompted.' Several of Mr McAngus's fellow passengers who had opened their mouths, shut them again.

Mr McAngus did not embark on his usual round of periphrases. He blinked twice at Alleyn and said: 'I am too upset to remember. If I tried I should only muddle myself and you. A dreadful tragedy has happened: I cannot begin to think of anything else.'

Alleyn, his hands in his coat pockets, said drily: 'Perhaps, after all, a little help is called for. May we go back to a complaint you made to Captain Bannerman before you went to bed. You said, I think, that somebody had been taking the hyacinths that Mrs Dillington-Blick gave you.'

'Oh, *yes.* Two. I noticed the second had gone this morning. I was *very* much distressed. And now – of course – even more so.'

'The hyacinths are growing, aren't they, in a basket which I think is underneath your porthole?'

'I keep them there for the fresh air.'

'Have you any idea who was responsible?'

Mr McAngus drew down his upper lip. 'I am very much averse,' he said, 'to making unwarranted accusations but I confess I *have* wondered about the steward. He is always admiring them. Or, then again he might have knocked one off by accident. But he denies it, you see. He denies it.'

'What colour was it?'

'White, a handsome spike. I believe the name is Virgin Queen.'

Alleyn withdrew his hand from his pocket, extended and opened it. His handkerchief was folded about an irregular object. He laid it on the table and opened it. A white hyacinth, scarcely wilted, was disclosed.

Mr McAngus gave a stifled cry, Jemima felt Tim's hand close on hers. She saw again in an instantaneous muddle, the mangled doll, the paragraphs in the newspapers and the basket of hyacinths that Dennis had brought in on – their first morning at sea. She heard Miss Abbott say: 'I *beg* you not to speak, Mrs Cuddy,' and Mrs Cuddy's inevitable cry of: 'Hyacinths! Fred!' And then she saw Mr McAngus rise, holding his lower lip between his thumb and forefinger.

'Is that it?' Alleyn asked.

Mr McAngus moved slowly to the table and stopped.

'Don't touch it, if you please.'

'It – it looks like it.'

Mrs Cuddy shrilly ejaculated: 'Wherever did you find it?'

Mr Cuddy said: 'Never mind, Eth,' but Mrs Cuddy's deductive capacity was under a hard drive. She stared, entranced, at the hyacinth. Everyone knew what she was about to say, no one was able to forestall it.

'My Gawd!' said Mrs Cuddy, 'you never found it on the corpse! My Gawd, Fred, it's the Flower Killer's done it. He's on the ship, Fred, and we can't get orf!'

Miss Abbott raised her large hands and brought them down heavily on her knees. 'We've been asked to keep quiet,' she cried out. 'Can't you, for pity's sake, hold your tongue!'

'Gently, my child,' Father Jourdain murmured.

'I'm not feeling gentle.'

Alleyn said: 'It will be obvious to all of you before long that this crime has been committed by the so-called Flower Murderer. At the moment, however, that's a matter which need not concern us. Now, Mr McAngus. You left this room, immediately after Mr and Mrs Cuddy. Did you go straight to your cabin?'

After a great deal of painstaking elucidation it was at last collected from Mr McAngus that he had strayed out through the double doors of the lounge to the deck, had walked round the passengers' block to the port side, had gazed into the heavens for a few addled minutes and had re-entered by the door into the interior passageway and thus arrived at his own quarters. 'My thoughts,' he said, 'were occupied by the film. I found it *very* moving. Not, perhaps, what one would have expected but nevertheless *exceedingly* disturbing.'

As he had not been seen by anybody else after he had left the lounge, his statement could only be set down for what it was worth and left to simmer.

Alleyn turned to Aubyn Dale.

Dale was slumped in his chair. He presented a sort of travesty of the splendid figure they had grown accustomed to. His white dinner-jacket was unbuttoned. His tie was crooked, his rope-soled shoes were unlatched, his hair was disordered and his eyes were imperfectly focused. His face was deadly pale.

Alleyn said: 'Now, Mr Dale, are you capable of giving me an account of yourself?'

Dale crossed his legs and with some difficulty joined the tips of his fingers. It was a sketch of his customary position before the cameras.

'Captain Bannerman,' he said, 'I think you realize I'm ver' close friend of the General Manager of y'r Company. He's going to hear juss how I've been treated in this ship and he's *not* going to be pleased about it.'

Captain Bannerman said: 'You won't get anywhere that road, Mr Dale. Not with me nor with anyone else.'

Dale threw up his hands in an uncoordinated gesture. '*All* right. On y'own head!'

Alleyn crossed the room and stood over him. 'You're drunk,' he said, 'and I'd very much rather you were sober. I'm going to ask you a question that may have a direct bearing on a charge of murder. This is not a threat: it is a statement of fact. In your own interest you'd better pull yourself together if you can and answer me. Can you do that?'

Dale said: 'I know I'm plastered. It's not fair. Doc', I'm plastered, aren't I?'

Alleyn looked at Tim. 'Can you do anything?'

'I can give him something, yes. It'll take a little time.'

'I don't want anything,' Dale said. He pressed the palms of his hands against his eyes, held them there for some seconds and then shook his head sharply. 'I'll be OK,' he muttered and actually did seem to have taken some sort of hold over himself. 'Go on,' he added with an air of heroic fortitude. 'I can take it.'

'Very well. After you left this room tonight you went out on deck. You went to the verandah. You stood beside the chaise-longue where the body was found. What were you doing there?'

Dale's face softened as if it had been struck. He said: 'You don't know what you're talking about.'

'Do you deny that you were there?'

'Refuse to answer.'

Alleyn glanced at Tim who went out.

'If you're capable of thinking,' Alleyn said, 'you must know where that attitude will take you. I'll give you a minute.'

'Tell you, I refuse.'

Dale looked from one of his fellow passengers to the other: the Cuddys, Jemima, Miss Abbott, Father Jourdain, Mr McAngus; and he found no comfort anywhere.

'You'll be saying presently,' he said with a sort of laugh, 'that I had something to do with it.'

'I'm saying now that I've found indisputable evidence that you stood beside the body. In your own interest don't you think you'd be well advised to tell me why you didn't at once report what you saw?'

'Suppose I deny it?'

'In your boots,' Alleyn said drily, 'I wouldn't.' He pointed to Dale's rope-soled shoes. 'They're still damp,' he said.

Dale drew his feet back as if he'd scorched them.

'Well, Mr Dale?'

'I – I didn't know – I didn't know there was anything the matter. I didn't know he – I mean she – was dead.'

'Really? Did you not say anything? Did you just stand there meekly and then run away?'

He didn't answer.

'I suggest that you had come into the verandah from the starboard side: the side opposite to that used by Mr Cuddy. I also suggest that you had been hiding by the end of the locker near the verandah corner.'

Unexpectedly Dale behaved in a manner that was incongruously, almost embarrassingly theatrical. He crossed his wrists, palms outward, before his face and then made a violent gesture of dismissal. 'No!' he protested, 'you don't understand. You frighten me. No!'

The door opened and Tim Makepiece returned. He stood, keeping it open and looking at Alleyn.

Alleyn nodded and Tim, turning his head to the passage, also nodded.

A familiar scent drifted into the stifled room. There was a tap of high heels in the passage. Through the door, dressed in a wonderful negligee, came Mrs Dillington-Blick.

Mrs Cuddy made a noise that was not loud but strangulated. Her husband and McAngus got to their feet, the latter looking as if he had seen a phantom and the former as if he was going to faint again. But if, in fact, they were about to say or do anything more they were forestalled. Jemima gave a shout of astonishment and relief and gratitude. She ran across the room and took Mrs Dillington-Blick's hands in hers and kissed her. She was half-crying, half-laughing. 'It wasn't you!' she stammered. 'You're all right. I'm so glad. I'm so terribly glad.'

Mrs Dillington-Blick gazed at her in amazement.

'You don't even know what's happened, do you?' Jemima went on. 'Something quite dreadful but – ' She stopped short. Tim had come to her and put his arm round her. 'Wait a moment, my darling,' he said and she turned to him.

'Wait a moment,' he repeated and drew her away.

Mrs Dillington-Blick looked in bewilderment at Aubyn Dale.

'What's all the fuss?' she asked. 'Have they found out?'

He floundered across the room and seized Mrs Dillington-Blick by the arms, shaking and threatening her.

'Ruby, don't speak!' he said. 'Don't say anything. Don't tell them. Don't you dare!'

'Has everybody gone mad?' asked Mrs Dillington-Blick. She wrenched herself out of Dale's grip. 'Don't!' she said and pushed away the hand that he actually tried to lay across her mouth. 'What's happened? *Have* they found out?' And after a moment, with a change of voice: 'Where's Dennis?'

'Dennis,' Alleyn said, 'has been murdered.'

III

It was, apparently, Mr Cuddy who was most disturbed by the news of Dennis's death but his was an inarticulate agitation. He merely stopped smiling, opened his mouth, developed a slight tremor of the hands and continued to gape incredulously at Mrs Dillington-Blick. His wife, always predictable, put her hand over his and was heard to say that someone was trying to be funny. Mr McAngus kept repeating: 'Thank God. I thank God!' in an unnatural voice. Miss Abbott said loudly: 'Why have we been misled! An abominable trick!' While Aubyn Dale crumpled back into his chair and buried his face in his hands.

'Mrs Dillington-Blick herself,' Alleyn thought, 'was bewildered and frightened.' She looked once at Aubyn Dale and away again, quickly. She turned helplessly towards Captain Bannerman who went to her and patted her shoulder.

'Never you fret,' he said and glared uneasily at Alleyn. 'You ought to have had it broken to you decently, not sprung on you without a word of warning. Never mind. No need to upset yourself.'

She turned from him to Alleyn and held out her hands. 'You make me nervous,' she said. 'It's not true, is it? Why are you behaving like this? You're angry, aren't you? Why have you brought me here?'

'If you'll sit down,' he said, 'I'll tell you.' She tried to take his hands. 'No, just sit down, please, and listen.'

Father Jourdain went to her. 'Come along,' he said and led her to a chair.

'He's a plain-clothes detective, Mrs Blick,' Mrs Cuddy announced with a kind of angry triumph. 'We've all been spied upon and made mock of and put in danger of our lives and now there's a murderer loose in the ship and he says it's one of us. In my opinion – '

'Mrs Cuddy,' Alleyn said, 'I must ask you for the moment to be quiet.'

Mr Cuddy automatically and for the last time on the voyage said: 'Steady, Ethel.'

'Indeed,' Alleyn went on, 'I must ask you all to be quiet and to listen carefully. You will understand that a state of emergency exists and that I have the authority to deal with it. The steward, Dennis, has been killed in the manner you have all discussed so often. He was clad in the Spanish dress Mrs Dillington-Blick bought in Las Palmas and the inference is that he was killed in mistake for her. He was lying in the chair in the unlit verandah. The upper part of his face was veiled and it was much too dark to see the mole at the corner of his mouth. In the hearing of all of the men in this room Mrs Dillington-Blick had said she was going to the verandah. She did go there. I met her there and went with her to the lower deck and from thence to her cabin door. She was wearing a black lace dress, not unlike the Spanish one. I returned here and almost immediately Mr Cuddy arrived announcing that he had discovered her and she was dead. Apparently he had been deceived by the dress. Dr Makepiece examined the body and says death had occurred no more than a few minutes before he did so. For reasons which I shall give you when we have time for them, there can be no question of his having been murdered by some member of the ship's complement. His death is the fourth in the series that you have so often discussed and one of the passengers is, in my opinion, undoubtedly responsible for all of them. For the moment you'll have to accept that.'

He waited. Aubyn Dale raised his head and suddenly demanded: 'Where's Merryman?'

There were excited ejaculations from the Cuddys.

'That's right!' Mr Cuddy said. 'Where is he! All this humbugging the rest of us about. Insinuations here and questions there! And Mister Know-all Merryman mustn't be troubled, I suppose?'

'Personally,' Mrs Cuddy added, 'I wouldn't trust him. I've always said there was something. Haven't I, dear?'

'Mr Merryman,' Alleyn said, 'is asleep in bed. He's been very unwell and I decided to leave him there until we actually needed him as, of course, we shall. I have not forgotten him.'

'He was well enough to go to the pictures,' Mrs Cuddy pointed out. 'I think the whole thing looks very funny. Very funny indeed.'

Jemima suddenly found herself exclaiming indignantly: 'Why do you say it looks "funny"? Mr Merryman has already pointed out what a maddeningly incorrect expression it is and he *is* ill and he only came to the pictures because he's naughty and obstinate and I think he's a poppet and certainly not a murderer and I'm sorry to interrupt but I do.'

Alleyn said, almost as Father Jourdain might have said: 'All right, my child. All right,' and Tim put his arm round Jemima.

'It will be obvious to you all,' Alleyn went on exactly as if there had been no interruption, 'that I must find out why the steward was there and why he was dressed in this manner. It is here that you, Mrs Dillington-Blick, can help us.'

'Ruby!' Dale whispered, but she was not looking at him.

'It was only a joke,' she said. 'We did it for a joke. How could we possibly know – ?'

'We? You mean you and Mr Dale, don't you?'

'And Dennis. Yes. It's no good, Aubyn. I can't not say.'

'Did you give Dennis the dress?'

'Yes.'

'After Las Palmas?'

'Yes. He'd been awfully obliging and he said – you know what an odd little creature he was – he admired it awfully and I, I told you, I took against it after the doll business. So I gave it to him. He said he wanted to dress up for a joke at some sort of birthday party the stewards were having.'

'On Friday night?'

'Yes. He wanted me not to say anything. That was why, when you asked me about the dress I didn't tell you. I wondered if you knew. Did you?'

Alleyn was careful not to look at Captain Bannerman. 'It doesn't arise at the moment,' he said.

The Captain made an indeterminate rumbling noise that culminated in utterance.

'Yes, it does!' he roared. 'Fair's fair and little though I may fancy the idea, I'm not a man to shirk my responsibilities.' He jerked his head at Alleyn. 'The superintendent,' he said, 'came to me and told me somebody had been seen fooling about the forward well-deck in that damned dress. He said he hadn't seen it himself and whoever did see it reckoned it was Mrs Dillington-Blick. And why not, I thought? Her dress, and why wouldn't she be wearing it? He asked me to make inquiries and stop a repetition. I didn't see my way to interfering and I wouldn't give my consent to him doing it on his own. All my time as Master, I've observed a certain attitude towards my passengers. I didn't see fit to change it. I was wrong. I didn't believe I'd shipped a murderer. Wrong again. Dead wrong. I don't want it overlooked or made light of. I was wrong.'

Alleyn said: 'That's a very generous statement,' and thought it best to carry on. 'I had not seen the figure in the Spanish dress,' he said. 'I had been told it was Mrs Dillington-Blick and there was no reason that anybody would accept to suppose it wasn't. I merely had a notion, unsupported by evidence, that the behaviour as reported was uncharacteristic.'

Jemima said: 'It was I who told about it. Mr Alleyn asked me if I was sure it was Mrs Dillington-Blick and I said I was.'

Mrs Dillington-Blick said: 'Dennis told me what he'd done. He said he'd always wanted to be a dancer.' She looked at Alleyn. 'When you asked me if I would wear the dress to dance by the light of the moon, I thought you'd seen him and mistaken him for me. I didn't tell you. I pretended it *was* me, because – ' her face crumpled and she began to cry, 'because we were planning the joke.'

'Well,' Alleyn said, 'there it was. And now I shall tell you what I think happened. I think, Mr Dale, that with your fondness for practical jokes, you suggested that it would be amusing to get the steward to dress up tonight and go to the verandah and that you arranged with Mrs Dillington-Blick to let it be understood that she herself was going to be there. Is that right?'

Aubyn Dale had sobered up considerably. Something of his old air of conventional decency had reappeared. He exhibited all the troubled concern of a good chap who is overwhelmed with self-reproach.

'Of course,' he said, 'I'll never forgive myself for this. It's going to haunt me for the rest of my life. But how could I know? How *could* I know! We – I mean, I – I take the whole responsibility,' he threw a glance, perhaps slightly reproachful, at Mrs Dillington-Blick. ' – I just thought it would be rather amusing to do it. The idea was that this poor little devil should – ' He hesitated and stole a look at

Mr McAngus and Mr Cuddy. ' – well, should go to the verandah as you say and, if anybody turned up he was just to sort of string them along a bit. I mean, putting it like that in cold blood after what's happened, it may sound rather poor but – '

He stopped and waved his hands.

Miss Abbott broke her self-imposed silence. She said: 'It sounds common, cheap and detestable.'

'I resent that, Miss Abbott.'

'You can resent it till you're purple in the face but the fact remains. To plot with the steward! To make a vulgar practical joke out of what may have been the wretched little creature's tragedy – his own private, inexorable weakness – his devil!'

'My child!' Father Jourdain said. 'You must stop.' But she pointed wildly and clumsily at Cuddy. 'To trick that man! To use his idiotic, hopeless infatuation! And the other – '

'No, no. Please!' Mr McAngus cried out. 'It doesn't matter. Please!'

Miss Abbott looked at him with what might have been a kind of compassion and turned on Mrs Dillington-Blick. 'And you,' she said, 'with your beauty and fascination, with everything that unhappy women long for: to lend yourself to such a thing! To give him your lovely dress, to allow him to so much as touch it! What were you thinking of!' She ground her heavy hands together: 'Beauty is sacred!' she said. 'It is sacred in its own right: you have committed sacrilege.'

'Katherine, you must come away. As your priest, I insist. You will do yourself irreparable harm. Come with me.'

For the first time she seemed to hear him. The familiar look of mulish withdrawal returned and she got up.

'Alleyn?' Father Jourdain asked.

'Yes, of course.'

'Come along,' he said and Miss Abbott let him take her away.

IV

'That woman's upset me,' Mrs Dillington-Blick said, angrily sobbing. 'I don't feel at all well. I feel awful.'

'Ruby, darling!'

'No! No, Aubyn, don't paw me. We shouldn't have done it. You shouldn't have started it. I feel ghastly.'

Captain Bannerman squared his shoulders and approached her. 'Nor you!' she said, and, perhaps for the first time in her adult life she appealed to someone of her own sex. 'Jemima!' she said. 'Tell me I needn't feel like this. It's not fair. I'm hating it.'

Jemima went to her. 'I can't tell you you needn't,' she said, 'but we all know you do and that's much better than not minding at all. At least – ' She appealed to Alleyn. ' – isn't it?'

'Of course it is.'

Mr McAngus, tying himself up in a sort of agonized knot of sympathy, said: 'You mustn't think about it. You mustn't reproach yourself. You are goodness itself. Oh, don't!'

Mrs Cuddy sniffed piercingly.

'It's this awful heat,' Mrs Dillington-Blick moaned. 'One can't *think.*' She had, in fact, gone very white. 'I – I feel faint.'

Alleyn opened the double doors. 'I was going to suggest,' he said, 'that we let a little air in.' Jemima put her arm round Mrs Dillington-Blick and Tim went over to her. 'Can you manage?' he asked. 'Come outside.'

They helped her through the doors. Alleyn moved Mr Merryman's chair so that its back was turned to the lounge and Mrs Dillington-Blick sank out of sight. 'Will you stay here?' Alleyn asked. 'When you feel more like it I should be glad of another word with you. I'll ask Dr Makepiece to come and see how you are. Perhaps, Miss Carmichael, you'd stay with Mrs Dillington-Blick. Would you?'

'Yes, of course.'

'All right?' Tim asked her.

'Perfectly.'

Alleyn had a further word with Tim and then the two men went back into the room.

Alleyn said: 'I'm afraid I must press on. I shall need all the men but if you, Mrs Cuddy, would rather go to your cabin, you may.'

'I prefer to stay with Mr Cuddy, thank you.'

Mr Cuddy moistened his lips and said: 'Look, Eth, you toddle off. It's not suitable for ladies.'

'I wouldn't fancy being there by myself.'

'You'll be OK, dear.'

'What about you, though?'

He didn't look at her. 'I'll be OK,' he said.

She was staring at him: expressionless as always. It was odd to see that her eyes were masked in tears. 'Oh, Fred,' Mrs Cuddy said, 'why did you do it?'

CHAPTER 11

Arrest

The four men in the lounge behaved exactly as if Mrs Cuddy had uttered an indecency. They looked everywhere but at the Cuddys, they said nothing and then after a moment eyed Alleyn surreptitiously as if they expected him to take drastic action.

His voice broke across the little void of silence.

'Why did he do what, Mrs Cuddy?'

'Eth,' Mr Cuddy said, 'for God's sake choose your words. They'll be thinking, things, Eth. Be careful.'

She didn't take her eyes off him and though she seemed to disregard completely what he had said to her, Alleyn thought that she was scarcely aware of anybody else in the room. Mr Cuddy returned her gaze with a look of terror.

'You know how I feel about it,' she said, 'and let you go on. Making an exhibition of yourself. I blame her, mind, more than I do you: she's a wicked woman, Fred. She's poking fun at you. I've seen her laughing behind your back with the others. I don't care,' Mrs Cuddy went on, raising her voice and indicating the inarticulate back of Mrs Dillington-Blick's deck-chair, 'if she hears what I say. What's happened is her fault: she's as good as responsible for it. And you had to go and chase after her and get yourself mixed up with a corpse. I hope it'll be a lesson to you.' A kind of spasm twitched at her mouth and her eyes overflowed. She ended as she had begun. 'Oh Fred,' Mrs Cuddy said again, 'why did you do it?'

'I'm sorry, dear. It was just a bit of fun.'

'Fun!' Her voice broke. She went up to him and made a curious gesture, a travesty of playfulness, shaking her fist at him. 'You old fool!' she said and without a word to anyone else bolted out of the room.

Mr Cuddy made a slight move as if to follow her but found himself confronted by Alleyn. He stood in the middle of the room, half-smiling, scanning the faces of the other men.

'You don't want to misunderstand Mrs Cuddy,' he ventured. 'I'm not a violent man. I'm quiet.'

Captain Bannerman cleared his throat. 'It looks to me,' he said, 'as if you'll have to prove that.' He glanced at the open doors to the deck, at the back of Mrs Dillington-Blick's chair and at Jemima who sat on the edge of the hatch with her chin in her hands.

'This is a man's job,' he said to Alleyn. 'For God's sake, keep the women out of it,' and with some emphasis, shut the doors.

Alleyn had been speaking to Tim. He said: 'Very well. For the moment.'

The Captain pulled chairs up to the biggest table in the room, motioning Alleyn to sit at one end and himself taking the other. 'I like to see things done shipshape,' he muttered and his longing for a boardroom could be sensed. Aubyn Dale and Mr McAngus at once took chairs. Tim, after a moment's hesitation, followed suit. Mr Cuddy hung off, winding the cord of his dressing-gown round his spatulate fingers. Mr McAngus, with trembling fingers, lit one of his medicated cigarettes.

Father Jourdain came back and in response to a gesture from the Captain, also sat at the table.

'That's more like it,' sighed Captain Bannerman and made a clumsy ducking movement at Alleyn.

'Carry on, if you please, Mr A'leen,' he said.

But Aubyn Dale who for some time had been casting fretful glances at the bar cut in. 'Look, I need a drink. Is there anything against my ringing for the steward?'

'Which steward?' Captain Bannerman asked, and Dale said: 'God, I forgot.'

'We'll do our drinking,' the Captain pronounced, 'later. Mr Cuddy, I'll thank you to take a seat.'

Mr Cuddy said: 'That's all right, Captain. Don't rush us. I'd still like to know why we don't send for Merryman,' and he pulled out his chair, sat back in it with an affectation of ease, and stared, nervously impertinent, at Alleyn.

Aubyn Dale said: 'I must say, seeing this gets more like a board-meeting every second, I don't see why Merryman should have leave-of-absence. Unless – ' He paused and the others stirred, suddenly alert and eager. 'Unless – '

Alleyn walked to the head of the table and surveyed its occupants. 'If this were a normal investigation,' he said, 'I would see each of you separately while the others were kept under observation. In these circumstances I can't do that: I am taking each of your statements now in the presence of you all. That being done I shall send for Mr Merryman.'

'Why the hell should he be the king pin?' Dale demanded and then took the plunge. 'Unless, by God, he did it.'

'Mr Merryman,' Alleyn rejoined, 'sat in the deck-chair now occupied by Mrs Dillington-Blick. He was still there when the men left this room. He commanded a view of the deck: each side of it. He could see both approaches to the verandah. He is, therefore, the key witness. His temperament is not complaisant. If he were here he'd try to run the whole show. I therefore prefer to let you account for yourselves now and bring him in a little later.'

'That's all very well,' Mr Cuddy said. 'But suppose he did it. Suppose he's the Flower Murderer. How about that?'

'In that case, being ignorant of what you have all told me, he may offer a statement that one of you can disprove.'

'So it'll be our word,' Dale said, 'against his?'

'With this reservation. That he was in a position to see you all and none of you, it seems, was able to see him or each other. He can speak about you all, I hope. Each of you can only speak for himself.'

Mr McAngus said: 'I don't know why you all want him: he makes *me* feel uncomfortable and silly.'

'Ah, for God's sake!' Dale ejaculated. 'Can't we get on with it!'

Alleyn, still standing, put his hands on the back of his chair and said: 'By all means. This is the position as far as we've gone. I suggest that you consider it.'

They were at once silent and uneasily attentive.

'Three of you,' Alleyn said, 'have given me statements about your movements during the crucial time – the time, a matter of perhaps eight minutes, between the moment when Mrs Dillington-Blick left this room and the moment when Mr Cuddy came back with an account of his discovery of the body. During those eight minutes the steward Dennis was strangled, I believe in mistake for Mrs Dillington-Blick. None of the three statements corroborates either of the other two. We have a picture of three individuals all moving about, out there in the semi-dark, without catching sight of each other. For myself, I was the first to go. I met Mrs Dillington-Blick by the verandah to which she went (I'm sorry to put it like this but there's no time for polite evasions) as a decoy. No doubt she assured herself that Dennis was there and she was about to take cover when I appeared. To get rid of me she asked me to help her down the port-side companion-ladder to the lower deck. I did so and then saw her to her cabin and returned here. Mr Cuddy, in the meantime, had changed, gone below and then to the pool by way of the starboard side on the lower deck. Miss Abbott, who left after he did, walked round this deck and stood for some minutes on the starboard side. She remembers that she saw somebody in the pool.

'Mr McAngus says he left by these double doors, stood for a time by the passengers' quarters on the port side and then went to his cabin and to bed. Nobody appeared to have noticed him.

'Mr Dale, I imagine, will now admit that his first statement to the effect that he went straight to his cabin, was untrue. On the contrary, he was on deck. He hid behind a locker on the starboard side near the verandah corner hoping to overhear some cruelly ludicrous scene of mistaken identity. He afterwards went to the verandah, presumably discovered the body, returned to his cabin and drank himself into a state from which he has at least partially recovered.'

'I resent the tone – ' Dale began.

'You'll have to lump the tone, I'm afraid. I now want to know what, if anything, you heard from your hiding-place and exactly what you did and saw when you went into the verandah. Do you propose to tell me?'

'Captain Bannerman – '

'No good coming at me,' said the Captain. 'You're in a tight spot, Mr Dale, and truth had better be your master.'

Dale smacked the palm of his hand down on the table. '*All right*! Turn on me. The whole gang of you, and much good may it do you.

You badger and threaten and get a man tied up in knots until he doesn't know what he's saying. I'm as anxious as anyone for this bloody murderer to be caught. If I could tell you anything that'd bring him to book I would. All right. I did what you say. I sat behind the locker. I heard Miss Abbott go past. Tramp, tramp. She walks like a man. I couldn't see her but I knew it was Miss Abbott because she was humming a churchy tune. I've heard her before. And then, it was quiet. And then, after a bit, somebody else went by. Going towards the verandah. Tip-toe. Furtive. I heard him turn the corner and I heard somebody – Dennis I suppose – it was rather high-pitched – make a little sound. And then – ' He wiped his hand across his mouth. 'Then there were other sounds. The chair legs scraped. Somebody cried out. Only once and it was cut short. Then there was another sort of bumping and scraping. Then nothing. I don't know for how long. Then the tip-toe footsteps passed again. A bit faster but not running and somebody singing like Cuddy said. "Pack Up Your Troubles." In a head-voice. Falsetto. Only a phrase of it and then nothing.'

'In tune?' Alleyn asked.

'I beg your pardon?'

'Was the voice in tune?'

Dale said: 'Well really! Oh, yes. Perfectly in tune,' and gave a half-laugh.

'Thank you. Go on. What did you do next?'

'I was going to come out but I heard another voice.'

He screwed round in his chair and jerked his head at Cuddy. 'You,' he said. 'It was your voice. Unmistakably. You said: "All alone?" ' He aped a mellifluous, arch inquiry. 'I heard you go in. Wet feet on the deck. And then, after a pause, you made a sort of retching noise and you ran out, and I suppose you bolted down the deck.'

'I've explained everything,' Mr Cuddy said. 'I've told them. I've concealed nothing.'

'Very well,' Alleyn said. 'Keep quiet. And then, Mr Dale?'

'I waited. Then I thought I'd just go round and ask what had happened. I must have had some sort of idea there was something wrong: I realize that now. It was – it was so deadly quiet.'

'Yes?'

'So I did. I went in. I said something, I don't remember what and there was no answer. So I – I got out my cigarette lighter and flashed it on – Oh, God, *God*!'

'Well?'

'I couldn't see much at first. It seemed funny he didn't say anything. I put the flame nearer and then I saw. It was hell. Like that doll. Broken. And the flowers. The deck was wet and slippery. I thought: "I've done this: it's my fault. I arranged it and she'll say I did. Let somebody else discover it!" Something like that. I'd had one or two drinks over the eight and I suppose that's why I panicked. I ran out and round the deck, past the locker. I heard Cuddy's voice and I saw him by the doors here. I ducked down behind the hatch and heard him tell you. Then I heard you walk past on the other side and I knew that you'd gone to look. I thought "It's too late for me to tell them. I'm here. I'll be involved." So I made for the forward end of the deck.'

'Father Jourdain,' Alleyn said, 'I think you must at that time have been by the entrance to this room looking after Mr Cuddy, who had fainted. Did you see Mr Dale?'

'No. But, as you say, I was stooping over Mr Cuddy. I think my back was turned to the hatch.'

'Yes,' Dale said. 'Yes, it was. I watched you. I don't remember much else except – my God, yes!'

'What have you remembered?'

Dale had been staring at his hands clasped before him on the table. He now raised his head. Mr McAngus sat opposite him. They seemed to be moved by some common resentment.

'Go on,' Alleyn said.

'It was when I'd gone round the passengers' block to the port side. I wanted a drink damn' badly, and I wanted to be by myself. I'd got as far as the entrance into the passage and waited for a bit to make sure nobody was about. Ruby – Mrs Dillington-Blick, was in her cabin. I could hear her slapping her face. I wondered if I'd tell her and then – then I smelt it.'

'Smelt what?'

Dale pointed at Mr McAngus. 'That. One of those filthy things he smokes. It was quite close.'

Mr McAngus said: 'I have already stated that I waited for a little on deck before I went to my cabin. I have said so.'

'Yes. But *where? Where* were you? I couldn't see you and yet you must have been quite close. I actually saw the smoke.'

'Well, Mr McAngus?' Alleyn asked.

'I – don't exactly remember where I stood. Why should I?' He ground out his cigarette. A little malodorous spiral rose from the butt.

Dale said excitedly: 'But the deck's open and there was the light from her porthole. Why couldn't I see him?'

'The door giving on the passage opens back on the outside bulk-head,' Alleyn said. 'Close to Mrs Dillington-Blick's porthole. Were you standing behind that door, Mr McAngus?'

'Hiding behind it, more like,' Mr Cuddy eagerly exclaimed.

'Well, Mr McAngus?'

The long indeterminate face under the dyed hair was unevenly pallid. 'I admit nothing,' said Mr McAngus. 'Nothing.'

'Are you sure?'

'Nothing.'

'Do you think he might have been there, Mr Dale?'

'Yes. Yes, I do. You see, I thought he must be in the passage and I waited and then I thought: "I've *had* this!" And I looked and there was nobody there. So I went straight in. My door's just on the left. I had a Scotch neat and I dare say it was a snorter. Then I had another. I was all anyhow. My nerves are shot to pieces. I've had a breakdown. I'm supposed,' Dale said in a trembling voice, 'to be on a rest cure. This has set me all back to hell.'

'Mr McAngus, did you hear Mr Cuddy when he came and told us of his discovery? He was hysterical and made a great noise. Did you hear him?'

Mr McAngus said: 'I heard something. It didn't matter.'

'Didn't matter?'

'I knew where she was.'

'Mrs Dillington-Blick?'

'I cannot answer you, sir.'

'You have yourself told us that you left this room by the deck doors, walked round the centrecastle block and then waited for some time on the port side. Do you stick to that statement?'

Mr McAngus, holding to the edge of the table as if for support, did not take his eyes off Alleyn. He had compressed his mouth so ruthlessly that drops of saliva oozed out of the corners. He inclined his head slightly.

'Very well then – '

'No! No, no!' Mr McAngus suddenly shouted. 'I refuse! What I have done, I have done under compulsion. I cannot discuss it. Never!'

'In that case,' Alleyn said, 'we have reached an impasse. Dr Makepiece, will you be so kind as to ask Mr Merryman if he will join us?'

II

Mr Merryman could be heard coming down the passage. His sharp voice was raised to its familiar pitch of indignation.

'I should have been informed of this,' he was saying, 'at once. Immediately. I demand an explanation. *Who* did you say the man is?'

An indistinguishable murmur from Tim.

'Indeed? *Indeed*! Then he has no doubt enjoyed the salutary experience popularly assigned to eavesdroppers. This is an opportunity,' the voice continued as its owner drew nearer, 'that I have long wished for. If I had been consulted at the outset, the typical, the all-too-familiar, pattern of official ineptitude might have – nay, would have been anticipated. But, of course, that was too much to hope for. I – '

The door was opened by Tim who came in, pulled an eloquent grimace at Alleyn and stood aside.

Mr Merryman made a not ineffective entrance. He was girded into his dressing-gown. His cockscomb was erect and his eyes glittered with the light of battle. He surveyed the party round the table with a Napoleonic eye.

Captain Bannerman half rose and said: 'Come in, Mr Merryman. Hope you're feeling well enough to join us. Take a chair.' He indicated the only vacant chair which faced the glass doors leading to the deck. Mr Merryman made a slight acknowledgement but no move. He was glaring at Alleyn. 'I dare say,' the Captain went on, 'that it's in order, under the circumstances, for me to make an introduction. This gentleman is in charge of the meeting. Superintendent A'leen.'

'The name,' Mr Merryman said at once, 'is Alleyn. *Alleyn,* my good sir. Al-*lane* is permissible. A'leen, never. It is, presumably, too much to expect that you should have so much as heard of the founder of Dulwich College: an Elizabethan actor who was unsurpassed in his day: Edward Alleyn. Or, less acceptably in my poor opinion, Al-*lain.* Good evening, sir,' Mr Merryman concluded, nodding angrily at Alleyn.

'Over to you,' the Captain muttered woodenly, 'Mr Allan.'

'No!' Mr Merryman objected on a rising inflexion.

'It's of no consequence,' Alleyn hastily intervened.

'Will you sit down, Mr Merryman?'

'Why not?' Mr Merryman said and did so.

'I believe,' Alleyn went on, 'that Dr Makepiece has told you what has happened?'

'I have been informed, in the baldest manner conceivable, that a felony has been committed. I assume that I am about to be introduced to the insupportable *longeurs* of a police investigation.'

'I'm afraid so,' Alleyn said cheerfully.

'Then perhaps you will be good enough to advise me of the nature of the crime and the circumstances under which it was committed and discovered. Unless, of course,' Mr Merryman added, throwing back his head and glaring at Alleyn from under his spectacles, 'you regard me as a suspect in which case you will no doubt attempt some elephantine piece of finesse. *Do* you, in fact, regard me as a suspect?'

'Yes,' Alleyn said coolly. 'Together with sundry others. I do. Why not?'

'Upon my word!' he said after a pause. 'It does not astonish me. And pray what am I supposed to have done? And to whom? And where? Enlighten me, I beg you.'

'You are supposed at this juncture to answer questions, and not to ask them. You will be good enough not to be troublesome, Mr Merryman. No,' Alleyn said as Mr Merryman opened his mouth, 'I really can't do with any more tantrums. This case is in the hands of the police. I am a policeman. Whatever you may think of the procedure you've no choice but to put up with it. And we'll all get along a great deal faster if you can contrive to do so gracefully. Behave yourself, Mr Merryman.'

Mr Merryman put on an expression of mild astonishment. He appeared to take thought. He folded his arms, flung himself back in his chair and stared at the ceiling. 'Very well,' he said. 'Let us plumb the depths. Continue.'

Alleyn did so. Without giving any indication whatever of the nature or locale of the crime, an omission which at once appeared to throw Mr Merryman into an extremity of annoyance, he merely asked for an account in detail of anything Mr Merryman may have seen from his vantage point in the deck-chair, facing the hatch.

'*May* I ask?' Mr Merryman said, still looking superciliously at the ceiling, '*why* you adopt this insufferable attitude? *Why* you elect to withhold the nature of your little problem? Do I detect a note of professional jealousy?'

'Let us assume that you do,' said Alleyn with perfect good nature.

'Ah! You are afraid – '

'I am afraid that if you were told what has happened you would try and run the show and I don't choose to let you. What did you see from your deck-chair, Mr Merryman?'

A faint, an ineffably complaisant smile played about Mr Merryman's lips. He closed his eyes.

'What did I see?' he ruminated and, as if they had joined the tips of their fingers and thumbs round the table, his listeners were involved in a current of heightened tension. Alleyn saw Aubyn Dale wet his lips. Cuddy yawned nervously and McAngus again hid his hands in his armpits. Captain Bannerman was glassy-eyed. Father Jourdain's head was inclined as if to hear a confession. Only Tim Makepiece kept his eyes on Alleyn rather than on Mr Merryman.

'What did I see?' Mr Merryman repeated. He hummed a meditative air and looked slyly round the table and said loudly: 'Nothing. Nothing at all.'

'Nothing?'

'For a very good reason. I was sound asleep.'

He broke into a triumphant cackle of laughter. Alleyn nodded to Tim who again went out.

McAngus, rather shockingly, joined in Mr Merryman's laughter: 'The key witness!' he choked out, hugging himself. 'The one who was to prove us all right or wrong. Fast asleep! What a farce!'

'It doesn't affect you,' Dale pointed out. 'He wouldn't have seen you anyway. You've still got to account for yourself.'

'That's right. That's dead right,' Mr Cuddy cried out.

'Mr Merryman,' Alleyn said, 'when did you wake up and go to your room?'

'I have no idea.'

'Which way did you go?'

'The direct way. To the entrance on the starboard side.'

'Who was in the lounge at that time?'

'I didn't look.'

'Did you meet anyone?'

'No.'

'May I just remind you of your position out there?'

Alleyn went to the double doors. He jerked the spring blinds and they flew up with a sharp rattle.

The lights were out on deck. In the glass doors only the reflection of the room and of the occupants appeared: faint, hollow-eyed and cadaverous as phantoms their own faces stared back at them.

From a region of darkness there emerged through these images, another. It moved towards the doors, gaining substance. Mrs Dillington-Blick was outside. Her hands were pressed against the glass. She looked in.

Mr Merryman screamed like a ferret in a trap.

His chair overturned. He was round the table before anyone could stop him. His hands scrabbled at the glass pane.

'No. No! Go away. Go away! Don't speak. If you speak I'll do it again. I'll kill you if you speak.'

Alleyn held him. It was quite clear to everybody that Mr Merryman's hands, scrabbling against the glass like fish in an aquarium, were ravenous for Mrs Dillington-Blick's throat.

CHAPTER 12

Cape Town

Cape Farewell steamed into Table Bay at dawn and hove-to awaiting the arrival of her pilot cutter and the police launch from Cape Town. Like all ships coming in to port she had begun to withdraw into herself, conserving her personality against the assaults that would be made upon it. She had been prepared. Her derricks were uncovered, her decks broken by orderly litter. Her servants, at their appointed stations, were ready to support her.

Alleyn looked across neatly scalloped waters at the butt-end of a continent and thought how unlikely it was that he would ever take such another voyage. At Captain Bannerman's invitation, he was on the bridge. Down on the dismantled boat-deck eight of the nine passengers were already assembled. They wore their shore-going clothes because *Cape Farewell* was to be at anchor for two days. Their deck-chairs had been stowed away, the hatch was uncovered and there was nowhere for them to sit. Sea-gulls, always a little too true to type, squawked and dived, squabbled and swooped about the bilge water of which *Cape Farewell* blandly relieved herself.

Two black accents appeared distantly on the surface of the Bay.

"There we are,' Captain Bannerman said, handing Alleyn his binoculars.

Alleyn said: 'If you don't mind I'm going to ask for the passengers to be sent to their sitting-room.'

'Do you expect any trouble?'

'None.'

'He won't – ' Captain Bannerman began and hesitated. 'You don't reckon he'll cut up rough?'

'He is longing,' Alleyn said, 'to be taken away.'

'Bloody monster,' the Captain muttered uneasily. He took a turn round the bridge, and came back to Alleyn.

'There's something I ought to say to you,' he said. 'It doesn't come easy and for that reason, I suppose, I haven't managed to get it out. But it's got to be said. I'm responsible for that boy's death. I know it. I should have let you act like you wanted.'

'I might just as easily have been wrong.'

'Ah! But you weren't, and there's the trouble.' The Captain fixed his gaze on the approaching black accents. 'Whisky,' he said, 'affects different men in different ways. Some, it makes affable, some it makes glum. Me, it makes pig-headed. When I'm on the whisky I can't stomach any man's notions but my own. How do you reckon we'd better handle this job?'

'Could we get it over before the pilot comes on board? My colleague from the Yard has flown here and will be with the Cape police. They'll take charge for the time being.'

'I'll have a signal sent.'

'Thank you, sir,' Alleyn said and went below.

A seaman was on guard outside the little hospital. When he saw Alleyn he unlocked the door and Alleyn went in.

Sitting on the unmade-up bed with its sharp mattress and smartly folded blankets, Mr Merryman had adopted an attitude quite unlike the one to which his fellow passengers had become accustomed. His spine curved forward and his head depended from it as if his whole structure had wilted. Only the hands, firmly padded and sinewed, clasped between the knees, retained their eloquence. When Alleyn came in, Mr Merryman looked up at him over the tops of his spectacles but said nothing.

'The police-launch,' Alleyn said, 'is sighted. I've come to tell you that I have packed your cases and will have the things you need sent with you. I shall not be coming in the launch but will see you later today. You will be given every opportunity to take legal advice in Cape Town or to cable instructions to your solicitors. You will return to England as soon as transport is available: probably by air. If you have changed your mind and wish to make a statement – '

Alleyn stopped. The lips had moved. After a moment, the voice, remotely tinged with arrogance, said:' – not in the habit of rescinding decisions – tedium of repetition. No.'

'Very well.'

He turned to go and was arrested by the voice.

' – a few observations. Now. No witnesses and without prejudice. Now.'

Alleyn said: 'I must warn you: the absence of witnesses doesn't mean that what you may tell me will not be given in evidence. It may be given in evidence. You understand that,' he added, as Mr Merryman raised his head and stared blankly at him, 'don't you?' He took out his notebook and opened it. 'You see, I shall write down anything that you say.'

Mr Merryman said with a vigour that a moment ago would have seemed impossible: 'Esmeralda. Ruby. Beryl. Bijou. Coralie. Majrguerite.'

He was still feverishly repeating these names when Inspector Fox from the Yard, with members of the Cape Town police force, came to take him off.

II

For a little while Alleyn watched the police launch dip and buck across the Bay. Soon the group of figures aboard her lost definition and she herself became no more than a receding dot. The pilot cutter was already alongside. He turned away and for the last time opened the familiar doors into the sitting-room.

They were all there, looking strange in their shore-going clothes.

Alleyn said: 'In about ten minutes we shall be alongside. I'm afraid I shall have to ask you all to come to the nearest police-station to make your depositions. Later on you will no doubt be summoned to give evidence and if that means an earlier return, arrangements will be made for transport. I'm sorry but that's how it is. In the meantime I feel that I owe you an explanation, and perhaps something of an apology.' He paused for a moment.

Jemima said: 'It seems to me the boot's on the other foot.'

'And to me,' said Tim.

'I'm not so sure,' Mrs Cuddy remarked. 'We've been treated in a very peculiar manner.'

Alleyn said: 'When I boarded this ship at Portsmouth I did so on the strength of as slight a piece of information as ever sent an investigating officer to sea. It consisted of the fragment of an embarkation notice for this ship and it was clutched in the hand of the girl who was killed on the wharf the night you sailed. It was at least arguable that this paper had been blown ashore or dropped or had come by some irrelevant means into the girl's hand. I didn't think so, your statements didn't suggest it, but it was quite possible. My superior officers ordered me to conceal my identity, to make what inquiries I could, entirely under cover, to take no action that did not meet with the Captain's approval and to prevent any further catastrophe. This last, of course, I have failed to do. If you consider them, these conditions may help to explain the events that followed. If the Flower Murderer was aboard, the obvious procedure was to discover which of you had an acceptable alibi for any of the times when these crimes were committed. I took the occasion of the fifteenth of January when Beryl Cohen was murdered. With Captain Bannerman's assistance I staged the alibi conversation.'

'Good lord!' Miss Abbott ejaculated. She turned dark red and added: 'Go on. Sorry.'

'The results were sent by radio to London and my colleagues there were able to confirm the alibis of Father Jourdain and Dr Makepiece. Mr Cuddy's and Mr McAngus's were unconfirmed but in the course of the conversation it transpired that Mr McAngus had been operated upon for a perforated appendix on the nineteenth of January which made him incapable of committing the crime of the twenty-fifth when Marguerite Slatters was murdered. If, of course, he was speaking the truth. Mr Cuddy, unless he was foxing, appeared to be unable to sing in tune and one of the few things we did know about our man was his ability to sing.'

Mrs Cuddy, who was holding her husband's hand, said: 'Well really, Mr Cuddy would be the last to pretend he was a performer! Wouldn't you, dear?'

'That's right, dear.'

'Mr Dale,' Alleyn went on, 'had no alibi for the fifteenth but it turned out that on the twenty-fifth he was in New York. That disposed of him as a suspect.'

'Then why the hell,' Dale demanded, 'couldn't you tell me what was up?'

'I'm afraid it was because I formed the opinion that you were not to be relied upon. You're a heavy drinker and you have been suffering from nervous strain. It would, I felt, be unsafe to trust to your discretion.'

'I must say!' Dale began angrily but Alleyn went on.

'It has never been supposed that a woman was responsible for these crimes but,' he smiled at Miss Abbott, 'one of the ladies, at least, had an alibi. She was in Paris on the twenty-fifth, at the same conference, incidentally, as Father Jourdain who was thus doubly cleared. Until I could hear that the remaining alibis were proved I couldn't take any of the passengers except Father Jourdain and Dr Makepiece into my confidence. I should like to say, now, that they have given me every possible help and I'm grateful as can be to both of them.'

Father Jourdain, who was very pale and withdrawn, raised his hand and let it fall again. Tim said they both felt they had failed at the crucial time. 'We were sceptical,' he said, 'about Mr Alleyn's interpretation of Jem's glimpse of the figure in the Spanish dress. We thought it must have been Mrs Dillington-Blick. We thought that with all the women accounted for, there was nothing to worry about.'

'I saw it,' Jemima said, 'and I told Mr Alleyn I was sure it was Mrs Dillington-Blick. That was my blunder.'

'I even heard the singing,' Father Jourdain said. 'How could I have been so tragically stupid!'

'I gave Dennis the dress and pretended I didn't,' Mrs Dillington-Blick lamented.

Aubyn Dale looked with something like horror at Mr Cuddy. 'And you and I, Cuddy,' he pointed out, 'listened to a murder and did nothing about it.'

Mr Cuddy, for once, was not smiling. He turned to his wife and said: 'Eth, I'm sorry. I'm cured, Eth. It won't occur again.'

Everybody tried to look as if they didn't know what he was talking about, especially Mrs Dillington-Blick.

'OK, dear,' said Mrs Cuddy, and herself, actually smiled.

Mr McAngus leant forward and said very earnestly: 'I can, of course, see that I have not behaved at all helpfully. Indeed, now I come to think of it I almost ask myself if I haven't been suffering from some complaint.' He looked wistfully at Mrs Dillington-Blick. 'A touch of the sun perhaps,' he murmured and made a little bob at her. 'It is,' he added after a moment's added reflection, 'very fussing to consider how one's actions go on and on having the most distressing results. For instance, when I ventured to buy the doll I never intended – '

A steamer hooted and there, outside, was a funnel sliding past and beyond it a confusion of shipping and the wharves themselves.

'I never intended,' Mr McAngus repeated but he had lost the attention of his audience and did not complete his sentence.

Miss Abbott said in her harsh way: 'It's no good any of us bemoaning our intentions. I dare say we've all behaved stupidly one way or another. I know I have. I started this trip in a stupid temper. I've made stupid scenes. If it's done nothing else it's shown me what a fool I was. Control!' announced Miss Abbott, 'and common sense! Complete lack of both leads to murder, it seems.'

'And of charity,' Father Jourdain added rather wearily.

That's right. And of charity,' Miss Abbott agreed snappishly. 'And of proportion and I dare say of a hundred other things we'd be the better for observing.'

'How right you are!' Jemima said so sombrely that Tim felt obliged to put his arm round her.

Alleyn moved over to the glass doors and looked out. 'We're alongside,' he said. 'I don't think there's anything more to say. I hope, when you go ashore, you still manage to find some sort of – what? compensation? – for all that has happened?'

Mrs Dillington-Blick approached him. She offered him her hand and when he took it leant towards him and murmured: 'I've had a blow to my vanity.'

'Surely not.'

'Were all your pretty ways purely professional?'

Alleyn suppressed a mad desire to reply: 'As surely as yours were not,' and merely said: 'Alas, I have no pretty ways. You're much too kind.' He shook her hand crisply and released it to find that Jemima and Tim were waiting for him.

Jemima said: 'I just wanted to tell you that I've discovered you haven't got it all your own way.'

'What does that mean?'

'You're not the only one to find the real thing on a sea voyage.'

'Really?'

'Really. *Dead* sure.'

'I'm so glad,' Alleyn said and shook hands with them.

After that the Cuddys and Mr McAngus came and made their odd little valedictions. Mr Cuddy said that he supposed it took all sorts to make a world and Mrs Cuddy said she'd always known there was something. Mr McAngus, scarlet and inextricably confused, made several false starts. He then advanced his long anxious face to within a few inches of Alleyn's and said in a rapid undertone: 'You were perfectly right, of course. But I didn't look in. No, no! I just stood with my back to the wall behind the door. It was something to be near her. Misleading, of course. That I *do* see. Goodbye.'

Aubyn Dale let Mr McAngus drift away and then pulled in his waist and with his frankest air came up to Alleyn and extended his hand.

'No hard thoughts, I hope, old boy?'

'Never a one.'

'Good man. Jolly good.' He shook Alleyn's hand with manly emphasis. 'All the same,' he said, 'dumb though it may be of me I still can *not* see why, at the end, you couldn't warn us men. Before you fetched him in.'

'A: because you were all lying like flatfish. As long as you thought he was the innocent observer who could prove you lied I had a chance of forcing the truth from you. And B: because one or more of you would undoubtedly have given the show away if you'd known he was guilty. He's extremely observant.'

Dale said: 'Well, I never pretended to be a diplomatic type,' and made it sound noble. Then, unexpectedly, he reddened. 'You're right about the drinks,' he said. 'I'm a fool. I'm going to lay off. If I can. See you later.' He went out. Miss Abbott marched up to Alleyn.

She said: 'I suppose what I'd like to say couldn't be of less importance. However, you'll just have to put up with it. Did you guess what was wrong with me, the night of the alibi conversation?'

'I fancied I did,' he said.

'So I supposed. Well, if it's any consolation, I'm cured. It's a mistake for a lonely woman to form an engrossing friendship. One

should have the courage of one's loneliness. This ghastly business
has at least taught me that.'

'Then,' Alleyn said gently, 'you may give thanks, mayn't you? In
a Gregorian chant?'

'Well, goodbye,' she said, and she too went out.

The others having all gone, Father Jourdain and Tim, who had
both waited at the far end of the room, came up to Alleyn.

Father Jourdain said: 'Alleyn, may I go to him? Will you let me
see him?'

Alleyn said that of course he would but added, as gently as he
could, that he didn't think Mr Merryman would respond graciously
to the visit.

'No, no. But I must go. He received Mass from me in a state of
deadly sin. I must go.'

'He was struggling with – ' Alleyn hesitated. 'With his devil. He
thought it might help.'

'I must tell him. He must be brought to a realization,' Father
Jourdain said. He went out on deck and stared, without seeing it, at
Table Mountain. Alleyn saw his hand go to his breast.

Tim said: 'Am I wanted?'

'I'm afraid you are. He's talked to me. It's pretty obvious that the
defence will call psychiatric opinions and yours may be crucial. I'll
tell you what he has said and then ask you to see him. If you can get
him to speak it may go some way in his favour.'

'You talk,' Tim said, 'as if you weren't a policeman.'

III

'So the priest and the psychiatrist are to do what they can,' Alleyn
wrote to his wife. 'Makepiece, of course, says he would need weeks
to arrive at a full report. He's professionally all steamed up over
Merryman's readiness to describe an incident that no doubt will be
advanced as the key to his obsession and is a sort of text-book
shining example of the Oedipus Complex and the whole blasted job.
Do you remember there was one curious link in all these wretched
crimes? It was the women's names. All jewels. Marguerite, of course,
means Pearl, and the doll's name Esmeralda, Emerald. It was bad

luck for Jemima Carmichael that her young man called her Jem. The sound was enough and she wore a pearl necklace. The necklaces were always twisted and broken. And, of course, there were the flowers. This is his story. When he was just seven years old his mother, a stupid woman whom he adored, had a birthday. It was in the early spring and he spent the contents of his money-box on a handful of hyacinths. He gave them to her but at the same time his father brought her a necklace. He fastened it round her neck with a display of uxoriousness which Merryman describes through his teeth. In raising her hands to his she dropped the hyacinths and in the subsequent embrace, trod on them. Makepiece says the pattern, from his point of view, is perfect – jewels, flowers, neck, amorousness and fury. The boy flew into a blind rage and went for her like a demon, twisted and broke the necklace and was dragged away and given a hiding by his father. This incident was followed at ten-day intervals by a series of something he calls fainting fits. Makepiece suspects *petit mal*. Here Merryman's story ends.

'It's as if the fact of his arrest had blown the stopper off a lifelong reticence, and as if, having once spoken, he can't stop but, with extraordinary vehemence, is obliged to go through with it again and again. But he won't carry his history an inch further and refuses to speak if any attempt is made to discuss the cases in hand. Makepiece thinks his mistaking Dennis for the woman has had a profound effect.

'There's no doubt that for years he has fought a lonely, frantic battle with his obsession, and to some extent may have beaten it off by segregating himself in a boys' school. Perhaps by substituting the lesser crime for the greater. He may have bought and destroyed necklaces and flowers for all one knows. But when his climacteric was reached and he retired from his school, the thing may have suddenly become malignant. I believe he took this voyage in an attempt to escape from it and might have done so if he hadn't encountered on the wharf a girl with flowers and those the most dangerous for him. The fact that her name was Coralie finished it. As for the earlier cases, I imagine that when his ten-day devil arose, he put on his false beard, went out on the hunt, buying flowers for the purpose, and picked up women with whom he got into conversation. He probably discarded many who didn't fit in with the pattern.

'He exhibits, to a marked degree, the murderer's vanity. I doubt if he has made one statement that was untrue throughout the voyage. He was eager to discuss these cases and others of their kind. Makepiece says he's a schizophrenic: I'm never absolutely certain what that means but no doubt it will be advanced at the trial and I hope to God it succeeds.

'Of course, almost from the beginning, I thought he was my man, if my man was aboard. If the others' alibis stood up, he was the only one left. But there were signs. His preferences in literature, for instance. Any Elizabethan play that concerned the murder of a woman was better than any that didn't. *The Duchess of Malfi* and *Othello* were the best because in each of these the heroine is strangled. He resented any suggestion that "sex monsters" might be unpleasant to look at. He carried bits of paper and sodamints in his waistcoat pocket. He spilt coffee all over himself when I uncovered the doll, and blamed Miss Abbott for it. He had been to a choir school and could therefore sing. He is an expert in make-up and no doubt bearded himself for the encounters. The beard, of course, went overboard after the event.

'But it was one thing to realize all this and a hell of another to sheet it home. When I saw him, as sound asleep as if he'd expiated a deadly crime instead of committing one, I realized there was only one chance of getting him. He had no doubt decided on the line he would take after the body had been found: I would have to give him the kind of shock that would jerk him off it. I fixed it up with Makepiece. When the right moment presented itself, we would confront Merryman and Mrs Dillington-Blick. He knew he'd made his kill and of course believed her to be his victim. He was relaxed, eased of his fever and immensely enjoying his act. She loomed up on the other side of the window and – it worked.

'The fact of the D-B being in her own style a *femme fatale* muddled the issues, since she quite deliberately went gunning for any male in sight and thus stirred up Cuddy and McAngus to the dizziest heights of middle-aged fatuity. Dale, of course, had merely settled down to a routine shipboard affair. She's a pretty consistent job-of-work, I must say, and I don't mind betting that when she's got over her vapours she'll take the whole thing as a sort of backhanded tribute.

'For my part, having from the outset been hamstrung by
Captain's orders, I hope never to be given such a job again. I can
even allow myself one brief bellyache: which is this. Why the hell
did the D-B have to dress up a queer steward and put him on the
verandah? And conversely why the hell couldn't she tell me about
it? It could have been turned without harm to advantage. Well,
there it is; by his death he brought about a denouement grotesque-
ly out-of-drawing to anything in his life.

'Well, my darling, an airmail goes out at noon and will bring you
this great wad of a letter. I'm staying in the ship until she sails and
will return with the official party. In the meantime – '

He finished his letter and went out on the bridge.

Cape Farewell was discharging cargo. At midnight, having got rid
of a bulldozer, four cars, three tons of unbleached calico and a murderer, she would continue her voyage to Durban.

He supposed he was unlikely ever to travel in her again.

False Scent

For
Jemima with love

Contents

CHAPTER 1

Pardoner's Place – 9.00 A.M.

When she died it was as if all the love she had inspired in so many people suddenly blossomed. She had never, of course, realized how greatly she was loved, never known that she was to be carried by six young men who would ask to perform this last courtesy: to bear her on their strong shoulders, so gently and with such dedication.

Quite insignificant people were there: her Old Ninn, the family nurse, with a face like a boot, grimly crying. And Florence, her dresser, with a bunch of primroses because of all flowers they were the ones she had best loved to see on her make-up table. And George, the stage doorkeeper at the Unicorn, sober as sober and telling anyone who would listen to him that there, if you liked, had been a great lady. Pinky Cavendish in floods and Maurice, very Guardee, with a stiff upper lip. Crowds of people whom she herself would have scarcely remembered but upon whom, at some time, she had bestowed the gift of her charm.

All the Knights and Dames, of course, and The Management, and Timon Gantry, the great producer, who had so often directed her. Bertie Saracen who had created her dresses since the days when she was a bit-part actress and who had, indeed, risen to his present eminence in the wake of her mounting fame. But it was not for her fame that they had come to say goodbye to her. It was because, quite simply, they had loved her.

And Richard? Richard was there, white and withdrawn. And – this was an afterthought – and, of course, Charles.

Miss Bellamy paused, bogged down in her own fantasy. Enjoyable tears started from her eyes. She often indulged herself with plans for her funeral and she never failed to be moved by them. The only catch was the indisputable fact that she wouldn't live to enjoy it. She would be, as it were, cheated of her own obsequies and she felt there was some injustice in this.

But perhaps, after all, she *would* know. Perhaps she would hover ambiguously over the whole show, employing her famous gift for making a party go without seeming to do anything about it. Perhaps – ? Feeling slightly uncomfortable, she reminded herself of her magnificent constitution and decided to think about something else.

There was plenty to think about. The new play. Her role: a fat part if ever she saw one. The long speech about keeping the old chin up and facing the future with a wry smile. Richard hadn't put it quite like that and she did sometimes wish he would write more simply. Perhaps she would choose her moment and suggest to him that a few homely phrases would do the trick much more effectively than those rather involved, rather *arid* sentences that were so bloody difficult to memorize. What was wanted – the disreputable word 'gimmick' rose to the surface and was instantly slapped down – what was wanted, when all was said and done, was the cosy human touch: a vehicle for her particular genius. She believed in humanity. Perhaps this morning would be the right occasion to talk to Richard. He would, of course, be coming to wish her many happy returns. Her birthday! That had to be thought of selectively and with a certain amount of care. She must at all costs exclude that too easy little sum whose answer would provide her age. She had, quite literally and by dint of a yogi-like discipline, succeeded in forgetting it. Nobody else that mattered knew except Florence who was utterly discreet and Old Ninn who, one must face it, was getting a bit garrulous, especially when she'd taken her glass or two of port. Please God she wouldn't forget herself this afternoon.

After all, it was how you felt and how you looked that mattered. She lifted her head from the pillows and turned it. There, across the room, she was, reflected in the tall glass above her dressing-table. Not bad, she thought, not half bad, even at that hour and with no make-up. She touched her face here and there, manipulating the skin above the temples and at the top of the jaw line. To lift or not to lift? Pinky Cavendish was all for it and said that nowadays there was no need

for the stretched look. But what about her famous triangular smile?
Maintaining the lift, she smiled. The effect was still triangular.

She rang her bell. It was rather touching to think of her little
household, oriented to her signal. Florence, Cookie, Gracefield, the
parlourmaid, the housemaid and the odd woman: all ready in
the kitchen and full of plans for the Great Day. Old Ninn, revelling
in her annual holiday, sitting up in bed with her *News of the World*
or perhaps putting the final touch to the bed-jacket she had
undoubtedly knitted and which would have to be publicly worn
for her gratification. And, of course, Charles. It was curious how
Miss Bellamy tended to leave her husband out of her meditations
because, after all, she was extremely fond of him. She hurriedly
inserted him. He would be waiting for Gracefield to tell him she was
awake and had rung. Presently he would appear, wearing a pink
scrubbed look and that plum-coloured dressing-gown that did so
little to help.

She heard a faint chink and a subdued rumble. The door opened
and Florence came in with her tray.

'Top of the morning, dear,' said Florence. 'What's it feel like to be
eighteen again?'

'You old fool,' Miss Bellamy said, and grinned at her. 'It feels fine.'

Florence built pillows up behind her and set the tray across her
knees. She then drew back the curtains and lit the fire. She was a
pale, small woman with black dyed hair and sardonic eyes. She had
been Miss Bellamy's dresser for twenty-five years and her personal
maid for fifteen. 'Three rousing cheers,' she said, 'it's a handsome-
looking morning.'

Miss Bellamy examined her tray. The basket-ends were full of
telegrams, a spray of orchids lay across the plate and beside it a
parcel in silver wrapping tied with pink ribbon.

'What's all this?' she asked, as she had asked for her last fifteen
birthdays, and took up the parcel.

'The flowers are from the colonel. He'll be bringing his present
later on as per usual, I suppose.'

'I wasn't talking about the flowers,' Miss Bellamy said and opened
the parcel. 'Florrie! Florrie, *darling*!'

Florence clattered the firearms. 'Might as well get in early,' she
muttered, 'or it'd never be noticed.'

It was a chemise, gossamer fine and exquisitely embroidered.

'Come *here!*' Miss Bellamy said, fondly bullying.

Florence walked over to the bed and suffered herself to be kissed. Her face became crimson. For a moment she looked at her employer with a devotion that was painful in its intensity and then turned aside, her eyes filmed with unwilling tears.

'But it's out of this world!' Miss Bellamy marvelled, referring to the chemise. 'That's all! It's just *made* my day for me.' She shook her head slowly from side to side, lost in wonderment. 'I can't wait,' she said and, indeed, she was very pleased with it.

'There's the usual mail,' Florence grunted. 'More, if anything.'

'Truly?'

'Outside on the trolley. Will I fetch it in here?'

'After my bath, darling, may we?'

Florence opened drawers and doors, and began to lay out the clothes her mistress had chosen to wear. Miss Bellamy, who was on a strict diet, drank her tea, ate her toast, and opened her telegrams, awarding each of them some pleased ejaculation. 'Darling, Bertie! Such a sweet muddled little message. And a cable, Florrie, from the Bantings in New York. Heaven of them!'

'That show's folding, I'm told,' Florence said, 'and small wonder. Dirty *and* dull, by all accounts. You mustn't be both.'

'You don't know anything about it,' Miss Bellamy absentmindedly observed. She was staring in bewilderment at the next telegram. 'This,' she said, 'isn't true. It's just not true. My dear Florrie, *will* you listen.' Modulating her lovely voice, Miss Bellamy read it aloud. ' "Her birth was of the womb of morning dew and her conception of the joyous prime." '

'Disgusting,' said Florence.

'I call it rather touching. But who in the wide world is Octavius Browne?'

'Search me, love.' Florence helped Miss Bellamy into a negligee designed by Bertie Saracen, and herself went into the bathroom. Miss Bellamy settled down to some preliminary work on her face.

There was a tap on the door connecting her room with her husband's and he came in. Charles Templeton was sixty years old, big and fair with a heavy belly. His eyeglass dangled over his dark-red dressing-gown, his hair, thin and babyishly fine, was carefully brushed and his face, which had the florid colouring associated with heart disease, was freshly shaved. He kissed his wife's hand and forehead and laid a small parcel before her. 'A very happy birthday to you, Mary, my dear,' he said. Twenty years ago, when she married him, she had told him that his voice was charming. If it was so, still, she no longer noticed it or, indeed, listened very attentively to much that he said.

But she let her birthday gaiety play about him and was enchanted with her present, a diamond and emerald bracelet. It was, even for Charles, quite exceptionally magnificent and for a fleeting moment she remembered that he, as well as Florence and Old Ninn, knew her age. She wondered if there was any intention of underlining this particular anniversary. There were some numerals that by their very appearance – stodgy and rotund – wore an air of horrid maturity. Five, for instance. She pulled her thoughts up short, and showed him the telegram. 'I should like to know what in the world you make of that,' she said and went into the bathroom, leaving the door open. Florence came back and began to make the bed with an air of standing none of its nonsense.

'Good morning, Florence,' Charles Templeton said. He put up his eyeglass and walked over to the bow window with the telegram.

'Good morning, sir,' Florence woodenly rejoined. Only when she was alone with her mistress did she allow herself the freedom of the dressing-room.

'Did you,' Miss Bellamy shouted from her bath, 'ever see anything quite like it?'

'But it's delightful,' he said, 'and how very nice of Octavius.'

'You don't mean to say you know who he is?'

'Octavius Browne? Of course I do. He's the old boy down below in the Pegasus bookshop. Up at the House, but a bit before my time. Delightful fellow.'

'Blow me down flat!' Miss Bellamy ejaculated, splashing luxuriously. 'You mean that dim little place with a fat cat in the window.'

'That's it. He specializes in pre-Jacobean literature.'

'Does that account for the allusion to wombs and conceptions? Of *what* can he be thinking, poor Mr Browne?'

'It's a quotation,' Charles said, letting his eyeglass drop. 'From Spenser. I bought a very nice Spenser from him last week. No doubt he supposes you've read it.'

'Then, of course, I must pretend I have. I shall call on him and thank him. Kind Mr Browne!'

'They're great friends of Richard's.'

Miss Bellamy's voice sharpened a little. 'Who? *They*?'

'Octavius Browne and his niece. A good-looking girl.' Charles glanced at Florence and after a moment's hesitation added: 'She's called Anelida Lee.'

Florence cleared her throat.

'Not true!' The voice in the bathroom gave a little laugh. 'A-nelly-da! It sounds like a face cream.'

'It's Chaucerian.'

'I suppose the cat's called Piers Plowman.'

'No. He's out of the prevailing period. He's called Hodge.'

'I've never heard Richard utter her name.'

Charles said: 'She's on the stage, it appears.'

'Oh, *God*!'

'In that new club theatre behind Walton Street. The Bonaventure.'

'You need say no more, my poor Charles. One knows the form.' Charles was silent and the voice asked impatiently: 'Are you still there?'

'Yes, my dear.'

'How do you know Richard's so thick with them?'

'I meet him there occasionally,' Charles said, and added lightly, 'I'm thick with them too, Mary.'

There was a further silence and then the voice, delightful and gay, shouted: 'Florrie! Bring me *you know what*.'

Florence picked up her own offering and went into the bathroom.

Charles Templeton stared through the window at a small London square, brightly receptive of April sunshine. He could just see the flower-woman at the corner of Pardoner's Row, sitting in a galaxy of tulips. There were tulips everywhere. His wife had turned the bow window into an indoor garden and had filled it with them and with a great mass of early-flowering azaleas, brought up in the conservatory and still in bud. He examined these absentmindedly and discovered among them a tin with a spray-gun mechanism. The tin was labelled 'Slaypest' and bore alarming captions about the lethal nature of its contents. Charles peered at them through his eyeglass.

'Florence,' he said, 'I don't think this stuff ought to be left lying about.'

'Just what I tell her,' Florence said, returning.

'There are all sorts of warnings. It shouldn't be used in enclosed places. *Is* it used like that?'

'It won't be for want of my telling her if it is.'

'Really, I *don't* like it. Could you lose it?'

'I'd get the full treatment meself if I did,' Florence grunted.

'Nevertheless,' Charles said, 'I think you should do so.'

Florence shot a resentful look at him and muttered under her breath.

'What did you say?' he asked.

'I said it wasn't so easy. She knows. She can read. I've told her.' She glowered at him and then said: 'I take my orders from her. Always have and always will.'

He waited for a moment. 'Quite so,' he said. 'But all the same . . .' And hearing his wife's voice, put the spray-gun down, gave a half-sigh and turned to confront the familiar room.

Miss Bellamy came into it wearing Florence's gift. There was a patch of sunshine in the room and she posed in it, expectant, unaware of its disobliging candour.

'Look at my smashing shift!' she cried. 'Florrie's present! A new birthday suit.'

She had 'made an entrance,' comic-provocative, skilfully French-farcical. She had no notion at all of the disservice she had done herself.

The voice that she had once called charming said: 'Marvellous. How kind of Florence.'

He was careful to wait a little longer before he said, 'Well, darling, I shall leave you to your mysteries,' and went down to his solitary breakfast.

II

There was no particular reason why Richard Dakers should feel uplifted that morning: indeed, there were many formidable reasons why he should not. Nevertheless, as he made his way by bus and on foot to Pardoner's Place, he did experience, very strongly, that upward kick of the spirit which lies in London's power of bestowal. He sat in the front seat at the prow of the bus and felt like a figure-head, cleaving the tide of the King's Road, masterfully above it, yet gloriously of it. The Chelsea shops were full of tulips and when, leaving the bus, he walked to the corner of Pardoner's Row, there was his friend the flower-woman with buckets of them, still pouted up in buds.

' 'Morning, dear,' said the flower-woman. 'Duck of a day, innit?'

'It's a day for the gods,' Richard agreed, 'and your hat fits you like a halo, Mrs Tinker.'

'It's me straw,' Mrs Tinker said. 'I usually seem to change to me straw on the second Sat. in April.'

'Aphrodite on her cockleshell couldn't say fairer. I'll take two dozen of the yellows.'

She wrapped them up in green paper. 'Ten bob to you,' said Mrs Tinker.

'Ruin!' Richard ejaculated, giving her eleven shillings.

'Destitution! But what the hell!'

'That's right, dear, we don' care, do we? Tulips, lady? Lovely tulips.'

Carrying his tulips and with his dispatch-case tucked under his arm, Richard entered Pardoner's Place and turned right. Three doors along he came to the Pegasus, a bow-fronted Georgian house that had been converted by Octavius Browne into a bookshop. In the window, tilted and open, lay a first edition of Beijer and Duchartre's *Premières Comédies Italiennes*. A little farther back, half in shadow, hung a negro marionette, very grand in striped silks. And in the watery depths of the interior Richard could just make out the shapes of the three beautifully polished old chairs, the lovely table and the vertical strata of rows and rows of books. He could see, too, the figure of Anelida Lee moving about among her uncle's treasure, attended by Hodge, their cat. In the mornings Anelida, when not rehearsing at her club theatre, helped her uncle. She hoped that she was learning to be an actress. Richard, who knew a good deal about it, was convinced that already she was one.

He opened the door and went in.

Anelida had been dusting and wore her black smock, an uncompromising garment. Her hair was tied up in a white scarf. He had

time to reflect that there was a particular beauty that most pleased
when it was least adorned and that Anelida was possessed of it.

'Hallo,' he said. 'I've brought you some tulips. Good morning,
Hodge.' Hodge stared at him briefly, jerked his tail, and walked away.

'How lovely! But it's not *my* birthday.'

'Never mind. It's because it's a nice morning and Mrs Tinker was
wearing her straw.'

'I couldn't be better pleased,' said Anelida. 'Will you wait while I
get a pot for them? There's a green jug.'

She went into a room at the back. He heard a familiar tapping
noise on the stairs. Her Uncle Octavius came down, leaning on his
black stick. He was a tall man of about sixty-three with a shock of
grey hair and a mischievous face. He had a trick of looking at people
out of the corners of his eyes as if inviting them to notice what a bad
boy he was. He was rather touchy, immensely learned and thin
almost to transparency.

'Good morning, my dear Dakers,' he said, and seeing the tulips
touched one of them with the tip of a bluish finger. 'Ah,' he said,
'"Art could not feign more simple grace, Nor Nature take a line
away." How very lovely and so pleasantly uncomplicated by any
smell. We have found something for you, by the way. Quite nice and
I hope in character, but it may be a little too expensive. You must tell
us what you think."

He opened a parcel on his desk and stood aside for Richard to look
at the contents.

'A tinsel picture, as you see,' he said, 'of Madame Vestris *en
travesti* in jockey's costume.' He looked sideways at Richard.
'Beguiling little breeches, don't you think? Do you suppose it would
appeal to Miss Bellamy?'

'I don't see how it could fail.'

'It's rare-ish. The frame's contemporary. I'm afraid it's twelve
guineas.'

'It's mine,' Richard said. 'Or rather, it's Mary's.'

'You're sure? Then, if you'll excuse me for a moment, I'll get Nell
to make a birthday parcel of it. There's a sheet of Victorian tinsel
somewhere. Nell, my dear! Would you – ?'

He tapped away and presently Anelida returned with the green
jug and his parcel, beautifully wrapped.

Richard put his hand on his dispatch-case. 'What do you suppose is in there?' he asked.

'Not – ? Not *the* play? Not *Husbandry in Heaven?*'

'Hot from the typist.' He watched her thin hands arrange the tulips. 'Anelida, I'm going to show it to Mary.'

'You couldn't choose a better day,' she said warmly and, when he didn't answer, 'What's the matter?'

'There isn't a part for her in it,' he blurted out.

After a moment she said: 'Well, no. But does that matter?'

'It might. If, of course, it ever comes to production. And, by the way, Timmy Gantry's seen it and makes agreeable noises. All the same, it's tricky about Mary.'

'But why? I don't see – '

'It's not all that easy to explain,' he mumbled.

'You've already written a new play for her and she's delighted with it, isn't she? This is something quite different.'

'And better? You've read it.'

'Immeasurably better. In another world. Everybody must see it.'

'Timmy Gantry likes it.'

'Well, there you are! It's special. Won't she see that?'

He said: 'Anelida, dear, you don't really know the theatre yet, do you? Or the way actors tick over?'

'Well, perhaps I don't. But I know how close you are to each other and how wonderfully she understands you. You've told me.'

'That's just it,' Richard said, and there followed a long silence.

'I don't believe,' he said at last, 'that I've ever told you exactly what she and Charles did?'

'No,' she agreed. 'Not exactly. But – '

'My parents, who were Australians, were friends of Mary's. They were killed in a car smash on the Grande Corniche when I was rising two. They were staying with Mary at the time. There was no money to speak of. She had me looked after by her own old nanny, the celebrated Ninn, and then, after she had married Charles, they took me over, completely. I owe everything to her. I like to think that, in a way, the plays have done something to repay. And now – you see what I go and do.'

Anelida finished her tulips and looked directly at him. 'I'm sure it'll work out,' she said gently. 'All very fine, I dare say, for me to say so, but you see, you've talked so much about her, I almost feel I know her.'

'I very much want you to know her. Indeed, this brings me to the main object of my pompous visit. Will you let me call for you at six and take you to see her? There's a party of sorts at half-past which I hope may amuse you, but I'd like you to meet her first. Will you, Anelida?'

She waited too long before she said: 'I don't think I can. I'm – I've booked myself up.'

'I don't believe you. Why won't you come?'

'But I can't. It's her birthday, and it's special to her and her friends. You can't go hauling in an unknown female. *And* an unknown actress, to boot.'

'Of course I can.'

'It wouldn't be comely.'

'What a fantastic word! And why the hell do you suppose it wouldn't be comely for the two people I like best in the world to meet each other?'

Anelida said: 'I didn't know – '

'Yes, you did,' he said crossly. 'You must have.'

'We scarcely know each other.'

'I'm sorry you feel like that about it.'

'I only meant – well, in point of time – '

'Don't hedge.'

'Now, look here – '

'I'm sorry. Evidently I've taken too much for granted.'

While they stared aghast at the quarrel that between them they had somehow concocted, Octavius came tapping back. 'By the way,' he said happily, 'I yielded this morning to a romantic impulse, Dakers. I sent your patroness a birthday greeting: one among hundreds, no doubt. The allusion was from Spenser. I hope she won't take it amiss.'

'How very nice of you, sir,' Richard said loudly. 'She'll be enchanted. She loves people to be friendly. Thank you for finding the picture.'

And forgetting to pay for it, he left hurriedly in a miserable frame of mind.

III

Mary Bellamy's house was next door to the Pegasus bookshop, but Richard was too rattled to go in. He walked round Pardoner's Place trying to sort out his thoughts. He suffered one of those horrid experiences, fortunately rare, in which the victim confronts himself as a stranger in an abrupt perspective. The process resembles that of pseudo-scientific films in which the growth of a plant, by mechanical skulduggery, is reduced from seven weeks to as many minutes and the subject is seen wavering, extending, elongating itself in response to some irresistible force until it breaks into its pre-ordained florescence.

The irresistible force in Richard's case had undoubtedly been Mary Bellamy. The end-product, after twenty-seven years of the treatment, was two successful West End comedies, a third in the bag, and (his hand tightened on his dispatch-case) a serious play.

He owed it all, as he had so repeatedly told her, to Mary. Well, perhaps not quite all. Not the serious play.

He had almost completed his round of the little Place and, not wanting to pass the shop window, turned back. Why in the world had he gone grand and huffy when Anelida refused to meet Mary? And why *did* she refuse? Any other girl in Anelida's boots, he thought uneasily, would have jumped at that sort of invitation: the great Mary Bellamy's birthday party. A tiny, hand-picked group from the topmost drawer in the London theatre. *The* Management. *The* producer. Any other girl . . . He fetched up short, not liking himself very much, conscious that if he followed his thoughts to their logical conclusion he would arrive at an uncomfortable position. What sort of man, he would have to ask himself, was Richard Dakers? Reality would disintegrate and he would find himself face-to-face with a stranger. It was a familiar experience and one he didn't enjoy. He shook himself free of it, made a sudden decision, walked quickly to the house and rang the bell.

Charles Templeton breakfasted in his study on the ground floor. The door was open and Richard saw him there, reading his *Times*, at home among his six so judiciously chosen pieces of *chinoiserie*, his three admirable pictures, his few distinguished chairs and lovely desk. Charles was fastidious about his surroundings and extremely knowledgeable. He could wait, sometimes for years, for the acquisition of a single treasure.

Richard went in. 'Charles!' he said. 'How are you?'

'Hallo, old boy. Come to make your devotions?'

'Am I the first?'

'The first in person. There are the usual massive offerings in kind. Mary'll be delighted to see you.'

'I'll go up,' Richard said, but still hovered. Charles lowered his newspaper. How often, Richard wondered, had he seen him make that gesture, dropping his eyeglass and vaguely smiling. Richard, still involved in the aftermath of his moment of truth, if that was its real nature, asked himself what he knew of Charles. How used he was to that even courtesy, that disengagement! What of Charles in other places? What of the reputedly implacable man of affairs who had built his own fortune? Or of the lover Charles must have been five-and-twenty years ago? Impossible to imagine, Richard thought, looking vaguely at an empty niche in the wall.

He said: 'Hallo! Where's the T'ang Musician?'

'Gone,' Charles said.

'Gone! Where? Not broken?'

'Chipped. The peg of her lute. Gracefield did it, I think. I've given her to Maurice Warrender.'

'But – even so – I mean, so often they're not absolutely perfect and you – it was your treasure.'

'Not now,' Charles said. 'I'm a perfectionist, you know.'

'That's what you say!' Richard exclaimed warmly. 'But I bet it was because Maurice always coveted her. You're so absurdly generous.'

'Oh, nonsense,' Charles said, and looked at his paper. Richard hesitated. He heard himself say:

'Charles, do I ever say thank you? To you and Mary?'

'My dear fellow, what for?'

'For everything.' He took refuge in irony. 'For befriending the poor orphan boy, you know, among other things.'

'I sincerely hope you're not making a vicarious birthday resolution.'

'It just struck me.'

Charles waited for a moment and then said: 'You've given us a tremendous interest and very much pleasure.' He again hesitated as if assembling his next sentence. 'Mary and I,' he said at last, 'look upon you as an achievement. And now, do go and make your pretty speeches to her.'

'Yes,' Richard said. 'I'd better, hadn't I? See you later.'

Charles raised his newspaper and Richard went slowly upstairs, wishing, consciously, for perhaps the first time in his life, that he was not going to visit Miss Bellamy.

She was in her room, dressed and enthroned among her presents. He slipped into another gear as he took her to his heart in a birthday embrace and then held her at arm's length to tell her how lovely she looked.

'Darling, darling, darling!' she cried joyously. 'How *perfect* of you to come. I've been hoping and hoping!'

It occurred to him that it would have been strange indeed if he hadn't performed this time-honoured observance, but he kissed her again and gave her his present.

It was early in the day and her reservoir of enthusiasm scarcely tapped. She was able to pour a freshet of praise over his tinsel picture and did so with many cries of gratitude and wonder. Where, she asked, where, *where* had he discovered the *one*, the *perfect* present?

It was an opening Richard had hoped for, but he found himself a little apprehensive nevertheless.

'I found it,' he said, 'at the Pegasus – or rather Octavius Browne found it for me. He says it's rareish.'

Her triangular smile didn't fade. Her eyes continued to beam into his, her hands to press his hands.

'Ah, yes!' she cried gaily. 'The old man in the bookshop! Believe it or not, darling, he sent me a telegram about my conception. Too sweet, but a little difficult to acknowledge.'

'He's very donnish,' Richard said. She made a comic face at him. 'He *was*, in fact, a don, but he found himself out of sympathy with angry young men and set up a bookshop instead.'

She propped up her tinsel picture on the dressing-table and gazed at it through half-closed eyes. 'Isn't there a daughter or something? I seem to have heard – '

'A niece,' Richard said. Maddeningly, his mouth had gone dry.

'Ought I,' she asked, 'to nip downstairs and thank him? One never quite knows with that sort of person.'

Richard kissed her hand. 'Octavius,' he said, 'is not that sort of person, darling. Do nip down: he'll be enchanted. And Mary – '

'What, my treasure?'

'I thought perhaps you might be terribly kind and ask them for a drink. If you find them pleasant, that is.'

She sat at her dressing-table and examined her face in the glass. 'I wonder,' she said, 'if I *really* like that new eyeshade.' She took up a heavy Venetian glass scent spray and used it lavishly. 'I hope some-one gives me some really superlative scent,' she said. 'This is almost gone.' She put it down. 'For a drink?' she said. 'When? Not today, of course.'

'*Not* today, you think?'

She opened her eyes very wide. 'My dear, we'd only embarrass them.'

'Well,' he murmured. 'See how you feel about it.'

She turned back to the glass and said nothing. He opened his dispatch-case and took out his typescript.

'I've brought something,' he said, 'for you to read. It's a surprise, Mary.' He laid it on the dressing-table. 'There.'

She looked at the cover-page. '*Husbandry in Heaven*. A play by Richard Dakers.'

'Dicky? Dicky, darling, *what* is all this?'

'Something I've kept for today,' he said and knew at once that he'd made a mistake. She gave him that special luminous gaze that meant she was deeply moved. 'Oh Dicky! ' she whispered. 'For me? My *dear*!'

He was panic-stricken.

'But when?' she asked him, slowly shaking her head in bewil-derment. 'When did you *do* it? With all the other work? I don't understand. I'm flabbergasted. Dicky!'

'I've been working on it for some time. It's – it's quite a different thing. Not a comedy. You may hate it.'

'Is it the great one – at last?' she whispered. 'The one that we always knew would happen? And all by yourself, Dicky? Not even with poor stupid, old, loving me to listen?'

She was saying all the things he would least have chosen for her to say. It was appalling.

'For all I know,' he said, 'it may be frighteningly bad. I've got to that state where one just can't tell. Anyway, don't let's burden the great day with it.'

'You couldn't have given me anything else that would make me half so happy.' She stroked the typescript with both eloquent, not very young hands. 'I'll shut myself away for an hour before lunch and wolf it up.'

'Mary,' he said desperately. 'Don't be so sanguine about it. It's not your sort of play.'

'I won't hear a word against it. You've written it for *me*, darling.'

He was hunting desperately for some way of telling her he had done nothing of the sort when she said gaily: 'All right! We'll see. I won't tease you. What were we talking about? Your funnies in the bookshop? I'll pop in this morning and see what I think of them, shall I? Will that do?'

Before he could answer two voices, one elderly and uncertain and the other a fluting alto, were raised outside in the passage:

'Happy birthday to you. Happy birthday to you.
Happy birthday, dear Mary,
Happy birthday to you.'

The door opened to admit Colonel Warrender and Mr Bertie Saracen.

IV

Colonel Warrender was sixty years old, a bachelor and a cousin of Charles Templeton whom, in a leaner, better-looking way, he slightly resembled. He kept himself fit, was well dressed and wore a moustache so neatly managed that it looked as if it had been ironed on his face. His manner was pleasant and his bearing soldierly.

Mr Bertie Saracen was also immaculate, but more adventurously so. The sleeves of his jacket were narrower and displayed a great deal of pinkish cuff. He had a Berlin-china complexion, wavy hair, blue eyes and wonderfully small hands. His air was gay and insouciant. He, too, was a bachelor and most understandably so.

They made a comic entrance together: Warrender good-naturedly self-conscious, Bertie Saracen revelling in his act of prima ballerina. He chasséd to right and left, holding aloft his votive offering and finally laid it at Miss Bellamy's feet.

'God, what a fool I must look!' he exclaimed. 'Take it, darling, quickly or we'll kill the laugh.'

A spate of greetings broke out and an examination of gifts: from Warrender, who had been abroad, gloves of Grenoble, and from Bertie a miniature group of five bathing beauties and a photographer all made of balsa-wood and scraps of cotton. 'It's easily the nicest present you'll get,' he said. 'And now I must enjoy a good jeer at all the others.'

He flitted about the room, making little darts at them. Warrender, a rather silent man, generally believed to entertain a long-standing and blameless adoration of Mary Bellamy, had a word with Richard, who liked him.

'Rehearsals started yet?' he asked. 'Mary tells me she's delighted with her new part.'

'Not yet. It's the mixture as before,' Richard rejoined.

Warrender gave him a brief look. 'Early days to settle into a routine, isn't it?' he said surprisingly. 'Leave that to the old hands, isn't it? ' He had a trick of ending his remarks with this colloquialism.

'I'm trying, on the side, to break out in a rash of serious writing.'

'Are you? Good. Afford to take risks, I'd have thought.'

'How pleasant,' Richard exclaimed, 'to hear somebody say that!'

Warrender looked at his shoes. 'Never does,' he said, 'to let yourself be talked into things. Not that I know anything about it.'

Richard thought with gratitude: 'That's exactly the kind of thing I wanted to be told,' but was prevented from saying so by the entrance of Old Ninn.

Old Ninn's real name was Miss Clara Plumtree, but she was given the courtesy title of 'Mrs'. She had been Mary Bellamy's nurse, and, from the time of his adoption by Mary and Charles, Richard's also. Every year she emerged from retirement for a fortnight to stay with her former charge. She was small, scarlet-faced and fantastically opinionated. Her age was believed to be eighty-one. Nannies being universally accepted as character-parts rather than people in their own right, Old Ninn was the subject of many of Mary Bellamy's funniest stories. Richard sometimes wondered if she played up to her own legend. In her old age she had developed a liking for port and under its influence made great mischief among the servants and kept up a sort of guerrilla warfare with Florence, with whom, nevertheless, she was on intimate terms. They were united, Miss Bellamy said, in their devotion to herself.

Wearing a cerise shawl and a bold floral print, for she adored bright colours, Old Ninn trudged across the room with the corners of her mouth turned down and laid a tissue paper parcel on the dressing-table.

'Happy birthday, m',' she said. For so small a person she had an alarmingly deep voice.

A great fuss was made over her. Bertie Saracen attempted Mercutian badinage and called her Nurse Plumtree. She ignored him and addressed herself exclusively to Richard.

'We don't see much of you these days,' she said and, by the sour look she gave him, proclaimed her affection.

'I've been busy, Ninn.'

'Still making up your plays, by all accounts.'

'That's it.'

'You always were a fanciful boy. Easy to see you've never grown out of it.'

Mary Bellamy had unwrapped the parcel and disclosed a knitted bed-jacket of sensible design. Her thanks were effusive, but Old Ninn cut them short.

'Four-ply,' she said. 'You require warmth when you're getting on in years and the sooner you face the fact the more comfortable you'll find yourself. Good morning, sir,' Ninn added, catching sight of Warrender. 'I dare say you'll bear me out. Well, I won't keep you.'

With perfect composure she trudged away, leaving a complete silence behind her.

'Out of this world!' Bertie said, with a shrillish laugh. 'Darling Mary, here I am *sizzling* with decorative fervour. *When* are we to tuck up our sleeves and lay all our plots and plans?'

'Now, darling, if you're ready. Dicky, treasure, will you and Maurice be able to amuse yourselves? We'll scream if we want any help. Come along, Bertie.'

She linked her arm in his. He sniffed ecstatically. 'You smell,' he said, 'like all, but *all*, of King Solomon's wives *and* concubines. In spring. *En avant!*'

They went downstairs. Warrender and Richard were left together in a room that still retained the flavour of her personality, as inescapably potent as the all-pervasive after-math of her scent.

It was an old-established custom that she and Bertie arranged the house for her birthday party. Her drawing-room was the first on the left on the ground floor. It was a long Georgian saloon with a door into the hall and with folding doors leading into the dining-room. This, in its turn opened both into the hall and into the conservatory, which was her especial pride. Beyond the conservatory lay a small formal garden. When all the doors were open an impressive vista was obtained. Bertie himself had 'done' the decor and had used a wealth of old French brocades. He had painted bunches of misty cabbage roses in the recesses above the doors and in the wall panels and had found some really distinguished chandeliers. This year the flowers were to be all white and yellow. He settled down with the greatest efficiency and determination to his task, borrowing one of Gracefield's, the butler's, aprons for the purpose. Miss Bellamy tied herself into a modish confection with a flounced bib, put on wash-leather gloves, and wandered happily about her conservatory, snipping off deadheads and rearranging groups of flowerpots. She was an enthusiastic gardener. They shouted at each other from room to room, exchanging theatre shop, and breaking every now and then into stage cockney: 'Whatseye, dear?' and 'Coo! You wouldn't credit it!' this mode of communication being sacred to the occasion. They enjoyed themselves enormously while from under Bertie's clever fingers emerged bouquets of white and gold and wonderful garlands for the table. In this setting, Miss Bellamy was at her best.

They had been at it for perhaps half an hour and Bertie had retired to the flower-room when Gracefield ushered in Miss Kate Cavendish, known to her intimates as Pinky.

Pinky was younger than her famous contemporary and less distinguished. She had played supporting roles in many Bellamy successes and their personal relationship, not altogether to her satisfaction, resembled their professional one. She had an amusing face, dressed plainly and well and possessed the gifts of honesty and direct thinking. She was, in fact, a charming woman.

'I'm in a tizzy,' she said. 'High as a rocket, darling, and in a minute I'll tell you why. Forty thousand happy returns, Mary, and may your silhouette never grow greater. Here's my offering.'

It was a flask of a new scent by a celebrated maker and was called 'Unguarded.' 'I got it smuggled over from Paris,' she said. 'It's not here yet. A lick on either lobe, I'm told, and the satellites reel in their courses.'

Miss Bellamy insisted on opening it. She dabbed the stopper on her wrists and sniffed. 'Pinky,' she said solemnly, 'it's *too* much! Darling, it opens the *floodgates!* Honestly!'

'It's good, isn't it?'

'Florrie shall put it into my spray. At once. Before Bertie can get at it. You know what he is.'

'Is Bertie here?' Pinky asked quickly.

'He's in the flower-room.'

'Oh.'

'Why? Have you fallen out with him?'

'Far from it,' Pinky said. 'Only – well, it's just that I'm not really meant to let my cat out of its bag as yet and Bertie's involved. But I really am, I fear, more than a little tiddly.'

'*You!* I thought you never touched a thing in the morning.'

'Nor I do. But this is an occasion, Mary. I've been drinking with The Management. Only two small ones, but on an empty turn: Bingo!'

Miss Bellamy said sharply: '*With The Management?*'

'That gives you pause, doesn't it?'

'And Bertie's involved?'

Pinky laughed rather wildly and said: 'If I don't tell somebody I'll spontaneously combust, so I'm going to tell you. Bertie can lump it, bless him, because why after all shouldn't I be audibly grateful.'

Mary Bellamy looked fixedly at her friend for a moment and then said: 'Grateful?'

'All right. I know I'm incoherent. Here it comes. Darling: I'm to have the lead in Bongo Dillon's new play. At the Unicorn. Opening in September. Swear you won't breathe it but it's true and it's settled and the contract's mine for the signing. My first lead, Mary. Oh, *God*, I'm so happy.'

A hateful and all too-familiar jolt under the diaphragm warned Miss Bellamy that she had been upset. Simultaneously she knew that somehow or another she must run up a flag of welcome, must show a responsive warmth, must override the awful, menaced, slipping feeling, the nausea of the emotions that Pinky's announcement had churned up.

'Sweetie-pie!' she said. 'How wonderful!' It wasn't, she reflected, much cop as an expression of delighted congratulation from an old chum, but Pinky was too excited to pay any attention. She went prancing on about the merits of her contract, the glories of the role, the nice behaviour of The Management (Miss Bellamy's Management, as she sickeningly noted), and the feeling that at last this was going to be It. All this gave Miss Bellamy a breather. She began to make fairly appropriate responses. Presently when Pinky drew breath, she was able to say with the right touch of down-to-earth honesty:

'Pinky, this is going to be your Great Thing.'

'I know it! I feel it myself,' Pinky said soberly and added: 'Please God, I'll have what it takes. Please God, I will.'

'My dear, you will,' she rejoined and for the life of her couldn't help adding, 'Of course, I haven't read the play.'

'The *purest* Bongo! Comedy with a twist. You know? Though I says it as shouldn't, it's right up my cul-de-sac. Bongo says he had me in mind all the time he was writing it.'

Miss Bellamy laughed. 'Darling! We do know our Bongo, don't we? The number of plays he's said he'd written for me and when one looked at them – !'

With one of her infuriating moments of penetration, Pinky said, 'Mary! Be pleased for me.'

'But, sweetie, *naturally* I'm pleased. It sounds like a wonderful bit of luck and I hope with all my heart it works out.'

'Of course, I know it means giving up my part in Richard's new one for you. But, face it, there wasn't much in it for me, was there? And nothing was really settled so I'm not letting the side down, am I?'

Miss Bellamy couldn't help it. 'My dear!' she said, with a kindly laugh, 'we'll lose no sleep over that little problem: the part'll cast itself in two seconds.'

'Exactly!' Pinky cried happily and Miss Bellamy felt one of her rare onsets of rage begin to stir. She said:

'But you were talking about Bertie, darling. Where does he come in?'

'Aha!' Pinky said maddeningly and shook her finger.

At this juncture Gracefield arrived with a drinks-tray.

Miss Bellamy controlled herself. 'Come on,' she said, 'I'm going to break my rule, too. We *must* have a drink on this, darling.'

'No, no, no!'

'Yes, yes, yes. A teeny one. Pink for Pinky?'

She stood between Pinky and the drinks and poured out one stiff and one negligible gin-and-bitters. She gave the stiff one to Pinky.

'To your wonderful future, darling,' she said. 'Bottoms up!'

'Oh, *dear*!' Pinky said. 'I shouldn't.'

'Never mind.'

They drank.

'And Bertie?' Miss Bellamy asked presently. 'Come on. You know I'm as silent as the grave.'

The blush that long ago had earned Pinky her nickname appeared in her cheeks. 'This really *is* a secret,' she said. 'Deep and deadly. But I'm sure he won't mind my telling *you*. You see, it's a part that has to be dressed up to the hilt – five changes and all of them grand as grand. Utterly beyond me and my little woman in Bayswater. Well! Bertie, being so much mixed up with The Management has heard all about it, and do you know, darling, he's offered, *entirely* of his own accord, to do my clothes. Designs, materials, making – *everything* from Saracen. And all completely free-ers. *Isn't* that kind?'

Wave after wave of fury chased each other like electrical frequencies through Miss Bellamy's nerves and brain. She had time to think: 'I'm going to throw a temperament and it's bad for me,' and then she arrived at the point of climax.

The explosion was touched off by Bertie himself who came tripping back with a garland of tuberoses twined round his person. When he saw Pinky he stopped short, looked from her to Miss Bellamy and turned rather white.

'Bertie,' Pinky said. 'I've split on you.'

'How could you!' he said. 'Oh, Pinky, how could you!'

Pinky burst into tears.

'I don't know!' she stammered. 'I didn't mean to, Bertie darling. Forgive me. I was high.'

'Stay me with flagons!' he said in a small voice. Miss Bellamy, employing a kind of enlargement of herself that was technically one of her most telling achievements, crossed to him and advanced her face to within four inches of his own.

'You rat, Bertie,' she said quietly. 'You little, two-timing, double-crossing, dirty rat.'

And she wound her hands in his garland, tore it off him and threw it in his face.

CHAPTER 2

Preparation for a Party

Mary Bellamy's temperaments were of rare occurrence but formidable in the extreme and frightening to behold. They were not those regulation theatre tantrums that seem to afford pleasure both to observer and performer; on the contrary they devoured her like some kind of migraine and left her exhausted. Their onset was sudden, their duration prolonged and their sequel incalculable.

Bertie and Pinky, both familiar with them, exchanged looks of despair. Miss Bellamy had not raised her voice, but a kind of stillness seemed to have fallen on the house. They themselves spoke in whispers. They also, out of some impulse of helpless unanimity, said the same thing at the same time.

'Mary!' they said. 'Listen! Don't!'

They knew very well that they had better have held their tongues. Their effort, feeble though it was, served only to inflame her. With an assumption of calmness that was infinitely more alarming than raging hysteria she set about them, concentrating at first on Bertie.

'I wonder,' she said, 'what it feels like to be you. I wonder if you enjoy your own cunning. I expect you do, Bertie. I expect you rather pride yourself on your talent for cashing in on other people's generosity. On mine, for instance.'

'Mary, *darling*! Please!'

'Let us,' she continued, trembling slightly, 'look at this thing quite calmly and objectively, shall we? I'm afraid it will not be a delicious experience but it has to be faced.'

Gracefield came in, took one look at his mistress and went out again. He had been with the family for some time.

'I am the last woman in the world,' Miss Bellamy explained, 'to remind people of their obligations. The last. However – '

She began to remind Bertie of his obligations. Of the circumstances under which she had discovered him – she did not, to his evident relief, say how many years ago – of how she had given him his first chance; of how, since then, he had never looked back; of how there had been an agreement – 'gentlemen's,' she added bitterly – that he would never design for another leading lady in The Management without first consulting her. He opened his mouth, but was obliged without utterance to shut it again. Had he not, she asked, risen to his present position entirely on the wings of her patronage? Besieged as she was by the importunities of the great fashion houses, had she not stuck resolutely to him through thick and thin? And now –

She executed a gesture, Siddons-like in its tragic implications, and began to pace to and fro while Pinky and Bertie hastily made room for her to do so. Her glance lighting for a moment on Pinky she began obliquely to attack her.

'I imagine,' she said, still to Bertie, 'that I shall not be accused of lack of generosity. I am generally said, I think, to be a good friend. Faithful and just,' she added, perhaps with some obscure recollection of Mark Antony. 'Over and over again for friendship's sake I've persuaded The Management to cast actresses who were unable to give me adequate support.'

'Now, look here – !' Pinky began warmly.

'– over and over again. Timmy said, only the other day: "Darling, you're sacrificing yourself on the altar of your personal loyalties!" He's said, over and over again, that he wouldn't for anybody else under the sun accept the casting as it stood. Only for me . . .'

'What casting?' Pinky demanded. Miss Bellamy continued to address herself exclusively to Bertie.

'Only for me, Timmy said, would he dream of taking into any production of his an artist whose spiritual home was weekly rep. in the ham-counties.'

'Timmy,' Pinky said dangerously, 'is producing my play. It's entirely due to him and the author that I've got the part. They told The Management they wanted me.'

Bertie said: 'I happen to know that's perfectly true.'

'Conspiracy!' Miss Bellamy shouted so loudly and suddenly that the others jumped in unison. She was ravaged by a terrible vision of Bertie, Pinky and Timmy all closeted with The Management and agreeing to say nothing to her of their plots and plans. In a Delphic fury she outlined this scene. Bertie, who had been moodily disengaging himself from the remnants of his garland, showed signs of fight. He waited his chance and cut in.

'Speaking,' he began, 'as a two-timing, double-crossing rat, which God knows I am *not*, I take leave to assure you, darling Mary, that you're wrecking yourself for nothing. I'm doing Pinky's gowns out of friendliness and my name isn't going to appear and I must say I'd have thought. . .'

He was allowed to get no further.

'It's not,' Miss Bellamy said, 'what you've done, both of you, but the revolting way you've done it. If you'd come to me in the first instance and said . . .' Then followed an exposition of what they should have said and of the generous response they would have enjoyed if they'd said it. For a moment it looked as if the row was going to degenerate into an aimless and repetitive wrangle. It would probably have done so if Pinky had not said abruptly:

'Now, look here, Mary! It's about time you faced up to yourself. You know jolly well that anything you've done for either of us has been paid back with interest. I know you've had a lot to do with my getting on The Management's short list and I'm grateful, but I also know that it's suited you very well to have me there. I'm a good foil to you. I know all your gimmicks. How you like to be fed lines. And when you dry, as nowadays you very often do, I can fill in like nobody's business. In the gentle art of letting myself be upstaged, cheated out of points and fiddled into nonentity I've done you proud and you'll find I'm damn' hard to replace.'

'My *God!* My *God!* That I should have to listen to this!'

'As for Bertie . . .'

'Never mind, Pinky,' he said quickly.

'I do mind. It's true you gave Bertie his start, but what hasn't he done for you? Your decor! Your clothes! Face it, Mary, without the Saracen Concealed Curve you'd be the Grand Old Lady of the Hip Parade.'

Bertie gave a hysterical hoot of laughter and looked terrified.

'The truth is,' Pinky said, 'you want it both ways, Mary. You want to boss everybody and use everybody for your own ends and at the same time you want us all to wallow in your wake saying how noble and generous and wonderful you are. You're a cannibal, Mary, and it's high time somebody had the guts to tell you so.'

A dead silence followed this unexampled speech.

Miss Bellamy walked to the door and turned. It was a movement with which they were familiar.

'After this,' she said very slowly, dead-panning her voice to a tortured monotone, 'there is only one thing for me to do and much as it hurts me, I shall do it. I shall see The Management. Tomorrow.'

She opened the door. They had a brief glimpse of Charles, Warrender and Richard, irresolute in the hall, before she swept out and shut the door behind her.

The room seemed very quiet after she had gone.

'Bertie,' Pinky said at last, 'if I've done you any harm I'm desperately sorry. I was high. I'll never, never forgive myself.'

'That's all right, dear.'

'You're so *kind*. Bertie – do you think she'll – do you think she can – ?'

'She'll try, dear. She'll try.'

'It took everything I've got, I promise you, to give battle. Honestly, Bertie, she frightened me. She looked murderous.'

'Horrid, wasn't it?'

Pinky stared absently at the great flask of the scent called 'Unguarded.' A ray of sunshine had caught it and it shone golden.

'What are *you* going to do?' she asked.

Bertie picked up a handful of tuberoses from the carpet.

'Get on with me bloody flowers, dear,' he said. 'Get on with me bloody flowers.'

II

Having effected her exit, Miss Bellamy swept like a sirocco past Richard, Warrender and her husband and continued upstairs. In her bedroom she encountered Florence who said: 'What have *you* been doing to yourself?'

'You shut up,' Miss Bellamy shouted and slammed the door.

'Whatever it is it's no good to you. Come on, dear. What's the story?'

'Bloody treachery's the story. Shut up. I don't want to tell you. My God, what friends I've got! My God, what friends!'

She strode about the room and made sounds of outrage and defeat. She flung herself on the bed and pummelled it.

Florence said: 'You know what'll be the end of this – party and all.'

Miss Bellamy burst into tears. 'I haven't,' she sobbed, 'a friend in the world. Not in the whole wide world. Except Dicky.'

A spasm of something that might have been chagrin twitched at Florence's mouth. 'Him!' she said under her breath.

Miss Bellamy abandoned herself to a passion of tears. Florence went into the bathroom and returned with sal volatile.

'Here,' she said. 'Try this. Come along now, dear.'

'I don't want that muck. Give me one of my tablets.'

'Not now.'

'*Now!*'

'You know as well as I do, the doctor said only at night.'

'I don't care what he said. Get me one.'

She turned her head and looked up at Florence, 'Did you hear what I said?'

'There aren't any left. I was going to send out.'

Miss Bellamy said through her teeth: 'I've had enough of this. You think you can call the tune here, don't you? You think you're indispensable. You never made a bigger mistake. You're not indispensable and the sooner you realize it, the better for you. Now, get out.'

'You don't mean that.'

'Get out!'

Florence stood quite still for perhaps ten seconds and then left the room.

Miss Bellamy stayed where she was. Her temperament, bereft of an audience, gradually subsided. Presently she went to her dressing-table, dealt with her face and gave herself three generous shots from her scent spray. At the fourth, it petered out. The bottle was empty.

She made an exasperated sound, stared at herself in the glass and for the first time since the onset of her rage, began to think collectedly.

At half-past twelve she went down to call on Octavius Browne and Anelida Lee.

Her motives in taking this action were mixed. In the first place her temperament, having followed the classic pattern of diminishing returns, had finally worked itself out and had left her restless. She was unwilling to stay indoors. In the second, she wanted very badly to prove to herself how grossly she had been misjudged by Pinky and Bertie and could this be better achieved than by performing an act of gracious consideration towards Richard? In the third place, she was burningly anxious to set her curiosity at rest in the matter of Anelida Lee.

On her way down she looked in at the drawing-room. Bertie, evidently, had finished the flowers and gone. Pinky had left a note saying she was sorry if she'd been too upsetting but not really hauling down her flag an inch. Miss Bellamy blew off steam to Charles, Richard and Warrender without paying much attention to their reactions. They withdrew, dismayed, to Charles's study from whence came the muted sound of intermittent conversation. Superbly dressed and gloved she let herself out and after pausing effectively for a moment in the sunshine, turned into the Pegasus.

Octavius was not in the shop. Anelida, having completed her cleaning, had a smudge across her cheek and grubby hands. She had cried a little after Richard went out in a huff and there had been no time to repair the damage. She was not looking her best.

Miss Bellamy was infinitely relieved.

She was charming to Anelida. Her husband and Richard Dakers, she said, had talked so much about the shop: it was so handy for them, funny old bookworms that they were, to have found one practically on the doorstep. She understood that Anelida was hoping to go on the stage. Anelida replied that she was working at the Bonaventure. With every appearance of infinite generosity Miss Bellamy said that, unlike most of her friends, she thought the little experimental club theatres performed a very useful function in showing plays that otherwise would never see the light of day. Anelida was quiet, well mannered and, Miss Bellamy supposed, much overcome by the honour that was being paid her. That was the kindest interpretation to put upon her somewhat ungushing response. 'Not much temperament *there*,' Miss Bellamy thought and from her this was not a complimentary assessment. She grew more and more cordial.

Octavius returned from a brief shopping expedition and was a success. On being introduced by Anelida – quite prettily, Miss Bellamy had to admit – he uncovered his dishevelled head and smiled so broadly that his face looked rather like a mask of comedy.

'But what a pleasure!' he said, shaping his words with exquisite precision. 'May we not exclaim "*Hic ver assiduum*" since April herself walks in at our door?'

Miss Bellamy got the general trend of this remark and her spirits rose. She thanked him warmly for his telegram and he at once looked extremely pleased with himself. 'Your husband and your ward,' he said, 'told us of the event and I thought, you know, of the many delicious hours you have given us and of how meagre a return is the mere striking together of one's hands.' He looked sideways at her. 'An old fogey's impulse,' he said and waved it aside. He made her a little bow and put his head on one side. Anelida wished he wouldn't.

'It was *heaven* of you,' said Miss Bellamy. '*So* much pleasure it gave: you can't think! And what's more I haven't thanked you for finding that *perfect* picture for Dicky to give me nor,' she improvised on the spur of the moment, 'for that heavenly copy of . . .' Maddeningly, she had forgotten the author of Charles's purchase and of the quotation in the telegram. She marked time with a gesture indicating ineffable pleasure and then mercifully remembered. 'Of Spenser,' she cried.

'You admired the Spenser? I'm very glad.'

'*So* much. And now,' she continued with an enchanting air of diffidence, 'I'm going to ask you something that you'll think quite preposterous. I've come with an invitation. You are, I know, *great* friends of my ward's – of Dicky's – and I, like you, am a creature of impulse. I want you both – *please* – to come to my little party this evening. Drinks and a handful of ridiculous chums at half-past six. Now, please be very sweet and spoil me on my birthday. Please, say yes.'

Octavius turned quite pink with gratification. He didn't hear his niece who came near to him and said hurriedly: 'Unk, I don't think we . . .'

'I have never,' Octavius said, 'in my life attended a theatrical party. It is something quite outside my experience. Really, it's extraordinarily kind of you to think of inviting us. My niece, no doubt, is an initiate. Though not at such an exalted level, I think, Nelly, my love?'

Anelida had began to say: ' It's terribly kind . . .' but Miss Bellamy was already in full spate. She had taken Octavius impulsively by the hands and was beaming into his face. 'You will? Now, *isn't* that *big* of you? I *was* so afraid I might be put in my place or that you would be booked up. And I'm *not!* And you *aren't!* Isn't that wonderful!'

'We are certainly free,' Octavius said. 'Anelida's theatre is not open on Monday evenings. She had offered to help me with our new catalogue. I shall be enchanted.'

'Wonderful!' Miss Bellamy gaily repeated. 'And now I must run. *Au revoir,* both of you. Till this evening!'

She did, almost literally, run out of the shop filled with a delicious sense of having done something altogether charming. 'Kind!' she thought. 'That's what I've been. Kind as kind. Dicky will be so touched. And when he sees that *rather* dreary *rather* inarticulate girl in his own setting – well, if there *has* been anything, it'll peter out on the spot.'

She saw the whole thing in a gratifying flash of clairvoyance: the last fumes of temperament subsided in the sunshine of her own loving-kindness. She returned to the house and found Richard in the hall.

'Darling!' she cried. 'All settled! I've seen your buddies and asked them. The old fuddy-duddy's heaven, isn't he? Out of this world. And the girl's the nicest little thing. Are you pleased?'

'But,' Richard said, amazed. 'Are they . . .? Did Anelida say they'd come?'

'My dear, you don't imagine, do you, that a bit-part fill-in at the Bonaventure is going to turn down an invitation to my birthday party!'

'It's not a bit-part,' Richard said. 'They're doing *Pygmalion* and she's playing Eliza.'

'Poor child.'

He opened his mouth and shut it again.

'There's something,' Miss Bellamy said, 'so endlessly depressing about those clubs. Blue jeans, beards and a snack-bar, no doubt.' He didn't answer and she said kindly:

'Well! We mustn't let them feel too lost, must we? I'll tell Maurice and Charles to be kind. And now, sweetie, I'm off to keep my date with the Great Play.'

Richard said hurriedly: ' There's something I wanted to alter. . . . Could we – ?'

'Darling! You're such heaven when you panic. I'll read it and then I'll put it in your study. Blessings!'

'Mary – Mary, thank you so much.'

She kissed him lightly and almost ran upstairs to read his play and to telephone Pinky and Bertie. She would tell them that she couldn't bear to think of any cloud of dissonance overshadowing her birthday and she would add that she expected them at six-thirty. That would show them how ungrudging she could be. 'After all,' she thought, 'they'll be in a tizzy because if I *did* do my stuff with The Management . . .' Reassured on all counts she went into her room.

Unfortunately, neither Bertie nor Pinky was at home but she left messages. It was now one o'clock. Half an hour before luncheon in which to relax and skim through Richard's play. Everything was going, in the event, very well. 'I'll put me boots up,' she said to herself in stage cockney and did so on the chaise-longue in the bow window of her room. She noticed that once again the azaleas were infected and reminded herself to spray them with Slaypest. She turned her attention, now growing languid, to the play. *Husbandry in Heaven. Not* a very good title, she thought. Wasn't it a quotation from something? The dialogue seemed to be quite unlike Dicky; a bit Sloane Square, in fact. The sort of dialogue that is made up of perfectly understandable phrases that taken together add up to a kind of egg-headed Goon show. Was it or was it not in verse? She read Dicky's description of the leading woman.

'*Mimi comes on. She might be nineteen or twenty-nine. Her beauty is bone-deep. Seductive without luxury. Virginal and dangerous.*' 'Hum!' thought Miss Bellamy. '*Hodge comes out of the Prompt corner. Wolf-whistles. Gestures unmistakably and with feline intensity.*'

Now, why had that line stirred up some obscure misgivings? She turned the pages. It was certainly an enormously long part.

'*Mimi: Can this be April, then, or have I, so early in the day, misinterpreted my directive?*'

'Hell!' thought Miss Bellamy.

But she read one or two of the lines aloud and decided that they might have something. As she flipped over the pages she became more and more satisfied that Dicky had tried to write a wonderful part for her. Different. It wouldn't do, of course, but at least the loving intention was there.

The typescript tipped over and fell across her chest. Her temperaments always left her tired. Just before she dropped off she suffered one of those mysterious jolts that briefly galvanize the body. She had been thinking about Pinky. It may be fanciful to suppose that her momentary discomfort was due to a spasm of hatred rather than to any physical cause. However that may be, she fell at last into an unenjoyable doze.

Florence came in. She had the flask of scent called 'Unguarded' in her hands. She tiptoed across the room, put it on the dressing-table and stood for a moment looking at Miss Bellamy. Beyond the chaise-longue in the bay window were ranks of tulips and budding azaleas and among them stood the tin of Slaypest. To secure it, Florence had to lean across her mistress. She did so, delicately, but Miss Bellamy, at that moment, stirred. Florence drew back and tiptoed out of the room.

Old Ninn was on the landing. She folded her arms and stared up at Florence.

'Asleep,' Florence said, with a jerk of her head. 'Gone to bye-byes.'

'Always the same after tantrums,' said Old Ninn. She added woodenly: 'She'll be the ruin of that boy.'

'She'll be the ruin of herself,' said Florence, 'if she doesn't watch her step.'

III

When Miss Bellamy had gone Anelida, in great distress, turned to her uncle. Octavius was humming a little Elizabethan catch and staring at himself in a Jacobean looking-glass above his desk.

'Captivating!' he said. 'Enchanting! Upon my word, Nell, it must be twenty years since a pretty woman made much of me. I feel, I promise you, quite giddily inclined. And the whole thing – so spontaneous: so touchingly impulsive! We have widened our horizon, my love.'

'Unk,' Anelida said rather desperately, 'you can't think, my poor blessing, what a muddle you've made.'

'A *muddle?*' He looked plaintively at her and she knew she was in for trouble. 'What do you mean? I accept an invitation, most graciously extended by a charming woman. Pray where is the muddle?' She didn't answer, and he said: ' There are certain matters, of course, to be considered. I do not, for instance, know what clothes are proper, nowadays, for cocktail parties. In my day one would have worn – '

'It's not a matter of clothes.'

'No? In any case, you shall instruct me.'

'I've already told Richard I can't go to the party.'

'Nonsense, my dear. Of course we can go,' Octavius said. 'What arc you thinking of?'

'It's so hard to explain, Unky. It's just that – well, it's partly because of me being in the theatre only so very much at the bottom of the ladder – less than the dust, you know, beneath Miss B.'s chariot wheels. I'd be like a corporal in the officers' mess.'

'That,' said Octavius, reddening with displeasure, 'seems to me to be a false analogy, if you'll forgive me for saying so, Nelly. And, my dear, when one quotes it is pleasant to borrow from reputable sources. The Indian Love lyrics, in my undergraduate days, were the scourge of the drawing-rooms.'

'I'm sorry.'

'It would be extremely uncivil to refuse so kind an invitation,' Octavius said, looking more and more like a spoilt and frustrated child. 'I *want* to accept it. What is the matter with you, Anelida?'

'The truth is,' Anelida said rather desperately, 'I don't quite know where I am with Richard Dakers.'

Octavius stared at her and experienced a moment of truth. ' Now that I consider it,' he said huffily, 'I realize that Dakers is paying his addresses to you. I wonder that it hasn't occurred to me before. Have you taken against him?'

To her dismay Anelida found herself on the brink of tears. 'No!' she cried. 'No! Nothing like that – really. I mean – I mean I just don't know . . .' She looked helplessly at Octavius. He was, she knew, hovering on the edge of one of his rare fits of temper. His vanity had been tickled by Miss Bellamy. He had almost strutted and preened before her. Anelida, who loved him very much, could have shaken him.

'Never mind,' she said. 'It's not worth another thought. But I'm sorry, darling, if you're put out over your lovely party.'

'I *am* put out,' Octavius said crossly. 'I want to go.'

'And you shall go. I'll do your tie and make you look beautiful.'

'My dear,' Octavius said, 'it is you who would have looked beautiful. It would have been a great pleasure to take you. I should have been proud.'

'Oh, hell! ' said Amelia. She rushed at him and gave him an exasperated hug. He was much puzzled and hit her gently several times on the shoulder blades.

The shop door opened.

'Here,' Octavius said over the top of Anelida's head, '*is* Dakers.'

Coming from the sunshine into the dark shop, Richard had been given a confused impression of Anelida collaring Octavius in a high tackle. He waited for her to emerge, which she did after some fumbling with her uncle's handkerchief.

Octavius said: 'If you'll excuse me, Nell. Really, one *must* get on with one's job.' He nodded to Richard and limped away into his back room.

Richard was careful not to look at Anelida. 'I came,' he said, 'first to apologize.'

'Not at all. I expect I behaved badly.'

'And to say how very glad I am. Mary told me you had decided for the party.'

'It was terribly kind of her to come. Unk was bewitched.'

'We are being polite to each other, aren't we?'

'Better than flying into rages.'

'May I call for you?'

'There's no need. Really. You'll be busy with the party. Unk will be proud to escort me. He said so.'

'So he well might.' Richard now looked directly at Anelida. 'You've been crying,' he said, 'and your face is dirty. Like a little girl's. Smudged.'

'All right. All right. I'm going to tidy it up.'

'Shall I?'

'No.'

'How old are you, Anelida?'

'Nineteen. Why?'

'I'm twenty-eight.'

'You've done very well,' Anelida said politely, 'for your age. Famous dramatist.'

'Playwright.'

'I think with the new one you may allow yourself to be a dramatist.'

'My God, you've got a cheek,' he said thoughtfully. After a moment he said: 'Mary's reading it. Now.'

'Was she pleased about it?'

'For the wrong reason. She thinks I wrote it for her.'

'But – how could she? Still, she'll soon find out.'

'As I mentioned before, you don't really know much as yet about theatre people.'

Anelida said, to her own astonishment: 'But I do know I can act.'

'Yes,' he agreed. 'Of course you do. You're a good actress.'

'You haven't seen me.'

'That's what you think.'

'Richard!'

'At least I've surprised you into calling me by name.'

'But when did you see me?'

'It slipped out. It's part of a deep-laid plan. You'll find out.'

'When?'

'At the party. I'm off, now. Au revoir, dear Anelida.'

When he had gone, Anelida sat perfectly still for quite a long time. She was bewildered, undecided and piercingly happy.

Richard, however, returned to the house with his mind made up. He went straight to Charles Templeton's study. He found Charles and Maurice Warrender there, rather solemn over a decanter of sherry. When he came in they both looked self-conscious.

'We were just talking about you,' Charles said. 'Have whatever it is you do have at this hour, Dicky. Lager?'

'Please. I'll get it. Should I make myself scarce so that you can go on talking about me?'

'No, no.'

'We'd finished,' Warrender said, 'I imagine. Hadn't we, Charles?'

'I suppose we had.'

Richard poured out his lager. 'As a matter of fact,' he said, 'I sidled in with the idea of boring you with a few observations under that very heading.'

Warrender muttered something about taking himself off. 'Not unless you have to, Maurice,' Richard said. 'It arises, in a way, out of what you said this morning.' He sat down and stared at his beer mug. 'This is going to be difficult,' he said.

They waited, Warrender looking owlish, Charles, as always, politely attentive.

'I suppose it's a question of divided allegiances,' Richard said at last. 'Partly that, anyway.' He went on, trying to put what he wanted to say as objectively as might be. He knew that he was floundering and almost at once began to regret his first impulse.

Charles kept turning his elderly freckled hand and looking at it. Warrender sipped his sherry and shot an occasional, almost furtive, glance at Richard.

Presently Charles said: 'Couldn't we come to the point?'

'I wish I could,' Richard rejoined. 'I'm making a mess of this, I know.'

'May I have a go at it? Is this what you're trying to tell us? You think you can write a different kind of play from the sort of thing that suits Mary. You have, in fact, written one. You think it's the best thing you've done but you're afraid Mary won't take kindly to the idea of your making a break. You've shown it to her and she's reading it now. You're afraid that she'll take it for granted that you see her in the lead. Right, so far?'

'Yes. That's it.'

'But,' Warrender demanded unexpectedly, 'she won't like this play, what!'

'I don't think she'll like it.'

'Isn't that your answer? ' Charles said. 'If she doesn't like it you can offer it elsewhere?'

'It isn't,' Richard said, 'as simple as that.' And looking at these two men, each old enough to be his father, each with thirty years' experience of Mary Bellamy, he saw that he was understood.

'There's been one row already this morning,' he said. 'A snorter.'

Warrender shot a look at Charles. 'I don't know if I'm imagining it,' he said, 'but I've fancied the rows come a bit oftener these days, isn't it?'

Charles and Richard were silent.

Warrender said: 'Fellow's got to live his own life. My opinion. Worst thing that can happen to a man's getting himself bogged down in a mistaken loyalty. Seen it happen. Man in my regiment. Sorry business.'

Charles said: 'We all have our mistaken loyalties.'

There was a further silence.

Richard said violently: 'But – I owe everything to her. The ghastly things I began to write at school. The first shamingly hopeless plays. Then the one that rang the bell. *She* made The Management take it. We talked everything over. Everything. And now – suddenly – I don't want to. I – don't – want – to. Why? *Why?*'

'Very well,' Charles said. Richard looked at him in surprise, but he went on very quietly. 'Writing plays is your business. You understand it. You're an expert. You should make your own decisions.'

'Yes. But Mary . . .'

'Mary holds a number of shares in companies that I direct, but I don't consult her about their policy or confine my interests to those companies only.'

'Surely it's not the same thing.'

'Isn't it?' Charles said placidly. 'I think it is. Sentiment,' he added, 'can be a disastrous guide in such matters. Mary doesn't understand your change of policy: the worst reason in the world for mistrusting it. She is guided almost entirely by emotion.'

Warrender said: 'Think *she's* changed? Sorry, Charles, I've no kind of business to ask.'

'She has changed,' her husband said. 'One does.'

'You can see,' Richard said, 'what happened with Pinky and Bertie. How much more will she mind with me! Was there anything so terrible about what they did? The truth is, of course, that they didn't confide in her because they didn't know how she'd take it. Well – you saw how she took it.'

'I suppose,' Warrender began dimly, 'as a woman gets older . . .' He faded out in a bass rumble.

'Charles,' Richard said, 'you may consider this a monstrous suggestion, but have you thought, lately, that there might be anything – anything – ?'

'Pathological? ' Charles said.

'It's so unlike her to be vindictive. *Isn't it?*' He appealed to both of them. 'Well, my God, *isn't* it?'

To his astonishment they didn't answer immediately. Presently Charles said with a suggestion of pain in his voice: 'The same thing has occurred to me. I – I asked Frank Harkness about it. He's looked after us both for years, as you know. He thinks she's been a bit nervy for some time, I gather, like many women of her – well, of her age. He thinks the high-pressure atmosphere of the theatre may have increased the tension. I got the impression he was under-stating his case. I don't mind telling you,' Charles added unhappily, 'it's been worrying me for some time. These – these ugly scenes.'

Warrender muttered: 'Vindictive,' and looked as if he regretted it.

Richard cried out: 'Her kindness! I've always thought she had the kindest eyes I'd ever seen in a woman.'

Warrender, who seemed this morning to be bent on speaking out of character, did so now. 'People,' he said, 'talk about eyes and mouths as if they had something to do with the way other people think and behave. Only bits of the body, aren't they? Like navels and knees and toenails. Arrangements.'

Charles glanced at him with amusement. 'My dear Maurice, you terrify me. So you discount our old friends the generous mouth, the frank glance, the open forehead. I wonder if you're right.'

'Right or wrong,' Richard burst out, 'it doesn't get me any nearer a decision.'

Charles put down his sherry and put up his eyeglass. 'If I were you, Dicky,' he said, 'I should go ahead.'

'Hear, hear!'

'Thank you, Maurice. Yes. I should go ahead. Offer your play in what you believe to be the best market. If Mary's upset it won't be for long, you know. You must keep a sense of perspective, my dear boy.'

Colonel Warrender listened to this with his mouth slightly open and a glaze over his eyes. When Charles had finished Warrender looked at his watch, rose and said he had a telephone call to make before luncheon. 'I'll do it from the drawing-room, if I may,' he said. He glared at Richard. 'Stick to your guns, isn't it?' he said. 'Best policy.' And went out.

Richard said: 'I've always wondered: just how simple *is* Maurice?'

'It would be the greatest mistake,' Charles said, 'to underrate him.'

IV

In their houses and flats, all within a ten-mile radius of Pardoner's Place, the guests for Mary Bellamy's birthday party made ready to present themselves. Timon (Timmy) Gantry, the famous director, made few preparations for such festivities. He stooped from his inordinate height to the cracked glass on his bathroom wall in order to brush his hair, which he kept so short that the gesture was redundant. He had changed into a suit which he was in the habit of calling his 'decent blue' and as a concession to Miss Bellamy, wore a waistcoat instead of a plum-coloured pullover. He looked rather like a retired policeman whose enthusiasm had never dwindled. He sang a snatch from *Rigoletto*, an opera he had recently directed and remembered how much he disliked cocktail parties.

'*Bell-a-mé-a, you're a bell of a bóre,*' he sang, improvising to the tune of *Bella Filia*. And it was true, he reflected. Mary was becoming more and more of a tiresome girl. It would probably be necessary to quarrel with her before her new play went on. She was beginning to jib at the physical demands made upon her by his production methods: he liked to keep his cast moving rather briskly through complicated, almost fugal patterns and Mary was not as sound in the wind as she used to be. Nor in the temper, he reflected. He rather thought that this play would be his last production for her.

'*For she's not my, not my cuppa tea at all,*' he sang.

This led him to think of her influence on other people, particularly on Richard Dakers. '*She's a seccuba,*' he chanted.' '*She's an o-ogress. She devours young men alive. Nasty Mary!*' He was delighted that Richard showed signs of breaking loose with his venture into serious dramatic writing. He had read *Husbandry in Heaven* to Gantry while it was still in manuscript. Gantry always made up his mind at once about a play and he did so about this one.

'If you go on writing slip-slop for Mary when you've got this sort of stuff under your thatch,' he had said, 'you deserve to drown in it. Parts of this thing are bloody awful and must come out. Other parts need a rewrite. Fix them and I'm ready to produce the piece.'

Richard had fixed them.

Gantry shoved his birthday present for Miss Bellamy into his pocket. It was a bit of pinchbeck he'd picked up for five bob on a street stall. He bought his presents in an inverse ratio to the monetary situation of the recipients and Miss Bellamy was rich.

As he strode along in the direction of Knightsbridge he thought with increasing enthusiasm about *Husbandry in Heaven* and of what he would do with it if he could persuade The Management to take it.

'The actors,' he promised himself, 'shall skip like young rams.'

At Hyde Park Corner he began to sing again. At the corner of Wilton Place a chauffeur-driven car pulled up alongside him. The Management in the person of Mr Montague Marchant, exquisitely dressed, with a gardenia in his coat, leaned from the window. His face and his hair were smooth, fair and pale, and his eyes wary.

'Timmy!' Mr Marchant shouted. '*Look* at you! *So* purposeful! Such *devouring* strides! Come in, do, for God's sake, and let us support each other on our approach to the shrine.'

Gantry said: 'I wanted to see you.' He doubled himself up like a camel and got into the car. It was his custom to plunge directly into whatever matter concerned him at the moment. He presented his ideas with the same ruthless precipitancy that he brought to his work in the theatre. It was a deceptive characteristic, because in Gantry impulse was subordinate to design.

He drew in his breath with an authoritative gasp. 'Listen!' he said. 'I have a proposition.'

All the way along Sloane Street and into the King's Road he thrust Richard's play at Marchant. He was still talking, very eloquently, as they turned up Pardoner's Row. Marchant listened with the undivided though guarded attention that The Management brought to bear only on the utterances of the elect.

'You will do this,' Gantry said as the car turned into Pardoner's Place, 'not for me and not for Dicky. You will do it because it's going to be a Thing for The Management. Mark my words. Here we are. Oh, misery, *how* I abominate grand parties!'

'I'd have you remember,' Marchant said as they went in, 'that I commit myself to nothing, Timmy.'

'Naturally, my dear man. But naturally. You *will* commit yourself, however, I promise you. You will.'

'Mary, *darling*!' they both exclaimed and were swallowed up by the party.

Pinky and Bertie had arranged to go together. They came to this decision after a long gloomy post-luncheon talk in which they weighed the dictates of proper pride against those of professional expediency.

'Face it, sweetie-pie,' Bertie had said, 'if we *don't* show up she'll turn plug-ugly again and go straight to The Management. You know what a fuss Monty makes about personal relationships. "A happy theatre is a successful theatre." Nobody – but *nobody* can afford to cut up rough. He loathes internal strife.'

Pinky, who was feeling the effects of her morning excesses, sombrely agreed. 'God knows,' she said, 'that at this juncture I can ill-afford to get myself the reputation of being difficult. After all, my contract isn't signed, Bertie.'

'It's as clear as daylight: magnanimity must be our watchword.'

'I'll be blowed if I crawl.'

'We shan't have to, dear. A pressure of the hand and a long, long gaze into the eyeballs will carry us through.'

'I resent having to.'

'Never mind. Rise above. Watch me: I'm a past master at it. Gird up the loins, dear, such as they are, and remember you're an actress.' He giggled. 'Looked at in the right way it'll be rather fun.'

'What shall I wear?'

'Black, and no jewellery. She'll be clanking.'

'I hate being at enmity, Bertie. What a beastly profession ours is. In some ways.'

'It's a jungle, darling. Face it – it's a jungle.'

'You,' Pinky said rather enviously, 'don't seem to be unduly perturbed, I must say.'

'My poorest girl, little do you know. I'm quaking.'

'Really? But could she actually do you any damage?'

'Can the boa-constrictor,' Bertie said, 'consume the rabbit?'

Pinky had thought it better not to press this matter any further. They had separated and gone to their several flats, where in due course they made ready for the party.

Anelida and Octavius also made ready. Octavius, having settled for a black coat, striped trousers and the complementary details that he considered appropriate to these garments, had taken up a good deal of his niece's attention. She had managed to have a bath and was about to dress when, for the fourth time, he tapped at her door and presented himself before her, looking anxious and unnaturally tidy. 'My hair,' he said. 'Having no unguent, I used a little olive oil. Do I smell like a salad?'

She reassured him, gave his coat a brush and begged him to wait for her in the shop. He had old-fashioned ideas about punctuality and had begun to fret. 'It's five-and-twenty minutes to seven. We were asked for half-past six, Nelly.'

'That means seven at the earliest, darling. Just take a furtive leer through the window and you'll see when people begin to come. And please, Unk, we can't go while I'm still in my dressing-gown, can we, now?'

'No, no, of course not. Half-past six *for* a quarter-to-seven? Or seven? I see. I see. In that case . . .'

He pottered downstairs.

Anelida thought: 'It's a good thing I've had some practice in quick changes.' She did her face and hair, and she put on a white dress that had been her one extravagance of the year, a large white hat with a black velvet crown, and new gloves. She looked in the glass, forcing herself to adopt the examining attitude she used in the theatre. 'And it might as well be a first night,' she thought, 'the way I'm feeling.' Did Richard like white? she wondered.

Heartened by the certainty of her dress being satisfactory and her hat becoming, Anelida began to daydream along time-honoured lines. She and Octavius arrived at the party. There was a sudden hush. Monty Marchant, The Management in person, would ejaculate to Timon Gantry, the great producer, 'Who are they?' and Timon Gantry, with the abrupt grasp which all actors, whether they had heard it or not, liked to imitate, would reply: 'I don't know, but by God, I'm going to find out.' The ranks would part as she and Octavius, escorted by Miss Bellamy, moved down the room to the

accompaniment of a discreet murmur. They would be the cynosure
of all eyes. What was a cynosure and why was it never mentioned
except in reference to eyes? All eyes on Anelida Lee. And there, rapt
in admiration, would be Richard. . . .

At this point Anelida stopped short, was stricken with shame, had
a good laugh at herself and became the prey of her own nerves.

She went to her window and looked down into Pardoner's Place.
Cars were now beginning to draw up at Miss Bellamy's house. Here
came a large black one with a very smart chauffeur. Two men got
out. Anelida's inside somersaulted. The one with the gardenia *was*
Monty Marchant and that incredibly tall, that unmistakably shabby
figure *was* the greatest of all directors, Timon Gantry.

'Whoops!' Anelida said. 'None of your nonsense, Cinderella.' She
counted sixty and then went downstairs.

Octavius was seated at his desk, reading, and Hodge was on his
knee. They both looked extraordinarily smug.

'Have you come over calm?' Anelida asked.

'What? Calm? Yes,' Octavius said. 'Perfectly, thank you. I have
been reading *The Gulls Hornbook.'*

'Have you been up to something, Unk?'

He rolled his eyes round at her. 'Up to something? I? What can
you mean?'

'You look as if butter wouldn't melt on your whiskers.'

'Really? I wonder why. Should we go?'

He displaced Hodge, who was moulting. Anelida was obliged to
fetch the clothes-brush again.

'I wouldn't change you,' she said, 'for the Grand Cham of Tartary.
Come on, darling, let's go.'

V

Miss Bellamy's preparation for the party occupied the best part of
ninety minutes and had something of the character of a restoration
salon, with Florence, truculently unaware of this distinction, in the
role of abigail.

It followed the after-luncheon rest and, in its early stages, was
conducted in the strictest privacy. She lay on her bed. Florence,

unspeaking and tight-mouthed, darkened the room and produced from the bathroom sundry bottles and pots. She removed the make-up from her mistress's face, put wet pads over her eyes and began to apply a layer of greenish astringent paste. Miss Bellamy attempted to make conversation and was unsuccessful. At last she demanded impatiently: 'What's the matter with *you?* Gone upstage?' Florence was silent. 'Oh, for heaven's *sake!*' Miss Bellamy ejaculated. ' You're not holding out on me because of this morning, are you?'

Florence slapped a layer across Miss Bellamy's upper lip. 'That stuff's stinging me,' Miss Bellamy mumbled with difficulty. 'You haven't mixed it properly.'

Florence completed the mask. From behind it Miss Bellamy attempted to say: 'All right, you can go to hell and sulk there,' but remembering she was not supposed to speak, lay fuming. She heard Florence go out of the room. Ten minutes later she returned, stood for some time looking down on the greenish, blinded face and then set about removing the mask.

The toilet continued in icy silence, proceeding through its manifold and exacting routines. The face was scrutinized like a microscopic slide. The hair was drilled. The person was subjected to masterful but tactful discipline. That which, unsubjected, declared itself centrally, was forced to make a less aggressive reappearance above the seventh rib where it was trapped, confined and imperceptibly distributed. And throughout these intimate manipulations, Florence and Miss Bellamy maintained an absolute and inimical silence. Only when they had been effected did Miss Bellamy open her door to her court.

In the past, Pinky and Bertie had attended: the former vaguely in the role of confidante, the latter to advise about the final stages of the ritual. Today they had not presented themselves and Miss Bellamy was illogically resentful. Though her initial fury had subsided it lay like a sediment at the bottom of her thoughts and it wouldn't take much, she realized, to stir it up.

Charles was the first to arrive and found her already dressed. She wore crimson chiffon, intricately folded and draped with loose panels that floated tactfully past her waist and hips. The décolletage plunged and at its lowest point contained orchids and diamonds. Diamonds appeared again at intervals in the form of brooches and clips, flashed in stalactites from her ears and encircled her neck and wrist in a stutter of brilliance: she was indeed magnificent.

'Well?' she said and faced her husband.

'My dear!' said Charles gently. 'I'm overwhelmed.'

Something in his voice irritated her. 'You don't like it,' she said. 'What's the matter with it?'

'It's quite superb. Dazzling.'

Florence had opened the new bottle of scent and was pouring it into the Venetian glass atomiser. The air was thickened with effluvium so strong that it almost gave the impression of being visible. Charles made the slightest of grimaces.

'Do you think I'm overdressed, Charles?' Miss Bellamy demanded.

'I have implicit faith in your judgment,' he said. 'And you look glorious.'

'Why did you make a face?'

'It's that scent. I find it a bit too much. It's – well – '

'Well! What is it?'

'I fancy indecent is the word I'm groping for.'

'It happens to be the most exclusive perfume on the market.'

'I don't much like the word "perfume," but in this case it seems to be entirely appropriate.'

'I'm sorry,' she said in a high voice, 'that you find my choice of words non-U.'

'My dear Mary! . . .'

Florence screwed the top on the atomiser and placed it, with the three-quarters emptied bottle on the dressing-table. She then retired to the bathroom.

Charles Templeton took his wife's hands in his and kissed them. 'Ah!' he said. 'That's your usual scent.'

'The last dregs.'

'I'll give you some more.'

She made as if to pull her hands away, but he folded them between his own.

'Do something for me,' he said. 'Will you? I never ask you.'

'My dear Charles!' she exclaimed impatiently. 'What?'

'Don't use that stuff. It's vulgar, Mary. The room stinks of it already.'

She stared at him with a kind of blank anger. His skin was mottled. The veins showed on his nose and his eyes were watery. It was an elderly face, and not very handsome.

'Don't be ridiculous,' she said and withdrew her hands.

Warrender tapped on the door and came in. When he saw Miss Bellamy he ejaculated 'What!' several times and was so clearly bowled over that her ill-humour modulated into a sort of petulant gratification. She made much of him and pointedly ignored her husband.

'You are the most fabulous, heavenly sweetie-pie,' she said and kissed his ear.

He turned purple and said: 'By George!'

Charles had walked over to the window. The tin of Slaypest was still there. At the same moment Florence reentered the room. Charles indicated the tin. Florence cast up her eyes.

He said: 'Mary, you do leave the windows open, don't you, when you use this stuff on your plants?'

'Oh, for heaven's *sake*!' she exclaimed. 'Have you got a secret Thing about sprays? You'd better get yourself psychoed, my poor Charles.'

'It's dangerous. I took the trouble to buy a text book on these things and what it has to say is damn' disquieting. I showed it to Maurice. Read it yourself, my dear, if you don't believe me. Ask Maurice. You don't think she ought to monkey about with it, do you, Maurice?'

Warrender picked up the tin and stared at the label with its red skull and crossbones and intimidating warning. 'Shouldn't put this sort of stuff on the market,' he said. 'My opinion.'

'Exactly. Let Florence throw it out, Mary.'

'Put it down!' she shouted. 'My God, Charles, what a bore you can be when you set your mind to it.'

Suddenly she thrust the scent atomiser into Warrender's hands. 'Stand there, darling,' she said. 'Far enough away for it not to make rivers or stain my dress. Just a delicious mist. Now! Spray madly.'

Warrender did as he was told. She stood in the redolent cloud with her chin raised and her arms extended.

'Go on, Maurice,' she said, shutting her eyes in a kind of ecstasy. 'Go on.'

Charles said, very quietly: 'My God!'

Warrender stared at him, blushed scarlet, put down the scent spray and walked out of the room.

Mary and Charles looked at each other in silence.

The whole room reeked of 'Unguarded.'

CHAPTER 3

Birthday Honours

Mr and Mrs Charles Templeton stood just inside their drawing-room door. The guests, on their entry, encountered a bevy of Press photographers, while a movie outfit was established at the foot of the stairs, completely blocking the first flight. New arrivals smiled or looked thoughtful as the flashlamps discovered them. Then, forwarded by the parlourmaid in the hall to Gracefield on the threshold, they were announced and, as it were, passed on to be neatly fielded by their hosts.

It was not an enormous party: perhaps fifty all told. It embraced the élite of the theatre world and it differed in this respect from other functions of its size. It was a little as if the guests gave rattling good performances of themselves arriving at a cocktail party. They did this to music, for Miss Bellamy, in an alcove of her great salon, had stationed a blameless instrumental trio.

Although, in the natural course of events, they met each other very often, there was a tendency among the guests to express astonishment, even rapture, at this particular encounter. Each congratulated Miss Bellamy on her birthday and her superb appearance. Some held her at arm's length the better to admire. Some expressed bewilderment and others a sort of matey reverence. Then in turn they shook hands with Charles and by the particular pains the nice ones took with him, they somehow established the fact that he was not quite of their own world.

When Pinky and Bertie arrived, Miss Bellamy greeted them with magnanimity.

'*So* glad,' she said to both of them, 'that you decided to come.' The kiss that accompanied this greeting was tinctured with forbearance and what passed with Miss Bellamy for charity. It also, in some ineffable manner, seemed to convey a threat. They were meant to receive it like a sacrament and (however reluctantly) they did so, progressing on the conveyor belt of hospitality to Charles, who was markedly cordial to both of them.

They passed on down the long drawing-room and were followed by two Dames, a Knight, three distinguished commoners, another Knight and his Lady, Montague Marchant and Timon Gantry.

Richard, filling his established role of a sort of unofficial son of the house, took over the guests as they came his way. He was expected to pilot them through the bottleneck of the intake and encourage them to move to the dining-room and conservatory. He also helped the hired barman and the housemaid with the drinks until Gracefield and the parlourmaid were able to carry on. He was profoundly uneasy. He had been out to lunch and late returning and had had no chance to speak to Mary before the first guests appeared. But he knew that all was not well. There were certain only-too-unmistakable signs, of which a slight twitch in Mary's triangular smile was the most ominous. 'There's been another temperament,' Richard thought, and he fancied he saw confirmation of this in Charles, whose hands were not quite steady and whose face was unevenly patched.

The rooms filled up. He kept looking towards the door and thinking he saw Anelida.

Timon Gantry came up to him. 'I've been talking to Monty,' he said. 'Have you got a typescript for him?'

'Timmy, how kind of you! Yes, of course.'

'Here?'

'Yes. Mary's got one. She said she'd leave it in my old room upstairs.'

''*Mary!* Why?'

'I always show her my things.'

Gantry looked at him for a moment, gave his little gasp and then said: 'I see I must speak frankly. Will Mary think you wrote the part for her?'

Richard said: 'I – that was not my intention . . .'

'Because you'd better understand at once, Dicky, that I wouldn't dream of producing this play with Mary in the lead. Nor would I dream of advising The Management to back it with Mary in the lead. Nor could it be anything but a disastrous flop with Mary in the lead. Is that clear?'

'Abundantly,' Richard said.

'Moreover,' Gantry said, 'I should be lacking in honesty and friendship if I didn't tell you it was high time you cut loose from those particular apron strings. Thank you, I would prefer whisky and water.'

Richard, shaken, turned aside to get it. As he made his way back to Gantry he was aware of one of those unaccountable lulls that sometimes fall across the insistent din of a cocktail party. Gantry, inches taller than anyone else in the room, was looking across the other guests towards the door. Several of them also had turned in the same direction, so that it was past the backs of heads and through a gap between shoulders that Richard first saw Anelida and Octavius come in.

It was not until a long time afterwards that he realized his first reaction had been one of simple gratitude to Anelida for being, in addition to everything else, so very beautiful.

He heard Timon Gantry say: 'Monty! Look.' Montague Marchant had come up to them.

'I am looking,' he said. 'Hard.'

And indeed they all three looked so hard at Anelida that none of them saw the smile dry out on Mary Bellamy's face and then re-appear as if it had been forcibly stamped there.

Anelida shook hands with her hostess, expected, perhaps, some brief return of the morning's excessive cordiality, heard a voice say: 'So kind of you to come,' and witnessed the phenomenon of the tri-angular smile. Followed by Octavius she moved on to Charles. And then she was face to face with Richard who, as quickly as he could, had made his way down the room to meet them.

'Well?' Timon Gantry said.

'Well,' Marchant repeated. 'What is it?'

'It's an actress.'

'Any good?'

'I'll answer that one,' Gantry said, 'a little later.'

'Are you up to something?'

'Yes.'

'What, for God's sake?'

'Patience, patience.'

'I sometimes wonder, Timmy, why we put up with you.'

'You needn't. You put up with me, dear boy, because I give The Management its particular brand of prestige.'

'So you say.'

'True?'

'I won't afford you the ignoble satisfaction of saying so.'

'All the same, to oblige me, stay where you are.'

He moved towards the group of three that was slowly making its way down the drawing-room.

Marchant continued to look at Anelida.

When Richard met Anelida and took her hand he found, to his astonishment, he was unable to say to her any of the things that for the last ten years he had so readily said to lovely ladies at parties. The usual procedure would have been to kiss her neatly on the cheek, tell her she looked marvellous and then pilot her by the elbow about the room. If she was his lady of the moment, he would contrive to spend a good deal of time in her company and they would probably dine somewhere after the party. How the evening then proceeded would depend upon a number of circumstances, none of which seemed to be entirely appropriate to Anelida. Richard felt, unexpectedly, that his nine years seniority were more like nineteen.

Octavius had found a friend. This was Miss Bellamy's physician, Dr Harkness, a contemporary of Octavius's Oxford days and up at the House with him. They could be left together, happily reminiscent, and Anelida could be given her dry Martini and introduced to Pinky and Bertie, who were tending to hunt together through the party.

Bertie said rapidly: 'I *do* congratulate you. *Do* swear to me on your *sacred* word of honour, *never* to wear anything but white and always, but *always* with your clever hat. *Ever!*'

'You mustn't take against Bertie,' Pinky said kindly. 'It's really a smashing compliment, coming from him.'

'I'll bear it in mind,' Anelida said. It struck her that they were both behaving rather oddly. They kept looking over her shoulder as if somebody or something behind her exerted a strange attraction over them. They did this so often that she felt impelled to follow their gaze and did so. It was Mary Bellamy at whom they had been darting their glances. She had moved farther into the room and stood quite close, surrounded by a noisy group of friends. She herself was talking. But to Anelida's embarrassment she found Miss Bellamy's eyes looked straight into her own, coldly and searchingly. It was not, she was sure, a casual or accidental affair. Miss Bellamy had been watching her and the effect was disconcerting. Anelida turned away only to meet another pair of eyes, Timon Gantry's. And beside him yet another pair, Montague Marchant's, speculative, observant. It was like an inversion of her ridiculous daydream and she found it disturbing. 'The cynosure of all eyes indeed! With a difference,' thought Anelida.

But Richard was beside her: not looking at her, his arm scarcely touching hers but *there*, to her great content. Pinky and Bertie talked with peculiar energy, making a friendly fuss over Anelida but conveying, nevertheless, a singular effect of nervous tension.

Presently Richard said: 'Here's somebody else who would like to meet you, Anelida.' She looked up at a brick-coloured Guardee face and a pair of surprised blue eyes. 'Colonel Warrender,' Richard said.

After his bumpy fashion, Warrender made conversation. 'Everybody always shouts at these things, isn't it? Haven't got up to pitch yet but will, of course. You're on the stage, isn't it?'

'Just.'

'Jolly good! What d'you think of Dicky's plays?'

Anelida wasn't yet accustomed to hearing Richard called Dicky or to being asked that sort of question in that sort of way.

She said: 'Well – immensely successful, of course.'

'Oh!' he said. 'Successful! Awfully successful! 'Course. And I like 'em, you know. I'm his typical audience: want something gay and 'musing, with a good part for Mary. Not up to intellectual drama. Point is, though: is *he* satisfied? What d'you think? Wasting himself or not? What?'

Anelida was greatly taken aback and much exercised in her mind. Did this elderly soldier know Richard very intimately or did all Richard's friends plunge on first acquaintance into analyses of each other's inward lives for the benefit of perfect strangers? And did Warrender know about *Husbandry in Heaven*?

Again she had the feeling of being closely watched.

She said: 'I hope he'll give us a serious play one of these days and I shouldn't have thought he'll be really satisfied until he does.'

'Ah!' Warrender ejaculated as if she'd made a dynamic observation. 'There you are! Jolly good! Keep him up to it. Will you?'

'I!' Anelida cried in a hurry. She was about to protest that she was in no position to keep Richard up to anything when it occurred to her surprisingly, that Warrender might consider any such disclaimer an affectation.

'But does he need "keeping up"?' she asked.

'Oh, lord, yes!' he said. 'What with one thing and another. You must know all about that.'

Anelida reminded herself she had only drunk half a dry Martini so she couldn't possibly be under the influence of alcohol. Neither, she would have thought, was Colonel Warrender. Neither, apparently, was Miss Bellamy or Charles Templeton or Miss Kate Cavendish or Mr Bertie Saracen. Nor it would seem was Mr Timon Gantry, to whom, suddenly, she was being introduced by Richard.

'Timmy,' Richard was saying. 'Here is Anelida Lee.'

To Anelida it was like meeting a legend.

'Good evening,' the so-often mimicked voice was saying. 'What is there for us to talk about? I know. You shall tell me precisely why you make that "throw-it-over-your-shoulder" gesture in your final speech and whether it is your own invention or a bit of producer's whimsy.'

'Is it wrong?' Anelida demanded. She then executed the mime that is known in her profession as a double-take. Her throat went dry, her eyes started and she crammed the knuckle of her gloved hand between her separated teeth. 'You haven't *seen* me!' she cried.

'But I have. With Dicky Dakers.'

'Oh, my God!' whispered Anelida and this was not an expression she was in the habit of using.

'Look out. You'll spill your drink. Shall we remove a little from this barnyard cacophony? The conservatory seems at the moment to be unoccupied.'

Anelida disposed of her drink by distractedly swallowing it. 'Come along,' Gantry said. He took her by the elbow and piloted her towards the conservatory. Richard, as if by sleight-of-hand, had disappeared. Octavius was lost to her.

'Good evening, Bunny. Good evening, my dear Paul. Good evening, Tony,' Gantry said with the omniscience of M. de Charlus. Celebrated faces responded to these greetings and drifted astern. They were in the conservatory and for the rest of her life the smell of freesias would carry Anelida back to it.

'There!' Gantry said, releasing her with a little pat. 'Now then.'

'Richard didn't tell me. Nobody said you were in front.'

'Nobody knew, dear. We came in during the first act and left before the curtain. I preferred it.'

She remembered, dimly, that this kind of behaviour was part of his legend.

'Why are you fussed?' Gantry inquired. 'Are you ashamed of your performance?'

'No,' Anelida said truthfully, and she added in a hurry, 'I know it's very bad in patches.'

'How old are you?'

'Nineteen.'

'What else have you played?'

'Only bits at the Bonaventure.'

'No *dra-mat-ic ac-ad-emy?*' he said, venomously spitting out the consonants. 'No agonizing in devoted little groups? No *depicting?* No going to bed with Stanislavsky and rising with Method?'

Anelida, who was getting her second wind, grinned at him.

'I admire Stanislavsky,' she said. 'Intensely.'

'Very well. Very well. Now, attend to me. I am going to tell you about your performance.'

He did so at some length and in considerable detail. He was waspish, didactic, devastating and overwhelmingly right. For the most part she listened avidly and in silence, but presently she ventured to ask for elucidation. He answered, and seemed to be pleased.

'Now,' he said, 'those are all the things that were amiss with your performance. You will have concluded that I wouldn't have told you about them if I didn't think you were an actress. Most of

your mistakes were technical. You will correct them. In the meantime I have a suggestion to make. Just that. No promises. It's in
reference to a play that may never go into production. I believe you
have already read it. You will do so again, if you please, and to that
end you will come to the Unicorn at ten o'clock next Thursday
morning. Hi! Monty!'

Anelida was getting used to the dream-like situation in which she
found herself. It had, in its own right, a kind of authenticity. When
The Management, that bourne to which all unknown actresses
aspired, appeared before her in the person of Montague Marchant,
she was able to make a reasonable response. How pale was Mr
Marchant, how matt his surface, how immense his aplomb! He
talked of the spring weather, of the flowers in the conservatory and,
through some imperceptible gradation, of the theatre. She was, he
understood, an actress.

'She's playing Eliza Doolittle,' Gantry remarked.

'Of course. Nice notices,' Marchant murmured and tidily smiled
at her. She supposed he must have seen them.

'I've been bullying her about the performance,' Gantry continued.

'What a bad man!' Marchant said lightly. 'Isn't he?'

'I suggest you take a look at it.'

'Now, you see, Miss Lee, he's trying to bully me.'

'You mustn't let him,' Anelida said.

'Oh, I'm well up to his tricks. Are you liking Eliza?'

'Very much indeed. It's a great stroke of luck for me to try my
hand at her.'

'How long is your season?'

'Till Sunday. We change every three weeks.'

'God, yes. Club policy.'

'That's it.'

'I see no good reason,' Gantry said, 'for fiddling about with this
conversation. You know the part I told you about in Dicky's new
play? She's going to read it for me. In the meantime, Monty, my
dear, you're going to look at the piece and then pay a call on the
Bonaventure.' He suddenly displayed the cock-eyed charm for
which he was famous. 'No promises made, no bones broken. Just a
certain amount of very kind trouble taken because you know I
wouldn't ask it idly. Come, Monty: do say you will.'

'I seem,' Marchant said, 'to be cornered,' and it was impossible to tell whether he really minded.

Anelida said: 'It's asking altogether too much – please *don't* be cornered.'

'I shall tell you quite brutally if I think you've wasted my time.'

'Yes, of course.'

'Ah, Dicky!' Marchant said. 'May I inquire if you're a party to this conspiracy?'

Richard was there again, beside her. 'Conspiracy?' he said. 'I'm up to my neck in it. Why?'

Gantry said: 'The cloak-and-dagger business is all mine, however. Dicky's a puppet.'

'Aren't we all!' Marchant said. 'I need another drink. So, I should suppose, do you.'

Richard had brought them. 'Anelida,' he asked, 'what have they been cooking?'

For the third time, Anelida listened to her own incredible and immediate future.

'I've turned bossy, Richard,' Gantry said. 'I've gone ahead on my own. This child's going to take a running jump at reading your wench in *Heaven*. Monty's going to have a look at the play and see her Eliza. I tell him he'll be pleased. Too bad if you think she can't make it.' He looked it Anelida and a very pleasant smile broke over his face. He dipped the brim of her hat with a thumb and forefinger. 'Nice hat,' he said.

Richard's hand closed painfully about her arm. 'Timmy!' he shouted. 'You're a *splendid* fellow! *Timmy!*'

'The author, at least,' Marchant said dryly, 'would appear to be pleased.'

'In that case,' Gantry proposed, 'let's drink to the unknown quantity. To your bright eyes, Miss Potential.'

'I may as well go down gracefully,' Marchant said. 'To your conspiracy, Timmy. In the person of Anelida Lee.'

They had raised their glasses to Anelida when a voice behind them said: 'I don't enjoy conspiracies in my own house, Monty, and I'm afraid I'm not mad about what I've heard of this one. Do let me in on it, won't you?'

It was Miss Bellamy.

II

Miss Bellamy had not arrived in the conservatory unaccompanied.
She had Colonel Warrender in attendance upon her. They had been
followed by Charles Templeton, Pinky Cavendish and Bertie
Saracen. These three had paused by Gracefield to replenish their
glasses and then moved from the dining-room into the conservatory,
leaving the door open. Gracefield, continuing his round, was about
to follow them. The conglomeration of voices in the rooms behind
had mounted to its extremity, but above it, high-pitched, edged with
emotion, a single voice rang out: Mary Bellamy's. There, in the conservatory she was, for all to see. She faced Anelida and leant slightly
towards her.

'No, no, no, my dear. That, really, is not quite good enough.'

A sudden lull, comparable to that which follows the lowering of
houselights in a crowded theatre, was broken by the more distant
babble in the farther room, and by the inconsequent, hitherto
inaudible excursions of the musicians. Heads were turned towards
the conservatory. Warrender came to the door. Gracefield found
himself moved to one side: Octavius was there, face to face with
Warrender. Gantry's voice said:

'Mary; this won't do.'

'I think,' Octavius said, 'if I may, I would like to go to my niece.'

'Not yet,' Warrender said. 'Do you mind? ' He shut the door and
cut off the voices in the conservatory.

For a moment the picture beyond the glass walls was held. Mary
Bellamy's lips worked. Richard faced her and was speaking. So were
Charles and Gantry. It was like a scene from a silent film. Then,
with a concerted movement, the figures of Gantry, Charles, Richard
and Warrender, their backs to their audience, hid Miss Bellamy and
Anelida.

'Ah, there you are, Occy!' a jovial, not quite sober voice exclaimed.
'I was going to ask you, old boy. D'you remember – ?'

It was Octavius's old acquaintance, Dr Harkness, now rather tight.
As if he had given a signal, everybody began to talk again very loudly
indeed. Charles broke from the group and came through the glass
door, shutting it quickly behind him. He put his hand on Octavius's
arm.

'It's all right, Browne, I assure you,' he said. 'It's nothing. Dicky is taking care of her. Believe me, it's all right.' He turned to Gracefield. 'Tell them to get on with it,' he said. 'At once.'

Gracefield gave his butler's inclination and moved away.

Octavius said: 'But all the same, I would prefer to join Anelida.'

Charles looked at him. 'How would you have liked,' he said, 'to have spent the greater part of your life among aliens?'

Octavius blinked. 'My dear Templeton,' he said, 'I don't know. But if you'll forgive me I find myself in precisely that situation at the moment and I should still like to go to my niece.'

'Here she is, now.'

The door had opened again and Anelida had come through with Richard. They were both very white. Again a single voice was heard. Miss Bellamy's. 'Do you suppose for one moment that I'm taken in?' And again Warrender shut the door.

'Well, Nelly, darling,' Octavius said. 'I promised to remind you that we must leave early. Are you ready?'

'Quite ready,' Anelida said. She turned to Charles Templeton and offered him her hand. 'I'm so sorry,' she said. 'We'll slip out under our own steam.'

'I'm coming,' Richard announced grimly.

'So there's nothing,' Charles said, 'to be done?'

'I'm afraid we must go,' Octavius said.

'We're running late as it is,' Anelida agreed. Her voice, to her own astonishment, was steady. 'Goodbye,' she said, and to Richard: 'No, don't come.'

'I am coming.'

Octavius put his hand on her shoulder and turned her towards the end of the room.

As he did so a cascade of notes sounded from a tubular gong. The roar of voices again died down, the musicians stood up and began to play that inevitable, that supremely silly air.

'Happy birthday *to* you,

'Happy birthday *to* you . . .'

The crowd in the far room surged discreetly through into the dining-room, completely blocking the exit. Richard muttered: 'This way. Quick,' and propelled them towards a door into the hall. Before they could reach it, it opened to admit a procession: the maids,

Gracefield with magnums of champagne, Florence, Cooky, in a white hat and carrying an enormously ornate birthday cake, and Old Ninn. They walked to the central table and moved ceremoniously to their appointed places. The cake was set down. Led by Dr Harkness the assembly broke into applause.

'Now,' Richard said.

And at last they were out of the room and in the hall. Anelida was conscious for the first time of her own heartbeat. It thudded in her throat and ears. Her mouth was dry and she trembled.

Octavius, puzzled and disturbed, touched her arm. 'Nelly, my love,' he said, 'shall we go?'

'Yes,' Anelida said, and turned to Richard. 'Don't come any farther. Goodbye.'

'I'm coming with you. I've got to.'

'Please not.'

He held her by the wrist. 'I don't insult you with apologies, Anelida, but I do beg you to be generous and let me talk to you.'

'Not now. Please, Richard, not now.'

'Now. You're cold and you're trembling. Anelida!' He looked into her face and his own darkened. 'Never again shall she speak to you like that. Do you hear me, Anelida? Never again.' She drew away from him.

The door opened. Pinky and Bertie came through. Pinky made a dramatic pounce at Anelida and laid her hand on her arm. 'Darling!' she cried incoherently. 'Forget it! Nothing! God, what a scene!' She turned distractedly to the stairs, found herself cut off by the cinema unit and doubled back into the drawing-room. The camera men began to move their equipment across the hall.

'*Too* much!' Bertie said. 'No! *Too* much.' He disappeared in the direction of the men's cloakroom.

Timon Gantry came out, 'Dicky,' he said, 'push off. I want a word with this girl. You won't do any good while you're in this frame of mind. Off!'

He took Anelida by the shoulders. 'Listen to me,' he said. 'You will rise above. You will not let this make the smallest difference. Go home, now, and sort yourself out. I shall judge you by this and I shall see you on Thursday. Understood?' He gave her a firm little shake and stood back.

Warrender appeared, shutting the door behind him. He glared wretchedly at Anelida and barked: 'Anything I can do – realize how distressed. . . . Isn't it?'

Octavius said: 'Very kind: I don't think, however . . .'

Richard announced loudly: 'I'll never forgive her for this. Never.'

Anelida thought: 'If I don't go now I'll break down.' She heard her own voice: 'Don't give it another thought. Come along, Unk.'

She turned and walked out of the house into the familiar square, and Octavius followed her.

'Richard,' Warrender said, 'I must have a word with you, boy. Come in here.'

'No,' Richard said and he, too, went out into the square.

Gantry stood for a moment looking after him.

'I find myself,' he observed, 'unable, any longer, to tolerate Mary Bellamy.'

A ripple of applause broke out in the dining-room. Miss Bellamy was about to cut her birthday cake.

III

Miss Bellamy was a conscientious, able and experienced actress. Her public appearances were the result of hard work as well as considerable talent and, if one principle above all others could be said to govern them, it was that which is roughly indicated in the familiar slogan 'The show must go on.' It was axiomatic with Miss Bellamy that whatever disrupting influences might attend her, even up to the moment when her hand was on the offstage door knob, they would have no effect whatsoever upon her performance.

They had none on the evening of her fiftieth birthday. She remained true to type.

When the procession with the cake appeared in the dining-room beyond the glass wall of the conservatory, she turned upon the persons with whom she had been doing battle and uttered the single and strictly professional order: 'Clear!'

They had done so. Pinky, Bertie, Warrender and Gantry had all left her. Charles had already gone. Only Marchant remained, according, as it were, to the script. It had been arranged that he escort Miss

Bellamy and make the birthday speech. They stood together in the conservatory, watching. Gracefield opened the champagne. There was a great deal of laughter and discreet skirmishing among the guests. Glasses were distributed and filled. Gracefield and the maids returned to their appointed places. Everybody looked towards the conservatory.

'This,' Marchant said, 'is it. You'd better bury the temperament, sweetie, for the time being.' He opened the door, adding blandly as he did so: 'Bitch into them, dear.'

'The hell I will,' said Miss Bellamy. She shot one malevolent glance at him, stepped back, collected herself, parted her lips in their triangular smile and made her entrance.

The audience, naturally, applauded.

Marchant, who had his own line in smiles, fingered his bowtie and then raised a deprecating hand.

'Mary, darling,' he said, pitching his voice, 'and everybody! Please!'

A Press photographer's lamp flashed.

Marchant's speech was short, graceful, bland and for the most part, highly appreciated. He made the point, an acceptable one to his audience, that nobody really understood the people of their wonderful old profession but they themselves. The ancient classification of 'rogues and vagabonds' was ironically recapitulated. The warmth, the dedication, the loyalties were reviewed and a brief but moving reference was made to 'our wonderful Mary's happy association with, he would not say Marchant and Company, but would use a more familiar and he hoped affectionate phrase – "The Management." ' He ended by asking them all to raise their glasses and drink 'to Mary.'

Miss Bellamy's behaviour throughout was perfect. She kept absolutely still and even the most unsympathetic observer would scarcely have noticed that she was anything but oblivious of her audience. She was, in point of fact, attentive to it and was very well aware of the absence of Richard, Pinky, Bertie, Warrender and Gantry: to say nothing of Anelida and Octavius. She also noticed that Charles, a late arrival in his supporting role of consort, looked pale and troubled. This irritated her. She saw that Old Ninn, well to the fore, was scarlet in the face, a sure sign of intemperance. No doubt there had been port-drinking parties with Florence and

Gracefield and further noggins on her own account. Infuriating of Old Ninn! Outrageous of Richard, Pinky, Bertie, Maurice and Timon to absent themselves from the speech! Intolerable, that on her birthday she should be subjected to slight after slight and deception after deception: culminating, my God, in their combined treachery over that boney girl from the bookshop! It was time to give Monty a look of misty gratitude. They were drinking her health.

She replied, as usual, very briefly. The suggestion was of thoughts too deep for words and the tone whimsical. She ended by making a special reference to the cake and said that on this occasion Cooky, if that were possible, had excelled herself and she called attention to the decorations.

There was a round of applause, during which Gantry, Pinky, Bertie and Warrender edged in through the far doorway. Miss Bellamy was about to utter her peroration, but before she could do so, Old Ninn loudly intervened. 'What's a cake without candles?' said Old Ninn.

A handful of guests laughed, nervously and indulgently. The servants looked scandalized and apprehensive.

'Fifty of them,' Old Ninn proclaimed. 'Oh, wouldn't they look lovely!' And broke into a disreputable chuckle.

Miss Bellamy took the only possible action. She topped Old Ninn's lines by snatching up the ritual knife and plunging it into the heart of the cake. The gesture, which may have had something of the character of a catharsis, was loudly applauded.

The Press photographers' lamps flashed.

The ceremony followed its appointed course. The cake was cut up and distributed. Glasses were refilled and the guests began to talk again at the tops of their voices. It was time for her to open the presents which had already been deposited on a conveniently placed table in the drawing-room. When that had been done they would go and the party would be over. But it would take a considerable time and all her resources. In the meantime, there was Old Ninn, purple-faced, not entirely steady on her pins and prepared to continue her unspeakable act for the benefit of anyone who would listen to her.

Miss Bellamy made a quick decision. She crossed to Old Ninn, put her arm about her shoulders and, gaily laughing, led her towards the door into the hall. In doing so she passed Warrender, Pinky, Bertie and

Timon Gantry. She ignored them, but shouted to Monty Marchant that she was going to powder her nose. Charles was in the doorway. She was obliged to stop for a moment. He said under his breath: 'You've done a terrible thing.' She looked at him with contempt.

'You're in my way. I want to go out.'

'I can't allow you to go on like this.'

'Get *out*!' she whispered and thrust towards him. In that over-heated room her scent engulfed him like a fog.

He said loudly: 'At least don't use any more of that stuff. At least don't do that. Mary, listen to me!'

'I think you must be mad.'

They stared at each other. He stood aside and she went out taking Old Ninn with her. In the hall she said: 'Ninn, go to your room and lie down. Do you hear me!'

Old Ninn looked her fully in the face, drew down the corners of her mouth and, keeping a firm hold on the banister, plodded upstairs.

Neither she nor Charles had noticed Florence, listening avidly, a pace or two behind them. She moved away down the hall and a moment later Richard came in by the front door. When he saw Miss Bellamy he stopped short.

'Where have you been?' she demanded.

'I've been trying, not very successfully, to apologize to my friends.'

'They've taken themselves off, it appears.'

'Would you have expected them to stay?'

'I should have thought them capable of anything.'

He looked at her with a sort of astonishment and said nothing.

'I've got to speak to you,' she said between her teeth.

'Have you? I wonder what you can find to say.'

'Now.'

'The sooner the better. But shouldn't you' – he jerked his head at the sounds beyond the doors – 'be in there?'

'*Now*.'

'Very well.'

'Not here.'

'Wherever you like, Mary.'

'In my room.'

She had turned to the stairs when a Press photographer, all smiles, emerged from the dining-room.

'Miss Bellamy, could I have a shot? By the door? With Mr Dakers perhaps? It's an opportunity. Would you mind?'

For perhaps five seconds, she hesitated. Richard said something under his breath.

'It's a bit crowded in there. We'd like to run a full-page spread,' said the photographer and named his paper.

'But, of course,' said Miss Bellamy.

Richard watched her touch her hair and re-do her mouth. Accustomed though he was to her professional technique he was filled with amazement. She put away her compact and turned brilliantly to the photographer. 'Where?' she asked.

'In the entrance, I thought. Meeting Mr Dakers.'

She moved down the hall to the front door. The photographer dodged round her. 'Not in the full glare,' she said and placed herself.

'Mr Dakers? ' said the photographer.

'Isn't it better as it is? ' Richard muttered.

'Don't pay any attention to him,' she said with ferocious gaiety. 'Come along, Dicky.'

'There's a new play on the skids, isn't there? If Mr Dakers could be showing it to you, perhaps? I've brought something in case.'

He produced a paper-bound quarto of typescript, opened it and put it in her hands.

'Just as if you'd come to one of those sure-fire laugh lines,' the photographer said. 'Pointing it out to him, you know? Right, Mr Dakers?'

Richard, nauseated, said: 'I'm photocatastrophic. Leave me out.'

'No!' said Miss Bellamy. Richard shook his head.

'You're too modest,' said the photographer. 'Just a little this way. Grand.'

She pointed to the opened script. 'And the great big smile,' he said. The bulb flashed. 'Wonderful. *Thank* you,' and he moved away.

'And now,' she said through her teeth, 'I'll talk to you.'

Richard followed her upstairs. On the landing they passed Old Ninn, who watched them go into Miss Bellamy's room. After the door had shut she stood outside and waited.

She was joined there by Florence who had come up by the back stairway. They communicated in a series of restrained gestures and brief whispers.

'You all right, Mrs Plumtree?'

'Why not!' Ninn countered austerely.

'You look flushed,' Florence observed dryly.

'The heat in those rooms is disgraceful.'

'Has She come up?'

'In there.'

'Trouble?' Florence asked, listening. Ninn said nothing. 'It's him, isn't it? Mr Richard? What's *he* been up to?'

'Nothing,' Ninn said, 'that wouldn't be a credit to him, Floy, and I'll thank you to remember it.'

'Oh, dear,' Florence said rather acidly. 'He's a man like the rest of them.'

'He's better than most.'

In the bedroom Miss Bellamy's voice murmured, rose sharply and died. Richard's scarcely audible, sounded at intervals. Then both together, urgent and expostulatory, mounted to some climax and broke off. There followed a long silence during which the two women stared at each other, and then a brief unexpected sound.

'What was that!' Florence whispered.

'Was she laughing?'

'It's left off now.'

Ninn said nothing. 'Oh, well,' Florence said, and had moved away when the door opened.

Richard came out, white to the lips. He walked past without seeing them, paused at the stairhead and pressed the palms of his hands against his eyes. They heard him fetch his breath with a harsh sound that might have been a sob. He stood there for some moments like a man who had lost his bearings and then struck his closed hand twice on the newel post and went quickly downstairs.

'What did I tell you,' Florence said. She stole nearer to the door. It was not quite shut. 'Trouble,' she said.

'None of his making.'

'How do you know?'

'The same way,' Ninn said, 'that I know how to mind my own business.'

Inside the room, perhaps beyond it, something crashed.

They stood there, irresolute, listening.

IV

At first Miss Bellamy had not been missed. Her party had reverted to its former style, a little more confused by the circulation of champagne. It spread through the two rooms and into the conservatory and became noisier and noisier. Everybody forgot about the ceremony of opening the birthday presents. Nobody noticed that Richard, too, was absent.

Gantry edged his way towards Charles who was in the drawing-room and stooped to make himself heard.

'Dicky,' he said, 'has made off.'

'Where to?'

'I imagine to do the best he can with the girl and her uncle.'

Charles looked at him with something like despair. 'There's nothing to be done,' he said; 'nothing. It was shameful.'

'Where is she?'

'I don't know. Isn't she in the next room?'

'I don't know,' Gantry said.

'I wish to God this show was over.'

'She ought to get on with the present-opening. They won't go till she does.'

Pinky had come up. 'Where's Mary? ' she said.

'We don't know,' Charles said. 'She ought to be opening her presents.'

'She won't miss her cue, my dear, you may depend upon it. Don't you feel it's time?'

'I'll find her,' Charles said. 'Get them mustered if you can, Gantry, will you?'

Bertie Saracen joined them, flushed and carefree. 'What goes on?' he inquired.

'We're waiting for Mary.'

'She went upstairs for running repairs,' Bertie announced and giggled. 'I *am* a poet and *don't* I know it!' he added.

'Did you see her? ' Gantry demanded.

'I heard her tell Monty. She's not uttering to poor wee me.'

Monty Marchant edged towards them. 'Monty, ducky,' Bertie cried, 'your speech was too poignantly right. Live for ever! *Oh*, I'm so tiddly.'

Marchant said: 'Mary's powdering her nose, Charles. Should we do a little shepherding?'

'I thought so.'

Gantry mounted a stool and used his director's voice: 'Attention, the cast!' It was a familiar summons and was followed by an obedient hush. 'To the table, please, everybody, and clear an entrance. Last act, ladies and gentlemen. Last act, please!'

They did so at once. The table with its heaped array of parcels had already been moved forward by Gracefield and the maids. The guests ranged themselves at both sides like a chorus in grand opera, leaving a passage to the principal door.

Charles said: 'I'll just see . . .' and went into the hall. He called up the stairs: 'Oh – Florence! Tell Miss Bellamy we're ready, will you?' and came back. 'Florence'll tell her,' he said.

There was a longish, expectant pause. Gantry drew in his breath with a familiar hiss.

'*I'll* tell her,' Charles said, and started off for the door.

Before he could reach it they all heard a door slam and running steps on the stairway. There was a relieved murmur and little indulgent laughter.

'First time Mary's ever missed an entrance,' someone said.

The steps ran across the hall. An irregular flutter of clapping broke out and stopped.

A figure appeared in the entrance and paused there.

It was not Mary Bellamy but Florence.

Charles said: 'Florence! Where's Miss Mary?'

Florence, breathless, mouthed at him. 'Not coming.'

'Oh, God!' Charles ejaculated. 'Not *now!*'

As if to keep the scene relentlessly theatrical, Florence cried out in a shrill voice:

'A doctor. For Christ's sake! Quick. Is there a doctor in the house?'

CHAPTER 4

Catastrophe

It might be argued that the difference between high tragedy and melodrama rests in the indisputable fact that the latter is more true to nature. People, even the larger-than-life-people of the theatre, tend at moments of tension to express themselves not in unexpected or memorable phrases but in clichés.

Thus, when Florence made her entrance, one or two voices in her audience ejaculated, 'My God, what's happened?' Bertie Saracen cried out shrilly, 'Does she mean Mary?' and somebody whose identity remained a secret said in an authoritative British voice: 'Quiet, everybody. No need to panic,' as if Florence had called for a fireman rather than a physician.

The only person to remain untouched was Dr Harkness, who was telling a long, inebriated story to Monty Marchant and whose voice droned on indecently in a far corner of the dining-room.

Florence stretched out a shaking hand towards Charles Templeton. 'Oh, for Christ's sake, sir!' she stammered. 'Oh, for Christ's sake, come quick.'

'– and this chap said to the other chap . . .' Dr Harkness recounted.

Charles said: 'Good God, what's the matter! Is it – ?'

'It's her, sir. Come quick.'

Charles thrust her aside, ran from the room and pelted upstairs.

'A doctor!' Florence said. 'My God, a doctor!'

It was Marchant who succeeded in bringing Dr Harkness into focus.

'You're wanted,' he said. 'Upstairs. Mary.'

'Eh? Bit of trouble?' Dr Harkness asked vaguely.

'Something's happened to Mary.'

Timon Gantry said: 'Pull yourself together, Harkness. You've got a patient.'

Dr Harkness had forgotten to remove his smile, but a sort of awareness now overtook him. 'Patient?' he said. 'Where? Is it Charles?'

'Upstairs. Mary.'

'Good gracious!' said Dr Harkness. 'Very good. I'll come.' He rocked slightly on his feet and remained stationary.

Maurice Warrender said to Florence: 'Is it bad?'

Her hand to her mouth, she nodded her head up and down like a mandarin.

Warrender took a handful of ice from a wine-cooler and suddenly thrust it down the back of Dr Harkness's collar.

'Come on,' he said. Harkness let out a sharp oath. He swung round as if to protest, lost his balance and fell heavily.

Florence screamed.

'I'm a' right,' Dr Harkness said from the floor. 'Tripped over something. Silly!'

Warrender and Gantry got him to his feet. 'I'm all *right*!' he repeated angrily. 'Gimme some water, will you?'

Gantry tipped some out of the ice bucket. Dr Harkness swallowed it down noisily and shuddered. 'Beastly stuff,' he said. 'Where's this patient?'

From the stairhead, Charles called in an unrecognizable voice: 'Harkness! *Harkness!*'

'Coming,' Warrender shouted. Harkness, gasping, was led out.

Florence looked wildly round the now completely silent company, wrung her hands and followed them.

Timon Gantry said: 'More ice, perhaps,' picked up the wine-cooler and overtook them on the stairs.

The party was left in suspension.

In Mary Bellamy's bedroom all the windows were open. An evening breeze stirred the curtains and the ranks of tulips. Dr Harkness knelt beside a pool of rose-coloured chiffon from which protruded, like rods, two legs finished with high-heeled shoes and two naked arms whose clenched hands glittered with diamonds.

Diamonds were spattered across the rigid plane of the chest and shone through a hank of disarranged hair. A length of red chiffon lay across the face and this was a good thing.

Dr Harkness had removed his coat. His ice-wet shirt stuck to his spine. His ear was laid against the place from which he had pulled away the red chiffon.

He straightened up, looked closely into the face, reveiled it and got to his feet.

'I'm afraid there's nothing whatever to be done,' he said.

Charles said: 'There must be. You don't know. There must be. Try. Try something. My God, try!'

Warrender, in his short-stepped, square-shouldered way, walked over to Harkness and looked down for a moment.

'No good,' he said. 'Have to face it. What?'

Charles sat on the bed and rubbed his freckled hand across his mouth. 'I can't believe it's happened,' he said. 'It's – there – it's happened. And I can't believe it.'

Florence burst noisily into tears.

Dr Harkness turned to her. 'You,' he said. 'Florence, isn't it? Try to control yourself, there's a good girl. Did you find her like this?'

Florence nodded and sobbed out something indistinguishable.

'But she was . . .' He glanced at Charles. 'Conscious?'

Florence said: 'Not to know me. Not to speak,' and broke down completely.

'Were the windows open?'

Florence shook her head.

'Did you open them?'

She shook her head again. 'I didn't think to – I got such a wicked shock – I didn't think. . . .'

'I opened them,' Charles said.

'First thing to be done,' Warrender muttered.

Gantry, who from the time of his entry had stood motionless near the door, joined the others. 'But what *was* it?' he asked. 'What happened?'

Warrender said unevenly: 'Perfectly obvious. She used that bloody spray thing there. I said it was dangerous. Only this morning.'

'What thing?'

Warrender stooped. The tin of Slaypest lay on its side close to the clenched right hand. A trickle of dark fluid stained the carpet. 'This,' he said.

'Better leave it,' Dr Harkness said sharply.

'What?'

'Better leave it where it is.' He looked at Gantry. 'It's some damned insecticide. For plants. The tin's smothered in warnings.'

'We told her,' Warrender said. 'Look at it.'

'I said don't touch it.'

Warrender straightened up. The blood had run into his face. 'Sorry,' he said, and then: 'Why not?'

'You're a bit too ready with your hands. I'm wet as hell and half-frozen.'

'You were tight. Best cure, my experience.'

They eyed each other resentfully. Dr Harkness looked at Charles who sat, doubled up with his hands on his chest. He went to him. 'Not too good?' he said. Timon Gantry put a hand on Charles's shoulder.

'I'm going to take you to your room, old boy. Next door, isn't it?'

'Yes,' Dr Harkness said. 'But not just yet. In a minute. Good idea.' He turned to Florence. 'Do you know where Mr Templeton keeps his tablets? Get them, will you? And you might bring some aspirin at the same time. Run along, now.' Florence went into the dressing-room. He sat beside Charles on the bed and took his wrist. 'Steady does it,' he said, and looked at Gantry. 'Brandy.'

'I know where it is,' Warrender said, and went out.

Gantry said: 'What about the mob downstairs?'

'They can wait.' He held the wrist a little longer and then laid Charles's hand on his knee keeping his own over it. 'We'll move you in a moment. You must let other people think for you. It's been a bad thing.'

'I can't . . .' Charles said. 'I can't . . .' And fetched his breath in irregular, tearing sighs.

'Don't try to work things out. Not just yet. Ah, here's Florence. Good. Now then: one of these.'

He gave Charles a tablet. Warrender came back with brandy. 'This'll help,' Dr Harkness said. They waited in silence.

'I'm all right,' Charles said presently.

'Fine. Now, an arm each and take it steady. His room's next door. Lie down, Charles, won't you?'

Charles nodded and Warrender moved towards him. 'No,' Charles said quite strongly, and turned to Gantry. 'I'm all right,' he repeated, and Gantry very efficiently supported him through the door into his dressing-room.

Warrender stood for a moment, irresolute, and then lifted his chin and followed them.

'Get him a hot bottle,' Harkness said to Florence.

When she'd gone he swallowed three aspirins, took up the bedside telephone and dialled a number.

'This is Dr Frank Harkness. I'm speaking from Number 2, Pardoner's Place. Mr Charles Templeton's house. There's been an accident. A fatality. Some sort of pest killer. Mrs Templeton. Yes. About fifty people – a party. Right. I'll wait.'

As he replaced the receiver Gantry came back. He stopped short when he saw Harkness. 'What now?' he asked.

'I've telephoned the police.'

'The *police*!'

'In cases like this,' Harkness said, 'one notifies the police.'

'Anybody would think . . .'

'Anybody will think anything,' Dr Harkness grunted. He turned back the elaborate counterpane and the blankets under it. 'I don't want to call the servants,' he said, 'and that woman's on the edge of hysteria. This sheet'll do.' He pulled it off, bundled it up and threw it to Gantry. 'Cover her up, old boy, will you?'

Gantry turned white round the mouth. 'I don't like this sort of thing,' he said. ' I've produced it often enough, but I've never faced the reality.' And he added with sudden violence: 'Cover her up yourself.'

'All right. All right,' sighed Dr Harkness. He took the sheet, crossed the room and busied himself with masking the body. The breeze from the open windows moved it as if, fantastically, it was stirred by what it covered.

'May as well shut them, now,' Dr Harkness said and did so. 'Can you straighten the bed at least?' he asked. Gantry did his best with the bed.

'Right,' said Dr Harkness, putting on his coat. 'Does this door lock? Yes. Will you come?'

As they went out Gantry said: 'Warrender's crocked up. Charles didn't seem to want him, so he flung a sort of poker-backed, stiff-lipped, blimp-type temperament and made his exit. I don't know where he's gone, but in his way,' Gantry said, 'he's wonderful. Terrifyingly ham, but wonderful. He's upset, though.'

'Serve him bloody well right. It won't be his fault if I escape pneumonia. My *head*!' Dr Harkness said, momentarily closing his eyes.

'You were high.'

'Not so high I couldn't come down.'

Old Ninn was on the landing. Her face had bleached round its isolated patches of crimson. She confronted Dr Harkness.

'What's she done to herself?' asked Old Ninn.

Dr Harkness once more summoned up his professional manner. He bent over her. 'You've got to be very sensible and good, Nanny,' he said, and told her briefly what had happened.

She looked fixedly into his face throughout the recital and at the end said: 'Where's Mr Templeton?'

Dr Harkness indicated the dressing-room.

'Who's looking after him?'

'Florence was getting him a hot bottle.'

'Her!' Ninn said with a brief snort, and without another word stumped to the door. She gave it a smart rap and let herself in.

'Wonderful character,' Gantry murmured.

'Remarkable.'

They turned towards the stairs. As they did so a figure moved out of the shadows at the end of the landing, but they did not notice her. It was Florence.

'And now, I suppose,' Dr Harkness said as they went downstairs, 'for the mob.'

'Get rid of them?' Gantry asked.

'Not yet. They're meant to wait. Police orders.'

'But . . .'

'Matter of form.'

Gantry said: 'At least we can boot the Press off, can't we?'

'Great grief, I'd forgotten that gang!'

'Leave them to me.'

The Press was collected about the hall. A light flashed as Gantry and Harkness came down and a young man who had evidently just arrived, advanced hopefully. 'Mr Timon Gantry? I wonder if you could – '

Gantry looking down from his great height, said: 'I throw you one item. And one only. Miss Mary Bellamy was taken ill this evening and died some minutes ago.'

'Doctor – er . . . Could you – ?'

'The cause,' Dr Harkness said, 'is at present undetermined. She collapsed and did not recover consciousness.'

'Is Mr Templeton – ?'

'No,' they said together. Gantry added: 'And that is all, gentlemen. Good evening to you.'

Gracefield appeared from the back of the hall, opened the front door, and said: 'Thank you, gentlemen. If you will step outside.'

They hung fire. A car drew up in the Place. From it emerged a heavily built man, wearing a bowler hat and a tidy overcoat. He walked into the house.

'Inspector Fox,' he said.

II

It has been said of Mr Fox that his arrival at any scene of disturbance has the effect of a large and almost silent vacuum cleaner.

Under his influence the gentlemen of the Press were tidied out into Pardoner's Place where they lingered restively for a long time. The guests, some of whom were attempting to leave, found themselves neatly mustered in the drawing-room. The servants waited quietly in the hall. Mr Fox and Dr Harkness went upstairs. A constable appeared and stood inside the front door.

'I locked the door,' Dr Harkness said, with the air of a schoolboy hoping for praise. He produced the key.

'Very commendable, Doctor,' said Fox comfortably.

'Nothing's been moved. The whole thing speaks for itself.'

'Quite so. Very sad.'

Fox laid his bowler on the bed, knelt by the sheet and turned it back. 'Strong perfume.' he said. He drew out his spectacles, placed them and looked closely into the dreadful face.

'You can see for yourself,' Dr Harkness said. 'Traces of the stuff all over her.'

'Quite so,' Fox repeated. 'Very profuse.'

He contemplated the Slaypest, but did not touch it. He rose and made a little tour of the room. He had very bright eyes for a middle-aged person.

'If it's convenient, sir,' he said, 'I'll have a word with Mr Templeton.'

'He's pretty well knocked out. His heart's dicky. I made him lie down.'

'Perhaps you'd just have a little chat with him yourself, Doctor. Would you be good enough to say I won't keep him more than a minute? No need to disturb him: I'll come to his room. Where would it be?'

'Next door.'

'Nice and convenient. I'll give you a minute with him and then I'll come in. Thank you, Doctor.'

Dr Harkness looked sharply at him, but he was restoring his spectacles to their case and had turned to contemplate the view from the window.

'Pretty square, this,' said Mr Fox.

Dr Harkness went out.

Fox quietly locked the door and went to the telephone. He dialled a number and asked for an extension.

'Mr Alleyn?' he said. 'Fox, here. It's about this case in Pardoner's Place. There are one or two little features . . .'

III

When Superintendent Alleyn had finished speaking to Inspector Fox, he went resignedly into action. He telephoned his wife with the routine information that he would not after all be home for dinner, summoned Detective-Sergeants Bailey and Thompson with their impedimenta, rang the police surgeon, picked up his homicide bag and went whistling to the car. 'A lady of the theatre,' he told his subordinates, 'appears to have looked upon herself as a common or garden pest and sprayed herself out of this world. She was mistaken as far as her acting was concerned. Miss Mary Bellamy. A comedienne of the naughty darling school and not a beginner. It's Mr Fox's considered opinion that somebody done her in.'

When they arrived at 2 Pardoner's Place, the tidying-up process had considerably advanced. Fox had been shown the guest list with addresses. He had checked it, politely dismissed those who had stayed throughout in what he called the reception area and mildly retained the persons who had left it 'prior' to quote Mr Fox, 'to the unfortunate event.' These were Timon Gantry, Pinky Cavendish, and Bertie Saracen who were closeted in Miss Bellamy's boudoir on the ground floor. Hearing that Colonel Warrender was a relation, Mr Fox suggested that he joined Charles Templeton, who had now come down to his study. Showing every sign of reluctance but obedient to authority, Warrender did so. Dr Harkness had sent out for a corpse-reviver for himself and gloomily occupied a chair in the conservatory. Florence having been interviewed and Old Ninn briefly surveyed, they had retired to their sitting-room in the top storey. Gracefield, the maids and the hired men had gone a considerable way towards removing the débris.

Under a sheet from her own bed on the floor of her locked room, Miss Bellamy began to stiffen.

Alleyn approached the front door to the renewed activity of the camera men. One of them called out: 'Give us a break, won't you, Super?'

'All in good time,' he said.

'What d'you know, Mr Alleyn?'

'Damn all,' Alleyn said, and rang the bell.

He was admitted by Fox. 'Sorry you've been troubled, sir,' Fox said.

'I dare say. What *is* all this?'

Fox told him in a few neatly worded sentences.

'All right,' Alleyn said. 'Let's have a look, shall we?'

They went upstairs to Miss Bellamy's bedroom.

He knelt by the body. 'Did she *bathe* in scent?' he wondered.

'Very strong, isn't it, sir?'

'Revolting. The whole room stinks of it.' He uncovered the head and shoulders. 'I see.'

'Not very nice,' Fox remarked.

'Not very.' Alleyn was silent for a moment or two. 'I saw her a week ago,' he said, ' on the last night of that play of Richard Dakers's that's been running so long. It was a flimsy, conventional comedy, but she filled it with her own kind of gaiety. And now – to this favour is she come.' He looked more closely. 'Could the stuff have blown back in her face? But you tell me they say the windows were shut?'

'That's right.'

'The face and chest are quite thickly spattered.'

'Exactly. I wondered,' Fox said, 'if the spray gun mechanism on the Slaypest affair was not working properly and she turned it towards her to see.'

'And it *did* work? Possible, I suppose. But she'd stop at once and look at her. Just look, Fox. There's a fine spray such as she'd get if she held the thing at arm's length and didn't use much pressure. And over that there are great blotches and runnels of the stuff, as if she'd held it close to her face and pumped it like mad.'

'People do these things.'

'They do. As a theory I don't fancy it. Nobody's handled the Slaypest tin? Since the event?'

'They say not,' Fox said.

'Bailey'll have to go over it for dabs, of course. Damn this scent. You can't get a whiff of anything else.'

Alleyn bent double and advanced his nose to the tin of Slaypest. 'I know this stuff,' he said. 'It's about as highly concentrated as they come, and in my opinion shouldn't be let loose on the public for all the warnings on the label. The basic ingredient seems to be hexa-ethyl-tetra-phosphate.'

'You don't say,' Fox murmured.

'It's a contact poison and very persistent.' He replaced the sheet, got up and examined the bank of growing plants in the bay window. 'Here it is again. They've got thrips and red spider.' He stared absently at Fox. 'So what does she do, Br'er Fox? She comes up here in the middle of her own party wearing her best red wisp of tulle and all her diamonds and sets about spraying her azaleas.'

'Peculiar,' Fox said. 'What I thought.'

'Very rum indeed.'

He wandered to the dressing-table. The central drawer was pulled out. Among closely packed ranks of boxes and pots was an open powder bowl. A piece of cotton-wool coloured with powder lay on the top of the table near a lipstick that had been imperfectly shut. Nearby was a bunch of Parma violets, already wilting.

'She *did* have a fiddle with her face,' Alleyn pointed out. 'She's got a personal maid, you say. The woman that found her.'

'Florence.'

'All right. Well, Florence would have tidied up any earlier goes at the powder and paint. And she'd have done something about these violets. Where do *they* come in? So this poor thing walks in, pulls out the drawer, does her running repairs and I should say from the smell, has a lavish whack at her scent.' He sniffed the atomiser. 'That's it. Quarter full and stinks like a civet cat, and here's the bottle it came from, empty. "Unguarded." Expensive maker. "Abominable" would be more like it. How women can use such muck passes my understanding.'

'I rather fancy it,' said Mr Fox. 'It's intriguing.'

Alleyn gave him a look. 'If we're to accept what appears to be the current explanation, she drenches her azaleas with hexa-ethyl-tetra-phosphate and then turns the spray gun full in her own face and kills herself. D'you believe that?'

'Not when you put it like that.'

'Nor I. Bailey and Thompson are down below and Dr Curtis is on his way. Get them up here. We'll want the complete treatment. Detailed pictures of the body and the room, tell Thompson. And Bailey'll need to take her prints and search the spray gun, the dressing-table and anything else that may produce dabs, latent or otherwise. We don't know what we're looking for, of course.' The bathroom door was open and he glanced in. 'Even this place reeks of scent. What's that on the floor? Broken picture.' He looked more closely. 'Rather nice tinsel picture. Madame Vestris, I fancy. Corner of the washbasin freshly chipped. Somebody's tramped broken glass over the floor. Did she drop her pretty picture? And why in the bathroom? Washing the glass? Or what? We don't disturb it.' He opened the bathroom cupboard. 'The things they take!' he muttered. 'The tablets. For insomnia. One with water on retiring. The unguents! The lotions! Here's some muck like green clay. Lifting mask. Apply with spatula and leave on for ten minutes. Do not move lips or facial muscles during treatment. Here *is* the spatula with some nice fresh dabs. Florence's, no doubt. And in the clothes basket, a towel with greenish smears. She had the full treatment before the party. Sal volatile bottle by the hand-basin. Did someone try to force sal volatile down her throat?'

'Not a chance, I should say, sir.'

'She must have taken it earlier in the day. Why? Very fancy loo, tarted up with a quilted cover, good lord! All right, Fox. Away we go. I'd better see the husband.'

'He's still in his study with a Colonel Warrender who seems to be a relative. Mr Templeton had a heart-attack after the event. The doctor says he's subject to them. Colonel Warrender and Mr Gantry took him into his dressing-room there, and then the colonel broke up and went downstairs. Mr Templeton was still lying in there when I came up, but I suggested the colonel should take him down to the study. They didn't seem to fancy the move, but I wanted to clear the ground. It's awkward,' Mr Fox said, 'having people next door to the body.'

Alleyn went into the dressing-room, leaving the door open. 'Change of atmosphere,' Fox heard him remark. 'Very masculine. Very simple. Very good. Who gave him a hot bottle?'

'Florence. The doctor says the old nurse went in later, to take a look at him. By all accounts she's a bossy old cup of tea and likes her drop of port wine.'

'This,' Alleyn said, 'is the house of a damn' rich man. And woman, I suppose.'

'He's a big name in the City, isn't he?'

'He is indeed. C. G. Templeton. He brought off that coup with Eastland Transport two years ago. Reputation of being an implacable chap to run foul of.'

'The servants seem to fancy him. The cook says he must have everything just so. One slip and you're out. But well liked. He's taken this very hard. Very shaky when I saw him but easy to handle. The colonel was tougher.'

'Either of them strike you as being the form for a woman poisoner?'

'Not a bit like it,' Fox said cheerfully.

'They tell me you never know?'

'That's right. So they say.'

They went out. Fox locked the door. 'Not that it makes all that difference,' he sighed. 'The keys on this floor are inter-changeable. As usual. However,' he added brightening, 'I've taken the liberty of removing all the others.'

'You'll get the sack one of these days. Come on.' They went downstairs.

'The remaining guests,' Fox said, 'are in the second room on the right. They're the lot who were with deceased up to the time she left the conservatory and the only ones who went outside the reception area before the speeches began. And, by the way, sir, up to the time the speeches started, there was a photographer and a moving camera unit blocking the foot of the stairs and for the whole period a kind of bar with a man mixing drinks right by the back stairs. I've talked to the man concerned and he says nobody but the nurse and Florence went up while he was on duty. This is deceased's sitting-room. Or boudoir. The study is the first on the right.'

'Where's the quack?'

'In the glasshouse with a hangover. Shall I stir him up?'

'Thank you.'

They separated. Alleyn tapped on the boudoir door and went in.

Pinky sat in an armchair with a magazine, Timon Gantry was finishing a conversation on the telephone and Bertie, petulant and flushed, was reading a rare edition of 'Tis Pity She's a Whore. When they saw Alleyn the two men got up and Pinky put down her magazine as if she was ashamed of it.

Alleyn introduced himself. 'This is just to say I'm very sorry to keep you waiting about.'

Gantry said: 'It's damned awkward. I've had to tell people over the telephone.'

'There's no performance involved, is there?'

'No. But there's a new play going into rehearsal. Opening in three weeks. One has to cope.'

'Of course,' Alleyn said. 'One does, indeed,' and went out.

'What a superb-looking man,' Bertie said listlessly and returned to his play.

Warrender and Charles had the air of silence about them. It was not, Alleyn fancied, the kind of silence that falls naturally between two cousins united in a common sorrow: they seemed at odds with each other. He could have sworn his arrival was a relief rather than an annoyance. He noticed that the study, like the dressing-room, had been furnished and decorated by a perfectionist with restraint judgment and a very great deal of money. There was a kind of relationship between the reserve of these two men and the setting in which he found them. He thought that they had probably been sitting there for a long time without speech. A full decanter and two untouched glasses stood between them on a small and exquisite table.

Charles began to rise. Alleyn said: 'Please, don't move,' and he sank heavily back again. Warrender stood up. His eyes were red and his face patched with uneven colour.

'Bad business, this,' he said. 'What?'

'Yes,' Alleyn said. 'Very bad.' He looked at Charles. 'I'm sorry, sir, that at the moment we're not doing anything to make matters easier.'

With an obvious effort Charles said: 'Sit down, won't you? Alleyn, isn't it? I know your name, of course.'

Warrender pushed a chair forward.

'Will you have a drink?' Charles asked.

'No, thank you very much. I won't trouble you longer than I can help. There's a certain amount of unavoidable business to be got through. There will be an inquest and, I'm afraid, a post-mortem. In addition to that we're obliged to check, as far as we're able, the events leading to the accident. All this, I know, is very distressing and I'm sorry.'

Charles lifted a hand and let it fall.

Warrender said: 'Better make myself scarce.'

'No,' Alleyn said. 'I'd be glad if you waited a moment.'

Warrender was looking fixedly at Alleyn. He tapped himself above the heart and made a very slight gesture towards Charles. Alleyn nodded.

'If I may,' he said to Charles, 'I'll ask Colonel Warrender to give me an account of the period before your wife left the party and went up to her room. If, sir, you would like to amend or question or add to anything he says, please do so.'

They waited for several moments and then without looking up Charles said: 'Very well. Though God knows what difference it can make.'

Warrender straightened his back, touched his Brigade of Guards tie, and made his report, with the care and, one would have said, the precision of experience.

He had, he said, been near to Mary Bellamy from the time she left her post by the door and moved through her guests towards the conservatory. She had spoken to one group after another. He gave several names. She had then joined a small party in the conservatory.

Alleyn was taking notes. At this point there was a pause. Warrender was staring straight in front of him. Charles had not moved.

'Yes?' Alleyn said.

'She stayed in there until the birthday cake was brought in,' Warrender said.

'And the other people in her group stayed there too?'

'No,' Charles said. 'I came out and – I spoke to two of our guests who – who were leaving early.'

'Yes? Did you return?'

He said wearily: 'I told Gracefield, our butler, to start the business with the cake. I stayed in the main rooms until they brought it in.'

Alleyn said: 'Yes. And then – ?'

'They came in with the cake,' Warrender said. 'And she came out and Marchant – her Management is Marchant & Company – Marchant gave the birthday speech.'

'And did the other people in the conservatory come out?'

'Yes.'

'With Miss Bellamy?'

Warrender said: 'Not with her.'

'After her?'

'No. Before. Some of them. I expect all of them, except Marchant.'

'You, yourself, sir? What did you do?'

'I came out before she did.'

'Did you stay in the main rooms?'

'No,' he said. 'I went into the hall for a moment.' Alleyn waited. 'To say goodbye,' Warrender said, 'to the two people who were leaving early.'

'Oh, yes. Who were they?'

'Feller called Browne and his niece.'

'And having done that you returned?'

'Yes,' he said.

'To the conservatory?'

'No. To the dining-room. That's where the speech was made.'

'Had it begun when you returned?'

Still looking straight before him, Warrender said: 'Finished. She was replying.'

'Really? You stayed in the hall for some time then?'

'Longer,' he said, 'than I'd intended. Didn't realize the ceremony had begun, isn't it?'

'Do you remember who the other people were? The ones who probably came out before Miss Bellamy from the conservatory?'

'Miss Cavendish and Saracen. And Timon Gantry, the producer-man. Your second-in-command went over all this and asked them to stay.'

'I'd just like, if you don't mind, to sort it out for myself. Anyone else? The two guests who left early, for instance. Were they in the conservatory party?'

'Yes.'

'And left – ?'

'First,' Warrender said loudly.

'So you caught them up in the hall. What were they doing in the hall, sir?'

'Talking. Leaving. I don't know exactly.'

'You don't remember to whom they were talking?'

'I cannot,' Charles said, 'for the very life of me see why these two comparative strangers, who were gone long before anything happened, should be of the remotest interest to you.'

Alleyn said quickly: 'I know it sounds quite unreasonable, but they do at the moment seem to have been the cause of other people's behaviour.'

He saw that for some reason this observation had disturbed Warrender. He looked at Alleyn as if the latter had said something outrageous and penetrating.

'You see,' Alleyn explained, 'in order to establish accident, one does have to make a formal inquiry into the movements of those persons who were nearest to Miss Bellamy up to the *time* of the accident.'

'Oh! ' Warrender said firmly. 'Yes. Possibly.'

'But – Mary – my wife – was *there*. Still *there*! Radiant. *There*, seen by everybody – I can't imagine . . .' Charles sank back in his chair. 'Never mind,' he murmured. 'Go on.'

Warrender said: 'Browne and his niece had, I think, been talking to Saracen and Miss Cavendish. When I came into the hall . . . They were – saying goodbye to Gantry.'

'I see. And nobody else was concerned in this leave-taking? In the hall?'

There was a long silence. Warrender looked as if somebody had tapped him smartly on the back of the head. His eyes started and he turned to Charles who leant forward grasping the arms of his chair.

'My God!' Warrender said. 'Where is he? What's become of him? *Where's Richard?*'

IV

Alleyn had been trained over a long period of time to distinguish between simulated and involuntary reactions in human behaviour. He was perhaps better equipped than many of his colleagues in this respect, being fortified by an instinct that he was particularly careful to mistrust. It seldom let him down. He thought now that, whereas Charles Templeton was quite simply astounded by his own forgetfulness, Warrender's reaction was much less easily defined. Alleyn had a notion that Warrender's reticence was of the formidable kind which conceals nothing but the essential.

It was Warrender, now, who produced an explanation.

'Sorry,' he said. 'Just remembered something. Extraordinary we should have forgotten. We're talking about Richard Dakers.'

'The playwright?'

'That's the man. He's – you may not know this – he was . . .' Warrender boggled inexplicably and looked at his boots. 'He's – he was my cousin's – he was the Templetons' ward.'

For the first time since Alleyn had entered the room, Charles Templeton looked briefly at Warrender.

'Does he know about this catastrophe?' Alleyn asked.

'No,' Warrender said, 'he can't know. Be a shock.'

Alleyn began to ask about Richard Dakers and found that they were both unwilling to talk about him. When had he last been seen? Charles remembered he had been in the conservatory. Warrender, pressed, admitted that Richard was in the hall when Browne and his niece went away. Odd, Alleyn thought, that, as the climax of the party approached, no less than five of Miss Bellamy's most intimate friends should turn their backs on her to say goodbye to two people whom her husband had described as comparative strangers. He hinted as much.

Warrender glanced at Charles and then said: 'Point of fact they're friends of Richard Dakers. His guests in a way. Naturally he wanted to see them off.'

'And having done so, he returned for the speeches and the cake-cutting ceremony?'

'I – ah . . . Not exactly,' Warrender said.

'No?'

'No. Ah, speaking out of school, isn't it? But I rather fancy there's an attraction. He – ah – he went out – they live in the next house.'

'Not,' Alleyn ejaculated, '*Octavius* Browne of the Pegasus?'

'Point of fact, yes,' Warrender said, looking astonished.

'And Mr Dakers went out with them?'

'After them.'

'But you think he meant to join them?'

'Yes,' he said woodenly.

'And is perhaps with them still?'

Warrender was silent.

'Wouldn't he mind missing the ceremony?' Alleyn asked.

Warrender embarked on an incomprehensible spate of broken phrases.

'If he's there,' Charles said to Alleyn, 'he ought to be told.'

'I'll go,' Warrender said, and moved to the door.

Alleyn said: 'One minute, if you please.'

'What?'

'Shall we just see if he *is* there? It'll save trouble, won't it? May I use the telephone?'

He was at the telephone before they could reply and looking up the number.

'I know Octavius quite well,' he said pleasantly. 'Splendid chap, isn't he?'

Warrender looked at him resentfully. 'If the boy's there,' he said, 'I'd prefer to tell him about this myself.'

'Of course,' Alleyn agreed heartily. 'Ah, here we are.' He dialled a number. They heard a voice at the other end.

'Hallo,' Alleyn said. 'Is Mr Richard Dakers there by any chance?'

'No,' the voice said. 'I'm sorry. He left some time ago.'

'Really? How long would you say?'

The voice replied indistinguishably.

'I see. Thank you so much. Sorry to have bothered you.'

He hung up. 'He was only with them for a very short time,' he said. 'He must have left, it seems, before this thing happened. They imagined he came straight back here.'

Warrender and Templeton were, he thought, at peculiar pains not to look at each other or at him. He said lightly: 'Isn't that a little odd? Wouldn't you suppose he'd be sure to attend the birthday speeches?'

Perhaps each of them waited for the other to reply. After a moment Warrender barked out two words. 'Lovers' tiff?' he suggested.

'You think it might be that?'

'I think it might be that?'

'I think,' Warrender said angrily, 'that whatever it was it's got nothing to do with this – this tragedy. Good lord. why should it?'

'I really do assure you,' Alleyn said, 'that I wouldn't worry you about these matters if I didn't think it was necessary.'

'Matter of opinion,' Warrender said.

'Yes. A matter of opinion and mine may turn out to be wrong.'

He could see that Warrender was on the edge of some outburst and was restrained, it appeared, only by the presence of Charles Templeton.

'Perhaps,' Alleyn said, 'we might just make quite sure that Mr Dakers didn't, in fact, come back. After all, it was a biggish party. Might he not have slipped in, unnoticed, and gone out again for some perfectly explainable reason? The servants might have noticed. If you would . . .'

Warrender jumped at this. 'Certainly! I'll come out with you.'
And after a moment: 'D'you mind, Charles?'

With extraordinary vehemence Charles said: 'Do what you like. If
he comes back I don't want to see him. I . . .' He passed an unsteady
hand across his eyes. 'Sorry,' he said, presumably to Alleyn. 'This has
been a bit too much for me.'

'We'll leave you to yourself,' Alleyn said. 'Would you like
Dr Harkness to come in?'

'No. No. No. If I might be left alone. That's all.'

'Of course.'

They went out. The hall was deserted except for the constable
who waited anonymously in a corner. Alleyn said: 'Will you excuse
me for a moment?' and went to the constable.

'Anybody come in?' he asked under his breath.

'No, sir.'

'Keep the Press out, but admit anyone else and don't let them go
again. Take the names and say there's been an accident in the
vicinity and we're doing a routine check.'

'Very good, sir.'

Alleyn returned to Warrender. 'No one's come in,' he said.
'Where can we talk?'

Warrender glanced at him. 'Not here,' he muttered, and led the
way into the deserted drawing-room, now restored to order but
filled with the flower-shop smell of Bertie Saracen's decorations and
the faint reek of cigarette smoke and alcohol. The connecting doors
into the dining-room were open and beyond them, in the conservatory, Dr Harkness could be seen, heavily asleep in a canvas chair and
under observation by Inspector Fox. When Fox saw them he came
out and shut the glass door. 'He's down to it,' he said, 'but rouseable.
I thought I'd leave him as he is till required.'

Warrender turned on Alleyn. 'Look here!' he demanded. 'What
is all this? Are you trying to make out there's been any – any . . .' he
boggled, 'any hanky-panky?'

'We can't take accident as a matter of course.'

'Why not? Clear as a pikestaff.'

'Our job,' Alleyn said patiently, 'is to collect all the available
information and present it to the coroner. At the moment we are not
drawing any conclusions. Come, sir,' he said as Warrender still

looked mulish, 'I'm sure that, as a soldier, you'll recognize the position. It's a matter of procedure. After all, to be perfectly frank about it, a great many suicides as well as homicides have been rigged to look like accidents.'

'Either suggestion's outrageous.'

'And will, we hope, soon turn out to be so.'

'But, good God, is there anything at all to make you suppose – ?' He stopped and jerked his hands ineloquently.

'Suppose what?'

'That it could be – either? Suicide – or murder?'

'Oh, yes,' Alleyn said. 'Could be. Could be.'

'What? What evidence – ?'

'I'm afraid I'm not allowed to discuss details.'

'Why the hell not?'

'God bless my soul!' Alleyn exclaimed. 'Do *consider*. Suppose it was murder – for all I know you might have done it. You can't expect me to make you a present of what may turn out to be the police case against you.'

'I think you must be dotty,' said Colonel Warrender profoundly.

'Dotty or sane, I must get on with my job. Inspector Fox and I propose to have a word with those wretched people we've cooped up over the way. Would you rather return to Mr Templeton, sir?'

'My God, no!' he ejaculated with some force and then looked hideously discomfited.

'Why not?' Alleyn asked coolly. 'Have you had a row with him?'

'No!'

'Well, I'm afraid it's a case of returning to him or staying with me.'

'I . . . God dammit, I'll stick to you.'

'Right. Here we go, then.'

Bertie, Pinky and Timon Gantry seemed hardly to have moved since he last saw them. Bertie was asleep in his chair and resembled an overdressed baby. Pinky had been crying. Gantry now was reading *'Tis Pity She's a Whore*. He laid it aside and rose to his feet.

'I don't want to be awkward,' Gantry said, 'but I take leave to ask why the hell we're being mewed up in this interminable and intolerable fashion.'

He used what was known in the theatre as The Terrifying Tone.
He moved towards Alleyn who was almost his own height.

'This room,' Bertie faintly complained as he opened his eyes,
'would appear to be inhabited by angry giants.'

'You're being mewed up,' Alleyn said with some evidence of
toughness, 'because of death. Death, for your information, with
what are known as unexplained features. I don't know how much
longer you'll be here. If you're hungry, we shall arrange for food to
be sent in. If you're stuffy you may walk in the garden. If you want
to talk, you may use the telephone and the usual offices are last on
the right at the far end of the hall.'

There was an appreciable pause.

'And the worst of it is, Timmy, angel,' Bertie said, 'you can't tell
him the casting's gone wrong and you'll let him know if he's
wanted.'

Pinky was staring at Alleyn. 'I never,' she muttered, 'could have
thought to see the day.'

There can be no dictator whose discomfiture will not bring some
slight degree of pleasure to his most ardent disciples. Bertie and
Pinky, involuntarily, had given this reaction. There was a suggestion
of repressed glee.

Gantry gave them the sort of look he would have thrown at an
inattentive actor. They made their faces blank.

He drew in his breath. 'So be it,' he said. 'One submits. Naturally.
Perhaps one would prefer to know a little more, but elucidation is
evidently *not* an ingredient of the Yardly mystique.'

From his ramrod station inside the door, Warrender said: 'Foul
play. What it amounts to. They're suggesting foul play.'

'Oh, my God!' cried Pinky and Bertie in unison. They turned
sheet-white and began to talk at the tops of their voices. Fox took
out his notebook.

Alleyn raised his hand and they petered out. 'It doesn't,' he said
crossly, 'amount to anything of the sort. The situation is precisely
as I have tried to define it. There are unexplained discrepancies.
They may add up to accident, suicide or homicide and I know no
better than any one of you what the answer will be. And now, if
you please, we will try to arrive at a few possibly unimportant
facts.'

To his surprise he found himself supported.

Timon Gantry said: 'We're being emotional and tedious. Pay no attention. Your facts?'

Alleyn said patiently: 'Without any overtones or suggestions of criminal intention, I would rather like to trace exactly the movements of the group of people who were in conversation with Miss Bellamy during the last ten minutes or so of her life. You have all heard, *ad nauseam,* I dare say, of police routine. This is an example of it. I know you were all with her in the conservatory. I know each one of you, before the climax of her party, came out into the hall with the intention, Colonel Warrender tells me, of saying goodbye to two comparative strangers who for some reason that has not yet been divulged were leaving just before this climax. Among you was Mr Richard Dakers, Miss Bellamy's ward. Mr Dakers left the house on the heels of those two guests. His reason for doing so may well be personal and, from my point of view, completely uninteresting. *But I've got to clear him up.* Now then. Any of you know why they left and why he left?'

'Certainly,' Gantry said promptly. 'He's catched with Anelida Lee. No doubt he wanted to see more of her.'

'At that juncture? All right!' Alleyn added quickly. 'We leave that one, do we? We take it that there was nothing remarkable about Octavius Browne and his niece sweeping out of the party, do we, and that it was the most natural thing in the world for Miss Bellamy's ward to turn his back on her and follow them? Do we? Or do we?'

'Oh, Lord, Lord, *Lord*!' Bertie wavered. 'The way you put things.'

Pinky said: 'I *did* hear the uncle remind her that they had to leave early.'

'Did he say why?'

'No.'

'Had any of you met them before?'

Silence.

'None of you? Why did you all feel it necessary to go into the hall to say goodbye to them?'

Pinky and Bertie looked at each other out of the corners of their eyes and Warrender cleared his throat. Gantry appeared to come to a decision.

'I don't usually discuss this sort of thing outside the theatre,' he said, 'but under the circumstances I suppose I'd better tell you. I've decided to hear Miss Lee read the leading role in' – he hesitated fractionally – 'in a new play.'

'Really? Wonderful luck for her,' Alleyn said. 'What play?'

'*Oops!*' Bertie said involuntarily.

'It's called *Husbandry in Heaven*.'

'By – ?'

Warrender barked: 'Does it matter?'

'Not that I know,' Alleyn murmured. 'Why should it? Let's find out.'

Pinky said boldly: 'I don't see a bit why it should matter. We all heard about it.'

'Did you?' Alleyn asked. 'When? At the party?'

She blushed scarlet. 'Yes. It was mentioned there.'

'In the conservatory?'

Bertie said in a hurry, 'Mentioned. Just mentioned.'

'And we haven't had the author's name yet, have we?'

Pinky said: 'It's a new play by Dicky Dakers, isn't it, Timmy?'

'Yes, dear,' Gantry agreed and refrained with some difficulty, Alleyn thought, from casting his eyes up to heaven. 'In the hall I had a word with her about reading the part for me,' he said.

'Right. And,' Alleyn pursued, 'might that not explain why Dakers also wanted to have a further word with Miss Lee?'

They agreed feverishly.

'Strange,' he continued, 'that this explanation didn't occur to any of you.'

Bertie laughed musically. 'Weren't we sillies?' he asked. 'Fancy!'

'Perhaps you *all* hurtled into the hall in order to offer your congratulations to Miss Lee?'

'That's right!' Bertie cried, opening his eyes very wide, 'So we did! And anyway,' he added, 'I wanted the loo. That was really why I came out. Anything else was purely incidental. I'd forgotten.'

'Well,' Alleyn remarked, 'since you're all so bad at remembering your motives, I suppose I'd better go on cooking them up for you.'

Pinky Cavendish made a quick expostulatory movement with her hands. 'Yes?' Alleyn asked her. 'What is it?'

'Nothing. Not really. Only – I wish you wouldn't make one feel shabby,' Pinky said.

'Do I? I'm sorry about that.'

'Look!' she said. 'We're all of us shocked and horrified about Mary. She was our friend: a great friend. No, Timmy, please let me. She was tricky and temperamental and exacting and she said and did things that we'd rather forget about now. The important thing to remember is that one way or another, at one time or another, we've all loved her. You couldn't help it,' Pinky said, 'or I couldn't. Perhaps I should only speak for myself.'

Alleyn asked gently: 'Are you trying to tell me that you are protecting her memory?'

'You might put it like that,' Pinky said.

'Nonsense, dear,' Gantry said impatiently. 'It doesn't arise.'

Alleyn decided to dig a little further.

'The farewells being accomplished,' he said, 'and the two guests departed, what did you all do? Miss Cavendish?'

'Oh, dear! What *did* I do? I know! I tried to nip upstairs but the camera men were all over the bottom steps so I returned to the party.'

'Mr Saracen?'

'The gents. Downstairs. Last, as you've observed, on the right. Then I beetled back, bright as a button, for the speeches.'

'Mr Gantry?'

'I returned to the drawing-room, heard the speeches, and helped Templeton clear the way for the' – he jibbed for a moment – 'for what would have been the last scene. The opening of the presents.'

'Colonel Warrender?'

Warrender was staring at some part of the wall above Alleyn's head. 'Went back,' he said.

'Where?'

'To the party.'

'Oo!' Bertie said.

'Yes, Mr Saracen?'

'Nothing,' Bertie said hurriedly. 'Pay no attention.'

Alleyn looked round at them all. 'Tell me,' he said, 'hasn't Richard Dakers, up till now, written his plays exclusively for Miss Bellamy? Light comedies? *Husbandry in Heaven* doesn't suggest a light comedy.'

He knew by their silence that he had struck home. Pinky's face alone would have told him as much. It was already too late when Warrender said defensively: 'No need to put all his eggs in one basket, isn't it?'

'Exactly,' Gantry agreed.

'Did Miss Bellamy hold this view?'

'I still fail to understand . . .' Warrender began, but Bertie Saracen cried out in a sort of rage:

'I really *don't* see, I don't for the *life* of me see why we should fiddle and fuss and fabricate! Honestly! It's all very well to be nice about poor Mary's memory and Dicky's dilemma and everybody madly loving everybody else, but sooner or later Mr Alleyn's going to find out and then we'll all look peculiar and I for one *won't* and I'm sorry, Timmy, but I'm going to spill beans and unbag cats galore and announce in a ringing headtone that Mary minded like *hell* and that she made a scene in the conservatory and insulted the girl and Dicky left in a rage and why not, because suppose somebody *did* do something frightful to Mary, it couldn't be Dicky because Dicky flounced out of the house while Mary was still fighting fit and cutting her cake. And one other thing. I don't know why Colonel Warrender should go all cagey and everything but he didn't go straight back to the party. He went out. At the front door. I *saw* him on my way back from the loo. Now then!'

He had got to his feet and stood there, blinking, but defiant.

Gantry said: '*Oh*, well!' and flung up his hands.

Pinky said: 'I'm on Bertie's side.'

But Warrender, purple in the face, advanced upon Bertie.

'Don't touch me!' Bertie shouted angrily.

'You little rat!' Warrender said, and seized his arm.

Bertie gave an involuntary giggle. 'That's what she called me,' he said.

'Take,' Warrender continued between his teeth, 'that damned impertinent grin off your face and hold your tongue, sir, or by God I'll give you something to make you.'

He grasped Bertie with his left hand. He had actually drawn back his right and Alleyn had moved in, when a voice from the door said: '*Will somebody be good enough to tell me what goes on in this house?*'

Warrender lowered his hand and let Bertie go, Gantry uttered a
short oath and Pinky, a stifled ejaculation. Alleyn turned.

A young man with a white face and distracted air confronted him
in the doorway.

'Thank God!' Bertie cried. 'Dicky!'

CHAPTER 5

Questions of Adherence

The most noticeable thing about Richard Dakers was his agitation. He was pale, his face was drawn and his hands were unsteady. During the complete silence that followed Bertie's ejaculation, Richard stood where he was, his gaze fixed with extraordinary concentration upon Colonel Warrender. Warrender, in his turn, looked at him with, as far as his soldierly blueprint of a face could express anything, the same kind of startled attention. In a crazy sort of way, each might have been the reflection of the other.

Warrender said: 'Can I have a word with you, old boy? Shall we – ?'

'No!' Richard said quickly, and then: 'I'm sorry. I don't understand. What's that damned bobby doing in the hall? What's happened? Where's everybody? Where's Mary?'

Alleyn said: 'One moment,' and went to him. 'You're Mr Richard Dakers, aren't you? I'm from Scotland Yard – Alleyn. . . . At the moment I'm in charge of a police inquiry here. Shall we find somewhere where I can tell you why?'

'I'll tell him,' Warrender said.

'I think not,' Alleyn rejoined and opened the door.

'Come along,' he said and looked at the others. 'You will stay here, if you please.'

Richard put his hand to his head. 'Yes. All right. But – why?' Perhaps out of force of habit he turned to Timon Gantry. 'Timmy?' he said. 'What *is* this?'

Gantry said: 'We must accept authority, Dicky. Go with him.'

Richard stared at him in amazement and walked out of the room, followed by Alleyn, and Fox.

'In here, shall we?' Alleyn suggested and led the way into the deserted drawing-room.

There, he told Richard, as briefly as possible and without emphasis, what had happened. Richard listened distractedly, making no interruption but once or twice wiping his hand over his face as if a cobweb lay across it. When Alleyn had finished he said haltingly: 'Mary? It's happened to Mary? How can I possibly believe it?'

'It *is* hard, isn't it?'

'But – *how*? *How* did it happen? With the plant spray?'

'It seems so.'

'But she's used it over and over again. For a long time. Why did it happen now?' He had the air, often observable in people who have suffered a shock, of picking over the surface of the matter and distractedly examining the first thing he came upon. 'Why now?' he repeated and appeared scarcely to attend to the answer.

'That's one of the things we've got to find out.'

'Of course,' Richard said, more, it seemed, to himself than to Alleyn, 'it *is* dangerous. We were always telling her.' He shook his head impatiently. 'But – I don't see – she went to her room just after the speeches and – '

'Did she? How do you know?'

Richard said quickly: 'Why, because . . .' And then, if possible, turned whiter than he had been before. He looked desperately at Alleyn, seemed to hover on the edge of an outburst and then said: 'She must have. You say she was found there.'

'Yes. She was found there.'

'But why? Why would she use the plant spray at that moment? It sounds so crazy.'

'I know. Very strange.'

Richard beat his hands together. 'I'm sorry,' he said, 'I can't get hold of myself. I'm sorry.'

Looking at him, Alleyn knew that he was in that particular state of emotional unbalance when he would be most vulnerable to pressure. He was a nice-looking chap, Alleyn thought. It was a sensitive face and yet, obscurely, it reminded him of one much less sensitive. But whose?'

He said: 'You yourself have noticed two aspects of this tragic business that are difficult to explain. Because of them and because of normal police procedure I have to check as fully as possible the circumstances surrounding the event.'

'Do you?' Richard asked vaguely and then seemed to pull himself together. 'Yes. Very well. What circumstances?'

'I'm told you left the house before the birthday speeches. Is that right?'

Unlike the others, Richard appeared to feel no resentment or suspicion. 'I?' he said. 'Oh, yes, I think I did. I don't think they'd started. The cake had just been taken in.'

'Why did you leave, Mr Dakers?'

'I wanted to talk to Anelida,' he said at once, and then:

'Sorry. You wouldn't know. Anelida Lee. She lives next door and . . .' He stopped.

'I do know that Miss Lee left early with her uncle. But it must have been a very important discussion, mustn't it? To take you away at that juncture?'

'Yes. It was. To me. It was private,' Richard added. 'A private matter.'

'A long discussion?'

'It didn't happen.'

'Not?'

'She wasn't – available.' He produced a palpable understatement. 'She wasn't – feeling well.'

'You saw her uncle?'

'Yes.'

'Was it about her part in your play – *Husbandry in Heaven*, isn't it? – that you wanted to talk to her?'

Richard stared at him and for the first time seemed to take alarm. 'Who told you about that?' he demanded.

'Timon Gantry.'

'*He* did!' Richard ejaculated and then, as if nothing could compete with the one overriding shock, added perfunctorily: 'How extraordinary.' But he was watching Alleyn now with a new awareness. 'It was partly to do with that,' he muttered.

Alleyn decided to fire point blank. 'Was Miss Bellamy displeased with the plans for this new play?' he asked. Richard's hands made a sharp involuntary movement which was at once checked. His voice shook.

'I told you this was a private matter,' he said. 'It is entirely private.'

'I'm afraid there is very little room for privacy in a police inquiry.'

Richard surprised him by suddenly crying out: '*You think she did it herself!* She didn't! I can't believe it! Never!'

'Is there any reason why she should?'

'No! My God, no! *No!*'

Alleyn waited for a little, visited, as was not unusual with him, by a distaste for this particular aspect of his job.

He said: 'What did you do when Miss Lee couldn't receive you?'

Richard moved away from him, his hands thrust down in his pockets. 'I went for a walk,' he said.

'Now, look here,' Alleyn said, 'you must see that this is a very odd story. Your guardian, as I believe Miss Bellamy was, reaches the top moment of her birthday party. You leave her cold, first in pursuit of Miss Lee and then to go for a stroll round Chelsea. Are you telling me that you've been strolling ever since?'

Without turning, Richard nodded.

Alleyn walked round him and looked him full in the face.

'Mr Dakers,' he said. 'Is that the truth? It's now five to nine. Do you give me your word that from about seven o'clock when you left this house you didn't return to it until you came in, ten minutes ago?'

Richard, looking desperately troubled, waited for so long that to Alleyn the scene became quite unreal. The two of them were fixed in the hiatus like figures in a suspended film sequence.

'Are you going to give me an answer?' Alleyn said at last.

'I – I – don't – think – I did actually – just after – she was . . .' A look of profound astonishment came into Richard's face. He crumpled into a faint at Alleyn's feet.

II

'He'll do,' Dr Harkness said, relinquishing Richard's pulse. He straightened up and winced a little in the process. 'You say he's been walking about on an empty stomach and two or three drinks. The shock coming on top of it did the trick for him, I expect. In half an hour he won't be feeling any worse than I do and that's medium to bloody awful. Here he comes.'

Richard had opened his eyes. He stared at Dr Harkness and then frowned. 'Lord, I'm sorry,' he said. 'I passed out, didn't I?'

'You're all right,' Dr Harkness said. 'Where's this sal volatile, Gracefield?'

Gracefield presented it on a tray. Richard drank it down and let his head fall back. They had put him on a sofa there in the drawing-room. 'I was talking to somebody,' he said. 'That man – God, yes! Oh, God.'

'It's all right,' Alleyn said, 'I won't worry you. We'll leave you to yourself, for a bit.'

He saw Richard's eyes dilate. He was looking past Alleyn towards the door. 'Yes,' he said loudly. 'I'd rather be alone.'

'*What is all this?*'

It was Warrender. He shut the door behind him and went quickly to the sofa. 'What the devil have you done to him? Dicky, old boy . . .'

'No!' Richard said with exactly the same inflexion as before. Warrender stood above him. For a moment, apparently, they looked at each other. Then Richard said: 'I forgot that letter you gave me to post. I'm sorry.'

Alleyn and Fox moved, but Warrender anticipated them, stooping over Richard and screening him.

'If you don't mind,' Richard said. 'I'd rather be by myself. I'm all right.'

'And I'm afraid,' Alleyn pointed out, 'that I must remind you of instructions, Colonel Warrender. I asked you to stay with the others. Will you please go back to them?'

Warrender stood like a rock for a second or two and then, without another word, walked out of the room. On a look from Alleyn, Fox followed him.

'We'll leave you,' Alleyn said. 'Don't get up.'

'No,' Dr Harkness said. 'Don't. I'll ask them to send you in a cup of tea. Where's that old nanny of yours? She can make herself useful. Can you find her, Gracefield?'

'Very good, sir,' Gracefield said.

Alleyn, coolly picking up Richard's dispatch-case, followed Gracefield into the hall.

'Gracefield.'

Gracefield, frigid, came to a halt.

'I want one word with you. I expect this business has completely disorganized your household and I'm afraid it can't be helped. But I think it may make things a little easier in your department if you know what the form will be.'

'Indeed, sir?'

'In a little while a mortuary van will come. It will be better if we keep everybody out of the way at that time. I don't want to worry Mr Templeton more than I can help, but I shall have to interview people and it would suit us all if we could find somewhere that would serve as an office for the purpose. Is that possible?'

'There is Mr Richard's old study, sir, on the first floor. It is unoccupied.'

'Splendid. Where exactly?'

'The third on the right along the passage, sir.'

'Good.' Alleyn glanced at the pallid and impassive face. 'For your information,' he said, 'it's a matter of clearing up the confusion that unfortunately always follows accidents of this sort. The further we can get, now, the less publicity at the inquest. You understand?'

'Quite so, sir,' said Gracefield, with a slight easing of manner.

'Very well. And I'm sorry you'll be put to so much trouble.'

Gracefield's hand curved in classic acceptance. There was a faint crackle.

'Thank you, Gracefield.'

'Thank you very much, sir,' said Gracefield. 'I will inform Mrs Plumtree and then ascertain if your room is in order.' He inclined his head and mounted the stairs.

Alleyn raised a finger and the constable by the front door came to him.

'What happened,' he asked, 'about Mr Dakers? As quick and complete as you can.'

'He arrived, sir, about three minutes after you left your instructions, according to which I asked for his name and let on it was because of an accident. He took it up it was something about a car.

He didn't seem to pay much attention. He was very excited and upset. He went upstairs and was there about eight to ten minutes. You and Mr Fox were with the two gentlemen and the lady in that little room, sir. When he came down he had a case in his hand. He went to the door to go out and I advised him it couldn't be done. He still seemed very upset, sir, and that made him more so. He said: 'Good God, what is all this?' and went straight to the room where you were, sir.'

'Good. Thank you. Keep going.'

'Sir,' said the constable.

'And Philpott.'

'Sir?'

'We've sent for another man. In the meantime I don't want any of the visitors in the house moving about from room to room. Get them all together in the drawing-room and keep them there, including Colonel Warrender and Mr Templeton if he's feeling fit enough. Mr Dakers can stay where he is. Put the new man on the door and you keep observation in the dining-room. We can't do anything about the lavatory, I suppose, but everywhere else had better be out of bounds. If Colonel Warrender wants to go to the lavatory, you go with him.'

'Sir.'

'And ask Mr Fox to join me upstairs.'

The constable moved off.

A heavy thumping announced the descent of Old Ninn. She came down one step at a time. When she got to the bottom of the stairs and saw Alleyn she gave him a look and continued on her way. Her face was flaming and her mouth drawn down. For a small person she emanated an astonishingly heavy aura of the grape.

'Mrs Plumtree?' Alleyn asked.

'Yes,' said Old Ninn. She halted and looked into his face. Her eyes, surprisingly, were tragic.

'You're going to look after Mr Richard, aren't you?'

'What's he been doing to himself?' she asked as if Richard had been playing roughly and had barked his knee.

'He fainted. The doctor thinks it was shock.'

'Always takes things to heart,' Old Ninn said.

'Did you bring him up?'

'From three months.' She continued to look fixedly at Alleyn. 'He was a good child,' she said as if she was abusing Richard, ' and he's grown into a good man. No harm in him and never was.'

'An orphan?' Alleyn ventured.

'Father and mother killed in a motor accident.'

'How very sad.'

'You don't,' Old Ninn said, 'feel the want of what you've never had.'

'And of course Miss Bellamy – Mrs Templeton – took him over.'

'She,' Old Ninn said, 'was a different type of child altogether. If you'll excuse me I'll see what ails him.' But she didn't move at once. She said very loudly: 'Whatever it is it'll be no discredit to him,' and then stumped heavily and purposefully on to her charge.

Alleyn waited for a moment, savouring her observations. There had been one rather suggestive remark, he thought.

Dr Harkness came out of the drawing-room, looking very wan.

'He's all right,' he said, 'and I wish I could say as much for myself. The secondary effects of alcoholic indulgence are the least supportable. By the way, can I go out to the car for my bag? It's just opposite the house. Charles Templeton's my patient, you know, and I'd like to run him over. Just in case. He's had a bad knock over this.'

'Yes, of course,' Alleyn said, and nodded to the constable at the door. 'Before you go, though – was Mrs Templeton your patient too?'

'She was,' Harkness agreed and looked wary.

'Would you have expected anything like this? Supposing it be a case of suicide?'

'No. I wouldn't.'

'Not subject to fits of depression? No morbid tendencies? Nothing like that?'

Harkness looked at his hands. 'It wasn't an equable disposition,' he said carefully. 'Far from it. She had "nervous" spells. The famous theatrical temperament, you know.'

'No more than that? ' Alleyn persisted.

'Well – I don't like discussing my patients and never do, of course, but – '

'I think you may say the circumstances warrant it.'

'I suppose so. As a matter of fact, I have been a bit concerned. The temperaments had become pretty frequent and increasingly violent. Hysteria, really. Partly the time of life, but she was getting over that. There was some occasion for anxiety. One or two little danger signals. One was keeping an eye on her. But nothing suicidal. On the contrary. What's more, you can take my word for it she was the last woman on earth to disfigure herself. The last.'

'Yes,' Alleyn said. 'That's a point, isn't it? I'll see you later.'

'I suppose you will,' Harkness said disconsolately and Alleyn went upstairs. He found that Miss Bellamy's room now had the familiar look of any area given over to police investigation: something between an improvised laboratory and a photographer's studio with its focal point that unmistakable sheeted form on the floor.

Dr Curtis, the police surgeon, had finished his examination of the body. Sergeant Bailey squatted on the bathroom floor employing the tools of his trade upon the tinsel picture and as Alleyn came in Sergeant Thompson, whistling between his teeth, uncovered Mary Bellamy's terrible face and advanced his camera, to within a few inches of it. The bulb flashed.

Fox was seated at the dressing-table completing his notes.

'Well, Curtis?' Alleyn asked.

'Well, now,' Dr Curtis said. 'It's quite a little problem, you know. I can't see a verdict of accident, Alleyn, unless the coroner accepts the idea of her presenting this spray gun thing at her own face and pumping away like mad at it to see how it works. The face is pretty well covered with the stuff. It's in the nostrils and mouth and all over the chest and dress.'

'Suicide?'

'I don't see it. Have to be an uncommon determined effort. Any motive?'

'Not so far unless you count a suspected bout of tantrums, but I don't yet know about that. I don't see it, either. Which leaves us with homicide. See here, Curtis. Suppose I picked up that tin of Slaypest, pointed it at you and fell to work on the spray gun – what'd you do?'

'Dodge.'

'And if I chased you up?'

'Either collar you low or knock it out of your hands or bolt, yelling blue murder.'

'Exactly. But wouldn't the immediate reaction, particularly in a woman, be to throw up her arms and hide her face?'

'I think it might, certainly. Yes.'

'Yes,' said Fox glancing up from his notes.

'It wasn't hers. There's next to nothing on the hands and arms. And look,' Alleyn went on, 'at the actual character of the spray. Some of it's fine, as if delivered from a distance. Some, on the contrary, is so coarse that it's run down in streaks. Where's the answer to that one?'

'I don't know,' said Dr Curtis.

'How long would it take to kill her?'

'Depends on the strength. This stuff is highly concentrated. Hexa-ethyl-tetra-phosphate of which the deadly ingredient is TEPP: tetra-ethyl-pyro-phosphate. Broken down, I'd say, with some vehicle to reduce the viscosity. The nozzle's a very fine job: designed for indoor use. In my opinion the stuff shouldn't be let loose on the market. If she got some in the mouth, and it's evident she did, it might only be a matter of minutes. Some recorded cases mention nausea and convulsions. In others, the subject had dropped down insensible and died a few seconds later.'

Fox said: 'When the woman – Florence – found her, she was on the floor in what Florence describes as a sort of fit.'

'I'll see Florence next,' Alleyn said.

'And when Dr Harkness and Mr Templeton arrived she was dead,' Fox concluded.

'Where *is* Harkness?' Dr Curtis demanded. 'He's pretty damn' casual, isn't he? He ought to have shown up at once.'

'He was flat out with a hangover among the exotics in the conservatory,' Alleyn said. 'I stirred him up to look at Mr Richard Dakers, who was in a great tizzy before he knew there was anything to have a tizzy about. When I talked to him he fainted.'

'What a mob!' Curtis commented in disgust.

'Curtis, if you've finished here I think you'll find your colleague in reasonably working order downstairs.'

'He'd better be. Everything is fixed now. I'll do the PM tonight.'

'Good. Fox, you and I had better press on. We've got an office. Third on the right from here.'

They found Gracefield outside the door looking scandalized.

'I'm very sorry, I'm sure, sir,' he said, 'but the keys on this landing appear to have been removed. If you require to lock up . . .'

' 'T, 't! ' Fox said, and dived in his pocket. 'Thoughtless of me! Try this one.'

Gracefield coldly accepted it. He showed Alleyn into a small pleasantly furnished study and left Fox to look after himself, which he did very comfortably.

'Will there be anything further, sir?' Gracefield asked Alleyn.

'Nothing. This will do admirably.'

'Thank you, sir.'

'Here,' Fox said, 'are the other keys. They're interchangeable which is why I took the liberty of removing them.'

Gracefield received them without comment and retired.

'I always seem to hit it off better,' Fox remarked, 'with the female servants.'

'No doubt they respond more readily to your unbridled bodyurge,' said Alleyn.

'That's one way of putting it, Mr Alleyn,' Fox primly conceded.

'And the other is that I tipped that antarctic monument. Never mind: you'll have full play in a minute with Florence. Take a look at this room. It was Mr Richard Dakers's study. I suppose he now inhabits a bachelor flat somewhere, but he was adopted and brought up by the Templetons. Here you have his boyhood, adolescence and early maturity in microcosm. The usual school groups on one wall. Note the early dramatic interest. On the other three, his later progress. O.U.D.S. Signed photographs of lesser lights succeeded by signed photographs of greater ones. Sketches from unknown designers followed by the full treatment from famous designers and topped up by Saracen. The last is for a production that opened three years ago and closed last week. Programme of Command Performance. Several framed photographs of Miss Mary Bellamy, signed with vociferous devotion. One small photograph of Mr Charles Templeton. A calendar on the desk to support the theory that he left the house a year ago. Books from E. Nesbit to Samuel Beckett. *Who's Who in the Theatre* and *Spotlight* and cast an eye at this one, will you?'

He pulled out a book and showed it to Fox. '*Handbook of Poisons by a Medical Practitioner.* Book plate: "Ex libris C. H. Templeton." Let's see if the medical practitioner has anything to say about pest killers. Here we are. Poisons of Vegetable Origin. Tobacco. Alkaloid of.' He read for a moment or two. 'Rather scanty. Only one case quoted. Gentleman who swallowed nicotine from a bottle and died quietly in thirty seconds after heaving a deep sigh. Warnings about agricultural use of. And here are the newer concoctions including HETP and TEPP. Exceedingly deadly and to be handled with the greatest care. Ah, well!'

He replaced the book.

'That'll be the husband's,' Fox said. 'Judging by the book plate.'

'The husband's. Borrowed by the ward and accessible to all and sundry. For what it's worth. Well, Foxkin, that about completes our tour of the room. Tabloid history of the tastes and career of Richard Dakers. Hallo! Look here, Fox.'

He was stooping over the writing-desk and had opened the blotter.

'This looks fresh,' he said. 'Green ink. Ink on desk dried up and anyway, blue.'

There was a small Georgian glass above the fireplace. Alleyn held the blotting-paper to it and they looked at the reflected image:

'I' . . . . . e . . ck to . . y . . at it w . u . d . e . o . se my . . . te . ding I. . . . n't . . . n . . ven a . . . rible shock . . . that I . . . 't get . t . . rted . . t . . t I'm sure . t . . ll . e . . . ter if we do .'t me . t. I c . . 't. hin . clea . . . now . ut at . . ast I. now I'll n. . . . for. . . e your tr. . . ment of An . . . d . this after . . on. I . . ould . ave been told everything from the beginning. R.'

Alleyn copied this fragmentary message on a second sheet of paper, carried the blotter back to the desk and very carefully removed the sheet in question.

'We'll put the experts on to this,' he said, 'but I'm prepared to take a sporting chance on the result, Br'er Fox. Are you?'

'I'd give it a go, Mr Alleyn.'

'See if you can find Florence, will you? I'll take a flying jump while you're at it.'

Fox went out. Alleyn put his copy of the message on the desk and looked at it.

The correct method of deciphering and completing a blotting-paper impression is by measurement, calculation and elimination but occasionally, for persons with a knack, the missing letters start up vividly in the mind and the scientific method is thus accurately anticipated. When he was on his game, Alleyn possessed this knack and he now made use of it. Without allowing himself any second thoughts he wrote rapidly within the copy and stared with disfavour at the result. He then opened Richard Dakers's dispatch-case and found it contained a typescript of a play, *Husbandry in Heaven*. He flipped the pages over and came across some alterations in green ink and in the same hand as the letter.

'Miss Florence Johnson,' said Fox opening the door and standing aside with something of the air of a large sporting dog retrieving a bird. Florence, looking not unlike an apprehensive fowl, came in.

Alleyn saw an unshapely little woman, with a pallid, tear-stained face and hair so remorselessly dyed that it might have been a raven wig. She wore that particular air of disillusionment that is associated with the Cockney and she reeked of backstage.

'The superintendent,' Fox told her, 'just wants to hear the whole story like you told it to me. Nothing to worry about.'

'Of course not,' Alleyn said. 'Come and sit down. We won't keep you long.'

Florence looked as if she might prefer to stand, but compromised by sitting on the edge of the chair Fox had pushed forward.

'This has been a sad business for you,' Alleyn said.

'That's right,' Florence said woodenly.

'And I'm sure you must want to have the whole thing cleared up as soon and as quietly as possible.'

'Clear enough, isn't it? She's dead. You can't have it much clearer than that.'

'You can't indeed. But you see it's our job to find out why.'

'Short of seeing it happen you wouldn't get much nearer, would you? If you can read, that is.'

'You mean the tin of Slaypest?'

'Well, it wasn't perfume,' Florence said impertinently. 'They put that in bottles.' She shot a glance at Alleyn and seemed to undergo a slight change of temper. Her lips trembled and she compressed them. 'It wasn't all that pleasant,' she said. 'Seeing what I seen. Finding her like that. You'd think I might be let alone.'

'So you will be if you behave like a sensible girl. You've been with her a long time, haven't you?'

'Thirty years, near enough.'

'You must have got along very well to have stayed together all that time.'

Florence didn't answer and he waited. At last she said: 'I knew her ways.'

'And you were fond of her?'

'She was all right. Others might have their own ideas. I know 'er. Inside out. She'd talk to me like she wouldn't to others. She was all right.'

It was, Alleyn thought, after its fashion, a tribute.

He said: 'Florence, I'm going to be very frank indeed with you. Suppose it wasn't an accident. You'd want to know, wouldn't you?'

'It's no good you thinking she did it deliberate. She never! Not she. Wouldn't.'

'I didn't mean suicide.'

Florence watched him for a moment. Her mouth, casually but emphatically painted, narrowed into a scarlet thread.

'If you mean murder,' she said flatly, 'that's different.'

'You'd want to know,' he repeated. 'Wouldn't you?'

The tip of her tongue showed for a moment in the corner of her mouth. 'That's right,' she said.

'So do we. Now, Inspector Fox has already asked you about this but never mind: I'm asking you again. I want you to tell me in as much detail as you can remember just what happened from the time when Miss Bellamy dressed for her party up to the time you entered her room and found her – as you did find her. Let's start with the preparations, shall we?'

She was a difficult subject. She seemed to be filled with some kind of resentment and everything had to be dragged out of her. After luncheon, it appeared, Miss Bellamy rested. At half-past four Florence went in to her. She seemed to be 'much as usual.'

'She hadn't been upset by anything during the day?'

'Nothing,' Florence muttered, after a further silence, 'to matter.'

'I only ask,' Alleyn said, 'because there's a bottle of sal volatile left out in the bathroom. Did you give her sal volatile at any stage?'

'This morning.'

'What was the matter, this morning? Was she faint?'

Florence said: 'Over excited.'

'About what?'

'I couldn't say,' Florence said, and shut her mouth like a trap.

'Very well,' he said patiently. 'Let's get on with the preparation for the party. Did you give her a facial treatment of some kind?'

She stared at him. 'That's correct,' she said. 'A mask.'

'What did she talk about, Florence?'

'Nothing. You don't with that stuff over your face. Can't.'

'And then?'

'She made up and dressed. The two gentlemen came in and I went out.'

'That would be Mr Templeton and – who?'

'The colonel.'

'Did either of them bring her Parma violets?'

She stared at him. 'Vi'lets? Them? No. She didn't like vi'lets.'

'There's a bunch on her dressing-table.'

'I never noticed,' she said. 'I don't know anything about vi'lets. There wasn't any when I left the room.'

'And you saw her again – when?'

'At the party.'

'Well, let's hear about it.'

For a second or two he thought she was going to keep mum. She had the least eloquent face he had ever seen. But she began to speak as if somebody had switched her on. She said that from the time she left her mistress and during the early part of the cocktail party she had been with Mrs Plumtree in their little sitting-room. When the gong sounded they went down to take their places in the procession. After the speeches were over Old Ninn had dropped her awful brick about candles. Florence recounted the incident with detachment, merely observing that Old Ninn was, in fact, very old and sometimes forgot herself. 'Fifty candles,' Florence said grimly. 'What a remark to pass!' It was the only piece of comment, so far, that she had proffered. She had realized, Alleyn gathered, that her mistress had been upset and thinking she might be wanted had gone into the hall. She heard her mistress speak for a moment to Mr Templeton, something about him asking her not to use her scent. Up to here Florence's statement had been about as emotional as a grocery list, but at this point she appeared to boggle. She looked sideways at Alleyn, seemed to lose her bearings and came to a stop.

Alleyn said: 'That's all perfectly clear so far. Then did Miss Bellamy and the nanny – Mrs Plumtree, isn't it? – go upstairs together?'

Florence, blankly staring, said: 'No.'

'They didn't? What happened exactly?'

Ninn, it appeared, had gone first.

'Why? What delayed Miss Bellamy?'

'A photographer come butting in.'

'He took a photograph of her, did he?'

'That's right. By the front door.'

'Alone?'

'*He* came in. The chap wanted him in too.'

'Who?'

Her hands ground together in her lap. After waiting for a moment he asked: 'Don't you want to answer that one?'

'I want to know,' Florence burst out, 'if it's murder. If it's murder I don't care who it was, I want to see 'er righted. Never mind who! You can be mistaken in people, as I often told her. Them you think nearest and dearest are likely as not the ones that you didn't ought to trust. What I told her. Often and often.'

How vindictive, Alleyn wondered, was Florence? Of what character, precisely, was her relationship with her mistress? She was looking at him now, guardedly but with a kind of arrogance. 'What I want to know,' she repeated, 'is it murder? Is it that?'

He said: 'I believe it may be.'

She muttered: 'You ought to know: being trained to it. They tell you the coppers always know.'

From what background had Florence emerged nearly thirty years ago into Miss Bellamy's dressing-room? She was speaking now like a Bermondsey girl. Fly and wary. Her voice, hitherto negative and respectable, had ripened into strong Cockney.

Alleyn decided to take a long shot. He said: 'I expect you know Mr Richard Dakers very well, don't you?'

'Hardly help meself, could I?'

'No, indeed. He was more like a son than a ward to her, I dare say.'

Florence stared at him out of two eyes that closely resembled, and were about as eloquent as, boot-buttons.

'Acted like it,' she said. 'If getting nothing but the best goes for anything. And taking it as if it was 'is right.'

'Well,' Alleyn said lightly, 'he's repaid her with two very successful plays, hasn't he?'

'Them! What'd they have been without her? See another actress in the lead! Oh, dear! What a change! She *made* them: he couldn't have touched it on 'is own. She'd have breathed life into a corpse,' Florence said, and then looked sick.

Alleyn said: 'Mr Dakers left the house before the speeches, I understand?'

'He did. What a way to behave!'

'But he came back, didn't he?'

'He's back now,' she said quickly. 'You seen 'im, didn't you?' Gracefield, evidently, had talked.

'I don't mean now. I mean between the time he first left before the speeches and the time when he returned about half an hour ago. Wasn't there another visit in between?'

'That's right,' she said under her breath.

'Before the birthday speech?'

'That's right.'

'Take the moment we're discussing. Mrs Plumtree had gone upstairs, Miss Bellamy was in the hall. You had come out to see if she needed you.' He waited for a moment and then took his gamble. 'Did he walk in at the front door? At that moment?'

He thought she was going to say 'No': she seemed to be struggling with some kind of doubt. Then she nodded.

'Did he speak to Miss Bellamy? ' She nodded again.

'What about, do you know?'

'I didn't catch. I was at the other end of the hall.'

'What happened then?'

'They were photographed and then they went upstairs.'

'And you?'

'I went up. By the back stairs,' said Florence.

'Where to?'

'I went along to the landing.'

'And did you go in to her?'

'Mrs Plumtree was on the landing,' Florence said abruptly. Alleyn waited. 'They was talking inside – him and The Lady. So I didn't disturb her.'

'And you could hear them talking?'

She said angrily: 'What say we could? We weren't snooping, if that's what you mean. We didn't hear a word. She laughed – once.'

'And then?'

'He came out and went downstairs.'

'And did you go in to Miss Bellamy?'

'No,' Florence said loudly.

'Why not?'

'I didn't reckon she'd want me.'

'But why?'

'I didn't reckon she would.'

'Had you,' he asked without emphasis, 'had a row of some sort with Miss Bellamy?'

She went very white. 'What are you getting at?' she demanded and then: 'I told you. I understood her. Better than anyone.'

'And there'd been no trouble between you?'

'No!' she said loudly.

He decided not to press this point. 'So what did you do?' he asked. 'You and Mrs Plumtree?'

'Stayed where we was. Until . . .'

'Yes?'

'Until we heard something.'

'What was that?'

'Inside her room. Something. Kind of a crash.'

'What was it, do you think?'

'I wouldn't know. I was going in to see, whether or no, when I heard Mr Templeton in the hall. Calling. I go down to the half-landing,' Florence continued, changing her tense for the narrative-present. 'He calls up, they're waiting for her. So I go back to fetch her. And . . .' For the first time her voice trembled. 'And I walk in.'

'Yes,' Alleyn said. 'Before we go on, Florence, will you tell me this? Did Mr Richard at this time seem at all upset?'

'That's right,' she said, again with the air of defiance.

'When he arrived?' She nodded. 'I see. And when he came out of Miss Bellamy's room?'

And now there was no mistaking Florence's tone. It was one of pure hatred.

' 'Im? 'E looked ghasterly. 'E looked,' said Florence, 'like death.'

III

As if, by this one outburst, she had bestowed upon herself some kind of emotional blood-letting, Florence returned to her earlier manner – cagey, grudging, implicitly resentful. Alleyn could get no more from her about Richard Dakers's behaviour. When he suggested, obliquely, that perhaps Old Ninn might be more forthcoming, Florence let fall a solitary remark. 'Her! ' she said. 'You won't get her to talk. Not about him!' and refused to elaborate.

He had learned to recognize the point at which persistence defeats its own end. He took her on to the time where she entered the bedroom and discovered her mistress. Here, Florence exhibited a characteristic attitude towards scenes of violence. It was, he thought, as if she recognized in her own fashion their epic value and was determined to do justice to the current example.

When she went into the room, Mary Bellamy was on her knees, her hands to her throat and her eyes starting. She had tried to speak but had succeeded only in making a terrible retching noise. Florence had attempted to raise her, to ask her what had happened, but her mistress, threshing about on the floor, had been as unresponsive to these ministrations as an animal in torment. Florence had thought she heard the word 'doctor.' Quite beside herself, she had rushed out of the room and downstairs. 'Queer,' she said. That was what she had felt. 'Queer.' It was 'queer' that at such a moment she should concern herself with Miss Bellamy's nonappearance at her party. It was 'queer' that a hackneyed theatre phrase should occur to her in such a crisis but it had and she remembered using it: 'Is there a doctor in the house?' though, of course, she knew, really, that Dr Harkness was one of the guests. On the subject of Dr Harkness she was violent.

'Him! Nice lot of help he give, I *don't* think I Silly with what he'd taken and knew it. Couldn't make up his mind where he was or what he was wanted for till the colonel shoved ice down his neck. Even then he was stupid-like and 'ad to be pushed upstairs. For all we know,' Florence said, ' 'e might of saved 'er. For all we know! But when 'e got there it was over and in my opinion 'e's got it on 'is conscience for the rest of 'is days. And that's no error. Dr Harkness!'

Alleyn asked her to describe, in detail, the state of the room when she first went into it. She remembered nothing but her mistress and when he pressed her to try, he thought she merely drew on what she saw after she returned.

He said: 'We've almost finished but there's one question I must ask you. Do you know of anyone who had cause to wish for her death?'

She thought this over, warily. ' There's plenty,' she said, 'that was jealous of her and there's some that acted treacherous. Some that called themselves friends.'

'In the profession?' Alleyn ventured.

'Ah! Miss Kate Cavendish who'd never have got farther than Brighton Pier in the off-season without The Lady hadn't looked after 'er! Mr Albert Smith, pardon the slip, I should of said Saracen. But for her 'e'd of stuck behind 'is counter in the Manchester department. Look what she done for them and how do they pay 'er back? Only this morning!'

'What happened this morning?'

'Sauce and treachery was what happened.'

'That doesn't really answer my question, does it?'

She stood up. 'It's all the answer you'll get. You know your own business best, I suppose. But if she's been murdered, there's only one that had the chance. Why waste your time?'

'Only one?' Alleyn said. 'Do you really think so?'

For the first time she looked frightened but her answer was unexpected. 'I don't want what I've said to go no further,' she said with a look at Fox, who had been quietly taking notes. 'I don't fancy being quoted, particularly in some quarters. There's some that'd turn very nasty if they knew what I said.'

'Old Ninn?' Alleyn suggested. 'For one?'

'Smart,' Florence said with spirit, 'aren't you? All right. Her for one. She's got her fancy like I had mine. Only mine,' Florence said, and her voice was desolate, 'mine's gone where it won't come back, and that's the difference.' A spasm of something that might have been hatred crossed her face and she cried out with violence: 'I'll never forgive her! Never. I'll be even with her no matter what comes out of it, see if I'm not. Clara Plumtree!'

'But what did she do?'

He thought she was going to jib, but suddenly it all came out. It had happened, she said, after the tragedy. Charles Templeton had been taken to his dressing-room and Ninn had appeared on the landing while Florence was taking him a hot bottle. Florence herself had been too agitated to tell her what had happened in any detail. She had given Mr Templeton the bottle and left him. He was terribly distressed and wanted to be left alone. She had returned to the landing and seen Dr Harkness and Timon Gantry come out of the bedroom and speak to Mrs Plumtree who had then gone into the dressing-room. Florence herself had been consumed with a single overwhelming desire.

'I wanted to see after *her*. I wanted to look after my Lady. I knew what she'd have liked me to do for her. The way they'd left her! The way she looked! I wasn't going to let them see her like that and take her away like that. I knew her better than anybody. She'd have wanted her old Floy to look after her.'

She gave a harsh sob but went on very doggedly. She had gone to the bedroom door and found it locked. This, Alleyn gathered, had roused a kind of fury in her. She had walked up and down the landing in an agony of frustration and had then remembered the communicating door between the bedroom and dressing-room. So she had stolen to the door from the landing into the dressing-room and had opened it very carefully, not wishing to disturb Mr Templeton. She had found herself face to face with Mrs Plumtree.

It must, Alleyn thought, have been an extraordinary scene. The two women had quarrelled in whispers. Florence had demanded to be allowed to go through into the bedroom. Mrs Plumtree had refused. Then Florence had told her what she wanted to do.

'I told her! I told her I was the only one to lay my poor girl out and make her look more like herself. She said I couldn't. She said she wasn't to be touched by doctor's orders. *Doctor's orders!* I'd of pulled her away and gone through. I'd got me hands on 'er to do it, but it was too late.'

She turned to Fox. 'He'd come in. He was coming upstairs. She said, "That's the police. D'you want to get yourself locked up?" I had to give over and I went to my room.'

'I'm afraid she was right, Florence.'

'*Are* you! That shows how much you know! *I* wasn't to touch the body! Me! Me, that loved her. All right! So what was Clara Plumtree doing in the bedroom? Now!'

'What!' Fox ejaculated. 'In the bedroom? Mrs Plumtree?'

'Ah!' Florence cried out in a kind of triumph. 'Her! She'd been in there herself and let her try and deny it!'

Alleyn said: 'How do you know she'd been in the bedroom?'

'How? Because I heard the tank filling and the basin tap running in the bathroom beyond. She'd been in there doing what it was my right to do. Laying her hands on my poor girl.'

'But why do you suppose this? Why?'

Her lips trembled and she rubbed her hand across them. '*Why! Why!* I'll tell you why. Because she smelt of that scent. Smelt of it, I tell you, so strong it would sicken you. So if you're going to lock anybody up, you can start on Clara Plumtree.'

Her mouth twisted. Suddenly she burst into tears and blundered out of the room.

Fox shut the door after her and removed his spectacles. 'A tartar,' he observed.

'Yes,' Alleyn agreed. 'A faithful, treacherous, jealous, pig-headed tartar. You never know how they'll cut up in a crisis. Never. And I fancy, for our pains, we've got a brace of them in this party.'

As if to confirm this opinion there was a heavy single bang on the door. It swung violently open and there, on the threshold was Old Ninn Plumtree with PC Philpott, only less red-faced than herself, towering in close attendance.

'Lay a finger on me, young man,' Old Ninn was saying, 'and I'll make a public example of you.'

'I'm sure I'm very sorry, sir,' said Philpott. 'The lady insists on seeing you and short of taking her in charge I don't seem to be able to prevent it.'

'All right, Philpott,' Alleyn said. 'Come in, Ninn. Come in.'

She did so. Fox resignedly shut the door. He put a chair behind Ninn, but she disregarded it. She faced Alleyn over her own folded arms. To look in his face she was obliged to tilt her own acutely backwards and in doing so gave out such an astonishingly potent effluvium that she might have been a miniature volcano smouldering with port and due to erupt. Her voice was sepulchral and her manner truculent.

'I fancied,' she said, 'I knew a gentleman when I saw one and I hope you're not going to be a disappointment. Don't answer me back: I prefer to form my own opinion.'

Alleyn did not answer her back.

'That Floy,' Old Ninn continued, 'has been at you. A bad background, if ever there was one. What's bred in the child comes out in the woman. Don't believe a word of what she tells you. What's she been saying about the boy?'

'About Mr Dakers?'

'Certainly. A man to you, seem he may; to me who knows him inside out, he's a boy. Twenty-eight and famous, I dare say, but no more harm in him than there ever has been, which is never. Sensitive, and fanciful, yes. Not practical, granted. Vicious, fiddle! Now. What's that Floy been putting about?'

'Nothing very terrible, Ninn.'

'Did she say he was ungrateful? Or bad mannered?

'Well . . .'

'He's nothing of the sort. What else?'

Alleyn was silent. Old Ninn unfolded her arms. She laid a tiny gnarled paw on Alleyn's hand. 'Tell me what else,' she said, glaring into his face, 'I've got to know. Tell me.'

'*You* tell *me*,' he said, and put his hand over hers. 'What was the matter between Mr Richard and Mrs Templeton? It's better I should know. What was it?'

She stared at him. Her lips moved but no sound came from them.

'You saw him,' Alleyn said, 'when he came out of her room. What was the matter? Florence told us . . .'

'*She* told you! *She* told you that!'

'I'd have found out, you know. Can you clear it up for us? Do, if you can.'

She shook her head in a very desolate manner. Her eyes were glazed with tears and her speech had become uncertain. He supposed she had fortified herself with an extra glass before tackling him and it was now taking full effect.

'I can't say,' she said indistinctly. 'I don't know. One of her tantrums. A tyrant from the time she could speak. The boy's never anything but good and patient.' And after a moment she added quite briskly: 'Doesn't take after *her* in that respect. More like the father.'

Fox looked up from his notes. Alleyn remained perfectly still. Old Ninn rocked very slightly on her feet and sat down.

'Mr Templeton?' Alleyn said.

She nodded two or three times with her eyes shut. 'You may well say so,' she murmured, 'you – may – well . . .' Her voice trailed into silence and she dozed.

Fox opened his mouth and Alleyn signalled him and he shut it again. There was a considerable pause. Presently Old Ninn gave a slight snore, moved her lips and opened her eyes.

Alleyn said: 'Does Mr Richard know about his parentage?'

She looked fixedly at him. 'Why shouldn't he?' she said. 'They were both killed in a motor accident and don't you believe anything you're told to the contrary. Name of Dakers.' She caught sight of Fox and his notebook. 'Dakers,' she repeated and spelt it out for him.

'Thank you very much,' said Fox.

Alleyn said: 'Did you think Mr Richard looked very much upset when he came out of her room?'

'She had the knack of upsetting him. He takes things to heart.'

'What did he do?'

'Went downstairs. Didn't look at me. I doubt if he saw me.'

'Florence,' Alleyn said, 'thought he looked like death.'

Ninn got to her feet. Her little hands clutched at his arm.

'What's she mean? What's she been hinting? Why didn't she say what I heard? After she went downstairs? I told her. Why didn't she tell you?

'What did you hear?'

'She knows! I told her. I didn't think anything of it at the time and now she won't admit it. Trying to lay the blame on the boy. She's a wicked girl and always has been.'

'What did you hear?'

'I heard The Lady using that thing. The poison thing. Hissing. *Heard* it! She killed herself,' Ninn said. 'Why, we'll never know and the sin's on her head for ever. She killed herself.'

IV

There was a long pause during which Ninn showed signs of renewed instability. Fox put his arm under hers. 'Steady does it,' he said comfortably.

'That's no way to talk,' she returned sharply and sat down again.

'Florence,' Alleyn said, 'tells us Miss Bellamy was incapable of any such thing.'

The mention of Florence instantly restored her.

'Florence said this and Florence said that,' she barked. 'And did Florence happen to mention she fell out with her Lady and as good as got her notice this morning? Did she tell you that?'

'No,' Alleyn murmured, 'she didn't tell us that.'

'Ah! There you are, you see!'

'What did you do after Mr Richard left the room and went downstairs? After Florence had gone and after you'd heard the spray?'

She had shut her eyes again and he had to repeat his questions. 'I retired,' she said with dignity, 'to my room.'

'When did you hear of the catastrophe?'

'There was a commotion. Floy with a hot bottle on the landing having hysterics. I couldn't get any sense out of her. Then the doctor came out and told me.'

'And after that, what did you do?'

He could have sworn that she made a considerable effort to collect herself and that his question had alarmed her. 'I don't remember,' she said, and then added: 'Went back to my room.' She had opened her eyes and was watching him very warily.

'Are you sure, Ninn? Didn't you have a look at Mr Templeton in the dressing-room?'

'I've forgotten. I might have. I believe I did. You can't think of everything,' she added crossly.

'How was he? How did you find him?'

'How would you expect him to be?' she countered. 'Very low. Didn't speak. Upset. Naturally. With his trouble, it might have been the death of him. The shock and all.'

'How long were you in the dressing-room?'

'I don't remember. Till the police came and ordered everybody about.'

'Did you,' Alleyn asked her, 'go into the bedroom?'

She waited for a long time. 'No,' she said at last.

'Are you sure? You didn't go through into the bathroom or begin to tidy the room?'

'No.'

'Or touch the body?'

'I didn't go into the bedroom.'

'And you didn't let Florence go in either?'

'*What's she been telling you?*'

'That she wanted to go in and that you – very properly – told her that the doctor had forbidden it.'

'She was hysterical. She's a silly girl. Bad in some ways.'

'Did Mr Templeton go into the bedroom?'

'He had occasion,' she said with great dignity, 'to pass through it in order to make use of the convenience. That is not forbidden, I hope?'

'Naturally not.'

'Very well then,' she stifled a hiccough and rose. 'I'm going to bed,' she said loudly and, as there was nothing further to be collected from her, they let her out.

Fox offered assistance but was rebuffed. She tacked rapidly towards the door.

He opened it quickly.

There, on the landing, looking remarkably uncomfortable, was Richard Dakers.

V

He had been caught, it was evident, in the act of moving away from the door. Now, he stood stockstill, an uncomfortable smile twitching at the corner of his mouth. Old Ninn stopped short when she saw him, appeared to get her bearings and went up to him.

'Ninn,' he said looking past her at Alleyn and speaking with most unconvincing jauntiness, 'what *have* you been up to!'

She stared into his face. 'Speak up for yourself,' she said. 'They'll put upon you if you don't.'

'Hadn't you better go to bed? You're not yourself, you know.'

'Exactly,' Ninn said with hauteur. 'I'm going.'

She made off at an uncertain gait towards the back stairs.

Alleyn said: 'Mr Dakers, what are you doing up here?'

'I wanted to get into my room.'

'I'm afraid we're occupying it at the moment. But if there's anything you need . . .'

'Oh, God!' Richard cried out. 'Is there to be no end to these indignities? No! No, there's nothing I need. Not now. I wanted to be by myself in my room where I could make some attempt to think.'

'You had it all on your own in the drawing-room,' Fox said crossly. 'Why couldn't you think down there? How did you get past the man on duty, sir?'

'He was coping with a clutch of pressmen at the front door and I nipped up the back stairs.'

'Well,' Alleyn said, 'you'd better nip down again to where you came from and if you're sick of the drawing-room, you can join the party next door. Unless, of course, you'd like to stay and tell us your real object in coming up here.'

Richard opened his mouth and shut it again. He then turned on his heels and went downstairs. He was followed by Fox, who returned looking portentous. 'I gave that chap in the hall a rocket,' he said. 'They don't know the meaning of keeping observation these days. Mr Dakers is back in the drawing-room. Why do you reckon he broke out, sir?'

'I think,' Alleyn said, 'he may have remembered the blotting-paper.'

'Ah, there is that. May be. Mrs Plumtree wasn't bad value, though, was she?'

'Not bad. But none of it proves anything, of course,' Alleyn said. 'Not a damn' thing.'

'Floy getting the sack's interesting. If true.'

'It may be a recurrent feature of their relationship for all we know. What about the sounds they both heard in the bedroom?'

'Do we take it,' Fox asked, 'that Floy's crash came before Mrs Plumtree's hiss?'

'I suppose so. Yes.'

'And that Florence retired after the crash?'

'While Ninn remained for the hiss. Precisely.'

'The inference being,' Fox pursued, 'that as soon as Mr Dakers left her, the lady fell with a deafening crash on the four-pile carpet.'

'And then sprayed herself all over with Slaypest.'

'Quite so, Mr Alleyn.'

'I prefer a less dramatic reading of the evidence.'

'All the same, it doesn't look very pleasant for Mr Dakers.' And as Alleyn didn't reply: 'D'you reckon Mrs Plumtree was talking turkey when she let out about his parentage?'

'I think it's at least possible that she believes it.'

'Born,' Fox speculated, 'out of wedlock and the parents subsequently married?'

'Your guess is as good as mine. Wait a bit.' He took down the copy of Who's Who in the Theatre. 'Here we are. Bellamy. Sumptuous entry. Birth, not given. Curtis says, fifty. Married 1932, Charles Gavin Templeton. Now, where's the playwright. Dakers. Richard. Very conservative entry. Born 1931. Educated Westminster and Trinity. List of three plays. That's all. Could be, Foxkin. I suppose we can dig it out if needs must.'

Fox was silent for a moment. 'There is this,' he then said. 'Mrs Plumtree was alone on the landing after Florence went downstairs?'

'So it seems.'

'And she says she heard deceased using the Slaypest. What say she went in and used it herself? On deceased.'

'All right. Suppose she did. Why?'

'Because of the way deceased treated her ward or son or whatever he is? Went in and let her have it and then made off before Florence came back.'

'Do you like it?'

'Not much,' Fox grunted. 'What about this story of Mrs Plumtree going into the bedroom and rearranging the remains?'

'She didn't. The body was as Harkness and Gantry left it. Unless Harkness is too much hungover to notice.'

'It might be something quite slight.'

'What, for pity's sake?'

'God knows,' Fox said. 'Could *you* smell scent on Mrs P?'

'I could smell nothing but rich old tawny port on Mrs P?'

'Might be a blind for the perfume. Ah, forget it!' Fox said disgustedly. 'It's silly. How about this crash they heard after Mr Dakers left the room?'

'Oh, that. That was the lady pitching Madame Vestris into the bathroom.'

'Why?'

'Professional jealousy? Or perhaps it was his birthday present to her and she was taking it out on the Vestris.'

'Talk about conjecture! We do nothing else,' Fox grumbled. 'All right. So what's the next step, sir?'

'We've got to clear the ground. We've got to check, for one thing, Mr Bertie Saracen's little outburst. And the shortest way with that one, I suppose, is to talk to Anelida Lee.'

'Ah, yes. You know the young lady, don't you, Mr Alleyn?'

'I've met her in her uncle's bookshop. She's a charming girl. I know Octavius quite well. I tell you what, Foxkin, you go round the camp, will you? Talk to the butler. Talk to the maids. Pick up anything that's offering on the general set-up. Find out the pattern of the day's events. Furious Floy suggested a dust-up of some sort with Saracen and Miss Cavendish. Get the strength of it. And see if you can persuade the staff to feed the troops. Hallo – what's that?'

He went out into the passage and along to the landing. The door of Miss Bellamy's room was open. Dr Curtis and Dr Harkness stood just inside it watching the activities of two white-coated men. They had laid Miss Bellamy's body on a stretcher and had neatly covered it in orthodox sheeting. PC Philpott from the half-landing said: 'OK, chaps,' and the familiar progress started. They crossed the landing, changed the angle of their burden and gingerly began the descent. Thus Miss Bellamy made her final journey downstairs. Alleyn heard a subdued noise somewhere above him. He moved to a position from which he could look up the narrower flight of stairs to the second-floor landing. Florence was there, scarcely to be seen in the shadows, and the sound he had heard was of her sobbing.

Alleyn followed the stretcher downstairs. He watched the mortuary van drive away, had a final word with his colleagues, and went next door to call on Octavius Browne.

Octavius, after hours, used his shop as his sitting-room. With the curtains drawn, the lamp on his reading-table glowing and the firelight shining on his ranks of books, the room was enchanting. So, in his way, was Octavius, sunk deep in a red morocco chair with his book in his hand and his cat on his knee.

He had removed his best suit and, out of habit, had changed into old grey trousers and a disreputable but becoming velvet coat. For about an hour after Richard Dakers left (Anelida having refused to see him), Octavius had been miserable. Then she had come down, looking pale but familiar, saying she was sorry she'd been tiresome. She had kissed the top of his head and made him an omelet for his supper and had settled in her usual Monday night place on the other side of the fireplace behind a particularly large file in which she was writing up their catalogue. Once, Octavius couldn't resist sitting up high in order to look at her and as usual she made a hideous face at him and he made one back at her, which was a private thing they did on such occasions. He was reassured but not entirely so. He had a very deep affection for Anelida, but he was one of those people in whom the distress of those they love begets a kind of compassionate irritation. He liked Anelida to be gay and dutiful and lovely to look at: when he suspected that she had been crying he felt at once distressed and helpless and the sensation bored him because he didn't understand it.

When Alleyn rang the bell Anelida answered it. He saw, at once, that she had done her eyes up to hide the signs of tears.

Many of Octavius's customers were also his friends and it was not unusual for them to call after hours. Anelida supposed that Alleyn's was that sort of visit and so did Octavius, who was delighted to see him. Alleyn sat down between them, disliking his job.

'You look so unrepentantly cosy and Dickensian,' he said, 'both of you, that I feel like an interloper.'

'My dear Alleyn, I do hope your allusion is not to that other and unspeakable little Nell and her drooling grandparent. No, I'm sure it's not. You are thinking of *Bleak House*, perhaps, and your fellow-investigator's arrival at his friend's fireside. I seem to remember, though, that his visit ended uncomfortably in an arrest. I hope you've left *your* manacles at the Yard.'

Alleyn said: 'As a matter of fact, Octavius, I *am* here on business, though not, I promise, to take either of you into custody.'

'Really? How very intriguing! A bookish reference perhaps? Some malefactor with a flair for the collector's item?'

'I'm afraid not,' Alleyn said. 'It's a serious business, Octavius, and indirectly it concerns you both. I believe you were at Miss Mary Bellamy's birthday party this evening, weren't you?'

Anelida and her uncle both made the same involuntary movement of their hands. 'Yes,' Octavius said. 'For a short time. We were.'

'When did you arrive?'

'At seven. We were asked,' Octavius said, 'for six-thirty, but Anelida informed me it is the "done thing" nowadays to be late.'

'We waited,' Anelida said, 'till other people had begun to stream in.'

'So you kept an eye on the earlier arrivals?'

'A bit. I did. They were rather intimidating.'

'Did you by any chance see anybody go in with a bunch of Parma violets?'

Octavius jerked his leg. 'Damn you, Hodge,' he ejaculated and added mildly: 'He makes bread on one's thigh. Unconscionable feline, be gone.'

He cuffed the cat and it leapt indignantly to the floor.

Alleyn said: 'I know you left early. I believe I know why.'

'Mr Alleyn,' Anelida said. 'What's happened? Why are you talking like this?'

Alleyn said: 'It *is* a serious matter.'

'Has Richard . . .?' she began and stopped. 'What are you trying to tell us?'

'He's all right. He's had a shock but he's all right.'

'My dear Alleyn . . .'

'Unk,' she said, 'we'd better just listen.'

And Alleyn told them, carefully and plainly, what had happened. He said nothing of the implications.

'I wonder,' he ended, 'that you haven't noticed the comings and goings outside.'

'Our curtains are drawn as you see,' Octavius said. 'We had no occasion to look out. Had we, Nelly?'

Anelida said: 'This will hurt Richard more than anything else that has ever happened to him.' And then with dismay: 'I wouldn't see him when he came in. I turned him away. He won't forgive me and I won't forgive myself.'

'My darling child, you had every cause to behave as you did. She was an enchanting creature but evidently not always prettily behaved,' Octavius said. 'I always think,' he added, 'that one does a great disservice to the dead when one praises them inaccurately. *Nil nisi*, if you will, but at least let the *bonum* be authentic.'

'I'm not thinking of her!' she cried out. 'I'm thinking of Richard.'

'Are you, indeed, my pet?' he said uncomfortably.

Anelida said: 'I'm sorry, Mr Alleyn. This is bad behaviour, isn't it? You must put it down to the well-known hysteria of theatre people.'

'I put it down to the natural result of shock,' Alleyn said, 'and believe me, from what I've seen of histrionic behaviour yours is in the last degree conservative. You must be a beginner.'

'How right you are!' she said and looked gratefully at him.

The point had been reached where he should tell them of the implications and he was helped by Octavius, who said: 'But why, my dear fellow, are you concerned in all this? Do the police in cases of accident – ?'

'That's just it,' Alleyn said. 'They do. They have to make sure.'

He explained why they had to make sure. When he said that he must know exactly what had happened in the conservatory, Anelida turned so pale that he wondered if she, too, was going to faint. But she waited for a moment, taking herself in hand, and then told him, very directly, what had happened.

Timon Gantry, Montague and Richard had been talking to her about her reading the leading role in *Husbandry in Heaven*. Mary Bellamy had come in, unnoticed by them, and had heard enough to make her realize what was afoot.

'She was very angry,' Anelida said steadily. 'She thought of it as a conspiracy and she accused me of – of . . .' Her voice faltered but in a moment she went on. 'She said I'd been setting my cap at Richard to further my own ends in the theatre. I don't remember everything she said. They all tried to stop her but that seemed to make her more angry. Kate Cavendish and Bertie Saracen had come in with Mr Templeton. When she saw them she attacked them as well. It was something about another new production. She accused them, too, of conspiracy. I could see Unk on the other side of the glass door: like somebody you want very badly in a nightmare and can't reach. And then Mr Templeton went out and spoke to him. And then I went out. And Unk behaved perfectly. And we came home.'

'Beastly experience,' Alleyn said. 'For both of you.'

'Oh, horrid,' Octavius agreed. 'And *very* puzzling. She was, to meet, you know, so perfectly enchanting. One is quite at a loss . . .' He rumpled his hair.

'Poor Unky!' Anelida said.

'Was Colonel Warrender in the conservatory?'

'That is Templeton's cousin, isn't it? One sees the likeness,' said Octavius. 'Yes, he was. He came into the hall and tried to say something pleasant, poor man.'

'So did the others,' Anelida said. 'I'm afraid I wasn't as responsive as I ought to have been. I – we just walked out.'

'And Richard Dakers walked out after you?'

'Yes,' she said. 'He did. And I went off to my room and wouldn't see him. Which is so awful.'

'So what did he do?' Alleyn asked Octavius.

'Do? Dakers? He was in a great taking-on. I felt sorry for him. Angry, you know, with *her*. He said a lot of hasty, unpleasant things which I feel sure he didn't mean.'

'What sort of things?'

'Oh! 'Octavius said. 'It was, as far as I recollect, to the effect that Mrs Templeton had ruined his life. All very extravagant and ill-considered. I was sorry to hear it.'

'Did he say what he meant to do when he left here?'

'Yes, indeed. He said he was going back to have it out with her. Though how he proposed to do anything of the sort in the middle of a party, one can't imagine. I went to the door with him, trying to calm him down, and I saw him go into the house.'

'And that was the last you saw of him?'

'In point of fact, yes. The telephone rang at that moment. It's in the back room as you'll remember. I answered it and when I returned here I thought for a moment he had done so, too. I suppose because he was so much in my mind.'

Anelida made a small ejaculation, but her uncle went on: 'A ludicrous mistake. It was dark in here by then – very – and he was standing in silhouette against the windows. I said, "My dear chap, what now?" or something of that sort, and he turned and then, of course, I saw it was Colonel Warrender, you know.'

'What had *he* come for?' Anelida asked rather desperately.

'Well, my dear, I suppose on behalf of his cousin and to repeat his vicarious apologies and to attempt an explanation. I felt it much better to make as little of the affair as possible: after all, we don't *know* Warrender and in any case it was really nothing to do with him. He meant very well, no doubt. I was, I hope, perfectly civil but I got rid of him in a matter of seconds.'

'Yes,' Alleyn said. 'I see. To side-track for a moment, I suppose you're by way of being an authority on Victorian tinsel pictures, aren't you? Do you go in for them? I seem to remember . . .'

'How *very* odd!' Octavius exclaimed. 'My dear fellow, I sold one this morning to young Dakers, as a birthday present for – oh, well, there you are! – for his guardian.'

'Madam Vestris?'

'You saw it then? Charming, isn't it?'

'Yes,' Alleyn said. 'Charming.'

Anelida had been watching Alleyn, as he was well aware, very closely. She now asked him the question he had expected.

'Mr Alleyn,' Anelida said. 'Do you think it was not an accident?'

He gave her the inevitable answer. 'We don't know. We're not sure.'

'But what do you believe? In your heart? I must know. I won't do anything silly or make a nuisance of myself. Do you believe she was murdered?'

Alleyn said: 'I'm afraid I do, Anelida.'

'Have you told Richard?'

'Not in so many words.'

'But he guessed?'

'I don't know,' Alleyn said carefully,' what he thought. I've left him to himself for a little.'

'Why?'

'He's had a very bad shock. He fainted.'

She looked steadily at him and then with a quick collected movement rose to her feet.

'Unk,' she said, 'don't wait up for me and don't worry.'

'My dear girl,' he said, in a fluster, 'what do you mean? Where are you going?'

'To Richard,' she said. 'Where else? Of course to Richard.'

CHAPTER 6

On The Scent

When Anelida rang the bell at 2 Pardoner's Place, it was answered, almost at once, by a policeman.

She said: 'It's Miss Lee. I've been talking to Superintendent Alleyn. He knows I'm here and I think is probably coming himself in a moment. I want to speak to Mr Richard Dakers.'

The policeman said: 'I see, miss. Well, now, if you'll wait a moment I'll just find out whether that'll be all right. Perhaps you'd take a chair.'

'No, thank you. I want to see him at once, please.'

'I'll ascertain . . .' he had begun rather austerely when Alleyn himself arrived.

'Sir?'

'Yes, all right. Is Mr Dakers still in the drawing-room? Good.' Alleyn looked at Anelida. 'Come along,' he said. She lifted her chin and went to him.

She was in a state of mind she had never before experienced. It was as if her thoughts and desires and behaviour had been abruptly simplified and were governed by a single intention. She knew that somewhere within herself she must be afraid, but she also knew that fear, as things had turned out, was inadmissible.

She followed Alleyn across the hall. He said: 'Here you are,' and opened a door. She went from the hall into the drawing-room.

Immediately inside the door was a tall leather screen. She walked round it and there, staring out of a window, was Richard. Anelida

moved a little towards him and halted. This gave her time to realize
how very much she liked the shape of his head and at once she felt
an immense tenderness for him and even a kind of exultation. In a
second, she would speak his name, she would put herself absolutely
on his side.

'Richard,' she said.

He turned. She noticed that his face had bleached, not conven-
tionally, over the cheekbone, but at the temples and down the
jaw-line.

'Anelida?'

'I had to come. I'm trying to make up for my bad behaviour. Here,
you see, I am.'

He came slowly to her and when he took her hands in his, did so
doubtfully. 'I can't believe my luck,' he said. 'I thought I'd lost you
quite irrevocably. Cause enough, God knows.'

'On the contrary, I assure you.'

He broke into an uncertain smile. 'The things you say! Such grand
phrases!' His hands tightened on hers. 'You know what's happened,
don't you? About Mary?'

'Yes. Richard, I'm so terribly sorry. And what a hopeless phrase
that is!'

'I shouldn't let you stay. It's not the place for you. This is a nightmare of a house.'

'Do you want me? Am I any good: being here?'

'I love you.' He lifted her hands to his face. 'Ah, no! Why did I tell
you? This isn't the time.'

'Are you all right now – to talk, I mean? To talk very seriously?'

'I'm all right. Come over here.'

They sat together on the sofa, Richard still holding her hands. 'He
told us you fainted,' said Anelida.

'Alleyn? Has he been worrying you?'

'Not really. But it's because of what he did say that I'm here. And
because – Richard, when I wouldn't see you and you went away –
did you come back here?'

'Yes,' he said. 'I did.'

'Did you see her?'

He looked down at their clasped hands. 'Yes.'

'Where?'

'In her room. Only for a few minutes. I – left her there.'

'Was anyone else with you?'

'Good God, no!' he cried out.

'And then? Then what?'

'I went away. I walked for heaven knows how long. When I came back – it was like this.'

There was a long silence. At last Richard said very calmly: 'I know what you're trying to tell me. They think Mary has been murdered and they wonder if I'm their man. Isn't it?'

Anelida leant towards him and kissed him. 'That's it,' she said. 'At least, I think so. We'll get it tidied up and disposed of in no time. But, I think, that's it.'

'It seems,' he said, 'so fantastic. Too fantastic to be frightening. You mustn't be frightened. You must go away, my darling heart, and leave me to – to do something about it.'

'I'll go when I think it'll make things easier for you. Not before.'

'I love you so much. I should be telling you how much, not putting this burden upon you.'

'They may not leave me with you for long. You must remember exactly what happened. Where you went. Who may have seen you. And, Richard, you must tell them what she was doing when you left.'

He released her hands and pressed the palms of his own to his eyes. 'She was laughing,' he said.

'Laughing? They'll want to know why, won't they? What you both said to make her laugh.'

'Never!' he said violently. 'Never!'

'But – they'll ask you.'

'They can ask and ask and ask again. Never!'

'You must!' she said desperately. 'Think! It's what one always reads – that innocent people hold out on the police and muddle everything up and put themselves in the wrong. Richard, think what they'll find out anyway! That she spoke as she did to me, that you were angry, that you said you'd never forgive her. Everyone in the hall heard you. Colonel Warrender . . .'

'He!' Richard said bitterly. 'He won't talk. He daren't.'

'What do you mean?'

'It doesn't matter.'

'Oh!' she cried out. 'You are frightening me! What's going to happen when they ask you about it? What'll they think when you won't tell them!'

'They can think what they like.' He got up and began to walk about the room. 'Too much has happened. I can't get it into perspective. You don't know what it's like. I've no right to load it on to you.'

'Don't *talk* like that,' Anelida said desperately. 'I love you. It's my right to share.'

'You're so young.'

'I've got all the sense I'm ever likely to have.'

'Darling!'

'Never mind about me! You needn't tell me anything you don't want to. It's what you're going to say to them that matters.'

'I will tell you – soon – when I can.'

'If it clears you they won't make any further to-do about it. That's all they'll worry about. Clearing it up. You must tell them what happened. Everything.'

'I can't.'

'My God, *why*?'

'Have you any doubts about me? Have you!'

She went to him. 'You must know I haven't.'

'Yes,' he said. 'I can see that.'

They stared at each other. He gave an inarticulate cry and suddenly she was in his arms.

Gracefield came through the folding doors from the dining-room.

'Supper is served, sir,' he said.

Alleyn rose from his uncomfortable seclusion behind the screen, slipped through the door into the hall, shut it soundlessly behind him and went up to their office.

II

'I've been talking,' Mr Fox remarked, 'to a Press photographer and the servants.'

'And I.' Alleyn said sourly, 'have been eavesdropping on a pair of lovers. How low can you get? Next stop, with Polonius behind the arras in a bedroom.'

'All for their good, I dare say,' Fox observed comfortably.

'There is that. Fox, that blasted playwright is holding out on us. And on his girl for a matter of that. But I'm damned if I like him as a suspect.'

'He seems,' Fox considered, 'a very pleasant young fellow.'

'What the devil happened between him and Mary Bellamy when he came back? He won't tell his girl. He merely says the interview ended in Miss Bellamy laughing. We've got the reports from those two intensely prejudiced women who both agree he looked ghastly. All right. He goes out. There's this crash Florence talked about. Florence goes down to the half-landing and Ninn hears a spray being used. Templeton comes out from the drawing-room to the foot of the stairs. He calls up to Florence to tell her mistress they're waiting for her. Florence goes up to the room and finds her mistress in her death throes. Dakers returns two hours after the death, comes up to this room, writes a letter and tries to go away. End of information. Next step: confront him with the letter?'

'Your reconstruction of it?'

'Oh,' Alleyn said. 'I fancy I can lay my hands on the original.'

Fox looked at him with placid approval and said nothing.

'What did you get from your Press photographer? And which photographer?' Alleyn asked.

'He was hanging about in the street and said he'd something to tell me. Put-up job to get inside, of course, but I thought I'd see what it was. He took a picture of deceased with Mr Dakers in the background at twenty to eight by the hall clock. He saw them go upstairs together. Gives us an approximate time for the demise for what it's worth.'

'About ten minutes later. What did you extract from the servants?'

'Not a great deal. It seems the deceased wasn't all that popular with the staff except Florence, who was hers, as the cook put it, body and soul. Gracefield held out on me for a bit, but he's taken quite a liking to you, sir, and I built on that with good results.'

'What the hell have you been saying?'

'Well, Mr Alleyn, you know as well as I do what snobs these high-class servants are.'

Alleyn didn't pursue the subject.

'There was a dust-up,' Fox continued, 'this morning with Miss Cavendish and Mr Saracen. Gracefield happened to overhear it.' He repeated Gracefield's account, which had been detailed and accurate.

'According to Anelida Lee this row was revived in the conservatory,' Alleyn muttered. 'What were they doing here this morning?'

'Mr Saracen had come to do the flowers, about which Gracefield spoke very sarcastically, and Miss Cavendish had brought the deceased that bottle of scent.'

'What! 'Alleyn ejaculated. 'Not the muck on her dressing-table? Not "Unguarded"? *This morning?*'

'That's right.'

Alleyn slapped his hand down on Richard's desk and got up. 'My God, what an ass I've been!' he said and then, sharply: 'Who opened it?'

'She did. In the dining-room.'

'And used it? Then?'

'Had a bit of a dab, Gracefield said. He happened to be glancing through the serving-hatch at the time.'

'What became of it after that?'

'Florence took charge of it. I'm afraid,' Fox said, 'I'm not with you, Mr Alleyn, in respect of the scent.'

'My dear old boy, think! Think of the bottle.'

'Very big,' Fox said judiciously.

'Exactly. Very big. Well, then – ?'

'Yes. Ah, yes,' Fox said, and then: 'Well, I'll be staggered!'

'And so you jolly well should. This could blow the whole damn' case wide open again.'

'Will I fetch them?'

'Do. And call on Florence, wherever she is. Get the whole story, Fox. Tactfully, as usual. Find out when the scent was decanted into the spray and when she used it. Watch the reactions, won't you? And see if there's anything in the Plumtree stories: about Richard Dakers's parentage and Florence being threatened with the sack.'

Fox looked at his watch. 'Ten o'clock,' he said. 'She may have gone to bed.'

'That'll be a treat for you. Leave me your notes. Away you go.'

While Fox was on this errand, Alleyn made a plot, according to information, of the whereabouts of Charles Templeton, the four guests, the servants and Richard Dakers up to the time when he himself arrived on the scene. Fox's spadework had been exhaustive, as usual, and a pretty complicated pattern emerged. Alleyn lifted an eyebrow over the result. How many of them had told the whole truth? Which of them had told a cardinal lie? He put a query against one name and was shaking his head over it when Fox returned.

'Bailey's finished with them,' Fox said, and placed on Richard's desk the scent spray, the empty 'Unguarded' bottle and the tin of Slaypest.

'What'd he find in the way of dabs?'

'Plenty. All sorts, but none that you wouldn't expect. He's identified the deceased's. Florence says she and Mr Templeton and Colonel Warrender all handled the exhibits during the day. She says the deceased got the colonel to operate the spray on her, just before the party. Florence had filled it from the bottle.'

'And how much was left in the bottle?'

'She thinks it was about a quarter full. She *was* in bed,' Fox added in a melancholy tone.

'That would tally,' Alleyn muttered. 'No sign of the bottle being knocked over and spilling, is there?'

'None.'

Alleyn began to tap the Slaypest tin with his pencil.

'About half-full. Anyone know when it was first used?'

'Florence reckons a week ago. Mr Templeton didn't like her using it and tried to get Florence to make away with it.'

'Why didn't she?'

'No chance according to her. She went into a great taking-on and asked me if I was accusing her of murder.'

'*Did* she get the sack, this morning?'

'When I asked her she went up like a rocket bomb, the story being that Mrs Plumtree has taken against her and let out something that was told in confidence.'

Alleyn put his head in his hands. 'Oh, *Lord*!' he said.

'You meet that kind of thing,' Mr Fox observed, 'in middle-aged ladies. Florence says that when Miss Bellamy or Mrs Templeton was out of humour, she would make out she was going to sack Florence,

but there was nothing in it. She says she only told Mrs Plumtree as
a joke. I kind of nudged in a remark about Mr Dakers's parentage,
but she wasn't having any of that. She turned around and accused
me of having a dirty mind and in the next breath had another go at
Mrs Plumtree. All the same,' Mr Fox added primly, 'I reckon there's
something in it. I reckon so from her manner. She appears to be very
jealous of anybody who was near the deceased and that takes in
Mr Templeton, Mr Dakers, Mrs Plumtree and the colonel.'

'Good old Florrie,' Alleyn said absentmindedly.

'You know, sir,' Fox continued heavily. 'I've been thinking about
the order of events. Take the latter part of the afternoon. Say, from
when the colonel used the scent spray on deceased. What happened
after *that*, now?'

'According to himself he went downstairs and had a quick one
with Mrs Templeton in the presence of the servants while Templeton
and Dakers were closeted in the study. All this up to the time when
the first guests began to come in. It looks good enough, but it's not
cast iron.'

'Whereas,' Fox continued, 'Florence and Mrs Plumtree were
upstairs. Either of them could have gone into Mrs Templeton's room,
and got up to the odd bit of hanky-panky, couldn't they, now?'

'The story is that they were together in their parlour until they
went downstairs to the party. They're at daggers-drawn. Do you
think that if one of them had popped out of the parlour, the other
would feel disposed to keep mum about it?'

'Ah. There is that, of course. But it might have been forgotten.'

'Come off it, Foxkin.'

'The same goes for Mr Templeton and Mr Dakers. They've said,
independently of each other, that they were together in the study. I
don't know how you feel about that one, Mr Alleyn, but I'm inclined
to accept it.'

'So am I. Entirely.'

'If we do accept all this, we've got to take it that the job was fixed
after the guests began to arrive. Now, up to the row in the conservatory the three gentlemen were all in the reception rooms. The
colonel was in attendance on the deceased. Mr Templeton was also
with her receiving the guests and Mr Dakers was on the look out for
his young lady.'

'What's more, there was a Press photographer near the foot of the stairs, a cinematographer half-way up, and a subsidiary bar at the foot of the back stairs with a caterer's man on duty throughout. He saw Florence and Ninn and nobody else go up. What's that leave us in the way of a roaring-hot suspect?'

'It means,' Fox said, 'either that one of those two women fixed it then . . .'

'But when? You mean before they met on the landing and tried to listen in on the famous scene?'

'I suppose I do. Yes. While the photograph was being taken.'

'Yes?'

'Alternatively someone else went up before that.'

'Again, when? It would have to be after the cinema unit moved away and before Mrs Templeton left the conservatory and came out into the hall where she was photographed with Dakers glowering in the background. And it would have to be before she took him upstairs.'

'Which restricts you to the entrance with the birthday cake and the speeches. I reckon someone could have slipped upstairs then.'

'The general attention being focused on the speakers and the stairs being clear? Yes. I agree with you. So far. But, see here, Fox; this expert didn't do the trick as simply as that. I'm inclined to think there was one more visit at least, more likely that there were two more, one before and one after the death. Tidying up, you know. If I'm right, there was a certain amount of tidying up.'

'My God,' Fox began with unwonted heat, 'what are you getting at, Mr Alleyn? It's tough enough as it is, d'you want to make it more difficult? What's the idea?'

'If it's any good it's going to make it easier. Much easier.'

Alleyn stood up.

'You know, Br'er Fox,' he said, 'I can see only one explanation that really fits. Take a look at what's offering. Suicide? Leave her party, go up to her bedroom and spray herself to death? They all scout the notion and so do I. Accident? We've had it: the objection being the inappropriateness of the moment for her to horticult and the nature of the stains. Homicide? All right. What's the jury asked to believe? That she stood stockstill while her murderer pumped a deluge of Slaypest into her face at long and then at short range?

Defending Counsel can't keep a straight face over that one. But if, by any giddy chance, I'm on the right track, there's an answer that still admits homicide. Now, listen, while I check over and see if you can spot a weakness.'

Mr Fox listened placidly to a succinct argument, his gaze resting thoughtfully the while on the tin, the bottle, and the scent spray.

'Yes,' he said when Alleyn had finished 'Yes. It adds up, Mr Alleyn. It fits. The only catch that I can see rests in the little difficulty of our having next-to-nothing to substantiate the theory.'

Alleyn pointed a long finger at the exhibits. 'We've got those,' he said, 'and it'll go damn' hard if we don't rake up something else in the next half-hour.'

'Motive?'

'Motive unknown. It may declare itself. Opportunity's our bird, Fox. Opportunity, my boy.'

'What's the next step?'

'I rather fancy shock tactics. They're all cooped up in the dining-room, aren't they?'

'All except Mr Templeton. He's still in the study. When I looked in they were having supper. He'd ordered it for them. Cold partridge,' Mr Fox said rather wistfully. 'A bit of a waste, really, as they didn't seem to have much appetite.'

'We'll see if we can stimulate it,' Alleyn said grimly, 'with these,' and waved his hand at the three exhibits.

III

Pinky Cavendish pushed her plate away and addressed herself firmly to her companions.

'I feel,' she said, 'completely unreal. It's not an agreeable sensa-tion.' She looked round the table. 'Is there any reason why we don't say what's in all our minds? Here we sit, pretending to eat: every man-jack of us pea-green with worry but cutting the whole thing dead. I can't do with it. Not for another second. I'm a loquacious woman and I want to talk.'

'Pinky,' Timon Gantry said. 'Your sense of timing! Never quite successfully co-ordinated, dear, is it?'

'But, *actually*,' Bertie Saracen plaintively objected, 'I do so feel Pinky's dead right. I mean we *are* all devastated and for my part, at least, terrified but there's no *real* future, is there, in maintaining a *charnel-house* decorum? It can't improve anything, or can it? And it's so excessively wearing. Dicky, dear, you won't misunderstand me, will you? The hearts, I promise you, are utterly in their right place which, speaking for myself, is in the boots.'

Richard, who had been talking in an undertone to Anelida, looked up. 'Why not talk,' he said, 'if you can raise something that remotely resembles normal conversation.'

Warrender darted a glance at him. 'Of course,' he said. 'Entirely agree.' But Richard wouldn't look at Warrender.

'Even abnormal conversation,' Pinky said, 'would be preferable to strangulated silence.'

Bertie, with an air of relief, said: 'Well, then, everybody, let's face it. We're *not* being herded together in a' – he swallowed – 'in a communal cell just out of constabular whimsy. Now *are* we?'

'No, Bertie,' Pinky said, 'we are not'

'Under hawk-like supervision,' Bertie added, 'if Sergeant Philpott doesn't mind my mentioning it.'

PC Philpott, from his post at the far end of the room, said: 'Not at all, sir,' and surreptitiously groped for his notebook.

'*Thank* you,' Bertie said warmly. Gracefield and a maid came in and cleared the table in a deathly silence. When they had gone Bertie broke out again. 'My God,' he said. 'Isn't it as clear as daylight that every one of us, except Anelida, is under suspicion for something none of us likes to mention?'

'I do,' Pinky said. 'I'm all for mentioning it and indeed if I don't mention it I believe I'll go off like a geyser.'

'No, you won't, dear,' Gantry firmly intervened. He was sitting next to Pinky and looked down upon her with a crane-like tilt of his head. 'You'll behave beautifully and not start any free-associating nonsense. This is not the time for it.'

'Timmy, darling, I'm sorry as sorry but I'm moved to defy you,' Pinky announced with a great show of spirit. 'In the theatre – never. Outside it and under threat of being accused of murder – yes. There!' she ejaculated. 'I've said it! Murder. And aren't you all relieved?'

Bertie Saracen said at once: 'Bless you, darling. Immeasurably.'

Timon Gantry and Colonel Warrender simultaneously looked at the back of Philpott's head and then exchanged glances: two men, Anelida felt, of authority at the mercy of an uncontrollable situation.

'Very well, then,' Pinky continued. 'The police think Mary was murdered and presumably they think one of us murdered her. It sounds monstrous but it appears to be true. The point is, does anyone here agree with them?'

'I don't,' Bertie said. He glanced at the serving-hatch and lowered his voice. 'After all,' he said uncomfortably, 'we're not the only ones.'

'If you mean the servants . . .' Richard said angrily.

'I don't mean anybody in particular,' Bertie protested in a great hurry.

'– it's quite unthinkable.'

'To my mind,' Pinky said, 'the whole thing's out of this world. I don't and can't and won't believe it of anybody in the house.'

'Heah, heah,' Warrender ejaculated lending a preposterously hearty note to the conversation. 'Ridiculous idea,' he continued loudly. 'Alleyn's behaving altogether too damn' high-handedly.' He looked at Richard, hesitated and with an obvious effort said: 'Don't you agree?'

Without turning his head, Richard said: 'He knows his own business, I imagine.'

There was a rather deadly little silence broken by Timon Gantry.

'For my part,' Gantry said, 'I feel the whole handling of the situation is so atrociously hard on Charles Templeton.'

A guilty look came into their faces, Anelida noticed: as if they were ashamed of forgetting Charles. They made sympathetic noises and were embarrassed.

'What I resent,' Pinky said suddenly, 'is being left in the dark. *What* happened? *Why* the mystery? *Why not* accident? All we've been told is that poor Mary died of a dose of pest killer. It's hideous and tragic and we're all shocked beyond words, but if we're being kept here under suspicion' – she brought her clenched fist down on the table – '*we've a right to know why!*'

She had raised her not inconsiderable voice to full projection point. None of them had heard the door from the hall open.

'Every right,' Alleyn said, coming forward. 'And I'm sorry that the explanation has been so long delayed.'

The men had half-risen but he lifted his hand and they sat back again. Anelida, for all her anxiety, had time to reflect that he was possessed of an effortless authority before which even Gantry, famous for this quality, became merely one of a controllable group. The attentive silence that descended upon them was of exactly the same kind as that which Gantry himself commanded at rehearsals. Even Colonel Warrender, though he raised his eyebrows, folded his arms and looked uncommonly portentous, found nothing to say.

'I think,' Alleyn said, 'that we will make this a round-the-table discussion.' He sat in the vacant chair at the end of the table. 'It gives one,' he explained, with a smile at Pinky Cavendish, 'a spurious air of importance. We shall need five more chairs, Philpott.'

PC Philpott placed them. Nobody spoke.

Fox came in from the hall bringing Florence and Old Ninn in his wake. Old Ninn was attired in a red flannel gown. Florence had evidently redressed herself rather sketchily and covered the deficiencies with an alpaca overall. Her hair was trapped in a tortuous system of tin curlers.

'Please sit down,' Alleyn said. 'I'm sorry about dragging you in again. It won't, I hope, be for long.'

Florence and Ninn, both looking angry and extremely reluctant and each cutting the other dead, sat on opposite sides of the table, leaving empty chairs between themselves and their nearest neighbours.

'Where's Dr Harkness, Fox?'

'Back in the conservatory, I believe, sir. We thought it better not to rouse him.'

'I'm afraid we must do so now.'

Curtains had been drawn across the conservatory wall. Fox disappeared behind them. Stertorous, unlovely and protesting noises were heard and presently he reappeared with Dr Harkness, now bloated with sleep and very tousled.

'Oh, torment!' he said in a thick voice. 'Oh, hideous condition!'

'Would you,' Alleyn asked, 'be very kind and see if you think Mr Templeton is up to joining us? If there's any doubt about it we won't disturb him. He's in the study.'

'Very well,' said Dr Harkness, trying to flatten his hair with both hands. 'Never, never, never, any of you, chase up four whiskies with three glasses of champagne. Don't *do it*!' he added furiously as if somebody had shown signs of taking this action. He went out.

'We'll wait,' Alleyn said composedly, 'for Mr Templeton,' and arranged his papers.

Warrender cleared his throat. 'Don't like the look of sawbones,' he said.

'Poor pet,' Bertie sighed. 'And yet I almost wish I were in his boots. A pitiable but *not* unenviable condition.'

'Bad show!' Warrender said. 'Fellar's on duty.'

'Are you true?' Gantry asked suddenly, gazing at Warrender with a kind of devotion.

'I beg your pardon, sir?'

Gantry clasped his hands and said ecstatically: 'One would never dare! Never! And yet people say one's productions tend towards caricature! You shall give them the lie in their teeth, Colonel. In your own person you shall refute them.'

'I'm damned if I know what you're talking about, Gantry, but if you're trying to be abusive . . .'

' "No abuse," ' Alleyn quoted unexpectedly. He was reading his notes. ' "No abuse in the world: no, faith, boys, none." '

They stared at him. Gantry, thrown off his stride, looked round the table as if calling attention to Alleyn's eccentricity.

Pinky, greatly disconcerted, had opened her mouth to reply but was prevented by the appearance of Charles Templeton. He had come in with Dr Harkness. He was a bad colour, seemed somehow to have shrunk and walked like the old man he actually was. But his manner was contained and he smiled faintly at them.

Alleyn got up and went to him. 'He's all right,' Dr Harkness said. 'He'll do. Won't you, Charles?'

'I'll do,' Charles repeated. 'Much better.'

'Would you rather sit in a more comfortable chair?' Alleyn suggested. 'As you see, we are making free with your dining-room table.'

'Of course. I hope you've got everything you want. I'll join you.'

He took the nearest chair. Richard had got up and now, gripping Charles's shoulders, leant over him. Charles turned his head and looked up at him. During that moment, Alleyn thought, he saw a resemblance.

Richard said: 'Are you well enough for all this?'

'Yes, yes. Perfectly.'

Richard returned to his place, Dr Harkness and Fox took the two remaining seats, and the table was full.

Alleyn clasped his hands over his papers, said: 'Well, now,' and wishing, not for the first time, that he could find some other introductory formula, addressed himself to his uneasy audience.

Anelida thought: 'Here we all sit like a committee meeting and the chairman thinks one of us is a murderer.' Richard, very straight in his chair, looked at the table. When she stirred a little he reached for her hand, gripped it and let it go.

Alleyn was talking.

'. . . I would like to emphasize that until the pathologist's report comes in, there can be no certainty, but in the meantime I think we must try to arrive at a complete pattern of events. There are a number of points still to be settled and to that end I have kept you so long and asked you to come here. Fox?'

Fox had brought a small case with him. He now opened it, produced the empty scent bottle and laid it on the table.

' "Unguarded," ' Alleyn said and turned to Pinky. 'Your birthday present, wasn't it?'

Pinky said angrily: 'What have you done with the scent? Sorry,' she added. 'It doesn't matter, of course. It's only that – well, it was full this morning.'

'When you gave it to Miss Bellamy? In this room?'

'That's right.'

Alleyn turned to Florence. 'Can you help us?'

'I filled her spray from it,' Florence said mulishly.

'That wouldn't account for the lot, Florry,' Pinky pointed out.

'Was the spray empty?' Alleyn asked.

'Just about. She didn't mind mixing them.'

'And how much was left in the bottle?'

'*He* asked me all this,' Florence said, jerking her head at Fox.

'And now I do.'

'About that much,' she muttered, holding her thumb and forefinger an inch apart.

'About a quarter. And the spray was full?'

She nodded.

Fox, with the expertise of a conjuror, produced the scent spray and placed it by the bottle.

'And only about "that much," 'Alleyn pointed out, 'is now in the spray. So we've got pretty well three-quarters of this large bottle of scent to account for, haven't we?'

'I fail utterly,' Warrender began, 'to see what you think you're driving at.'

'Perhaps you can help. I understand, sir, that you actually used this thing earlier in the day.'

'Not on myself, God damn it!' Warrender ejaculated and then shot an uneasy glance at Charles Templeton.

Gantry gave a snort of delight.

'On Miss Bellamy?' Alleyn suggested.

'Naturally.'

'And did you happen to notice how much was left?'

'It was over three-quarters full. What!' Warrender demanded, appealing to Charles.

'I didn't notice,' he said, and put his hand over his eyes.

'Do you mind telling me, sir, how you came to do this?'

'Not a bit: why should I?' Warrender rejoined, and with every appearance of exquisite discomfort added: 'She asked me to. Didn't she, Charles?'

He nodded.

Alleyn pressed for more detail and got an awkward account of the scene with a grudging confirmation from Florence and a leaden one from Charles.

'Did you use a great deal of the scent?' he asked.

'Fair amount. She *asked* me to,' Warrender angrily repeated.

Charles shuddered and Alleyn said: 'It's very strong, isn't it? Even the empty bottle seems to fill the room if one takes the stopper out.'

'Don't!' Charles exclaimed. But Alleyn had already removed it. The smell, ponderable, sweet and improper, was disturbingly strong.

'Extraordinary!' Gantry ejaculated. 'She only wore it for an afternoon and yet – the association.'

'*Will* you be quiet, sir!' Warrender shouted. 'My God, what sort of a cad do you call yourself? Can't you see . . .' He made a jerky, ineloquent gesture.

Alleyn replaced the stopper.

'Did you, do you think,' he asked Warrender, 'use so much that the spray could then accommodate what was left in the bottle?'

'I wouldn't have thought so.'

'No,' said Florence.

'And even if it was filled up again, the spray itself now only contains about that same amount. Which means, to insist on the point, that somehow or another three-quarters of the whole amount of scent has disappeared.'

'That's impossible,' Pinky said bluntly. 'Unless it was spilt.'

'No,' said Florence again. Alleyn turned to her.

'And the spray and bottle were on the dressing-table when you found Miss Bellamy?'

'Must of been. I didn't stop,' Florence said bitterly, 'to tidy up the dressing-table.'

'And the tin of Slaypest was on the floor?'

Fox placed the tin beside the other exhibits and they looked at it with horror.

'Yes?' Alleyn asked.

'Yes,' said Warrender, Harkness and Gantry together and Charles suddenly beat with his hand on the table.

'Yes, yes, *yes*,' he said violently. 'My God, must we have all this!'

'I'm very sorry, sir, but I'm afraid we must.'

'Look here,' Gantry demanded, 'are you suggesting that – what the hell are you suggesting?'

'I suggest nothing. I simply want to try and clear up a rather odd state of affairs. Can anybody offer an explanation?'

'She herself – Mary – must have done something about it. Knocked it over perhaps.'

'Which?' Alleyn asked politely. 'The bottle or the spray?'

'I don't know,' Gantry said irritably. 'How should I? The spray, I suppose. And then filled it up.'

'There's no sign of a spill, as Florence has pointed out.'

'I know!' Bertie Saracen began. 'You think it was used as a sort of blind *to* – to . . .'

'To what, Mr Saracen?'

'Ah, no,' Bertie said in a hurry. 'I – thought – no, I was muddling. I don't know.'

'I think I do,' Pinky said, and turned very white.

'Yes?' Alleyn said.

'I won't go on. I can't. It's not clear enough. Please.'

She looked Alleyn straight in the eyes. 'Mr Alleyn,' Pinky said. 'If you prod and insist you'll winkle out all sorts of odd bits of information about – about arguments and rows. Inside the theatre and out. Mostly inside. Like a good many other actresses, Mary did throw the odd temperament. She threw one,' Pinky went on against an almost palpable surge of consternation among her listeners, 'for a matter of that, this morning.'

'*Pinky!*' Gantry warned her on a rising note.

'Timmy, why not? I dare say Mr Alleyn already knows,' she said wearily.

'How very wise you are,' Alleyn exclaimed. 'Thank you for it. Yes, we do know, in a piecemeal sort of way, as you've suggested, that there were ructions. We *have* winkled them out. We know, for instance, that there was a difference of opinion, on professional grounds, here in this room. This morning. We know it was resurrected with other controversial matters during the party. We know that you and Mr Saracen were involved and when I say that, I'm quite sure you're both much too sensible to suppose I'm suggesting anything more. Fox and I speak only of facts. We'll be nothing but grateful if you can help us discard as many as possible of the awkward load of facts that we've managed to accumulate.'

'All this,' Gantry said, 'sounds mighty fine. We're on foreign ground, Pinky, and may well make fools of ourselves. You watch your step, my girl.'

'I don't believe you,' she said, and still looking full at Alleyn: 'What do you want to know?'

'First of all, what your particular row was about.'

She said: 'All right with you, Bertie?'

'Oh, Christmas!' he said. 'I suppose so.'

'You're a fool, Bertie,' Timon Gantry said angrily.

'These things can't be controlled. You don't know where you'll fetch up.'

'But then you see, Timmy, dear, I never do,' Bertie rejoined with a sad little giggle.

Gantry rounded on Pinky Cavendish. 'You might care to remember that other people are involved.'

'I don't forget, Timmy, I promise you.' She turned to Alleyn. 'This morning's row,' she said, 'was because I told Mary I was going to play the lead in a new play. She felt I was deserting her. Later on, during the party when we were all' – she indicated the conservatory – 'in there, she brought it up again.'

'And was still very angry?'

Pinky looked unhappily at Charles. 'It was pretty hot while it lasted. Those sorts of dusts-up always were, with Mary.'

'You were involved, Mr Saracen?'

'Not 'alf!' Bertie said and explained why.

'And you, Mr Gantry?'

'Very well – yes. In so far as I am to produce the comedy.'

'But you copped it both ways, Timmy,' Bertie pointed out with some relish. 'You were involved in the other one, too. About Dicky's "different" play and Anelida being asked to do the lead. She was angrier about that than anything. She was livid.'

'Mr Alleyn knows,' Anelida said, and they looked uneasily at her.

'Never mind, dear,' Gantry said rather bossily. 'None of this need concern you. Don't get involved.'

'She *is* involved,' Richard said, looking at her. 'With me. Permanently, I hope.'

'*Really?*' Pinky cried out in her warmest voice and beamed at Anelida. 'How lovely! Bertie! Timmy! Isn't that lovely! Dicky, *darling!* Anelida!'

They made enthusiastic noises. It was impossible, Anelida found, not to be moved by their friendliness but it struck her as quite extraordinary that they could switch so readily to this congratulatory vein. She caught a look of – what? Surprise? Resignation? in Alleyn's eye and was astounded when he gave her the faintest shadow of a wink.

'Delightful though it is to refresh ourselves with this news,' he said, 'I'm afraid I must bring you back to the matter in hand. How did the row in the conservatory arise?'

Pinky and Bertie gave him a look in which astonishment mingled with reproach.

Richard said quickly: 'Mary came into the conservatory while we were discussing the casting of my play, *Husbandry in Heaven*. I should have told her – warned her. I didn't and she felt I hadn't been frank about it.'

'I'm sorry, but I shall have to ask you exactly what she said.'

He saw at once that Pinky, Saracen and Gantry were going to refuse. They looked quickly at one another and Gantry said rather off-handedly: 'I imagine none of us remembers in any detail. When Mary threw a temperament she said all sorts of things that everybody knew she didn't mean.'

'Did she, for instance, make threats of any sort?'

Gantry stood up. 'For the last time,' he said, 'I warn you all that you're asking for every sort of trouble if you let yourselves be led into making ill-considered statements about matters that are entirely beside the point. For the last time I suggest that you consider your obligations to your profession and your careers. Keep your tongues behind your teeth or, by God, you'll regret it.'

Bertie, looking frightened, said to Pinky: 'He's right, you know. Or isn't he?'

'I suppose so,' she agreed unhappily. 'There is a limit – I suppose. All the same . . .'

'If ever you've trusted yourself to my direction,' Gantry said, 'you'll do so now.'

'All right.' She looked at Alleyn. 'Sorry.'

Alleyn said: 'Then I must ask Colonel Warrender and Mr Templeton. Did Miss Bellamy utter threats of any sort?'

Warrender said: 'In my opinion, Charles, this may be a case for a solicitor. One doesn't know what turn things may take. Meantime, wait and see, isn't it?'

'Very well,' Charles said. 'Very well.'

'Mr Dakers?' Alleyn asked.

'I'm bound by the general decision,' Richard said and Anelida, after a troubled look at him, added reluctantly:

'And I by yours.'

'In that case,' Alleyn said, 'there's only one thing to be done. We must appeal to the sole remaining witness.'

'Who the hell's that!' Warrender barked out.

'Will you see if you can get him, Fox? Mr Montague Marchant,' said Alleyn.

IV

On Pinky and Bertie's part little attempt was made to disguise their consternation. It was obvious that they desired, more than anything else, an opportunity to consult together. Gantry, however, merely folded his arms, lay back in his chair and looked at the ceiling. He might have been waiting to rise in protest at a conference of Actors' Equity. Warrender, for his part, resembled a senior member at a club committee meeting. Charles fetched a heavy sigh and rested his head on his hand.

Fox went out of the room. As he opened the door into the hall a grandfather clock at the foot of the stairs was striking eleven. It provoked an involuntary ejaculation from the persons Alleyn had brought together round the table. Several of them glanced in despair at their watches.

'In the meantime,' Alleyn said, 'shall we try to clear up the position of Mr Richard Dakers?'

Anelida's heart suddenly thudded against her ribs as if drawing attention to its disregarded sovereignty. She had time to think: 'I'm involved, almost without warning, in a monstrous situation. I'm committed, absolutely, to a man of whom I know next to nothing. It's a kind of dedication and I'm not prepared for it.' She turned to look at Richard and, at once, knew that her allegiance, active or helpless, was irrevocable. 'So this,' Anelida thought in astonishment, 'is what it's like to be in love.'

Alleyn, aware of the immediate reactions, saw Old Ninn's hands move convulsively in her lap. He saw Florence look at her with a flash of something that might have been triumph and he saw the colour fade unevenly from Warrender's heavy face.

He went over the ground again up to the time of Richard's final return to the house.

'As you will see,' he said, 'there are blank passages. We don't know what passed between Mr Dakers and Miss Bellamy in her room. We do know that, whatever it was, it seemed to distress him.

We know he then went out and walked about Chelsea. We know he returned. We don't know why.'

'I wanted,' Richard said, 'to pick up a copy of my play.'

'Good. Why didn't you say so before?'

'I clean forgot,' he said and looked astonished.

'Do you now remember what else you did?'

'I went up to my old study to get it.'

'And did you do anything else while you were there?'

There was no answer. Alleyn said: 'You wrote a letter, didn't you?'

Richard stared at him with a sort of horror. 'How do you – why should you . . . ?' He made a small desperate gesture and petered out.

'To whom?'

'It was private. I prefer not to say.'

'Where is it, now? You've had no opportunity to post it.'

'I – haven't got it.'

'What have you done with it?'

'I got rid of it.' Richard raised his voice. 'I hope it's destroyed. It had nothing whatever to do with all this. I've told you it was private.'

'If that's true I can promise you it will remain so. Will you tell me – in private – what it was about?'

Richard looked at him, hesitated, and then said: 'I'm sorry. I can't.'

Alleyn drew a folded paper from his pocket. 'Will you read this, if you please? Perhaps you would rather take it to the light.'

'I can . . . All right,' Richard said. He took the paper, left the table and moved over to a wall-lamp. The paper rustled as he opened it. He glanced at it, crushed it in his hand, strode to the far end of the table and flung it down in front of Warrender.

'Did you *have* to do this?' he said. 'My God, what sort of a man are you!' He went back to his place beside Anelida.

Warrender, opening and closing his hands, sheet-white and speaking in an unrecognizable voice, said: 'I don't understand. I've done nothing. What do you mean?'

His hand moved shakily towards the inside pocket of his coat. 'No! It's not . . . It can't be.'

'Colonel Warrender,' Alleyn said to Richard, 'has not shown me the letter. I came by its content in an entirely different way. The thing I have shown you is a transcription. The original, I imagine, is still in his pocket.'

Warrender and Richard wouldn't look at each other. Warrender said: 'Then how the hell . . .' And stopped.

'Evidently,' Alleyn said, 'the transcription is near enough to the original. I don't propose at the moment to make it generally known. I will only put it to you that when you, Mr Dakers, returned the second time, you went to your study, wrote the original of this letter and subsequently, when you were lying on the sofa in the drawing-room, passed it to Colonel Warrender, saying, for my benefit, that you had forgotten to post it for him. Do you agree?'

'Yes.'

'I suggest that it refers to whatever passed between you and Mrs Templeton when you were alone with her in her room a few minutes before she died and that you wished to make Colonel Warrender read it. I'm still ready to listen to any statement you may care to make to me in private.'

To Anelida the silence seemed interminable.

'Very well,' Alleyn said. 'We shall have to leave it for the time being.'

None of them looked at Richard. Anelida suddenly and horribly remembered something she had once heard Alleyn tell her uncle. 'You always know, in a capital charge, if the jury are going to bring in a verdict of guilty: they never look at the accused when they come back.' With a sense of doing something momentous she turned, looked Richard full in the face and found she could smile at him.

'It'll be all right,' he said gently.

'All right!' Florence bitterly ejaculated. 'It doesn't strike me as being all right, and I wonder you've the nerve to say so!'

As if Florence had put a match to her, Old Ninn exploded into fury. 'You're a bad girl, Floy,' she said, trembling very much and leaning across the table. 'Riddled through and through with wickedness and jealousy and always have been.'

'Thank you very much, I'm sure, Mrs Plumtree,' Florence countered with a shrill outbreak of laughter.

'Everyone knows where your favour lies, Mrs Plumtree, especially when you've had a drop of port wine. You wouldn't stop short of murder to back it up.'

'Ninn,' Richard said, before she could speak, 'for the love of Mike, darling, shut up.'

She reached out her small knotted hands to Charles Templeton. 'You speak for him, sir. Speak for him.'

Charles said gently: 'You're making too much of this, Ninn. There's no need.'

'There shouldn't be the need!' she cried. 'And *she* knows it as well as I do.' She appealed to Alleyn. 'I've told you. *I've told you.* After Mr Richard came out I heard her. That wicked woman, there, knows as well as I do.' She pointed a gnarled finger at the spray gun. 'We heard her using that thing after everyone had warned her against it.'

'How do you know it was the spray gun, Ninn?'

'What else could it have been?'

Alleyn said: 'It might have been her scent, you know.'

'If it was! If it was, that makes no difference.'

'I'm afraid it would,' Alleyn said. 'If the scent spray had been filled up with Slaypest.'

CHAPTER 7

Re-entry of Mr Marchant

The scent spray, the bottle and the Slaypest tin had assumed star quality. There they stood in a neat row, three inarticulate objects, thrust into the spotlight. They might have been so many stagehands, yanked out of their anonymity and required to give an account of themselves before an unresponsive audience. They met with a frozen reception.

Timon Gantry was the first to speak. 'Have you,' he asked, 'any argument to support your extraordinary assumption?'

'I have,' Alleyn rejoined, 'but I don't propose to advance it in detail. You might call it a *reductio ad absurdum*. Nothing else fits. One hopes,' he added, 'that a chemical analysis of the scent spray will do something to support it. The supposition is based on a notion that while Mrs Templeton had very little reason, after what seems to have been a stormy interview, to deluge her plants and herself with insecticide, she may more reasonably be pictured as taking up her scent spray, and using that.'

'Not full on her face,' Bertie said unexpectedly. 'She'd never use it on her face. Not directly. Not after she was made up. Would she, Pinky? Pinky – would she?'

But Pinky was not listening to him. She was watching Alleyn.

'Well, anyway,' Bertie said crossly. 'She wouldn't.'

'Oh, yes, she would, Mr Saracen,' Florence said tartly.

'And did. Quite regular. Standing far enough off to get the fine spray only, which was what she done, as the colonel and Mr Templeton will bear me out, this afternoon.'

'The point,' Alleyn said, 'is well taken, but it doesn't, I think, affect the argument. Shall we leave it for the time being? I'm following, by the way, a very unorthodox line over this inquiry and I see no reason for not telling you why. Severally, I believe you will all go on withholding information that may be crucial. Together I have hopes that you may find these tactics impracticable.' And while they still gaped at him he added: 'I may be wrong about this, of course, but it does seem to me that each of you, with one exception, is most mistakenly concealing something. I say mistakenly because I don't for a moment believe that there has been any collusion in this business. I believe that one of you, under pressure of an extraordinary emotional upheaval, has acted in a solitary and an extraordinary way. It's my duty to find out who this person is. So let's press on, shall we?' He looked at Charles. 'There's a dictionary of poisons in Mr Dakers's former study. I believe it belongs to you, sir.'

Charles lifted a hand, saw that it trembled, and lowered it again. 'Yes,' he said. 'I bought it a week ago. I wanted to look up plant sprays.'

'Oh, my goodness me!' Bertie ejaculated and stared at him. There was a general shocked silence.

'This specific spray?' Alleyn asked, pointing to the Slaypest.

'Yes. It gives the formula. I wanted to look it up.'

'For God's sake, Charles,' Warrender ejaculated, 'why the devil can't you make yourself understood?' Charles said nothing and he waved his hands at Alleyn. 'He was worried about the damned muck!' he said. 'Told Mary. Showed it . . .'

'Yes?' Alleyn said as he came to a halt. 'Showed it to whom?'

'To me, blast it! We'd been trying to persuade her not to use the stuff. Gave it to me to read.'

'Did you read it?'

''Course I did. Lot of scientific mumbo-jumbo but it showed how dangerous it was.'

'What did you do with the book?'

'*Do* with it? I dunno. Yes, I do, though. I gave it to Florence. Asked her to get Mary to look at it. Didn't I, Florence?'

'I don't,' said Florence, 'remember anything about it, sir. You might have.'

'Please try to remember,' Alleyn said. 'Did you, in fact, show the book to Mrs Templeton?'

'Not me. She wouldn't have given me any thanks.' She slewed round in her chair and looked at Old Ninn. 'I remember now. I showed it to Mrs Plumtree. Gave it to her.'

'Well, Ninn? What did you do with the book?'

Old Ninn glared at him. 'Put it by,' she said. 'It was unwholesome.'

'Where?'

'I don't recollect.'

'In the upstairs study?'

'Might have been. I don't recollect.'

'So much for the book,' Alleyn said wryly, and turned to Warrender. 'You, sir, tell us that you actually used the scent spray, lavishly, on Mrs Templeton before the party. There were no ill-effects. What did you do after that?'

'Do? Nothing. I went out.'

'Leaving Mr and Mrs Templeton alone together?'

'Yes. At least . . . ' His eyes slewed round to look at her. 'There was Florence.'

'No, there wasn't. If you'll pardon my mentioning it, sir,' Florence again intervened. 'I left, just after you did, not being required any further.'

'Do you agree?' Alleyn asked Charles Templeton. He drew his hand across his eyes.

'I? Oh, yes. I think so.'

'Do you mind telling me what happened then? Between you and your wife?'

'We talked for a moment or two. Not long.'

'About?'

'I asked her not to use the scent I'm afraid I was in a temper about it.' He glanced at Pinky. 'I'm sorry, Pinky, I just – didn't like it. I expect my taste is hopelessly old fashioned.'

'That's all right, Charles. My God,' Pinky added in a low voice, 'I never want to smell it again, myself, as long as I live.'

'Did Mrs Templeton agree not to use it again?'

'No,' he said at once. 'She didn't. She thought me unreasonable.'

'Did you talk about anything else?'

'About nothing that I care to recall.'

'Is that final?'

'Final,' Charles said.

'Did it concern, in some way, Mr Dakers and Colonel Warrender?'

'Damn it!' Warrender shouted. 'He's said he's not going to tell you, isn't it!'

'It did not concern them,' Charles said.

'Where did you go when this conversation ended?'

'I went downstairs to my study. Richard came in at about that time and was telephoning. We stayed there until the first guests arrived.'

'And you, Colonel Warrender? Where were you at this time? What did you do when you left the bedroom?'

'Ah – I was in the drawing-room. She – ah – Mary – came in. She wanted a rearrangement of the tables. Gracefield and the other fella did it and she and I had a drink.'

'Did she seem quite herself, did you think?'

'Rather nervy. Bit on edge.'

'Why?'

'Been a trying day, isn't it?'

'Anything in particular?'

He glanced at Richard. 'No,' he said. 'Nothing else.'

Fox returned. 'Mr Marchant will be here in about a quarter of an hour, sir,' he said.

There were signs of consternation from Pinky, Bertie and Timon Gantry.

'Right,' Alleyn got up, walked to the far end of the table and picked up the crumpled paper that still lay where Richard had thrown it down. 'I must ask Colonel Warrender and Mr Dakers to give me a word or two in private. Perhaps we may use the study.'

They both rose with the same abrupt movement and followed him from the room, stiffly erect.

He ushered them into the study and turned to Fox who had come into the hall.

'I'd better take this one solus, I think, Fox. Will you get the exhibits sent at once for analysis. Say it's first priority and we're looking for a trace of Slaypest in the scent spray. They needn't expect to find more than a trace, I fancy. I want the result as soon as possible. Then go back to the party in there. See you later.'

In Charles Templeton's study, incongruously friendly and comfortable, Warrender and Richard Dakers faced Alleyn, still not looking at each other.

Alleyn said: 'I've asked you in here, without witnesses, to confirm or deny the conclusion I have drawn from the case-history, as far as it goes. Which is not by any means all the way. If I'm wrong, one or both of you can have a shot at knocking me down or hitting me across the face or performing any other of the conventional gestures. But I don't advise you to try.'

They stared at him apparently in horrified astonishment.

'Well,' he said, 'here goes. My idea, such as it is, is based on this business of the letter, which, since you seem to accept my pot shot at it, runs like this.'

He smoothed out the crumpled sheet of paper. 'It's pieced together, by the way,' he said, 'from the impression left on the blotting-paper.' He looked at Richard. 'The original was written, I believe, by you to Mrs Templeton when you returned, finally, to the house. I'm going to read this transcription aloud. If it's wrong anywhere, I hope you'll correct me.'

Warrender said: 'There's no need.'

'Perhaps not. Would you prefer to show me the original?'

With an air of diffidence that sat very ill on him, Warrender appealed to Richard. 'Whatever you say,' he muttered.

Richard said: 'Very well! Go on. Go on. Show him'

Warrender put his hand inside his coat and drew out an envelope. He dropped it on Charles Templeton's desk, crossed to the fireplace and stood there with his back turned to them.

Alleyn picked up the envelope. The word 'Mary' was written on it in green ink. He took out the enclosure and laid his transcription beside it on the desk. As he read it through to himself the room seemed monstrously quiet. The fire settled in the grate. A car or two drove past and the clock in the hall told the half-hour.

'*I've come back,*' Alleyn read, '*to say that it would be no use my pretending I haven't been given a terrible shock and that I can't get it sorted out but I'm sure it will be better if we don't meet. I can't think clearly now but at least I know I'll never forgive your treatment of Anelida this afternoon. I should have been told everything from the beginning. R.*'

He folded the two papers and put them aside. 'So they do correspond,' he said. 'And the handwriting is Mr Dakers's.'

Neither Richard nor Warrender moved nor spoke.

'I think,' Alleyn said, 'that you came back for the last time, you went up to your study and wrote this letter with the intention of putting it under her door. When you were about to do so you heard voices in the room, since two of my men were working there. So you came downstairs and were prevented from going out by the constable on duty. It was then that you came into the room where I was interviewing the others. The letter was in your breast pocket. You wanted to get rid of it and you wanted Colonel Warrender to know what was in it. So you passed it to him when you were lying on the sofa in the drawing-room. Do you agree?'

Richard nodded and turned away.

'This evening,' Alleyn went on, 'after Mr Dakers left the Pegasus bookshop, you, Colonel Warrender, also paid a call on Octavius Browne. Dusk had fallen but you were standing in the window when Octavius came in and seeing you against it he mistook you for his earlier visitor, who he thought must have returned. He was unable to say why he made this mistake, but I think I can account for it. Your heads are very much the same shape. The relative angles and distances from hairline to the top of the nose, from there to the tip and from the tip to the chin are almost identical. Seen in silhouette with the other features obliterated, your profiles must be strikingly alike. In full-face the resemblance disappears. Colonel Warrender has far greater width and a heavier jawline.'

They were facing him now. He looked from one to the other.

'In these respects,' he said, 'Mr Dakers, I think, takes after his mother.'

II

'Well,' Alleyn said at last, after a long silence, 'I'm glad, at least, that it seems I am not going to be knocked down.'

Warrender said: 'I've nothing to say. Unless it's to point out that, as things have come about, I've had no opportunity to speak to' – he lifted his head – 'to my son.'

Richard said: 'I don't want to discuss it. I should have been told from the beginning.'

'Whereas,' Alleyn said, 'you were told, weren't you, by your mother this afternoon. You went upstairs with her when you returned from the Pegasus and she told you then.'

'*Why!*' Warrender cried out. 'Why, why, *why*?'

'She was angry,' Richard said. 'With me.' He looked at Alleyn. 'You've heard or guessed most of it, apparently. She thought I'd conspired against her.'

'Yes?'

'Well – that's all. That's how it was.'

Alleyn waited. Richard drove his hands through his hair.

'All right!' he cried out. 'All right! I'll tell you. I suppose I've got to, haven't I? She accused me of ingratitude and disloyalty. I said I considered I owed her no more than I had already paid. I wouldn't have said that if she hadn't insulted Anelida. Then she came quite close to me and – it was horrible – I could see a nerve jumping under her cheek. She kept repeating that I owed her everything – everything, and that I'd insulted her by going behind her back. Then I said she'd no right to assume a controlling interest in either my friendships or my work. She said she had every right. And then it all came out. Everything. It happened because of our anger. We were both very angry. When she'd told me, she laughed as if she'd scored with the line of climax in a big scene. If she hadn't done that I might have felt some kind of compassion or remorse or something. I didn't. I felt cheated and sick and empty. I went downstairs and out into the streets and walked about trying to find an appropriate emotion. There was nothing but a sort of faint disgust.' He moved away and then turned on Alleyn. 'But I didn't murder my' – he caught his breath – 'my brand-new mother. I'm not, it appears, that kind of bastard.'

Warrender said: 'For God's sake, Dicky!'

'Just for the record,' Richard said, '*were* there two people called Dakers? A young married couple, killed in a car on the Riviera? Australians, I've always been given to understand.'

'It's – it's a family name. My mother was a Dakers.'

'I see,' Richard said. 'I just wondered. It didn't occur to you to marry her, evidently.' He stopped short and a look of horror crossed his face. 'I'm sorry! I'm sorry!' he cried out. 'Forgive me, Maurice, it wasn't I who said that.'

'My dear chap, of course I wanted to marry her. She wouldn't have it! She was at the beginning of her career. What could I give her? A serving ensign on a very limited allowance. She – naturally – she wasn't prepared to throw up her career and follow the drum.'

'And – Charles?'

'He was in a different position. Altogether.'

'Rich? Able to keep her in the style to which she would like to become accustomed?'

'There's no need,' Warrender muttered, 'to put it like that.'

'Poor Charles!' Richard said and then suddenly: 'Did he know?'

Warrender turned a painful crimson. 'No.' he said. 'It was – it was all over by then.'

'Did he believe in the Dakers story?'

'I think,' Warrender said after a pause, 'he believed everything Mary told him.'

'Poor Charles!' Richard repeated, and then turned on Alleyn. 'He's not going to be told? Not now! It'd kill him. There's no need – is there?'

'None,' Alleyn said, 'that I can see.'

'And you!' Richard demanded of Warrender.

'Oh, for God's sake, Dicky!'

'No, Naturally. Not you.'

There was a long silence.

'I remember,' Richard said at last, 'that she once told me it was you who brought them together. What ambivalent roles you both contrived to play. Restoration Comedy at its most elaborate.'

Evidently they had forgotten Alleyn. For the first time they looked fully at each other.

'Funny,' Richard said. 'I have wondered if Charles was my father. Some pre-marital indiscretion, I thought it might have been. I fancied I saw a likeness – the family one, of course. You and Charles are rather alike, aren't you? I must say I never quite believed in the Dakers. But why did it never occur to me that she was my mother? It really was very clever of her to put herself so magnificently out of bounds.'

'I don't know,' Warrender exclaimed, 'what to say to you. There's nothing I can say.'

'Never mind.'

'It need make no difference. To your work. Or to your marrying.'

'I really don't know how Anelida will feel about it. Unless . . .' He turned, as if suddenly aware of him, to Alleyn. 'Unless, of course Mr Alleyn is going to arrest me for matricide, which will settle everything very neatly, won't it?'

'I shouldn't,' Alleyn said, 'depend upon it. Suppose you set about clearing yourself if you can. Can you?'

'How the hell do I know? What am I supposed to have done?'

'It's more a matter of finding out what you couldn't have done. Where did you lunch? Here?'

'No. At the Garrick. It was a business luncheon.'

'And after that?'

'I went to my flat and did some work. I'd got a typist in.'

'Until when?'

'Just before six. I was waiting for a long-distance call from Edinburgh. I kept looking at the time because I was running late. I was meant to be here at six to organize the drinks. At last I fixed it up for the call to be transferred to this number. As it was I ran late and Mary – and she was coming downstairs. The call came through at a quarter to seven just as I arrived.'

'Where did you take it?'

'Here in the study. Charles was there. He looked ill and I was worried about him. He didn't seem to want to talk. I kept getting cut off. It was important, and I had to wait. She – wasn't very pleased about that. The first people were arriving when I'd finished.'

'So what did you do?'

'Went into the drawing-room with Charles and did my stuff.'

'Had you brought her some Parma violets?'

'I? No. She hated violets.'

'Did you see them in her room?'

'I didn't go up to her room. I've told you – I was here in the study.'

'When had you last been in her room?'

'This morning.'

'Did you visit it between then and the final time when you returned from the Pegasus and this disturbing scene took place?'

'I've told you. How could I? I . . . ' His voice changed. 'I was with Anelida until she left and I followed her into the Pegasus.'

'Well,' Alleyn said after a pause, 'if all this is provable, and I don't see why it shouldn't be, you're in the clear.'

Warrender gave a sharp ejaculation and turned quickly, but Richard said flatly: 'I don't understand.'

'If our reading of the facts is the true one, this crime was to all intents and purposes committed between the time (somewhere about six o'clock) when Mrs Templeton was sprayed with scent by Colonel Warrender and the time fixed by a Press photographer at twenty-five minutes to eight when she returned to her room with you. She never left her room and died in it a few minutes after you had gone.'

Richard flinched at the last phrase but seemed to have paid little attention to the earlier part. For the first time, he was looking at his father who had turned his back to them.

'Colonel Warrender,' Alleyn said, 'why did you go to the Pegasus?'

Without moving he said: 'Does it matter? I wanted to get things straight. With the gel.'

'But you didn't see her?'

'No.'

'Maurice,' Richard said abruptly.

Colonel Warrender faced him.

'I call you that still,' Richard went on. 'I suppose it's not becoming but I can't manage anything else. There are all sorts of adjustments to be arranged, aren't there? I know I'm not making this easy for either of us. You see one doesn't know how one's meant to behave. But I hope in time to do better: you'll have to give me time.'

'I'll do that,' Warrender said unevenly.

He made a slight movement as if to hold out his hand, glanced at Alleyn and withdrew it.

'I think,' Alleyn said, 'that I should get on with my job. I'll let you know when we need you.'

And he went out, leaving them helplessly together.

In the hall he encountered Fox.

'Peculiar party in there,' he said. 'Boy meets father. Both heavily embarrassed. They manage these things better in France. What goes on at your end of the table?'

'I came out to tell you, sir. Mr Templeton's come over very poorly again, and Dr Harkness thinks he's had about as much as he can take. He's lying down in the drawing-room, but as soon as he can manage it the doctor wants to get him into bed. The idea is to make one up in his study and save the stairs. I thought the best thing would be to let those two – Florence and Mrs Plumtree – fix it up. The doctor'll help him when the time comes.'

'Yes. All right. What a hell of a party this is, by and large. All right. But they'll have to bung the mixed-up playwright and his custom-built poppa out of it. Where? Into mama-deceased's boudoir, I suppose. Or they can rejoin that Goon show round the dining-room table. *I* don't know. Nobody tells me a thing. What else?'

'None of them will own up to knowing anything about the Parma violets. They all say she had no time for violets.'

'Blast and stink! Then who the devil put them on her dressing-table? The caterer in a fit of frustrated passion? Why the devil should we be stuck with a bunch of Parma violets wilting on our plates.'

Like Scheherazade, Fox discreetly fell silent.

'Pardon me, sir, but did I hear you mention violets?'

It was Gracefield, wan in the countenance, who had emerged from the far end of the hall.

'You did indeed,' Alleyn said warmly.

'If it is of any assistance, sir, a bunch of violets was brought in immediately prior to the reception. I admitted the gentleman myself, sir, and he subsequently presented them to madam on the first floor landing.'

'You took his name, I hope, Gracefield?'

'Quite so, sir. It was the elderly gentleman from the bookshop. The name is Octavius Browne.'

III

'And what the merry hell,' Alleyn ejaculated when Gracefield had withdrawn, 'did Octavius think he was up to, prancing about with violets at that hour of the day? Damnation, I'll have to find out, and Marchant's due any minute. Come on.'

They went out at the front door. Light still glowed behind the curtains at the Pegasus.

'You hold the fort here, Fox, for five minutes. Let them get Templeton settled down in the study and, if Marchant turns up, keep him till I'm back. Don't put him in with that horde of extroverts in the dining-room. Save him up. What a go!'

He rang the bell and Octavius opened the door.

'You again!' he said. 'How late! I thought you were Anelida.'

'Well, I'm not and I'm sorry it's late but you'll have to let me in.'

'Very well,' Octavius said, standing aside. 'What's up, now?'

'Why,' Alleyn asked, as soon as the door was shut, 'did you take violets to Mrs Templeton?'

Octavius blushed. 'A man with a handcart,' he said, 'went past the window. They came from the Channel Islands.'

'I don't give a damn where they came from. It's where they went to that matters. When did the cart go past?'

Octavius, disconcerted and rather huffy, was bustled into telling his story. Anelida had sent him downstairs while she got ready for the party. He was fretful because they'd been asked for half-past six and it was now twenty-five to seven and he didn't believe her story of the need to arrive late. He saw the handcart with the Parma violets and remembered that in his youth these flowers had been considered appropriate adjuncts to ladies of the theatre. So he went out and bought some. He then, Alleyn gathered, felt shy about presenting them in front of Anelida. The door of Miss Bellamy's house was open. The butler was discernible in the hall. Octavius mounted the steps. 'After all,' he said, 'one preferred to give her the opportunity of attaching them in advance if she chose to do so.'

He was in the act of handing them over to Gracefield when he heard a commotion on the first landing and a moment later Miss Bellamy shouted out at the top of her voice: 'Which only shows how wrong you were. You can get out whenever you like, my friend, and the sooner the better.'

For a moment Octavius was extremely flustered, imagining that he himself was thus addressed but the next second she appeared above him on the stairs. She stopped short and gazed down at him in astonishment. 'A vision,' Octavius said. 'Rose-coloured or more accurately, geranium, but with the air, I must confess, of a Fury.'

This impression, however, was almost at once dissipated. Miss Bellamy seemed to hesitate, Gracefield murmured an explanation which Octavius himself elaborated. 'And then, you know,' he said, 'suddenly she was all graciousness. Overwhelmingly so. She' – he blushed again – 'asked me to come up and I went. I presented my little votive offering. And then, in point of fact, she invited me into her room: a pleasing and Gallic informality. I was not unmoved by it. She laid the flowers on her dressing-table and told me she had just given an old bore the sack. Those were her words. I gathered that it was somebody who had been in her service for a long period. What did you say?'

'Nothing. Go on. You interest me strangely.'

'Do I? Well. At that juncture there were sounds of voices downstairs – the door, naturally, remained open – and she said, "Wait a moment, will you?" And left me.'

'Well?' Alleyn said after a pause.

'Well, I did wait. Nothing happened. I bethought me of Nelly, who would surely be ready by now. Rightly or wrongly,' Octavius said, with a sidelong look at Alleyn,

'I felt that Nelly would be not entirely in sympathy with my impulsive little *sortie* and I was therefore concerned to return before I could be missed. So I went downstairs and there *she* was, speaking to Colonel Warrender in the drawing-room. They paid no attention to me. I don't think they saw me. Warrender, I thought, looked very much put out. There seemed nothing to do but go away. So I went. A curious and not unintriguing experience.'

'Thank you, Octavius,' Alleyn said, staring thoughtfully at him. 'Thank you very much. And now I, too, must leave you. Goodnight.'

As he went out he heard Octavius saying rather fretfully that he supposed he might as well go to bed.

A very grand car had drawn up beside Miss Bellamy's house and Mr Montague Marchant was climbing out of it. His blond head gleamed, his overcoat was impeccable and his face exceedingly pale.

'Wait,' he said to his chauffeur.

Alleyn introduced himself. The anticipated remark was punctually delivered.

'This is a terrible business,' said Mr Marchant.

'Very bad,' Alleyn said. 'Shall we go in?'

Fox was in the hall.

'I just don't quite understand,' Marchant said, 'why I've been sent for. Naturally, we – her management – want to give every assistance but at the same time . . . ' He waved his pearly gloves.

Alleyn said: 'It's very simple. There are one or two purely business matters to be settled and it looks as if you are our sole authority.'

'I should have thought . . .'

'Of course you would,' Alleyn rejoined. 'But there is some need for immediate action. Miss Bellamy has been murdered.'

Marchant unsteadily passed his hand over the back of his head. 'I don't believe you,' he said.

'You may as well, because it happens to be true. Would you like to take your coat off? No? Then, shall we go in?'

Fox said: 'We've moved into the drawing-room, sir, it being more comfortable. The doctor is with Mr Templeton but will be coming in later.'

'Where's Florence?'

'She helped Mrs Plumtree with the bed making and they're both waiting in the boudoir in case required.'

'Right. In here, if you will, Mr Marchant. I'll just have a look at the patient and then I'll join you.'

He opened the door. After a moment's hesitation, Marchant went through and Fox followed him.

Alleyn went to the study, tapped on the door and went in.

Charles was in bed, looking very drawn and anxious. Dr Harkness sat in a chair at a little distance, watching him. When he saw Alleyn he said: 'We can't have any further upsets.'

'I know,' Alleyn rejoined and walked over to the bed. 'I've only come in to inquire,' he said.

Charles whispered: 'I'm sorry about this. I'm all right. I could have carried on.'

'There's no need. We can manage.'

'There you are, Charles,' Harkness said. 'Stop fussing.'

'But I want to know, Harkness! How can I stop fussing! My God, what a thing to say! I want to know what they're thinking and saying. I've a right to know. Alleyn, for God's sake tell me. You don't suspect – anyone close to her, do you? I can stand anything but that. Not – not the boy?'

'As things stand,' Alleyn said, 'there's no case against him.'

'Ah!' Charles sighed and closed his eyes. 'Thank God for that.' He moved restlessly and his breath came short.

'It's all these allusions and hints and evasions . . . ' he began excitedly. 'Why can't I be told things! Why not? Do you suspect *me*! Do you? Then for Christ's sake let's have it and be done with it.'

Harkness came over to the bed. 'This won't do at all,' he said, and to Alleyn: 'Out.'

'Yes, of course,' Alleyn said, and went out. He heard Charles panting: 'But I *want* to talk to him,' and Harkness trying to reassure him.

When Marchant went into the drawing-room Timon Gantry, Colonel Warrender, Pinky Cavendish and Bertie Saracen were sitting disconsolately in armchairs before a freshly tended fire. Richard and Anelida were together at some remove from the others and PC Philpott attended discreedly in the background. When Marchant came in, Pinky and Bertie made a little dash at him and Richard stood up. Marchant kissed Pinky with ritual solemnity, squeezed Bertie's arm, nodded at Gantry, and advanced upon Richard with soft extended hand.

'Dear boy! 'he said. 'What can one say! Oh, my *dear* Dicky!'

Richard appeared to permit, rather than return, a long pressure of his hand. Marchant added a manly grip of his shoulder and moved on to acknowledge, more briefly, Anelida and Colonel Warrender. His prestige was unmistakable. He said any number of highly appropriate things. They listened to him dolefully and appeared to be relieved when at last Alleyn came in.

Alleyn said: 'Before going any further, Mr Marchant, I think I should make it quite clear that any questions I may put to you will be raised with the sole object of clearing innocent persons of suspicion and of helping towards the solution of an undoubted case of homicide. Mary Bellamy has been murdered; I believe by someone who is now in this house. You will understand that matters of personal consideration or professional reticence can't be allowed to obstruct an investigation of this sort. Any attempt to withhold information may have disastrous results. On the other hand, information that turns out to be irrelevant, as yours, of course, may, will be entirely wiped out. Is that understood?'

Gantry said: 'In my opinion, Monty, we should take legal advice.'

Marchant looked thoughtfully at him.

'You are at liberty to do so,' Alleyn said. 'You are also at liberty to refuse to answer any or all questions until the arrival of your solicitor. Suppose you hear the questions and then decide.'

Marchant examined his hands, lifted his gaze to Alleyn's face and said: 'What are they?'

There was a restless movement among the others.

'First. What exactly was Mrs Templeton's, or perhaps in this connection I should say Miss Bellamy's, position in the firm of Marchant & Company?'

Marchant raised his eyebrows. 'A leading and distinguished artist who played exclusively for our management.'

'Any business connection other than that?'

'Certainly,' he said at once. 'She had a controlling interest.'

'*Monty*! ' Bertie cried out.

'Dear boy, an examination of our shareholders list would give it.'

'Has she held this position for some time?'

'Since 1956. Before that it was vested in her husband, but he transferred his holdings to her in that year.'

'I had no idea he had financial interests in the theatre world.'

'These were his only ones, I believe. After the war we were in considerable difficulties. Like many other managements we were threatened with a complete collapse. You may say that he saved us.'

'In taking this action was he influenced by his wife's connection with The Management?'

'She brought the thing to his notice, but fundamentally I should say he believed in the prospect of our recovery and expansion. In the event he proved to be fully justified.'

'Why did he transfer his share to her, do you know?'

'I don't know, but I can conjecture. His health is precarious. He's – he was – a devoted husband. He may have been thinking of death duties.'

'Yes, I see.'

Marchant said: 'It's so warm in here,' and unbuttoned his overcoat. Fox helped him out of it. He sat down, very elegantly and crossed his legs. The others watched him anxiously.

The door opened and Dr Harkness came in. He nodded at Alleyn and said: 'Better, but he's had as much as he can take.'

'Anyone with him?'

'The old nurse. He'll settle down now. No more visits, mind.'

'Right.'

Dr Harkness sat heavily on the sofa and Alleyn turned again to Marchant.

'Holding, as you say, a controlling interest,' he said, 'she must have been a power to reckon with, as far as other employees of The Management were concerned.'

The lids drooped a little over Marchant's very pale eyes. 'I really don't think I follow you,' he said.

'She was, everyone agrees, a temperamental woman. For instance, this afternoon, we are told, she cut up very rough indeed. In the conservatory.'

The heightened tension of his audience could scarcely have been more apparent, if they'd all begun to twang like bowstrings, but none of them spoke.

'She would throw a temperament,' Marchant said coolly, 'if she felt the occasion for it.'

'And she felt the occasion in this instance?'

'Quite so.'

'Suppose, for the sake of argument, she had pressed for the severance of some long-standing connection with your management? Would she have carried her point?'

'I'm afraid I don't follow that either.'

'I'll put it brutally. If she'd demanded that you sign no more contracts with, say, Mr Gantry or Mr Saracen or Miss Cavendish, would you have had to toe the line?'

'I would have talked softly and expected her to calm down.'

'But if she'd stuck to it?' Alleyn waited for a moment and then took his risk. 'Come,' he said. 'She did issue an ultimatum this afternoon.'

Saracen scrambled to his feet. 'There!' he shouted. 'What did I tell you! Somebody's blown the beastly gaff and now we're to suffer for it. I *said* we should talk first, ourselves, and be frank and forthcoming and see how right I was!'

Gantry said: 'For God's sake hold your tongue, Bertie.'

'What do we get for holding our tongues?' He pointed to Warrender. 'We get an outsider giving the whole thing away with both hands. I bet you, Timmy. I bet you anything you like.'

'Utter balderdash!' Warrender exclaimed. 'I don't know what you think you're talking about, Saracen.'

'Oh, pooh! You've told the Inspector or Commander or Great Panjandrum or whatever he is. You've *told* him.'

'On the contrary,' Gantry said, 'you've told him yourself. You *fool*, Bertie.'

Pinky Cavendish, in what seemed to be an agony of exasperation, cried out: 'Oh, *why*, for God's sake, can't we all admit we're no good at this sort of hedging! *I* can! Freely *and* without prejudice to the rest of you, if that's what you're all afraid of. And what's more, I'm going to. Look here, Mr Alleyn, this is what happened to me in the conservatory. Mary accused me of conspiring against her and told Monty it was either her or me as far as The Management was concerned. Just that. And if it really came to the point I can assure you it'd be her and not me. You know, Monty, and we *all* know, that with her name and star-ranking, Mary was worth a damn' sight more than me at the box office *and* in the firm. All right! This very morning you'd handed me my first real opportunity with The Management. She was well able, if she felt like it, to cook my goose. But I'm no more capable of murdering her than I am of taking her place with her own particular public. And when you hear an actress admit that kind of thing,' Pinky added, turning to Alleyn, 'you can bet your bottom dollar she's talking turkey.'

Alleyn said: 'Produce this sort of integrity on the stage, Miss Cavendish, and nobody will be able to cook your goose for you.' He looked round at Pinky's deeply perturbed audience. 'Has anybody got anything to add to this?' he asked.

After a pause, Richard said: 'Only that I'd like to endorse what Pinky said and to add that, as you and everybody else know, I was just as deeply involved as she. More so.'

'Dicky, darling!' Pinky said warmly. 'No! Where you are now! Offer a comedy on the open market and watch the managements bay like ravenous wolves.'

'Without Mary!' Marchant asked of nobody in particular.

'It's quite true,' Richard said, 'that I wrote specifically for Mary.'

'Not always. And no reason,' Gantry intervened, 'why you shouldn't write now for somebody else.' Once again he bestowed his most disarming smile on Anelida.

'Why not indeed!' Pinky cried warmly and laid her hand on Anelida's.

'Ah!' Richard said, putting his arm about her. 'That's another story. Isn't it, darling?'

Wave after wave of unconsidered gratitude flowed through Anelida. 'These are my people,' she thought. 'I'm in with them for the rest of my life.'

'The fact remains, however,' Gantry was saying to Alleyn, 'that Bertie, Pinky and Richard all stood to lose by Mary's death. A point you might care to remember.'

'Oh, lawks!' Bertie ejaculated. '*Aren't* we all suddenly generous and noble-minded! Everybody loves everybody! Safety in numbers, or so they say. Or do they?'

'In this instance,' Alleyn said, 'they well might.' He turned to Marchant. 'Would you agree that, with the exception of her husband, yourself and Colonel Warrender, Miss Bellamy issued some kind of ultimatum against each member of the group in the conservatory?'

'Would I?' Marchant said easily. 'Well, yes. I think I would.'

'To the effect that it was either they or she and you could take your choice?'

'More or less,' he murmured, looking at his fingernails.

Gantry rose to his enormous height and stood over Marchant.

'It would be becoming in you, Monty,' he said dangerously, 'if you acknowledged that as far as I enter into the picture the question of occupational anxiety does not arise. I choose my managements: they do not choose me.'

Marchant glanced at him. 'Nobody questions your prestige, I imagine, Timmy. I certainly don't.'

'Or mine, I hope,' said Bertie, rallying. 'The offers I've turned down for The Management! Well, I mean to say! Face it, Monty, dear, if Mary *had* bullied you into breaking off with Dicky and Timmy and Pinky and me, you'd have been in a very pretty pickle yourself.'

'I am not,' Marchant said, 'a propitious subject for bullying.'

'No,' Bertie agreed. 'Evidently.' And there followed a deadly little pause. 'I'd be obliged to everybody,' he added rather breathlessly, 'if they wouldn't set about reading horrors of any sort into what was an utterly unmeaningful little observation.'

'In common,' Warrender remarked, 'with the rest of your conversation.'

'Oh, but what a catty big colonel we've got!' Bertie said.

Marchant opened his cigarette case. 'It seems,' he observed, 'incumbent on me to point out that, unlike the rest of you, I am ignorant of the circumstances. After Mary's death, I left this house at the request of' – he put a cigarette between his lips and turned his head slightly to look at Fox – 'yes – at the request of this gentleman, who merely informed me that there had been a fatal accident. Throughout the entire time that Mary was absent until Florence made her announcement, I was in full view of about forty guests and those of you who had not left the drawing-room. I imagine I do *not* qualify for the star role.' He lit his cigarette. 'Or am I wrong?' he asked Alleyn.

'As it turns out, Monty,' Gantry intervened, 'you're dead wrong. It appears that the whole thing was laid on before Mary went to her room.'

Marchant waited for a moment, and then said: 'You astonish me.'

'Fancy!' Bertie exclaimed and added in an exasperated voice: '*I do* wish, oh, *how* I do wish, dearest Monty, that you would stop being a parody of your smooth little self and get down to tin-tacks (*why* tin-tacks, one wonders?) and admit that, like all the rest of us, you qualify for the homicide stakes.'

'And what,' Alleyn asked, 'have you got to say to that, Mr Marchant?'

An uneven flush mounted over Marchant's cheekbones. 'Simply,' he said, 'that I think everybody has, most understandably, become overwrought by this tragedy and that, as a consequence, a great deal of nonsense is being bandied about on all hands. And, as an afterthought, that I agree with Timon Gantry. I prefer to take no further part in this discussion until I have consulted my solicitor.'

'By all means,' Alleyn said. 'Will you ring him up? The telephone is over there in the corner.'

Marchant leant a little farther back in his chair. 'I'm afraid that's quite out of the question,' he said. 'He lives in Buckinghamshire. I can't possibly call him up at this time of night.'

'In that case you will give me your own address, if you please, and I shan't detain you any longer.'

'My address is in the telephone book and I can assure you that you are not detaining me now nor are you likely to do so in the future.' He half-closed his eyes. 'I resent,' he said, 'the tone of this interview, but I prefer to keep observation – if that is the accepted police jargon – upon its sequel. I'll leave when it suits me to do so.'

'You can't,' Colonel Warrender suddenly announced in a parade-ground voice, 'take that tone with the police, sir.'

'Can't I?' Marchant murmured. 'I promise you, my dear Colonel, I can take whatever tone I bloody well choose with whoever I bloody well like.'

Into the dead silence that followed this announcement, there intruded a distant but reminiscent commotion. A door slammed and somebody came running up the hall.

'My *God*, what now!' Bertie Saracen cried out. With the exception of Marchant and Dr Harkness they were all on their feet when Florence, grotesque in tin curling pins, burst into the room.

In an appalling parody of her fatal entrance she stood there, mouthing at them.

Alleyn strode over to her and took her by the wrist. 'What is it?' he said. 'Speak up.'

And Florence, as if in moments of catastrophe she was in command of only one phrase, gabbled: 'The doctor! Quick! For Christ's sake! Is the doctor in the house!'

CHAPTER 8

Pattern Completed

Charles Templeton lay face down, as if he had fallen forward with his head towards the foot of the bed that had been made up for him in the study. One arm hung to the floor, the other was outstretched beyond the end of the bed. The back of his neck was empurpled under its margin of thin white hair. His pyjama jacket was dragged up, revealing an expanse of torso; old, white and flaccid. When Alleyn raised him and held him in a sitting position, his head lolled sideways, his mouth and eyes opened and a flutter of sound wavered in his throat. Dr Harkness leant over him, pinching up the skin of his forearm to admit the needle. Fox hovered nearby. Florence, her knuckles clenched between her teeth, stood just inside the door. Charles seemed to be unaware of these four onlookers; his gaze wandered past them, fixed itself in terror on the fifth; the short person who stood, pressed back against the wall in shadow at the end of the room.

The sound in his throat was shaped with great difficulty into one word. 'No!' it whispered. 'No! No!'

Dr Harkness withdrew the needle.

'What is it?' Alleyn said. 'What do you want to tell us?'

The eyes did not blink or change their direction, but after a second or two they lost focus, glazed, and remained fixed. The jaw dropped, the body quivered and sank.

Dr Harkness leant over it for some time and then drew back.

'Gone,' he said

Alleyn laid his burden down and covered it.

In a voice that they had not heard from him before, Dr Harkness said: 'He was all right ten minutes ago. Settled. Quiet. Something's gone wrong here and I've got to hear what it was.' He turned on Florence. 'Well?'

Florence, with an air that was half-combative, half-frightened, moved forward, keeping her eyes on Alleyn.

'Yes,' Alleyn said, answering her look, 'we must hear from you. You raised the alarm. What happened?'

'That's what I'd like to know!' she said at once. 'I did the right thing, didn't I? I called the doctor. Now!'

'You'll do the right thing again, if you please, by telling me what happened before you called him.'

She darted a glance at the small motionless figure in shadow at the end of the room and wetted her lips.

'Come on, now,' Fox said. 'Speak up.'

Standing where she was, a serio-comic figure under her panoply of tin hair curlers, she did tell her story.

After Dr Harkness had given his orders, she and – again that side-long glance – she and Mrs Plumtree had made up the bed in the study. Dr Harkness had helped Mr Templeton undress and had seen him into bed and they had all waited until he was settled down, comfortably. Dr Harkness had left after giving orders that he was to be called if wanted. Florence had then gone to the pantry to fill a second hot-water bottle. This had taken some time as she had been obliged to boil a kettle. When she returned to the hall she had heard voices raised in the study. It seemed that she had paused outside the door. Alleyn had a picture of her, a hot-water bottle under her arm, listening avidly. She had heard Mrs Plumtree's voice, but had been unable to distinguish any words. Then, she said, she had heard Mr Templeton ejaculate: 'No!' three times, just as he did before he died, only much louder; as if, Florence said, he was frightened. After that there had been a clatter and Mrs Plumtree had suddenly become audible. She had shouted, Florence reported, at the top of her voice: 'I'll put a stop to it,' Mr Templeton had given a loud cry and Florence had burst into the room.

'All right,' Alleyn said. 'And what did you find?'

A scene, it appeared, of melodrama. Mrs Plumtree with the poker grasped and upraised, Mr Templeton sprawled along the bed, facing her.

'And when they seen me,' Florence said, 'she dropped the poker in the hearth and he gasped, "Florrie, don't let 'er" and then he took a turn for the worse and I see he was very bad. So I said, "Don't you touch 'im. Don't you dare," and I fetched the doctor like you saw. And God's my witness,' Florence concluded, 'if she isn't the cause of his death! As good as if she'd struck him down, ill and all as he was, and which she'd of done if I hadn't come in when I did and which she'd do to me now if it wasn't for you gentlemen.'

She stopped breathless. There was a considerable pause. 'Well!' she demanded. 'Don't you believe it? All right, then. Ask her. Go on. Ask her!'

'Everything in its turn,' Alleyn said. 'That will do from you for the moment. Stay where you are.' He turned to the short motionless figure in the shadows. 'Come along,' he said. 'You can't avoid it, you know. Come along.'

She moved out into the light. Her small nose and the areas over her cheekbones were still patched with red, but otherwise her face was a dreadful colour. She said, automatically, it seemed: 'You're a wicked girl, Floy.'

'Never mind about that,' Alleyn said. 'Are *you* going to tell me what happened?'

She looked steadily up into his face. Her mouth was shut like a trap, but her eyes were terrified.

'Look here, Ninn,' Dr Harkness began very loudly. Alleyn raised a finger and he stopped short.

'Has Florence,' Alleyn asked, 'spoken the truth? I mean as to facts. As to what she saw and heard when she came back to this room?'

She nodded, very slightly.

'You had the poker in your hand. You dropped it when she came in. Mr Templeton said, "Florrie, don't let her." That's true, isn't it?'

'Yes.'

'And before she came in you had said, very loudly, to Mr Templeton, "I'll put a stop to it?" Did you say this?'

'Yes.'

'What were you going to put a stop to?'

Silence.

'Was it something Mr Templeton had said he would do?'

She shook her head.

For a lunatic second or two Alleyn was reminded of a panel game on television. He saw the Plumtree face in close-up; tight-lipped, inimical, giving nothing away, winning the round.

He looked at Fox. 'Would you take Florence into the hall? You too, Dr Harkness, if you will?'

'I'm not going,' Florence said. 'You can't make me.'

'Oh, yes, I can,' Alleyn rejoined tranquilly, 'but you'd be very foolish to put it to the test. Out you go, my girl.'

Fox approached her. 'You keep your hands off me!' she said.

'Now, now!' Fox rumbled cosily. He opened the door. For a moment she looked as if she would show fight and then, with a lift of her chin, she went out. Fox followed her.

Dr Harkness said: 'There are things to be done. I mean . . .' He gestured at the covered form on the bed.

'I know. I don't expect to be long. Wait for me in the hall, will you, Harkness?'

The door shut behind them.

For perhaps ten seconds Alleyn and that small, determined and miserable little woman looked at each other.

Then he said: 'It's got to come out, you know. You've been trying to save him, haven't you?'

Her hands moved convulsively, and she looked in terror at the bed.

'No, no,' Alleyn said. 'Not there. I'm not talking about him. You didn't care about him. You were trying to shield the boy, weren't you? You did what you did for Richard Dakers.'

She broke into a passion of weeping and from then until the end of the case he had no more trouble with Ninn.

II

When it was over he sent her up to her room.

'Well,' he said to Fox, 'now for the final and far from delectable scene. We should, of course, have prevented all this but I'm damned if I see how. We couldn't arrest on what we'd got. Unless they find some trace of Slaypest in the scent spray my reading of the case will never be anything but an unsupported theory.'

'They ought to be coming through with the result before long.'

'You might ring up and see where they've got to.'

Fox dialled a number. There was a tap at the door and Philpott looked in. He stared at the covered body on the bed.

'Yes,' Alleyn said. 'A death. Mr Templeton.'

'By violence, sir?'

'Not by physical violence. Heart disease. What is it, Philpott?'

'It's that lot in there, sir. They're getting very restive, especially Mr Dakers and the colonel. Wondering what was wrong with' – he looked again at the bed – ' with him, sir.'

'Yes. Will you ask Mr Dakers and Colonel Warrender to go into the small sitting-room next door. I'll be there in a moment. Oh, and Philpott, I think you might ask Miss Lee to come too. And you may tell the others they will have very little longer to wait.'

'Sir,' said Philpott and withdrew.

Fox was talking into the telephone. 'Yes. Yes. I'll tell him. He'll be very much obliged. Thank you.'

He hung up. 'They were just going to ring. They've found an identifiable trace inside the bulb of the scent spray.'

'Have they, indeed? That provides the complete answer.'

'So you were right, Mr Alleyn.'

'And what satisfaction,' Alleyn said wryly, 'is to be had out of that?'

He went to the bed and turned back the sheet. The eyes, unseeing, still stared past him. The imprint of a fear already non-existent, still disfigured the face. Alleyn looked down at it for a second or two. 'What unhappiness!' he said and closed the eyes.

'He had a lot to try him,' Fox observed with his customary simplicity.

'He had indeed, poor chap.'

'So did they all, if it comes to that. She must have been a very vexing sort of lady. There'll have to be a PM, Mr Alleyn.'

'Yes, of course. All right. I'll see these people next door.'

He recovered the face and went out.

Dr Harkness and Florence were in the hall, watched over by a Yard reinforcement. Alleyn said: 'I think you'd better come in with me, if you will, Harkness.' And to Florence: 'You'll stay where you are for the moment, if you please.'

Harkness followed him into the boudoir.

It had been created by Bertie Saracen in an opulent mood and contrasted strangely with the exquisite austerity of the study. 'Almost indecently *you*, darling!' Bertie had told Miss Bellamy and, almost indecently, it was so.

Its present occupants – Richard, Anelida and Warrender – were standing awkwardly in the middle of this room, overlooked by an enormous and immensely vivacious portrait in pastel of Mary Bellamy. Charles, photographed some twenty years ago, gazed mildly from the centre of an occasional table. To Alleyn there was something atrociously ironic in this circumstance.

Richard demanded at once: 'What is it? What's happened? Is Charles – ?'

'Yes,' Alleyn said. 'It's bad news. He collapsed a few minutes ago.'

'But . . .? You don't mean . . .?'

'I'm afraid so.'

Richard said: 'Anelida! It's Charles. He means Charles has died. Doesn't he?'

'Why,' she said fiercely, 'must these things happen to you. *Why!*'

Dr Harkness went up to him. 'Sorry, old boy,' he said, 'I tried but it was no good. It might have happened any time during the last five years, you know.'

Richard stared blankly at him. 'My God! 'he cried out. 'You can't talk like that!'

'Steady, old chap. You'll realize, when you think it over. Any time.'

'I don't believe you. It's because of everything else. It's because of Mary and . . .' Richard turned on Alleyn. 'You'd no right to subject him to all this. It's killed him. You'd no right. If it hadn't been for you it needn't have happened.'

Alleyn said very compassionately: 'That may be true. He was in great distress. It may even be that for him this was the best solution.'

'How dare you say that! 'Richard exclaimed and then: 'What do you mean?'

'Don't you think he'd pretty well got to the end of his tether? He'd lost the thing he most valued in life, hadn't he?'

'I – I want to see him.'

Alleyn remembered Charles's face. 'Then you shall,' he promised, 'presently.'

'Yes,' Harkness agreed quickly. 'Presently.'

'For the moment,' Alleyn said, turning to Anelida, 'I suggest that you take him up to his old room and give him a drink. Will you do that?'

'Yes,' Anelida said. 'That's the thing.' She put her hand in Richard's. 'Coming?'

He looked down at her. 'I wonder,' he said, 'what on earth I should do without you, Anelida.'

'Come on,' she said, and they went out together.

Alleyn nodded to Harkness and he too went out.

An affected little French clock above the fireplace cleared its throat, broke into a perfect frenzy of silvery chimes and then struck midnight. Inspector Fox came into the room and shut the door.

Alleyn looked at Maurice Warrender.

'And now,' he said, 'there must be an end to equivocation. I must have the truth.'

'I don't know what you mean,' said Warrender and could scarcely have sounded less convincing.

'I wonder why people always say that when they know precisely what one does mean. However, I'd better tell you. A few minutes ago, immediately after Charles Templeton died, I talked to the nanny, Mrs Plumtree, who had been alone with him at the moment of his collapse. I told her that I believed she had uttered threats, that she had acted in this way because she thought Templeton was with-holding information which would clear your son from suspicion of murder and that under the stress of this scene, Templeton suffered the heart attack from which he died. I told her your son was in no danger of arrest and she then admitted the whole story. I now tell you, too, that your son is in no danger. If you have withheld infor-mation for fear of incriminating him you may understand that you have acted mistakenly.'

Warrender seemed to be on the point of speaking but instead turned abruptly away and stood very still.

'You refused to tell me of the threats Mrs Templeton uttered in the conservatory and I got them, after great difficulty it's true, from the other people who were there. When I asked you if you had quarrelled with Charles Templeton you denied it. I believe that, in fact, you *had* quarrelled with him and that it happened while you were together in the study before I saw you for the first time. For the whole of that interview you scarcely so much as looked at each other. He was obviously distressed by your presence and you were violently opposed to rejoining him there. I must ask you again: had you quarrelled?'

Warrender muttered: 'If you call it a quarrel.'

'Was it about Richard Dakers?' Alleyn waited. 'I think it was,' he said, 'but of course that's mere speculation and open, if you like, to contradiction.'

Warrender squared his shoulders. 'What's all this leading up to?' he demanded. 'An arrest?'

'Surely you've heard of the usual warning. Come, sir, you did have a scene with Charles Templeton and I believe it was about Richard Dakers. Did you tell Templeton you were the father?'

'I did not,' he said quickly.

'Did he know you were the father?'

'Not . . . We agreed from the outset that it was better that he shouldn't know. That nobody should know. Better on all counts.'

'You haven't really answered my question, have you? Shall I put it this way? Did Templeton learn for the first time, this afternoon, that Dakers is your son?'

'Why should you suppose anything of the sort?'

'Your normal relationship appears to have been happy, yet at this time, when one would have expected you all to come together in your common trouble, he showed a vehement disinclination to see Dakers – or you.'

Warrender made an unexpected gesture. He flung out his hands and lifted his shoulders. 'Very well,' he said.

'And *you* didn't tell him.' Alleyn walked up to him and looked him full in the face. 'She told him,' he said. 'Didn't she? Without consulting you, without any consideration for you or the boy. Because she was in one of those tantrums that have become less and less controllable. She made you spray that unspeakable scent over her in his presence, I suppose to irritate him. You went out and left them together. And she broke the silence of thirty years and told him.'

'You can't possibly know.'

'When she left the room a minute or two later she shouted at the top of her voice: "Which only shows how wrong you were. You can get out whenever you like, my friend, and the sooner the better." Florence had gone. You had gone. She was speaking to her husband. Did she tell you?'

'Tell *me!* What the hell. ..'

'Did she tell you what she'd said to Templeton?'

Warrender turned away to the fireplace, leant his arm on the shelf and hid his face.

'All right!' he stammered. 'All right! What does it matter, now. All right.'

'Was it during the party?'

He made some kind of sound, apparently in assent.

'Before or after the row in the conservatory?'

'After.' He didn't raise his head and his voice sounded as if it didn't belong to him. 'I tried to stop her attacking the girl.'

'And that turned her against you? Yes, I see.'

'I was following them, the girl and her uncle, and she whispered it. "Charles knows about Dicky." It was quite dreadful to see her look like that. I – I simply walked out – I . . . ' He raised his head and looked at Alleyn. 'It was indescribable.'

'And your great fear after that was that she would tell the boy?'

He said nothing.

'As, of course, she did. Her demon was let loose. She took him up to her room and told him. They were, I dare say, the last words she spoke.'

Warrender said: 'You assume – you say these things – you . . . ' And was unable to go on. His eyes were wet and bloodshot and his face grey. He looked quite old. 'I don't know what's come over me,' he said.

Alleyn thought he knew.

'It's not much cop,' he said, 'when a life's preoccupation turns out to have been misplaced. It seems to me that a man in such a position would rather see the woman dead than watch her turning into a monster.'

'Why do you say these things to me? *Why!*'

'Isn't it so?'

With a strange parody of his habitual mannerism he raised a shaking hand to his tie and pulled at it.

'I understand,' he said. 'You've been very clever, I suppose.'

'Not very, I'm afraid.'

Warrender looked up at the beaming portrait of Mary Bellamy. 'There's nothing left,' he said. 'Nothing. What do you want me to do?'

'I must speak to Dakers and then to those people in there. I think I must ask you to join us.'

'Very well,' Warrender said.

'Would you like a drink?'

'Thank you. If I may.'

Alleyn looked at Fox who went out and returned with a tumbler and the decanter that Alleyn had seen on the table between Warrender and Charles at his first encounter with them.

'Whisky,' Fox said. 'If that's agreeable. Shall I pour it out, sir?'

Warrender took it neat and in one gulp. 'I'm very much obliged to you,' he said, and straightened his back. The ghost of a smile distorted his mouth. 'One more,' he said, 'and I shall be ready for anything, isn't it?'

Alleyn said: 'I am going to have a word with Dakers before I see the others.'

'Are you going to – to tell him?'

'I think it best to do so, yes.'

'Yes. I see. Yes.'

'When you are ready, Fox,' Alleyn said, and went out.

'He'll make it as easy as possible, sir,' Fox said comfortably. 'You may be sure of that.'

'Easy!' said Warrender and made a sound that might have been a laugh. 'Easy!'

III

The persons sitting in the drawing-room were assembled there for the last time. In a few weeks Mary Bellamy's house would be transformed into the West End offices of a new venture in television, and a sedan chair, for heaven knows what reason, would adorn the hall. Bertie Saracen's decor, taken over in toto, would be the background for the frenzied bandying about of new gimmicks and Charles Templeton's study a waiting-room for disengaged actors.

At the moment it had an air of stability. Most of its occupants, having exhausted each in his or her own kind their capacity for anxiety, anger or compassion, had settled down into apathy. They exchanged desultory remarks, smoked continuously and occasionally helped themselves, rather self-consciously to the drinks that Gracefield had provided. PC Philpott remained alert in his corner.

It was Dr Harkness who, without elaboration, announced Charles Templeton's death and that indeed shook them into a state of flabbergasted astonishment. When Richard came in, deathly pale, with Anelida, they all had to pull themselves together before they found anything at all to say to him. They did, indeed, attempt appropriate remarks, but it was clear to Anelida that their store of consolatory offerings was spent. However heartfelt their sympathy, they were obliged to fall back on their technique in order to express it. Pinky Cavendish broke into this unreal state of affairs by suddenly giving Richard a kiss and saying warmly: 'It's no good, darling. There really is just literally nothing we can say or do, but we wish with all our hearts that there was and Anelida must be your comfort. There!'

'Pinky,' Richard said unevenly, 'you really are no end of a darling. I'm afraid I can't – I can't, . . . I'm sorry. I'm just not reacting much to anything.'

'Exactly,' Marchant said. 'How well one understands. The proper thing, of course, would be for one to leave you to yourself, which unfortunately this Yard individual at the moment won't allow.'

'He *did* send to say it wouldn't be long now,' Bertie pointed out nervously.

'Do you suppose,' Pinky asked, 'that means he's going to arrest somebody?'

'Who can tell! Do you know *what?*' Bertie continued very rapidly and in an unnatural voice. 'I don't mind betting every man Jack of us is madly wondering what all the others think about him. Or her. I know I am. I keep saying to myself, "*Can* any of them think I darted upstairs instead of into the loo, and did it!" I suppose it's no use asking you all for a frank opinion, is it? It would be taking an advantage.'

'*I* don't think it of you,' Pinky said at once. 'I promise you, darling.'

'Pinky! Nor I of you. Never for a moment. And I don't believe it of Anelida or Richard. Do you?'

'Never for a moment,' she said firmly. 'Absolutely not.'

'Well,' Bertie continued, inspired by Pinky's confidence, 'I should like to know if any of you *does* suppose it might be me.' Nobody answered. 'I can't help feeling immensely gratified,' Bertie said. 'Thank you. Now. Shall I tell you which of you I think *could – just* – under *frightful* provocation – do something violent all of a sudden?'

'Me, I suppose,' Gantry said. 'I'm a hot-tempered man.'

'Yes, Timmy, dear, you! But *only* in boiling hot blood with one blind swipe, not really meaning to. And that doesn't seem to fit the bill at all. One wants a calculating iceberg of a person for this job, doesn't one?'

There followed a period of hideous discomfort during which nobody looked at anybody else.

'An idle light of speculation, I'm afraid, Bertie,' said Marchant. 'Would you be very kind and bring me a drink?'

'But of course,' said Bertie, and did so.

Gantry glanced at Richard and said: 'Obviously there's no connection – apart from the shock of Mary's death having precipi-tated it – between Charles's tragedy – and hers.' Nobody spoke and he added half-angrily: 'Well, is there! Harkness – you were there.'

Dr Harkness said quickly: 'I don't know what's in Alleyn's mind.'

'Where's that monumental, that superb old ham, the colonel? Why's he gone missing all of a sudden?' Gantry demanded. 'Sorry, Dicky, he's a friend of yours, isn't he?'

'He's . . . Yes,' Richard said after a long pause. 'He is. I think he's with Alleyn.'

'Not,' Marchant coolly remarked, 'under arrest, one trusts.'

'I believe not,' Richard said. He turned his back on Marchant and sat beside Anelida on the sofa.

'Oh, lud!' Bertie sighed, 'how *wearing* has been this long, long day and how frightened in a vague sort of way I continue to feel. Never mind. *Toujours l'audace.*'

The handle of the door into the hall was heard to turn. Everybody looked up. Florence walked round the leather screen. 'If you'll just wait, miss,' the constable said and retired. Philpott cleared his throat.

Richard said: 'Come in, Floy. Come and sit down.'

She glared stonily at him, walked into the farthest corner of the room and sat on the smallest chair. Pinky looked as if she'd like to say something friendly to her, but the impulse came to nothing and a heavy silence again fell upon the company.

It was broken by the same sound and a heavier tread. Bertie half-rose from his seat, gave a little cry of frustration and sank back again as Colonel Warrender made his entry, very erect and looking at no one in particular.

'We were just talking about you,' said Bertie fretfully.

Richard stood up. 'Come and join us,' he said, and pushed a chair towards the sofa.

'Thank you, old boy,' Warrender said awkwardly, and did so.

Anelida leant towards him and after a moment's hesitation put her hand on his knee. 'I intend,' she said under her breath, 'to bully Richard into marrying me. Will you be on my side and give us your blessing?'

He drew his brows together and stared at her. He made an unsuccessful attempt to speak, hit her hand painfully hard with his own and ejaculated: 'Clumsy ass. Hurt you, isn't it? Ah – bless you.'

'OK,' said Anelida and looked at Richard. 'Now, you see, darling, you're sunk.'

There was a sound of masculine voices in the hall, Pinky said: 'Oh, *dear!*' and Gantry: 'Ah, for God's sake!' Marchant finished his drink quickly and PC Philpott rose to his feet. So, after a mulish second or two, did Florence.

This time it was Alleyn who came round the leather screen.

There was only one place in the room from which he could take them all in at one glance, and that was the hearthrug. Accordingly, he went to it and stood there like the central figure in some ill-assembled conversation piece.

'I'm sorry,' he said, 'to have kept you hanging about. It was unavoidable and it won't be for much longer. Until a short time ago you were still, all of you, persons of importance. From the police point of view, I mean, of course. It was through you that we hoped to assemble the fragments and fit them into their pattern. The pattern is now complete and our uncomfortable association draws to its end. Tomorrow there will be an inquest and you will be required, most of you, to appear at it. The coroner's jury will hear your evidence and mine and one can only guess at what they will make of it. But you have all become too far involved for me to use any sort of evasion. Already some of you are suspecting others who are innocent. In my opinion this is one of those cases where the truth, at any cost, is less damaging in the long run, to vague, festering conjecture. For you all must know,' Alleyn went on, 'you *must* know even if you won't acknowledge it . . . ' his glance rested fleetingly on Richard – 'that this has been a case of homicide.'

He waited. Gantry said: 'I don't accept that,' but without much conviction.

'You will, I think, when I tell you that the Home Office analyst has found a trace of Slaypest in the bulb of the scent spray.'

'Oh,' Gantry said faintly, as if Alleyn had made some quite unimportant remark. 'I see. That's different.'

'It's conclusive. It clears up all the extraneous matter. The professional rows, the threats that you were all so reluctant to admit, the evasions and half-lies. The personal bickerings and antagonisms. They are all tidied away by this single fact.'

Marchant, whose hands were joined in front of his face, lifted his gaze for a moment to Alleyn. 'You are not making yourself particularly clear,' he said.

'I hope to do so. This one piece of evidence explains a number of indisputable facts. Here they are. The scent spray was harmless when Colonel Warrender used it on Mrs Templeton. At some time before she went up to her room with Mr Dakers, enough Slaypest was transferred to the scent spray to kill her. At some time after she was killed the scent spray was emptied and washed out and the remaining scent from the original bottle was poured into it I think there were two, possibly three, persons in the house at that time who could have committed these actions. They are all familiar with the room and its appointments and surroundings. The presence of any one of them in her room would, under normal circumstances, have been unremarkable.'

A voice from outside the group violently demanded: 'Where is she? Why hasn't she been brought down to face it?' And then, with satisfaction: 'Has she been taken away? *Has* she?'

Florence advanced into the light.

Richard cried out: 'What do you mean, Floy? Be quiet! You don't know what you're saying.'

'*Where's Clara Plumtree?*'

'She will appear,' Alleyn said, 'if the occasion arises. And you *had* better be quiet, you know.'

For a moment she looked as if she would defy him, but seemed to change her mind. She stood where she was and watched him.

'There is, however,' Alleyn said, 'a third circumstance. You will all remember that after the speeches you waited down here for Mrs Templeton to take her part in the ceremony of opening the presents. Mr Dakers had left her in her room, passing Florence and Mrs Plumtree on his way downstairs. Mrs Plumtree had then gone to her room, leaving Florence alone on the landing. Mr Templeton went from here into the hall. From the foot of the stairs he saw Florence on the landing and called up to her that you were all waiting for her mistress. He then rejoined the party here. A minutes or so later Florence ran downstairs into this room and, after a certain amount of confused ejaculation, made it known that her mistress was desperately ill. Mr Templeton rushed upstairs. Dr Harkness, after a short delay, followed. With Florence, Colonel Warrender and Mr Gantry hard on his heels.

'They found Mrs Templeton lying dead on the floor of her room. The overturned tin of Slaypest lay close beside her right hand. The scent spray was on the dressing table. That has been agreed to, but I am going to ask for a further confirmation.'

Dr Harkness said: 'Certainly. That's how it was.'

'You'd make a statement on oath to that effect?'

'I would.' He looked at Gantry and Warrender. 'Wouldn't you?'

They said uneasily that they would.

'Well, Florence?' Alleyn asked.

'I said before: I didn't notice. I was too upset.'

'But you don't disagree?'

'No,' she admitted grudgingly.

'Very well. Now, you will see, I think, all of you, that the whole case turns on this one circumstance. The tin of Slaypest on the floor. The scent spray and the empty bottle on the dressing-table.'

'Isn't it awful?' Pinky said suddenly. 'I know it must be childishly obvious, but I just can't bring myself to think.'

'Can't you?' Gantry said grimly. 'I can.'

'Not having been involved in the subsequent discussions,' Marchant remarked to nobody in particular, 'the nicer points must be allowed, I hope, to escape me.'

'Let me bring you up to date,' Alleyn said. 'There was poison in the scent spray. Nobody, I imagine, will suggest that she put it there herself or that she used the Slaypest on herself. The sound of a spray in action was heard a minute or so before she died. By Ninn – Mrs Plumtree.'

'So she says,' Florence interjected.

Alleyn went on steadily: 'Mrs Templeton was alone in her room. Very well. Having used the lethal scent spray, did she replace it on the dressing-table and put the Slaypest on the floor?'

Florence said: 'What did I tell you? Clara Plumtree! After I went. Say she *did* hear the thing being used. She done it! She went in and fixed it all. What did I tell you!'

'On your own evidence,' Alleyn said, 'and on that of Mr Templeton, you were on the landing when he called up to you. You returned at once to the bedroom. Do you think that in those few seconds, Mrs Plumtree, who moves very slowly, could have darted into the room, rearranged the scent spray, and Slaypest, darted out again and got out of sight?'

'She could've hid in the dressing-room. Like she done afterwards when she wouldn't let me in.'

Alleyn said: 'I'm afraid that won't quite do. Which brings me to the fourth point. I won't go into all the pathological details, but there is clear evidence that the spray was used in the normal way – at about arm's length and without undue pressure – and then at very close quarters and with maximum pressure. Her murderer, finding she was not dead, made sure that she would die. Mrs Plumtree would certainly not have had an opportunity to do it. There is only one person who could have committed that act and the three other necessary acts as well. Only one.'

'*Florence!*' Gantry cried out.

'No. Not Florence. Charles Templeton.'

IV

The drawing-room now seemed strangely deserted. Pinky Cavendish, Montague Marchant, Dr Harkness, Bertie Saracen and Timon Gantry had all gone home. Charles Templeton's body had been carried away. Old Ninn was in her bed. Florence had retired to adjust her resentments and nurse her heartache as best she could. Mr Fox was busy with routine arrangements. Only Alleyn, Richard, Anelida and Warrender remained in the drawing-room.

Richard said: 'Ever since you told me and all through that last scene with them, I've been trying to see why. Why *should* he, having put up with so much for so long, do such a monstrous thing? It's – it's . . . I've always thought him – he was so . . . ' Richard drove his fingers through his hair. 'Maurice! You knew him. Better than any of us.'

Warrender, looking at his clasped hands, muttered unhappily: 'What's that word they use nowadays? Perfectionist?'

'But what do you . . . Yes. All right. He was a perfectionist, I suppose.'

'Couldn't stand anything that wasn't up to his own standard. Look at those T'ang figures. Little lady with a flute and little lady with a lute. Lovely little creatures. Prized them more than anything else in the house. But when the parlourmaid or somebody knocked the end off one of the little lute pegs, he wouldn't have it. Gave it to me, by God!' said Warrender.

Alleyn said: 'That's illuminating, isn't it?'

'But it's one thing to feel like that and another to . . . No!' Richard exclaimed. 'It's a nightmare. You can't reduce it to that size. It's irreducible. Monstrous!'

'It's happened,' Warrender said flatly.

'Mr Alleyn,' Anelida suggested, 'would you tell us what you think? Would you take the things that led up to it out of their background and put them in order for us? Might that help, do you think, Richard?'

'I think it might, darling. If anything can.'

'Well,' Alleyn said, 'shall I try? First of all, then, there's her personal history. There are the bouts of temperament that have increased in severity and frequency: to such a degree that they have begun to suggest a serious mental condition. You're all agreed about that, aren't you? Colonel Warrender?'

'I suppose so. Yes.'

'What was she like thirty years ago, when he married her?'

Warrender looked at Richard. 'Enchanting. Law unto herself. Gay. Lovely.' He raised his hand and let it fall. 'Ah, well! There it is. Never mind.'

'Different? From these days?' Alleyn pursued.

'My God, yes!'

'So the musician's lute was broken? The perfect had become imperfect?'

'Very well. Go on.'

'May we think back to yesterday, the day of the party? You must tell me if I'm all to blazes but this is how I see it. My reading, by the way, is pieced together from the statements Fox and I have collected from all of you and from the servants who, true to form, knew more than any of you might suppose. Things began to go wrong quite early, didn't they? Wasn't it in the morning that she learnt for the first time that her . . .' He hesitated for a moment.

'It's all right,' Richard said. 'Anelida knows. Everything. She says she doesn't mind.'

'Why on earth should I?' Anelida asked of the world at large. 'We're not living in the reign of King Lear. In any case, Mr Alleyn's talking about *Husbandry in Heaven* and me and how your mamma didn't much fancy the idea that you'd taken up with me and still less the idea of my reading for the part.'

'Which she'd assumed was written for her. That's it,' Alleyn said. 'That exacerbated a sense of being the victim of a conspiracy, which was set up by the scene in which she learnt that Miss Cavendish was to play the lead in another comedy and that Gantry and Saracen were in the "plot." She was a jealous, ageing actress, abnormally possessive.'

'But not always,' Richard protested. 'Not anything like always.'

'Getting more so,' Warrender muttered.

'Exactly. And perhaps because of that her husband, the perfectionist, may have transferred his ruling preoccupation from her to the young man whom he believed to be his son and on whom she was loath to relinquish her hold.'

'But *did* he?' Richard cried out. 'Maurice, did he think that?'

'She'd – let him assume it.'

'I see. And in those days, as you've told us, he believed everything she said. I understand, now,' Richard said to Alleyn, 'why you agreed that there was no need to tell him about me. He already knew, didn't he?'

'She herself,' Alleyn went on, 'told Colonel Warrender, after the flare-up in the conservatory, that she had disillusioned her husband.'

'Did Charles,' Richard asked Warrender, 'say anything to you, afterwards? Did he?'

'When we were boxed up together in the study. He hated my being there. It came out. He was . . .' Warrender seemed to search for an appropriate phrase. 'I've never seen a man so angry,' he said at last. 'So sick with anger.'

'Oh, God! 'Richard said.

'And then,' Alleyn continued, 'there was the row over the scent. He asked her not to use it. She made you, Colonel Warrender, spray it lavishly over her, in her husband's presence. You left the room. You felt, didn't you, that there was going to be a scene?'

'I shouldn't have done it. She could always make me do what she would,' Warrender said. 'I knew at the time but — isn't it?'

'Never mind,' Richard said, and to Alleyn: 'Was it then she told him?'

'I think it was at the climax of this scene. As he went out she was heard to shout after him: "Which only shows how wrong you were. You can get out whenever you like, my friend, and the sooner the better." She was not, as the hearer supposed, giving a servant the sack: she was giving it to him.'

'And half an hour later,' Richard said to Anelida, 'there he was — standing beside her, shaking hands with her friends. I thought, when I was telephoning, he looked ill. I told you. He wouldn't speak.'

'And then,' Anelida said to Alleyn, 'came the scene in the conservatory.'

'Exactly. And, you see, he knew she had the power to make good her threats. Hard on the heels of the blow she had dealt him, he had to stand by and listen to her saying what she did say to all of you.'

'Richard,' Anelida said, 'can you see? He'd loved her and he was watching her disintegrate. Anything to stop it!'

'I can see, darling, but I can't accept it. Not that.'

'To put it very brutally,' Alleyn said, 'the treasured possession was not only hideously flawed, but possessed of a devil. She reeked of the scent he'd asked her not to wear. I don't think it would be too much to say that at that moment it symbolized for him the full horror of his feeling for her.'

'D'you mean it was then that he did it?' Warrender asked.

'Yes. Then. It must have been then. During all the movement and excitement just before the speeches. He went upstairs, emptied out some of the scent and filled up the atomiser with Slaypest. He returned during the speeches. As she left the drawing-room she came face to face with him. Florence heard him ask her not to use the scent.'

Warrender gave an exclamation. 'Yes?' Alleyn asked.

'Good God, d'you mean it was a – kind of gamble? If she did as he'd asked – like those gambles on suicide? Fella with a revolver. Half-live, half-blank cartridges.'

'Exactly that. Only this time it was a gamble in murder.' Alleyn looked at them. 'It may seem strange that I tell you in detail so much that is painful and shocking. I do so because I believe that it is less damaging in the long run to know rather than to doubt.'

'Of course it is,' Anelida said quickly. 'Richard, my dear, isn't it?'

'Yes,' Richard said. 'I expect it is. Yes, it is.'

'Well, then,' Alleyn said. 'Immediately after he'd spoken to her, you came in. The photographs were taken and you went upstairs together. You tackled her about her treatment of Anelida, didn't you?'

'It would be truer to say she attacked me. But, yes – we were both terribly angry. I've told you.'

'And it ended in her throwing your parentage in your teeth?'

'It ended with that.'

'When you'd gone she hurled your birthday present into the bathroom where it smashed to pieces. Instead of at once returning downstairs she went through an automatic performance. She powdered her face and painted her mouth. And then – well, then it happened. She used her scent spray, holding it at arm's length. The windows were shut. It had an immediate effect, but not the effect he'd anticipated.'

'What d'you mean?' Warrender asked.

'You've read the dictionary of poisons he bought. You may remember it gives a case of instant and painless death. But it doesn't always act in that way.'

'He thought it would?'

'Probably. In this case, she became desperately ill. Florence came in and found her so. Do you remember what Charles Templeton said when Florence raised the alarm?'

Warrender thought for a moment. 'Yes. I do. He said "My God, not *now*!" I thought he meant: ' Not a temperament at this juncture."'

'Whereas he meant: "Not *now*. Not so soon." He then rushed upstairs. There was some delay in getting Harkness under way, wasn't there?'

'Tight. Bad show. I put ice down his neck.'

'And by the time you all arrived on the scene, the Slaypest was on the floor and the atomiser on the dressing-table. And she was dead. He had found her as Florence had left her. Whether she'd been able to say anything that showed she knew what he'd done is a matter of conjecture. Panic, terror, a determination to end it at all costs – we don't know. He *did* end it as quickly as he could and by the only means he had.'

There was a long silence. Anelida broke it. 'Perhaps,' she said, 'if it hadn't happened as it did, he would have changed his mind and not let it happen.'

'Yes. It's possible, indeed. As it was he had to protect himself. He had to improvise. It must have been a nightmare. He'd had a bad heart-turn and had been settled down in his dressing-room. As soon as he was alone, he went through the communicating door, emptied the atomiser into the lavatory, washed it out as best he could and poured in what was left of the scent.'

'But how do you *know*,' Richard protested.

'As he returned, old Ninn came into the dressing-room. She took it for granted he had been in the bathroom for the obvious reason. But later, when I developed my theory of the scent spray, she remembered. She suspected the truth, particularly as he had smelt of "Unguarded." So strongly that when Florence stood in the open doorway of the dressing-room she thought it was Ninn, and that she had been attempting to do the service which Florence regarded as her own right.'

'My poor Old Ninn!' Richard ejaculated.

'She, as you know, was not exactly at the top of her form. There had been certain potations, hadn't there? Florence, who in her anger and sorrow, was prepared to accuse anybody of anything, made some very damaging remarks about you.'

'There's no divided allegiance,' Richard said, 'about Floy.'

'Nor about Ninn. She was terrified. Tonight, she went into the study after Templeton had been put to bed there, and told him that if there was any chance of suspicion falling on you, she would tell her story. He was desperately ill but he made some kind of attempt to get at her. She made to defend herself. He collapsed and died.'

Richard said: 'One can't believe these things of people one has loved. For Charles to have died like that.'

'Isn't it better?' Alleyn asked. 'It *is* better. Because, as you know, we would have gone on. We would have brought him to trial. As it is, it's odds on that the coroner's jury will find it an accident. A rider will be added pointing out the dangers of indoor pest killers. That's all.'

'It is better,' Anelida said, and, after a moment: 'Mightn't one say that he brought about his own retribution?' She turned to Richard and was visited by a feeling of great tenderness and strength. 'We'll cope,' she said, 'with the future. Won't we?'

'I believe we will, darling,' Richard said. 'We must, mustn't we?'

Alleyn said: 'You've suffered a great shock and will feel it for some time. It's happened and can't be forgotten. But the hurt *will* grow less.'

He saw that Richard was not listening to him. He had his arm about Anelida and had turned her towards him.

'You'll do,' Alleyn said, unheeded.

He went up to Anelida and took her hand. 'True,' he said. 'Believe me. He'll be all right. To my mind he has nothing to blame himself for. And that,' Alleyn said, 'is generally allowed to be a great consolation. Goodnight.'

V

Miss Bellamy's funeral was everything that she would have wished.

All the Knights and Dames, of course, and The Management and Timon Gantry who had so often directed her. Bertie Saracen who had created her dresses since the days when she was a bit-part actress. Pinky Cavendish in floods, and Maurice, very Guardee, with a stiff upper lip.

Quite insignificant people, too: her Old Ninn with a face like a boot and Florence with a bunch of primroses. Crowds of people whom she herself would have scarcely remembered, but upon whom, as a columnist in a woman's magazine put it, she had at some time bestowed the gift of her charm. And it was not for her fame, the celebrated clergyman pointed out in his address, that they had come to say goodbye to her. It was, quite simply, because they had loved her.

And Richard Dakers was there, very white and withdrawn, with a slim, intelligent-looking girl beside him.

Everybody.

Except, of course, her husband. It was extraordinary how little he was missed. The lady columnist could not, for the life of her, remember his name.

Charles Templeton had, as he would have wished, a private funeral.

My Poor Boy

My Poor Boy was written for a talk on New Zealand Radio in 1959 and was subsequently printed in the *Listener*.

My Poor Boy,

So you want to be an author. O, my poor boy. I wonder *why* you want to be an author. Your letter, in common with almost all the, I'm afraid, very many other similar letters that I have been sent, tells me everything but that. It says that in your schooldays you frequently discovered the encomium V.G. written in the margins of your essays. It says that you would like me to tell you how you can find a publisher for the novel that you have in mind but of which you have not yet written the opening chapter. You add that whenever you think about beginning your novel you feel disheartened because you can't be sure it will ever see the light of day and that, as often as you are visited by this depressing notion, the fount of your inspiration dries up and you are unable to make a beginning. You say in parenthesis that your sister, who sounds a detestable girl, has a habit of picking up your poems and of reading them aloud with grotesque gestures and serio-comic inflexions to the ill-concealed amusement of your family. You ask if I think this is fair. You enclose a piece you have written on the sexual behaviour of blind eels which you submitted without success for publication in a New Zealand monthly. You say that you dislike your present job. Finally, you offer to collaborate with me in the writing of a detective novel for which you have an original plot. You say that on receiving my acceptance of your offer you will be glad to arrange a meeting, outline this plot and come to an appropriate business arrangement. O my poor boy.

Shall I try to answer your letter in reverse, beginning with its con-cluding offer? To this offer my answer is no. I hope the reason for my refusal will declare itself as I go on and shall merely point out that if your plot is as good as you believe it to be and you do in fact want to become a professional writer, it would be an excellent point of departure. Why not use it for an attempt at your own first detec-tive novel? Believe me, one can't enter this particular arena on the back of one of the old-stagers. Either you go in under your own steam, as every published writer has had to do in the beginning, or you decide that you don't feel like taking the risk of working very hard for no reward. In which case you are not, even potentially, a writer.

You dislike your present job. That's a depressing state of affairs but it doesn't necessarily mean that the alternative is authorship. Please don't entertain for a moment the utterly mistaken idea that there is no drudgery in writing. There is a great deal of drudgery in even the most inspired, the most noble, the most distinguished writing. Read what the great ones have said about their jobs; how they never sit down to their work without a sigh of distress and never get up from it without a sigh of relief. Do you imagine that your Muse is forever flamelike – breathing the inspired word, the wonderful situation, the superb solution into your attentive ear? Not at all. She can just as often appear as some acidulated school-marm, some nagging, shrill-voiced spouse or sulking girlfriend. 'You got yourself into this mess,' she points out. 'All right. Get yourself out of it. How many words have you written today? What's the latest excuse for taking a day off? You're not, I hope, depending on *me* to do it for you? I'm your Muse not your stand-in and I'll thank you to remember it.' Believe me, my poor boy, if you wait for inspiration in our set-up, you'll wait for ever. It's true that on good days the minor miracles do tend to crop up but one generally finds in the long run that one's best work is the stuff that has been ground out between the upper and nether millstones of self-criticism and hard labour. Of the antics of your sister I have little to say. Unless, with your indulgence, I may tell you that I wrote one of my most successful stories within the bosom of a family whose favourite pastime was to add chunks of nonsense to my manuscripts and shout aloud, with shrieks of laughter, the words they read over my shoulder as I was writing them.

Which brings us up to your not-yet-begun novel. What I have to say about this follows upon what I have already said. If you wait for fair weather, inspiration and no external interference, you will never begin it. You *may* be able to write a novel, you may *not*. You will never know until you have worked very hard indeed and written at least part of it. You will never *really* know until you have written the whole of it and submitted it for publication. You talk about detective fiction so I will assume that it is in this field, or an associated one, that you hope to work. May I draw your attention to one or two points? Nowadays, a good plot, an amusing anecdote and a string of lively episodes laced with a certain amount of factual information will not get you very far in any field of writing. These are essential ingredients but they can be ruined in the hands of a bad cook. In other words, you must be a craftsman – I will not say an artist since my purpose is to avoid the grandiose. You must be able to write. You must have a sense of form, of pattern, of design. You must have a respect for and a mastery over words. The writer of a thriller has no need to haul down his stylistic flag a quarter of an inch. Indeed, he has every reason not to do so. He will be read by persons of the educated sort – by university dons, by professors, doctors, clergymen, scientists, serious novelists, poets, journalists and members of the nobility. He will not be read by people whose interest in the written word is confined solely to the racing news, the football results and the scandal columns. Quite on the contrary. He is writing in a genre and an exacting, difficult genre at that.

Do you think you can do this? All I have to go by is your rejected article on the sex habits of blind eels. I have read it and I have also read a copy of the New Zealand journal that rejected it. Now, in the first place, literary merit apart, it is by no means the kind of thing these people are looking for. So, however well you may or may not have written it, you have made your initial mistake in sending it to the wrong market. But suppose you sent it to some appropriate scientific publication. Is it sufficiently well-informed and authoritative to find a home there? Knowing nothing of blind eels, I venture to suggest that it is not. So perhaps you have written an unsaleable article. Never mind. It was an exercise. Let us examine it purely as a piece of writing. To my mind it contains two sentences that have some distinction, some feeling for your instrument, some flavour of individuality. Two sentences are not enough to make it a good piece of writing but they are enough to make one wonder if, after all, you may not have a gift of words. Let us suppose that you have.

We arrive at your first question. How can you hope to find a publisher? My poor boy, by doing in a big way precisely what you have already done in a small one. By writing your novel. By sweating it out. By setting yourself the highest standard and by re-writing whenever you have fallen away from that standard. By preparing yourself to take the mortification of rejection slips. And also by remembering one or two points about publication which I shall now try to set out.

Publishers are continually on the look-out for authors. They do not exist in a constant state of haughty rejection. They yearn for authors. Every spring and every autumn they lavish thousands of pounds upon launching a new author in whom they have faith. They are even prepared to lose terrifying sums of money on a first novel if they think the author will ultimately command a public. Contrary to some opinions, they also have a standard to maintain and, in many cases, the standard of a great tradition. They are not unapproachable.

On the other hand, most publishing houses are not prepared to risk launching more than a limited number of unknown authors in a year. So that, suppose, my poor boy, you send your first novel off to Messrs Format and Serif and they think it well up to publishing standard, they may still reject it on the grounds that they have already signed up as many new authors as they can comfortably manage for the publishing season.

If, however, you entrust your book to a reputable agent he will know which publishers are on the lookout for a new author and will offer your book to them. He will not undertake to handle it unless he thinks he has a good chance of selling it. He will, if he succeeds in doing so, take 10% of everything you earn. If, in the ripeness of time, he finds an American publisher, he will watch your contracts there and protect you from piracy and raw deals. He will also try to get pre-publication serial rights and will have an eye on broadcasting, television and the cinema. He is an expert. There are reputable agents and there are disreputable ones. The good agents are listed in the *Authors and Composers Year Book*, a publication you will be well advised to study. I have always dealt with an agent. He sold my first novel 25 years ago and has, I consider, done me proud ever since.

And so we have worked out way back to this one thing you have not told me about yourself. Why do you want to become an author? I will accept only one answer. If it is because you feel you can write better than you can do anything else then go ahead and do it without frills and flourishes. Stick to your present job and write in your spare time: but do it as if it is a whole time job. Depend on nobody but yourself. Don't talk about what you are doing – something goes wrong if you talk – because writing is a lonely job. If you are very lucky you may find one friend with whom it is good to discuss your work while it is in process. But be sure you *have* found the right one before you open your mouth. If you think journalism will help – and I'm not committing myself there except to say that good journalism is a very different thing from journalese – try your hand at freelance articles but find out the sort of thing that is wanted before you start. Above all things – read. Read the great stylists who cannot be copied rather than the successful writers who must not be copied. Don't try and turn yourself into a Hemingway, rather listen to E. M. Forster or V. S. Pritchett or Proust or Daniel Defoe. Read what people like Maugham have to say about style and what people like Maurice Richardson have to say about Maugham.

And write simply. And re-write and write again and – O my poor boy,

  I remain, with compassion,
   Yours sincerely,